*The Editor*

ANNE E. FERNALD is Professor of English and Women's, Gender, and Sexuality Studies at Fordham University. She is the author of *Virginia Woolf: Feminism and the Reader* and editor of a textual edition of *Mrs. Dalloway* for Cambridge University Press. Her articles have appeared in *Feminist Studies, Modern Fiction Studies, Guernica, Open Letters Monthly,* and multiple edited collections.

## NORTON CRITICAL EDITIONS
### Modernist & Contemporary Eras

ANDERSON, Winesburg, Ohio
AZUELA, The Underdogs
BURGESS, A Clockwork Orange
CATHER, My Ántonia
CATHER, O Pioneers!
CONRAD, Heart of Darkness
CONRAD, Lord Jim
CONRAD, The Secret Agent
CONRAD, The Secret Sharer and Other Stories
CUMMINGS, E. E. Cummings: Selected Works
Eight Modern Plays
ELIOT, The Waste Land
FAULKNER, As I Lay Dying
FAULKNER, The Sound and the Fury
FITZGERALD, The Great Gatsby
FORD, The Good Soldier
FORSTER, Howards End
FORSTER, A Passage to India
FRIEDAN, The Feminine Mystique
HIGHSMITH, The Price of Salt
JOHNSON, The Autobiography of an Ex-Colored Man
JOYCE, Dubliners
JOYCE, A Portrait of the Artist as a Young Man
KAFKA, Kafka's Selected Stories
KAFKA, The Metamorphosis
LARSEN, Passing
LARSEN, Quicksand
MANN, Death in Venice
MANSFIELD, Katherine Mansfield's Selected Stories
Modern African Drama
Modern and Contemporary Irish Drama
PROUST, Swann's Way
RHYS, Wide Sargasso Sea
RICH, Adrienne Rich: Poetry and Prose
SHAW, George Bernard Shaw's Plays
SOYINKA, Death and the King's Horseman
STEIN, Three Lives and Q.E.D.
TOOMER, Cane
WATSON, The Double Helix
WHARTON, The Age of Innocence
WHARTON, Ethan Frome
WHARTON, The House of Mirth
WOOLF, Jacob's Room
WOOLF, Mrs. Dalloway
YEATS, Yeats's Poetry, Drama, and Prose

For a complete list of Norton Critical Editions, visit
wwnorton.com/nortoncriticals

A NORTON CRITICAL EDITION

# Virginia Woolf
# MRS. DALLOWAY

AUTHORITATIVE TEXT
CONTEXTS
CRITICISM

*Edited by*

ANNE E. FERNALD
FORDHAM UNIVERSITY

**W. W. NORTON & COMPANY**
*Independent Publishers Since 1923*

W. W. Norton & Company has been independent since its founding in 1923, when William Warder Norton and Mary D. Herter Norton first published lectures delivered at the People's Institute, the adult education division of New York City's Cooper Union. The firm soon expanded its program beyond the Institute, publishing books by celebrated academics from America and abroad. By mid-century, the two major pillars of Norton's publishing program—trade books and college texts—were firmly established. In the 1950s, the Norton family transferred control of the company to its employees, and today—with a staff of five hundred and hundreds of trade, college, and professional titles published each year—W. W. Norton & Company stands as the largest and oldest publishing house owned wholly by its employees.

Composition: Westchester Publishing Services
Manufacturing: Maple Press
Production manager: Stephen Sajdak
Cartography: Adrian Kitzinger

**Library of Congress Cataloging-in-Publication Data**
Names: Woolf, Virginia, 1882–1941, author. | Fernald, Anne E., editor.
Title: Mrs. Dalloway : authoritative text, contexts, criticism / Virginia
    Woolf ; edited by Anne E. Fernald.
Description: First edition. | New York, N.Y. : W. W. Norton & Company,
    [2021] | Series: A Norton critical edition | Includes bibliographical references.
Identifiers: LCCN 2020036690 | ISBN 9780393655995 (paperback) |
    ISBN 9780393540147 (epub)
Subjects: LCSH: Triangles (Interpersonal relations)--Fiction. | Middle-aged
    women--Fiction. | Married women--Fiction. | Suicide victims--Fiction. |
    Woolf, Virginia, 1882–1941. Mrs. Dalloway.
Classification: LCC PR6045.O72 M7 2021b | DDC 823/.912--dc23
LC record available at https://lccn.loc.gov/2020036690

**ISBN: 978-0-393-65599-5 (pbk)**

W. W. Norton & Company, Inc., 500 Fifth Avenue, New York, NY 10110
wwnorton.com
W. W. Norton & Company Ltd., 15 Carlisle Street, London W1D 3BS

2   3   4   5   6   7   8   9   0

# Contents

Introduction     ix
A Note on the Text     xxix
Acknowledgments     xxx
MAP: The London of *Mrs. Dalloway*     xxxi

## The Text of *Mrs. Dalloway*     1

## Contexts     139

   AUTOBIOGRAPHICAL SOURCES     141
   Early Writings     141
     Hyde Park Gate News • Cristmas Number, vol. i, No. 51
     (December 1891)     141
       • [Mrs Leslie Stephen], vol. ii, No. 25 (July 4, 1892)     143
       • [The Dog], vol. ii, No. 43 (November 7, 1892)     144
     Early Diary Entry • Giggleswick 1906     145
     Diary     146
       • February 1, 1915 [A violent explosion]     146
       • December 14, 1917 [A quiet man]     147
       • April 9, 1918 [My father was a German]     147
       • May 1, 1918 [The Equator]     148
       • May 28, 1918 [An enormous pocket knife]     149
       • June 8, 1920 [A complete case of servant's hysteria]     151
       • September 15, 1920 [Especially the satire of
       the Dalloways]     152
       • October 25, 1920 [A little strip of pavement over
       an abyss]     154
       • April 18, 1921 [Lunching with a cabinet minister]     155
       • June 2, 1921 [Actually under this roof]     157
       • October 4, 1922 [I like reading my own writing]     158
       • October 8, 1922 [Kitty Maxse's death]     159
       • June 19, 1923 [Feeling things deeply]     160
       • August 6, 1923 [Hollyhocks, decapitated, swam
       in a bowl]     162
       • April 5, 1924 [Angelica's accident]     164
       • November 18, 1924 [The mad chapters of Mrs D]     166
       • January 6, 1925 [Proofs will come next week]     168

- April 19, 1925 [Mrs Dalloway is a success] — 169
- June 18, 1925 [Lytton does not like Mrs Dalloway] — 170

Letters — 171

To Emma Vaughan, April 1899 [How I do love London] — 171

To Thoby Stephen, November 5, 1901
[No true Shakespearian] — 173

To Madge Vaughan, early January 1905 [Teaching in the
Waterloo Road] — 175

To Violet Dickinson, mid-February 1905 [Dr Savage's
dinner] — 175

To Violet Dickinson, October 1, 1907 [The poet Keats] — 177

To Vanessa Bell, August 20, 1908 [I have no wish to perish] — 177

To T. S. Eliot, April 14, 1922 [As for my own story] — 179

To Gerald Brenan, December 25, 1922 [You said you
were very wretched] — 180

To Vita Sackville-West, August 19, 1924
[London and the marshes] — 183

SELECTED SHORT STORIES — 184

Mrs Dalloway in Bond Street — 184

The Introduction — 191

The Man Who Loved His Kind — 195

SELECTED NONFICTION — 201

Review of Dorothy Richardson's *The Tunnel* (1919) — 201

*From* 22 Hyde Park Gate (1920) — 203

*From* Old Bloomsbury (1922) — 205

On Not Knowing Greek (1925) — 207

Modern Fiction (1925) — 218

Introduction to Modern Library Edition of
*Mrs. Dalloway* (1928) — 224

LITERARY SOURCES — 227

Homer • *From* The Odyssey, Book 5 (late-eighth-to
late-seventh-century B.C.E.) — 227

King James Bible • *From* The Book of Ruth
(c. fourth century B.C.E.) — 229

William Shakespeare • *From* Richard II (1595) — 230
• *From* Othello (1604) — 231
• *From* Cymbeline (1610) — 232

Alexander Pope • *From* The Rape of the Lock (1717) — 233

John Keats • *From* Ode to a Nightingale (1819) — 233

Hermann Von Gilm • Allerseelen — 234
All Souls' Day (c. 1863) — 235

H. G. Wells • *From* Ann Veronica:
A Modern Romance (1909) — 235

Rupert Brooke • The Soldier (1915) — 237

T. S. Eliot • *From* The Waste Land (1922)                238
Katherine Mansfield • The Garden Party (1922)            239
HISTORICAL CONTEXTS                                      252
W. H. R. Rivers • The Repression of War
    Experience (1917)                                    252
May Sinclair • The Novels of Dorothy Richardson (1918)  270
Ted Bogacz • [The War Office Committee of Enquiry
    into "Shell-Shock"] (1989)                           277
Trudi Tate • [*Mrs Dalloway* and the Armenians] (1998)  288
Alison Light • *From* Mrs. Woolf and the Servants (2007) 294
Elizabeth Outka • [*Mrs. Dalloway* and the Influenza
    Pandemic] (2015)                                     301

# Criticism                                              311

EARLY REVIEWS                                            313
Anonymous • A Long, Long Chapter
    [Review of *Mrs. Dalloway*] (1925)                   313
Anonymous • A Novelist's Experiment [Review of
    *Mrs. Dalloway*] (1925)                              313
E. W. Hawkins • The Stream of Consciousness
    Novel (1926)                                         315
RECENT CRITICISM                                         318
Christine Froula • Sex, Lies, and Selling Out:
    Women and Civilization's Discontents (2002)          318
Molly Hite • [Tonal Cues and Character in
    *Mrs. Dalloway*] (2010)                              327
Sara Ahmed • *From* Feminist Killjoys (2010)             333
Paul K. Saint-Amour • *Mrs. Dalloway* and the Gaze of
    Total War (2015)                                     339
Celia Marshik • [Miss Kilman's Mackintosh] (2016)       350

Virginia Woolf and *Mrs. Dalloway*: A Chronology         359
Selected Bibliography                                    363

# Introduction

## Woolf and Modernism

"Mrs. Dalloway said she would buy the flowers herself." This opening sentence sticks with us, in part, because it tells us so much about the novel that follows in just nine words. The "Mrs." tells us that our protagonist is already a wife, foreclosing one of the commonest plots for novels about women: the marriage plot. This will be a book about a married woman. We know she must be wealthy, for only the wealthy have servants to whom they might ordinarily delegate an errand such as buying flowers (already a luxury purchase). Most of us, if we have enough money to buy flowers, have no one to tell that we will do so. This sentence also tells us that Mrs. Dalloway lives in a city, where one buys flowers, rather than the country, where one gathers them. The sentence is neither direct discourse, which crisply delineates narration from speech, as if she had written "Mrs. Dalloway said, 'I'll buy the flowers myself,'" nor indirect discourse, which reports speech without quoting it, "Mrs. Dalloway said that she would buy the flowers." Instead, Woolf's sentence hovers between direct quotation and narration, so that we can almost, but not quite, hear her words. Woolf's use of free indirect discourse here signals both a debt to Jane Austen, who used the technique, and announces Woolf's participation in the modern experiments of interior monologue and stream of consciousness. In this one sentence, then, we already know that we are reading the story of a wealthy, married woman going about her day in a modern city, and that the story will be told in a new way.

On the first page of *Mrs. Dalloway* we are plunged into Clarissa Dalloway's past as she plunges into her day. Where Woolf's third novel, *Jacob's Room* (1922), revolved around the difficulty of knowing someone, *Mrs. Dalloway* attempts to help us gain that knowledge. While composing the novel, Woolf wrote of "my discovery, how I dig out beautiful caves behind my characters; I think that gives exactly what I want; humanity, humour, depth. The idea is that the caves shall connect, & each comes to daylight at the present moment—."[1] Woolf never explains what she means by these caves, but the image of depth suggests the desire to make writing, a nearly motionless activity, evoke the duration, breadth, and depth of life. In that, the image of caves, like the image of a "fin in a waste of waters"[2] that inspired *The Waves* or Terence Hewet's desire to write a novel about silence, "the things people don't say,"[3] in *The Voyage Out*, participates in Woolf's interest in asking fiction to convey the important but ineffable aspects of life, the very things that language might seem least well suited to convey.

This tunneling method is almost immediately apparent in the way the novel uses the characters' memories to add depth to their day. Clarissa thinks "What a lark! What a plunge! For so it had always seemed to her, when, with a little squeak of the hinges, which she could hear now, she had burst open the French windows and plunged at Bourton into the open air,"[4] and we see the same woman as girl and middle-aged woman at once. The act of buying flowers combined with our double vision of her as young and older also begins a pattern of allusion to the myth of Demeter and Persephone, a myth which we might understand as two manifestations of the same woman, much as the novel shows us a young and an older woman. So, not only does Woolf "tunnel" back to Clarissa's youth, but she connects her to a classical antecedent and the heroine of an eighteenth-century novel.[5] All of these details place Clarissa Dalloway precisely in London on a June day of 1923, as a character in the history of literature, and someone whom we come to know and understand despite only spending a single day with her.

The techniques of interior monologue, including our access to Clarissa's memories, and stream of consciousness are indelibly associated with literary modernism, the movement with which we most associate Woolf's writing. The term "stream of consciousness" itself was coined by the American psychologist and philosopher William James (1842–1910). In *Principles of Psychology* (1890), James uses the phrase to describe the experience of thinking: "Consciousness . . . does not appear to itself chopped up in bits. . . . It is nothing jointed; it flows. A 'river' or a 'stream' are the metaphors by which it is most naturally described. *In talking of it hereafter, let us call it the stream of thought, of consciousness.*"[6] James's metaphor for what it feels like to think captured the imagination of

---

1. Diary, vol. 2, p. 263.
2. Diary, vol. 4, p. 10.
3. Virginia Woolf, *The Voyage Out*, 1915 (New York: Harcourt, 1948), p. 216.
4. See below, p. 3.
5. *Clarissa* (1747–48) is an epistolary novel by Samuel Richardson. Woolf's father greatly admired it, although Woolf herself did not read *Clarissa* until 1926.
6. William James, *Principles of Psychology*, vol. 1, 239 (New York: Henry Holt, 1890).

writers, which is not entirely surprising. His brother, Henry, was a novelist and a friend of Woolf's father. Woolf emerged as a writer during a time of great experiment with stream of consciousness techniques. Marcel Proust, a writer whom Woolf admired greatly and from whom she learned much, began publishing his master-piece *A la recherche du temps perdu* (*In Search of Lost Time*) in 1913. (He completed it in 1927.) The following year, James Joyce's *Portrait of the Artist as a Young Man* was published. In 1915, Virginia Woolf published her first novel, *The Voyage Out*, and Dorothy Richardson published *Pointed Roofs*, the first volume of her multi-volume novel, *Pilgrimage*, also with Woolf's half-brother's press, Duckworth. The first use of the phrase "stream of consciousness" to apply to fiction was in a 1918 review of Richardson by another experimental woman novelist, May Sinclair:

> Nothing happens. It is just life going on and on. It is Miriam Henderson's stream of consciousness going on and on. . . . In identifying herself with . . . Miriam's stream of consciousness, Miss Richardson produces her effect of being the first, of getting closer to reality than any of our novelists who are trying so desperately to get close.[7]

Sinclair praises the "stream of consciousness" for "getting closer to reality." Woolf, too, wanted to find a new way to capture "reality" in her fiction, to capture what she called the workings of "an ordinary mind on an ordinary day." Woolf consulted Sinclair's essay for her own review of Richardson in 1919.[8] So, when Woolf published *Mrs. Dalloway* six years later, she was already deeply engaged in a conversation about how a literary technique might offer a new approach to representing reality in fiction. Not only had she already published experimental fiction, including the short stories "Kew Gardens" and "The Mark on the Wall," and her third novel, *Jacob's Room* (1922), but she had also reviewed other writers' work—including Richardson's—and discussed how best to pursue these experiments with her friend, the New Zealand–born writer Katherine Mansfield.

In March 1919, about a month after Woolf's review of Richardson's *The Tunnel* appeared in the *Times Literary Supplement*, Woolf discussed Richardson with Mansfield "with the greatest freedom & animation on both sides until I had to catch my train."[9] The following November, however, Katherine Mansfield wrote a painfully negative review of Woolf's second novel, *Night and Day*. In the

---

7. May Sinclair, "The Novels of Dorothy Richardson." *The Egoist* 5.4 (April 1918): 58. See below, p. 275.
8. See below, pp. 201–03.
9. *Diary*, vol. 1, p. 257.

review, Mansfield compares Woolf to Jane Austen, implying that Woolf is old-fashioned, and describes the novel as "old and chill," "a novel in the tradition of the English novel . . . we had never thought to look upon its like again."[1] Mansfield's judgment cast a pall on Woolf's friendship with her, but also on Woolf's willingness to review subsequent work not only by Mansfield, but by Richardson, too: "The truth is that when I looked at it, I felt myself looking for faults; hoping for them. And they would have bent my pen, I know."[2] Today, Woolf is by far the best known of these women, but in the early twentieth century, she was part of a group of women writers collaborating, competing, and striving to change the way novels were written. As the diary entry reminds us, competition is complicated. Nevertheless, these four women, Dorothy Richardson, May Sinclair, Katherine Mansfield, and Virginia Woolf, were at the forefront of English-language experiments with the stream of consciousness, an experiment which might be said to culminate in *Mrs. Dalloway.*

## *Mrs. Dalloway* and World War I

The subject matter of *Mrs. Dalloway* is not, on its face, promising nor does it seem to bear much connection to World War I. We do not meet the shell-shocked veteran, Septimus Warren Smith, for many pages, and the novel's two main characters never meet each other. Instead, for much of the book we follow Clarissa Dalloway, a wealthy London hostess, in her early fifties, wife to a Conservative Member of Parliament, and mother of an eighteen-year-old girl. She is throwing a party. It is a provocatively trivial subject. She buys flowers, comes home, rests, mends her dress, sees an old friend, and invites him to the party, too. All of this is set on an unusually hot Wednesday in June 1923, on which Clarissa Dalloway thinks, in the novel's opening pages, "the war was over. Thank god, over, except for . . ."[3] and that "except for" is the key to the novel's continuing relevance. *Mrs. Dalloway* is, among other things, a war novel. In centering on Clarissa Dalloway, Woolf explores the extent of the ongoing reverberations of World War I.

When we announce that something is over, as Clarissa does in the opening pages, we are also inviting in a trace of doubt: when things are truly, fully, and completely over, they are so far from our thoughts, we do not think to announce them. It quickly becomes

---

1. Katherine Mansfield. "A Ship Comes Into the Harbour" (rev. of *Night and Day*). *The Athenaeum* (November 21, 1919): 1227.
2. *Diary*, vol. 1, p. 315.
3. See p. 4.

clear that Clarissa's thought—"the war was over. Thank god, over,"—
is more a wish than a truth. The war is not really over, as even this
cosseted, wealthy woman perceives. Before the echoes of the
thought have died from her mind, she thinks of two friends who
still pay for the war. The first woman is Mrs. Foxcroft, an acquaintance whom she has seen at a party; she must be a widow, because
we learn that, since her son has died (and because, at this time,
women did not ordinarily inherit property), she will also lose her
home. The second, Lady Bexborough, "the woman she admired
most,"[4] lost her favorite son in the war. So, on this June day, four
years after the Armistice, these friends of Clarissa's are still griev-
ing their lost sons. In Mrs. Foxcroft's case, her grief is compounded
by economic danger: she is about to lose her home. Clarissa, however, seems untouched by the war. In 1914, when World War I
began, she was already the married mother of a young child, and
such women, when wealthy, were not expected to contribute to the
War effort much beyond opening bazaars—something Lady Bexborough does—and offering other generic patriotic support. Moreover, her only child was a daughter, just five when the war began,
barred by her sex from serving, and by her age from even considering the kind of volunteer work that led some young women, such as
Vera Brittain, Winifred Holtby,[5] and many others, to become nurses
and ambulance drivers. With her husband already middle-aged and
serving in politics, she did not even bear the worry that he might be
conscripted. The Dalloways' Conservative Party affiliation further
protects them from social scorn from within their social class. In
short, World War I was as far from Mrs. Dalloway as from almost
any person in England.

   In choosing Clarissa Dalloway as her protagonist, Virginia Woolf
set herself an ambitious challenge. How can she get readers to care
about the life of a wealthy married woman whose biggest adventure
is a trip to the florist? Woolf uses Clarissa's distance from the war
to show the vast ripple effects of war, far beyond the space of the
battlefield or the time of the conflict itself. One key to that demonstration of war's ongoing wound comes in Clarissa's surprising and
unspoken sympathy with Septimus Warren Smith, the novel's second main character. The novel traces his day in London alongside
Clarissa's. Although the two never meet, Woolf shows them to be in
sympathy with each other, giving them similar thoughts and perceptions: their mutual distaste for Sir William Bradshaw and their

---

4. See p. 8.
5. Writers Vera Brittain (1893–1970) and Winifred Holtby (1898–1935) both volunteered
during the war. They met in college, became best friends, and lectured on peace
together until Holtby's early death. Holtby wrote one of the first book-length studies of
Virginia Woolf.

mutual admiration for a song in Shakespeare's lesser-known play
*Cymbeline*. When she hears Septimus has died, Clarissa knows,
without being told, that he "plunged," a word associated positively
with her on the novel's opening page.

Readers often associate Woolf with Clarissa Dalloway. But Woolf
based Clarissa not so much on herself as on her mother, her half-
sister Stella Duckworth, and the kind of woman her mother wanted
her to be. Falsely associating Woolf with Clarissa leads to another
oversight. Readers often fail to appreciate the many, many ways in
which Woolf felt the impact of the War, far beyond what her character does. It is natural to imagine that writers are somehow "like"
their characters, and, of course, as characters emerge out of their
creator's imaginations, similarities will always exist. Woolf's character comes from the world of Woolf's upper-middle-class childhood—
the one she sought to escape after her parents died and she moved
from conventional Kensington to arty, intellectual, and cosmopolitan Bloomsbury. Where Woolf was in her early thirties during the
war, her character is a decade older. This difference utterly changes
the impact the war had on Virginia Woolf's life. Woolf was a pacifist and still young enough to be friends both with men who served
and men who objected to the war. Some of her male friends, notably Lytton Strachey, claimed conscientious objector status, appearing in court to refuse service on moral grounds. Her friend, the
hostess Ottoline Morrell, turned her country estate into a kind of
working farm where objectors could go and work—work that was
often mocked as less than serious—in lieu of fighting. Woolf's husband, Leonard, was exempted from service not on account of his
politics (although he, too, opposed the war), but on account of a serious physical tremor, a disability which made holding a rifle unsafe, if
not nearly impossible. His brothers Philip and Cecil served. Cecil
Woolf was killed in action by a shell that also wounded Philip. In
Woolf's diary she describes a visit from Philip shortly after Cecil's
death, observing that he seems stunned by his inability to "feel
more,"[6] an experience and observation that became key to her depiction of the soldier Septimus Smith.

Septimus has many fictional and literary antecedents. In November 1922, Woolf wrote in a notebook, "S's character. founded on
R.?" and later on the same page, "can be partly R.; partly me."[7] If "S"
is Septimus, who is "R"? "R" might refer to either Rupert Brooke
(1887–1915) or Ralph Partridge (1894–1960). Brooke had been a
close friend of Woolf's from childhood vacations at St. Ives. When

---

6. *Diary*, vol. 1, p. 92.
7. *The Hours: The British Museum Manuscript of* Mrs. Dalloway. Transcribed and edited
   by Helen Wussow (New York: Pace UP, 2010), p. 418.

Woolf visited Brooke at Grantchester in 1911, they went skinny-dipping and she provided him with a line for his poem "Town and Country." Both Woolf and Brooke had precocious literary talent and both struggled with mental health (Brooke suffered from a nervous breakdown in 1913). Woolf was outraged and disgusted by the way in which Brooke's good looks, his patriotic poetry, and his death early in the war (not in battle, but of blood poisoning) were used to recruit more troops.[8] Woolf was also close to Ralph Partridge, another soldier and possible referent for "R.," in the early 1920s, both as his supervisor at the Hogarth Press and as a friend, having advocated for his marriage to the painter Dora Carrington (1893–1932). But frustrations with Partridge—who proved an exasperating friend at work and in love—color our sense of one backdrop for Woolf's environment during the early drafting of Mrs. Dalloway, although they seem to bear little on the character of Septimus himself. After all, Rezia admires him for being controlled, quiet.[9]

In her draft of the novel, Woolf also proposes another soldier, Gerald Brenan (1894–1987), as a model. Brenan fought in World War I alongside Partridge. Brenan, who lived in a remote Spanish village, was also in love with Carrington, but he was more cerebral, and his friendship with Woolf, conducted by letter and strengthened during her and Leonard's visit to Spain in 1923, suggests how Woolf understood the sensitive, literary war veteran:

> Why not have something of G. B. in him? The young man who has gone into business after the war: takes life to heart: seeks truth—revelations—some reason; yet of course it is insanity. His insensibility to other people's feelings—that is to say he must have the masculine feelings. selfishness: egoism; but has also an extreme insight, & humility.[1]

Woolf was close to Brenan at this time and her correspondence with him offers biographical support for the ineffable connection between Clarissa and Septimus. On Christmas Day of 1922, Woolf wrote him a reassuring letter about madness, isolation, age, and success.[2] In this letter, Woolf tries to create a circuit of sympathetic understanding between herself and her suffering male friend, twelve years her junior. She reminds him of her own feelings of despair and holds out the promise that, soon enough, his depression may abate as hers has. In doing so, she repeats her metaphor of pavement for a kind of precarious safety: "Why is life so tragic; so like

---

8. See "Rupert Brooke" (*Essays*, vol. 2, pp. 277–84). For further discussion, see Karen Levenback, *Virginia Woolf and the Great War* (Syracuse, NY: Syracuse UP, 1999).
9. See, for example, p. 63.
1. *The Hours*, p. 419.
2. *Letters*, vol. 2, pp. 597–600; see below, pp. 180–82.

a little strip of pavement over an abyss. I look down."[3] Woolf returns to a version of this idea in *Mrs. Dalloway*, where Septimus finds himself "rooted to the pavement,"[4] clinging to that strip of concrete.

*Mrs. Dalloway* records and asks us to attend to the long aftermath of war. While the novel's attention is primarily on the empathetic—almost telepathic—connection between Clarissa and Septimus, it also acknowledges the value of generous civic action in Richard Dalloway. At a time when many still saw shell shock as cowardice, Richard is working on a bill that would address the deferred effects of shell shock—the very thing that took Septimus's life. Clarissa's difficult recovery from influenza, Rezia's challenges as an immigrant who met her husband in wartime, and Clarissa's refusal to learn the difference between Albanians and Armenians all bring postwar geopolitical and social changes into the novel.

This last refusal to understand the Armenian crisis warrants greater attention. Decades ago, Clarissa's willful ignorance of the Armenian Genocide was seen as part of her independence within her marriage. It is partly that: we know she chose Richard over Peter in part because Richard did not demand that everything be gone into. However, Trudi Tate's work, excerpted in this volume, reminds us of England's role in the Armenian Genocide (both in efforts to curtail it and a final abandonment of support for an independent Armenia). Woolf had studied the conflict at length, working with her husband, Leonard, and was aware of Turkish-Armenian tensions from at least her first visit to Turkey in 1906. She noted in her diary how hard it is to wrap one's mind around the scale of genocide. For Clarissa to fail to know the difference between Armenians and Albanians suggests a surprising degree of disengagement from current events and further complicates our vision of her. As much as the war continues to affect even Clarissa, she still has a privilege which Septimus and Rezia do not share: to ignore some of its reverberating consequences, consequences the novel invites us to see.

## Virginia Woolf's Life

Virginia Woolf, the author of *Mrs. Dalloway*, was a writer almost as early as she was a reader. As a little girl of six, she wrote a letter to her godfather, the American poet James Russell Lowell, asking him, "have you been to the Adirondacks and have you seen lots of

3. *Diary*, vol. 2, p. 72.
4. See p. 12.

wild beasts and a lot of birds in their nests?"[5] At ten, Virginia took the lead in writing articles for the family newspaper, *Hyde Park Gate News*,[6] named for their street in London. The paper covered such topics as sports, the family dog, and servants' gossip. Woolf's leadership in writing the paper is all the more striking because she was seventh of eight children in the large Stephen family. Her father, Leslie Stephen, a widower, had a daughter (Laura) from his first marriage; her mother, Julia Prinsep Duckworth Stephen, a widow, had two sons and a daughter from her first marriage (George, Gerald, and Stella). They had four children together—Vanessa, Thoby, Virginia, and Adrian.

So, in 1882, Virginia Woolf was born into an already large family, and a prominent one. Her father was a public intellectual who had given up his fellowship at Cambridge when he felt that it was wrong to pretend to believe in God and perform the religious duties then required of faculty. Her mother, famous for her beauty, was born into an artistic family. With summers by the sea in the village of St. Ives in Cornwall and the rest of the year in London, Leslie and Julia created a bustling Victorian household that found time for and valued intense industry—both parents were inclined to work themselves sick. Neither of her parents supported women's rights, and her mother actively opposed the vote for women, agreeing with those Victorian women who argued that a woman's most important role was domestic. Her extended family included many prominent men and women: a pioneering Victorian photographer (Julia Margaret Cameron), a colonial administrator (Sir James Stephen), a Quaker activist for peace and other social causes (Caroline Emilia Stephen), and a judge (Sir James Fitzjames Stephen). Writers, artists, and politicians from England and America were frequent guests in her childhood home and, throughout her life, Woolf continued her parents' gift for social connection, talk, and mixing art with politics.

This busy childhood life changed abruptly when her mother died in 1895. Virginia was just thirteen and the loss was devastating to all. In that deep grief, her father, Leslie Stephen, saw that Vanessa had art lessons and Virginia got tutored in classical Greek, pursuits which proved instrumental in setting them on the path to their later careers as painter and writer. While brothers Thoby and Adrian went to Cambridge, Leslie Stephen did not provide university degrees for his daughters. Although women's colleges had been around since the 1860s, they were not yet the norm for even the daughters of educated men, an inequity that frustrated and angered

5. *Letters*, vol. 1, p. 2.
6. See selections below, pp. 141–45.

Woolf. In addition to learning Greek at home, Woolf took classes at King's College London, and taught classes to working men and women in the Waterloo Road, much as Miss Isabel Pole would teach Septimus here. Her mother's death was not her only loss, however. More deaths—of her half-sister Stella, her brother Thoby, and her elderly father—followed in the next few years.

Virginia's life changed again when her late brother Thoby's friend Leonard Woolf came home from Sri Lanka (then the British colony of Ceylon) on leave and proposed marriage. They married in 1912, when she was thirty. As Virginia Woolf, she published her first two novels, and in 1917 she and Leonard started the Hogarth Press, in part to get away from her first publisher, Duckworth House, which was owned by her half-brother, Gerald. That move to her own press was crucial: it finalized her separation from the half-brother who had abused her as a child,[7] and it gave her the creative license to pursue modernism without fear of a conservative editor who had also been her tormentor.

With the publication of *Mrs. Dalloway*, Woolf's fourth novel, Woolf was twenty years into her career as a published writer and ten into her career as a novelist. Her most experimental work (*The Waves*, 1931) and her most explicit declaration of her feminism (*A Room of One's Own*, 1929) were yet to come. During the composition of *Mrs. Dalloway*, the Woolfs moved from suburban Richmond back to London. Specifically, they returned to Bloomsbury, a neighborhood that is home to the British Museum, the British Library, and many universities. Central and bustling, Bloomsbury is also dotted with many park-like squares, giving the urban neighborhood its character. Many of the large houses there were already, in Woolf's time, divided into rooming houses for international students. Visitors to England from Sri Lanka, India, and the rest of the world were occasional guests in the Woolfs' home as both Leonard and Virginia took a keen interest in international government, Labour Party politics, workers' education, and peace work.

The Woolfs had an active social life both in London and at their Sussex country home, Monks House (now a National Trust site). While the parties they gave and attended were very different from Clarissa's party, Virginia Woolf loved parties, despite often feeling anxious about attending them. She valued friendship, gossip, and socializing, and she saw, too, how the work of making these good and fun things happen often falls to women, who then get teased for being so silly as to like the very parties they are asked to throw.

---

7. For Woolf's account of her sexual abuse, see the autobiographical essays collected in *A Sketch of the Past*. While both half-brothers abused her, it was George whose abuse was ongoing and more serious.

Woolf went on to write many more novels after *Mrs. Dalloway*. She was nearly done with her last, the great 1941 novel *Between the Acts*, also set on a single day, when fearing her own sanity and an encroaching Nazi invasion, she committed suicide in the spring of 1941, at one of bleakest moments of the war for England.

## London and *Mrs. Dalloway*

*Mrs. Dalloway* is a London novel. Every street and landmark named in the book is real and conveys all the significance that such landmarks convey to city-dwellers. It is possible to trace the characters' various walks on a map and to infer from where they live, wander, and shop things about their class and affinities. With a commanding view of all is Big Ben, more heard than seen, the giant clock tower near the Houses of Parliament, whose bell keeps the time. Although we do not hear every hour toll, Woolf ensures that we hear not only noon, but eleven o'clock, a sober reference to the end of the war at eleven o'clock in the morning on November 11, 1918, still marked annually in England by a moment of silence.

In adulthood, Woolf repeated her childhood pattern of moving between city and country, spending most of her time in London, but summers and weekends in her home in Rodmell, Sussex (much nearer to London than the remote Cornwall of her childhood). However, she wrote *Mrs. Dalloway* during the only period in her life when she lived in the suburbs, and we might imagine we hear some of her longing to return to London in Clarissa's enthusiasm for walking in the city. (Leonard and Virginia moved back to London in 1924.) Woolf shared Clarissa's enthusiasm. In her essay "Street-Haunting" (1927) and the six essays published in *Good Housekeeping* in 1931–32 as *The London Scene*, she writes more on the pleasures of being a Londoner, of wandering and exploring city streets. As she wrote in a letter to Vita Sackville-West, "How could I think mountains and climbing romantic? Wasn't I brought up with alpenstocks in my nursery, and a raised map of the Alps, showing every peak my father had climbed? Of course, London and the marshes are the places I like best."[8]

The freedom Woolf valued so highly and which she celebrates in *Mrs. Dalloway* was new for women. When Woolf was a little girl, she had to accompany her sister Stella on visits: it was considered improper for a young woman of her social class to walk the city alone. So, when Clarissa takes joy in her London walk, or Elizabeth enjoys riding the bus to an unfamiliar (and poorer) part of

---

8. *Letters*, vol. 3, pp. 125–26. See p. 183 below.

London, they are enjoying a new freedom. That freedom, however, is not without its dangers, as the novel hints. The minor character Maisie Johnson, who sees Rezia and Septimus in the park, has clearly worked to persuade her parents to let her move to the city. Peter Walsh uses the freedom of movement men have long enjoyed to follow a young woman a few blocks, down the aptly named Cockspur Street. Peter's London adventure, unlike Clarissa's and Elizabeth's, is one that likely feels different to the unnamed young woman whom he follows. This scene is, in fact, the mirror image of a scene early in H. G. Wells's 1909 feminist novel *Ann Veronica*, in which the title character delights in the newfound possibility of wandering the city only to have her adventure spoiled by a man following her.

The differences between how men and women experience walking through London is but one of the ways in which *Mrs. Dalloway*'s London is both timeless and utterly specific to the 1920s. The skywriting scene, in which Londoners come together to gaze upward at a plane advertising something, is the first-ever literary description of this twentieth-century mode of advertising. For Gillian Beer, in "The Island and the Aeroplane," it contrasts sharply with the mysterious motor car which has just passed. The car seems to call everyone to their roles—ready to serve Crown and Empire; while, by contrast, the airplane is democratizing—everyone, regardless of rank, looks up together.[9] This shared looking, however, is not without threat. As the startling sound of a backfiring car has also suggested, London in 1923 is a city that still remembers the first air-raid drills of World War I. And, as Paul K. Saint-Amour argues, London between the wars is anxious with the recognition that it will likely become a target again, as indeed it did in World War II.[1]

Woolf would develop her argument about the troubling patriarchal legacy of the British Empire four years later in *A Room of One's Own* (1929), where she notes that, for women, walking past the imposing government buildings of Whitehall is an uncomfortable reminder of *men's* power, not the stirring sign of the *nation's* power that men may feel it to be. Here, in *Mrs. Dalloway*, we get hints of the arguments to come. So, it is Peter Walsh, gentle, intelligent, and kind, but also an underachiever and a colonial official, who thinks self-satisfied thoughts about the statues of military heroes. He notices that the boys laying a

9. Gillian Beer, "The Island and the Aeroplane: The Case of Virginia Woolf." First published in *Nation and Narration*, ed. Homi Bhabha (London: Routledge, 1990), pp. 265–90. Repr. *Virginia Woolf: The Common Ground* (Edinburgh: Edinburgh UP, 1996), pp. 149–78.
1. Paul K. Saint-Amour, *Tense Future*. See below, pp. 339–50.

wreath on the Cenotaph, London's stark and haunting monument to the unknown soldier, are weak, and yet he cannot keep up with them.

*Mrs. Dalloway* notices the palaces and monuments, but it celebrates life on a human scale. We hear Big Ben's chime and we also hear the bells of St. Margaret's coming in "like a hostess" who "finds her guests there already."[2] We see shop window displays and Woolf lets us glimpse the small relationships between shopkeepers and their customers, and among patrons in a restaurant. The novel also depicts London's great network of parks, where people meet and mix with Londoners whom they would not ordinarily meet. These Londoners, many of whom are names but only appear for a paragraph or even just a line, make a kind of Greek chorus for the novel, so that London itself becomes a key supporting character in the book. Woolf returned to the Greek she had studied so intensively as a young woman while she was writing *Mrs. Dalloway*. One of the questions she asked herself, as she was rereading Greek plays, was how a novel might capture the functions of a chorus: commenting on the main action, representing the ideas of the people. We see her thinking on this topic most explicitly in the essay "On Not Knowing Greek," and we see it in action throughout *Mrs. Dalloway*.

## Literary Allusions[3]

The twentieth century saw a flowering of highly self-conscious, self-referential writing of texts about other texts, but allusions in Woolf tend not to announce themselves as loudly as allusions in other writers of the period, especially T. S. Eliot and James Joyce. Nevertheless, readers interested in chasing down literary allusions in Woolf will find abundant resources. *The Cambridge Edition of Woolf* and Harcourt's annotated editions identify Woolf's chief allusions. The publication of Woolf's letters and diaries in the 1970s made it possible for critics to recover valuable material about Woolf's writing process as well as sources for her fiction. In the early 1980s, three works deepened our understanding of Woolf's literary sources: Beverly Ann Schlack's *Continuing Presences* identifies many of the major allusions in Woolf's novels; Elizabeth Steele's two volumes list the books cited and alluded to in the more than 400 essays and reviews Woolf wrote; and Brenda

---

2. See p. 36.
3. Parts of this section are adapted from my chapter "Woolf and Intertextuality," in *Virginia Woolf in Context*, ed. Susan Sellers and Jane Goldman (Cambridge UP, 2012), pp. 52–64.

Silver's book detailing the contents of Woolf's "reading notebooks" (distinct from her diary, these are notes for reviews and essays). Schlack, Steele, and Silver offered irrefutable archival proof of Woolf's lifelong reading. Washington State University houses what remains of Leonard and Virginia Woolf's private library (much of which was destroyed when their London home was bombed in the war). The online catalog of their books makes it possible to check some of what they owned, enabling the researcher to confirm hunches.

This Norton Critical Edition includes many of the literary sources upon which Woolf drew for *Mrs. Dalloway*. Four allusions in particular bear study for the light they shed on *Mrs. Dalloway*. The first, to Shakespeare's *Cymbeline*, is also one of the few allusions set off as a quotation. One of the main ways Woolf teaches us to read her is by planting direct quotations and mentions of an author's name early in a novel. That quoted author typically turns out to be a crucial touchstone and reference point for the remainder of the book. We see this most dramatically here when Clarissa sees a copy of Shakespeare's play *Cymbeline* in a bookstore window, reads a few lines, and they run through her head for the rest of the day. Separately and significantly, Septimus, with no external prompting, thinks about this song, too, and their mutual admiration for Shakespeare bonds them for us, the readers. *Cymbeline* is not as odd a choice as it may seem: the late Victorians revived the play, said to have been a favorite of Tennyson, who was reading it on his deathbed. This song, "Fear No More the Heat of the Sun,"[4] is particularly apt for linking Septimus and Clarissa as it is a funeral song, offering a way to grieve over what appears to be the dead body of a young man, but is really a married woman in disguise.

The second allusion is buried more deeply, but it, too, is set off as a quotation. When Rezia and Peter encounter an old homeless woman, singing at the entrance to a Tube (or subway) station, her words seem like nonsense; "ee um fa um so," she sings. However, the quoted phrases and images that follow come directly from a nineteenth-century German poem set to music by Richard Strauss. The poem, translated as "All Soul's Day," mirrors the book's plot. Where *Mrs. Dalloway* shows us the tragic and troubled young marriage of the Warren Smiths on a June day, the song is sung by a woman on All Soul's Day (November 1), thinking back on the flowers her lover once gave her in May.

4. See below, pp. 234–35.

In one of his most terrifying hallucinations, Septimus feels him-self "macerated . . . like a veil upon a rock."[5] The imagery of this passage draws heavily on Book Five of *The Odyssey*. There, Odys-seus, in his protracted journey home from the Trojan War, finally escapes Calypso and builds a raft, but his enemy Poseidon sends a storm, preventing his landing in Phaeacia. The goddess Ino appears from the waves, tossing him an enchanted veil which protects him, allowing him to land on the rocky shore: "His skin / would have been ripped away, and his bones smashed, / had not Athena given him a thought."[6] Odysseus remains unconscious until awakened by Nausicaa and her handmaidens. Woolf reread *The Odyssey* in prep-aration for her essay "On Not Knowing Greek," which she wrote alongside *Mrs. Dalloway*. In her reading notes she wrote, "At last he was dashed against rocks; a very odd image comes—his skin was torn off by the rocks."[7]

If Septimus resembles Odysseus, the lost and broken soldier, struggling to make it home, Rezia's character bears traces of a fig-ure from the Bible. When Rezia drifts off in a drugged sleep after Septimus's death, this city-bred hat maker imagines herself running through a field of corn, an allusion to Keats's Ruth, "in tears amid the alien corn,"[8] a line Woolf admired and quoted more than once. Like Ruth, Rezia is a young widow in a strange land, and this Keat-sian allusion heightens the poignancy of her position even as the novel bids her farewell. In the Biblical book of Ruth, Ruth is from Moab and a widow. When her mother-in-law, Naomi, also a widow, wants to return home to Bethlehem, Ruth follows her to a land where she will be poor and a stranger. Ruth remains loyal to her mother-in-law, humbly gleaning corn from the fields. Keats revisits the story of the young widow in a foreign land in "Ode to a Nightin-gale": "Perhaps the self-same song that found a path / Through the sad heart of Ruth, when, sick for home, / She stood in tears amid the alien corn" (lines 65–67). Woolf mentions the "sad heart of Ruth" in a 1919 review of Washington Irving and again in "Craftsmanship."[9] You will find excerpts from the literary sources to these four allu-sions—to *Cymbeline*, Hermann von Gilm's poem "Allerseelen" (in German and English), *The Odyssey*, and the Bible—in this volume, as well as many others.

Equally important to the books that contributed to *Mrs. Dalloway* were the people whose personalities, quirks, and beliefs contributed

5. See p. 49.
6. Homer (Wilson trans.), 5.425–27. See below, pp. 227–29.
7. Berg Collection, New York Public Library, Reading Notebook 25, p. 80.
8. Keats, "Ode to a Nightingale," l.67. See below, pp. 233–34.
9. For Washington Irving, see *Essays*, vol. 3, p. 29; for "Craftsmanship," see *Essays*, vol. 6, pp. 91–102. "Craftsmanship" was recorded for the BBC, and you can find online the only extant recording of Woolf's voice reading part of this essay.

to the novel. The minor character of Hugh Whitbread is a good example. Shortly after the novel was published, Woolf wrote to a friend, "There were originals for some of the people in *Mrs. Dalloway*: but very far away—people I last saw 10 years ago."[1] In fact, in 1915, her diary records an encounter with Walter Lamb, then secretary to the Royal Academy of Arts. Woolf writes:

> I was sitting typewriting this morning when there came a rap at the door; . . . it was Walter Lamb . . . fresh from the King. Whenever he has seen the King he comes to tell us. He insisted that we should go for a walk with him in Richmond Park. . . . On our doorstep he burst at length into an account of the last Royal visit, when the King, who now treats him as a friend (or rather, as Leonard says, like a superior footman). . . .[2]

This scene, in which a slightly ridiculous, self-important man, whose worth derives from his proximity to the palace, strides across a park, returns, a decade later, in the opening pages of *Mrs. Dalloway*: "who should be coming along with his back against the Government buildings, most appropriately, carrying a despatch box stamped with the Royal Arms, who but Hugh Whitbread; her old friend Hugh—the admirable Hugh!"[3]

Harder to identify are the larger-scale resonances that link texts by genre and theme. The title *Mrs. Dalloway* announces Woolf's direct and distinctively modern engagement with other novels. Novels often carry the name of the protagonist in the title (*Tom Jones, Clarissa, Emma, Amelia, David Copperfield*), and, *Moll Flanders* aside, for women, the surname is often left off: after all, a traditional female-centered novel ends with the heroine's marriage, and thus, until recently, the changing of her last name. The "Mrs." announces *Mrs. Dalloway* as a novel about middle age. It also makes it resonate with Gustave Flaubert's *Madame Bovary*, a key precursor text for the modernists and a novel about a woman fatally unhappy in her marriage. Meanwhile, Clarissa's first name associates her with the heroine of Samuel Richardson's *Clarissa*, a young woman who makes a fatally poor choice of husband. The deaths of Emma Bovary and Clarissa Harlowe may render credence to Woolf's post-publication claim that she had initially planned for Clarissa to die at the novel's end.[4] Clarissa Dalloway in her attic reading of the retreat from Moscow recalls the many scenes of Clarissa Harlowe writing letters to Lovelace in secret: a place of cruel confinement and violation for Clarissa Harlowe

1. *Letters*, vol. 3, p. 195.
2. *Diary*, vol. 1, p. 14.
3. See p. 5.
4. See her 1928 Introduction below, pp. 224–26.

becomes, for Clarissa Dalloway, a place of retreat, power, and resumed virginity. Clarissa's highly allusive, hyper-feminine name (which she also shares with the scissors-wielding character in Alexander Pope's *The Rape of the Lock*[5]) puts her in an ironic relationship to her own fate; by the standards of her class, Clarissa's marriage to a kindly, if dull, conservative member of Parliament is anything but disastrous. The disappointments are small in the public sense, and yet, through her name and the novel's tide, Woolf signals that Clarissa's dissatisfaction is just as great as that of those other heroines. Similarly, something strange is afoot when Clarissa keeps accidentally calling Richard Dalloway "Wickham."[6] In *Pride and Prejudice,* Elizabeth Bennett initially finds Wickham attractive before learning of his deceptions and falling in love with Mr. Darcy. In *Mrs. Dalloway,* Peter Walsh is the novel's structural Wickham (the first, inappropriate suitor whom the heroine must reject to find true love), and he also immediately sees that Richard is Clarissa's match. In calling Richard "Wickham," Clarissa announces her attraction (and, perhaps, her desire for adventure and her desire to pretend that marrying Richard *is* an adventure), and Woolf signals, with heavy irony, that the marriage will not be a happy one. Thus, in addition to all these direct allusions, and to what Woolf learned from her contemporaries (especially Proust, T. S. Eliot, and Katherine Mansfield), Flaubert, Richardson, and Austen all shimmer behind *Mrs. Dalloway.*

## The Hours and the Text of Mrs. Dalloway

We have quite a bit of information about how Woolf wrote *Mrs. Dalloway.* From the very first ideas for the plot and characters, through the composition, when it was called *The Hours,* to the revisions she made just before publication. This Norton Critical Edition includes selections from letters, diary entries, short stories, and essays that form part of the story of the novel's long genesis and afterlife.

When Woolf prepared *Mrs. Dalloway* for publication, she mailed a typed copy of the book to her printer in Edinburgh. (The Hogarth Press was her publisher, but their printing press was too small to handle full-length novels.) The printer then sent proofs back to Woolf. At this point, any correction beyond typos could set the publication back, something Woolf knew, and she took care to keep her revisions minimal at this stage. However, one major revision to the

5. See below, p. 233.
6. See p. 44.

proofs occurs in Septimus's final moments. Woolf wrote, canceled, and then added back in his thought process about how to kill himself and cause the least trouble. When she received the page proofs, she typed and added, "Getting up rather unsteadily, hopping indeed from foot to foot, he considered Mrs. Filmer's nice clean bread knife with 'Bread' carved on the handle. Ah, but one mustn't spoil that. The gas fire? But it was too late now. Holmes was coming. Razors he might have got, but Rezia, who always did that sort of thing, had packed them."[7] It is a substantial change at a very late stage, but it is also a change that returns to something she had written in an earlier draft. Still, it is interesting to know that up until the final moments of writing, Woolf was considering how best to compose this scene.

The Cambridge Edition of the novel details over four hundred small differences between the American and British editions, but the overwhelming majority of these are small enough to go undetected by most readers. Two differences, however, bear mention. When Clarissa retreats from her party to contemplate Septimus's death, she thinks, "He made her feel the beauty; made her feel the fun"[8] in the American edition, but not the British. The uncorrected proofs have, "He made her feel the beauty; the fun," eliminating the grounds for arguing that Woolf over-explained Clarissa's feelings for an American audience. On the contrary, the uncorrected proofs show that two of the three most authoritative versions of the novel contain a version of this sentence, a sentence that intensifies the language of sacrifice elsewhere and that complicates our sense of Clarissa's emotional response to the news of this stranger's death. Such observations might seem to support adopting this reading, but mitigating against this choice is a factor at least as important: the presence of a section break on this page in the first British, but not the first American, edition. Woolf did not call for a break on the American proofs here as she did elsewhere. As a publisher herself, Woolf was keenly aware of the need to ensure that corrections to the proofs maintain spacing: she had to choose between the section break and the sentence to keep the pagination. While all American editions have the sentence, the first British edition has a two-line-wide section break after "And she came in from the little room." This break does as much to signal the significance of the moment as the omitted sentence, and it does something much more: it gives *Mrs. Dalloway* precisely twelve sections, one for each hour.

7. See p. 105.
8. See p. 131.

# Reviews, Criticism, and Continuing Relevance

*Mrs. Dalloway* came out simultaneously in England and the United States on May 14, 1925. It was Woolf's first novel to have simultaneous American and English publication, a sign of her growing fame throughout the English-speaking world. In December 1924, Woolf had predicted that "[t]he reviewers will say that it is disjointed because of the mad scenes not connecting with the Dalloway scenes."[9] A sense of two disjunctive narratives was not the predominant note among the early reviews. Reviewers praised Woolf's depiction of London, while an early reviewer complained about the lack of chapters: "we like to have places which we can dog-ear when we go to bed."[1] By and large, reviewers focused on the novel's participation in a modern experimental strain. Woolf's experimentation was the basis for the somewhat muted praise of the *Times Literary Supplement*, where the reviewer compares her single-day novel to James Joyce's *Ulysses*, noting that she "escapes disaster" but that ultimately "it remains experimental in so far as we are uncertain what more can be done with it." Other reviewers compared Woolf's novel to the work of Dorothy Richardson, May Sinclair, as well as James Joyce. This cautious sense that an experiment had reached its limits was characteristic of many early reviews.

As was her habit, Woolf noted sales, reviews, and the reactions of friends in her diary. The day after publication, she notes the jarring coincidence of "Two unfavourable reviews of Mrs D . . . & a letter from a young man in Earls Court"[2] lavishing praise. The success of *Mrs. Dalloway* and *The Common Reader* secured Woolf's stature as among the greatest of living novelists in Britain. It led to commissions for articles from British *Vogue* and it led *Vogue's* fashion editor, Madge Garland, to undertake the task of choosing clothes for Woolf. Winifred Holtby's celebratory and astute 1932 book-length study continued the comparisons to Proust and Joyce that begin with early reviews, but she distinguishes Woolf because of her intense engagement with Greek literature and her feminism. American Ruth Gruber completed a doctoral thesis on Virginia Woolf in Germany in 1935. As is true of Holtby's study, Gruber's *Virginia Woolf: The Will to Create as a Woman* has a strong feminist perspective. In her discussion of *Mrs. Dalloway*, she focuses on Woolf's interest in women's lives, her poetic prose, and her impressionistic, woman-centered depictions of time. The period just after *Mrs. Dalloway* also

---

9. *Diary*, vol. 2, p. 323.
1. See below, p. 313.
2. *Diary*, vol. 3, p. 21.

marks the beginning of Woolf's international reputation. A German translation by Theresia Mutzenbecher appeared in 1928. *Mrs. Dalloway* (translated by Andre Maurois) and *To the Lighthouse* (translated by Maurice Lanoire) were both published in French in 1929 and, by 1932, Woolf was the subject of a book-length study in French by Floris Delattre. Spanish translations came out of Argentina's Collecíon Sur, spurred by the feminist publisher Victoria Ocampo and including early translations by Jorge Luis Borges. At the time of Woolf's death, obituaries more commonly noted *The Waves* and *The Common Reader* as her masterpieces, and included *Mrs. Dalloway* among a list of her publications rather than as a favorite.

This Norton Critical Edition of *Mrs. Dalloway* was designed to spark your curiosity, whatever direction your interests take you. Included here are a rich selection of diary entries and letters related to the composition of the novel, essays, short stories, autobiographical excerpts, and the only introduction Woolf ever wrote to any of her novels. There is also a wide array of contextual material by other writers, including several literary passages that influenced her art. A selection of historical contexts includes material from Woolf's lifetime: an early medical study on the best method for treating shell shock (far more compassionate than any of the doctors in the novel) and the first appearance of the phrase "stream of consciousness" as applied to fiction. This section also includes more recent historical considerations of war trauma, the Armenian Genocide, the role of servants in the period, and the influenza pandemic of 1918.

The criticism selection includes several early reviews as well as more recent work. The latter selection, drawn from the abundant secondary material on *Mrs. Dalloway*, offers ways to think about some of the most important issues raised by the novel: women's narrow life options, how Woolf subtly shapes our view of characters through tone, a feminist reading of Clarissa's unhappiness, the cultural connotations of fashion (and unfashionable clothes) in the novel, and how the novel manifests ongoing cultural anxiety about war—both past and to come.

# A Note on the Text

*Mrs. Dalloway* was published in both the United States and England on May 14, 1925. This was the first of Woolf's novels to have simultaneous American and English publication, a sign of Woolf's growing international reputation. All of her subsequent books would have simultaneous publication. The text of this edition follows the first American edition. While there are over four hundred differences between the two versions, most of these are so small as to be nearly undetectable: a missing comma, a spelling variant. The most significant difference lies in the section breaks: there are more in the English edition. Most notably, the English edition has a section break toward the novel's end where the American edition has, instead, the sentence "He made her feel the beauty; made her feel the fun."

Following prior editors, throughout the excerpts from her diaries and letters, I have preserved Woolf's original spelling and punctuation. It was often slapdash, with liberal use of "&" for "and" and lots of long dashes, and to regularize it would lose some of the energy at the heart of this more private writing.

# Acknowledgments

I have been living with *Mrs. Dalloway* for a long time. This novel, about an ordinary woman with a gift of gathering people, continues to work its magic, bringing many lovely and intelligent people to my life. I owe a debt of tremendous gratitude to Jane Goldman and Susan Sellers, series editors, and to Ray Ryan of Cambridge University Press. For them, I edited a textual edition of *Mrs. Dalloway*. I drew upon what I learned in the years of preparing that edition to prepare this one.

The community of Woolf's scholars and feminist modernists worldwide has been a source of inspiration and learning for decades. For sustaining conversation, brilliant advice, and laughter, I thank in particular Melissa Bradshaw, Jane Garrity, Tamar Katz, Celia Marshik, Allison Pease, and Julie Vandivere.

Every day I am grateful for my students at Fordham University. In the preparation of this edition, I am especially grateful to my students in the Fall 2019 section of my Virginia Woolf class, who enthusiastically and patiently shared all their questions, helping me better understand what students everywhere might want to learn. I feel extraordinarily fortunate that one of those students, Hector Maccise, chose to do an independent study on *Mrs. Dalloway* with me. He worked tirelessly, with great enthusiasm and deep curiosity. During our many conversations about the novel, we weighed which literary and historical sources would be the most exciting for future students to encounter in this volume. Our conversations kept me inspired.

I am grateful to my editors at W. W. Norton, Carol Bemis and Rachel Goodman, for their patient guidance and their enthusiasm. I am continually impressed by and grateful for Norton books and thrilled to be working on one again.

My family continues to be a source of joy and sustenance. I thank my daughters, Olivia and Izzy, who fill me with pride and wonder every day. Their delight in language and their growing gift for making others feel at home in the world continue the best of both Woolf's gifts and Clarissa Dalloway's talents. My husband, Bill, is my rock and my beloved. I am grateful to him.

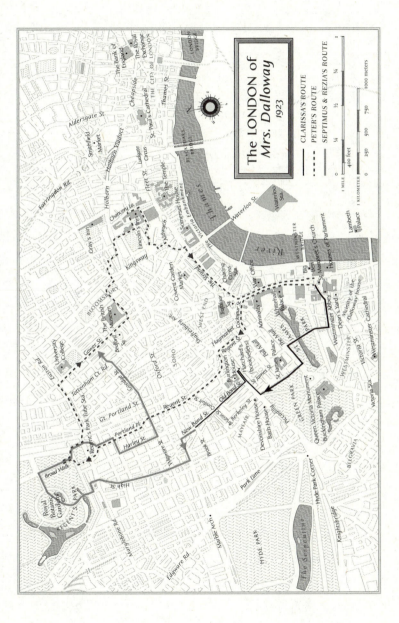

The LONDON of
*Mrs. Dalloway*
1923

CLARISSA'S ROUTE
PETER'S ROUTE
SEPTIMUS & REZIA'S ROUTE

# The Text of
# MRS. DALLOWAY

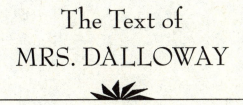

Mrs. Dalloway said she would buy the flowers herself.

For Lucy had her work cut out for her. The doors would be taken off their hinges; Rumpelmayer's men were coming. And then, thought Clarissa Dalloway, what a morning—fresh as if issued to children on a beach.

What a lark! What a plunge! For so it had always seemed to her, when, with a little squeak of the hinges, which she could hear now, she had burst open the French windows and plunged at Bourton into the open air. How fresh, how calm, stiller than this of course, the air was in the early morning; like the flap of a wave; the kiss of a wave; chill and sharp and yet (for a girl of eighteen as she then was) solemn, feeling as she did, standing there at the open window, that something awful was about to happen; looking at the flowers, at the trees with the smoke winding off them and the rooks rising, falling; standing and looking until Peter Walsh said, "Musing among the vegetables?"—was that it?—"I prefer men to cauliflowers"—was that it? He must have said it at breakfast one morning when she had gone out on to the terrace—Peter Walsh. He would be back from India[1] one of these days, June or July, she forgot which, for his letters were awfully dull; it was his sayings one remembered; his eyes, his pocket-knife, his smile, his grumpiness and, when millions of things had utterly vanished—how strange it was!—a few sayings like this about cabbages.

She stiffened a little on the kerb, waiting for Durtnall's van to pass. A charming woman, Scrope Purvis thought her (knowing her as one does know people who live next door to one in Westminster); a touch of the bird about her, of the jay, blue-green, light, vivacious, though she was over fifty, and grown very white since her illness. There she perched, never seeing him, waiting to cross, very upright.

---

1. Peter works as a colonial administrator in India, which was an important British colony at the time, with a growing movement for independence during the 1920s; India gained its independence in 1947.

3

For having lived in Westminster—how many years now? over
twenty,—one feels even in the midst of the traffic, or waking at
night, Clarissa was positive, a particular hush, or solemnity; an
indescribable pause; a suspense (but that might be her heart,
affected, they said, by influenza)[2] before Big Ben[3] strikes. There!
Out it boomed. First a warning, musical; then the hour, irrevocable. The leaden circles dissolved in the air. Such fools we are, she
thought, crossing Victoria Street. For Heaven only knows why one
loves it so, how one sees it so, making it up, building it round one,
tumbling it, creating it every moment afresh; but the veriest
frumps, the most dejected of miseries sitting on doorsteps (drink
their downfall) do the same; can't be dealt with, she felt positive,
by Acts of Parliament for that very reason: they love life. In people's
eyes, in the swing, tramp, and trudge; in the bellow and the uproar;
the carriages, motor cars, omnibuses, vans, sandwich men[4] shuffling and swinging; brass bands; barrel organs; in the triumph and
the jingle and the strange high singing of some aeroplane overhead
was what she loved; life; London; this moment of June.

For it was the middle of June.[5] The War was over, except for some
one like Mrs. Foxcroft at the Embassy last night eating her heart
out because that nice boy was killed and now the old Manor House
must go to a cousin; or Lady Bexborough who opened a bazaar,[6]
they said, with the telegram in her hand, John, her favourite, killed;
but it was over; thank Heaven—over. It was June. The King and
Queen were at the Palace.[7] And everywhere, though it was still so
early, there was a beating, a stirring of galloping ponies, tapping of
cricket bats; Lords, Ascot, Ranelagh[8] and all the rest of it; wrapped

2. The 1918 influenza pandemic killed 228,917 Britons and more than 20 million people
   worldwide. A severe case of influenza can turn hair permanently white; it can also
   damage the heart, as it seems to have done in Clarissa's case. See Outka, 301–09.
3. The nickname for the bell, and by extension the clock, within the clock tower of the
   Houses of Parliament. The clock tower rises above Westminster Palace, which contains the Houses of Parliament. From December 31, 1923, onward, Big Ben's chime
   was broadcast over the radio to mark the hour. The tolling of bells was the common
   way to mark the beginning of the moments of silence, first observed at 11:00 A.M. on
   Armistice Day, November 11, 1919. Woolf takes care that we hear the clocks chime
   "eleven times" (16).
4. That is, men wearing "sandwich boards" or large advertising placards around their
   necks, front and back, like walking easels.
5. In June of 1923, World War I had been over for more than four years. Active fighting
   ceased on Armistice Day, November 11, 1918, and the Treaty of Versailles had been
   signed on June 28, 1919; thus the novel takes place about a week before that anniversary. Later, Peter thinks "those five years—1918 to 1923—had been, he suspected,
   somehow very important" (51).
6. That is, a fundraiser for a parish church or a village hall. Bazaars usually include some
   combination of food and used goods for sale and games. Opening a bazaar was an
   appropriate public activity for an aristocratic woman.
7. A flag flying over a royal palace, such as Buckingham Palace in this case, indicated the
   King and Queen's presence there.
8. Most likely refers to the Hurlingham Club, a polo grounds in London; Lord's (Woolf
   left out the apostrophe): a cricket ground in the north of London; Ascot: a horse-racing

in the soft mesh of the grey-blue morning air, which, as the day wore on, would unwind them, and set down on their lawns and pitches the bouncing ponies, whose forefeet just struck the ground and up they sprung, the whirling young men, and laughing girls in their transparent muslins who, even now, after dancing all night, were taking their absurd woolly dogs for a run; and even now, at this hour, discreet old dowagers were shooting out in their motor cars on errands of mystery; and the shopkeepers were fidgeting in their windows with their paste and diamonds, their lovely old sea-green brooches in eighteenth-century settings to tempt Americans (but one must economise, not buy things rashly for Elizabeth), and she, too, loving it as she did with an absurd and faithful passion, being part of it, since her people were courtiers once in the time of the Georges,[9] she, too, was going that very night to kindle and illu-minate; to give her party. But how strange, on entering the Park, the silence; the mist; the hum; the slow-swimming happy ducks; the pouched birds waddling; and who should be coming along with his back against the Government buildings, most appropriately, carrying a despatch box[1] stamped with the Royal Arms, who but Hugh Whitbread; her old friend Hugh—the admirable Hugh!

"Good-morning to you, Clarissa!" said Hugh, rather extrava-gantly, for they had known each other as children. "Where are you off to?"

"I love walking in London," said Mrs. Dalloway. "Really it's better than walking in the country."

They had just come up—unfortunately—to see doctors. Other people came to see pictures; go to the opera; take their daughters out; the Whitbreads came "to see doctors." Times without number Clarissa had visited Evelyn Whitbread in a nursing home. Was Eve-lyn ill again? Evelyn was a good deal out of sorts, said Hugh, inti-mating by a kind of pout or swell of his very well-covered, manly, extremely handsome, perfectly upholstered body (he was almost too well dressed always, but presumably had to be, with his little job at Court) that his wife had some internal ailment, nothing seri-ous, which, as an old friend, Clarissa Dalloway would quite under-stand without requiring him to specify. Ah yes, she did of course; what a nuisance; and felt very sisterly and oddly conscious at the same time of her hat. Not the right hat for the early morning, was that it? For Hugh always made her feel, as he bustled on, raising his

---

course. Polo, cricket, and horse-racing are all common summer sports in England. Woolf went to see a polo match while writing *Mrs. Dalloway*.

9. That is, any time during the reigns of the British kings George I–IV (1714–1830).

1. A large boxy, leather briefcase for transporting files, used by lawyers and government officials. As Hugh works at the Palace, his would have the King's Coat of Arms embossed on it.

hat rather extravagantly and assuring her that she might be a girl of eighteen, and of course he was coming to her party to-night, Evelyn absolutely insisted, only a little late he might be after the party at the Palace to which he had to take one of Jim's boys,—she always felt a little skimpy beside Hugh; schoolgirlish; but attached to him, partly from having known him always, but she did think him a good sort in his own way, though Richard was nearly driven mad by him, and as for Peter Walsh, he had never to this day forgiven her for liking him.

She could remember scene after scene at Bourton—Peter furious; Hugh not, of course, his match in any way, but still not a positive imbecile as Peter made out; not a mere barber's block. When his old mother wanted him to give up shooting or to take her to Bath he did it, without a word; he was really unselfish, and as for saying, as Peter did, that he had no heart, no brain, nothing but the manners and breeding of an English gentleman, that was only her dear Peter at his worst; and he could be intolerable; he could be impossible; but adorable to walk with on a morning like this.

(June had drawn out every leaf on the trees. The mothers of Pimlico gave suck to their young. Messages were passing from the Fleet to the Admiralty. Arlington Street and Piccadilly seemed to chafe the very air in the Park and lift its leaves hotly, brilliantly, on waves of that divine vitality which Clarissa loved. To dance, to ride, she had adored all that.)

For they might be parted for hundreds of years, she and Peter; she never wrote a letter and his were dry sticks; but suddenly it would come over her, If he were with me now what would he say?—some days, some sights bringing him back to her calmly, without the old bitterness; which perhaps was the reward of having cared for people; they came back in the middle of St. James's Park on a fine morning—indeed they did. But Peter—however beautiful the day might be, and the trees and the grass, and the little girl in pink—Peter never saw a thing of all that. He would put on his spectacles, if she told him to; he would look. It was the state of the world that interested him; Wagner, Pope's poetry,[2] people's characters eternally, and the defects of her own soul. How he scolded her! How they argued! She would marry a Prime Minister and stand at the top of a staircase; the perfect hostess he called her (she had cried over it in her bedroom), she had the makings of the perfect hostess, he said.

So she would still find herself arguing in St. James's Park, still making out that she had been right—and she had too—not to marry him. For in marriage a little licence, a little independence there must be between people living together day in day out in the

---

2. Richard Wagner (1813–1883), German composer noted for his operas. Alexander Pope (1688–1744), English poet and satirist, author of "The Rape of the Lock" (see p. 233).

same house; which Richard gave her, and she him. (Where was he this morning for instance? Some committee, she never asked what.) But with Peter everything had to be shared; everything gone into. And it was intolerable, and when it came to that scene in the little garden by the fountain, she had to break with him or they would have been destroyed, both of them ruined, she was convinced; though she had borne about with her for years like an arrow sticking in her heart the grief, the anguish; and then the horror of the moment when some one told her at a concert that he had married a woman met on the boat going to India! Never should she forget all that! Cold, heartless, a prude, he called her. Never could she understand how he cared. But those Indian women[3] did presumably—silly, pretty, flimsy nincompoops. And she wasted her pity. For he was quite happy, he assured her—perfectly happy, though he had never done a thing that they talked of; his whole life had been a failure. It made her angry still.

She had reached the Park gates. She stood for a moment, looking at the omnibuses in Piccadilly.

She would not say of any one in the world now that they were this or were that. She felt very young; at the same time unspeakably aged. She sliced like a knife through everything; at the same time was outside, looking on. She had a perpetual sense, as she watched the taxi cabs, of being out, out, far out to sea and alone; she always had the feeling that it was very, very dangerous to live even one day. Not that she thought herself clever, or much out of the ordinary. How she had got through life on the few twigs of knowledge Fräulein Daniels gave them she could not think. She knew nothing; no language, no history; she scarcely read a book now, except memoirs in bed; and yet to her it was absolutely absorbing; all this; the cabs passing; and she would not say of Peter, she would not say of herself, I am this, I am that.

Her only gift was knowing people almost by instinct, she thought, walking on. If you put her in a room with some one, up went her back like a cat's; or she purred. Devonshire House, Bath House, the house with the china cockatoo,[4] she had seen them all lit up once; and remembered Sylvia, Fred, Sally Seton—such hosts of people; and dancing all night; and the waggons plodding past to market; and driving home across the Park. She remembered once throwing a shilling into the Serpentine. But every one remembered; what she loved was this, here, now, in front of her; the fat lady in the cab. Did it matter then, she asked herself, walking towards Bond Street,

---

3. That is, British (and therefore, at this time, white) women living in India, often as wives of soldiers or colonial administrators.
4. Each a grand private house and the setting for high-society parties, all on or near Clarissa's route east on Piccadilly.

did it matter that she must inevitably cease completely; all this must go on without her; did she resent it; or did it not become consoling to believe that death ended absolutely? but that somehow in the streets of London, on the ebb and flow of things, here, there, she survived, Peter survived, lived in each other, she being part, she was positive, of the trees at home; of the house there, ugly, rambling all to bits and pieces as it was; part of people she had never met; being laid out like a mist between the people she knew best, who lifted her on their branches as she had seen the trees lift the mist, but it spread ever so far, her life, herself. But what was she dreaming as she looked into Hatchards' shop window? What was she trying to recover? What image of white dawn in the country, as she read in the book spread open:

> Fear no more the heat o' the sun
> Nor the furious winter's rages.[5]

This late age of the world's experience had bred in them all, all men and women, a well of tears. Tears and sorrows; courage and endurance; a perfectly upright and stoical bearing. Think, for example, of the woman she admired most, Lady Bexborough, opening the bazaar.

There were Jorrocks' *Jaunts and Jollities*; there were *Soapy Sponge* and Mrs. Asquith's *Memoirs* and *Big Game Shooting in Nigeria*,[6] all spread open. Ever so many books there were; but none that seemed exactly right to take to Evelyn Whitbread in her nursing home. Nothing that would serve to amuse her and make that indescribably dried-up little woman look, as Clarissa came in, just for a moment cordial; before they settled down for the usual interminable talk of women's ailments. How much she wanted it—that people should look pleased as she came in, Clarissa thought and turned and walked back towards Bond Street, annoyed, because it was silly to have other reasons for doing things. Much rather would she have been one of those people like Richard who did things for themselves, whereas, she thought, waiting to cross, half the time she did things not simply, not for themselves; but to make people think this or that; perfect idiocy she knew (and now the policeman held up his

5. Beginning of the song in Shakespeare's *Cymbeline* (see pp. 232–33) and the first of five allusions to this song in the novel (see also pp. 22, 29, 99, and 131).
6. All books that might have been in the window of Hatchard's bookshop in 1923. (Woolf misplaced the apostrophe.) *Jorrocks' Jaunts and Jollities* (1838) is the best known of Robert Smith Surtees' comic novels of English sporting life; *Soapy Sponge* (i.e., *Mr Sponge's Sporting Tour*, 1853), is a later novel of the same type. Mrs. Asquith was Emma Alice Margaret, Countess of Oxford and Asquith, née Tennant (1864–1945), the second wife of former prime minister Herbert Henry Asquith (Liberal, in office 1908–16). Woolf met her. Her *Autobiography* was published in 1920 and 1922. *Big Game Shooting in Nigeria* is an invented title, but is in keeping with the other hunting, sporting, and society books in Hatchard's window.

hand) for no one was ever for a second taken in. Oh if she could have had her life over again! she thought, stepping on to the pavement, could have looked even differently!

She would have been, in the first place, dark like Lady Bexborough, with a skin of crumpled leather and beautiful eyes. She would have been, like Lady Bexborough, slow and stately; rather large; interested in politics like a man; with a country house; very dignified, very sincere. Instead of which she had a narrow pea-stick figure; a ridiculous little face, beaked like a bird's. That she held herself well was true; and had nice hands and feet; and dressed well, considering that she spent little. But often now this body she wore (she stopped to look at a Dutch picture), this body, with all its capacities, seemed nothing—nothing at all. She had the oddest sense of being herself invisible; unseen; unknown; there being no more marrying, no more having of children now, but only this astonishing and rather solemn progress with the rest of them, up Bond Street, this being Mrs. Dalloway; not even Clarissa any more; this being Mrs. Richard Dalloway.

Bond Street fascinated her; Bond Street early in the morning in the season; its flags flying; its shops; no splash; no glitter; one roll of tweed in the shop where her father had bought his suits for fifty years; a few pearls; salmon on an iceblock.

"That is all," she said, looking at the fishmonger's. "That is all," she repeated, pausing for a moment at the window of a glove shop where, before the War, you could buy almost perfect gloves. And her old Uncle William used to say a lady is known by her shoes and her gloves. He had turned on his bed one morning in the middle of the War. He had said, "I have had enough." Gloves and shoes; she had a passion for gloves; but her own daughter, her Elizabeth, cared not a straw for either of them.

Not a straw, she thought, going on up Bond Street to a shop where they kept flowers for her when she gave a party. Elizabeth really cared for her dog most of all. The whole house this morning smelt of tar. Still, better poor Grizzle than Miss Kilman; better distemper and tar and all the rest of it than sitting mewed in a stuffy bedroom with a prayer book! Better anything, she was inclined to say. But it might be only a phase, as Richard said, such as all girls go through. It might be falling in love. But why with Miss Kilman? who had been badly treated of course; one must make allowances for that, and Richard said she was very able, had a really historical mind. Anyhow they were inseparable, and Elizabeth, her own daughter, went to Communion; and how she dressed, how she treated people who came to lunch she did not care a bit, it being her experience that the religious ecstasy made people callous (so did causes); dulled their feelings, for Miss Kilman would do anything for the Russians, starved herself for the Austrians,[7] but in private inflicted positive torture, so insensitive was she, dressed in a green mackintosh coat. Year in year out she wore that coat; she perspired; she was never in the room five minutes without making you feel her superiority, your inferiority; how poor she was; how rich you were; how she lived in a slum without a cushion or a bed or a rug or whatever it might be, all her soul rusted with that grievance sticking in it, her dismissal from school during the War—poor embittered unfortunate creature! For it was not her one hated but the idea of her, which undoubtedly had gathered in to itself a great deal that was not Miss Kilman; had become one of those spectres with which one battles in the night; one of those spectres who stand astride us and suck up half our life-blood, dominators and tyrants; for no doubt with another throw of the dice, had the black been uppermost and not the white, she would have loved Miss Kilman! But not in this world. No.

It rasped her, though, to have stirring about in her this brutal monster! to hear twigs cracking and feel hooves planted down in the depths of that leaf-encumbered forest, the soul; never to be content quite, or quite secure, for at any moment the brute would be stirring, this hatred, which, especially since her illness, had power to make her feel scraped, hurt in her spine; gave her physical pain, and made all pleasure in beauty, in friendship, in being well, in being loved and making her home delightful rock, quiver, and bend as if indeed there were a monster grubbing at the roots, as if the whole panoply of content were nothing but self love! this hatred!

Nonsense, nonsense! she cried to herself, pushing through the swing doors of Mulberry's the florists.

She advanced, light, tall, very upright, to be greeted at once by button-faced Miss Pym, whose hands were always bright red, as if they had been stood in cold water with the flowers.

There were flowers: delphiniums, sweet peas, bunches of lilac; and carnations, masses of carnations. There were roses; there were irises. Ah yes—so she breathed in the earthy garden sweet smell as she stood talking to Miss Pym who owed her help, and thought her kind, for kind she had been years ago; very kind, but she looked older, this year, turning her head from side to side among the irises and roses and nodding tufts of lilac with her eyes half closed, snuffing in, after the street uproar, the delicious scent, the exquisite coolness. And then, opening her eyes, how fresh like frilled linen clean from a laundry laid in wicker trays the roses looked; and dark

---

7. Both Russia and Austria were experiencing economic hardship following, respectively, the Russian Revolution of 1917; the Russian Civil War, which ensued (1918–22); and the breakup of the Austro-Hungarian Empire after its defeat in World War I.

and prim the red carnations, holding their heads up; and all the sweet peas spreading in their bowls, tinged violet, snow white, pale—as if it were the evening and girls in muslin frocks came out to pick sweet peas and roses after the superb summer's day, with its almost blue-black sky, its delphiniums, its carnations, its arum lilies was over; and it was the moment between six and seven when every flower—roses, carnations, irises, lilac—glows; white, violet, red, deep orange; every flower seems to burn by itself, softly, purely in the misty beds; and how she loved the grey-white moths spinning in and out, over the cherry pie, over the evening primroses!

And as she began to go with Miss Pym from jar to jar, choosing, nonsense, nonsense, she said to herself, more and more gently, as if this beauty, this scent, this colour, and Miss Pym liking her, trusting her, were a wave which she let flow over her and surmount that hatred, that monster, surmount it all; and it lifted her up and up when—oh! a pistol shot in the street outside!

"Dear, those motor cars," said Miss Pym, going to the window to look, and coming back and smiling apologetically with her hands full of sweet peas, as if those motor cars, those tyres of motor cars, were all *her* fault.

The violent explosion which made Mrs. Dalloway jump and Miss Pym go to the window and apologise came from a motor car which had drawn to the side of the pavement precisely opposite Mulberry's shop window. Passers-by who, of course, stopped and stared, had just time to see a face of the very greatest importance against the dove-grey upholstery, before a male hand drew the blind and there was nothing to be seen except a square of dove grey.

Yet rumours were at once in circulation from the middle of Bond Street to Oxford Street on one side, to Atkinson's scent shop on the other, passing invisibly, inaudibly, like a cloud, swift, veil-like upon hills, falling indeed with something of a cloud's sudden sobriety and stillness upon faces which a second before had been utterly disorderly. But now mystery had brushed them with her wing; they had heard the voice of authority; the spirit of religion was abroad with her eyes bandaged tight and her lips gaping wide. But nobody knew whose face had been seen. Was it the Prince of Wales's, the Queen's, the Prime Minister's? Whose face was it? Nobody knew.

Edgar J. Watkiss, with his roll of lead piping round his arm, said audibly, humorously of course: "The Proime Minister's kyar."

Septimus Warren Smith, who found himself unable to pass, heard him.

Septimus Warren Smith, aged about thirty, pale-faced, beak-nosed, wearing brown shoes and a shabby overcoat, with hazel eyes which had that look of apprehension in them which makes complete strangers apprehensive too. The world has raised its whip; where will it descend?

Everything had come to a standstill. The throb of the motor engines sounded like a pulse irregularly drumming through an entire body. The sun became extraordinarily hot because the motor car had stopped outside Mulberry's shop window; old ladies on the tops of omnibuses spread their black parasols; here a green, here a red parasol opened with a little pop. Mrs. Dalloway, coming to the window with her arms full of sweet peas, looked out with her little pink face pursed in enquiry. Every one looked at the motor car. Septimus looked. Boys on bicycles sprang off. Traffic accumulated. And there the motor car stood, with drawn blinds, and upon them a curious pattern like a tree, Septimus thought, and this gradual drawing together of everything to one centre before his eyes, as if some horror had come almost to the surface and was about to burst into flames, terrified him. The world wavered and quivered and threatened to burst into flames. It is I who am blocking the way, he thought. Was he not being looked at and pointed at; was he not weighted there, rooted to the pavement, for a purpose? But for what purpose?

"Let us go on, Septimus," said his wife, a little woman, with large eyes in a sallow pointed face; an Italian girl.

But Lucrezia herself could not help looking at the motor car and the tree pattern on the blinds. Was it the Queen in there—the Queen going shopping?

The chauffeur, who had been opening something, turning something, shutting something, got on to the box.

"Come on," said Lucrezia.

But her husband, for they had been married four, five years now, jumped, started, and said, "All right!" angrily, as if she had interrupted him.

People must notice; people must see. People, she thought, looking at the crowd staring at the motor car; the English people, with their children and their horses and their clothes, which she admired in a way; but they were "people" now, because Septimus had said, "I will kill myself"; an awful thing to say. Suppose they had heard him? She looked at the crowd. Help, help! she wanted to cry out to butchers' boys and women. Help! Only last autumn she and Septimus had stood on the Embankment wrapped in the same cloak and, Septimus reading a paper instead of talking, she had snatched it from him and laughed in the old man's face who saw them! But failure one conceals. She must take him away into some park.

"Now we will cross," she said.

She had a right to his arm, though it was without feeling. He would give her, who was so simple, so impulsive, only twenty-four, without friends in England, who had left Italy for his sake, a piece of bone.

The motor car with its blinds drawn and an air of inscrutable reserve proceeded towards Piccadilly, still gazed at, still ruffling the faces on both sides of the street with the same dark breath of veneration whether for Queen, Prince, or Prime Minister nobody knew. The face itself had been seen only once by three people for a few seconds. Even the sex was now in dispute. But there could be no doubt that greatness was seated within; greatness was passing, hidden, down Bond Street, removed only by a hand's-breadth from ordinary people who might now, for the first and last time, be within speaking distance of the majesty of England, of the enduring symbol of the state which will be known to curious antiquaries, sifting the ruins of time, when London is a grass-grown path and all those hurrying along the pavement this Wednesday morning are but bones with a few wedding rings mixed up in their dust and the gold stoppings of innumerable decayed teeth. The face in the motor car will then be known.

It is probably the Queen, thought Mrs. Dalloway, coming out of Mulberry's with her flowers; the Queen. And for a second she wore a look of extreme dignity standing by the flower shop in the sunlight while the car passed at a foot's pace, with its blinds drawn. The Queen going to some hospital; the Queen opening some bazaar, thought Clarissa.

The crush was terrific for the time of day. Lords, Ascot, Hurlingham, what was it? she wondered, for the street was blocked. The British middle classes sitting sideways on the tops of omnibuses with parcels and umbrellas, yes, even furs on a day like this, were, she thought, more ridiculous, more unlike anything there has ever been than one could conceive; and the Queen herself held up; the Queen herself unable to pass. Clarissa was suspended on one side of Brook Street; Sir John Buckhurst, the old Judge on the other, with the car between them (Sir John had laid down the law for years and liked a well-dressed woman) when the chauffeur, leaning ever so slightly, said or showed something to the policeman, who saluted and raised his arm and jerked his head and moved the omnibus to the side and the car passed through. Slowly and very silently it took its way.

Clarissa guessed; Clarissa knew of course; she had seen something white, magical, circular,[8] in the footman's hand, a disc inscribed with a name,—the Queen's, the Prince of Wales's, the Prime Minister's?—which, by force of its own lustre, burnt its way

8. Likely a kind of pass that would permit the holder to move quickly through stalled traffic.

through (Clarissa saw the car diminishing, disappearing), to blaze among candelabras, glittering stars, breasts stiff with oak leaves, Hugh Whitbread and all his colleagues, the gentlemen of England, that night in Buckingham Palace. And Clarissa, too, gave a party. She stiffened a little; so she would stand at the top of her stairs.

The car had gone, but it had left a slight ripple which flowed through glove shops and hat shops and tailors' shops on both sides of Bond Street. For thirty seconds all heads were inclined the same way—to the window. Choosing a pair of gloves—should they be to the elbow or above it, lemon or pale grey?—ladies stopped; when the sentence was finished something had happened. Something so trifling in single instances that no mathematical instrument, though capable of transmitting shocks in China, could register the vibration; yet in its fulness rather formidable and in its common appeal emotional; for in all the hat shops and tailors' shops strangers looked at each other and thought of the dead; of the flag; of Empire. In a public house in a back street a Colonial insulted the House of Windsor[9] which led to words, broken beer glasses, and a general shindy, which echoed strangely across the way in the ears of girls buying white underlinen threaded with pure white ribbon for their weddings. For the surface agitation of the passing car as it sunk grazed something very profound.

Gliding across Piccadilly, the car turned down St. James's Street. Tall men, men of robust physique, well-dressed men with their tail-coats and their white slips and their hair raked back who, for reasons difficult to discriminate, were standing in the bow window of Brooks's with their hands behind the tails of their coats, looking out, perceived instinctively that greatness was passing, and the pale light of the immortal presence fell upon them as it had fallen upon Clarissa Dalloway. At once they stood even straighter, and removed their hands, and seemed ready to attend their Sovereign, if need be, to the cannon's mouth, as their ancestors had done before them. The white busts and the little tables in the background covered with copies of the *Tatler* and syphons of soda water seemed to approve; seemed to indicate the flowing corn and the manor houses of England; and to return the frail hum of the motor wheels as the walls of a whispering gallery return a single voice expanded and made sonorous by the might of a whole cathedral. Shawled Moll Pratt with her flowers on the pavement wished the dear boy well (it

9. That is, someone from one of the colonies or former colonies of the British Empire makes an anti-monarchist remark. In this case, the colonial is likely from a majority-white settler colony such as Australia or Canada. The royal family assumed the name Windsor in 1917 by proclamation of King George V, whose lineage was German and whose family name had been Saxe-Coburg-Gotha. The change reflects the family's reaction to anti-German sentiment common in England during World War I.

was the Prince of Wales for certain) and would have tossed the
price of a pot of beer—a bunch of roses—into St. James's Street out
of sheer light-heartedness and contempt of poverty had she not
seen the constable's eye upon her, discouraging an old Irishwom-
an's loyalty.[1] The sentries at St. James's saluted; Queen Alexandra's
policeman approved.

A small crowd meanwhile had gathered at the gates of Buckingham Palace. Listlessly, yet confidently, poor people all of them, they
waited; looked at the Palace itself with the flag flying; at Victoria,
billowing on her mound, admired her shelves of running water, her
geraniums; singled out from the motor cars in the Mall first this
one, then that; bestowed emotion, vainly, upon commoners out for
a drive; recalled their tribute to keep it unspent while this car
passed and that; and all the time let rumour accumulate in their
veins and thrill the nerves in their thighs at the thought of Royalty
looking at them; the Queen bowing; the Prince saluting; at the
thought of the heavenly life divinely bestowed upon Kings; of the
equerries and deep curtsies; of the Queen's old doll's house; of
Princess Mary married to an Englishman, and the Prince—ah! the
Prince! who took wonderfully, they said, after old King Edward, but
was ever so much slimmer. The Prince lived at St. James's; but he
might come along in the morning to visit his mother.

So Sarah Bletchley said with her baby in her arms, tipping her
foot up and down as though she were by her own fender in Pimlico, but keeping her eyes on the Mall, while Emily Coates ranged
over the Palace windows and thought of the housemaids, the
innumerable housemaids, the bedrooms, the innumerable bedrooms. Joined by an elderly gentleman with an Aberdeen terrier,
by men without occupation, the crowd increased. Little Mr. Bowley, who had rooms in the Albany and was sealed with wax over
the deeper sources of life but could be unsealed suddenly, inap-
propriately, sentimentally, by this sort of thing—poor women
waiting to see the Queen go past—poor women, nice little
children, orphans, widows, the War—tut-tut—actually had tears
in his eyes. A breeze flaunting ever so warmly down the Mall
through the thin trees, past the bronze heroes, lifted some flag
flying in the British breast of Mr. Bowley and he raised his hat as
the car turned into the Mall and held it high as the car approached;
and let the poor mothers of Pimlico press close to him, and stood
very upright. The car came on.

1. Moll Pratt's continuing loyalty to the British Crown is anachronistic. The novel is set
   in 1923, a rocky period in Anglo-Irish relations, following the bloody Easter Rising
   against British rule (1916) and a bitter civil war. As a result of a 1921 treaty, the Irish
   Free State had dominion status in the British Commonwealth, while Northern Ireland
   remained part of Britain. This compromise outraged many Irish people.

Suddenly Mrs. Coates looked up into the sky. The sound of an aeroplane bored ominously into the ears of the crowd. There it was coming over the trees, letting out white smoke from behind, which curled and twisted, actually writing something! making letters in the sky![2] Every one looked up.

Dropping dead down the aeroplane soared straight up, curved in a loop, raced, sank, rose, and whatever it did, wherever it went, out fluttered behind it a thick ruffled bar of white smoke which curled and wreathed upon the sky in letters. But what letters? A C was it? an E, then an L? Only for a moment did they lie still; then they moved and melted and were rubbed out up in the sky, and the aeroplane shot further away and again, in a fresh space of sky, began writing a K, an E, a Y perhaps?

"Glaxo," said Mrs. Coates in a strained, awe-stricken voice, gazing straight up, and her baby, lying stiff and white in her arms, gazed straight up.

"Kreemo," murmured Mrs. Bletchley, like a sleep-walker. With his hat held out perfectly still in his hand, Mr. Bowley gazed straight up. All down the Mall people were standing and looking up into the sky. As they looked the whole world became perfectly silent, and a flight of gulls crossed the sky, first one gull leading, then another, and in this extraordinary silence and peace, in this pallor, in this purity, bells struck eleven times,[3] the sound fading up there among the gulls.

The aeroplane turned and raced and swooped exactly where it liked, swiftly, freely, like a skater—

"That's an E," said Mrs. Bletchley—or a dancer—

"It's toffee," murmured Mr. Bowley—(and the car went in at the gates and nobody looked at it), and shutting off the smoke, away and away it rushed, and the smoke faded and assembled itself round the broad white shapes of the clouds.

It had gone; it was behind the clouds. There was no sound. The clouds to which the letters E, G, or L had attached themselves moved freely, as if destined to cross from West to East on a mission of the greatest importance which would never be revealed, and yet certainly so it was—a mission of the greatest importance. Then suddenly, as a train comes out of a tunnel, the aeroplane rushed out of the clouds again, the sound boring into the ears of all people in the Mall, in the Green Park, in Piccadilly, in Regent Street, in Regent's Park, and the bar of smoke curved behind and it dropped

---

2. The first-ever demonstration of skywriting occurred over London in 1922. This is likely the first description of it in fiction.
3. On November 11, 1919, the government introduced the two-minute silence at 11:00 A.M. to commemorate the first anniversary of the Armistice. Church bells commonly signaled the start of the silence.

down, and it soared up and wrote one letter after another—but what word was it writing?

Lucrezia Warren Smith, sitting by her husband's side on a seat in Regent's Park in the Broad Walk, looked up.

"Look, look, Septimus!" she cried. For Dr. Holmes had told her to make her husband (who had nothing whatever seriously the matter with him but was a little out of sorts) take an interest in things outside himself.

So, thought Septimus, looking up, they are signalling to me. Not indeed in actual words; that is, he could not read the language yet; but it was plain enough, this beauty, this exquisite beauty, and tears filled his eyes as he looked at the smoke words languishing and melting in the sky and bestowing upon him in their inexhaustible charity and laughing goodness one shape after another of unimaginable beauty and signalling their intention to provide him, for nothing, for ever, for looking merely, with beauty, more beauty! Tears ran down his cheeks.

It was toffee; they were advertising toffee, a nursemaid told Rezia. Together they began to spell t . . . o . . . f . . .

"K . . . R . . ." said the nursemaid, and Septimus heard her say "Kay Arr" close to his ear, deeply, softly, like a mellow organ, but with a roughness in her voice like a grasshopper's, which rasped his spine deliciously and sent running up into his brain waves of sound which, concussing, broke. A marvellous discovery indeed—that the human voice in certain atmospheric conditions (for one must be scientific, above all scientific) can quicken trees into life! Happily Rezia put her hand with a tremendous weight on his knee so that he was weighted down, transfixed, or the excitement of the elm trees rising and falling, rising and falling with all their leaves alight and the colour thinning and thickening from blue to the green of a hollow wave, like plumes on horses' heads, feathers on ladies', so proudly they rose and fell, so superbly, would have sent him mad. But he would not go mad. He would shut his eyes; he would see no more.

But they beckoned; leaves were alive; trees were alive. And the leaves being connected by millions of fibres with his own body, there on the seat, fanned it up and down; when the branch stretched he, too, made that statement. The sparrows fluttering, rising, and falling in jagged fountains were part of the pattern; the white and blue, barred with black branches. Sounds made harmonies with premeditation; the spaces between them were as significant as the sounds. A child cried. Rightly far away a horn sounded. All taken together meant the birth of a new religion—

"Septimus!" said Rezia. He started violently. People must notice.

"I am going to walk to the fountain and back," she said.

For she could stand it no longer. Dr. Holmes might say there was nothing the matter. Far rather would she that he were dead! She could not sit beside him when he stared so and did not see her and made everything terrible; sky and tree, children playing, dragging carts, blowing whistles, falling down; all were terrible. And he would not kill himself; and she could tell no one. "Septimus has been working too hard"—that was all she could say to her own mother. To love makes one solitary, she thought. She could tell nobody, not even Septimus now, and looking back, she saw him sitting in his shabby overcoat alone, on the seat, hunched up, staring. And it was cowardly for a man to say he would kill himself, but Septimus had fought; he was brave; he was not Septimus now. She put on her lace collar. She put on her new hat and he never noticed; and he was happy without her. Nothing could make her happy without him! Nothing! He was selfish. So men are. For he was not ill. Dr. Holmes said there was nothing the matter with him. She spread her hand before her. Look! Her wedding ring slipped—she had grown so thin. It was she who suffered—but she had nobody to tell.

Far was Italy and the white houses and the room where her sisters sat making hats, and the streets crowded every evening with people walking, laughing out loud, not half alive like people here, huddled up in Bath chairs, looking at a few ugly flowers stuck in pots!

"For you should see the Milan gardens," she said aloud. But to whom?

There was nobody. Her words faded. So a rocket fades. Its sparks, having grazed their way into the night, surrender to it, dark descends, pours over the outlines of houses and towers; bleak hillsides soften and fall in. But though they are gone, the night is full of them; robbed of colour, blank of windows, they exist more ponderously, give out what the frank daylight fails to transmit—the trouble and suspense of things conglomerated there in the darkness; huddled together in the darkness; reft of the relief which dawn brings when, washing the walls white and grey, spotting each window-pane, lifting the mist from the fields, showing the red-brown cows peacefully grazing, all is once more decked out to the eye; exists again. I am alone; I am alone! she cried, by the fountain in Regent's Park (staring at the Indian and his cross), as perhaps at midnight, when all boundaries are lost, the country reverts to its ancient shape, as the Romans saw it, lying cloudy, when they landed, and the hills had no names and rivers wound they knew not where—such was her darkness; when suddenly, as if a shelf were shot forth and she stood on it, she said how she was his wife, married years ago in Milan, his wife, and would never, never tell that he was mad! Turning, the shelf fell; down, down she dropped. For

he was gone, she thought—gone, as he threatened, to kill himself—
to throw himself under a cart! But no; there he was; still sitting
alone on the seat, in his shabby overcoat, his legs crossed, staring,
talking aloud.

Men must not cut down trees. There is a God. (He noted such
revelations on the backs of envelopes.) Change the world. No one
kills from hatred. Make it known (he wrote it down). He waited. He
listened. A sparrow perched on the railing opposite chirped Septimus, Septimus, four or five times over and went on, drawing its
notes out, to sing freshly and piercingly in Greek words how there
is no crime and, joined by another sparrow, they sang in voices prolonged and piercing in Greek words, from trees in the meadow of
life beyond a river where the dead walk, how there is no death.

There was his hand; there the dead. White things were assembling behind the railings opposite. But he dared not look. Evans
was behind the railings!

"What are you saying?" said Rezia suddenly, sitting down by him.
Interrupted again! She was always interrupting.

Away from people—they must get away from people, he said
(jumping up), right away over there, where there were chairs
beneath a tree and the long slope of the park dipped like a length of
green stuff with a ceiling cloth of blue and pink smoke high above,
and there was a rampart of far irregular houses hazed in smoke, the
traffic hummed in a circle, and on the right, dun-coloured animals
stretched long necks over the Zoo palings, barking, howling. There
they sat down under a tree.

"Look," she implored him, pointing at a little troop of boys carrying cricket stumps, and one shuffled, spun round on his heel and
shuffled, as if he were acting a clown at the music hall.

"Look," she implored him, for Dr. Holmes had told her to make
him notice real things, go to a music hall, play cricket—that was
the very game, Dr. Holmes said, a nice out-of-door game, the very
game for her husband.

"Look," she repeated.

Look the unseen bade him, the voice which now communicated
with him who was the greatest of mankind, Septimus, lately taken
from life to death, the Lord who had come to renew society, who lay
like a coverlet, a snow blanket smitten only by the sun, for ever
unwasted, suffering for ever, the scapegoat, the eternal sufferer,
but he did not want it, he moaned, putting from him with a wave of
his hand that eternal suffering, that eternal loneliness.

"Look," she repeated, for he must not talk aloud to himself out of
doors.

"Oh look," she implored him. But what was there to look at? A
few sheep. That was all.

The way to Regent's Park Tube station—could they tell her the way to Regent's Park Tube station—Maisie Johnson wanted to know. She was only up from Edinburgh two days ago.

"Not this way—over there!" Rezia exclaimed, waving her aside, lest she should see Septimus.

Both seemed queer,[4] Maisie Johnson thought. Everything seemed very queer. In London for the first time, come to take up a post at her uncle's in Leadenhall Street, and now walking through Regent's Park in the morning, this couple on the chairs gave her quite a turn; the young woman seeming foreign, the man looking queer; so that should she be very old she would still remember and make it jangle again among her memories how she had walked through Regent's Park on a fine summer's morning fifty years ago. For she was only nineteen and had got her way at last, to come to London; and now how queer it was, this couple she had asked the way of, and the girl started and jerked her hand, and the man—he seemed awfully odd; quarrelling, perhaps; parting for ever, perhaps; something was up, she knew; and now all these people (for she returned to the Broad Walk), the stone basins, the prim flowers, the old men and women, invalids most of them in Bath chairs—all seemed, after Edinburgh, so queer. And Maisie Johnson, as she joined that gently trudging, vaguely gazing, breeze-kissed company—squirrels perching and preening, sparrow fountains fluttering for crumbs, dogs busy with the railings, busy with each other, while the soft warm air washed over them and lent to the fixed unsurprised gaze with which they received life something whimsical and mollified—Maisie Johnson positively felt she must cry Oh! (for that young man on the seat had given her quite a turn. Something was up, she knew.)

Horror! horror! she wanted to cry. (She had left her people; they had warned her what would happen.)

Why hadn't she stayed at home? she cried, twisting the knob of the iron railing.

That girl, thought Mrs. Dempster (who saved crusts for the squirrels and often ate her lunch in Regent's Park), don't know a thing yet; and really it seemed to her better to be a little stout, a little slack, a little moderate in one's expectations. Percy drank. Well, better to have a son, thought Mrs. Dempster. She had had a hard time of it, and couldn't help smiling at a girl like that. You'll get married, for you're pretty enough, thought Mrs. Dempster. Get

---

4. As a provincial young woman, Maisie is likely to be using *queer* in the sense of "odd" or "strange." However, during the War, *queer* was just beginning to be used as a pejorative term for homosexuality. The reappropriation of *queer* as a term of pride for gender nonconformity comes much later (c. 1980s). Maisie Johnson bears some similarity to H. G. Wells's heroine Ann Veronica (see pp. 235–37).

married, she thought, and then you'll know. Oh, the cooks, and so on. Every man has his ways. But whether I'd have chosen quite like that if I could have known, thought Mrs. Dempster, and could not help wishing to whisper a word to Maisie Johnson; to feel on the creased pouch of her worn old face the kiss of pity. For it's been a hard life, thought Mrs. Dempster. What hadn't she given to it? Roses; figure; her feet too. (She drew the knobbed lumps beneath her skirt.)

Roses, she thought sardonically. All trash, m'dear. For really, what with eating, drinking, and mating, the bad days and good, life had been no mere matter of roses, and what was more, let me tell you, Carrie Dempster had no wish to change her lot with any woman's in Kentish Town! But, she implored, pity. Pity, for the loss of roses. Pity she asked of Maisie Johnson, standing by the hyacinth beds.

Ah, but that aeroplane! Hadn't Mrs. Dempster always longed to see foreign parts? She had a nephew, a missionary. It soared and shot. She always went on the sea at Margate, not out o' sight of land, but she had no patience with women who were afraid of water. It swept and fell. Her stomach was in her mouth. Up again. There's a fine young feller aboard of it, Mrs. Dempster wagered, and away and away it went, fast and fading, away and away the aeroplane shot; soaring over Greenwich and all the masts; over the little island of grey churches, St. Paul's and the rest till, on either side of London, fields spread out and dark brown woods where adventurous thrushes hopping boldly, glancing quickly, snatched the snail and tapped him on a stone, once, twice, thrice.

Away and away the aeroplane shot, till it was nothing but a bright spark; an aspiration; a concentration; a symbol (so it seemed to Mr. Bentley, vigorously rolling his strip of turf at Greenwich) of man's soul; of his determination, thought Mr. Bentley, sweeping round the cedar tree, to get outside his body, beyond his house, by means of thought, Einstein, speculation, mathematics, the Mendelian theory—away the aeroplane shot.

Then, while a seedy-looking nondescript man carrying a leather bag stood on the steps of St. Paul's Cathedral, and hesitated, for within was what balm, how great a welcome, how many tombs with banners waving over them, tokens of victories not over armies, but over, he thought, that plaguy spirit of truth seeking which leaves me at present without a situation, and more than that, the cathedral offers company, he thought, invites you to membership of a society; great men belong to it; martyrs have died for it; why not enter in, he thought, put this leather bag stuffed with pamphlets before an altar, a cross, the symbol of something which has soared beyond seeking and questing and knocking of words together and

has become all spirit, disembodied, ghostly—why not enter in? he
thought and while he hesitated out flew the aeroplane over Ludgate
Circus.

It was strange; it was still. Not a sound was to be heard above the
traffic. Unguided it seemed; sped of its own free will. And now,
curving up and up, straight up, like something mounting in ecstasy,
in pure delight, out from behind poured white smoke looping, writing a T, an O, an F.

"What are they looking at?" said Clarissa Dalloway to the maid who
opened her door.

The hall of the house was cool as a vault. Mrs. Dalloway raised
her hand to her eyes, and, as the maid shut the door to, and she
heard the swish of Lucy's skirts, she felt like a nun who has left the
world and feels fold round her the familiar veils and the response to
old devotions. The cook whistled in the kitchen. She heard the
click of the typewriter. It was her life, and, bending her head over
the hall table, she bowed beneath the influence, felt blessed and
purified, saying to herself, as she took the pad with the telephone
message on it, how moments like this are buds on the tree of life,
flowers of darkness they are, she thought (as if some lovely rose had
blossomed for her eyes only); not for a moment did she believe in
God; but all the more, she thought, taking up the pad, must one
repay in daily life to servants, yes, to dogs and canaries, above all to
Richard her husband, who was the foundation of it—of the gay
sounds, of the green lights, of the cook even whistling, for
Mrs. Walker was Irish and whistled all day long—one must pay
back from this secret deposit of exquisite moments, she thought,
lifting the pad, while Lucy stood by her, trying to explain how

"Mr. Dalloway, ma'am"—

Clarissa read on the telephone pad, "Lady Bruton wishes to know
if Mr. Dalloway will lunch with her to-day."

"Mr. Dalloway, ma'am, told me to tell you he would be lunching
out."

"Dear!" said Clarissa, and Lucy shared as she meant her to her
disappointment (but not the pang); felt the concord between them;
took the hint; thought how the gentry love; gilded her own future
with calm; and, taking Mrs. Dalloway's parasol, handled it like a
sacred weapon which a Goddess, having acquitted herself honour-
ably in the field of battle, sheds, and placed it in the umbrella stand.

"Fear no more," said Clarissa. Fear no more the heat o' the sun;
for the shock of Lady Bruton asking Richard to lunch without her
made the moment in which she had stood shiver, as a plant on the
river-bed feels the shock of a passing oar and shivers: so she rocked:
so she shivered.

Millicent Bruton, whose lunch parties were said to be extraordinarily amusing, had not asked her. No vulgar jealousy could separate her from Richard. But she feared time itself, and read on Lady Bruton's face, as if it had been a dial cut in impassive stone, the dwindling of life; how year by year her share was sliced; how little the margin that remained was capable any longer of stretching, of absorbing, as in the youthful years, the colours, salts, tones of existence, so that she filled the room she entered, and felt often as she stood hesitating one moment on the threshold of her drawing-room, an exquisite suspense, such as might stay a diver before plunging while the sea darkens and brightens beneath him, and the waves which threaten to break, but only gently split their surface, roll and conceal and encrust as they just turn over the weeds with pearl.

She put the pad on the hall table. She began to go slowly upstairs, with her hand on the bannisters, as if she had left a party, where now this friend now that had flashed back her face, her voice; had shut the door and gone out and stood alone, a single figure against the appalling night, or rather, to be accurate, against the stare of this matter-of-fact June morning; soft with the glow of rose petals for some, she knew, and felt it, as she paused by the open staircase window which let in blinds flapping, dogs barking, let in, she thought, feeling herself suddenly shrivelled, aged, breastless, the grinding, blowing, flowering of the day, out of doors, out of the window, out of her body and brain which now failed, since Lady Bruton, whose lunch parties were said to be extraordinarily amusing, had not asked her.

Like a nun withdrawing, or a child exploring a tower, she went upstairs, paused at the window, came to the bathroom. There was the green linoleum and a tap dripping. There was an emptiness about the heart of life; an attic room. Women must put off their rich apparel. At midday they must disrobe. She pierced the pincushion and laid her feathered yellow hat on the bed. The sheets were clean, tight stretched in a broad white band from side to side. Narrower and narrower would her bed be. The candle was half burnt down and she had read deep in Baron Marbot's *Memoirs*. She had read late at night of the retreat from Moscow. For the House sat so long that Richard insisted, after her illness, that she must sleep undisturbed. And really she preferred to read of the retreat from Moscow. He knew it. So the room was an attic; the bed narrow; and lying there reading, for she slept badly, she could not dispel a virginity preserved through childbirth which clung to her like a sheet. Lovely in girlhood, suddenly there came a moment—for example on the river beneath the woods at Clieveden—when, through some contraction of this cold spirit, she had failed him. And then at Constantinople, and again and again. She could see what she lacked. It was not beauty; it was not mind. It was something central which

permeated; something warm which broke up surfaces and rippled the
cold contact of man and woman, or of women together. For *that* she
could dimly perceive. She resented it, had a scruple picked up Heaven
knows where, or, as she felt, sent by Nature (who is invariably wise);
yet she could not resist sometimes yielding to the charm of a woman,
not a girl, of a woman confessing, as to her they often did, some
scrape, some folly. And whether it was pity, or their beauty, or that she
was older, or some accident—like a faint scent, or a violin next door
(so strange is the power of sounds at certain moments), she did
undoubtedly then feel what men felt. Only for a moment; but it was
enough. It was a sudden revelation, a tinge like a blush which one
tried to check and then, as it spread, one yielded to its expansion, and
rushed to the farthest verge and there quivered and felt the world
come closer, swollen with some astonishing significance, some pressure of rapture, which split its thin skin and gushed and poured with
an extraordinary alleviation over the cracks and sores! Then, for that
moment, she had seen an illumination; a match burning in a crocus;
an inner meaning almost expressed. But the close withdrew; the hard
softened. It was over—the moment. Against such moments (with
women too) there contrasted (as she laid her hat down) the bed and
Baron Marbot and the candle half-burnt. Lying awake, the floor
creaked; the lit house was suddenly darkened, and if she raised her
head she could just hear the click of the handle released as gently as
possible by Richard, who slipped upstairs in his socks and then, as
often as not, dropped his hot-water bottle and swore! How she laughed!

But this question of love (she thought, putting her coat away),
this falling in love with women. Take Sally Seton; her relation in
the old days with Sally Seton. Had not that, after all, been love?

She sat on the floor—that was her first impression of Sally—she
sat on the floor with her arms round her knees, smoking a cigarette.
Where could it have been? The Mannings? The Kinloch-Jones's? At
some party (where, she could not be certain), for she had a distinct
recollection of saying to the man she was with, "Who is *that?*" And
he had told her, and said that Sally's parents did not get on (how
that shocked her—that one's parents should quarrel!). But all that
evening she could not take her eyes off Sally. It was an extraordinary beauty of the kind she most admired, dark, large-eyed, with
that quality which, since she hadn't got it herself, she always
envied—a sort of abandonment, as if she could say anything, do anything; a quality much commoner in foreigners than in Englishwomen.
Sally always said she had French blood in her veins, an ancestor had
been with Marie Antoinette,[5] had his head cut off, left a ruby ring.

5. Austrian-born queen of France (1755–1793), wife of King Louis XVI, known for her
extravagance, guillotined during the French Revolution.

Perhaps that summer she came to stay at Bourton, walking in quite unexpectedly without a penny in her pocket, one night after dinner, and upsetting poor Aunt Helena to such an extent that she never forgave her. There had been some quarrel at home. She literally hadn't a penny that night when she came to them—had pawned a brooch to come down. She had rushed off in a passion. They sat up till all hours of the night talking. Sally it was who made her feel, for the first time, how sheltered the life at Bourton was. She knew nothing about sex—nothing about social problems. She had once seen an old man who had dropped dead in a field—she had seen cows just after their calves were born. But Aunt Helena never liked discussion of anything (when Sally gave her William Morris,[6] it had to be wrapped in brown paper). There they sat, hour after hour, talking in her bedroom at the top of the house, talking about life, how they were to reform the world. They meant to found a society to abolish private property, and actually had a letter written, though not sent out. The ideas were Sally's, of course—but very soon she was just as excited—read Plato[7] in bed before breakfast; read Morris; read Shelley[8] by the hour.

Sally's power was amazing, her gift, her personality. There was her way with flowers, for instance. At Bourton they always had stiff little vases all the way down the table. Sally went out, picked hollyhocks, dahlias—all sorts of flowers that had never been seen together—cut their heads off, and made them swim on the top of water in bowls. The effect was extraordinary—coming in to dinner in the sunset. (Of course Aunt Helena thought it wicked to treat flowers like that.) Then she forgot her sponge, and ran along the passage naked. That grim old housemaid, Ellen Atkins, went about grumbling—"Suppose any of the gentlemen had seen?" Indeed she did shock people. She was untidy, Papa said.

The strange thing, on looking back, was the purity, the integrity, of her feeling for Sally. It was not like one's feeling for a man. It was completely disinterested, and besides, it had a quality which could only exist between women, between women just grown up. It was protective, on her side; sprang from a sense of being in league together, a presentiment of something that was bound to part them (they spoke of marriage always as a catastrophe), which led to this chivalry, this protective feeling which was much more on her side than Sally's. For in those days she was completely reckless; did the most idiotic things out of bravado; bicycled round the parapet on the terrace; smoked cigars. Absurd, she was—very absurd. But the

6. Poet and social activist (1834–1896).
7. Athenian philosopher (429–347 B.C.E.); saw the philosopher-ruler as humanity's best hope.
8. Percy Bysshe Shelley (1792–1822), poet, socialist, habitually unfaithful lover.

charm was overpowering, to her at least, so that she could remember standing in her bedroom at the top of the house holding the
hot-water can in her hands and saying aloud, "She is beneath this
roof. . . . She is beneath this roof!"

No, the words meant absolutely nothing to her now. She could
not even get an echo of her old emotion. But she could remember
going cold with excitement, and doing her hair in a kind of ecstasy
(now the old feeling began to come back to her, as she took out her
hairpins, laid them on the dressing-table, began to do her hair),
with the rooks flaunting up and down in the pink evening light, and
dressing, and going downstairs, and feeling as she crossed the hall
"if it were now to die 'twere now to be most happy."[9] That was her
feeling—Othello's feeling, and she felt it, she was convinced, as
strongly as Shakespeare meant Othello to feel it, all because she
was coming down to dinner in a white frock to meet Sally Seton!

She was wearing pink gauze—was that possible? She *seemed*,
anyhow, all light, glowing, like some bird or air ball that has flown
in, attached itself for a moment to a bramble. But nothing is so
strange when one is in love (and what was this except being in
love?) as the complete indifference of other people. Aunt Helena
just wandered off after dinner; Papa read the paper. Peter Walsh
might have been there, and old Miss Cummings; Joseph Breitkopf
certainly was, for he came every summer, poor old man, for weeks
and weeks, and pretended to read German with her, but really
played the piano and sang Brahms without any voice.

All this was only a background for Sally. She stood by the fire-
place talking, in that beautiful voice which made everything she
said sound like a caress, to Papa, who had begun to be attracted
rather against his will (he never got over lending her one of his
books and finding it soaked on the terrace), when suddenly she
said, "What a shame to sit indoors!" and they all went out on to the
terrace and walked up and down. Peter Walsh and Joseph Breitkopf
went on about Wagner. She and Sally fell a little behind. Then
came the most exquisite moment of her whole life passing a stone
urn with flowers in it. Sally stopped; picked a flower; kissed her on
the lips. The whole world might have turned upside down! The
others disappeared; there she was alone with Sally. And she felt
that she had been given a present, wrapped up, and told just to keep
it, not to look at it—a diamond, something infinitely precious,
wrapped up, which, as they walked (up and down, up and down),
she uncovered, or the radiance burnt through, the revelation, the
religious feeling!—when old Joseph and Peter faced them:

"Star-gazing?" said Peter.

---

9. Othello's words upon reuniting with Desdemona (see pp. 231–32).

It was like running one's face against a granite wall in the darkness! It was shocking; it was horrible!

Not for herself. She felt only how Sally was being mauled already, maltreated; she felt his hostility; his jealousy; his determination to break into their companionship. All this she saw as one sees a landscape in a flash of lightning—and Sally (never had she admired her so much!) gallantly taking her way unvanquished. She laughed. She made old Joseph tell her the names of the stars, which he liked doing very seriously. She stood there: she listened. She heard the names of the stars.

"Oh this horror!" she said to herself, as if she had known all along that something would interrupt, would embitter her moment of happiness.

Yet, after all, how much she owed to him later. Always when she thought of him she thought of their quarrels for some reason—because she wanted his good opinion so much, perhaps. She owed him words: "sentimental," "civilised"; they started up every day of her life as if he guarded her. A book was sentimental; an attitude to life sentimental. "Sentimental," perhaps she was to be thinking of the past. What would he think, she wondered, when he came back?

That she had grown older? Would he say that, or would she see him thinking when he came back, that she had grown older? It was true. Since her illness she had turned almost white.

Laying her brooch on the table, she had a sudden spasm, as if, while she mused, the icy claws had had the chance to fix in her. She was not old yet. She had just broken into her fifty-second year. Months and months of it were still untouched. June, July, August! Each still remained almost whole, and, as if to catch the falling drop, Clarissa (crossing to the dressing-table) plunged into the very heart of the moment, transfixed it, there—the moment of this June morning on which was the pressure of all the other mornings, seeing the glass, the dressing-table, and all the bottles afresh, collecting the whole of her at one point (as she looked into the glass), seeing the delicate pink face of the woman who was that very night to give a party; of Clarissa Dalloway; of herself.

How many million times she had seen her face, and always with the same imperceptible contraction! She pursed her lips when she looked in the glass. It was to give her face point. That was her self—pointed; dartlike; definite. That was her self when some effort, some call on her to be her self, drew the parts together, she alone knew how different, how incompatible and composed so for the world only into one centre, one diamond, one woman who sat in her drawing-room and made a meeting-point, a radiancy no doubt in some dull lives, a refuge for the lonely to come to, perhaps; she had helped young people, who were grateful to her; had tried to be the

same always, never showing a sign of all the other sides of her—
faults, jealousies, vanities, suspicions, like this of Lady Bruton not
asking her to lunch; which, she thought (combing her hair finally),
is utterly base! Now, where was her dress?

Her evening dresses hung in the cupboard. Clarissa, plunging her
hand into the softness, gently detached the green dress and carried it
to the window. She had torn it. Some one had trod on the skirt. She
had felt it give at the Embassy party at the top among the folds. By
artificial light the green shone, but lost its colour now in the sun. She
would mend it. Her maids had too much to do. She would wear it to-
night. She would take her silks, her scissors,[1] her—what was it?—her
thimble, of course, down into the drawing-room, for she must also
write, and see that things generally were more or less in order.

Strange, she thought, pausing on the landing, and assembling
that diamond shape, that single person, strange how a mistress
knows the very moment, the very temper of her house! Faint sounds
rose in spirals up the well of the stairs; the swish of a mop; tapping;
knocking; a loudness when the front door opened; a voice repeating
a message in the basement; the chink of silver on a tray; clean silver
for the party. All was for the party.

(And Lucy, coming into the drawing-room with her tray held out,
put the giant candlesticks on the mantelpiece, the silver casket in
the middle, turned the crystal dolphin towards the clock. They
would come; they would stand; they would talk in the mincing
tones which she could imitate, ladies and gentlemen. Of all, her
mistress was loveliest—mistress of silver, of linen, of china, for the
sun, the silver, doors off their hinges, Rumpelmayer's men, gave her
a sense, as she laid the paper-knife on the inlaid table, of something
achieved. Behold! Behold! she said, speaking to her old friends in
the baker's shop, where she had first seen service at Caterham, prying into the glass. She was Lady Angela, attending Princess Mary,
when in came Mrs. Dalloway.)

"Oh Lucy," she said, "the silver does look nice!"

"And how," she said, turning the crystal dolphin to stand straight,
"how did you enjoy the play last night?" "Oh, they had to go before
the end!" she said. "They had to be back at ten!" she said. "So they
don't know what happened," she said. "That does seem hard luck,"
she said (for her servants stayed later, if they asked her). "That does
seem rather a shame," she said, taking the old bald-looking cushion
in the middle of the sofa and putting it in Lucy's arms, and giving
her a little push, and crying:

1. Clarissa shares a name with the character who provides the scissors in Alexander
   Pope's *The Rape of the Lock* (1717) (see p. 233). These scenes of her in her dressing
   room also echo the opening lines of "The Game of Chess" section of T. S. Eliot's *The
   Waste Land* (see pp. 238–39).

"Take it away! Give it to Mrs. Walker with my compliments! Take it away!" she cried.

And Lucy stopped at the drawing-room door, holding the cushion, and said, very shyly, turning a little pink, Couldn't she help to mend that dress?

But, said Mrs. Dalloway, she had enough on her hands already, quite enough of her own to do without that.

"But, thank you, Lucy, oh, thank you," said Mrs. Dalloway, and thank you, thank you, she went on saying (sitting down on the sofa with her dress over her knees, her scissors, her silks), thank you, thank you, she went on saying in gratitude to her servants generally for helping her to be like this, to be what she wanted, gentle, generous-hearted. Her servants liked her. And then this dress of hers—where was the tear? and now her needle to be threaded. This was a favourite dress, one of Sally Parker's, the last almost she ever made, alas, for Sally had now retired, living at Ealing, and if ever I have a moment, thought Clarissa (but never would she have a moment any more), I shall go and see her at Ealing. For she was a character, thought Clarissa, a real artist. She thought of little out-of-the-way things; yet her dresses were never queer. You could wear them at Hatfield; at Buckingham Palace. She had worn them at Hatfield; at Buckingham Palace.

Quiet descended on her, calm, content, as her needle, drawing the silk smoothly to its gentle pause, collected the green folds together and attached them, very lightly, to the belt. So on a summer's day waves collect, overbalance, and fall; collect and fall; and the whole world seems to be saying "that is all" more and more ponderously, until even the heart in the body which lies in the sun on the beach says too, That is all. Fear no more, says the heart. Fear no more, says the heart, committing its burden to some sea, which sighs collectively for all sorrows, and renews, begins, collects, lets fall. And the body alone listens to the passing bee; the wave breaking; the dog barking, far away barking and barking.

"Heavens, the front-door bell!" exclaimed Clarissa, staying her needle. Roused, she listened.

"Mrs. Dalloway will see me," said the elderly man in the hall. "Oh yes, she will see *me*," he repeated, putting Lucy aside very benevolently, and running upstairs ever so quickly. "Yes, yes, yes," he muttered as he ran upstairs. "She will see me. After five years in India, Clarissa will see me."

"Who can—what can," asked Mrs. Dalloway (thinking it was outrageous to be interrupted at eleven o'clock on the morning of the day she was giving a party), hearing a step on the stairs. She heard a hand upon the door. She made to hide her dress, like a virgin protecting chastity, respecting privacy. Now the brass knob slipped.

Now the door opened, and in came—for a single second she could not remember what he was called! so surprised she was to see him, so glad, so shy, so utterly taken aback to have Peter Walsh come to her unexpectedly in the morning! (She had not read his letter.)

"And how are you?" said Peter Walsh, positively trembling; taking both her hands; kissing both her hands. She's grown older, he thought, sitting down. I shan't tell her anything about it, he thought, for she's grown older. She's looking at me, he thought, a sudden embarrassment coming over him, though he had kissed her hands. Putting his hand into his pocket, he took out a large pocket-knife and half opened the blade.

Exactly the same, thought Clarissa; the same queer look; the same check suit; a little out of the straight his face is, a little thinner, dryer, perhaps, but he looks awfully well, and just the same.

"How heavenly it is to see you again!" she exclaimed. He had his knife out. That's so like him, she thought.

He had only reached town last night, he said; would have to go down into the country at once; and how was everything, how was everybody—Richard? Elizabeth?

"And what's all this?" he said, tilting his penknife towards her green dress.

He's very well dressed, thought Clarissa; yet he always criticises *me*.

Here she is mending her dress; mending her dress as usual, he thought; here she's been sitting all the time I've been in India; mending her dress; playing about; going to parties; running to the House and back and all that, he thought, growing more and more irritated, more and more agitated, for there's nothing in the world so bad for some women as marriage, he thought; and politics; and having a Conservative husband, like the admirable Richard. So it is, so it is, he thought, shutting his knife with a snap.

"Richard's very well. Richard's at a Committee," said Clarissa.

And she opened her scissors, and said, did he mind her just finishing what she was doing to her dress, for they had a party that night?

"Which I shan't ask you to," she said. "My dear Peter!" she said.

But it was delicious to hear her say that—my dear Peter! Indeed, it was all so delicious—the silver, the chairs; all so delicious!

Why wouldn't she ask him to her party? he asked.

Now of course, thought Clarissa, he's enchanting! perfectly enchanting! Now I remember how impossible it was ever to make up my mind—and why did I make up my mind—not to marry him? She wondered, that awful summer?

"But it's so extraordinary that you should have come this morning!" she cried, putting her hands, one on top of another, down on her dress.

"Do you remember," she said, "how the blinds used to flap at Bourton?"

"They did," he said; and he remembered breakfasting alone, very awkwardly, with her father; who had died; and he had not written to Clarissa. But he had never got on well with old Parry, that querulous, weak-kneed old man, Clarissa's father, Justin Parry.

"I often wish I'd got on better with your father," he said.

"But he never liked any one who—our friends," said Clarissa; and could have bitten her tongue for thus reminding Peter that he had wanted to marry her.

Of course I did, thought Peter; it almost broke my heart too, he thought; and was overcome with his own grief, which rose like a moon looked at from a terrace, ghastly beautiful with light from the sunken day. I was more unhappy than I've ever been since, he thought. And as if in truth he were sitting there on the terrace he edged a little towards Clarissa; put his hand out; raised it; let it fall. There above them it hung, that moon. She too seemed to be sitting with him on the terrace, in the moonlight.

"Herbert has it now," she said. "I never go there now," she said.

Then, just as happens on a terrace in the moonlight, when one person begins to feel ashamed that he is already bored, and yet as the other sits silent, very quiet, sadly looking at the moon, does not like to speak, moves his foot, clears his throat, notices some iron scroll on a table leg, stirs a leaf, but says nothing—so Peter Walsh did now. For why go back like this to the past? he thought. Why make him think of it again? Why make him suffer, when she had tortured him so infernally? Why?

"Do you remember the lake?" she said, in an abrupt voice, under the pressure of an emotion which caught her heart, made the muscles of her throat stiff, and contracted her lips in a spasm as she said "lake." For she was a child, throwing bread to the ducks, between her parents, and at the same time a grown woman coming to her parents who stood by the lake, holding her life in her arms which, as she neared them, grew larger and larger in her arms, until it became a whole life, a complete life, which she put down by them and said, "This is what I have made of it! This!" And what had she made of it? What, indeed? sitting there sewing this morning with Peter.

She looked at Peter Walsh; her look, passing through all that time and that emotion, reached him doubtfully; settled on him tearfully; and rose and fluttered away, as a bird touches a branch and rises and flutters away. Quite simply she wiped her eyes.

"Yes," said Peter. "Yes, yes, yes," he said, as if she drew up to the surface something which positively hurt him as it rose. Stop! Stop! he wanted to cry. For he was not old; his life was not over; not by any means. He was only just past fifty. Shall I tell her, he thought, or not? He would like to make a clean breast of it all. But she is too

cold, he thought; sewing, with her scissors; Daisy would look ordinary beside Clarissa. And she would think me a failure, which I am
in their sense, he thought; in the Dalloways' sense. Oh yes, he had
no doubt about that; he was a failure, compared with all this—the
inlaid table, the mounted paper-knife, the dolphin and the candlesticks, the chair-covers and the old valuable English tinted prints—
he was a failure! I detest the smugness of the whole affair he
thought; Richard's doing, not Clarissa's; save that she married him.
(Here Lucy came into the room, carrying silver, more silver, but
charming, slender, graceful she looked, he thought, as she stooped
to put it down.) And this has been going on all the time! he thought;
week after week; Clarissa's life; while I—he thought; and at once
everything seemed to radiate from him; journeys; rides; quarrels;
adventures; bridge parties; love affairs; work; work, work! and he
took out his knife quite openly—his old horn-handled knife which
Clarissa could swear he had had these thirty years—and clenched
his fist upon in.

What an extraordinary habit that was, Clarissa thought; always
playing with a knife. Always making one feel, too, frivolous; empty-
minded; a mere silly chatterbox, as he used. But I too, she thought,
and, taking up her needle, summoned, like a Queen whose guards
have fallen asleep and left her unprotected (she had been quite
taken aback by this visit—it had upset her) so that any one can
stroll in and have a look at her where she lies with the brambles
curving over her, summoned to her help the things she did; the
things she liked; her husband; Elizabeth; her self, in short, which
Peter hardly knew now, all to come about her and beat off the
enemy.

"Well, and what's happened to you?" she said. So before a battle
begins, the horses paw the ground; toss their heads; the light shines
on their flanks; their necks curve. So Peter Walsh and Clarissa, sitting side by side on the blue sofa, challenged each other. His powers chafed and tossed in him. He assembled from different quarters
all sorts of things; praise; his career at Oxford; his marriage, which
she knew nothing whatever about; how he had loved; and altogether
done his job.

"Millions of things!" he exclaimed, and, urged by the assembly of
powers which were now charging this way and that and giving him
the feeling at once frightening and extremely exhilarating of being
rushed through the air on the shoulders of people he could no longer see, he raised his hands to his forehead.

Clarissa sat very upright; drew in her breath.

"I am in love," he said, not to her however, but to some one raised
up in the dark so that you could not touch her but must lay your
garland down on the grass in the dark.

"In love," he repeated, now speaking rather dryly to Clarissa Dalloway; "in love with a girl in India." He had deposited his garland. Clarissa could make what she would of it.

"In love!" she said. That he at his age should be sucked under in his little bow-tie by that monster! And there's no flesh on his neck; his hands are red; and he's six months older than I am! her eye flashed back to her; but in her heart she felt, all the same, he is in love. He has that, she felt; he is in love.

But the indomitable egotism which for ever rides down the hosts opposed to it, the river which says on, on, on; even though, it admits, there may be no goal for us whatever, still on, on; this indomitable egotism charged her cheeks with colour; made her look very young; very pink; very bright-eyed as she sat with her dress upon her knee, and her needle held to the end of green silk, trembling a little. He was in love! Not with her. With some younger woman, of course.

"And who is she?" she asked.

Now this statue must be brought from its height and set down between them.

"A married woman, unfortunately," he said; "the wife of a Major in the Indian Army."[2]

And with a curious ironical sweetness he smiled as he placed her in this ridiculous way before Clarissa.

(All the same, he is in love, thought Clarissa.)

"She has," he continued, very reasonably, "two small children; a boy and a girl; and I have come over to see my lawyers about the divorce."

There they are! he thought. Do what you like with them, Clarissa! There they are! And second by second it seemed to him that the wife of the Major in the Indian Army (his Daisy) and her two small children became more and more lovely as Clarissa looked at them; as if he had set light to a grey pellet on a plate and there had risen up a lovely tree in the brisk sea-salted air of their intimacy (for in some ways no one understood him, felt with him, as Clarissa did)—their exquisite intimacy.

She flattered him; she fooled him, thought Clarissa; shaping the woman, the wife of the Major in the Indian Army, with three strokes of a knife. What a waste! What a folly! All his life long Peter had been fooled like that; first getting sent down from Oxford; next marrying the girl on the boat going out to India; now the wife of a Major in the Indian Army—thank Heaven she had refused to marry him! Still, he was in love; her old friend, her dear Peter, he was in love.

2. The British Army in India.

"But what are you going to do?" she asked him. Oh the lawyers and solicitors, Messrs. Hooper and Grateley of Lincoln's Inn, they were going to do it, he said. And he actually pared his nails with his pocket-knife.

For Heaven's sake, leave your knife alone! she cried to herself in irrepressible irritation; it was his silly unconventionality, his weakness; his lack of the ghost of a notion what any one else was feeling that annoyed her, had always annoyed her; and now at his age, how silly!

I know all that, Peter thought; I know what I'm up against, he thought, running his finger along the blade of his knife, Clarissa and Dalloway and all the rest of them; but I'll show Clarissa—and then to his utter surprise, suddenly thrown by those uncontrollable forces thrown through the air, he burst into tears; wept; wept without the least shame, sitting on the sofa, the tears running down his cheeks.

And Clarissa had leant forward, taken his hand, drawn him to her, kissed him,—actually had felt his face on hers before she could down the brandishing of silver flashing—plumes like pampas grass in a tropic gale in her breast, which, subsiding, left her holding his hand, patting his knee and, feeling as she sat back extraordinarily at her ease with him and light-hearted, all in a clap it came over her, If I had married him, this gaiety would have been mine all day!

It was all over for her. The sheet was stretched and the bed narrow. She had gone up into the tower alone and left them blackberrying in the sun. The door had shut, and there among the dust of fallen plaster and the litter of birds' nests how distant the view had looked, and the sounds came thin and chill (once on Leith Hill, she remembered), and Richard, Richard! she cried, as a sleeper in the night starts and stretches a hand in the dark for help. Lunching with Lady Bruton, it came back to her. He has left me; I am alone for ever, she thought, folding her hands upon her knee.

Peter Walsh had got up and crossed to the window and stood with his back to her, flicking a bandanna handkerchief from side to side. Masterly and dry and desolate he looked, his thin shoulder-blades lifting his coat slightly; blowing his nose violently. Take me with you, Clarissa thought impulsively, as if he were starting directly upon some great voyage; and then, next moment, it was as if the five acts of a play that had been very exciting and moving were now over and she had lived a lifetime in them and had run away, had lived with Peter, and it was now over.

Now it was time to move, and, as a woman gathers her things together, her cloak, her gloves, her opera-glasses, and gets up to go out of the theatre into the street, she rose from the sofa and went to Peter.

And it was awfully strange, he thought, how she still had the power, as she came tinkling, rustling, still had the power as she came across the room, to make the moon, which he detested, rise at Bourton on the terrace in the summer sky.

"Tell me," he said, seizing her by the shoulder. "Are you happy, Clarissa? Does Richard—"

The door opened.

"Here is my Elizabeth," said Clarissa, emotionally, histrionically, perhaps.

"How d'y do?" said Elizabeth coming forward.

The sound of Big Ben striking the half-hour struck out between them with extraordinary vigour, as if a young man, strong, indifferent, inconsiderate, were swinging dumb-bells this way and that.

"Hullo, Elizabeth!" cried Peter, stuffing his handkerchief into his pocket, going quickly to her, saying "Good-bye, Clarissa" without looking at her, leaving the room quickly, and running downstairs and opening the hall door.

"Peter! Peter!" cried Clarissa, following him out on to the landing. "My party to-night! Remember my party to-night!" she cried, having to raise her voice against the roar of the open air, and, overwhelmed by the traffic and the sound of all the clocks striking, her voice crying "Remember my party to-night!" sounded frail and thin and very far away as Peter Walsh shut the door.

Remember my party, remember my party, said Peter Walsh as he stepped down the street, speaking to himself rhythmically, in time with the flow of the sound, the direct downright sound of Big Ben striking the half-hour. (The leaden circles dissolved in the air.) Oh these parties, he thought; Clarissa's parties. Why does she give these parties, he thought. Not that he blamed her or this effigy of a man in a tail-coat with a carnation in his button-hole coming towards him. Only one person in the world could be as he was, in love. And there he was, this fortunate man, himself, reflected in the plate-glass window of a motor-car manufacturer in Victoria Street. All India lay behind him; plains, mountains; epidemics of cholera; a district twice as big as Ireland; decisions he had come to alone—he, Peter Walsh; who was now really for the first time in his life, in love. Clarissa had grown hard, he thought; and a trifle sentimental into the bargain, he suspected, looking at the great motor-cars capable of doing—how many miles on how many gallons? For he had a turn for mechanics; had invented a plough in his district, had ordered wheel-barrows from England, but the coolies[3] wouldn't use them, all of which Clarissa knew nothing whatever about.

3. In 1925, the use of this word for a hired laborer, especially in India but also in China, was widely accepted; the word is now recognized as a racial slur. The derogatory sense of *coolie* for any person of Asian descent was also current from the mid-nineteenth century (*OED*).

The way she said "Here is my Elizabeth!"—that annoyed him. Why not "Here's Elizabeth" simply? It was insincere. And Elizabeth didn't like it either. (Still the last tremors of the great booming voice shook the air round him; the half-hour; still early; only half-past eleven still.) For he understood young people; he liked them. There was always something cold in Clarissa, he thought. She had always, even as a girl, a sort of timidity, which in middle age becomes conventionality, and then it's all up, it's all up, he thought, looking rather drearily into the glassy depths, and wondering whether by calling at that hour he had annoyed her; overcome with shame suddenly at having been a fool; wept; been emotional; told her everything, as usual, as usual.

As a cloud crosses the sun, silence falls on London; and falls on the mind. Effort ceases. Time flaps on the mast. There we stop; there we stand. Rigid, the skeleton of habit alone upholds the human frame. Where there is nothing, Peter Walsh said to himself; feeling hollowed out, utterly empty within. Clarissa refused me, he thought. He stood there thinking, Clarissa refused me.

Ah, said St. Margaret's, like a hostess who comes into her drawing-room on the very stroke of the hour and finds her guests there already. I am not late. No, it is precisely half-past eleven, she says. Yet, though she is perfectly right, her voice, being the voice of the hostess, is reluctant to inflict its individuality. Some grief for the past holds it back; some concern for the present. It is half-past eleven, she says, and the sound of St. Margaret's glides into the recesses of the heart and buries itself in ring after ring of sound, like something alive which wants to confide itself, to disperse itself, to be, with a tremor of delight, at rest—like Clarissa herself, thought Peter Walsh, coming down the stairs on the stroke of the hour in white. It is Clarissa herself, he thought, with a deep emotion, and an extraordinarily clear, yet puzzling, recollection of her, as if this bell had come into the room years ago, where they sat at some moment of great intimacy, and had gone from one to the other and had left, like a bee with honey, laden with the moment. But what room? What moment? And why had he been so profoundly happy when the clock was striking? Then, as the sound of St. Margaret's languished, he thought, She has been ill, and the sound expressed languor and suffering. It was her heart, he remembered; and the sudden loudness of the final stroke tolled for death that surprised in the midst of life, Clarissa falling where she stood, in her drawing-room. No! No! he cried. She is not dead! I am not old, he cried, and marched up Whitehall, as if there rolled down to him, vigorous, unending, his future.

He was not old, or set, or dried in the least. As for caring what they said of him—the Dalloways, the Whitbreads, and their set, he cared not a straw—not a straw (though it was true he would have, some time or other, to see whether Richard couldn't help him to some job). Striding, staring, he glared at the statue of the Duke of Cambridge. He had been sent down from Oxford—true. He had been a Socialist, in some sense a failure—true. Still the future of civilisation lies, he thought, in the hands of young men like that; of young men such as he was, thirty years ago; with their love of abstract principles; getting books sent out to them all the way from London to a peak in the Himalayas; reading science; reading philosophy. The future lies in the hands of young men like that, he thought.

A patter like the patter of leaves in a wood came from behind, and with it a rustling, regular thudding sound, which as it overtook him drummed his thoughts, strict in step, up Whitehall, without his doing. Boys in uniform, carrying guns, marched with their eyes ahead of them, marched, their arms stiff, and on their faces an expression like the letters of a legend written round the base of a statue praising duty, gratitude, fidelity, love of England.

It is, thought Peter Walsh, beginning to keep step with them, a very fine training. But they did not look robust. They were weedy for the most part, boys of sixteen, who might, to-morrow, stand behind bowls of rice, cakes of soap on counters. Now they wore on them unmixed with sensual pleasure or daily preoccupations the solemnity of the wreath which they had fetched from Finsbury Pavement to the empty tomb. They had taken their vow. The traffic respected it; vans were stopped.

I can't keep up with them, Peter Walsh thought, as they marched up Whitehall, and sure enough, on they marched, past him, past every one, in their steady way, as if one will worked legs and arms uniformly, and life, with its varieties, its irreticences, had been laid under a pavement of monuments and wreaths and drugged into a stiff yet staring corpse by discipline. One had to respect it; one might laugh; but one had to respect it, he thought. There they go, thought Peter Walsh, pausing at the edge of the pavement; and all the exalted statues, Nelson, Gordon, Havelock,[4] the black, the spectacular images of great soldiers stood looking ahead of them, as if they too had made the same renunciation (Peter Walsh felt he too had made it, the great renunciation), trampled under the same temptations, and achieved at length a marble stare. But the stare Peter Walsh did not want for himself in the least; though he could respect it in others. He could respect it in boys. They don't know

---

4. Military heroes whose statues are in Trafalgar Square. Horatio Nelson (1758–1805) was the victor at the Battle of Trafalgar (1805), during which he was mortally wounded. Charles George Gordon (1833–1885) died in the Siege of Khartoum. Sir Henry Havelock (1795–1857) died of dysentery at Lucknow in November 1857.

the troubles of the flesh yet, he thought, as the marching boys disappeared in the direction of the Strand—all that I've been through, he thought, crossing the road, and standing under Gordon's statue, Gordon whom as a boy he had worshipped; Gordon standing lonely with one leg raised and his arms crossed,—poor Gordon, he thought.

And just because nobody yet knew he was in London, except Clarissa, and the earth, after the voyage, still seemed an island to him, the strangeness of standing alone, alive, unknown, at half-past eleven in Trafalgar Square overcame him. What is it? Where am I? And why, after all, does one do it? he thought, the divorce seeming all moonshine. And down his mind went flat as a marsh, and three great emotions bowled over him; understanding; a vast philanthropy; and finally, as if the result of the others, an irrepressible, exquisite delight; as if inside his brain by another hand strings were pulled, shutters moved, and he, having nothing to do with it, yet stood at the opening of endless avenues, down which if he chose he might wander. He had not felt so young for years.

He had escaped! was utterly free—as happens in the downfall of habit when the mind, like an unguarded flame, bows and bends and seems about to blow from its holding. I haven't felt so young for years! thought Peter, escaping (only of course for an hour or so) from being precisely what he was, and feeling like a child who runs out of doors, and sees, as he runs, his old nurse waving at the wrong window. But she's extraordinarily attractive, he thought, as, walking across Trafalgar Square in the direction of the Haymarket, came a young woman who, as she passed Gordon's statue, seemed, Peter Walsh thought (susceptible as he was), to shed veil after veil, until she became the very woman he had always had in mind; young, but stately; merry, but discreet; black, but enchanting.

Straightening himself and stealthily fingering his pocket-knife he started after her to follow this woman,[5] this excitement, which seemed even with its back turned to shed on him a light which connected them, which singled him out, as if the random uproar of the traffic had whispered through hollowed hands his name, not Peter, but his private name which he called himself in his own thoughts. "You," she said, only "you," saying it with her white gloves and her shoulders. Then the thin long cloak which the wind stirred as she walked past Dent's shop in Cockspur Street blew out with an enveloping kindness, a mournful tenderness, as of arms that would open and take the tired—

5. Peter's actions here mirror those of the older man who follows the heroine in the opening pages of H. G. Wells's *Ann Veronica* (1909) (see pp. 235–37).

But she's not married; she's young; quite young, thought Peter, the red carnation he had seen her wear as she came across Trafalgar Square burning again in his eyes and making her lips red. But she waited at the kerbstone. There was a dignity about her. She was not worldly, like Clarissa; not rich, like Clarissa. Was she, he wondered as she moved, respectable? Witty, with a lizard's flickering tongue, he thought (for one must invent, must allow oneself a little diversion), a cool waiting wit, a darting wit; not noisy.

She moved; she crossed; he followed her. To embarrass her was the last thing he wished. Still if she stopped he would say "Come and have an ice," he would say, and she would answer, perfectly simply, "Oh yes."

But other people got between them in the street, obstructing him, blotting her out. He pursued; she changed. There was colour in her cheeks; mockery in her eyes; he was an adventurer, reckless, he thought, swift, daring, indeed (landed as he was last night from India) a romantic buccaneer, careless of all these damned proprieties, yellow dressing-gowns, pipes, fishing-rods, in the shop windows; and respectability and evening parties and spruce old men wearing white slips beneath their waistcoats. He was a buccaneer. On and on she went, across Piccadilly, and up Regent Street, ahead of him, her cloak, her gloves, her shoulders combining with the fringes and the laces and the feather boas in the windows to make the spirit of finery and whimsy which dwindled out of the shops on to the pavement, as the light of a lamp goes wavering at night over hedges in the darkness.

Laughing and delightful, she had crossed Oxford Street and Great Portland Street and turned down one of the little streets, and now, and now, the great moment was approaching, for now she slackened, opened her bag, and with one look in his direction, but not at him, one look that bade farewell, summed up the whole situation and dismissed it triumphantly, for ever, had fitted her key, opened the door, and gone! Clarissa's voice saying, Remember my party, Remember my party, sang in his ears. The house was one of those flat red houses with hanging flower-baskets of vague impropriety. It was over.

Well, I've had my fun; I've had it, he thought, looking up at the swinging baskets of pale geraniums. And it was smashed to atoms—his fun, for it was half made up, as he knew very well; invented, this escapade with the girl; made up, as one makes up the better part of life, he thought—making oneself up; making her up; creating an exquisite amusement, and something more. But odd it was, and quite true; all this one could never share—it smashed to atoms.

He turned; went up the street, thinking to find somewhere to sit, till it was time for Lincoln's Inn—for Messrs. Hooper and Grateley.

Where should he go? No matter. Up the street, then, towards
Regent's Park. His boots on the pavement struck out "no matter";
for it was early, still very early.

It was a splendid morning too. Like the pulse of a perfect heart,
life struck straight through the streets. There was no fumbling—no
hesitation. Sweeping and swerving, accurately, punctually, noise-
lessly, there, precisely at the right instant, the motor-car stopped at
the door. The girl, silk-stockinged, feathered, evanescent, but not
to him particularly attractive (for he had had his fling), alighted.
Admirable butlers, tawny chow dogs, halls laid in black and white
lozenges with white blinds blowing, Peter saw through the opened
door and approved of. A splendid achievement in its own way, after
all, London; the season; civilisation. Coming as he did from a
respectable Anglo-Indian family which for at least three generations had administered the affairs of a continent (it's strange, he
thought, what a sentiment I have about that, disliking India, and
empire, and army as he did), there were moments when civilisation,
even of this sort, seemed dear to him as a personal possession;
moments of pride in England; in butlers; chow dogs; girls in their
security. Ridiculous enough, still there it is, he thought. And the
doctors and men of business and capable women all going about
their business, punctual, alert; robust, seemed to him wholly admirable, good fellows, to whom one would entrust one's life, companions in the art of living, who would see one through. What with one
thing and another, the show was really very tolerable; and he would
sit down in the shade and smoke.

There was Regent's Park. Yes. As a child he had walked in
Regent's Park—odd, he thought, how the thought of childhood
keeps coming back to me—the result of seeing Clarissa, perhaps;
for women live much more in the past than we do, he thought. They
attach themselves to places; and their fathers—a woman's always
proud of her father. Bourton was a nice place, a very nice place, but
I could never get on with the old man, he thought. There was quite
a scene one night—an argument about something or other, what,
he could not remember. Politics presumably.

Yes, he remembered Regent's Park; the long straight walk; the
little house where one bought air-balls to the left; an absurd statue
with an inscription somewhere or other. He looked for an empty
seat. He did not want to be bothered (feeling a little drowsy as he
did) by people asking him the time. An elderly grey nurse, with a
baby asleep in its perambulator—that was the best he could do for
himself; sit down at the far end of the seat by that nurse.

She's a queer-looking girl, he thought, suddenly remembering
Elizabeth as she came into the room and stood by her mother.
Grown big; quite grown-up, not exactly pretty; handsome rather;

and she can't be more than eighteen. Probably she doesn't get on with Clarissa. "There's my Elizabeth"—that sort of thing—why not "Here's Elizabeth" simply?—trying to make out, like most mothers, that things are what they're not. She trusts to her charm too much, he thought. She overdoes it.

The rich benignant cigar smoke eddied coolly down his throat; he puffed it out again in rings which breasted the air bravely for a moment; blue, circular—I shall try and get a word alone with Elizabeth to-night, he thought—then began to wobble into hour-glass shapes and taper away; odd shapes they take, he thought. Suddenly he closed his eyes, raised his hand with an effort, and threw away the heavy end of his cigar. A great brush swept smooth across his mind, sweeping across it moving branches, children's voices, the shuffle of feet, and people passing, and humming traffic, rising and falling traffic. Down, down he sank into the plumes and feathers of sleep, sank, and was muffled over.

The grey nurse resumed her knitting as Peter Walsh, on the hot seat beside her, began snoring. In her grey dress, moving her hands indefatigably yet quietly, she seemed like the champion of the rights of sleepers, like one of those spectral presences which rise in twilight in woods made of sky and branches. The solitary traveller, haunter of lanes, disturber of ferns, and devastator of great hemlock plants, looking up, suddenly sees the giant figure at the end of the ride.

By conviction an atheist perhaps, he is taken by surprise with moments of extraordinary exaltation. Nothing exists outside us except a state of mind, he thinks; a desire for solace, for relief, for something outside these miserable pigmies,[6] these feeble, these ugly, these craven men and women. But if he can conceive of her, then in some sort she exists, he thinks, and advancing down the path with his eyes upon sky and branches he rapidly endows them with womanhood; sees with amazement how grave they become; how majestically, as the breeze stirs them, they dispense with a dark flutter of the leaves charity, comprehension, absolution, and then, flinging themselves suddenly aloft, confound the piety of their aspect with a wild carouse.

Such are the visions which proffer great cornucopias full of fruit to the solitary traveller, or murmur in his ear like sirens lolloping away on the green sea waves, or are dashed in his face like bunches

---

6. The word 'pigmy' or more usually 'pygmy' is a now archaic term for both a tribe of hunter-gatherers from equatorial Africa who have an average male height of not above 150 cm (4 ft. 11 in.) and a race of tiny people, possibly mythical, said to inhabit Ethiopia or India (OED). While both usages were common in 1925, they are no longer accepted due to the negative racial connotation the term carries. Here, it is used in what was then the colloquial sense of any tiny or insignificant person.

of roses, or rise to the surface like pale faces which fishermen flounder through floods to embrace.

Such are the visions which ceaselessly float up, pace beside, put their faces in front of, the actual thing; often overpowering the solitary traveller and taking away from him the sense of the earth, the wish to return, and giving him for substitute a general peace, as if (so he thinks as he advances down the forest ride) all this fever of living were simplicity itself; and myriads of things merged in one thing; and this figure, made of sky and branches as it is, had risen from the troubled sea (he is elderly, past fifty now) as a shape might be sucked up out of the waves to shower down from her magnificent hands compassion, comprehension, absolution. So, he thinks, may I never go back to the lamplight; to the sitting-room; never finish my book; never knock out my pipe; never ring for Mrs. Turner to clear away; rather let me walk straight on to this great figure, who will, with a toss of her head, mount me on her streamers and let me blow to nothingness with the rest.

Such are the visions. The solitary traveller is soon beyond the wood; and there, coming to the door with shaded eyes, possibly to look for his return, with hands raised, with white apron blowing, is an elderly woman who seems (so powerful is this infirmity) to seek, over a desert, a lost son; to search for a rider destroyed; to be the figure of the mother whose sons have been killed in the battles of the world. So, as the solitary traveller advances down the village street where the women stand knitting and the men dig in the garden, the evening seems ominous; the figures still; as if some august fate, known to them, awaited without fear, were about to sweep them into complete annihilation.

Indoors among ordinary things, the cupboard, the table, the window-sill with its geraniums, suddenly the outline of the landlady, bending to remove the cloth, becomes soft with light, an adorable emblem which only the recollection of cold human contacts forbids us to embrace. She takes the marmalade: she shuts it in the cupboard.

"There is nothing more to-night, sir?"

But to whom does the solitary traveller make reply?

So the elderly nurse knitted over the sleeping baby in Regent's Park. So Peter Walsh snored.

He woke with extreme suddenness, saying to himself, "The death of the soul."

"Lord, Lord!" he said to himself out loud, stretching and opening his eyes. "The death of the soul." The words attached themselves to some scene, to some room, to some past he had been dreaming of. It became clearer; the scene, the room, the past he had been dreaming of.

It was at Bourton that summer, early in the 'nineties, when he was so passionately in love with Clarissa. There were a great many people there, laughing and talking, sitting round a table after tea and the room was bathed in yellow light and full of cigarette smoke. They were talking about a man who had married his housemaid, one of the neighbouring squires, he had forgotten his name. He had married his housemaid, and she had been brought to Bourton to call—an awful visit it had been. She was absurdly over-dressed, "like a cockatoo," Clarissa had said, imitating her, and she never stopped talking. On and on she went, on and on. Clarissa imitated her. Then somebody said—Sally Seton it was—did it make any real difference to one's feelings to know that before they'd married she had had a baby? (In those days, in mixed company, it was a bold thing to say.) He could see Clarissa now, turning bright pink; somehow contracting; and saying, "Oh, I shall never be able to speak to her again!" Whereupon the whole party sitting round the tea-table seemed to wobble. It was very uncomfortable.

He hadn't blamed her for minding the fact, since in those days a girl brought up as she was, knew nothing, but it was her manner that annoyed him; timid; hard; something arrogant; unimaginative; prudish. "The death of the soul." He had said that instinctively, ticketing the moment as he used to do—the death of her soul.

Every one wobbled; every one seemed to bow, as she spoke, and then to stand up different. He could see Sally Seton, like a child who has been in mischief, leaning forward, rather flushed, wanting to talk, but afraid, and Clarissa did frighten people. (She was Clarissa's greatest friend, always about the place, totally unlike her, an attractive creature, handsome, dark, with the reputation in those days of great daring and he used to give her cigars, which she smoked in her bedroom. She had either been engaged to somebody or quarrelled with her family and old Parry disliked them both equally, which was a great bond.) Then Clarissa, still with an air of being offended with them all, got up, made some excuse, and went off, alone. As she opened the door, in came that great shaggy dog which ran after sheep. She flung herself upon him, went into raptures. It was as if she said to Peter—it was all aimed at him, he knew—"I know you thought me absurd about that woman just now; but see how extraordinarily sympathetic I am; see how I love my Rob!"

They had always this queer power of communicating without words. She knew directly he criticised her. Then she would do something quite obvious to defend herself, like this fuss with the dog—but it never took him in, he always saw through Clarissa. Not that he said anything, of course; just sat looking glum. It was the way their quarrels often began.

She shut the door. At once he became extremely depressed. It all seemed useless—going on being in love; going on quarrelling; going on making it up, and he wandered off alone, among outhouses, stables, looking at the horses. (The place was quite a humble one; the Parrys were never very well off; but there were always grooms and stable-boys about—Clarissa loved riding—and an old coachman—what was his name?—an old nurse, old Moody, old Goody, some such name they called her, whom one was taken to visit in a little room with lots of photographs, lots of bird-cages.)

It was an awful evening! He grew more and more gloomy, not about that only; about everything. And he couldn't see her; couldn't explain to her; couldn't have it out. There were always people about—she'd go on as if nothing had happened. That was the devilish part of her—this coldness, this woodenness, something very profound in her, which he had felt again this morning talking to her; an impenetrability. Yet Heaven knows he loved her. She had some queer power of fiddling on one's nerves, turning one's nerves to fiddle-strings, yes.

He had gone in to dinner rather late, from some idiotic idea of making himself felt, and had sat down by old Miss Parry—Aunt Helena—Mr. Parry's sister, who was supposed to preside. There she sat in her white Cashmere shawl, with her head against the window—a formidable old lady, but kind to him, for he had found her some rare flower, and she was a great botanist, marching off in thick boots with a black collecting-box slung between her shoulders. He sat down beside her, and couldn't speak. Everything seemed to race past him; he just sat there, eating. And then half-way through dinner he made himself look across at Clarissa for the first time. She was talking to a young man on her right. He had a sudden revelation. "She will marry that man," he said to himself. He didn't even know his name.

For of course it was that afternoon, that very afternoon, that Dalloway had come over; and Clarissa called him "Wickham";[7] that was the beginning of it all. Somebody had brought him over; and Clarissa got his name wrong. She introduced him to everybody as Wickham. At last he said "My name is Dalloway!"—that was his first view of Richard—a fair young man, rather awkward, sitting on a deck-chair, and blurting out "My name is Dalloway!" Sally got hold of it; always after that she called him "My name is Dalloway!"

He was a prey to revelations at that time. This one—that she would marry Dalloway—was blinding—overwhelming at the moment. There was a sort of—how could he put it?—a sort of ease

7. In Jane Austen's *Pride and Prejudice* (1813), "Wickham" is the name of a feckless young man who initially seems attractive.

in her manner to him; something maternal; something gentle. They were talking about politics. All through dinner he tried to hear what they were saying.

Afterwards he could remember standing by old Miss Parry's chair in the drawing-room. Clarissa came up, with her perfect manners, like a real hostess, and wanted to introduce him to some one—spoke as if they had never met before, which enraged him. Yet even then he admired her for it. He admired her courage; her social instinct; he admired her power of carrying things through. "The perfect hostess," he said to her, whereupon she winced all over. But he meant her to feel it. He would have done anything to hurt her after seeing her with Dalloway. So she left him. And he had a feeling that they were all gathered together in a conspiracy against him—laughing and talking—behind his back. There he stood by Miss Parry's chair as though he had been cut out of wood, he talking about wild flowers. Never, never had he suffered so infernally! He must have forgotten even to pretend to listen; at last he woke up; he saw Miss Parry looking rather disturbed, rather indignant, with her prominent eyes fixed. He almost cried out that he couldn't attend because he was in Hell! People began going out of the room. He heard them talking about fetching cloaks; about its being cold on the water, and so on. They were going boating on the lake by moonlight—one of Sally's mad ideas. He could hear her describing the moon. And they all went out. He was left quite alone.

"Don't you want to go with them?" said Aunt Helena—old Miss Parry!—she had guessed. And he turned round and there was Clarissa again. She had come back to fetch him. He was overcome by her generosity—her goodness.

"Come along," she said. "They're waiting."

He had never felt so happy in the whole of his life! Without a word they made it up. They walked down to the lake. He had twenty minutes of perfect happiness. Her voice, her laugh, her dress (something floating, white, crimson), her spirit, her adventurousness; she made them all disembark and explore the island; she startled a hen; she laughed; she sang. And all the time, he knew perfectly well, Dalloway was falling in love with her; she was falling in love with Dalloway; but it didn't seem to matter. Nothing mattered. They sat on the ground and talked—he and Clarissa. They went in and out of each other's minds without any effort. And then in a second it was over. He said to himself as they were getting into the boat, "She will marry that man," dully, without any resentment; but it was an obvious thing. Dalloway would marry Clarissa.

Dalloway rowed them in. He said nothing. But somehow as they watched him start, jumping on to his bicycle to ride twenty miles through the woods, wobbling off down the drive, waving his hand

and disappearing, he obviously did feel, instinctively, tremendously, strongly, all that; the night; the romance; Clarissa. He deserved to have her.

For himself, he was absurd. His demands upon Clarissa (he could see it now) were absurd. He asked impossible things. He made terrible scenes. She would have accepted him still, perhaps, if he had been less absurd. Sally thought so. She wrote him all that summer long letters; how they had talked of him; how she had praised him, how Clarissa burst into tears! It was an extraordinary summer—all letters, scenes, telegrams—arriving at Bourton early in the morning, hanging about till the servants were up; appalling *tête-à-têtes* with old Mr. Parry at breakfast; Aunt Helena formidable but kind; Sally sweeping him off for talks in the vegetable garden; Clarissa in bed with headaches.

The final scene, the terrible scene which he believed had mattered more than anything in the whole of his life (it might be an exaggeration—but still so it did seem now) happened at three o'clock in the afternoon of a very hot day. It was a trifle that led up to it—Sally at lunch saying something about Dalloway, and calling him "My name is Dalloway"; whereupon Clarissa suddenly stiffened, coloured, in a way she had, and rapped out sharply, "We've had enough of that feeble joke." That was all; but for him it was precisely as if she had said, "I'm only amusing myself with you; I've an understanding with Richard Dalloway." So he took it. He had not slept for nights. "It's got to be finished one way or the other," he said to himself. He sent a note to her by Sally asking her to meet him by the fountain at three. "Something very important has happened," he scribbled at the end of it.

The fountain was in the middle of a little shrubbery, far from the house, with shrubs and trees all round it. There she came, even before the time, and they stood with the fountain between them, the spout (it was broken) dribbling water incessantly. How sights fix themselves upon the mind! For example, the vivid green moss.

She did not move. "Tell me the truth, tell me the truth," he kept on saying. He felt as if his forehead would burst. She seemed contracted, petrified. She did not move. "Tell me the truth," he repeated, when suddenly that old man Breitkopf popped his head in carrying the *Times*; stared at them; gaped; and went away. They neither of them moved. "Tell me the truth," he repeated. He felt that he was grinding against something physically hard; she was unyielding. She was like iron, like flint, rigid up the backbone. And when she said, "It's no use. It's no use. This is the end"—after he had spoken for hours, it seemed, with the tears running down his cheeks—it was as if she had hit him in the face. She turned, she left him, went away.

"Clarissa!" he cried. "Clarissa!" But she never came back. It was over. He went away that night. He never saw her again.

It was awful, he cried, awful, awful!

Still, the sun was hot. Still, one got over things. Still, life had a way of adding day to day. Still, he thought, yawning and beginning to take notice—Regent's Park had changed very little since he was a boy, except for the squirrels—still, presumably there were compensations—when little Elise Mitchell, who had been picking up pebbles to add to the pebble collection which she and her brother were making on the nursery mantelpiece, plumped her handful down on the nurse's knee and scudded off again full tilt into a lady's legs. Peter Walsh laughed out.

But Lucrezia Warren Smith was saying to herself, It's wicked; why should I suffer? she was asking, as she walked down the broad path. No; I can't stand it any longer, she was saying, having left Septimus, who wasn't Septimus any longer, to say hard, cruel, wicked things, to talk to himself, to talk to a dead man, on the seat over there; when the child ran full tilt into her, fell flat, and burst out crying.

That was comforting rather. She stood her upright, dusted her frock, kissed her.

But for herself she had done nothing wrong; she had loved Septimus; she had been happy; she had had a beautiful home, and there her sisters lived still, making hats. Why should she suffer?

The child ran straight back to its nurse, and Rezia saw her scolded, comforted, taken up by the nurse who put down her knitting, and the kind-looking man gave her his watch to blow open to comfort her—but why should she be exposed? Why not left in Milan? Why tortured? Why?

Slightly waved by tears the broad path, the nurse, the man in grey, the perambulator, rose and fell before her eyes. To be rocked by this malignant torturer was her lot. But why? She was like a bird, sheltering under the thin hollow of a leaf, who blinks at the sun when the leaf moves; starts at the crack of a dry twig. She was exposed; she was surrounded by the enormous trees, vast clouds of an indifferent world, exposed; tortured; and why should she suffer? Why?

She frowned; she stamped her foot. She must go back again to Septimus since it was almost time for them to be going to Sir William Bradshaw. She must go back and tell him, go back to him sitting there on the green chair under the tree, talking to himself, or to that dead man Evans, whom she had only seen once for a moment in the shop. He had seemed a nice quiet man; a great friend of Septimus's, and he had been killed in the War. But such things happen to every one. Every one has friends who were killed in the War. Every one gives up something when they marry. She had given up her home. She had come to live here, in this awful city. But Septimus let himself think about horrible things, as she could too, if she tried. He had grown stranger and stranger. He said people were talking behind the bedroom walls. Mrs. Filmer thought it odd. He saw things too— he had seen an old woman's head in the middle of a fern. Yet he could be happy when he chose. They went to Hampton Court[8] on top of a bus, and they were perfectly happy. All the little red and yellow flowers were out on the grass, like floating lamps he said, and talked and chattered and laughed, making up stories. Suddenly he said, "Now we will kill ourselves," when they were standing by the river, and he looked at it with a look which she had seen in his eyes when a train went by, or an omnibus—a look as if something fascinated him; and she felt he was going from her and she caught him by the arm. But going home he was perfectly quiet—perfectly reasonable. He would argue with her about killing themselves; and explain how wicked people were; how he could see them making up lies as they passed in the street. He knew all their thoughts, he said; he knew everything. He knew the meaning of the world, he said.

Then when they got back he could hardly walk. He lay on the sofa and made her hold his hand to prevent him from falling down, down, he cried, into the flames! and saw faces laughing at him, calling him horrible disgusting names, from the walls, and hands pointing round the screen. Yet they were quite alone. But he began to talk aloud, answering people, arguing, laughing, crying, getting very excited and making her write things down. Perfect nonsense it was; about death; about Miss Isabel Pole. She could stand it no longer. She would go back.

She was close to him now, could see him staring at the sky, muttering, clasping his hands. Yet Dr. Holmes said there was nothing the matter with him. What then had happened—why had he gone, then, why, when she sat by him, did he start, frown at her, move away, and point at her hand, take her hand, look at it terrified?

Was it that she had taken off her wedding ring? "My hand has grown so thin," she said. "I have put it in my purse," she told him.

He dropped her hand. Their marriage was over, he thought, with agony, with relief. The rope was cut; he mounted; he was free, as it was decreed that he, Septimus, the lord of men, should be free; alone (since his wife had thrown away her wedding ring; since she had left him), he, Septimus, was alone, called forth in advance of the mass of men to hear the truth, to learn the meaning, which

8. Royal palace, begun in 1514 on the banks of the Thames River, about fifteen miles southwest of London. Queen Victoria opened it to the public, and it has been a popular day trip from the city since 1851.

now at last, after all the toils of civilisation—Greeks, Romans, Shakespeare, Darwin, and now himself—was to be given whole to. . . . "To whom?" he asked aloud. "To the Prime Minister," the voices which rustled above his head replied. The supreme secret must be told to the Cabinet; first that trees are alive; next there is no crime; next love, universal love, he muttered, gasping, trembling, painfully drawing out these profound truths which needed, so deep were they, so difficult, an immense effort to speak out, but the world was entirely changed by them for ever.

No crime; love; he repeated, fumbling for his card and pencil, when a Skye terrier snuffed his trousers and he started in an agony of fear. It was turning into a man! He could not watch it happen! It was horrible, terrible to see a dog become a man! At once the dog trotted away.

Heaven was divinely merciful, infinitely benignant. It spared him, pardoned his weakness. But what was the scientific explanation (for one must be scientific above all things)? Why could he see through bodies, see into the future, when dogs will become men? It was the heat wave presumably, operating upon a brain made sensitive by eons of evolution. Scientifically speaking, the flesh was melted off the world. His body was macerated until only the nerve fibres were left. It was spread like a veil upon a rock.[9]

He lay back in his chair, exhausted but upheld. He lay resting, waiting, before he again interpreted, with effort, with agony, to mankind. He lay very high, on the back of the world. The earth thrilled beneath him. Red flowers grew through his flesh; their stiff leaves rustled by his head. Music began clanging against the rocks up here. It is a motor horn down in the street, he muttered; but up here it cannoned from rock to rock, divided, met in shocks of sound which rose in smooth columns (that music should be visible was a discovery) and became an anthem, an anthem twined round now by a shepherd boy's piping (That's an old man playing a penny whistle by the public-house, he muttered) which, as the boy stood still came bubbling from his pipe, and then, as he climbed higher, made its exquisite plaint while the traffic passed beneath. This boy's elegy is played among the traffic, thought Septimus. Now he withdraws up into the snows, and roses hang about him—the thick red roses which grow on my bedroom wall, he reminded himself. The music stopped. He has his penny, he reasoned it out, and has gone on to the next public-house.

But he himself remained high on his rock, like a drowned sailor on a rock. I leant over the edge of the boat and fell down, he

9. Septimus's sense of having nearly drowned, saved only by a veil, alludes to Odysseus's situation, in Book Five of *The Odyssey*, where he is saved from drowning by the goddess Ino (see pp. 227–29).

thought. I went under the sea. I have been dead, and yet am now alive, but let me rest still; he begged (he was talking to himself again—it was awful, awful!); and as, before waking, the voices of birds and the sound of wheels chime and chatter in a queer harmony, grow louder and louder and the sleeper feels himself drawing to the shores of life, so he felt himself drawing towards life, the sun growing hotter, cries sounding louder, something tremendous about to happen.

He had only to open his eyes; but a weight was on them; a fear. He strained; he pushed; he looked; he saw Regent's Park before him. Long streamers of sunlight fawned at his feet. The trees waved, brandished. We welcome, the world seemed to say; we accept; we create. Beauty, the world seemed to say. And as if to prove it (scientifically) wherever he looked at the houses, at the railings, at the antelopes stretching over the palings, beauty sprang instantly. To watch a leaf quivering in the rush of air was an exquisite joy. Up in the sky swallows swooping, swerving, flinging themselves in and out, round and round, yet always with perfect control as if elastics held them; and the flies rising and falling; and the sun spotting now this leaf, now that, in mockery, dazzling it with soft gold in pure good temper; and now and again some chime (it might be a motor horn) tinkling divinely on the grass stalks—all of this, calm and reasonable as it was, made out of ordinary things as it was, was the truth now; beauty, that was the truth now. Beauty was everywhere.

"It is time," said Rezia.

The word "time" split its husk; poured its riches over him; and from his lips fell like shells, like shavings from a plane, without his making them, hard, white, imperishable words, and flew to attach themselves to their places in an ode to Time; an immortal ode to Time. He sang. Evans answered from behind the tree. The dead were in Thessaly, Evans sang, among the orchids. There they waited till the War was over, and now the dead, now Evans himself—

"For God's sake don't come!" Septimus cried out. For he could not look upon the dead.

But the branches parted. A man in grey was actually walking towards them. It was Evans! But no mud was on him; no wounds; he was not changed. I must tell the whole world, Septimus cried, raising his hand (as the dead man in the grey suit came nearer), raising his hand like some colossal figure who has lamented the fate of man for ages in the desert alone with his hands pressed to his forehead, furrows of despair on his cheeks, and now sees light on the desert's edge which broadens and strikes the iron-black figure (and Septimus half rose from his chair), and with legions of men prostrate behind him he, the giant mourner, receives for one moment on his face the whole—

"But I am so unhappy, Septimus," said Rezia trying to make him sit down.

The millions lamented; for ages they had sorrowed. He would turn round, he would tell them in a few moments, only a few moments more, of this relief, of this joy, of this astonishing revelation—

"The time, Septimus," Rezia repeated. "What is the time?"

He was talking, he was starting, this man must notice him. He was looking at them.

"I will tell you the time," said Septimus, very slowly, very drowsily, smiling mysteriously. As he sat smiling at the dead man in the grey suit the quarter struck—the quarter to twelve.

And that is being young, Peter Walsh thought as he passed them. To be having an awful scene—the poor girl looked absolutely desperate—in the middle of the morning. But what was it about, he wondered, what had the young man in the overcoat been saying to her to make her look like that; what awful fix had they got themselves into, both to look so desperate as that on a fine summer morning? The amusing thing about coming back to England, after five years, was the way it made, anyhow the first days, things stand out as if one had never seen them before; lovers squabbling under a tree; the domestic family life of the parks. Never had he seen London look so enchanting—the softness of the distances; the richness; the greenness; the civilization, after India, he thought, strolling across the grass.

This susceptibility to impressions had been his undoing no doubt. Still at his age he had, like a boy or a girl even, these alternations of mood; good days, bad days, for no reason whatever, happiness from a pretty face, downright misery at the sight of a frump. After India of course one fell in love with every woman one met. There was a freshness about them; even the poorest dressed better than five years ago surely; and to his eye the fashions had never been so becoming; the long black cloaks; the slimness; the elegance; and then the delicious and apparently universal habit of paint. Every woman, even the most respectable, had roses blooming under glass; lips cut with a knife; curls of Indian ink; there was design, art, everywhere; a change of some sort had undoubtedly taken place. What did the young people think about? Peter Walsh asked himself.

Those five years—1918 to 1923—had been, he suspected, somehow very important. People looked different. Newspapers seemed different. Now for instance there was a man writing quite openly in one of the respectable weeklies about water-closets.[1] That you couldn't have done ten years ago—written quite openly about water-closets in a respectable weekly. And then this taking out a

1. That is, toilets.

stick of rouge, or a powder-puff and making up in public. On board
ship coming home there were lots of young men and girls—Betty
and Bertie he remembered in particular—carrying on quite openly;
the old mother sitting and watching them with her knitting, cool as
a cucumber. The girl would stand still and powder her nose in
front of every one. And they weren't engaged; just having a good time;
no feelings hurt on either side. As hard as nails she was—Betty
What'shername—; but a thorough good sort. She would make a very
good wife at thirty—she would marry when it suited her to marry;
marry some rich man and live in a large house near Manchester.

Who was it now who had done that? Peter Walsh asked himself,
turning into the Broad Walk,—married a rich man and lived in a
large house near Manchester? Somebody who had written him a
long, gushing letter quite lately about "blue hydrangeas." It was seeing blue hydrangeas that made her think of him and the old days—
Sally Seton, of course! It was Sally Seton—the last person in the
world one would have expected to marry a rich man and live in a
large house near Manchester, the wild, the daring, the romantic
Sally!

But of all that ancient lot, Clarissa's friends—Whitbreads,
Kinderleys, Cunninghams, Kinloch-Jones's—Sally was probably
the best. She tried to get hold of things by the right end anyhow.
She saw through Hugh Whitbread anyhow—the admirable Hugh—
when Clarissa and the rest were at his feet.

"The Whitbreads?" he could hear her saying. "Who are the Whitbreads? Coal merchants. Respectable tradespeople."

Hugh she detested for some reason. He thought of nothing but
his own appearance, she said. He ought to have been a Duke. He
would be certain to marry one of the Royal Princesses. And of
course Hugh had the most extraordinary, the most natural, the
most sublime respect for the British aristocracy of any human being
he had ever come across. Even Clarissa had to own that. Oh, but he
was such a dear, so unselfish, gave up shooting to please his old
mother—remembered his aunts' birthdays, and so on.

Sally, to do her justice, saw through all that. One of the things
he remembered best was an argument one Sunday morning at
Bourton about women's rights (that antediluvian topic),[2] when
Sally suddenly lost her temper, flared up, and told Hugh that he
represented all that was most detestable in British middle-class
life. She told him that she considered him responsible for the
state of "those poor girls in Piccadilly"[3]—Hugh, the perfect

---

2. The British suffrage movement obtained the vote for women thirty and older in 1918,
   just five years before the novel takes place. Women twenty-one to twenty-nine had to
   wait until 1928 for the vote. Women's rights was hardly an ancient topic in 1923.
3. That is, prostitutes. See Froula, pp. 318–26.

gentleman, poor Hugh!—never did a man look more horrified!
She did it on purpose she said afterwards (for they used to get
together in the vegetable garden and compare notes). "He's read
nothing, thought nothing, felt nothing," he could hear her saying
in that very emphatic voice which carried so much farther than
she knew. The stable boys had more life in them than Hugh, she
said. He was a perfect specimen of the public school type, she said.
No country but England could have produced him. She was really
spiteful, for some reason; had some grudge against him. Something had happened—he forgot what—in the smoking-room. He
had insulted her—kissed her? Incredible! Nobody believed a word
against Hugh of course. Who could? Kissing Sally in the smoking-
room! If it had been some Honourable Edith or Lady Violet, perhaps; but not that ragamuffin Sally without a penny to her name,
and a father or a mother gambling at Monte Carlo. For of all the
people he had ever met Hugh was the greatest snob—the most
obsequious—no, he didn't cringe exactly. He was too much of a
prig for that. A first-rate valet was the obvious comparison—
somebody who walked behind carrying suit cases; could be trusted
to send telegrams—indispensable to hostesses. And he'd found
his job—married his Honourable Evelyn; got some little post at
Court, looked after the King's cellars, polished the Imperial shoe-
buckles, went about in knee-breeches and lace ruffles. How
remorseless life is! A little job at Court!

He had married this lady, the Honourable Evelyn, and they lived
hereabouts, so he thought (looking at the pompous houses over-
looking the Park), for he had lunched there once in a house which
had, like all Hugh's possessions, something that no other house
could possibly have—linen cupboards it might have been. You had
to go and look at them—you had to spend a great deal of time
always admiring whatever it was—linen cupboards, pillow-cases,
old oak furniture, pictures, which Hugh had picked up for an old
song. But Mrs. Hugh sometimes gave the show away. She was one
of those obscure mouse-like little women who admire big men. She
was almost negligible. Then suddenly she would say something
quite unexpected—something sharp. She had the relics of the
grand manner perhaps. The steam coal was a little too strong for
her—it made the atmosphere thick. And so there they lived, with
their linen cupboards and their old masters and their pillow-cases
fringed with real lace at the rate of five or ten thousand a year presumably, while he, who was two years older than Hugh, cadged for
a job.

At fifty-three he had to come and ask them to put him into some
secretary's office, to find him some usher's job teaching little boys
Latin, at the beck and call of some mandarin in an office,

something that brought in five hundred a year; for if he married
Daisy, even with his pension, they could never do on less. Whitbread could do it presumably; or Dalloway. He didn't mind what he
asked Dalloway. He was a thorough good sort; a bit limited; a bit
thick in the head; yes; but a thorough good sort. Whatever he took
up he did in the same matter-of-fact sensible way; without a touch
of imagination, without a spark of brilliancy, but with the inexpli-
cable niceness of his type. He ought to have been a country gentleman—he was wasted on politics. He was at his best out of doors,
with horses and dogs—how good he was, for instance, when that
great shaggy dog of Clarissa's got caught in a trap and had its paw
half torn off, and Clarissa turned faint and Dalloway did the whole
thing; bandaged, made splints; told Clarissa not to be a fool. That
was what she liked him for perhaps—that was what she needed.
"Now, my dear, don't be a fool. Hold this—fetch that," all the time
talking to the dog as if it were a human being.

But how could she swallow all that stuff about poetry? How could
she let him hold forth about Shakespeare? Seriously and solemnly
Richard Dalloway got on his hind legs and said that no decent man
ought to read Shakespeare's sonnets because it was like listening at
keyholes (besides the relationship was not one that he approved).
No decent man ought to let his wife visit a deceased wife's sister.
Incredible! The only thing to do was to pelt him with sugared
almonds—it was at dinner. But Clarissa sucked it all in; thought it
so honest of him; so independent of him; Heaven knows if she
didn't think him the most original mind she'd ever met!

That was one of the bonds between Sally and himself. There was
a garden where they used to walk, a walled-in place, with rose-
bushes and giant cauliflowers—he could remember Sally tearing
off a rose, stopping to exclaim at the beauty of the cabbage leaves in
the moonlight (it was extraordinary how vividly it all came back to
him, things he hadn't thought of for years,) while she implored him,
half laughing of course, to carry off Clarissa, to save her from the
Hughs and the Dalloways and all the other "perfect gentlemen"
who would "stifle her soul" (she wrote reams of poetry in those
days), make a mere hostess of her, encourage her worldliness. But
one must do Clarissa justice. She wasn't going to marry Hugh anyhow. She had a perfectly clear notion of what she wanted. Her emotions were all on the surface. Beneath, she was very shrewd—a far
better judge of character than Sally, for instance, and with it all,
purely feminine; with that extraordinary gift, that woman's gift, of
making a world of her own wherever she happened to be. She came
into a room; she stood, as he had often seen her, in a doorway with
lots of people round her. But it was Clarissa one remembered. Not
that she was striking; not beautiful at all; there was nothing

picturesque about her; she never said anything specially clever; there she was, however; there she was.

No, no, no! He was not in love with her any more! He only felt, after seeing her that morning, among her scissors and silks, making ready for the party, unable to get away from the thought of her; she kept coming back and back like a sleeper jolting against him in a railway carriage; which was not being in love, of course; it was thinking of her, criticising her, starting again, after thirty years, trying to explain her. The obvious thing to say of her was that she was worldly; cared too much for rank and society and getting on in the world—which was true in a sense; she had admitted it to him. (You could always get her to own up if you took the trouble; she was honest.) What she would say was that she hated frumps, fogies, failures, like himself presumably; thought people had no right to slouch about with their hands in their pockets; must do something, be something; and these great swells, these Duchesses, these hoary old Countesses one met in her drawing-room, unspeakably remote as he felt them to be from anything that mattered a straw, stood for something real to her. Lady Bexborough, she said once, held herself upright (so did Clarissa herself; she never lounged in any sense of the word; she was straight as a dart, a little rigid in fact). She said they had a kind of courage which the older she grew the more she respected. In all this there was a great deal of Dalloway, of course; a great deal of the public-spirited, British Empire, tariff-reform, governing-class spirit, which had grown on her, as it tends to do. With twice his wits, she had to see things through his eyes—one of the tragedies of married life. With a mind of her own, she must always be quoting Richard—as if one couldn't know to a tittle what Richard thought by reading the *Morning Post* of a morning! These parties for example were all for him, or for her idea of him (to do Richard justice he would have been happier farming in Norfolk). She made her drawing-room a sort of meeting-place; she had a genius for it. Over and over again he had seen her take some raw youth, twist him, turn him, wake him up; set him going. Infinite numbers of dull people conglomerated round her of course. But odd unexpected people turned up; an artist sometimes; sometimes a writer; queer fish in that atmosphere. And behind it all was that network of visiting, leaving cards, being kind to people; running about with bunches of flowers, little presents; So-and-so was going to France—must have an air-cushion; a real drain on her strength; all that interminable traffic that women of her sort keep up; but she did it genuinely, from a natural instinct.

Oddly enough, she was one of the most thorough-going sceptics he had ever met, and possibly (this was a theory he used to make up to account for her, so transparent in some ways, so inscrutable in others), possibly she said to herself, As we are a doomed race, chained to a sinking ship (her favourite reading as a girl was Huxley and Tyndall, and they were fond of these nautical metaphors), as the whole thing is a bad joke, let us, at any rate, do our part; mitigate the sufferings of our fellow-prisoners (Huxley again); decorate the dungeon with flowers and air-cushions; be as decent as we possibly can. Those ruffians, the Gods, shan't have it all their own way,—her notion being that the Gods, who never lost a chance of hurting, thwarting and spoiling human lives were seriously put out if, all the same, you behaved like a lady. That phase came directly after Sylvia's death—that horrible affair. To see your own sister killed by a falling tree (all Justin Parry's fault—all his carelessness) before your very eyes, a girl too on the verge of life, the most gifted of them, Clarissa always said, was enough to turn one bitter. Later she wasn't so positive perhaps; she thought there were no Gods; no one was to blame; and so she evolved this atheist's religion of doing good for the sake of goodness.

And of course she enjoyed life immensely. It was her nature to enjoy (though goodness only knows, she had her reserves; it was a mere sketch, he often felt, that even he, after all these years, could make of Clarissa). Anyhow there was no bitterness in her; none of that sense of moral virtue which is so repulsive in good women. She enjoyed practically everything. If you walked with her in Hyde Park now it was a bed of tulips, now a child in a perambulator, now some absurd little drama she made up on the spur of the moment. (Very likely, she would have talked to those lovers, if she had thought them unhappy.) She had a sense of comedy that was really exquisite, but she needed people, always people, to bring it out, with the inevitable result that she frittered her time away, lunching, dining, giving these incessant parties of hers, talking nonsense, saying things she didn't mean, blunting the edge of her mind, losing her discrimination. There she would sit at the head of the table taking infinite pains with some old buffer who might be useful to Dalloway—they knew the most appalling bores in Europe—or in came Elizabeth and everything must give way to *her*. She was at a High School, at the inarticulate stage last time he was over, a round-eyed, pale-faced girl, with nothing of her mother in her, a silent stolid creature, who took it all as a matter of course, let her mother make a fuss of her, and then said "May I go now?" like a child of four; going off, Clarissa explained, with that mixture of amusement and pride which Dalloway himself seemed to rouse in her, to play hockey. And now Elizabeth was "out,"[4] presumably; thought him an

---

4. Peter presumes that Elizabeth, as a member of an elite set, would by now have been presented at Court (and thus "out" in society) and would be participating in an active social season, June and July being the season's busiest months.

old fogy, laughed at her mother's friends. Ah well, so be it. The compensation of growing old, Peter Walsh thought, coming out of Regent's Park, and holding his hat in hand, was simply this; that the passions remain as strong as ever, but one has gained—at last!—the power which adds the supreme flavour to existence,—the power of taking hold of experience, of turning it round, slowly, in the light.

A terrible confession it was (he put his hat on again), but now, at the age of fifty-three one scarcely needed people any more. Life itself, every moment of it, every drop of it, here, this instant, now, in the sun, in Regent's Park, was enough. Too much indeed. A whole lifetime was too short to bring out, now that one had acquired the power, the full flavour; to extract every ounce of pleasure, every shade of meaning; which both were so much more solid than they used to be, so much less personal. It was impossible that he should ever suffer again as Clarissa had made him suffer. For hours at a time (pray God that one might say these things without being overheard!), for hours and days he never thought of Daisy.

Could it be that he was in love with her then, remembering the misery, the torture, the extraordinary passion of those days? It was a different thing altogether—a much pleasanter thing—the truth being, of course, that now *she* was in love with *him*. And that perhaps was the reason why, when the ship actually sailed, he felt an extraordinary relief, wanted nothing so much as to be alone; was annoyed to find all her little attentions—cigars, notes, a rug for the voyage—in his cabin. Every one if they were honest would say the same; one doesn't want people after fifty; one doesn't want to go on telling women they are pretty; that's what most men of fifty would say, Peter Walsh thought, if they were honest.

But then these astonishing accesses of emotion—bursting into tears this morning, what was all that about? What could Clarissa have thought of him? thought him a fool presumably, not for the first time. It was jealousy that was at the bottom of it—jealousy which survives every other passion of mankind, Peter Walsh thought, holding his pocket-knife at arm's length. She had been meeting Major Orde, Daisy said in her last letter; said it on purpose he knew; said it to make him jealous; he could see her wrinkling her forehead as she wrote, wondering what she could say to hurt him; and yet it made no difference; he was furious! All this pother of coming to England and seeing lawyers wasn't to marry her, but to prevent her from marrying anybody else. That was what tortured him, that was what came over him when he saw Clarissa so calm, so cold, so intent on her dress or whatever it was; realising what she might have spared him, what she had reduced him to—a whimpering, snivelling old ass. But women, he thought, shutting his pocket-knife, don't know what passion is. They don't know the meaning of

it to men. Clarissa was as cold as an icicle. There she would sit on
the sofa by his side, let him take her hand, give him one kiss—Here
he was at the crossing.

A sound interrupted him; a frail quivering sound, a voice bubbling up without direction, vigour, beginning or end, running
weakly and shrilly and with an absence of all human meaning into

> ee um fah um so
> foo swee too eem oo—[5]

the voice of no age or sex, the voice of an ancient spring spouting
from the earth; which issued, just opposite Regent's Park Tube station from a tall quivering shape, like a funnel, like a rusty pump,
like a wind-beaten tree for ever barren of leaves which lets the wind
run up and down its branches singing

> ee um fah um so
> foo swee too eem oo

and rocks and creaks and moans in the eternal breeze.

Through all ages—when the pavement was grass, when it was
swamp, through the age of tusk and mammoth, through the age of
silent sunrise, the battered woman—for she wore a skirt—with her
right hand exposed, her left clutching at her side, stood singing of
love—love which has lasted a million years, she sang, love which
prevails, and millions of years ago, her lover, who had been dead
these centuries, had walked, she crooned, with her in May; but in
the course of ages, long as summer days, and flaming, she remembered, with nothing but red asters, he had gone; death's enormous
sickle had swept those tremendous hills, and when at last she laid
her hoary and immensely aged head on the earth, now become a
mere cinder of ice, she implored the Gods to lay by her side a bunch
of purple heather, there on her high burial place which the last rays
of the last sun caressed; for then the pageant of the universe would
be over.

As the ancient song bubbled up opposite Regent's Park Tube station still the earth seemed green and flowery; still, though it issued
from so rude a mouth, a mere hole in the earth, muddy too, matted
with root fibres and tangled grasses, still the old bubbling burbling
song, soaking through the knotted roots of infinite ages, and skele-
tons and treasure, streamed away in rivulets over the pavement and
all along the Marylebone Road, and down towards Euston, fertilis-
ing, leaving a damp stain.

---

5. While these words sound like nonsense, the images and quoted language in the following
paragraphs—a May lover, asters, "look in my eyes"—draw from a poem, "Allerseelen," by
Herman von Gilm, famously set to music by Richard Strauss (see pp. 234–35).

Still remembering how once in some primeval May she had walked with her lover, this rusty pump, this battered old woman with one hand exposed for coppers the other clutching her side, would still be there in ten million years, remembering how once she had walked in May, where the sea flows now, with whom it did not matter—he was a man, oh yes, a man who had loved her. But the passage of ages had blurred the clarity of that ancient May day; the bright petalled flowers were hoar and silver frosted; and she no longer saw, when she implored him (as she did now quite clearly) "look in my eyes with thy sweet eyes intently," she no longer saw brown eyes, black whiskers or sunburnt face but only a looming shape, a shadow shape, to which, with the bird-like freshness of the very aged she still twittered "give me your hand and let me press it gently" (Peter Walsh couldn't help giving the poor creature a coin as he stepped into his taxi), "and if some one should see, what matter they?" she demanded; and her fist clutched at her side, and she smiled, pocketing her shilling, and all peering inquisitive eyes seemed blotted out, and the passing generations—the pavement was crowded with bustling middle-class people—vanished, like leaves, to be trodden under, to be soaked and steeped and made mould of by that eternal spring—

> ee um fah um so
> foo swee too eem oo

"Poor old woman," said Rezia Warren Smith, waiting to cross. Oh poor old wretch!

Suppose it was a wet night? Suppose one's father, or somebody who had known one in better days had happened to pass, and saw one standing there in the gutter? And where did she sleep at night?

Cheerfully, almost gaily, the invincible thread of sound wound up into the air like the smoke from a cottage chimney, winding up clean beech trees and issuing in a tuft of blue smoke among the topmost leaves. "And if some one should see, what matter they?"

Since she was so unhappy, for weeks and weeks now, Rezia had given meanings to things that happened, almost felt sometimes that she must stop people in the street, if they looked good, kind people, just to say to them "I am unhappy"; and this old woman singing in the street "if some one should see, what matter they?" made her suddenly quite sure that everything was going to be right. They were going to Sir William Bradshaw; she thought his name sounded nice; he would cure Septimus at once. And then there was a brewer's cart, and the grey horses had upright bristles of straw in their tails; there were newspaper placards. It was a silly, silly dream, being unhappy.

So they crossed, Mr. and Mrs. Septimus Warren Smith, and was there, after all, anything to draw attention to them, anything to make a passer-by suspect here is a young man who carries in him the greatest message in the world, and is, moreover, the happiest man in the world, and the most miserable? Perhaps they walked more slowly than other people, and there was something hesitating, trailing, in the man's walk, but what more natural for a clerk, who has not been in the West End on a weekday at this hour for years, than to keep looking at the sky, looking at this, that and the other, as if Portland Place were a room he had come into when the family are away, the chandeliers being hung in holland bags, and the care-taker, as she lets in long shafts of dusty light upon deserted, queer-looking armchairs, lifting one corner of the long blinds, explains to the visitors what a wonderful place it is; how wonderful, but at the same time, he thinks, as he looks at chairs and tables, how strange.

To look at, he might have been a clerk, but of the better sort; for he wore brown boots; his hands were educated; so, too, his profile—his angular, big-nosed, intelligent, sensitive profile; but not his lips altogether, for they were loose; and his eyes (as eyes tend to be), eyes merely; hazel, large; so that he was, on the whole, a border case, neither one thing nor the other, might end with a house at Purley and a motor car, or continue renting apartments in back streets all his life; one of those half-educated, self-educated men whose education is all learnt from books borrowed from public libraries, read in the evening after the day's work, on the advice of well-known authors consulted by letter.

As for the other experiences, the solitary ones, which people go through alone, in their bedrooms, in their offices, walking the fields and the streets of London, he had them; had left home, a mere boy, because of his mother; she lied; because he came down to tea for the fiftieth time with his hands unwashed; because he could see no future for a poet in Stroud; and so, making a confidant of his little sister, had gone to London leaving an absurd note behind him, such as great men have written, and the world has read later when the story of their struggles has become famous.

London has swallowed up many millions of young men called Smith; thought nothing of fantastic Christian names like Septimus with which their parents have thought to distinguish them. Lodg-ing off the Euston Road, there were experiences, again experiences, such as change a face in two years from a pink innocent oval to a face lean, contracted, hostile. But of all this what could the most observant of friends have said except what a gardener says when he opens the conservatory door in the morning and finds a new blos-som on his plant:—It has flowered; flowered from vanity, ambition, idealism, passion, loneliness, courage, laziness, the usual seeds,

which all muddled up (in a room off the Euston Road), made him
shy, and stammering, made him anxious to improve himself, made
him fall in love with Miss Isabel Pole, lecturing in the Waterloo
Road upon Shakespeare.

Was he not like Keats? she asked; and reflected how she might
give him a taste of *Antony and Cleopatra*[6] and the rest; lent him
books; wrote him scraps of letters; and lit in him such a fire as
burns only once in a lifetime, without heat, flickering a red gold
flame infinitely ethereal and insubstantial over Miss Pole; *Antony
and Cleopatra*; and the Waterloo Road. He thought her beautiful,
believed her impeccably wise; dreamed of her, wrote poems to her,
which, ignoring the subject, she corrected in red ink; he saw her,
one summer evening, walking in a green dress in a square. "It has
flowered," the gardener might have said, had he opened the door;
had he come in, that is to say, any night about this time, and found
him writing; found him tearing up his writing; found him finishing
a masterpiece at three o'clock in the morning and running out to
pace the streets, and visiting churches, and fasting one day, drinking another, devouring Shakespeare, Darwin, *The History of Civilisation*, and Bernard Shaw.

Something was up, Mr. Brewer knew; Mr. Brewer, managing
clerk at Sibleys and Arrowsmiths, auctioneers, valuers, land and
estate agents; something was up, he thought, and, being paternal
with his young men, and thinking very highly of Smith's abilities,
and prophesying that he would, in ten or fifteen years, succeed to
the leather arm-chair in the inner room under the skylight with the
deed-boxes round him, "if he keeps his health," said Mr. Brewer,
and that was the danger—he looked weakly; advised football,
invited him to supper and was seeing his way to consider recom-
mending a rise of salary, when something happened which threw
out many of Mr. Brewer's calculations, took away his ablest young
fellows, and eventually, so prying and insidious were the fingers of
the European War, smashed a plaster cast of Ceres, ploughed a
hole in the geranium beds, and utterly ruined the cook's nerves at
Mr. Brewer's establishment at Muswell Hill.

Septimus was one of the first to volunteer. He went to France to
save an England which consisted almost entirely of Shakespeare's
plays and Miss Isabel Pole in a green dress walking in a square.
There in the trenches the change which Mr. Brewer desired when he
advised football was produced instantly; he developed manliness; he

6. Woolf's rough draft was explicit about the risks of a woman teacher sharing this play
   with her student. The play depicts, among other things, how Cleopatra, Queen of
   Egypt, baits Marc Antony to fight. When their fight fails, both lovers die by their own
   hand. In naming this play, Woolf suggests that Miss Isabel Pole inspires Septimus to
   enlist in a war that will be dangerous for him.

was promoted; he drew the attention, indeed the affection of his
officer, Evans by name. It was a case of two dogs playing on a
hearth-rug; one worrying a paper screw, snarling, snapping, giving
a pinch, now and then, at the old dog's ear; the other lying somno-
lent, blinking at the fire, raising a paw, turning and growling good-
temperedly. They had to be together, share with each other, fight
with each other, quarrel with each other. But when Evans (Rezia
who had only seen him once called him "a quiet man," a sturdy red-
haired man, undemonstrative in the company of women), when
Evans was killed, just before the Armistice, in Italy, Septimus, far
from showing any emotion or recognising that here was the end of
a friendship, congratulated himself upon feeling very little and very
reasonably. The War had taught him. It was sublime. He had gone
through the whole show, friendship, European War, death, had
won promotion, was still under thirty and was bound to survive. He
was right there. The last shells missed him. He watched them
explode with indifference. When peace came he was in Milan, bil-
leted in the house of an innkeeper with a courtyard, flowers in
tubs, little tables in the open, daughters making hats, and to Lucrezia, the younger daughter, he became engaged one evening when
the panic was on him—that he could not feel.

For now that it was all over, truce signed, and the dead buried, he
had, especially in the evening, these sudden thunder-claps of fear.
He could not feel. As he opened the door of the room where the
Italian girls sat making hats, he could see them; could hear them;
they were rubbing wires among coloured beads in saucers; they
were turning buckram shapes this way and that; the table was all
strewn with feathers, spangles, silks, ribbons; scissors were rapping
on the table; but something failed him; he could not feel. Still, scissors rapping, girls laughing, hats being made protected him; he was
assured of safety; he had a refuge. But he could not sit there all
night. There were moments of waking in the early morning. The
bed was falling; he was falling. Oh for the scissors and the lamp-
light and the buckram shapes! He asked Lucrezia to marry him, the
younger of the two, the gay, the frivolous, with those little artist's
fingers that she would hold up and say "It is all in them." Silk,
feathers, what not were alive to them.

"It is the hat that matters most," she would say, when they walked
out together. Every hat that passed, she would examine; and the
cloak and the dress and the way the woman held herself. Ill-
dressing, over-dressing she stigmatised, not savagely, rather with
impatient movements of the hands, like those of a painter who puts
from him some obvious well-meant glaring imposture; and then,
generously, but always critically, she would welcome a shop-girl
who had turned her little bit of stuff gallantly, or praise, wholly,

with enthusiastic and professional understanding, a French lady descending from her carriage, in chinchilla, robes, pearls.

"Beautiful!" she would murmur, nudging Septimus, that he might see. But beauty was behind a pane of glass. Even taste (Rezia liked ices, chocolates, sweet things) had no relish to him. He put down his cup on the little marble table. He looked at people outside; happy they seemed, collecting in the middle of the street, shouting, laughing, squabbling over nothing. But he could not taste, he could not feel. In the tea-shop among the tables and the chattering waiters the appalling fear came over him—he could not feel. He could reason; he could read, Dante[7] for example, quite easily ("Septimus, do put down your book," said Rezia, gently shutting the *Inferno*), he could add up his bill; his brain was perfect; it must be the fault of the world then—that he could not feel.

"The English are so silent," Rezia said. She liked it, she said. She respected these Englishmen, and wanted to see London, and the English horses, and the tailor-made suits, and could remember hearing how wonderful the shops were, from an Aunt who had married and lived in Soho.[8]

It might be possible, Septimus thought, looking at England from the train window, as they left Newhaven; it might be possible that the world itself is without meaning.

At the office they advanced him to a post of considerable responsibility. They were proud of him; he had won crosses. "You have done your duty; it is up to us—" began Mr. Brewer; and could not finish, so pleasurable was his emotion. They took admirable lodgings off the Tottenham Court Road.

Here he opened Shakespeare once more. That boy's business of the intoxication of language—*Antony and Cleopatra*—had shrivelled utterly. How Shakespeare loathed humanity—the putting on of clothes, the getting of children, the sordidity of the mouth and the belly! This was now revealed to Septimus; the message hidden in the beauty of words. The secret signal which one generation passes, under disguise, to the next is loathing, hatred, despair. Dante the same. Aeschylus[9] (translated) the same. There Rezia sat at the table trimming hats. She trimmed hats for Mrs. Filmer's friends; she trimmed hats by the hour. She looked pale, mysterious, like a lily, drowned, under water, he thought.

---

7. Dante Alighieri (1265–1321), Italian poet best known for *The Inferno* (1321).
8. Central London district; through the twentieth century it was densely populated with immigrants, many of them French, German, Swiss, or Italian in origin.
9. Poet and dramatist (515–456 B.C.E.). See Woolf's essay "On Not Knowing Greek," pp. 207–18, where she discusses him.

"The English are so serious," she would say, putting her arms round Septimus, her cheek against his.

Love between man and woman was repulsive to Shakespeare. The business of copulation was filth to him before the end. But, Rezia said, she must have children. They had been married five years.

They went to the Tower together; to the Victoria and Albert Museum; stood in the crowd to see the King open Parliament. And there were the shops—hat shops, dress shops, shops with leather bags in the window, where she would stand staring. But she must have a boy.

She must have a son like Septimus, she said. But nobody could be like Septimus; so gentle; so serious; so clever. Could she not read Shakespeare too? Was Shakespeare a difficult author? she asked.

One cannot bring children into a world like this. One cannot perpetuate suffering, or increase the breed of these lustful animals, who have no lasting emotions, but only whims and vanities, eddying them now this way, now that.

He watched her snip, shape, as one watches a bird hop, flit in the grass, without daring to move a finger. For the truth is (let her ignore it) that human beings have neither kindness, nor faith, nor charity beyond what serves to increase the pleasure of the moment. They hunt in packs. Their packs scour the desert and vanish screaming into the wilderness. They desert the fallen. They are plastered over with grimaces. There was Brewer at the office, with his waxed moustache, coral tiepin, white slip, and pleasurable emotions—all coldness and clamminess within,—his geraniums ruined in the War—his cook's nerves destroyed; or Amelia What'shername, handing round cups of tea punctually at five—a leering, sneering obscene little harpy; and the Toms and Berties in their starched shirt fronts oozing thick drops of vice. They never saw him drawing pictures of them naked at their antics in his notebook. In the street, vans roared past him; brutality blared out on placards; men were trapped in mines; women burnt alive; and once a maimed file of lunatics being exercised or displayed for the diversion of the populace (who laughed aloud), ambled and nodded and grinned past him, in the Tottenham Court Road, each half apologetically, yet triumphantly, inflicting his hopeless woe. And would *he* go mad?

At tea Rezia told him that Mrs. Filmer's daughter was expecting a baby. *She* could not grow old and have no children! She was very lonely, she was very unhappy! She cried for the first time since they were married. Far away he heard her sobbing; he heard it accurately, he noticed it distinctly; he compared it to a piston thumping. But he felt nothing.

His wife was crying, and he felt nothing; only each time she sobbed in this profound, this silent, this hopeless way, he descended another step into the pit.

At last, with a melodramatic gesture which he assumed mechanically and with complete consciousness of its insincerity, he dropped his head on his hands. Now he had surrendered; now other people must help him. People must be sent for. He gave in.

Nothing could rouse him. Rezia put him to bed. She sent for a doctor—Mrs. Filmer's Dr. Holmes. Dr. Holmes examined him. There was nothing whatever the matter, said Dr. Holmes. Oh, what a relief! What a kind man, what a good man! thought Rezia. When he felt like that he went to the Music Hall, said Dr. Holmes. He took a day off with his wife and played golf. Why not try two tabloids of bromide dissolved in a glass of water at bedtime? These old Bloomsbury houses, said Dr. Holmes, tapping the wall, are often full of very fine panelling, which the landlords have the folly to paper over. Only the other day, visiting a patient, Sir Somebody Something in Bedford Square—

So there was no excuse; nothing whatever the matter, except the sin for which human nature had condemned him to death; that he did not feel. He had not cared when Evans was killed; that was worst; but all the other crimes raised their heads and shook their fingers and jeered and sneered over the rail of the bed in the early hours of the morning at the prostrate body which lay realising its degradation; how he had married his wife without loving her; had lied to her; seduced her; outraged Miss Isabel Pole, and was so pocked and marked with vice that women shuddered when they saw him in the street. The verdict of human nature on such a wretch was death.

Dr. Holmes came again. Large, fresh coloured, handsome, flicking his boots, looking in the glass, he brushed it all aside—headaches, sleeplessness, fears, dreams—nerve symptoms and nothing more, he said. If Dr. Holmes found himself even half a pound below eleven stone six,[1] he asked his wife for another plate of porridge at breakfast. (Rezia would learn to cook porridge.) But, he continued, health is largely a matter in our own control. Throw yourself into outside interests; take up some hobby. He opened Shakespeare— *Antony and Cleopatra*; pushed Shakespeare aside. Some hobby, said Dr. Holmes, for did he not owe his own excellent health (and he worked as hard as any man in London) to the fact that he could always switch off from his patients on to old furniture? And what a

1. Overfeeding was a common treatment for mental illness at the time. A stone is commonly used in England as a measure of weight. One stone equals 14 pounds, thus 11 stones is 154 pounds.

very pretty comb, if he might say so, Mrs. Warren Smith was wearing!

When the damned fool came again, Septimus refused to see him. Did he indeed? said Dr. Holmes, smiling agreeably. Really he had to give that charming little lady, Mrs. Smith, a friendly push before he could get past her into her husband's bedroom.

"So you're in a funk," he said agreeably, sitting down by his patient's side. He had actually talked of killing himself to his wife, quite a girl, a foreigner, wasn't she? Didn't that give her a very odd idea of English husbands? Didn't one owe perhaps a duty to one's wife? Wouldn't it be better to do something instead of lying in bed? For he had had forty years' experience behind him; and Septimus could take Dr. Holmes's word for it—there was nothing whatever the matter with him. And next time Dr. Holmes came he hoped to find Smith out of bed and not making that charming little lady his wife anxious about him.

Human nature, in short, was on him—the repulsive brute, with the blood-red nostrils. Holmes was on him. Dr. Holmes came quite regularly every day. Once you stumble, Septimus wrote on the back of a postcard, human nature is on you. Holmes is on you. Their only chance was to escape, without letting Holmes know; to Italy— anywhere, anywhere, away from Dr. Holmes.

But Rezia could not understand him. Dr. Holmes was such a kind man. He was so interested in Septimus. He only wanted to help them, he said. He had four little children and he had asked her to tea, she told Septimus.

So he was deserted. The whole world was clamouring: Kill yourself, kill yourself, for our sakes. But why should he kill himself for their sakes? Food was pleasant; the sun hot; and this killing oneself, how does one set about it, with a table knife, uglily, with floods of blood,— by sucking a gaspipe? He was too weak; he could scarcely raise his hand. Besides, now that he was quite alone, condemned, deserted, as those who are about to die are alone, there was a luxury in it, an isolation full of sublimity; a freedom which the attached can never know. Holmes had won of course; the brute with the red nostrils had won. But even Holmes himself could not touch this last relic straying on the edge of the world, this outcast, who gazed back at the inhabited regions, who lay, like a drowned sailor, on the shore of the world.

It was at that moment (Rezia gone shopping) that the great revelation took place. A voice spoke from behind the screen. Evans was speaking. The dead were with him.

"Evans, Evans!" he cried.

Mr. Smith was talking aloud to himself, Agnes the servant girl cried to Mrs. Filmer in the kitchen. "Evans, Evans," he had said as she brought in the tray. She jumped, she did. She scuttled downstairs.

And Rezia came in, with her flowers, and walked across the room, and put the roses in a vase, upon which the sun struck directly, and it went laughing, leaping round the room.

She had had to buy the roses, Rezia said, from a poor man in the street. But they were almost dead already, she said, arranging the roses.

So there was a man outside; Evans presumably; and the roses, which Rezia said were half dead, had been picked by him in the fields of Greece. "Communication is health; communication is happiness, communication—" he muttered.

"What are you saying, Septimus?" Rezia asked, wild with terror, for he was talking to himself.

She sent Agnes running for Dr. Holmes. Her husband, she said, was mad. He scarcely knew her.

"You brute! You brute!" cried Septimus, seeing human nature, that is Dr. Holmes, enter the room.

"Now what's all this about?" said Dr. Holmes in the most amiable way in the world. "Talking nonsense to frighten your wife?" But he would give him something to make him sleep. And if they were rich people, said Dr. Holmes, looking ironically round the room, by all means let them go to Harley Street; if they had no confidence in him, said Dr. Holmes, looking not quite so kind.[2]

It was precisely twelve o'clock; twelve by Big Ben; whose stroke was wafted over the northern part of London; blent with that of other clocks, mixed in a thin ethereal way with the clouds and wisps of smoke, and died up there among the seagulls—twelve o'clock struck as Clarissa Dalloway laid her green dress on her bed, and the Warren Smiths walked down Harley Street. Twelve was the hour of their appointment. Probably, Rezia thought, that was Sir William Bradshaw's house with the grey motor car in front of it. The leaden circles dissolved in the air.

Indeed it was—Sir William Bradshaw's motor car; low, powerful, grey with plain initials interlocked on the panel, as if the pomps of heraldry were incongruous, this man being the ghostly helper, the priest of science; and, as the motor car was grey, so to match its sober suavity, grey furs, silver grey rugs were heaped in it, to keep her ladyship warm while she waited. For often Sir William would travel sixty miles or more down into the country to visit the rich, the afflicted, who could afford the very large fee which Sir William very properly charged for his advice. Her ladyship waited with the rugs about her knees an hour or more, leaning back, thinking sometimes of the patient, sometimes, excusably, of the wall of gold, mounting minute by minute while she waited; the wall of gold that

2. The British edition has a section break after this line, making the stroke of twelve mark a new section.

was mounting between them and all shifts and anxieties (she had borne them bravely; they had had their struggles) until she felt wedged on a calm ocean, where only spice winds blow; respected, admired, envied, with scarcely anything left to wish for, though she regretted her stoutness; large dinner-parties every Thursday night to the profession; an occasional bazaar to be opened; Royalty greeted; too little time, alas, with her husband, whose work grew and grew; a boy doing well at Eton;[3] she would have liked a daughter too; interests she had, however, in plenty; child welfare; the after-care of the epileptic, and photography, so that if there was a church building, or a church decaying, she bribed the sexton, got the key and took photographs, which were scarcely to be distinguished from the work of professionals, while she waited.

Sir William himself was no longer young. He had worked very hard; he had won his position by sheer ability (being the son of a shopkeeper); loved his profession; made a fine figurehead at ceremonies and spoke well—all of which had by the time he was knighted given him a heavy look, a weary look (the stream of patients being so incessant, the responsibilities and privileges of his profession so onerous), which weariness, together with his grey hairs, increased the extraordinary distinction of his presence and gave him the reputation (of the utmost importance in dealing with nerve cases) not merely of lightning skill, and almost infallible accuracy in diagnosis but of sympathy; tact; understanding of the human soul. He could see the first moment they came into the room (the Warren Smiths they were called); he was certain directly he saw the man; it was a case of extreme gravity. It was a case of complete breakdown—complete physical and nervous breakdown, with every symptom in an advanced stage, he ascertained in two or three minutes (writing answers to questions, murmured discreetly, on a pink card).

How long had Dr. Holmes been attending him?

Six weeks.

Prescribed a little bromide? Said there was nothing the matter? Ah yes (those general practitioners! thought Sir William. It took half his time to undo their blunders. Some were irreparable).

"You served with great distinction in the War?"

The patient repeated the word "war" interrogatively.

He was attaching meanings to words of a symbolical kind. A serious symptom, to be noted on the card.

"The War?" the patient asked. The European War—that little shindy of schoolboys with gunpowder? Had he served with distinction? He really forgot. In the War itself he had failed.

---

3. One of the largest, oldest, and most famous English public schools, founded in 1440. A "public" school in England is a fee-based (i.e., private) secondary school.

"Yes, he served with the greatest distinction," Rezia assured the doctor; "he was promoted."

"And they have the very highest opinion of you at your office?" Sir William murmured, glancing at Mr. Brewer's very generously worded letter. "So that you have nothing to worry you, no financial anxiety, nothing?"

He had committed an appalling crime and been condemned to death by human nature.

"I have—I have," he began, "committed a crime—"

"He has done nothing wrong whatever," Rezia assured the doctor. If Mr. Smith would wait, said Sir William, he would speak to Mrs. Smith in the next room. Her husband was very seriously ill, Sir William said. Did he threaten to kill himself?

Oh, he did, she cried. But he did not mean it, she said. Of course not. It was merely a question of rest, said Sir William; of rest, rest, rest; a long rest in bed. There was a delightful home down in the country where her husband would be perfectly looked after. Away from her? she asked. Unfortunately, yes; the people we care for most are not good for us when we are ill. But he was not mad, was he? Sir William said he never spoke of "madness"; he called it not having a sense of proportion. But her husband did not like doctors. He would refuse to go there. Shortly and kindly Sir William explained to her the state of the case. He had threatened to kill himself. There was no alternative. It was a question of law.[4] He would lie in bed in a beautiful house in the country. The nurses were admirable. Sir William would visit him once a week. If Mrs. Warren Smith was quite sure she had no more questions to ask—he never hurried his patients—they would return to her husband. She had nothing more to ask—not of Sir William.

So they returned to the most exalted of mankind; the criminal who faced his judges; the victim exposed on the heights; the fugitive; the drowned sailor; the poet of the immortal ode; the Lord who had gone from life to death; to Septimus Warren Smith, who sat in the arm-chair under the skylight staring at a photograph of Lady Bradshaw in Court dress,[5] muttering messages about beauty.

"We have had our little talk," said Sir William.

"He says you are very, very ill," Rezia cried.

---

4. Suicide remained illegal in England until 1961, so threats of suicide could result in criminal investigation as a suicide attempt could be seen as attempted self-murder.
5. For a woman in 1923, Court dress meant a ball gown in a rigidly codified cut and style, often consciously archaic, and deemed fitting for wear at formal court occasions, including presentations to the monarch. At the time, this included the dictum that women wear three feathers, after the Prince of Wales's crest, toward the left side of the head.

"We have been arranging that you should go into a home," said Sir William.

"One of Holmes's homes?" sneered Septimus.

The fellow made a distasteful impression. For there was in Sir William, whose father had been a tradesman, a natural respect for breeding and clothing, which shabbiness nettled; again, more profoundly, there was in Sir William, who had never had time for reading, a grudge, deeply buried, against cultivated people who came into his room and intimated that doctors, whose profession is a constant strain upon all the highest faculties, are not educated men.

"One of *my* homes, Mr. Warren Smith," he said, "where we will teach you to rest."

And there was just one thing more.

He was quite certain that when Mr. Warren Smith was well he was the last man in the world to frighten his wife. But he had talked of killing himself.

"We all have our moments of depression," said Sir William.

Once you fall, Septimus repeated to himself, human nature is on you. Holmes and Bradshaw are on you. They scour the desert. They fly screaming into the wilderness. The rack and the thumbscrew are applied. Human nature is remorseless.

"Impulses came upon him sometimes?" Sir William asked, with his pencil on a pink card.

That was his own affair, said Septimus.

"Nobody lives for himself alone," said Sir William, glancing at the photograph of his wife in Court dress.

"And you have a brilliant career before you," said Sir William. There was Mr. Brewer's letter on the table. "An exceptionally brilliant career."

But if he confessed? If he communicated? Would they let him off then, his torturers?

"I—I—" he stammered.

But what was his crime? He could not remember it.

"Yes?" Sir William encouraged him. (But it was growing late.)

Love, trees, there is no crime—what was his message?

He could not remember it.

"I—I—" Septimus stammered.

"Try to think as little about yourself as possible," said Sir William kindly. Really, he was not fit to be about.

Was there anything else they wished to ask him? Sir William would make all arrangements (he murmured to Rezia) and he would let her know between five and six that evening he murmured.

"Trust everything to me," he said, and dismissed them.

Never, never had Rezia felt such agony in her life! She had asked for help and been deserted! He had failed them! Sir William Bradshaw was not a nice man.

The upkeep of that motor car alone must cost him quite a lot, said Septimus, when they got out into the street.

She clung to his arm. They had been deserted.

But what more did she want?

To his patients he gave three-quarters of an hour; and if in this exacting science which has to do with what, after all, we know nothing about—the nervous system, the human brain—a doctor loses his sense of proportion, as a doctor he fails. Health we must have; and health is proportion; so that when a man comes into your room and says he is Christ (a common delusion), and has a message, as they mostly have, and threatens, as they often do, to kill himself, you invoke proportion; order rest in bed; rest in solitude; silence and rest; rest without friends, without books, without messages; six months' rest; until a man who went in weighing seven stone six comes out weighing twelve.

Proportion, divine proportion, Sir William's goddess, was acquired by Sir William walking hospitals, catching salmon, begetting one son in Harley Street by Lady Bradshaw, who caught salmon herself and took photographs scarcely to be distinguished from the work of professionals. Worshipping proportion, Sir William not only prospered himself but made England prosper, secluded her lunatics, forbade childbirth, penalised despair, made it impossible for the unfit to propagate their views until they, too, shared his sense of proportion—his, if they were men, Lady Bradshaw's if they were women (she embroidered, knitted, spent four nights out of seven at home with her son), so that not only did his colleagues respect him, his subordinates fear him, but the friends and relations of his patients felt for him the keenest gratitude for insisting that these prophetic Christs and Christesses, who prophesied the end of the world, or the advent of God, should drink milk in bed, as Sir William ordered; Sir William with his thirty years' experience of these kinds of cases, and his infallible instinct, this is madness, this sense; in fact, his sense of proportion.

But Proportion has a sister, less smiling, more formidable, a Goddess even now engaged—in the heat and sands of India, the mud and swamp of Africa, the purlieus of London, wherever in short the climate or the devil tempts men to fall from the true belief which is her own—is even now engaged in dashing down shrines, smashing idols, and setting up in their place her own stern countenance. Conversion is her name and she feasts on the wills of the weakly, loving to impress, to impose, adoring her own features stamped on the face of the populace. At Hyde Park Corner on a tub

she stands preaching; shrouds herself in white and walks peniten-
tially disguised as brotherly love through factories and parliaments;
offers help, but desires power; smites out of her way roughly the
dissentient, or dissatisfied; bestows her blessing on those who,
looking upward, catch submissively from her eyes the light of their
own. This lady too (Rezia Warren Smith divined it) had her dwell-
ing in Sir William's heart, though concealed, as she mostly is, under
some plausible disguise; some venerable name; love, duty, self sacrifice. How he would work—how toil to raise funds, propagate
reforms, initiate institutions! But conversion, fastidious Goddess,
loves blood better than brick, and feasts most subtly on the human
will. For example, Lady Bradshaw. Fifteen years ago she had gone
under. It was nothing you could put your finger on; there had been
no scene, no snap; only the slow sinking, water-logged, of her will
into his. Sweet was her smile, swift her submission; dinner in Harley Street, numbering eight or nine courses, feeding ten or fifteen
guests of the professional classes, was smooth and urbane. Only as
the evening wore on a very slight dulness, or uneasiness perhaps, a
nervous twitch, fumble, stumble and confusion indicated, what it
was really painful to believe—that the poor lady lied. Once, long
ago, she had caught salmon freely: now, quick to minister to the
craving which lit her husband's eye so oilily for dominion, for
power, she cramped, squeezed, pared, pruned, drew back, peeped
through; so that without knowing precisely what made the evening
disagreeable, and caused this pressure on the top of the head
(which might well be imputed to the professional conversation, or
the fatigue of a great doctor whose life, Lady Bradshaw said, "is not
his own but his patients'") disagreeable it was: so that guests, when
the clock struck ten, breathed in the air of Harley Street even with
rapture; which relief, however, was denied to his patients.
    There in the grey room, with the pictures on the wall, and the
valuable furniture, under the ground glass skylight, they learnt the
extent of their transgressions; huddled up in arm-chairs, they
watched him go through, for their benefit, a curious exercise with
the arms, which he shot out, brought sharply back to his hip, to
prove (if the patient was obstinate) that Sir William was master of
his own actions, which the patient was not. There some weakly
broke down; sobbed, submitted; others, inspired by Heaven knows
what intemperate madness, called Sir William to his face a damnable humbug; questioned, even more impiously, life itself. Why
live? they demanded. Sir William replied that life was good. Certainly Lady Bradshaw in ostrich feathers hung over the mantelpiece, and as for his income it was quite twelve thousand a year.
But to us, they protested, life has given no such bounty. He acqui-
esced. They lacked a sense of proportion. And perhaps, after all,

there is no God? He shrugged his shoulders. In short, this living or not living is an affair of our own? But there they were mistaken. Sir William had a friend in Surrey where they taught, what Sir William frankly admitted was a difficult art—a sense of proportion. There were, moreover, family affection; honour; courage; and a brilliant career. All of these had in Sir William a resolute champion. If they failed him, he had to support police and the good of society, which, he remarked very quietly, would take care, down in Surrey, that these unsocial impulses, bred more than anything by the lack of good blood, were held in control. And then stole out from her hiding-place and mounted her throne that Goddess whose lust is to override opposition, to stamp indelibly in the sanctuaries of others the image of herself. Naked, defenceless, the exhausted, the friendless received the impress of Sir William's will. He swooped; he devoured. He shut people up. It was this combination of decision and humanity that endeared Sir William so greatly to the relations of his victims.

But Rezia Warren Smith cried, walking down Harley Street, that she did not like that man.

Shredding and slicing, dividing and subdividing, the clocks of Harley Street nibbled at the June day, counselled submission, upheld authority, and pointed out in chorus the supreme advantages of a sense of proportion, until the mound of time was so far diminished that a commercial clock, suspended above a shop in Oxford Street, announced, genially and fraternally, as if it were a pleasure to Messrs. Rigby and Lowndes to give the information gratis, that it was half-past one.

Looking up, it appeared that each letter of their names stood for one of the hours; subconsciously one was grateful to Rigby and Lowndes for giving one time ratified by Greenwich; and this gratitude (so Hugh Whitbread ruminated, dallying there in front of the shop window), naturally took the form later of buying off Rigby and Lowndes socks or shoes. So he ruminated. It was his habit. He did not go deeply. He brushed surfaces; the dead languages, the living, life in Constantinople, Paris, Rome; riding, shooting, tennis, it had been once. The malicious asserted that he now kept guard at Buckingham Palace, dressed in silk stockings and knee-breeches, over what nobody knew. But he did it extremely efficiently. He had been afloat on the cream of English society for fifty-five years. He had known Prime Ministers. His affections were understood to be deep. And if it were true that he had not taken part in any of the great movements of the time or held important office, one or two humble reforms stood to his credit; an improvement in public shelters was one; the protection of owls in Norfolk another; servant girls had reason to be grateful to him; and his name at the end of

letters to the *Times*, asking for funds, appealing to the public to
protect, to preserve, to clear up litter, to abate smoke, and stamp
out immorality in parks, commanded respect.

A magnificent figure he cut too, pausing for a moment (as the
sound of the half hour died away) to look critically, magisterially, at
socks and shoes; impeccable, substantial, as if he beheld the world
from a certain eminence, and dressed to match; but realised the
obligations which size, wealth, health, entail, and observed punc-
tiliously even when not absolutely necessary, little courtesies, old-
fashioned ceremonies which gave a quality to his manner,
something to imitate, something to remember him by, for he would
never lunch, for example, with Lady Bruton, whom he had known
these twenty years, without bringing her in his outstretched hand a
bunch of carnations and asking Miss Brush, Lady Bruton's secretary, after her brother in South Africa, which, for some reason,
Miss Brush, deficient though she was in every attribute of female
charm, so much resented that she said "Thank you, he's doing very
well in South Africa," when, for half a dozen years, he had been
doing badly in Portsmouth.

Lady Bruton herself preferred Richard Dalloway, who arrived at
the next moment. Indeed they met on the doorstep.

Lady Bruton preferred Richard Dalloway of course. He was made
of much finer material. But she wouldn't let them run down her
poor dear Hugh. She could never forget his kindness—he had been
really remarkably kind—she forgot precisely upon what occasion.
But he had been—remarkably kind. Anyhow, the difference between
one man and another does not amount to much. She had never seen
the sense of cutting people up, as Clarissa Dalloway did—cutting
them up and sticking them together again; not at any rate when one
was sixty-two. She took Hugh's carnations with her angular grim
smile. There was nobody else coming, she said. She had got them
there on false pretences, to help her out of a difficulty—

"But let us eat first," she said.

And so there began a soundless and exquisite passing to and fro
through swing doors of aproned white-capped maids, handmaidens
not of necessity, but adepts in a mystery or grand deception practised by hostesses in Mayfair from one-thirty to two, when, with a
wave of the hand, the traffic ceases, and there rises instead this
profound illusion in the first place about the food—how it is not
paid for; and then that the table spreads itself voluntarily with glass
and silver, little mats, saucers of red fruit; films of brown cream
mask turbot; in casseroles severed chickens swim; coloured, undo-
mestic, the fire burns; and with the wine and the coffee (not paid
for) rise jocund visions before musing eyes; gently speculative eyes;
eyes to whom life appears musical, mysterious; eyes now kindled to

observe genially the beauty of the red carnations which Lady Bruton (whose movements were always angular) had laid beside her
plate, so that Hugh Whitbread, feeling at peace with the entire universe and at the same time completely sure of his standing, said,
resting his fork,

"Wouldn't they look charming against your lace?"

Miss Brush resented this familiarity intensely. She thought him
an underbred fellow. She made Lady Bruton laugh.

Lady Bruton raised the carnations, holding them rather stiffly
with much the same attitude with which the General held the scroll
in the picture behind her; she remained fixed, tranced. Which was
she now, the General's great-grand-daughter? great-great-grand-
daughter? Richard Dalloway asked himself. Sir Roderick, Sir Miles,
Sir Talbot—that was it. It was remarkable how in that family the
likeness persisted in the women. She should have been a general of
dragoons herself. And Richard would have served under her, cheerfully; he had the greatest respect for her; he cherished these romantic views about well-set-up old women of pedigree, and would have
liked, in his good-humoured way, to bring some young hot-heads of
his acquaintance to lunch with her; as if a type like hers could be
bred of amiable tea-drinking enthusiasts! He knew her country. He
knew her people. There was a vine, still bearing, which either
Lovelace or Herrick—she never read a word poetry of herself, but
so the story ran—had sat under. Better wait to put before them the
question that bothered her (about making an appeal to the public;
if so, in what terms and so on), better wait until they have had their
coffee, Lady Bruton thought; and so laid the carnations down
beside her plate.

"How's Clarissa?" she asked abruptly.

Clarissa always said that Lady Bruton did not like her. Indeed,
Lady Bruton had the reputation of being more interested in politics
than people; of talking like a man; of having had a finger in some
notorious intrigue of the eighties, which was now beginning to be
mentioned in memoirs. Certainly there was an alcove in her
drawing-room, and a table in that alcove, and a photograph upon
that table of General Sir Talbot Moore, now deceased, who had
written there (one evening in the eighties) in Lady Bruton's presence, with her cognisance, perhaps advice, a telegram ordering the
British troops to advance upon an historical occasion. (She kept the
pen and told the story.) Thus, when she said in her offhand way
"How's Clarissa?" husbands had difficulty in persuading their wives
and indeed, however devoted, were secretly doubtful themselves, of
her interest in women who often got in their husbands' way, prevented them from accepting posts abroad, and had to be taken to
the seaside in the middle of the session to recover from influenza.

Nevertheless her inquiry, "How's Clarissa?" was known by women infallibly, to be a signal from a well-wisher, from an almost silent companion, whose utterances (half a dozen perhaps in the course of a lifetime) signified recognition of some feminine comradeship which went beneath masculine lunch parties and united Lady Bruton and Mrs. Dalloway, who seldom met, and appeared when they did meet indifferent and even hostile, in a singular bond.

"I met Clarissa in the Park this morning," said Hugh Whitbread, diving into the casserole, anxious to pay himself this little tribute, for he had only to come to London and he met everybody at once; but greedy, one of the greediest men she had ever known, Milly Brush thought, who observed men with unflinching rectitude, and was capable of everlasting devotion, to her own sex in particular, being knobbed, scraped, angular, and entirely without feminine charm.

"D'you know who's in town?" said Lady Bruton suddenly bethinking her. "Our old friend, Peter Walsh."

They all smiled. Peter Walsh! And Mr. Dalloway was genuinely glad, Milly Brush thought; and Mr. Whitbread thought only of his chicken.

Peter Walsh! All three, Lady Bruton, Hugh Whitbread, and Richard Dalloway, remembered the same thing—how passionately Peter had been in love; been rejected; gone to India; come a cropper;[6] made a mess of things; and Richard Dalloway had a very great liking for the dear old fellow too. Milly Brush saw that; saw a depth in the brown of his eyes; saw him hesitate; consider; which interested her, as Mr. Dalloway always interested her, for what was he thinking, she wondered, about Peter Walsh?

That Peter Walsh had been in love with Clarissa; that he would go back directly after lunch and find Clarissa; that he would tell her, in so many words, that he loved her. Yes, he would say that.

Milly Brush once might almost have fallen in love with these silences; and Mr. Dalloway was always so dependable; such a gentleman too. Now, being forty, Lady Bruton had only to nod, or turn her head a little abruptly, and Milly Brush took the signal, however deeply she might be sunk in these reflections of a detached spirit, of an uncorrupted soul whom life could not bamboozle, because life had not offered her a trinket of the slightest value; not a curl, smile, lip, cheek, nose; nothing whatever; Lady Bruton had only to nod, and Perkins was instructed to quicken the coffee.

"Yes; Peter Walsh has come back," said Lady Bruton. It was vaguely flattering to them all. He had come back, battered, unsuccessful, to their secure shores. But to help him, they reflected, was

6. To fall headlong, as from a horse, and thus, figuratively, to fail.

impossible; there was some flaw in his character. Hugh Whitbread said one might of course mention his name to So-and-so. He wrinkled lugubriously, consequentially, at the thought of the letters he would write to the heads of Government offices about "my old friend, Peter Walsh," and so on. But it wouldn't lead to anything— not to anything permanent, because of his character.

"In trouble with some woman," said Lady Bruton. They had all guessed that *that* was at the bottom of it.

"However," said Lady Bruton, anxious to leave the subject, "we shall hear the whole story from Peter himself."

(The coffee was very slow in coming.)

"The address?" murmured Hugh Whitbread; and there was at once a ripple in the grey tide of service which washed round Lady Bruton day in, day out, collecting, intercepting, enveloping her in a fine tissue which broke concussions, mitigated interruptions, and spread round the house in Brook Street a fine net where things lodged and were picked out accurately, instantly, by grey-haired Perkins, who had been with Lady Bruton these thirty years and now wrote down the address; handed it to Mr. Whitbread, who took out his pocket-book, raised his eyebrows, and slipping it in among documents of the highest importance, said that he would get Evelyn to ask him to lunch.

(They were waiting to bring the coffee until Mr. Whitbread had finished.)

Hugh was very slow, Lady Bruton thought. He was getting fat, she noticed. Richard always kept himself in the pink of condition. She was getting impatient; the whole of her being was setting positively, undeniably, domineeringly brushing aside all this unnecessary trifling (Peter Walsh and his affairs) upon that subject which engaged her attention, and not merely her attention, but that fibre which was the ramrod of her soul, that essential part of her without which Millicent Bruton would not have been Millicent Bruton; that project for emigrating young people of both sexes born of respectable parents and setting them up with a fair prospect of doing well in Canada.[7] She exaggerated. She had perhaps lost her sense of proportion. Emigration was not to others the obvious remedy, the sublime conception. It was not to them (not to Hugh, or Richard, or even to devoted Miss Brush) the liberator of the pent egotism, which a strong martial woman, well nourished, well descended, of direct impulses, downright feelings, and little introspective power (broad and simple—why could not every one be broad and simple?

---

7. Woolf here satirizes arguments that appeared in the *Times* in 1922–23 calling for eugenically sound emigrants to Canada. The British felt indebted to the Canadians for their help and sacrifices in World War I. Beginning in 1919, the government funded the Society for the Oversea Settlement of British Women.

she asked) feels rise within her, once youth is past, and must eject
upon some object—it may be Emigration, it may be Emancipation;
but whatever it be, this object round which the essence of her soul
is daily secreted, becomes inevitably prismatic, lustrous, half
looking-glass, half precious stone; now carefully hidden in case
people should sneer at it; now proudly displayed. Emigration had
become, in short, largely Lady Bruton.

But she had to write. And one letter to the *Times*, she used to say
to Miss Brush, cost her more than to organise an expedition to
South Africa (which she had done in the war). After a morning's
battle beginning, tearing up, beginning again, she used to feel the
futility of her own womanhood as she felt it on no other occasion,
and would turn gratefully to the thought of Hugh Whitbread who
possessed—no one could doubt it—the art of writing letters to the
*Times*.

A being so differently constituted from herself, with such a command of language; able to put things as editors like them put; had
passions which one could not call simply greed. Lady Bruton often
suspended judgement upon men in deference to the mysterious
accord in which they, but no woman, stood to the laws of the universe; knew how to put things; knew what was said; so that if Richard advised her, and Hugh wrote for her, she was sure of being
somehow right. So she let Hugh eat his soufflé; asked after poor
Evelyn; waited until they were smoking, and then said,

"Milly, would you fetch the papers?"

And Miss Brush went out, came back; laid papers on the table;
and Hugh produced his fountain pen; his silver fountain pen, which
had done twenty years' service, he said, unscrewing the cap. It was
still in perfect order; he had shown it to the makers; there was no
reason, they said, why it should ever wear out; which was somehow
to Hugh's credit, and to the credit of the sentiments which his pen
expressed (so Richard Dalloway felt) as Hugh began carefully writing capital letters with rings round them in the margin, and thus
marvellously reduced Lady Bruton's tangles to sense, to grammar
such as the editor of the *Times*, Lady Bruton felt, watching the
marvellous transformation, must respect. Hugh was slow. Hugh
was pertinacious. Richard said one must take risks. Hugh proposed
modifications in deference to people's feelings, which, he said
rather tartly when Richard laughed, "had to be considered," and
read out "how, therefore, we are of opinion that the times are
ripe . . . the superfluous youth of our ever-increasing population . . . what we owe to the dead . . ." which Richard thought all
stuffing and bunkum, but no harm in it, of course, and Hugh went
on drafting sentiments in alphabetical order of the highest nobility,
brushing the cigar ash from his waistcoat, and summing up now

and then the progress they had made until, finally, he read out the draft of a letter which Lady Bruton felt certain was a masterpiece. Could her own meaning sound like that?

Hugh could not guarantee that the editor would put it in; but he would be meeting somebody at luncheon.

Whereupon Lady Bruton, who seldom did a graceful thing, stuffed all Hugh's carnations into the front of her dress, and flinging her hands out called him "My Prime Minister!" What she would have done without them both she did not know. They rose. And Richard Dalloway strolled off as usual to have a look at the General's portrait, because he meant, whenever he had a moment of leisure, to write a history of Lady Bruton's family.

And Millicent Bruton was very proud of her family. But they could wait, they could wait, she said, looking at the picture; meaning that her family, of military men, administrators, admirals, had been men of action, who had done their duty; and Richard's first duty was to his country, but it was a fine face, she said; and all the papers were ready for Richard down at Aldmixton whenever the time came; the Labour Government she meant. "Ah, the news from India!"[8] she cried.

And then, as they stood in the hall taking yellow gloves from the bowl on the malachite table and Hugh was offering Miss Brush with quite unnecessary courtesy some discarded ticket or other compliment, which she loathed from the depths of her heart and blushed brick red, Richard turned to Lady Bruton, with his hat in his hand, and said,

"We shall see you at our party to-night?" whereupon Lady Bruton resumed the magnificence which letter-writing had shattered. She might come; or she might not come. Clarissa had wonderful energy. Parties terrified Lady Bruton. But then, she was getting old. So she intimated, standing at her doorway; handsome; very erect; while her chow stretched behind her, and Miss Brush disappeared into the background with her hands full of papers.

And Lady Bruton went ponderously, majestically, up to her room, lay, one arm extended, on the sofa. She sighed, she snored, not that she was asleep, only drowsy and heavy, drowsy and heavy, like a field of clover in the sunshine this hot June day, with the bees going round and about and the yellow butterflies. Always she went back to those fields down in Devonshire, where she had jumped the brooks on Patty, her pony, with Mortimer and Tom, her brothers. And there were the dogs; there were the rats; there were her father and mother on the lawn under the trees, with the tea-things out,

8. In June 1923, this would have been largely news of the growing movement for Indian independence (not achieved until 1947).

and the beds of dahlias, the hollyhocks, the pampas grass; and they, little wretches, always up to some mischief! stealing back through the shrubbery, so as not to be seen, all bedraggled from some roguery. What old nurse used to say about her frocks!

Ah dear, she remembered—it was Wednesday in Brook Street. Those kind good fellows, Richard Dalloway, Hugh Whitbread, had gone this hot day through the streets whose growl came up to her lying on the sofa. Power was hers, position, income. She had lived in the forefront of her time. She had had good friends; known the ablest men of her day. Murmuring London flowed up to her, and her hand, lying on the sofa back, curled upon some imaginary baton such as her grandfathers might have held, holding which she seemed, drowsy and heavy, to be commanding battalions marching to Canada, and those good fellows walking across London, that territory of theirs, that little bit of carpet, Mayfair.

And they went further and further from her, being attached to her by a thin thread (since they had lunched with her) which would stretch and stretch, get thinner and thinner as they walked across London; as if one's friends were attached to one's body, after lunching with them, by a thin thread, which (as she dozed there) became hazy with the sound of bells, striking the hour or ringing to service, as a single spider's thread is blotted with rain-drops, and, burdened, sags down. So she slept.

And Richard Dalloway and Hugh Whitbread hesitated at the corner of Conduit Street at the very moment that Millicent Bruton, lying on the sofa, let the thread snap; snored. Contrary winds buffeted at the street corner. They looked in at a shop window; they did not wish to buy or to talk but to part, only with contrary winds buffeting the street corner, with some sort of lapse in the tides of the body, two forces meeting in a swirl, morning and afternoon, they paused. Some newspaper placard went up in the air, gallantly, like a kite at first, then paused, swooped, fluttered; and a lady's veil hung. Yellow awnings trembled. The speed of the morning traffic slackened, and single carts rattled carelessly down half-empty streets. In Norfolk, of which Richard Dalloway was half thinking, a soft warm wind blew back the petals; confused the waters; ruffled the flowering grasses. Haymakers, who had pitched beneath hedges to sleep away the morning toil, parted curtains of green blades; moved trembling globes of cow parsley to see the sky; the blue, the steadfast, the blazing summer sky.

Aware that he was looking at a silver two-handled Jacobean mug, and that Hugh Whitbread admired condescendingly with airs of connoisseurship a Spanish necklace which he thought of asking the price of in case Evelyn might like it—still Richard was torpid; could not think or move. Life had thrown up this wreckage; shop

windows full of coloured paste, and one stood stark with the leth-
argy of the old, stiff with the rigidity of the old, looking in. Evelyn
Whitbread might like to buy this Spanish necklace—so she might.
Yawn he must. Hugh was going into the shop.

"Right you are!" said Richard, following.

Goodness knows he didn't want to go buying necklaces with
Hugh. But there are tides in the body. Morning meets afternoon.
Borne like a frail shallop on deep, deep floods, Lady Bruton's great-
grandfather and his memoir and his campaigns in North America
were whelmed and sunk. And Millicent Bruton too. She went
under. Richard didn't care a straw what became of Emigration;
about that letter, whether the editor put it in or not. The necklace
hung stretched between Hugh's admirable fingers. Let him give it
to a girl, if he must buy jewels—any girl, any girl in the street. For
the worthlessness of this life did strike Richard pretty forcibly—
buying necklaces for Evelyn. If he'd had a boy he'd have said, Work,
work. But he had his Elizabeth; he adored his Elizabeth.

"I should like to see Mr. Dubonnet," said Hugh in his curt worldly
way. It appeared that this Dubonnet had the measurements of
Mrs. Whitbread's neck, or, more strangely still, knew her views
upon Spanish jewellery and the extent of her possessions in that
line (which Hugh could not remember). All of which seemed to
Richard Dalloway awfully odd. For he never gave Clarissa presents,
except a bracelet two or three years ago, which had not been a success. She never wore it. It pained him to remember that she never
wore it. And as a single spider's thread after wavering here and
there attaches itself to the point of a leaf, so Richard's mind, recovering from its lethargy, set now on his wife, Clarissa, whom Peter
Walsh had loved so passionately; and Richard had had a sudden
vision of her there at luncheon; of himself and Clarissa; of their life
together; and he drew the tray of old jewels towards him, and taking
up first this brooch then that ring, "How much is that?" he asked,
but doubted his own taste. He wanted to open the drawing-room
door and come in holding out something; a present for Clarissa.
Only what? But Hugh was on his legs again. He was unspeakably
pompous. Really, after dealing here for thirty-five years he was not
going to be put off by a mere boy who did not know his business. For
Dubonnet, it seemed, was out, and Hugh would not buy anything
until Mr. Dubonnet chose to be in; at which the youth flushed and
bowed his correct little bow. It was all perfectly correct. And yet
Richard couldn't have said that to save his life! Why these people
stood that damned insolence he could not conceive. Hugh was
becoming an intolerable ass. Richard Dalloway could not stand
more than an hour of his society. And, flicking his bowler hat by
way of farewell, Richard turned at the corner of Conduit Street

eager, yes, very eager, to travel that spider's thread of attachment between himself and Clarissa; he would go straight to her, in Westminster.

But he wanted to come in holding something. Flowers? Yes, flowers, since he did not trust his taste in gold; any number of flowers, roses, orchids, to celebrate what was, reckoning things as you will, an event; this feeling about her when they spoke of Peter Walsh at luncheon; and they never spoke of it; not for years had they spoken of it; which, he thought, grasping his red and white roses together (a vast bunch in tissue paper), is the greatest mistake in the world. The time comes when it can't be said; one's too shy to say it, he thought, pocketing his sixpence or two of change, setting off with his great bunch held against his body to Westminster to say straight out in so many words (whatever she might think of him), holding out his flowers, "I love you." Why not? Really it was a miracle thinking of the war, and thousands of poor chaps, with all their lives before them, shovelled together, already half forgotten; it was a miracle. Here he was walking across London to say to Clarissa in so many words that he loved her. Which one never does say, he thought. Partly one's lazy; partly one's shy. And Clarissa—it was difficult to think of her; except in starts, as at luncheon, when he saw her quite distinctly; their whole life. He stopped at the crossing; and repeated—being simple by nature, and undebauched, because he had tramped, and shot; being pertinacious and dogged, having championed the down-trodden and followed his instincts in the House of Commons; being preserved in his simplicity yet at the same time grown rather speechless, rather stiff—he repeated that it was a miracle that he should have married Clarissa; a miracle—his life had been a miracle, he thought; hesitating to cross. But it did make his blood boil to see little creatures of five or six crossing Piccadilly alone.[9] The police ought to have stopped the traffic at once. He had no illusions about the London police. Indeed, he was collecting evidence of their malpractices; and those costermongers, not allowed to stand their barrows in the streets; and prostitutes, good Lord, the fault wasn't in them, nor in young men either, but in our detestable social system and so forth; all of which he considered, could be seen considering, grey, dogged, dapper, clean, as he walked across the Park to tell his wife that he loved her.

For he would say it in so many words, when he came into the room. Because it is a thousand pities never to say what one feels, he thought, crossing the Green Park and observing with pleasure how in the shade of the trees whole families, poor families, were sprawling;

9. Traffic lights were being introduced in London at this time. Although electric, they had to be changed manually by a police officer.

children kicking up their legs; sucking milk; paper bags thrown about, which could easily be picked up (if people objected) by one of those fat gentlemen in livery; for he was of opinion that every park, and every square, during the summer months should be open to children (the grass of the park flushed and faded, lighting up the poor mothers of Westminster and their crawling babies, as if a yellow lamp were moved beneath). But what could be done for female vagrants like that poor creature, stretched on her elbow (as if she had flung herself on the earth, rid of all ties, to observe curiously, to speculate boldly, to consider the whys and the wherefores, impudent, loose-lipped, humorous), he did not know. Bearing his flowers like a weapon, Richard Dalloway approached her; intent he passed her; still there was time for a spark between them—she laughed at the sight of him, he smiled good-humouredly, considering the problem of the female vagrant; not that they would ever speak. But he would tell Clarissa that he loved her, in so many words. He had, once upon a time, been jealous of Peter Walsh; jealous of him and Clarissa. But she had often said to him that she had been right not to marry Peter Walsh; which, knowing Clarissa, was obviously true; she wanted support. Not that she was weak; but she wanted support.

As for Buckingham Palace (like an old prima donna facing the audience all in white) you can't deny it a certain dignity, he considered, nor despise what does, after all, stand to millions of people (a little crowd was waiting at the gate to see the King drive out) for a symbol, absurd though it is; a child with a box of bricks could have done better, he thought; looking at the memorial to Queen Victoria (whom he could remember in her horn spectacles driving through Kensington), its white mound, its billowing motherliness; but he liked being ruled by the descendant of Horsa; he liked continuity; and the sense of handing on the traditions of the past. It was a great age in which to have lived. Indeed, his own life was a miracle; let him make no mistake about it; here he was, in the prime of life, walking to his house in Westminster to tell Clarissa that he loved her. Happiness is this he thought.

It is this, he said, as he entered Dean's Yard. Big Ben was beginning to strike, first the warning, musical; then the hour, irrevocable. Lunch parties waste the entire afternoon, he thought, approaching his door.

The sound of Big Ben flooded Clarissa's drawing-room, where she sat, ever so annoyed, at her writing-table; worried; annoyed. It was perfectly true that she had not asked Ellie Henderson to her party; but she had done it on purpose. Now Mrs. Marsham wrote "she had told Ellie Henderson she would ask Clarissa—Ellie so much wanted to come."

But why should she invite all the dull women in London to her parties? Why should Mrs. Marsham interfere? And there was Elizabeth closeted all this time with Doris Kilman. Anything more nauseating she could not conceive. Prayer at this hour with that woman. And the sound of the bell flooded the room with its melancholy wave; which receded, and gathered itself together to fall once more, when she heard, distractingly, something fumbling, something scratching at the door. Who at this hour? Three, good Heavens! Three already! For with over-powering directness and dignity the clock struck three; and she heard nothing else; but the door handle slipped round and in came Richard! What a surprise! In came Richard, holding out flowers. She had failed him, once at Constantinople; and Lady Bruton, whose lunch parties were said to be extraordinarily amusing, had not asked her. He was holding out flowers—roses, red and white roses. (But he could not bring himself to say he loved her; not in so many words.)

But how lovely, she said, taking his flowers. She understood; she understood without his speaking; his Clarissa. She put them in vases on the mantelpiece. How lovely they looked! she said. And was it amusing, she asked? Had Lady Bruton asked after her? Peter Walsh was back. Mrs. Marsham had written. Must she ask Ellie Henderson? That woman Kilman was upstairs.

"But let us sit down for five minutes," said Richard.

It all looked so empty. All the chairs were against the wall. What had they been doing? Oh, it was for the party; no, he had not forgotten, the party. Peter Walsh was back. Oh yes; she had had him. And he was going to get a divorce; and he was in love with some woman out there. And he hadn't changed in the slightest. There she was, mending her dress. . . .

"Thinking of Bourton," she said.

"Hugh was at lunch," said Richard. She had met him too! Well, he was getting absolutely intolerable. Buying Evelyn necklaces; fatter than ever; an intolerable ass.

"And it came over me 'I might have married you,'" she said, thinking of Peter sitting there in his little bow-tie; with that knife, opening it, shutting it. "Just as he always was, you know."

They were talking about him at lunch, said Richard. (But he could not tell her he loved her. He held her hand. Happiness is this, he thought.) They had been writing a letter to the *Times* for Millicent Bruton. That was about all Hugh was fit for.

"And our dear Miss Kilman?" he asked. Clarissa thought the roses absolutely lovely; first bunched together; now of their own accord starting apart.

"Kilman arrives just as we've done lunch," she said. "Elizabeth turns pink. They shut themselves up. I suppose they're praying."

Lord! He didn't like it; but these things pass over if you let them.

"In a mackintosh with an umbrella," said Clarissa.

He had not said "I love you"; but he held her hand. Happiness is this, is this, he thought.

"But why should I ask all the dull women in London to my parties?" said Clarissa. And if Mrs. Marsham gave a party, did *she* invite her guests?

"Poor Ellie Henderson," said Richard—it was a very odd thing how much Clarissa minded about her parties, he thought.

But Richard had no notion of the look of a room. However—what was he going to say?

If she worried about these parties he would not let her give them. Did she wish she had married Peter? But he must go.

He must be off, he said, getting up. But he stood for a moment as if he were about to say something; and she wondered what? Why? There were the roses.

"Some Committee?" she asked, as he opened the door.

"Armenians," he said; or perhaps it was "Albanians."[1]

And there is a dignity in people; a solitude; even between husband and wife a gulf; and that one must respect, thought Clarissa, watching him open the door; for one would not part with it oneself, or take it, against his will, from one's husband, without losing one's independence, one's self-respect—something, after all, priceless.

He returned with a pillow and a quilt.

"An hour's complete rest after luncheon," he said. And he went.

How like him! He would go on saying "An hour's complete rest after luncheon" to the end of time, because a doctor had ordered it once. It was like him to take what doctors said literally; part of his adorable, divine simplicity, which no one had to the same extent; which made him go and do the thing while she and Peter frittered their time away bickering. He was already halfway to the House of Commons, to his Armenians, his Albanians, having settled her on the sofa, looking at his roses. And people would say, "Clarissa Dalloway is spoilt." She cared much more for her roses than for the Armenians. Hunted out of existence, maimed, frozen, the victims of cruelty and injustice (she had heard Richard say so over and over

---

1. Albania was in the news at this time. By 1921, Albania was bankrupt, having been at war continuously since 1910. The discovery of oil led the British-based Anglo-Persian Oil Company to send significant financial support to Ahmed Zogu, who was elected prime minister in 1922, then president in 1925. In 1928, Albania became a monarchy and Zogu its king, Zog I. Armenians: Richard's meeting almost certainly concerns the Armenians in Eastern Anatolia or Asia Minor (now northeastern Turkey). The Armenians, a Christian ethnic minority in the Ottoman Empire, had been victims of intercommunal violence and massacres throughout the second half of the nineteenth century, culminating in the Armenian Genocide of 1915. Two thirds of the Armenian population was driven out, and, from 1915 to 1920, one million Armenians were either killed or died of starvation. See Tate, pp. 288–94.

again)—no, she could feel nothing for the Albanians, or was it the Armenians? but she loved her roses (didn't that help the Armenians?)—the only flowers she could bear to see cut. But Richard was already at the House of Commons; at his Committee, having settled all her difficulties. But no; alas, that was not true. He did not see the reasons against asking Ellie Henderson. She would do it, of course, as he wished it. Since he had brought the pillows, she would lie down. . . . But—but—why did she suddenly feel, for no reason that she could discover, desperately unhappy? As a person who has dropped some grain of pearl or diamond into the grass and parts the tall blades very carefully, this way and that, and searches here and there vainly, and at last spies it there at the roots, so she went through one thing and another; no, it was not Sally Seton saying that Richard would never be in the Cabinet because he had a second-class brain (it came back to her); no, she did not mind that; nor was it to do with Elizabeth either and Doris Kilman; those were facts. It was a feeling, some unpleasant feeling, earlier in the day perhaps; something that Peter had said, combined with some depression of her own, in her bedroom, taking off her hat; and what Richard had said had added to it, but what had he said? There were his roses. Her parties! That was it! Her parties! Both of them criticised her very unfairly, laughed at her very unjustly, for her parties. That was it! That was it!

Well, how was she going to defend herself? Now that she knew what it was, she felt perfectly happy. They thought, or Peter at any rate thought, that she enjoyed imposing herself; liked to have famous people about her; great names; was simply a snob in short. Well, Peter might think so. Richard merely thought it foolish of her to like excitement when she knew it was bad for her heart. It was childish, he thought. And both were quite wrong. What she liked was simply life.

"That's what I do it for," she said, speaking aloud, to life.

Since she was lying on the sofa, cloistered, exempt, the presence of this thing which she felt to be so obvious became physically existent; with robes of sound from the street, sunny, with hot breath, whispering, blowing out the blinds. But suppose Peter said to her, "Yes, yes, but your parties—what's the sense of your parties?" all she could say was (and nobody could be expected to understand): They're an offering; which sounded horribly vague. But who was Peter to make out that life was all plain sailing?—Peter always in love, always in love with the wrong woman? What's your love? she might say to him. And she knew his answer; how it is the most important thing in the world and no woman possibly understood it. Very well. But could any man understand what she meant either? about life? She could not imagine Peter or Richard taking the trouble to give a party for no reason whatever.

But to go deeper, beneath what people said (and these judge-
ments, how superficial, how fragmentary they are!) in her own
mind now, what did it mean to her, this thing she called life? Oh, it
was very queer. Here was So-and-so in South Kensington; some one
up in Bayswater; and somebody else, say, in Mayfair. And she felt
quite continuously a sense of their existence; and she felt what a
waste; and she felt what a pity; and she felt if only they could be
brought together; so she did it. And it was an offering; to combine,
to create; but to whom?

An offering for the sake of offering, perhaps. Anyhow, it was her
gift. Nothing else had she of the slightest importance; could not
think, write, even play the piano. She muddled Armenians and
Turks; loved success; hated discomfort; must be liked; talked
oceans of nonsense: and to this day, ask her what the Equator was,
and she did not know.

All the same, that one day should follow another; Wednesday,
Thursday, Friday, Saturday; that one should wake up in the morning;
see the sky; walk in the park; meet Hugh Whitbread; then suddenly
in came Peter; then these roses; it was enough. After that, how unbe-
lievable death was!—that it must end; and no one in the whole world
would know how she had loved it all; how, every instant . . .

The door opened. Elizabeth knew that her mother was resting.
She came in very quietly. She stood perfectly still. Was it that some
Mongol had been wrecked on the coast of Norfolk (as Mrs. Hilbery
said), had mixed with the Dalloway ladies, perhaps, a hundred
years ago? For the Dalloways, in general, were fair-haired; blue-
eyed; Elizabeth, on the contrary, was dark; had Chinese eyes in a
pale face; an Oriental mystery; was gentle, considerate, still.[2] As a
child, she had had a perfect sense of humour; but now at seventeen,
why, Clarissa could not in the least understand, she had become
very serious; like a hyacinth, sheathed in glossy green, with buds
just tinted, a hyacinth which has had no sun.

She stood quite still and looked at her mother; but the door was
ajar, and outside the door was Miss Kilman, as Clarissa knew; Miss
Kilman in her mackintosh, listening to whatever they said.

Yes, Miss Kilman stood on the landing, and wore a mackintosh;
but had her reasons. First, it was cheap; second, she was over forty;
and did not, after all, dress to please. She was poor, moreover;
degradingly poor. Otherwise she would not be taking jobs from
people like the Dalloways; from rich people, who liked to be kind.
Mr. Dalloway, to do him justice, had been kind. But Mrs. Dalloway
had not. She had been merely condescending. She came from the

---

2. These musings on Elizabeth's appearance reflect stereotypes now recognized as racist.
Woolf's large social circle included several East and South Asians.

most worthless of all classes—the rich, with a smattering of culture. They had expensive things everywhere; pictures, carpets, lots of servants. She considered that she had a perfect right to anything that the Dalloways did for her.

She had been cheated. Yes, the word was no exaggeration, for surely a girl has a right to some kind of happiness? And she had never been happy, what with being so clumsy and so poor. And then, just as she might have had a chance at Miss Dolby's school, the war came; and she had never been able to tell lies. Miss Dolby thought she would be happier with people who shared her views about the Germans. She had had to go. It was true that the family was of German origin; spelt the name Kiehlman in the eighteenth century; but her brother had been killed. They turned her out because she would not pretend that the Germans were all villains— when she had German friends, when the only happy days of her life had been spent in Germany! And after all, she could read history. She had had to take whatever she could get. Mr. Dalloway had come across her working for the Friends.[3] He had allowed her (and that was really generous of him) to teach his daughter history. Also she did a little Extension lecturing[4] and so on. Then Our Lord had come to her (and here she always bowed her head). She had seen the light two years and three months ago. Now she did not envy women like Clarissa Dalloway; she pitied them.

She pitied and despised them from the bottom of her heart, as she stood on the soft carpet, looking at the old engraving of a little girl with a muff. With all this luxury going on, what hope was there for a better state of things? Instead of lying on a sofa—"My mother is resting," Elizabeth had said—she should have been in a factory; behind a counter; Mrs. Dalloway and all the other fine ladies!

Bitter and burning, Miss Kilman had turned into a church two years three months ago. She had heard the Rev. Edward Whittaker preach; the boys sing; had seen the solemn lights descend, and whether it was the music, or the voices (she herself when alone in the evening found comfort in a violin; but the sound was excruciating; she had no ear), the hot and turbulent feelings which boiled and surged in her had been assuaged as she sat there, and she had wept copiously, and gone to call on Mr. Whittaker at his private house in Kensington. It was the hand of God, he said. The Lord had shown her the way. So now, whenever the hot and painful feelings boiled within her, this hatred of Mrs. Dalloway, this grudge

---

3. The Religious Society of Friends (founded 1610), or the Quakers, are pacifists. Quakers refuse military service but often serve in the ambulance and medical corps and in charitable work. Virginia Woolf's aunt Caroline Emilia Stephen was a Quaker.
4. University Extension lecturing was in 1923 another name for public lecturing for nondegree candidates (often women) at the Universities of London and Oxford.

against the world, she thought of God. She thought of Mr. Whittaker. Rage was succeeded by calm. A sweet savour filled her veins, her lips parted, and, standing formidable upon the landing in her mackintosh, she looked with steady and sinister serenity at Mrs. Dalloway, who came out with her daughter.

Elizabeth said she had forgotten her gloves. That was because Miss Kilman and her mother hated each other. She could not bear to see them together. She ran upstairs to find her gloves.

But Miss Kilman did not hate Mrs. Dalloway. Turning her large gooseberry-coloured eyes upon Clarissa, observing her small pink face, her delicate body, her air of freshness and fashion, Miss Kilman felt, Fool! Simpleton! You who have known neither sorrow nor pleasure; who have trifled your life away! And there rose in her an overmastering desire to overcome her; to unmask her. If she could have felled her it would have eased her. But it was not the body; it was the soul and its mockery that she wished to subdue; make feel her mastery. If only she could make her weep; could ruin her; humiliate her; bring her to her knees crying, You are right! But this was God's will, not Miss Kilman's. It was to be a religious victory. So she glared; so she glowered.

Clarissa was really shocked. This a Christian—this woman! This woman had taken her daughter from her! She in touch with invisible presences! Heavy, ugly, commonplace, without kindness or grace, she know the meaning of life!

"You are taking Elizabeth to the Stores?" Mrs. Dalloway said.

Miss Kilman said she was. They stood there. Miss Kilman was not going to make herself agreeable. She had always earned her living. Her knowledge of modern history was thorough in the extreme. She did out of her meagre income set aside so much for causes she believed in; whereas this woman did nothing, believed nothing; brought up her daughter—but here was Elizabeth, rather out of breath, the beautiful girl.

So they were going to the Stores.[5] Odd it was, as Miss Kilman stood there (and stand she did, with the power and taciturnity of some prehistoric monster armoured for primeval warfare), how, second by second, the idea of her diminished, how hatred (which was for ideas, not people) crumbled, how she lost her malignity, her size, became second by second merely Miss Kilman, in a mackintosh, whom Heaven knows Clarissa would have liked to help.

At this dwindling of the monster, Clarissa laughed. Saying goodbye, she laughed.

Off they went together, Miss Kilman and Elizabeth, downstairs.

5. The Army and Navy Stores opened in 1871 as a cooperative run by military officers to supply inexpensive goods to military families.

With a sudden impulse, with a violent anguish, for this woman was taking her daughter from her, Clarissa leant over the bannisters and cried out, "Remember the party! Remember our party tonight!"

But Elizabeth had already opened the front door; there was a van passing; she did not answer.

Love and religion! thought Clarissa, going back into the drawing-room, tingling all over. How detestable, how detestable they are! For now that the body of Miss Kilman was not before her, it over-whelmed her—the idea. The cruelest things in the world, she thought, seeing them clumsy, hot, domineering, hypocritical, eavesdropping, jealous, infinitely cruel and unscrupulous, dressed in a mackintosh coat, on the landing; love and religion. Had she ever tried to convert any one herself? Did she not wish everybody merely to be themselves? And she watched out of the window the old lady opposite climbing upstairs. Let her climb upstairs if she wanted to; let her stop; then let her, as Clarissa had often seen her, gain her bedroom, part her curtains, and disappear again into the background. Somehow one respected that—that old woman look-ing out of the window, quite unconscious that she was being watched. There was something solemn in it—but love and religion would destroy that, whatever it was, the privacy of the soul. The odious Kilman would destroy it. Yet it was a sight that made her want to cry.

Love destroyed too. Everything that was fine, everything that was true went. Take Peter Walsh now. There was a man, charming, clever, with ideas about everything. If you wanted to know about Pope, say, or Addison, or just to talk nonsense, what people were like, what things meant, Peter knew better than any one. It was Peter who had helped her; Peter who had lent her books. But look at the women he loved—vulgar, trivial, commonplace. Think of Peter in love—he came to see her after all these years, and what did he talk about? Himself. Horrible passion! she thought. Degrading passion! she thought, thinking of Kilman and her Elizabeth walk-ing to the Army and Navy Stores.

Big Ben struck the half-hour.

How extraordinary it was, strange, yes, touching, to see the old lady (they had been neighbours ever so many years) move away from the window, as if she were attached to that sound, that string. Gigantic as it was, it had something to do with her. Down, down, into the midst of ordinary things the finger fell making the moment solemn. She was forced, so Clarissa imagined, by that sound, to move, to go—but where? Clarissa tried to follow her as she turned and disappeared, and could still just see her white cap moving at the back of the bedroom. She was still there moving about at the other end of the room. Why creeds and prayers and mackintoshes?

when, thought Clarissa, that's the miracle, that's the mystery; that old lady, she meant, whom she could see going from chest of drawers to dressing-table. She could still see her. And the supreme mystery which Kilman might say she had solved, or Peter might say he had solved, but Clarissa didn't believe either of them had the ghost of an idea of solving, was simply this: here was one room; there another. Did religion solve that, or love?

Love—but here the other clock, the clock which always struck two minutes after Big Ben, came shuffling in with its lap full of odds and ends, which it dumped down as if Big Ben were all very well with his majesty laying down the law, so solemn, so just, but she must remember all sorts of little things besides—Mrs. Marsham, Ellie Henderson, glasses for ices—all sorts of little things came flooding and lapping and dancing in on the wake of that solemn stroke which lay flat like a bar of gold on the sea. Mrs. Marsham, Ellie Henderson, glasses for ices. She must telephone now at once.

Volubly, troublously, the late clock sounded, coming in on the wake of Big Ben, with its lap full of trifles. Beaten up, broken up by the assault of carriages, the brutality of vans, the eager advance of myriads of angular men, of flaunting women, the domes and spires of offices and hospitals, the last relics of this lap full of odds and ends seemed to break, like the spray of an exhausted wave, upon the body of Miss Kilman standing still in the street for a moment to mutter "It is the flesh."

It was the flesh that she must control. Clarissa Dalloway had insulted her. That she expected. But she had not triumphed; she had not mastered the flesh. Ugly, clumsy, Clarissa Dalloway had laughed at her for being that; and had revived the fleshly desires, for she minded looking as she did beside Clarissa. Nor could she talk as she did. But why wish to resemble her? Why? She despised Mrs. Dalloway from the bottom of her heart. She was not serious. She was not good. Her life was a tissue of vanity and deceit. Yet Doris Kilman had been overcome. She had, as a matter of fact, very nearly burst into tears when Clarissa Dalloway laughed at her. "It is the flesh, it is the flesh," she muttered (it being her habit to talk aloud) trying to subdue this turbulent and painful feeling as she walked down Victoria Street. She prayed to God. She could not help being ugly; she could not afford to buy pretty clothes. Clarissa Dalloway had laughed—but she would concentrate her mind upon something else until she had reached the pillar-box. At any rate she had got Elizabeth. But she would think of something else; she would think of Russia;[6] until she reached the pillar-box.

6. Since the Communist Revolution of 1917, Russia had stood for an alternative civilization founded on revolutionary grounds.

How nice it must be, she said, in the country, struggling, as Mr. Whittaker had told her, with that violent grudge against the world which had scorned her, sneered at her, cast her off, beginning with this indignity—the infliction of her unlovable body which people could not bear to see. Do her hair as she might, her forehead remained like an egg, bald, white. No clothes suited her. She might buy anything. And for a woman, of course, that meant never meeting the opposite sex. Never would she come first with any one. Sometimes lately it had seemed to her that, except for Elizabeth, her food was all that she lived for; her comforts; her dinner, her tea; her hot-water bottle at night. But one must fight; vanquish; have faith in God. Mrs. Whittaker had said she was there for a purpose. But no one knew the agony! He said, pointing to the crucifix, that God knew. But why should she have to suffer when other women, like Clarissa Dalloway, escaped? Knowledge comes through suffering, said Mr. Whittaker.

She had passed the pillar-box, and Elizabeth had turned into the cool brown tobacco department of the Army and Navy Stores while she was still muttering to herself what Mr. Whittaker had said about knowledge coming through suffering and the flesh. "The flesh," she muttered.

What department did she want? Elizabeth interrupted her.

"Petticoats," she said abruptly, and stalked straight on to the lift.

Up they went. Elizabeth guided her this way and that; guided her in her abstraction as if she had been a great child, an unwieldy battleship. There were the petticoats, brown, decorous, striped, frivolous, solid, flimsy; and she chose, in her abstraction, portentously, and the girl serving thought her mad.

Elizabeth rather wondered, as they did up the parcel, what Miss Kilman was thinking. They must have their tea, said Miss Kilman, rousing, collecting herself. They had their tea.

Elizabeth rather wondered whether Miss Kilman could be hungry. It was her way of eating, eating with intensity, then looking, again and again, at a plate of sugared cakes on the table next them; then, when a lady and a child sat down and the child took the cake, could Miss Kilman really mind it? Yes, Miss Kilman did mind it. She had wanted that cake—the pink one. The pleasure of eating was almost the only pure pleasure left her, and then to be baffled even in that!

When people are happy, they have a reserve, she had told Elizabeth, upon which to draw, whereas she was like a wheel without a tyre (she was fond of such metaphors), jolted by every pebble, so she would say staying on after the lesson standing by the fire-place with her bag of books, her "satchel," she called it, on a Tuesday morning, after the lesson was over. And she talked too about the war. After all, there were people who did not think the English invariably right. There were books. There were meetings. There were other points of view. Would Elizabeth like to come with her to listen to So-and-so (a most extraordinary looking old man)? Then Miss Kilman took her to some church in Kensington and they had tea with a clergyman. She had lent her books. Law, medicine, politics, all professions are open to women of your generation,[7] said Miss Kilman. But for herself, her career was absolutely ruined and was it her fault? Good gracious, said Elizabeth, no.

And her mother would come calling to say that a hamper had come from Bourton and would Miss Kilman like some flowers? To Miss Kilman she was always very, very nice, but Miss Kilman squashed the flowers all in a bunch, and hadn't any small talk, and what interested Miss Kilman bored her mother, and Miss Kilman and she were terrible together; and Miss Kilman swelled and looked very plain. But then Miss Kilman was frightfully clever. Elizabeth had never thought about the poor. They lived with everything they wanted,—her mother had breakfast in bed every day; Lucy carried it up; and she liked old women because they were Duchesses, and being descended from some Lord. But Miss Kilman said (one of those Tuesday mornings when the lesson was over), "My grandfather kept an oil and colour shop[8] in Kensington." Miss Kilman made one feel so small.

Miss Kilman took another cup of tea. Elizabeth, with her oriental bearing, her inscrutable mystery, sat perfectly upright; no, she did not want anything more. She looked for her gloves—her white gloves. They were under the table. Ah, but she must not go! Miss Kilman could not let her go! this youth, that was so beautiful, this girl, whom she genuinely loved! Her large hand opened and shut on the table.

But perhaps it was a little flat somehow, Elizabeth felt. And really she would like to go.

But said Miss Kilman, "I've not quite finished yet."

Of course, then, Elizabeth would wait. But it was rather stuffy in here.

"Are you going to the party to-night?" Miss Kilman said. Elizabeth supposed she was going; her mother wanted her to go. She must not let parties absorb her, Miss Kilman said, fingering the last two inches of a chocolate éclair.

She did not much like parties, Elizabeth said. Miss Kilman opened her mouth, slightly projected her chin, and swallowed down

7. The Sex Disqualification (Removal) Act of 1919 was an early attempt to address sexual discrimination in the workplace. It was an attempt to remove policies that automatically disqualified job candidates on the basis of their sex.
8. That is, a shop selling oil paints.

the last inches of the chocolate éclair, then wiped her fingers, and washed the tea round in her cup.

She was about to split asunder, she felt. The agony was so terrific. If she could grasp her, if she could clasp her, if she could make her hers absolutely and forever and then die; that was all she wanted. But to sit here, unable to think of anything to say; to see Elizabeth turning against her; to be felt repulsive even by her—it was too much; she could not stand it. The thick fingers curled inwards.

"I never go to parties," said Miss Kilman, just to keep Elizabeth from going. "People don't ask me to parties"—and she knew as she said it that it was this egotism that was her undoing; Mr. Whittaker had warned her; but she could not help it. She had suffered so horribly. "Why should they ask me?" she said. "I'm plain, I'm unhappy." She knew it was idiotic. But it was all those people passing—people with parcels who despised her, who made her say it. However, she was Doris Kilman. She had her degree. She was a woman who had made her way in the world. Her knowledge of modern history was more than respectable.

"I don't pity myself," she said. "I pity"—she meant to say "your mother" but no, she could not, not to Elizabeth. "I pity other people," she said, "more."

Like some dumb creature who has been brought up to a gate for an unknown purpose, and stands there longing to gallop away, Elizabeth Dalloway sat silent. Was Miss Kilman going to say anything more?

"Don't quite forget me," said Doris Kilman; her voice quivered. Right away to the end of the field the dumb creature galloped in terror.

The great hand opened and shut.

Elizabeth turned her head. The waitress came. One had to pay at the desk, Elizabeth said, and went off, drawing out, so Miss Kilman felt, the very entrails in her body, stretching them as she crossed the room, and then, with a final twist, bowing her head very politely, she went.

She had gone. Miss Kilman sat at the marble table among the éclairs, stricken once, twice, thrice by shocks of suffering. She had gone. Mrs. Dalloway had triumphed. Elizabeth had gone. Beauty had gone, youth had gone.

So she sat. She got up, blundered off among the little tables, rocking slightly from side to side, and somebody came after her with her petticoat, and she lost her way, and was hemmed in by trunks specially prepared for taking to India; next got among the accouchement sets, and baby linen; through all the commodities of the world, perishable and permanent, hams, drugs, flowers, stationery, variously smelling, now sweet, now sour she lurched; saw herself thus lurching with her hat askew, very red in the face, full length in a looking-glass; and at last came out into the street.

The tower of Westminster Cathedral rose in front of her, the habitation of God. In the midst of the traffic, there was the habitation of God. Doggedly she set off with her parcel to that other sanctuary, the Abbey, where, raising her hands in a tent before her face, she sat beside those driven into shelter too; the variously assorted worshippers, now divested of social rank, almost of sex, as they raised their hands before their faces; but once they removed them, instantly reverent, middle class, English men and women, some of them desirous of seeing the wax works.

But Miss Kilman held her tent before her face. Now she was deserted; now rejoined. New worshippers came in from the street to replace the strollers, and still, as people gazed round and shuffled past the tomb of the Unknown Warrior, still she barred her eyes with her fingers and tried in this double darkness, for the light in the Abbey was bodiless, to aspire above the vanities, the desires, the commodities, to rid herself both of hatred and of love. Her hands twitched. She seemed to struggle. Yet to others God was accessible and the path to Him smooth. Mr. Fletcher, retired, of the Treasury, Mrs. Gorham, widow of the famous K.C., approached Him simply, and having done their praying, leant back, enjoyed the music (the organ pealed sweetly), and saw Miss Kilman at the end of the row, praying, praying, and, being still on the threshold of their underworld, thought of her sympathetically as a soul haunting the same territory; a soul cut out of immaterial substance; not a woman, a soul.

But Mr. Fletcher had to go. He had to pass her, and being himself neat as a new pin, could not help being a little distressed by the poor lady's disorder; her hair down; her parcel on the floor. She did not at once let him pass. But, as he stood gazing about him, at the white marbles, grey window panes, and accumulated treasures (for he was extremely proud of the Abbey), her largeness, robustness, and power as she sat there shifting her knees from time to time (it was so rough the approach to her God—so tough her desires) impressed him, as they had impressed Mrs. Dalloway (she could not get the thought of her out of her mind that afternoon), the Rev. Edward Whittaker, and Elizabeth too.

And Elizabeth waited in Victoria Street for an omnibus. It was so nice to be out of doors. She thought perhaps she need not go home just yet. It was so nice to be out in the air. So she would get on to an omnibus. And already, even as she stood there, in her very well cut clothes, it was beginning. . . . People were beginning to compare her to poplar trees, early dawn, hyacinths, fawns, running water, and garden lilies; and it made her life a burden to her, for she so much preferred being left alone to do what she liked in the country, but they would compare her to lilies, and she had to go to parties, and London was so dreary compared with being alone in the country with her father and the dogs.

Buses swooped, settled, were off—garish caravans, glistening with red and yellow varnish. But which should she get on to? She had no preferences. Of course, she would not push her way. She inclined to be passive. It was expression she needed, but her eyes were fine, Chinese, oriental, and, as her mother said, with such nice shoulders and holding herself so straight, she was always charming to look at; and lately, in the evening especially, when she was interested, for she never seemed excited, she looked almost beautiful, very stately, very serene. What could she be thinking? Every man fell in love with her, and she was really awfully bored. For it was beginning. Her mother could see that—the compliments were beginning. That she did not care more about it—for instance for her clothes—sometimes worried Clarissa, but perhaps it was as well with all those puppies and guinea pigs about having distemper, and it gave her a charm. And now there was this odd friendship with Miss Kilman. Well, thought Clarissa about three o'clock in the morning, reading Baron Marbot for she could not sleep, it proves she has a heart.

Suddenly Elizabeth stepped forward and most competently boarded the omnibus, in front of everybody. She took a seat on top. The impetuous creature—a pirate—started forward, sprang away; she had to hold the rail to steady herself, for a pirate it was, reckless, unscrupulous, bearing down ruthlessly, circumventing dangerously, boldly snatching a passenger, or ignoring a passenger, squeezing eel-like and arrogant in between, and then rushing insolently all sails spread up Whitehall. And did Elizabeth give one thought to poor Miss Kilman who loved her without jealousy, to whom she had been a fawn in the open, a moon in a glade? She was delighted to be free. The fresh air was so delicious. It had been so stuffy in the Army and Navy Stores. And now it was like riding, to be rushing up Whitehall; and to each movement of the omnibus the beautiful body in the fawn-coloured coat responded freely like a rider, like the figure-head of a ship, for the breeze slightly disarrayed her; the heat gave her cheeks the pallor of white painted wood; and her fine eyes, having no eyes to meet, gazed ahead, blank, bright, with the staring incredible innocence of sculpture.

It was always talking about her own sufferings that made Miss Kilman so difficult. And was she right? If it was being on committees and giving up hours and hours every day (she hardly ever saw him in London) that helped the poor, her father did that, goodness knows,—if that was what Miss Kilman meant about being a Christian; but it was so difficult to say. Oh, she would like to go a little further. Another penny was it to the Strand? Here was another penny then. She would go up the Strand.

She liked people who were ill. And every profession is open to the women of your generation, said Miss Kilman. So she might be a doctor. She might be a farmer. Animals are often ill. She might own a thousand acres and have people under her. She would go and see them in their cottages. This was Somerset House. One might be a very good farmer—and that, strangely enough though Miss Kilman had her share in it, was almost entirely due to Somerset House. It looked so splendid, so serious, that great grey building. And she liked the feeling of people working. She liked those churches, like shapes of grey paper, breasting the stream of the Strand. It was quite different here from Westminster, she thought, getting off at Chancery Lane. It was so serious; it was so busy. In short, she would like to have a profession. She would become a doctor, a farmer, possibly go into Parliament, if she found it necessary, all because of the Strand.

The feet of those people busy about their activities, hands putting stone to stone, minds eternally occupied not with trivial chatterings (comparing women to poplars—which was rather exciting, of course, but very silly), but with thoughts of ships, of business, of law, of administration, and with it all so stately (she was in the Temple), gay (there was the river), pious (there was the Church), made her quite determined, whatever her mother might say, to become either a farmer or a doctor. But she was, of course, rather lazy.

And it was much better to say nothing about it. It seemed so silly. It was the sort of thing that did sometimes happen, when one was alone—buildings without architects' names, crowds of people coming back from the city having more power than single clergymen in Kensington, than any of the books Miss Kilman had lent her, to stimulate what lay slumberous, clumsy, and shy on the mind's sandy floor to break surface, as a child suddenly stretches its arms; it was just that, perhaps, a sigh, a stretch of the arms, an impulse, a revelation, which has its effects for ever, and then down again it went to the sandy floor. She must go home. She must dress for dinner. But what was the time?—where was a clock?

She looked up Fleet Street. She walked just a little way towards St. Paul's, shyly, like some one penetrating on tiptoe, exploring a strange house by night with a candle, on edge lest the owner should suddenly fling wide his bedroom door and ask her business, nor did she dare wander off into queer alleys, tempting bye-streets, any more than in a strange house open doors which might be bedroom doors, or sitting-room doors, or lead straight to the larder. For no Dalloways came down the Strand daily; she was a pioneer, a stray, venturing, trusting.

In many ways, her mother felt, she was extremely immature, like a child still, attached to dolls, to old slippers; a perfect baby; and that was charming. But then, of course, there was in the Dalloway family the tradition of public service. Abbesses, principals, head mistresses, dignitaries, in the republic of women—without being brilliant, any of them, they were that. She penetrated a little further in the direction of St. Paul's. She liked the geniality, sisterhood, motherhood, brotherhood of this uproar. It seemed to her good. The noise was tremendous; and suddenly there were trumpets (the unemployed) blaring, rattling about in the uproar; military music; as if people were marching; yet had they been dying—had some woman breathed her last and whoever was watching, opening the window of the room where she had just brought off that act of supreme dignity, looked down on Fleet Street, that uproar, that military music would have come triumphing up to him, consolatory, indifferent.

It was not conscious. There was no recognition in it of one fortune, or fate, and for that very reason even to those dazed with watching for the last shivers of consciousness on the faces of the dying, consoling. Forgetfulness in people might wound, their ingratitude corrode, but this voice, pouring endlessly, year in year out, would take whatever it might be; this vow; this van; this life; this procession, would wrap them all about and carry them on, as in the rough stream of a glacier the ice holds a splinter of bone, a blue petal, some oak trees, and rolls them on.

But it was later than she thought. Her mother would not like her to be wandering off alone like this. She turned back down the Strand.

A puff of wind (in spite of the heat, there was quite a wind) blew a thin black veil over the sun and over the Strand. The faces faded; the omnibuses suddenly lost their glow. For although the clouds were of mountainous white so that one could fancy hacking hard chips off with a hatchet, with broad golden slopes, lawns of celestial pleasure gardens, on their flanks, and had all the appearance of settled habitations assembled for the conference of gods above the world, there was a perpetual movement among them. Signs were interchanged, when, as if to fulfil some scheme arranged already, now a summit dwindled, now a whole block of pyramidal size which had kept its station inalterably advanced into the midst or gravely led the procession to fresh anchorage. Fixed though they seemed at their posts, at rest in perfect unanimity, nothing could be fresher, freer, more sensitive superficially than the snow-white or gold-kindled surface; to change, to go, to dismantle the solemn assemblage was immediately possible; and in spite of the grave fixity, the accumulated robustness and solidity, now they struck light to the earth, now darkness.

Calmly and competently, Elizabeth Dalloway mounted the Westminster omnibus.

Going and coming, beckoning, signalling, so the light and shadow which now made the wall grey, now the bananas bright yellow, now made the Strand grey, now made the omnibuses bright yellow, seemed to Septimus Warren Smith lying on the sofa in the sitting-room; watching the watery gold glow and fade with the astonishing sensibility of some live creature on the roses, on the wallpaper. Outside the trees dragged their leaves like nets through the depths of the air; the sound of water was in the room and through the waves came the voices of birds singing. Every power poured its treasures on his head, and his hand lay there on the back of the sofa, as he had seen his hand lie when he was bathing, floating, on the top of the waves, while far away on shore he heard dogs barking and barking far away. Fear no more, says the heart in the body; fear no more.

He was not afraid. At every moment Nature signified by some laughing hint like that gold spot which went round the wall—there, there, there—her determination to show, by brandishing her plumes, shaking her tresses, flinging her mantle this way and that, beautifully, always beautifully, and standing close up to breathe through her hollowed hands Shakespeare's words, her meaning.

Rezia, sitting at the table twisting a hat in her hands, watched him; saw him smiling. He was happy then. But she could not bear to see him smiling. It was not marriage; it was not being one's husband to look strange like that, always to be starting, laughing, sitting hour after hour silent, or clutching her and telling her to write. The table drawer was full of those writings; about war; about Shakespeare; about great discoveries; how there is no death. Lately he had become excited suddenly for no reason (and both Dr. Holmes and Sir William Bradshaw said excitement was the worst thing for him), and waved his hands and cried out that he knew the truth! He knew everything! That man, his friend who was killed, Evans, had come, he said. He was singing behind the screen. She wrote it down just as he spoke it. Some things were very beautiful; others sheer nonsense. And he was always stopping in the middle, changing his mind; wanting to add something; hearing something new; listening with his hand up.

But she heard nothing.

And once they found the girl who did the room reading one of these papers in fits of laughter. It was a dreadful pity. For that made Septimus cry out about human cruelty—how they tear each other to pieces. The fallen, he said, they tear to pieces. "Holmes is on us," he would say, and he would invent stories about Holmes; Holmes eating porridge; Holmes reading Shakespeare—making himself roar with laughter or rage, for Dr. Holmes seemed to stand for something horrible to him. "Human nature," he called him. Then there were the visions. He was drowned, he used to say, and lying on a cliff with the gulls screaming over him. He would look over the edge of the sofa down into the sea. Or he was hearing music. Really it was only a barrel organ or some man crying in the street. But "Lovely!" he used to cry, and the tears would run down his cheeks, which was to her the most dreadful thing of all, to see a man like Septimus, who had fought, who was brave, crying. And he would lie listening until suddenly he would cry that he was fall-ing down, down into the flames! Actually she would look for flames, it was so vivid. But there was nothing. They were alone in the room. It was a dream, she would tell him and so quiet him at last, but sometimes she was frightened too. She sighed as she sat sewing.

Her sigh was tender and enchanting, like the wind outside a wood in the evening. Now she put down her scissors; now she turned to take something from the table. A little stir, a little crin-kling, a little tapping built up something on the table there, where she sat sewing. Through his eyelashes he could see her blurred out-line; her little black body; her face and hands; her turning move-ments at the table, as she took up a reel, or looked (she was apt to lose things) for her silk. She was making a hat for Mrs. Filmer's married daughter, whose name was—he had forgotten her name.

"What is the name of Mrs. Filmer's married daughter?" he asked.

"Mrs. Peters," said Rezia. She was afraid it was too small, she said, holding it before her. Mrs. Peters was a big woman; but she did not like her. It was only because Mrs. Filmer had been so good to them. "She gave me grapes this morning," she said—that Rezia wanted to do something to show that they were grateful. She had come into the room the other evening and found Mrs. Peters, who thought they were out, playing the gramophone.

"Was it true?" he asked. She was playing the gramophone? Yes; she had told him about it at the time; she had found Mrs. Peters playing the gramophone.

He began, very cautiously, to open his eyes, to see whether a gramophone was really there. But real things—real things were too exciting. He must be cautious. He would not go mad. First he looked at the fashion papers on the lower shelf, then, gradually at the gramophone with the green trumpet. Nothing could be more exact. And so, gathering courage, he looked at the sideboard; the plate of bananas; the engraving of Queen Victoria and the Prince Consort; at the mantelpiece, with the jar of roses. None of these things moved. All were still; all were real.

"She is a woman with a spiteful tongue," said Rezia.

"What does Mr. Peters do?" Septimus asked.

"Ah," said Rezia, trying to remember. She thought Mrs. Filmer had said that he travelled for some company. "Just now he is in Hull," she said.

"Just now!" She said that with her Italian accent. She said that herself. He shaded his eyes so that he might see only a little of her face at a time, first the chin, then the nose, then the forehead, in case it were deformed, or had some terrible mark on it. But no, there she was, perfectly natural, sewing, with the pursed lips that women have, the set, the melancholy expression, when sewing. But there was nothing terrible about it, he assured himself, looking a second time, a third time at her face, her hands, for what was frightening or disgusting in her as she sat there in broad daylight, sewing? Mrs. Peters had a spiteful tongue. Mr. Peters was in Hull. Why then rage and prophesy? Why fly scourged and outcast? Why be made to tremble and sob by the clouds? Why seek truths and deliver messages when Rezia sat sticking pins into the front of her dress, and Mr. Peters was in Hull? Miracles, revelations, agonies, loneliness, falling through the sea, down, down into the flames, all were burnt out, for he had a sense, as he watched Rezia trimming the straw hat for Mrs. Peters, of a coverlet of flowers.

"It's too small for Mrs. Peters," said Septimus.

For the first time for days he was speaking as he used to do! Of course it was—absurdly small, she said. But Mrs. Peters had chosen it.

He took it out of her hands. He said it was an organ grinder's monkey's hat.

How it rejoiced her that! Not for weeks had they laughed like this together, poking fun privately like married people. What she meant was that if Mrs. Filmer had come in, or Mrs. Peters or anybody they would not have understood what she and Septimus were laughing at.

"There," she said, pinning a rose to one side of the hat. Never had she felt so happy! Never in her life!

But that was still more ridiculous, Septimus said. Now the poor woman looked like a pig at a fair. (Nobody ever made her laugh as Septimus did.)

What had she got in her work-box? She had ribbons and beads, tassels, artificial flowers. She tumbled them out on the table. He began putting odd colours together—for though he had no fingers, could not even do up a parcel, he had a wonderful eye, and often he was right, sometimes absurd, of course, but sometimes wonderfully right.

"She shall have a beautiful hat!" he murmured, taking up this and that, Rezia kneeling by his side, looking over his shoulder. Now it was finished—that is to say the design; she must stitch it together. But she must be very, very careful, he said, to keep it just as he had made it.

So she sewed. When she sewed, he thought, she made a sound like a kettle on the hob; bubbling, murmuring, always busy, her strong little pointed fingers pinching and poking; her needle flashing straight. The sun might go in and out, on the tassels, on the wall-paper, but he would wait, he thought, stretching out his feet, looking at his ringed sock at the end of the sofa; he would wait in this warm place, this pocket of still air, which one comes on at the edge of a wood sometimes in the evening, when, because of a fall in the ground, or some arrangement of the trees (one must be scientific above all, scientific), warmth lingers, and the air buffets the cheek like the wing of a bird.

"There it is," said Rezia, twirling Mrs. Peters' hat on the tips of her fingers. "That'll do for the moment. Later . . ." her sentence bubbled away drip, drip, drip, like a contented tap left running.

It was wonderful. Never had he done anything which made him feel so proud. It was so real, it was so substantial, Mrs. Peters' hat.

"Just look at it," he said.

Yes, it would always make her happy to see that hat. He had become himself then, he had laughed then. They had been alone together. Always she would like that hat.

He told her to try it on.

"But I must look so queer!" she cried, running over to the glass and looking first this side then that. Then she snatched it off again, for there was a tap at the door. Could it be Sir William Bradshaw? Had he sent already?

No! it was only the small girl with the evening paper.

What always happened, then happened—what happened every night of their lives. The small girl sucked her thumb at the door; Rezia went down on her knees; Rezia cooed and kissed; Rezia got a bag of sweets out of the table drawer. For so it always happened. First one thing, then another. So she built it up, first one thing and then another. Dancing, skipping, round and round the room they went. He took the paper. Surrey was all out, he read. There was a heat wave. Rezia repeated: Surrey was all out. There was a heat wave, making it part of the game she was playing with Mrs. Filmer's grandchild, both of them laughing, chattering at the same time, at their game. He was very tired. He was very happy. He would sleep. He shut his eyes. But directly he saw nothing the sounds of the game became fainter and stranger and sounded like the cries of people seeking and not finding, and passing further and further away. They had lost him!

He started up in terror. What did he see? The plate of bananas on the sideboard. Nobody was there (Rezia had taken the child to its mother. It was bedtime). That was it: to be alone forever. That was the doom pronounced in Milan when he came into the room and saw them cutting out buckram shapes with their scissors; to be alone forever.

He was alone with the sideboard and the bananas. He was alone, exposed on this bleak eminence, stretched out—but not on a hill-top; not on a crag; on Mrs. Filmer's sitting-room sofa. As for the visions, the faces, the voices of the dead, where were they? There was a screen in front of him, with black bulrushes and blue swallows. Where he had once seen mountains, where he had seen faces, where he had seen beauty, there was a screen.

"Evans!" he cried. There was no answer. A mouse had squeaked, or a curtain rustled. Those were the voices of the dead. The screen, the coal-scuttle, the sideboard remained to him. Let him then face the screen, the coal-scuttle and the sideboard . . . but Rezia burst into the room chattering.

Some letter had come. Everybody's plans were changed. Mrs. Filmer would not be able to go to Brighton after all. There was no time to let Mrs. Williams know, and really Rezia thought it very, very annoying, when she caught sight of the hat and thought . . . perhaps . . . she . . . might just make a little. . . . Her voice died out in contented melody.

"Ah, damn!" she cried (it was a joke of theirs, her swearing), the needle had broken. Hat, child, Brighton, needle. She built it up; first one thing, then another, she built it up, sewing.

She wanted him to say whether by moving the rose she had improved the hat. She sat on the end of the sofa.

They were perfectly happy now, she said, suddenly, putting the hat down. For she could say anything to him now. She could say whatever came into her head. That was almost the first thing she had felt about him, that night in the café when he had come in with his English friends. He had come in, rather shyly, looking round him, and his hat had fallen when he hung it up. That she could remember. She knew he was English, though not one of the large Englishmen her sister admired, for he was always thin; but he had a beautiful fresh colour; and with his big nose, his bright eyes, his way of sitting a little hunched made her think, she had often told him, of a young hawk, that first evening she saw him, when they were playing dominoes, and he had come in—of a young hawk; but with her he was always very gentle. She had never seen him wild or drunk, only suffering sometimes through this terrible war, but even so, when she came in, he would put it all away. Anything, anything in the whole world, any little bother with her work, anything that struck her to say she would tell him, and he understood at once. Her own family even were not the same. Being older than she was and being so clever—how serious he was, wanting her to read Shakespeare before she could even read a child's story in English!— being so much more experienced, he could help her. And she too could help him.

But this hat now. And then (it was getting late) Sir William Bradshaw.

She held her hands to her head, waiting for him to say did he like the hat or not, and as she sat there, waiting, looking down, he could feel her mind, like a bird, falling from branch to branch, and always alighting, quite rightly; he could follow her mind, as she sat there in one of those loose lax poses that came to her naturally and, if he should say anything, at once she smiled, like a bird alighting with all its claws firm upon the bough.

But he remembered Bradshaw said, "The people we are most fond of are not good for us when we are ill." Bradshaw said, he must be taught to rest. Bradshaw said they must be separated.

"Must," "must," why "must"? What power had Bradshaw over him? "What right has Bradshaw to say 'must' to me?" he demanded.

"It is because you talked of killing yourself," said Rezia. (Mercifully, she could now say anything to Septimus.)

So he was in their power! Holmes and Bradshaw were on him! The brute with the red nostrils was snuffing into every secret place! "Must" it could say! Where were his papers? the things he had written?

She brought him his papers, the things he had written, things she had written for him. She tumbled them out on to the sofa. They looked at them together. Diagrams, designs, little men and women brandishing sticks for arms, with wings—were they?—on their backs; circles traced round shillings and sixpences—the suns and stars; zigzagging precipices with mountaineers ascending roped together, exactly like knives and forks; sea pieces with little faces laughing out of what might perhaps be waves: the map of the world. Burn them! He cried. Now for his writings; how the dead sing behind rhododendron bushes; odes to Time; conversations with Shakespeare; Evans, Evans, Evans—his messages from the dead; do not cut down trees; tell the Prime Minister. Universal love: the meaning of the world. Burn them! he cried.

But Rezia laid her hands on them. Some were very beautiful, she thought. She would tie them up (for she had no envelope) with a piece of silk.

Even if they took him, she said, she would go with him. They could not separate them against their wills, she said.

Shuffling the edges straight, she did up the papers, and tied the parcel almost without looking, sitting beside him, he thought, as if all her petals were about her. She was a flowering tree; and through her branches looked out the face of a lawgiver, who had reached a sanctuary where she feared no one; not Holmes; not Bradshaw; a miracle, a triumph, the last and greatest. Staggering he saw her mount the appalling staircase, laden with Holmes and Bradshaw, men who never weighed less than eleven stone six, who sent their wives to Court, men who made ten thousand a year and talked of proportion; who different in their verdicts (for Holmes said one thing, Bradshaw another), yet judges they were; who mixed the vision and the sideboard; saw nothing clear, yet ruled, yet inflicted. "Must" they said. Over them she triumphed.

"There!" she said. The papers were tied up. No one should get at them. She would put them away.

And, she said, nothing should separate them. She sat down beside him and called him by the name of that hawk or crow which being malicious and a great destroyer of crops was precisely like him. No one could separate them, she said.

Then she got up to go into the bedroom to pack their things, but hearing voices downstairs and thinking that Dr. Holmes had perhaps called, ran down to prevent him coming up.

Septimus could hear her talking to Holmes on the staircase.

"My dear lady, I have come as a friend," Holmes was saying.

"No. I will not allow you to see my husband," she said.

He could see her, like a little hen, with her wings spread barring his passage. But Holmes persevered.

"My dear lady, allow me . . ." Holmes said, putting her aside (Holmes was a powerfully built man).

Holmes was coming upstairs. Holmes would burst open the door. Holmes would say "In a funk, eh?" Holmes would get him. But no; not Holmes; not Bradshaw. Getting up rather unsteadily, hopping indeed from foot to foot, he considered Mrs. Filmer's nice clean bread knife with "Bread" carved on the handle. Ah, but one mustn't spoil that. The gas fire? But it was too late now. Holmes was coming. Razors he might have got, but Rezia, who always did that sort of thing, had packed them. There remained only the window, the large Bloomsbury-lodging house window, the tiresome, the troublesome, and rather melodramatic business of opening the window and throwing himself out. It was their idea of tragedy, not his or Rezia's (for she was with him). Holmes and Bradshaw like that sort of thing. (He sat on the sill.) But he would wait till the very last moment. He did not want to die. Life was good. The sun hot. Only human beings—what did *they* want? Coming down the staircase opposite an old man stopped and stared at him. Holmes was at the door. "I'll give it you!" he cried, and flung himself vigorously, violently down on to Mrs. Filmer's area railings.

"The coward!" cried Dr. Holmes, bursting the door open. Rezia ran to the window, she saw; she understood. Dr. Holmes and Mrs. Filmer collided with each other. Mrs. Filmer flapped her apron and made her hide her eyes in the bedroom. There was a great deal of running up and down stairs. Dr. Holmes came in— white as a sheet, shaking all over, with a glass in his hand. She must be brave and drink something, he said (What was it? Something sweet), for her husband was horribly mangled, would not recover consciousness, she must not see him, must be spared as much as possible, would have the inquest to go through, poor young woman. Who could have foretold it? A sudden impulse, no one was in the least to blame (he told Mrs. Filmer). And why the devil he did it, Dr. Holmes could not conceive.

It seemed to her as she drank the sweet stuff that she was opening long windows, stepping out into some garden. But where? The clock was striking—one, two, three: how sensible the sound was; compared with all this thumping and whispering; like Septimus himself. She was falling asleep. But the clock went on striking, four, five, six and Mrs. Filmer waving her apron (they wouldn't bring the body in here, would they?) seemed part of that garden; or a flag. She had once seen a flag slowly rippling out from a mast when she stayed with her aunt at Venice. Men killed in battle were thus saluted, and Septimus had been through the War. Of her memories, most were happy.

She put on her hat, and ran through cornfields[9]—where could it have been?—on to some hill, somewhere near the sea, for there were ships, gulls, butterflies; they sat on a cliff. In London too, there they sat, and, half dreaming, came to her through the bedroom door, rain falling, whisperings, stirrings among dry corn, the caress of the sea, as it seemed to her, hollowing them in its arched shell and murmuring to her laid on shore, strewn she felt, like flying flowers over some tomb.

"He is dead," she said, smiling at the poor old woman who guarded her with her honest light-blue eyes fixed on the door. (They wouldn't bring him in here, would they?) But Mrs. Filmer pooh-poohed. Oh no, oh no! They were carrying him away now. Ought

---

9. This is an odd image for a Milanese hatmaker to imagine. It recalls Ruth's situation in the Bible, a poor immigrant, gleaning the cornfields for food. Woolf admired this image. See the Book of Ruth and Keats below (pp. 229–30 and 233–34).

she not to be told? Married people ought to be together, Mrs. Filmer thought. But they must do as the doctor said.

"Let her sleep," said Dr. Holmes, feeling her pulse. She saw the large outline of his body standing dark against the window. So that was Dr. Holmes.

One of the triumphs of civilisation, Peter Walsh thought. It is one of the triumphs of civilisation, as the light high bell of the ambulance sounded. Swiftly, cleanly the ambulance sped to the hospital, having picked up instantly, humanely, some poor devil; some one hit on the head, struck down by disease, knocked over perhaps a minute or so ago at one of these crossings, as might happen to oneself. That was civilisation. It struck him coming back from the East—the efficiency, the organisation, the communal spirit of London. Every cart or carriage of its own accord drew aside to let the ambulance pass. Perhaps it was morbid; or was it not touching rather, the respect which they showed this ambulance with its victim inside—busy men hurrying home yet instantly bethinking them as it passed of some wife; or presumably how easily it might have been them there, stretched on a shelf with a doctor and a nurse. . . . Ah, but thinking became morbid, sentimental, directly one began conjuring up doctors, dead bodies; a little glow of pleasure, a sort of lust too over the visual impression warned one not to go on with that sort of thing any more—fatal to art, fatal to friendship. True. And yet, thought Peter Walsh, as the ambulance turned the corner though the light high bell could be heard down the next street and still farther as it crossed the Tottenham Court Road, chiming constantly, it is the privilege of loneliness; in privacy one may do as one chooses. One might weep if no one saw. It had been his undoing— this susceptibility—in Anglo-Indian society; not weeping at the right time, or laughing either. I have that in me, he thought standing by the pillar-box, which could now dissolve in tears. Why, Heaven knows. Beauty of some sort probably, and the weight of the day, which beginning with that visit to Clarissa had exhausted him with its heat, its intensity, and the drip, drip, of one impression after another down into that cellar where they stood, deep, dark, and no one would ever know. Partly for that reason, its secrecy, complete and inviolable, he had found life like an unknown garden, full of turns and corners, surprising, yes; really it took one's breath away, these moments; there coming to him by the pillar-box opposite the British Museum one of them, a moment, in which things came together; this ambulance; and life and death. It was as if he were sucked up to some very high roof by that rush of emotion and the rest of him, like a white shell-sprinkled beach, left bare. It had been his undoing in Anglo-Indian society—this susceptibility.

Clarissa once, going on top of an omnibus with him some-where, Clarissa superficially at least, so easily moved, now in despair, now in the best of spirits, all aquiver in those days and such good company, spotting queer little scenes, names, people from the top of a bus, for they used to explore London and bring back bags full of treasures from the Caledonian market—Cla-rissa had a theory in those days—they had heaps of theories, always theories, as young people have. It was to explain the feel-ing they had of dissatisfaction; not knowing people; not being known. For how could they know each other? You met every day; then not for six months, or years. It was unsatisfactory, they agreed, how little one knew people. But she said, sitting on the bus going up Shaftesbury Avenue, she felt herself everywhere; not "here, here, here"; and she tapped the back of the seat; but everywhere. She waved her hand, going up Shaftesbury Avenue. She was all that. So that to know her, or any one, one must seek out the people who completed them; even the places. Odd affini-ties she had with people she had never spoken to, some woman in the street, some man behind a counter—even trees, or barns. It ended in a transcendental theory which, with her horror of death, allowed her to believe, or say that she believed (for all her scepti-cism), that since our apparitions, the part of us which appears, are so momentary compared with the other, the unseen part of us, which spreads wide, the unseen might survive, be recovered somehow attached to this person or that, or even haunting cer-tain places after death . . . perhaps—perhaps.

Looking back over that long friendship of almost thirty years her theory worked to this extent. Brief, broken, often painful as their actual meetings had been what with his absences and interruptions (this morning, for instance, in came Elizabeth, like a long-legged colt, handsome, dumb, just as he was beginning to talk to Clarissa) the effect of them on his life was immeasurable. There was a mys-tery about it. You were given a sharp, acute, uncomfortable grain— the actual meeting; horribly painful as often as not; yet in absence, in the most unlikely places, it would flower out, open, shed its scent, let you touch, taste, look about you, get the whole feel of it and understanding, after years of lying lost. Thus she had come to him; on board ship; in the Himalayas; suggested by the oddest things (so Sally Seton, generous, enthusiastic goose! thought of *him* when she saw blue hydrangeas). She had influenced him more than any person he had ever known. And always in this way coming before him without his wishing it, cool, lady-like, critical; or ravish-ing, romantic, recalling some field or English harvest. He saw her most often in the country, not in London. One scene after another at Bourton. . . .

He had reached his hotel. He crossed the hall, with its mounds of reddish chairs and sofas, its spike-leaved, withered-looking plants. He got his key off the hook. The young lady handed him some letters. He went upstairs—he saw her most often at Bourton, in the late summer, when he stayed there for a week, or fortnight even, as people did in those days. First on top of some hill there she would stand, hands clapped to her hair, her cloak blowing out, pointing, crying to them—she saw the Severn beneath. Or in a wood, making the kettle boil—very ineffective with her fingers; the smoke curtseying, blowing in their faces; her little pink face showing through; begging water from an old woman in a cottage, who came to the door to watch them go. They walked always; the others drove. She was bored driving, disliked all animals, except that dog. They tramped miles along roads. She would break off to get her bearings, pilot him back across country; and all the time they argued, discussed poetry, discussed people, discussed politics (she was a Radical then); never noticing a thing except when she stopped, cried out at a view or a tree, and made him look with her; and so on again, through stubble fields, she walking ahead, with a flower for her aunt, never tired of walking for all her delicacy; to drop down on Bourton in the dusk. Then, after dinner, old Breitkopf would open the piano and sing without any voice, and they would lie sunk in arm-chairs, trying not to laugh, but always breaking down and laughing, laughing—laughing at nothing. Breitkopf was supposed not to see. And then in the morning, flirting up and down like a wagtail in front of the house. . . .

Oh it was a letter from her! This blue envelope; that was her hand. And he would have to read it. Here was another of those meetings, bound to be painful! To read her letter needed the devil of an effort. "How heavenly it was to see him. She must tell him that." That was all.

But it upset him. It annoyed him. He wished she hadn't written it. Coming on top of his thoughts, it was like a nudge in the ribs. Why couldn't she let him be? After all, she had married Dalloway, and lived with him in perfect happiness all these years.

These hotels are not consoling places. Far from it. Any number of people had hung up their hats on those pegs. Even the flies, if you thought of it, had settled on other people's noses. As for the cleanliness which hit him in the face, it wasn't cleanliness, so much as bareness, frigidity; a thing that had to be. Some arid matron made her rounds at dawn sniffing, peering, causing blue-nosed maids to scour, for all the world as if the next visitor were a joint of meat to be served on a perfectly clean platter. For sleep, one bed; for sitting in, one arm-chair; for cleaning one's teeth and shaving one's chin, one tumbler, one looking-glass. Books, letters, dressing-gown,

slipped about on the impersonality of the horsehair like incongruous impertinences. And it was Clarissa's letter that made him see
all this. "Heavenly to see you. She must say so!" He folded the
paper; pushed it away; nothing would induce him to read it again!

To get that letter to him by six o'clock she must have sat down and
written it directly he left her; stamped it; sent somebody to the post.[1]
It was, as people say, very like her. She was upset by his visit. She
had felt a great deal; had for a moment, when she kissed his hand,
regretted, envied him even, remembered possibly (for he saw her
look it) something he had said—how they would change the world if
she married him perhaps; whereas, it was this; it was middle age; it
was mediocrity; then forced herself with her indomitable vitality to
put all that aside, there being in her a thread of life which for tough-
ness, endurance, power to overcome obstacles, and carry her triumphantly through he had never known the like of. Yes; but there
would come a reaction directly he left the room. She would be
frightfully sorry for him; she would think what in the world she
could do to give him pleasure (short always of the one thing) and he
could see her with the tears running down her cheeks going to her
writing-table and dashing off that one line which he was to find
greeting him. . . . "Heavenly to see you!" And she meant it.

Peter Walsh had now unlaced his boots.

But it would not have been a success, their marriage. The other
thing, after all, came so much more naturally.

It was odd; it was true; lots of people felt it. Peter Walsh, who had
done just respectably, filled the usual posts adequately, was liked,
but thought a little cranky, gave himself airs—it was odd that *he*
should have had, especially now that his hair was grey, a contented
look; a look of having reserves. It was this that made him attractive
to women who liked the sense that he was not altogether manly.
There was something unusual about him, or something behind
him. It might be that he was bookish—never came to see you without taking up the book on the table (he was now reading, with his
bootlaces trailing on the floor); or that he was a gentleman, which
showed itself in the way he knocked the ashes out of his pipe, and in
his manners of course to women. For it was very charming and quite
ridiculous how easily some girl without a grain of sense could twist
him round her finger. But at her own risk. That is to say, though he
might be ever so easy, and indeed with his gaiety and good-breeding
fascinating to be with, it was only up to a point. She said something—no, no; he saw through that. He wouldn't stand that—no,
no. Then he could shout and rock and hold his sides together over

---

1. In London in the 1920s there were several mail deliveries a day, making it possible to
write a letter and have it be received the same day.

some joke with men. He was the best judge of cooking in India. He was a man. But not the sort of man one had to respect—which was a mercy; not like Major Simmons, for instance; not in the least like that, Daisy thought, when, in spite of her two small children, she used to compare them.

He pulled off his boots. He emptied his pockets. Out came with his pocket-knife a snapshot of Daisy on the verandah; Daisy all in white, with a fox-terrier on her knee; very charming, very dark; the best he had ever seen of her. It did come, after all so naturally; so much more naturally than Clarissa. No fuss. No bother. No finicking and fidgeting. All plain sailing. And the dark, adorably pretty girl on the verandah exclaimed (he could hear her). Of course, of course she would give him everything! she cried (she had no sense of discretion) everything he wanted! she cried, running to meet him, whoever might be looking. And she was only twenty-four. And she had two children. Well, well!

Well indeed he had got himself into a mess at his age. And it came over him when he woke in the night pretty forcibly. Suppose they did marry? For him it would be all very well, but what about her? Mrs. Burgess, a good sort and no chatterbox, in whom he had confided, thought this absence of his in England, ostensibly to see lawyers might serve to make Daisy reconsider, think what it meant. It was a question of her position, Mrs. Burgess said; the social barrier; giving up her children. She'd be a widow with a past one of these days, draggling about in the suburbs, or more likely, indiscriminate (you know, she said, what such women get like, with too much paint). But Peter Walsh pooh-poohed all that. He didn't mean to die yet. Anyhow she must settle for herself; judge for herself, he thought, padding about the room in his socks, smoothing out his dress-shirt, for he might go to Clarissa's party, or he might go to one of the Halls, or he might settle in and read an absorbing book written by a man he used to know at Oxford. And if he did retire, that's what he'd do—write books. He would go to Oxford and poke about in the Bodleian. Vainly the dark, adorably pretty girl ran to the end of the terrace; vainly waved her hand; vainly cried she didn't care a straw what people said. There he was, the man she thought the world of, the perfect gentleman, the fascinating, the distinguished (and his age made not the least difference to her), padding about a room in an hotel in Bloomsbury, shaving, washing, continuing, as he took up cans, put down razors, to poke about in the Bodleian, and get at the truth about one or two little matters that interested him. And he would have a chat with whoever it might be, and so come to disregard more and more precise hours for lunch, and miss engagements, and when Daisy asked him, as she would, for a kiss, a scene, fail to come up to the scratch (though he was genuinely devoted to her)—in short it might be happier, as Mrs. Burgess said, that she should forget him, or merely remember him as he was in August 1922, like a figure standing at the cross roads at dusk, which grows more and more remote as the dog-cart spins away, carrying her securely fastened to the back seat, though her arms are outstretched, and as she sees the figure dwindle and disappear still she cries out how she would do anything in the world, anything, anything, anything. . . .

He never knew what people thought. It became more and more difficult for him to concentrate. He became absorbed; he became busied with his own concerns; now surly, now gay; dependent on women, absent-minded, moody, less and less able (so he thought as he shaved) to understand why Clarissa couldn't simply find them a lodging and be nice to Daisy; introduce her. And then he could just—just do what? just haunt and hover (he was at the moment actually engaged in sorting out various keys, papers), swoop and taste, be alone, in short, sufficient to himself; and yet nobody of course was more dependent upon others (he buttoned his waist-coat); it had been his undoing. He could not keep out of smoking-rooms, liked colonels, liked golf, liked bridge, and above all women's society, and the fineness of their companionship, and their faithful-ness and audacity and greatness in loving which though it had its drawbacks seemed to him (and the dark, adorably pretty face was on top of the envelopes) so wholly admirable, so splendid a flower to grow on the crest of human life, and yet he could not come up to the scratch, being always apt to see round things (Clarissa had sapped something in him permanently), and to tire very easily of mute devotion and to want variety in love, though it would make him furious if Daisy loved anybody else, furious! for he was jealous, uncontrollably jealous by temperament. He suffered tortures! But where was his knife; his watch; his seals, his note-case, and Claris-sa's letter which he would not read again but liked to think of, and Daisy's photograph? And now for dinner.

They were eating.

Sitting at little tables round vases, dressed or not dressed, with their shawls and bags laid beside them, with their air of false com-posure, for they were not used to so many courses at dinner, and confidence, for they were able to pay for it, and strain, for they had been running about London all day shopping, sightseeing; and their natural curiosity, for they looked round and up as the nice-looking gentleman in horn-rimmed spectacles came in, and their good nature, for they would have been glad to do any little service, such as lend a time-table or impart useful information, and their desire, pulsing in them, tugging at them subterraneously, somehow to establish connections if it were only a birthplace (Liverpool, for example) in common or friends of the same name; with their furtive glances, odd silences, and sudden withdrawals into family jocularity and isolation; there they sat eating dinner when Mr. Walsh came in and took his seat at a little table by the curtain.

It was not that he said anything, for being solitary he could only address himself to the waiter; it was his way of looking at the menu, of pointing his forefinger to a particular wine, of hitching himself up to the table, of addressing himself seriously, not gluttonously to dinner, that won him their respect; which, having to remain unexpressed for the greater part of the meal, flared up at the table where the Morrises sat when Mr. Walsh was heard to say at the end of the meal, "Bartlett pears." Why he should have spoken so moderately yet firmly, with the air of a disciplinarian well within his rights which are founded upon justice, neither young Charles Morris, nor old Charles, neither Miss Elaine nor Mrs. Morris knew. But when he said, "Bartlett pears," sitting alone at his table, they felt that he counted on their support in some lawful demand; was champion of a cause which immediately became their own, so that their eyes met his eyes sympathetically, and when they all reached the smoking-room simultaneously, a little talk between them became inevitable.

It was not very profound—only to the effect that London was crowded; had changed in thirty years; that Mr. Morris preferred Liverpool; that Mrs. Morris had been to the Westminster flowershow, and that they had all seen the Prince of Wales. Yet, thought Peter Walsh, no family in the world can compare with the Morrises; none whatever; and their relations to each other are perfect, and they don't care a hang for the upper classes, and they like what they like, and Elaine is training for the family business, and the boy has won a scholarship at Leeds, and the old lady (who is about his own age) has three more children at home; and they have two motor cars, but Mr. Morris still mends the boots on Sunday: it is superb, it is absolutely superb, thought Peter Walsh, swaying a little backwards and forwards with his liqueur glass in his hand among the hairy red chairs and ash-trays, feeling very well pleased with himself, for the Morrises liked him. Yes, they liked a man who said, "Bartlett pears." They liked him, he felt.

He would go to Clarissa's party. (The Morrises moved off; but they would meet again.) He would go to Clarissa's party, because he wanted to ask Richard what they were doing in India—the conservative duffers. And what's being acted? And music. . . . Oh yes, and mere gossip.

For this is the truth about our soul, he thought, our self, who fish-like inhabits deep seas and plies among obscurities threading her way between the boles of giant weeds, over sun-flickered spaces and on and on into gloom, cold, deep, inscrutable; suddenly she shoots to the surface and sports on the wind-wrinkled waves; that is, has a positive need to brush, scrape, kindle herself, gossiping. What did the Government mean—Richard Dalloway would know—to do about India?

Since it was a very hot night and the paper boys went by with placards proclaiming in huge red letters that there was a heat-wave, wicker chairs were placed on the hotel steps and there, sipping, smoking, detached gentlemen sat. Peter Walsh sat there. One might fancy that day, the London day, was just beginning. Like a woman who had slipped off her print dress and white apron to array herself in blue and pearls, the day changed, put off stuff, took gauze, changed to evening, and with the same sigh of exhilaration that a woman breathes, tumbling petticoats on the floor, it too shed dust, heat, colour; the traffic thinned; motor cars, tinkling, darting, succeeded the lumber of vans; and here and there among the thick foliage of the squares an intense light hung. I resign, the evening seemed to say, as it paled and faded above the battlements and prominences, moulded, pointed, of hotel, flat, and block of shops, I fade, she was beginning, I disappear, but London would have none of it, and rushed her bayonets into the sky, pinioned her, constrained her to partnership in her revelry.

For the great revolution of Mr. Willett's summer time had taken place since Peter Walsh's last visit to England. The prolonged evening was new to him. It was inspiriting, rather. For as the young people went by with their despatch-boxes, awfully glad to be free, proud too, dumbly, of stepping this famous pavement, joy of a kind, cheap, tinselly, if you like, but all the same rapture, flushed their faces. They dressed well too; pink stockings; pretty shoes. They would now have two hours at the pictures. It sharpened, it refined them, the yellow-blue evening light; and on the leaves in the square shone lurid, livid—they looked as if dipped in sea water—the foliage of a submerged city. He was astonished by the beauty; it was encouraging too, for where the returned Anglo-Indian sat by rights (he knew crowds of them) in the Oriental Club biliously summing up the ruin of the world, here was he, as young as ever; envying young people their summer time and the rest of it, and more than suspecting from the words of a girl, from a housemaid's laughter—intangible things you couldn't lay your hands on—that shift in the whole pyramidal accumulation which in his youth had seemed immovable. On top of them it had pressed; weighed them down, the women especially, like those flowers Clarissa's Aunt Helena used to press between sheets of grey blotting-paper with Littré's dictionary on top, sitting under the lamp after dinner. She was dead now. He had heard of her, from Clarissa, losing the sight of one eye. It

seemed so fitting—one of nature's masterpieces—that old Miss
Parry should turn to glass. She would die like some bird in a frost
gripping her perch. She belonged to a different age, but being so
entire, so complete, would always stand up on the horizon, stone-
white, eminent, like a lighthouse marking some past stage on this
adventurous, long, long voyage, this interminable (he felt for a copper to buy a paper and read about Surrey and Yorkshire—he had
held out that copper millions of times. Surrey was all out once
more)—this interminable life. But cricket was no mere game.
Cricket was important. He could never help reading about cricket.
He read the scores in the stop press first, then how it was a hot day;
then about a murder case. Having done things millions of times
enriched them, though it might be said to take the surface off. The
past enriched, and experience, and having cared for one or two
people, and so having acquired the power which the young lack, of
cutting short, doing what one likes, not caring a rap what people
say and coming and going without any very great expectations (he
left his paper on the table and moved off), which however (and he
looked for his hat and coat) was not altogether true of him, not to-
night, for here he was starting to go to a party, at his age, with the
belief upon him that he was about to have an experience. But what?

Beauty anyhow. Not the crude beauty of the eye. It was not beauty
pure and simple—Bedford Place leading into Russell Square. It was
straightness and emptiness of course; the symmetry of a corridor;
but it was also windows lit up, a piano, a gramophone sounding; a
sense of pleasure-making hidden, but now and again emerging
when, through the uncurtained window, the window left open, one
saw parties sitting over tables, young people slowly circling, conversations between men and women, maids idly looking out (a strange
comment theirs, when work was done), stockings drying on top
ledges, a parrot, a few plants. Absorbing, mysterious, of infinite
richness, this life. And in the large square where the cabs shot and
swerved so quick, there were loitering couples, dallying, embracing,
shrunk up under the shower of a tree; that was moving; so silent, so
absorbed, that one passed, discreetly, timidly, as if in the presence
of some sacred ceremony to interrupt which would have been impi-
ous. That was interesting. And so on into the flare and glare.

His light overcoat blew open, he stepped with indescribable idio-
syncrasy, lent a little forward, tripped, with his hands behind his
back and his eyes still a little hawklike; he tripped through London,
towards Westminster, observing.

Was everybody dining out, then? Doors were being opened here
by a footman to let issue a high-stepping old dame, in buckled
shoes, with three purple ostrich feathers in her hair. Doors were
being opened for ladies wrapped like mummies in shawls with

bright flowers on them, ladies with bare heads. And in respectable quarters with stucco pillars through small front gardens lightly swathed with combs in their hair (having run up to see the children), women came; men waited for them, with their coats blowing open, and the motor started. Everybody was going out. What with these doors being opened, and the descent and the start, it seemed as if the whole of London were embarking in little boats moored to the bank, tossing on the waters, as if the whole place were floating off in carnival. And Whitehall was skated over, silver beaten as it was, skated over by spiders, and there was a sense of midges round the arc lamps; it was so hot that people stood about talking. And here in Westminster was a retired Judge, presumably, sitting four square at his house door dressed all in white. An Anglo-Indian presumably.

And here a shindy of brawling women, drunken women; here only a policeman and looming houses, high houses, domed houses, churches, parliaments, and the hoot of a steamer on the river, a hollow misty cry. But it was her street, this, Clarissa's; cabs were rushing round the corner, like water round the piers of a bridge, drawn together, it seemed to him because they bore people going to her party, Clarissa's party.

The cold stream of visual impressions failed him now as if the eye were a cup that overflowed and let the rest run down its china walls unrecorded. The brain must wake now. The body must contract now, entering the house, the lighted house, where the door stood open, where the motor cars were standing, and bright women descending: the soul must brave itself to endure. He opened the big blade of his pocket-knife.

Lucy came running full tilt downstairs, having just nipped in to the drawing-room to smooth a cover, to straighten a chair, to pause a moment and feel whoever came in must think how clean, how bright, how beautifully cared for, when they saw the beautiful silver, the brass fire-irons, the new chair-covers, and the curtains of yellow chintz: she appraised each; heard a roar of voices; people already coming up from dinner; she must fly!

The Prime Minister was coming, Agnes said: so she had heard them say in the dining-room, she said, coming in with a tray of glasses. Did it matter, did it matter in the least, one Prime Minister more or less? It made no difference at this hour of the night to Mrs. Walker among the plates, saucepans, cullenders, frying-pans, chicken in aspic, ice-cream freezers, pared crusts of bread, lemons, soup tureens, and pudding basins which, however hard they washed up in the scullery seemed to be all on top of her, on the kitchen table, on chairs, while the fire blared and roared, the electric lights

glared, and still supper had to be laid. All she felt was, one Prime
Minister more or less made not a scrap of difference to Mrs. Walker.

The ladies were going upstairs already, said Lucy; the ladies were
going up, one by one, Mrs. Dalloway walking last and almost always
sending back some message to the kitchen, "My love to Mrs. Walker,"
that was it one night. Next morning they would go over the dishes—
the soup, the salmon; the salmon, Mrs. Walker knew, as usual
underdone, for she always got nervous about the pudding and left it
to Jenny; so it happened, the salmon was always underdone. But
some lady with fair hair and silver ornaments had said, Lucy said,
about the entrée, was it really made at home? But it was the salmon
that bothered Mrs. Walker, as she spun the plates round and round,
and pulled in dampers and pulled out dampers; and there came a
burst of laughter from the dining-room; a voice speaking; then
another burst of laughter—the gentlemen enjoying themselves
when the ladies had gone. The tokay, said Lucy running in. Mr. Dalloway had sent for the tokay, from the Emperor's cellars, the Imperial Tokay.

It was borne through the kitchen. Over her shoulder Lucy
reported how Miss Elizabeth looked quite lovely; she couldn't take
her eyes off her; in her pink dress, wearing the necklace Mr. Dalloway had given her. Jenny must remember the dog, Miss Elizabeth's fox-terrier, which, since it bit, had to be shut up and might,
Elizabeth thought, want something. Jenny must remember the dog.
But Jenny was not going upstairs with all those people about. There
was a motor at the door already! There was a ring at the bell—and
the gentlemen still in the dining-room, drinking tokay!

There, they were going upstairs; that was the first to come, and
now they would come faster and faster, so that Mrs. Parkinson
(hired for parties) would leave the hall door ajar, and the hall would
be full of gentlemen waiting (they stood waiting, sleeking down
their hair) while the ladies took their cloaks off in the room along
the passage; where Mrs. Barnet helped them, old Ellen Barnet, who
had been with the family for forty years, and came every summer to
help the ladies, and remembered mothers when they were girls, and
though very unassuming did shake hands; said "milady" very
respectfully, yet had a humorous way with her, looking at the young
ladies, and ever so tactfully helping Lady Lovejoy, who had some
trouble with her underbodice. And they could not help feeling, Lady
Lovejoy and Miss Alice, that some little privilege in the matter of
brush and comb, was awarded them having known Mrs. Barnet—
"thirty years, milady," Mrs. Barnet supplied her. Young ladies did
not use to rouge, said Lady Lovejoy, when they stayed at Bourton in
the old days. And Miss Alice didn't need rouge, said Mrs. Barnet,
looking at her fondly. There Mrs. Barnet would sit, in the

cloakroom, patting down the furs, smoothing out the Spanish shawls, tidying the dressing-table, and knowing perfectly well, in spite of the furs and the embroideries, which were nice ladies, which were not. The dear old body, said Lady Lovejoy, mounting the stairs, Clarissa's old nurse.

And then Lady Lovejoy stiffened. "Lady and Miss Lovejoy," she said to Mr. Wilkins (hired for parties). He had an admirable manner, as he bent and straightened himself, bent and straightened himself and announced with perfect impartiality "Lady and Miss Lovejoy . . . Sir John and Lady Needham . . . Miss Weld . . . Mr. Walsh." His manner was admirable; his family life must be irreproachable, except that it seemed impossible that a being with greenish lips and shaven cheeks could ever have blundered into the nuisance of children.

"How delightful to see you!" said Clarissa. She said it to every one. How delightful to see you! She was at her worst—effusive, insincere. It was a great mistake to have come. He should have stayed at home and read his book, thought Peter Walsh; should have gone to a music hall; he should have stayed at home, for he knew no one.

Oh dear, it was going to be a failure; a complete failure, Clarissa felt it in her bones as dear old Lord Lexham stood there apologizing for his wife who had caught cold at the Buckingham Palace garden party. She could see Peter out of the tail of her eye, criticising her, there, in that corner. Why, after all, did she do these things? Why seek pinnacles and stand drenched in fire? Might it consume her anyhow! Burn her to cinders! Better anything, better brandish one's torch and hurl it to earth than taper and dwindle away like some Ellie Henderson! It was extraordinary how Peter put her into these states just by coming and standing in a corner. He made her see herself; exaggerate. It was idiotic. But why did he come, then, merely to criticize? Why always take, never give? Why not risk one's one little point of view? There he was wandering off, and she must speak to him. But she would not get the chance. Life was that—humiliation, renunciation. What Lord Lexham was saying was that his wife would not wear her furs at the garden party because "my dear, you ladies are all alike"—Lady Lexham being seventy-five at least! It was delicious, how they petted each other, that old couple. She did like old Lord Lexham. She did think it mattered, her party, and it made her feel quite sick to know that it was all going wrong, all falling flat. Anything, any explosion, any horror was better than people wandering aimlessly, standing in a bunch at a corner like Ellie Henderson, not even caring to hold themselves upright.

Gently the yellow curtain with all the birds of Paradise blew out and it seemed as if there were a flight of wings into the room, right out, then sucked back. (For the windows were open.) Was it draughty, Ellie Henderson wondered? She was subject to chills. But it did not matter that she should come down sneezing to-morrow; it was the girls with their naked shoulders she thought of, being trained to think of others by an old father, an invalid, late vicar of Bourton, but he was dead now; and her chills never went to her chest, never. It was the girls she thought of, the young girls with their bare shoulders, she herself having always been a wisp of a creature, with her thin hair and meagre profile; though now, past fifty, there was beginning to shine through some mild beam, something purified into distinction by years of self-abnegation but obscured again, perpetually, by her distressing gentility, her panic fear, which arose from three hundred pounds' income, and her weaponless state (she could not earn a penny) and it made her timid, and more and more disqualified year by year to meet well-dressed people who did this sort of thing every night of the season, merely telling their maids "I'll wear so and so," whereas Ellie Henderson ran out nervously and bought cheap pink flowers, half a dozen, and then threw a shawl over her old black dress. For her invitation to Clarissa's party had come at the last moment. She was not quite happy about it. She had a sort of feeling that Clarissa had not meant to ask her this year.

Why should she? There was no reason really, except that they had always known each other. Indeed, they were cousins. But naturally they had rather drifted apart, Clarissa being so sought after. It was an event to her, going to a party. It was quite a treat just to see the lovely clothes. Wasn't that Elizabeth, grown up, with her hair done in the fashionable way, in the pink dress? Yet she could not be more than seventeen. She was very, very handsome. But girls when they first came out didn't seem to wear white as they used. (She must remember everything to tell Edith.) Girls wore straight frocks, perfectly tight, with skirts well above the ankles. It was not becoming, she thought.

So, with her weak eyesight, Ellie Henderson craned rather forward, and it wasn't so much she who minded not having any one to talk to (she hardly knew anybody there), for she felt that they were all such interesting people to watch; politicians presumably; Richard Dalloway's friends; but it was Richard himself who felt that he could not let the poor creature go on standing there all the evening by herself.

"Well, Ellie, and how's the world treating *you*?" he said in his genial way, and Ellie Henderson, getting nervous and flushing and feeling that it was extraordinarily nice of him to come and talk to her, said that many people really felt the heat more than the cold.

"Yes, they do," said Richard Dalloway. "Yes."

But what more did one say?

"Hullo, Richard," said somebody, taking him by the elbow, and, good Lord, there was old Peter, old Peter Walsh. He was delighted to see him—ever so pleased to see him! He hadn't changed a bit. And off they went together walking right across the room, giving each other little pats, as if they hadn't met for a long time, Ellie Henderson thought, watching them go, certain she knew that man's face. A tall man, middle aged, rather fine eyes, dark, wearing spectacles, with a look of John Burrows. Edith would be sure to know.

The curtain with its flight of birds of Paradise blew out again. And Clarissa saw—she saw Ralph Lyon beat it back, and go on talking. So it wasn't a failure after all! it was going to be all right now—her party. It had begun. It had started. But it was still touch and go. She must stand there for the present. People seemed to come in a rush.

Colonel and Mrs. Garrod . . . Mr. Hugh Whitbread . . . Mr. Bowley . . . Mrs. Hilbery . . . Lady Mary Maddox . . . Mr. Quin . . . intoned Wilkin. She had six or seven words with each, and they went on, they went into the rooms; into something now, not nothing, since Ralph Lyon had beat back the curtain.

And yet for her own part, it was too much of an effort. She was not enjoying it. It was too much like being—just anybody, standing there; anybody could do it; yet this anybody she did a little admire, couldn't help feeling that she had, anyhow, made this happen, that it marked a stage, this post that she felt herself to have become, for oddly enough she had quite forgotten what she looked like, but felt herself a stake driven in at the top of her stairs. Every time she gave a party she had this feeling of being something not herself, and that every one was unreal in one way; much more real in another. It was, she thought, partly their clothes, partly being taken out of their ordinary ways, partly the background, it was possible to say things you couldn't say anyhow else, things that needed an effort; possible to go much deeper. But not for her; not yet anyhow.

"How delightful to see you!" she said. Dear old Sir Harry! He would know every one.

And what was so odd about it was the sense one had as they came up the stairs one after another, Mrs. Mount and Celia, Herbert Ainsty, Mrs. Dakers—oh and Lady Bruton!

"How awfully good of you to come!" she said, and she meant it—it was odd how standing there one felt them going on, going on, some quite old, some . . .

*What* name? Lady Rosseter? But who on earth was Lady Rosseter?

"Clarissa!" That voice! It was Sally Seton! Sally Seton! after all these years! She loomed through a mist. For she hadn't looked like *that*, Sally Seton, when Clarissa grasped the hot water can, to think of her under this roof, under this roof! Not like that!

All on top of each other, embarrassed, laughing, words tumbled out—passing through London; heard from Clara Haydon; what a chance of seeing you! So I thrust myself in—without an invitation. . . .

One might put down the hot water can quite composedly. The lustre had gone out of her. Yet it was extraordinary to see her again, older, happier, less lovely. They kissed each other, first this cheek then that, by the drawing-room door, and Clarissa turned, with Sally's hand in hers, and saw her rooms full, heard the roar of voices, saw the candlesticks, the blowing curtains, and the roses which Richard had given her.

"I have five enormous boys," said Sally.

She had the simplest egotism, the most open desire to be thought first always, and Clarissa loved her for being still like that. "I can't believe it!" she cried, kindling all over with pleasure at the thought of the past.

But alas, Wilkins; Wilkins wanted her; Wilkins was emitting in a voice of commanding authority as if the whole company must be admonished and the hostess reclaimed from frivolity, one name:

"The Prime Minister," said Peter Walsh.

The Prime Minister? Was it really? Ellie Henderson marvelled. What a thing to tell Edith!

One couldn't laugh at him. He looked so ordinary. You might have stood him behind a counter and bought biscuits—poor chap, all rigged up in gold lace. And to be fair, as he went his rounds, first with Clarissa then with Richard escorting him, he did it very well. He tried to look somebody. It was amusing to watch. Nobody looked at him. They just went on talking, yet it was perfectly plain that they all knew, felt to the marrow of their bones, this majesty passing; this symbol of what they all stood for, English society. Old Lady Bruton, and she looked very fine too, very stalwart in her lace, swam up, and they withdrew into a little room which at once became spied upon, guarded, and a sort of stir and rustle rippled through every one, openly: the Prime Minister!

Lord, lord, the snobbery of the English! thought Peter Walsh, standing in the corner. How they loved dressing up in gold lace and doing homage! There! That must be, by Jove it was, Hugh Whitbread, snuffing round the precincts of the great, grown rather fatter, rather whiter, the admirable Hugh!

He looked always as if he were on duty, thought Peter, a privileged, but secretive being, hoarding secrets which he would die to defend, though it was only some little piece of tittle-tattle dropped by a court footman, which would be in all the papers tomorrow. Such were his rattles, his baubles, in playing with which he had grown white, come to the verge of old age, enjoying the respect and affection of all who had the privilege of knowing this type of the English public school man. Inevitably one made up things like that about Hugh; that was his style; the style of those admirable letters which Peter had read thousands of miles across the sea in the *Times*, and had thanked God he was out of that pernicious hubble-bubble if it were only to hear baboons chatter and coolies beat their wives. An olive-skinned youth from one of the Universities stood obsequiously by. Him he would patronise, initiate, teach how to get on. For he liked nothing better than doing kindnesses, making the hearts of old ladies palpitate with the joy of being thought of in their age, their affliction, thinking themselves quite forgotten, yet here was dear Hugh driving up and spending an hour talking of the past, remembering trifles, praising the home-made cake, though Hugh might eat cake with a Duchess any day of his life, and, to look at him, probably did spend a good deal of time in that agreeable occupation. The All-judging, the All-merciful, might excuse. Peter Walsh had no mercy. Villains there must be, and God knows the rascals who get hanged for battering the brains of a girl out in a train do less harm on the whole than Hugh Whitbread and his kindness. Look at him now, on tiptoe, dancing forward, bowing and scraping, as the Prime Minister and Lady Bruton emerged, intimating for all the world to see that he was privileged to say something, something private, to Lady Bruton as she passed. She stopped. She wagged her fine old head. She was thanking him presumably for some piece of servility. She had her toadies, minor officials in Government offices who ran about putting through little jobs on her behalf, in return for which she gave them luncheon. But she derived from the eighteenth century. She was all right.

And now Clarissa escorted her Prime Minister down the room, prancing, sparkling, with the stateliness of her grey hair. She wore ear-rings, and a silver-green mermaid's dress. Lolloping on the waves and braiding her tresses she seemed, having that gift still; to be; to exist; to sum it all up in the moment as she passed; turned, caught her scarf in some other woman's dress, unhitched it, laughed, all with the most perfect ease and air of a creature floating in its element. But age had brushed her; even as a mermaid might behold in her glass the setting sun on some very clear evening over the waves. There was a breath of tenderness; her severity, her prudery, her woodenness were all warmed through now, and she had about her as she said good-bye to the thick gold-laced man who was doing his best, and good luck to him, to look important, an inexpressible dignity; an exquisite cordiality; as if she wished the whole world well, and must now, being on the very verge and rim of things, take her leave. So she made him think. (But he was not in love.)

Indeed, Clarissa felt, the Prime Minister had been good to come. And, walking down the room with him, with Sally there and Peter there and Richard very pleased, with all those people rather inclined, perhaps, to envy, she had felt that intoxication of the moment, that dilatation of the nerves of the heart itself till it seemed to quiver, steeped, upright;—yes, but after all it was what other people felt, that; for, though she loved it and felt it tingle and sting, still these semblances, these triumphs (dear old Peter, for example, thinking her so brilliant), had a hollowness; at arm's length they were, not in the heart; and it might be that she was growing old but they satisfied her no longer as they used; and suddenly, as she saw the Prime Minister go down the stairs, the gilt rim of the Sir Joshua picture of the little girl with a muff brought back Kilman with a rush; Kilman her enemy. That was satisfying; that was real. Ah, how she hated her—hot, hypocritical, corrupt; with all that power; Elizabeth's seducer; the woman who had crept in to steal and defile (Richard would say, What nonsense!). She hated her: she loved her. It was enemies one wanted, not friends— not Mrs. Durrant and Clara, Sir William and Lady Bradshaw, Miss Truelock and Eleanor Gibson (whom she saw coming upstairs). They must find her if they wanted her. She was for the party!

There was her old friend Sir Harry.

"Dear Sir Harry!" she said, going up to the fine old fellow who had produced more bad pictures than any other two Academicians in the whole of St. John's Wood (they were always of cattle, standing in sunset pools absorbing moisture, or signifying, for he had a certain range of gesture, by the raising of one foreleg and the toss of the antlers, "the Approach of the Stranger"—all his activities, dining out, racing, were founded on cattle standing absorbing moisture in sunset pools).

"What are you laughing at?" she asked him. For Willie Titcomb and Sir Harry and Herbert Ainsty were all laughing. But no. Sir Harry could not tell Clarissa Dalloway (much though he liked her; of her type he thought her perfect, and threatened to paint her) his stories of the music hall stage. He chaffed her about her party. He missed his brandy. These circles, he said, were above him. But he liked her; respected her, in spite of her damnable, difficult upperclass refinement, which made it impossible to ask Clarissa Dalloway to sit on his knee. And up came that wandering will-o'-the-wisp, that vagulous phosphorescence, old Mrs. Hilbery, stretching her hands to the blaze of his laughter (about the Duke and the Lady), which, as she heard it across the room, seemed to reassure her on a point which sometimes bothered her if she woke early in the morning and did not like to call her maid for a cup of tea; how it is certain we must die.

"They won't tell us their stories," said Clarissa.

"Dear Clarissa!" exclaimed Mrs. Hilbery. She looked to-night, she said, so like her mother as she first saw her walking in a garden in a grey hat.

And really Clarissa's eyes filled with tears. Her mother, walking in a garden! But alas, she must go.

For there was Professor Brierly, who lectured on Milton,[2] talking to little Jim Hutton (who was unable even for a party like this to compass both tie and waistcoat or make his hair lie flat), and even at this distance they were quarrelling, she could see. For Professor Brierly was a very queer fish. With all those degrees, honours, lectureships between him and the scribblers he suspected instantly an atmosphere not favourable to his queer compound; his prodigious learning and timidity; his wintry charm without cordiality; his innocence blent with snobbery; he quivered if made conscious by a lady's unkempt hair, a youth's boots, of an underworld, very creditable doubtless, of rebels, of ardent young people; of would-be geniuses, and intimated with a little toss of the head, with a sniff—Humph!—the value of moderation; of some slight training in the classics in order to appreciate Milton. Professor Brierly (Clarissa could see) wasn't hitting it off with little Jim Hutton (who wore red socks,[3] his black being at the laundry) about Milton. She interrupted.

She said she loved Bach. So did Hutton. That was the bond between them, and Hutton (a very bad poet) always felt that Mrs. Dalloway was far the best of the great ladies who took an interest in art. It was odd how strict she was. About music she was purely impersonal. She was rather a prig. But how charming to look at! She made her house so nice if it weren't for her Professors. Clarissa had half a mind to snatch him off and set him down at the piano in the back room. For he played divinely.

"But the noise!" she said. "The noise!"

"The sign of a successful party." Nodding urbanely, the Professor stepped delicately off.

"He knows everything in the whole world about Milton," said Clarissa.

"Does he indeed?" said Hutton, who would imitate the Professor throughout Hampstead; the Professor on Milton; the Professor on moderation; the Professor stepping delicately off.

---

2. John Milton (1608–1674), English poet and intellectual, best known for *Paradise Lost* (1667).
3. Hutton commits a surprising breach of decorum at a party this formal, where one would expect men to wear unremarkable black socks.

But she must speak to that couple, said Clarissa, Lord Gayton and Nancy Blow.

Not that *they* added perceptibly to the noise of the party. They were not talking (perceptibly) as they stood side by side by the yellow curtains. They would soon be off elsewhere, together; and never had very much to say in any circumstances. They looked; that was all. That was enough. They looked so clean, so sound, she with an apricot bloom of powder and paint, but he scrubbed, rinsed, with the eyes of a bird, so that no ball could pass him or stroke surprise him. He struck, he leapt, accurately, on the spot. Ponies' mouths quivered at the end of his reins. He had his honours, ancestral monuments, banners hanging in the church at home. He had his duties; his tenants; a mother and sisters; had been all day at Lords, and that was what they were talking about—cricket, cousins, the movies—when Mrs. Dalloway came up. Lord Gayton liked her most awfully. So did Miss Blow. She had such charming manners.

"It is angelic—it is delicious of you to have come!" she said. She loved Lords; she loved youth, and Nancy, dressed at enormous expense by the greatest artists in Paris, stood there looking as if her body had merely put forth, of its own accord, a green frill.

"I had meant to have dancing," said Clarissa.

For the young people could not talk. And why should they? Shout, embrace, swing, be up at dawn; carry sugar to ponies; kiss and caress the snouts of adorable chows; and then all tingling and streaming, plunge and swim. But the enormous resources of the English language, the power it bestows, after all, of communicating feelings (at their age, she and Peter would have been arguing all the evening), was not for them. They would solidify young. They would be good beyond measure to the people on the estate, but alone, perhaps, rather dull.

"What a pity!" she said. "I had hoped to have dancing."

It was so extraordinarily nice of them to have come! But talk of dancing! The rooms were packed.

There was old Aunt Helena in her shawl. Alas, she must leave them—Lord Gayton and Nancy Blow. There was old Miss Parry, her aunt.

For Miss Helena Parry was not dead: Miss Parry was alive. She was past eighty. She ascended staircases slowly with a stick. She was placed in a chair (Richard had seen to it). People who had known Burma in the 'seventies were always led up to her. Where had Peter got to? They used to be such friends. For at the mention of India, or even Ceylon, her eyes (only one was glass) slowly deepened, became blue, beheld, not human beings—she had no tender memories, no proud illusions about Viceroys, Generals, Mutinies—it was orchids she saw, and mountain passes and herself carried on the backs of coolies in the 'sixties over solitary peaks; or descending to uproot orchids (startling blossoms, never beheld before) which she painted in water-colour; an indomitable Englishwoman, fretful if disturbed by the War, say, which dropped a bomb at her very door, from her deep meditation over orchids and her own figure journeying in the 'sixties in India—but here was Peter.

"Come and talk to Aunt Helena about Burma," said Clarissa.

And yet he had not had a word with her all the evening!

"We will talk later," said Clarissa, leading him up to Aunt Helena, in her white shawl, with her stick.

"Peter Walsh," said Clarissa.

That meant nothing.

Clarissa had asked her. It was tiring; it was noisy; but Clarissa had asked her. So she had come. It was a pity that they lived in London—Richard and Clarissa. If only for Clarissa's health it would have been better to live in the country. But Clarissa had always been fond of society.

"He has been in Burma," said Clarissa.

Ah. She could not resist recalling what Charles Darwin[4] had said about her little book on the orchids of Burma.

(Clarissa must speak to Lady Bruton.)

No doubt it was forgotten now, her book on the orchids of Burma, but it went into three editions before 1870, she told Peter. She remembered him now. He had been at Bourton (and he had left her, Peter Walsh remembered, without a word in the drawing-room that night when Clarissa had asked him to come boating).

"Richard so much enjoyed his lunch party," said Clarissa to Lady Bruton.

"Richard was the greatest possible help," Lady Bruton replied. "He helped me to write a letter. And how are you?"

"Oh, perfectly well!" said Clarissa. (Lady Bruton detested illness in the wives of politicians.)

"And there's Peter Walsh!" said Lady Bruton (for she could never think of anything to say to Clarissa; though she liked her. She had lots of fine qualities; but they had nothing in common—she and Clarissa. It might have been better if Richard had married a woman with less charm, who would have helped him more in his work. He had lost his chance of the Cabinet). "There's Peter Walsh!" she said, shaking hands with that agreeable sinner, that very able fellow who should have made a name for himself but hadn't (always in difficulties with women), and, of course, old Miss Parry. Wonderful old lady!

---

4. English naturalist (1809–1882), best known for his contribution to the theory of evolution as articulated in *The Origin of Species* (1859).

Lady Bruton stood by Miss Parry's chair, a spectral grenadier, draped in black, inviting Peter Walsh to lunch; cordial; but without small talk, remembering nothing whatever about the flora or fauna of India. She had been there, of course; had stayed with three Viceroys; thought some of the Indian civilians uncommonly fine fellows; but what a tragedy it was—the state of India! The Prime Minister had just been telling her (old Miss Parry huddled up in her shawl, did not care what the Prime Minister had just been telling her), and Lady Bruton would like to have Peter Walsh's opinion, he being fresh from the centre, and she would get Sir Sampson to meet him, for really it prevented her from sleeping at night, the folly of it, the wickedness she might say, being a soldier's daughter. She was an old woman now, not good for much. But her house, her servants, her good friend Milly Brush—did he remember her?— were all there only asking to be used if—if they could be of help, in short. For she never spoke of England, but this isle of men, this dear, dear land, was in her blood (without reading Shakespeare), and if ever a woman could have worn the helmet and shot the arrow, could have led troops to attack, ruled with indomitable justice barbarian hordes and lain under a shield noseless in a church, or made a green grass mound on some primeval hillside, that woman was Millicent Bruton. Debarred by her sex and some truancy, too, of the logical faculty (she found it impossible to write a letter to the *Times*), she had the thought of Empire always at hand, and had acquired from her association with that armoured goddess her ramrod bearing, her robustness of demeanour, so that one could not figure her even in death parted from the earth or roaming territories over which, in some spiritual shape, the Union Jack had ceased to fly. To be not English even among the dead—no, no![5] Impossible!

But was it Lady Bruton (whom she used to know)? Was it Peter Walsh grown grey? Lady Rosseter asked herself (who had been Sally Seton). It was old Miss Parry certainly—the old aunt who used to be so cross when she stayed at Bourton. Never should she forget running along the passage naked, and being sent for by Miss Parry! And Clarissa! oh Clarissa! Sally caught her by the arm.

Clarissa stopped beside them.

"But I can't stay," she said. "I shall come later. Wait," she said, looking at Peter and Sally. They must wait, she meant, until all these people had gone.

"I shall come back," she said, looking at her old friends, Sally and Peter, who were shaking hands, and Sally, remembering the past no doubt, was laughing.

---

5. An allusion to Rupert Brooke's "The Soldier" (see p. 237).

But her voice was wrung of its old ravishing richness; her eyes not aglow as they used to be, when she smoked cigars, when she ran down the passage to fetch her sponge bag, without a stitch of clothing on her, and Ellen Atkins asked, What if the gentlemen had met her? But everybody forgave her. She stole a chicken from the larder because she was hungry in the night; she smoked cigars in her bedroom; she left a priceless book in the punt. But everybody adored her (except perhaps Papa). It was her warmth; her vitality—she would paint, she would write. Old women in the village never to this day forgot to ask after "your friend in the red cloak who seemed so bright." She accused Hugh Whitbread, of all people (and there he was, her old friend Hugh, talking to the Portuguese Ambassador), of kissing her in the smoking-room to punish her for saying that women should have votes. Vulgar men did, she said. And Clarissa remembered having to persuade her not to denounce him at family prayers—which she was capable of doing with her daring, her recklessness, her melodramatic love of being the centre of everything and creating scenes, and it was bound, Clarissa used to think, to end in some awful tragedy; her death; her martyrdom; instead of which she had married, quite unexpectedly, a bald man with a large buttonhole who owned, it was said, cotton mills at Manchester. And she had five boys!

She and Peter had settled down together. They were talking: it seemed so familiar—that they should be talking. They would discuss the past. With the two of them (more even than with Richard) she shared her past; the garden; the trees; old Joseph Breitkopf singing Brahms without any voice; the drawing-room wallpaper; the smell of the mats. A part of this Sally must always be; Peter must always be. But she must leave them. There were the Bradshaws, whom she disliked. She must go up to Lady Bradshaw (in grey and silver, balancing like a sea-lion at the edge of its tank, barking for invitations, Duchesses, the typical successful man's wife), she must go up to Lady Bradshaw and say . . .

But Lady Bradshaw anticipated her.

"We are shockingly late, dear Mrs. Dalloway, we hardly dared to come in," she said.

And Sir William, who looked very distinguished, with his grey hair and blue eyes, said yes; they had not been able to resist the temptation. He was talking to Richard about that Bill probably, which they wanted to get through the Commons. Why did the sight of him, talking to Richard, curl her up? He looked what he was, a great doctor. A man absolutely at the head of his profession, very powerful, rather worn. For think what cases came before him— people in the uttermost depths of misery; people on the verge of insanity; husbands and wives. He had to decide questions of appalling difficulty. Yet—what she felt was, one wouldn't like Sir William to see one unhappy. No; not that man.

"How is your son at Eton?" she asked Lady Bradshaw.

He had just missed his eleven,[6] said Lady Bradshaw, because of the mumps. His father minded even more than he did, she thought "being," she said, "nothing but a great boy himself."

Clarissa looked at Sir William, talking to Richard. He did not look like a boy—not in the least like a boy. She had once gone with some one to ask his advice. He had been perfectly right; extremely sensible. But Heavens—what a relief to get out to the street again! There was some poor wretch sobbing, she remembered, in the waiting-room. But she did not know what it was—about Sir William; what exactly she disliked. Only Richard agreed with her, "didn't like his taste, didn't like his smell." But he was extraordinarily able. They were talking about this Bill. Some case, Sir William was mentioning, lowering his voice. It had its bearing upon what he was saying about the deferred effects of shell shock.[7] There must be some provision in the Bill.

Sinking her voice, drawing Mrs. Dalloway into the shelter of a common femininity, a common pride in the illustrious qualities of husbands and their sad tendency to overwork, Lady Bradshaw (poor goose—one didn't dislike her) murmured how, "just as we were starting, my husband was called up on the telephone, a very sad case. A young man (that is what Sir William is telling Mr. Dalloway) had killed himself. He had been in the army." Oh! thought Clarissa, in the middle of my party, here's death, she thought.

She went on, into the little room where the Prime Minister had gone with Lady Bruton. Perhaps there was somebody there. But there was nobody. The chairs still kept the impress of the Prime Minister and Lady Bruton, she turned deferentially, he sitting four-square, authoritatively. They had been talking about India. There was nobody. The party's splendour fell to the floor, so strange it was to come in alone in her finery.

What business had the Bradshaws to talk of death at her party? A young man had killed himself. And they talked of it at her party—the Bradshaws, talked of death. He had killed himself—but how? Always her body went through it first, when she was told, suddenly, of an accident; her dress flamed, her body burnt. He had thrown himself from a window. Up had flashed the ground; through him, blundering, bruising, went the rusty spikes. There he lay with a

---

6. That is, the cricket team of his school boarding house.
7. Perhaps a reference to the War Office Committee of Enquiry into Shell-Shock, which met from 1920 to 1922. Woolf may also be referring to the War Pensions Act of 1921, which permitted very limited benefits to some veterans whose disabilities were latent or less obvious.

thud, thud, thud in his brain, and then a suffocation of blackness. So she saw it. But why had he done it? And the Bradshaws talked of it at her party!

She had once thrown a shilling into the Serpentine, never anything more. But he had flung it away. They went on living (she would have to go back; the rooms were still crowded; people kept on coming). They (all day she had been thinking of Bourton, of Peter, of Sally), they would grow old. A thing there was that mattered; a thing, wreathed about with chatter, defaced, obscured in her own life, let drop every day in corruption, lies, chatter. This he had preserved. Death was defiance. Death was an attempt to communicate; people feeling the impossibility of reaching the centre which, mystically, evaded them; closeness drew apart; rapture faded, one was alone. There was an embrace in death.

But this young man who had killed himself—had he plunged holding his treasure? "If it were now to die, 'twere now to be most happy," she had said to herself once, coming down in white.

Or there were the poets and thinkers. Suppose he had had that passion, and had gone to Sir William Bradshaw, a great doctor yet to her obscurely evil, without sex or lust, extremely polite to women, but capable of some indescribable outrage—forcing your soul, that was it—if this young man had gone to him, and Sir William had impressed him, like that, with his power, might he not then have said (indeed she felt it now), Life is made intolerable; they make life intolerable, men like that?

Then (she had felt it only this morning) there was the terror; the overwhelming incapacity, one's parents giving it into one's hands, this life, to be lived to the end, to be walked with serenely; there was in the depths of her heart an awful fear. Even now, quite often if Richard had not been there reading the *Times*, so that she could crouch like a bird and gradually revive, send roaring up that immeasurable delight, rubbing stick to stick, one thing with another, she must have perished. But that young man had killed himself.

Somehow it was her disaster—her disgrace. It was her punishment to see sink and disappear here a man, there a woman, in this profound darkness, and she forced to stand here in her evening dress. She had schemed; she had pilfered. She was never wholly admirable. She had wanted success. Lady Bexborough and the rest of it. And once she had walked on the terrace at Bourton.

It was due to Richard; she had never been so happy. Nothing could be slow enough; nothing last too long. No pleasure could equal, she thought, straightening the chairs, pushing in one book on the shelf, this having done with the triumphs of youth, lost herself in the process of living, to find it, with a shock of delight, as the sun rose, as the day sank. Many a time had she gone, at Bourton when they were all talking, to look at the sky; or seen it between people's shoulders at dinner; seen it in London when she could not sleep. She walked to the window.

It held, foolish as the idea was, something of her own in it, this country sky, this sky above Westminster. She parted the curtains; she looked. Oh, but how surprising!—in the room opposite the old lady stared straight at her! She was going to bed. And the sky. It will be a solemn sky, she had thought, it will be a dusky sky, turning away its cheek in beauty. But there it was—ashen pale, raced over quickly by tapering vast clouds. It was new to her. The wind must have risen. She was going to bed, in the room opposite. It was fascinating to watch her, moving about, that old lady, crossing the room, coming to the window. Could she see her? It was fascinating, with people still laughing and shouting in the drawing-room, to watch that old woman, quite quietly, going to bed. She pulled the blind now. The clock began striking. The young man had killed himself; but she did not pity him; with the clock striking the hour, one, two, three, she did not pity him, with all this going on. There! the old lady had put out her light! the whole house was dark now with this going on, she repeated, and the words came to her, Fear no more the heat of the sun.[8] She must go back to them. But what an extraordinary night! She felt somehow very like him—the young man who had killed himself. She felt glad that he had done it; thrown it away. The clock was striking. The leaden circles dissolved in the air. He made her feel the beauty; made her feel the fun.[9] But she must go back. She must assemble. She must find Sally and Peter. And she came in from the little room.

"But where is Clarissa?" said Peter. He was sitting on the sofa with Sally. (After all these years he really could not call her "Lady Rosseter.") "Where's the woman gone to?" he asked. "Where's Clarissa?"

Sally supposed, and so did Peter for the matter of that, that there were people of importance, politicians, whom neither of them knew unless by sight in the picture papers, whom Clarissa had to be nice to, had to talk to. She was with them. Yet there was Richard Dalloway not in the Cabinet. He hadn't been a success, Sally supposed? For herself, she scarcely ever read the papers. She sometimes saw his name mentioned. But then—well, she lived a very solitary life, in the wilds, Clarissa would say, among great merchants, great manufacturers, men, after all, who did things. She had done things too!

"I have five sons!" she told him.

Lord, Lord, what a change had come over her! the softness of motherhood; its egotism too. Last time they met, Peter remembered,

8. The fifth and final allusion to the dirge from *Cymbeline*.
9. This sentence, which was in the page proofs, does not appear in the British edition. Instead, there is a section break at the end of this paragraph.

had been among the cauliflowers in the moonlight, the leaves "like rough bronze" she had said, with her literary turn; and she had picked a rose. She had marched him up and down that awful night, after the scene by the fountain; he was to catch the midnight train. Heavens, he had wept!

That was his old trick, opening a pocket-knife, thought Sally, always opening and shutting a knife when he got excited. They had been very, very intimate, she and Peter Walsh, when he was in love with Clarissa, and there was that dreadful, ridiculous scene over Richard Dalloway at lunch. She had called Richard "Wickham." Why not call Richard "Wickham"? Clarissa had flared up! and indeed they had never seen each other since, she and Clarissa, not more than half a dozen times perhaps in the last ten years. And Peter Walsh had gone off to India, and she had heard vaguely that he had made an unhappy marriage, and she didn't know whether he had any children, and she couldn't ask him, for he had changed. He was rather shrivelled-looking, but kinder, she felt, and she had a real affection for him, for he was connected with her youth, and she still had a little Emily Brontë he had given her, and he was to write, surely? In those days he was to write.

"Have you written?" she asked him, spreading her hand, her firm and shapely hand, on her knee in a way he recalled.

"Not a word!" said Peter Walsh, and she laughed.

She was still attractive, still a personage, Sally Seton. But who was this Rosseter? He wore two camellias on his wedding day—that was all Peter knew of him. "They have myriads of servants, miles of conservatories," Clarissa wrote; something like that. Sally owned it with a shout of laughter.

"Yes, I have ten thousand a year"—whether before the tax was paid or after, she couldn't remember, for her husband, "whom you must meet," she said, "whom you would like," she said, did all that for her.

And Sally used to be in rags and tatters. She had pawned her grandmother's ring which Marie Antoinette had given her great-grandfather to come to Bourton.

Oh yes, Sally remembered; she had it still, a ruby ring which Marie Antoinette had given her great-grandfather. She never had a penny to her name in those days, and going to Bourton always meant some frightful pinch. But going to Bourton had meant so much to her—had kept her sane, she believed, so unhappy had she been at home. But that was all a thing of the past—all over now, she said. And Mr. Parry was dead; and Miss Parry was still alive. Never had he had such a shock in his life! said Peter. He had been quite certain she was dead. And the marriage had been, Sally supposed, a success? And that very handsome, very self-possessed young woman was Elizabeth, over there, by the curtains, in red.

(She was like a poplar, she was like a river, she was like a hyacinth, Willie Titcomb was thinking. Oh how much nicer to be in the country and do what she liked! She could hear her poor dog howling, Elizabeth was certain.) She was not a bit like Clarissa, Peter Walsh said.

"Oh, Clarissa!" said Sally.

What Sally felt was simply this. She had owed Clarissa an enormous amount. They had been friends, not acquaintances, friends, and she still saw Clarissa all in white going about the house with her hands full of flowers—to this day tobacco plants made her think of Bourton. But—did Peter understand?—she lacked something. Lacked what was it? She had charm; she had extraordinary charm. But to be frank (and she felt that Peter was an old friend, a real friend—did absence matter? did distance matter? She had often wanted to write to him, but torn it up, yet felt he understood, for people understand without things being said, as one realises growing old, and old she was, had been that afternoon to see her sons at Eton, where they had the mumps), to be quite frank then, how could Clarissa have done it?—married Richard Dalloway? a sportsman, a man who cared only for dogs. Literally, when he came into the room he smelt of the stables. And then all this? She waved her hand.

Hugh Whitbread it was, strolling past in his white waistcoat, dim, fat, blind, past everything he looked, except self-esteem and comfort.

"He's not going to recognise *us*," said Sally, and really she hadn't the courage—so that was Hugh! the admirable Hugh!

"And what does he do?" she asked Peter.

He blacked the King's boots or counted bottles at Windsor, Peter told her. Peter kept his sharp tongue still! But Sally must be frank, Peter said. That kiss now, Hugh's.

On the lips, she assured him, in the smoking-room one evening. She went straight to Clarissa in a rage. Hugh didn't do such things! Clarissa said, the admirable Hugh! Hugh's socks were without exception the most beautiful she had ever seen—and now his evening dress. Perfect! And had he children?

"Everybody in the room has six sons at Eton," Peter told her, except himself. He, thank God, had none. No sons, no daughters, no wife. Well, he didn't seem to mind, said Sally. He looked younger, she thought, than any of them.

But it had been a silly thing to do, in many ways, Peter said, to marry like that; "a perfect goose she was," he said, but, he said, "we had a splendid time of it," but how could that be? Sally wondered;

what did he mean? and how odd it was to know him and yet not know a single thing that had happened to him. And did he say it out of pride? Very likely, for after all it must be galling for him (though he was an oddity, a sort of sprite, not at all an ordinary man), it must be lonely at his age to have no home, nowhere to go to. But he must stay with them for weeks and weeks. Of course he would; he would love to stay with them, and that was how it came out. All these years the Dalloways had never been once. Time after time they had asked them. Clarissa (for it was Clarissa of course) would not come. For, said Sally, Clarissa was at heart a snob—one had to admit it, a snob. And it was that that was between them, she was convinced. Clarissa thought she had married beneath her, her husband being—she was proud of it—a miner's son. Every penny they had he had earned. As a little boy (her voice trembled) he had carried great sacks.

(And so she would go on, Peter felt, hour after hour; the miner's son; people thought she had married beneath her; her five sons; and what was the other thing—plants, hydrangeas, syringas, very, very rare hibiscus lilies that never grow north of the Suez Canal, but she, with one gardener in a suburb near Manchester, had beds of them, positively beds! Now all that Clarissa had escaped, unmaternal as she was.)

A snob was she? Yes, in many ways. Where was she, all this time? It was getting late.

"Yet," said Sally, "when I heard Clarissa was giving a party, I felt I couldn't *not* come—must see her again (and I'm staying in Victoria Street, practically next door). So I just came without an invitation. But," she whispered, "tell me, do. Who is this?"

It was Mrs. Hilbery, looking for the door. For how late it was getting! And, she murmured, as the night grew later, as people went, one found old friends; quiet nooks and corners; and the loveliest views. Did they know, she asked, that they were surrounded by an enchanted garden? Lights and trees and wonderful gleaming lakes and the sky. Just a few fairy lamps, Clarissa Dalloway had said, in the back garden! But she was a magician! It was a park. . . . And she didn't know their names, but friends she knew they were, friends without names, songs without words, always the best. But there were so many doors, such unexpected places, she could not find her way.

"Old Mrs. Hilbery," said Peter; but who was that? that lady standing by the curtain all the evening, without speaking? He knew her face; connected her with Bourton. Surely she used to cut up underclothes at the large table in the window? Davidson, was that her name?

"Oh, that is Ellie Henderson," said Sally. Clarissa was really very hard on her. She was a cousin, very poor. Clarissa *was* hard on people.

She was rather, said Peter. Yet, said Sally, in her emotional way, with a rush of that enthusiasm which Peter used to love her for, yet dreaded a little now, so effusive she might become—how generous to her friends Clarissa was! and what a rare quality one found it, and how sometimes at night or on Christmas Day, when she counted up her blessings, she put that friendship first. They were young; that was it. Clarissa was pure-hearted; that was it. Peter would think her sentimental. So she was. For she had come to feel that it was the only thing worth saying—what one felt. Cleverness was silly. One must say simply what one felt.

"But I do not know," said Peter Walsh, "what I feel."

Poor Peter, thought Sally. Why did not Clarissa come and talk to them? That was what he was longing for. She knew it. All the time he was thinking only of Clarissa, and was fidgeting with his knife.

He had not found life simple, Peter said. His relations with Clarissa had not been simple. It had spoilt his life, he said. (They had been so intimate—he and Sally Seton, it was absurd not to say it.) One could not be in love twice, he said. And what could she say? Still, it is better to have loved (but he would think her sentimental—he used to be so sharp). He must come and stay with them in Manchester. That is all very true, he said. All very true. He would love to come and stay with them, directly he had done what he had to do in London.

And Clarissa had cared for him more than she had ever cared for Richard. Sally was positive of that.

"No, no, no!" said Peter (Sally should not have said that—she went too far). That good fellow—there he was at the end of the room, holding forth, the same as ever, dear old Richard. Who was he talking to? Sally asked, that very distinguished-looking man? Living in the wilds as she did, she had an insatiable curiosity to know who people were. But Peter did not know. He did not like his looks, he said, probably a Cabinet Minister. Of them all, Richard seemed to him the best, he said—the most disinterested.

"But what has he done?" Sally asked. Public work, she supposed. And were they happy together? Sally asked (she herself was extremely happy); for, she admitted, she knew nothing about them, only jumped to conclusions, as one does, for what can one know even of the people one lives with every day? she asked. Are we not all prisoners? She had read a wonderful play about a man who scratched on the wall of his cell, and she had felt that was true of life—one scratched on the wall.[1] Despairing of human relationships (people were so difficult), she often went into her garden and got from her flowers a peace which men and women never gave her.

1. An allusion to Shakespeare's *Richard II* (see pp. 230–31).

But no; he did not like cabbages; he preferred human beings, Peter said. Indeed, the young are beautiful, Sally said, watching Elizabeth cross the room. How unlike Clarissa at her age! Could he make anything of her? She would not open her lips. Not much, not yet, Peter admitted. She was like a lily, Sally said, a lily by the side of a pool. But Peter did not agree that we know nothing. We know everything, he said; at least he did.

But these two, Sally whispered, these two coming now (and really she must go, if Clarissa did not come soon), this distinguished-looking man and his rather common-looking wife who had been talking to Richard—what could one know about people like that?

"That they're damnable humbugs," said Peter, looking at them casually. He made Sally laugh.

But Sir William Bradshaw stopped at the door to look at a picture. He looked in the corner for the engraver's name. His wife looked too. Sir William Bradshaw was so interested in art.

When one was young, said Peter, one was too much excited to know people. Now that one was old, fifty-two to be precise (Sally was fifty-five, in body, she said, but her heart was like a girl's of twenty); now that one was mature then, said Peter, one could watch, one could understand, and one did not lose the power of feeling, he said. No, that is true, said Sally. She felt more deeply, more passionately, every year. It increased, he said, alas, perhaps, but one should be glad of it—it went on increasing in his experience. There was some one in India. He would like to tell Sally about her. He would like Sally to know her. She was married, he said. She had two small children. They must all come to Manchester, said Sally—he must promise before they left.

There's Elizabeth, he said, she feels not half what we feel, not yet. But, said Sally, watching Elizabeth go to her father, one can see they are devoted to each other. She could feel it by the way Elizabeth went to her father.

For her father had been looking at her, as he stood talking to the Bradshaws, and he had thought to himself, Who is that lovely girl? And suddenly he realised that it was his Elizabeth, and he had not recognised her, she looked so lovely in her pink frock! Elizabeth had felt him looking at her as she talked to Willie Titcomb. So she went to him and they stood together, now that the party was almost over, looking at the people going, and the rooms getting emptier and emptier, with things scattered on the floor. Even Ellie Henderson was going, nearly last of all, though no one had spoken to her, but she had wanted to see everything, to tell Edith. And Richard and Elizabeth were rather glad it was over, but Richard was proud of his daughter. And he had not meant to tell her, but he could not help telling her. He had looked at her, he said, and he had wondered, Who is that lovely girl? and it was his daughter! That did make her happy. But her poor dog was howling.

"Richard has improved. You are right," said Sally. "I shall go and talk to him. I shall say good-night. What does the brain matter," said Lady Rosseter, getting up, "compared with the heart?"

"I will come," said Peter, but he sat on for a moment. What is this terror? What is this ecstasy? he thought to himself. What is it that fills me with extraordinary excitement?

It is Clarissa, he said.

For there she was.

**THE END**

# CONTEXTS

# Autobiographical Sources

## EARLY WRITINGS

### Hyde Park Gate News[†]

VOL. I, No. 51 Cristmas Number[1]

WE here give a picture of the celebrated author Mr Leslie Stephen

The drawing-room of No 22 H.P.G. was crowded last Sunday with Christmas presents which the benignant Mrs Leslie Stephen was about to bestow on her friends.

Mrs Jackson[2] has as no doubt our readers know brought her canary with her to H.P.G. It far excels in singing Miss Vanessa Stephens bird.
N.B. Miss Vanessa puts in her paper in whiteness of plumage instead of singing.

GHOST STORY
In the north of the little town St Ives Cornwall there are two houses said to be haunted. In the year 1789 a young gentleman visited St Ives he could get no lodging except the haunted house but he being a bold young chap said "Half a loaf is better than no bread" and accordingly went to the haunted house. He went

† From *Hyde Park Gate News: The Stephen Family Newspaper*, ed. Gill Lowe (London: Hesperus Press, 2005), pp. 18–20, 79, 136–37. © The Estates of Virginia Woolf, Vanessa Bell, and Thoby Stephen, 2005. Illustrations © Ekaterina Aplin. Reprinted by permission of The Society of Authors and DACS on behalf of the Estates. Notes are by the editor of this Norton Critical Edition. The Stephen family had a house at Hyde Park Gate, and the *Hyde Park Gate News* was a family paper, largely written by young Virginia Stephen, with assistance from her older brother Thoby and sister Vanessa.
1. This special "Cristmas number," with "Christmas" misspelled, is from 1891, a month before Virginia turned ten.
2. Virginia Woolf's maternal grandmother, Maria Jackson (1818–1892).

upstairs and found a spacious bedroom with a large airy bed in it. He got into it but was soon disturbed by a continual knocking underneath the bed and at intervals a hoarse voice said "Get out of my bed" Soon he got enraged and siezing an old blunderbuss looked under the bed there he saw a skeleton whose face was dis torted with anger.

N.B. It got bloged by mistake. He fired of the blunderbuss and the skeleton arose and seized him by the throat the young man vainly struglled to loose himself from the skeleton's grasp The skeleton grinned in his ferocious pleasure and gave a long low whistle instantly a huge black cat appeared who at his masters

bidding fetched a multitude of dead mice and with these suffocated the young man In the morning all trace of cat, mice, and skeleton had disappeared but the dead man remained.

Story not needing words Moral Don't be cheeky and don't get waxy

Her Ladyship the lady of the Lake arrived here on Monday 21st to the joy and delight of her family.

## A Poem

In the darkness of the night
When no house showed a light
A man with a drawn knife
Seeking to take an innocent life
For ten thousand pounds' sake
Up a back staircase his way
does take
And opens a gentlemans bed-
room door
From which proceeds a heavy
snore
Showing that his victim is wrapt
in sleep
And soon will be killed like a
butchered sheep
He sticks his knife right deeply in
And thinks nought of the awful
sin
But soon he hears a womans call
And hears some hurried foot-
steps fall
And then before he can turn
round
A Policeman pulls him to the
ground
And binds his arm with rope
And now has fled his faintest hope
Next day he's raised on gallows
high
And there like a carrion crow
does die.
N.B. The gentleman's wife
had just come home from
a party when she saw
the murderer going upstairs
so she went to fetch
a policeman.

J.T.S.[3]

CORESPONDENCE
Her Ladyship the Lady of the
Lake wishes to know what
colour to have for a pair of slippers. This is rather an embar-
rassing question and we should
like to leave it to her own
choice.

Miss A.V.S.[4] wants to know
what the average hieght of men
in central Australia is it is a very
big one being 5ft 11 inches

G.H.D.[5] wants to know if
woman should vote in
parliament

\* \* \*

## VOL. II, No. 25 Monday, 4th July 1892

### [MRS LESLIE STEPHEN]

Mrs Leslie Stephen though she
is an ardent lover of rats is
somewhat "riled" by the way in
which her favourites eat her
provisions and therefore she has
determined to get a dog. "Not
for pleasure but for business" as
she told her offsprings. She has
employed Mr Gerald Duck-
worth to buy a suitable one. Mr
Gerald Duckworth wrote her a
loving letter saying that he has
his eye on a promising Iris terrier. Mrs Stephen has requested
that it shall not be a dog like
some others of her acquaintance "frinstance" (to use Master Adrian Stephen's favourite
phrase) Pepper as Mrs Stephen
is sure that if another Pepper
were to come she would have
the police down on her.

3. Julian Thoby Stephen, called Thoby (1880–1906), Woolf's older brother.
4. Adeline Virginia Stephen, called Virginia, later Woolf.
5. George Herbert Duckworth (1868–1934), Woolf's half-brother, the child of her mother's first marriage to Herbert Duckworth.

Mr Leslie Stephen on account of ill health was prevented from going to Dublin to receive his honours which we mentioned in our last number. Mr Stephen is a botanist on the minor scale. He is now endeavouring to teach his children the names of the plants in the neighbourhood.

Mrs Leslie Stephen who adores birds scatters crumbs in front of the drawing room window which speedily entice the feathered favourites. It is amusing and pretty to see the way in which some audacious little fellow will hop inside the room to see if there are more crumbs there. Greatly to Mrs Stephen's delight Mr Paddy the gardener has found a nest with 3 young birds in it.

\* \* \*

### VOL. II, No. 43. Monday, 7th November 1892

#### [THE DOG]

On the 1st of November an advent happened which was and doubtless is still a source of mingled joy and sorrow to the children of 22 Hyde Park Gate. For on the morning of this memorable day as the youngsters were taking their "constitutional" a small but valuable dog (as they were afterwards informed) was seen walking about with that look of vagueness and wistfulness which comes into a lost dog's eyes. Having followed the lost dog right into High Street they were much dismayed to see him coolly trot over to the other side. They stood gaping presenting a most extraordinary appearance in the civilised street. Miss Duckworth[6] who came up at this moment was after some little time enlightened as to why the children were staring at the other side and gesticulating. She could see nothing but a small and to her uninteresting dog. But when the state of affairs was made clear to her she showed the natural generosity and kindness of heart which is never absent from this humane offspring of Eve. Miss Duckworth at once took a hansom cab and the dog being thrown into it by a sympathizing "cabby" she started off amid the many approving glances which the pleased juveniles bestowed upon her. Never dreaming of vulgar reward but of the great moral reward of virtue Miss Duckworth went on with her errand of mercy and as soon as the cab arrived Miss Duckworth walked up to the butler who was standing at the open door and said with her usual dignity that she had come in a cab with the dog all the way from Kensington Gardens. The only answer she got was "I'm sure we're very much obliged to you." She returned poorer in money but richer in virtue.

A surprising instance of a poodle's affection for his home was shown by Mrs Cooke's dog. Mrs

6. Stella Duckworth (1869–1897), Woolf's older half-sister.

Cooke moved to a new house and took her dog with her. He was however heard barking for admittance at nine o'clock in the morning after their departure. This shows that a dog has sometimes as strong home affections as a cat.

# Early Diary Entry[†]

*Giggleswick 1906*

\* \* \*

Again I have accomplished a day of partial solitude; except that I begin to make conversation with Mrs. Turner when she brings me my meal. But she is polite rather than communicative.

The unhappy spell of holiday [Easter] is still upon us: the roads are almost impassable. So, dragging Gurth on a chain, I crossed the road, & took the pathway shown me at the back of the wood, & so on to that high moor, with its pale side of ash gray rock. It was a curious walk. I followed a narrow pathway, on the ridge of the moor, protected by a stone wall, from a sheer drop of I don't know how many feet. The road wound directly beneath, so that a motor car even might be followed for some distance, squirming back on the white road.

Then I found a less precipitous place, where I might descend from these rather bleak altitudes. But it was not easy walking. The side of the hill, which is sufficiently steep to need an almost sitting posture, is strewn with a thick layer of loose gray stones; some of considerable size. As you walk they slip beneath you & rattle down, in a miniature avalanche, to the bottom. And if one looked down, the sight was a little giddy: so I clambered somehow, unseen happily & caught at trees & bushes till the descent was over. And after that I found me a grass seat beneath a rock, & lay in the sun, looking at that skeleton like hill before me, & others rising grand & tragic behind it & far away into the distance. A walk here, I find, tends to be rather an heroic undertaking. I amused myself with planning the countryside into Bloomsbury & Piccadilly, & setting St James Streets & Marble Arches on all the hills & valleys. Thus my domestic life passes like some very placid hours on a lake without a wave.

All the trees here are red & purple, but not green yet. It is not a country that is very sensitive to changes of the season I imagine. In

† From *A Passionate Apprentice: The Early Journals, 1897–1909*, ed. Mitchell A. Leaska (San Diego: Harcourt Brace Jovanovich, 1990), pp. 302–03. Copyright © 1990 by Quentin Bell and Angelica Garnett. Reprinted by permission of Houghton Mifflin Harcourt Publishing Company, Penguin Random House UK, and the Society of Authors on behalf of the Estate of Virginia Woolf. All rights reserved. In this April 1906 entry, the twenty-four-year-old Virginia Stephen describes imagining London during the pleasant solitude of a visit to her friends in the countryside.

winter it looked much the same. Two thousand years ago it looked
as it did this afternoon; in that continuity lies its singular grandeur
& stability perhaps. Two thousand years again may leave it equally
unchanged.

* * *

# DIARY

## Monday 1 February [1915][†]

### [*A violent explosion*]

I had to go out shopping this morning, so I called in on Chancellors.
They say that Mrs Wontner makes conditions about taking on
Hogarth,[1] so that it is possible that she won't take it—So here we are
on the seesaw again. Mrs Le Grys, also, told me this morning of a
house on the Green, 3 doors off, which is to let in March. The rent is
£65 & they want £75 premium. We went to look at it after luncheon,
but, being a boarding house, couldn't see over it. What we saw was
defaced in every possible way; but a nice substantial house, without
the charms of Hogarth, but then with the addition of the Green. We
went up to London—L.[2] to the London Library: I to Days. I walked
with him across the Green Park. In St James Street there was a terrific explosion; people came running out of Clubs; stopped still &
gazed about them. But there was no Zeppelin or aeroplane—only, I
suppose, a very large tyre burst. But it is really an instinct with me, &
most people, I suppose, to turn any sudden noise, or dark object in
the sky into an explosion, or a German aeroplane. And it always
seems utterly impossible that one should be hurt.

I was annoyed in the usual way at Days by the afternoon party of
fashionable ladies, looking for books. We have just been rung up by
Chancellors, who wish us to see the owner of Hogarth tomorrow, &
possibly by our presence & respectability outwit Mrs Wontner,
whose demands have annoyed Chancellors. In fact it seems quite

---

[†] This and the following entries are from the Virginia Woolf collection of papers, 1882–
1984, The Henry W. and Albert A. Berg Collection of English and American Literature, The New York Public Library, Astor, Lenox and Tilden Foundations. Reprinted by
permission of the Society of Authors on behalf of the Estate of Virginia Woolf. Notes
are by the editor of this Norton Critical Edition.

1. The name of the house the Woolfs rented in Richmond, a Thames River suburb of
London. They signed a five-year lease on February 25, 1915, and lived there until 1924.
Their publishing house was named for the Hogarth House, and Woolf wrote much of
*Mrs. Dalloway* here, moving back to London late in the composition of the novel.

2. Leonard Woolf, her husband.

likely at this moment that we shall get Hogarth! I wish it were
tomorrow. I am certain it is the best house to take.

## Friday 14 December [1917]

### [A quiet man]

Today we went to see Philip[3] at Fishmongers Hall. Rather a strange
place a few feet from London Bridge. A pompous hall, with a porter, a gigantic fire for that porter, a German gun; & within banisters
draped with crimson folds of stuff, as if for a royal visit; Nelson's
flag in a glass case; Dick Whittington in plaster standing in an
alcove; a branching staircase taking one to a great gallery now
divided into cubicles. Two or three nurses sat sewing outside. We
found Philip up; his chair by the open window, looking into the
street, which was noisy, & just catching sight of the river. I saw a
notice warning patients not to throw cigarette ends out, or they
might catch inflammable bales upon the wharf. To me, Philip
looked well; though there was that absentmindedness which one
sees in Nick. I suppose to Philip these days pass in a dream from
which he finds himself detached. I can imagine that he is puzzled
why he doesn't feel more. He still talks of "we" & "our" things. I
thought he must look to going back again with something like hope.
But he talked very easily & cheerfully—about horses & books & so
on—Another man—a great burly cavalry officer was reading his
book in a far corner; unused to reading books, I should think.
Nurses seemed very kindly. A feeling of the uselessness of it all,
breaking these people & mending them again, was in the air, I
thought. We asked Philip to Asheham, when he can move.

\* \* \*

## Tuesday 9 April [1918]

### [My father was a German]

This is most curious weather; also most unpleasant. Rain descends
at intervals from a dark grey sky; even when it isn't raining the sky
is still grey. Its warm, damp, & the young leaves have a lurid look in
the winter atmosphere; the green is as if seen at night by electric
lights. We quarrelled yesterday, about my jug of cream; & L. was
unreasonable, & I was generous. The quarrel ended at 4.25 sharp.

3. Philip Woolf, one of Leonard's brothers, had been wounded by a shell that killed their
brother, Cecil, earlier in the month.

At 4.30 Miss Mattaei arrived.[4] I remember her at Newnham. She has left, we understand, "under a cloud". It is easy to see from her limp, apologetic attitude that the cloud has sapped her powers of resistance. We skirted round the war, but she edged away from it, & it seemed altogether odious that anyone should be afraid to declare her opinions—as if a dog used to excessive beating, dreaded even the raising of a hand. She & L. discussed their business, which has to do with W[ar]. & P[eace]. & may result in an offer to her of a place on the staff. She has to earn her living. "I must tell you one thing, she said, when the talk was over, my father was a German. I find it makes a good deal of difference—it is a distinct hindrance commercially." L. agreed that it was. She is a lanky gawky unattractive woman, about 35, with a complexion that blotches red & shiny suddenly; dressed in her best, which was inconceivably stiff & ugly. But she has a quick mind, & is an enthusiast; said she loved writing.

## Wednesday 1 May [1918]

### [*The Equator*]

There's a fate in saying that we're safe from raids; On Friday [26 *April*] I went to the Hippodrome, to see life; L. seeing a different variety of it at the 17 Club. The incredible, pathetic stupidity of the music hall, (for surely we could have risen higher, & only politeness made us laugh,) almost made me uncomfortable; but the humour of Harry Tate, though a low grade was still the queer English humour; something natural to the race, which makes us all laugh; why I don't know; & you can't help feeling its the real thing, as, in Athens one might have felt that poetry was. Home about 11. At 12 the usual maroons, & even extra whistling. The fine night made this likely; we bundled our bedding into the kitchen & took up our appointed stations; L. and I lying by the grate; N. & Lottie whispering in the cellar. After 20 minutes, I thought I heard bugles. One's ears can imagine so much that I said nothing. Ten minutes later Nelly burst out "The bugles!" So they were. We went upstairs, inclined to blame some clerk whose ears played him tricks which the night made into certainties. But Desmond tells us that 3 American aeroplanes crossing the coast without giving the signal caused

---

4. Louise Ernestine Matthei (1880–1969) was a classical scholar at Newnham College. She had lost her job because of her German background.

the false alarm, which woke the whole of London, though ignored
by the press.

On Saturday [27 *April*] we went to Hampton Court, the first visit
for a long time. But this weather (I am unjust though; Saturday was
fine). We had a tremendous talk about the Equator. In the middle
of a demonstration with two pebbles, Jack Radcliffe passed (or so I
thought). This diverted my attention. A serious reprimand had to be
administered. It was discovered that I took the Equator to be a circular mark, coloured dull red, upon the end of a football. The ignorance & inattention combined displayed in this remark seemed so
crass that for about 20 minutes we couldn't speak. However, I was
forgiven, & told about the tropics of Cancer & Capricorn. The
question originally was about the time of moon & sun rise & setting
in different months.

⁎ ⁎ ⁎

## Tuesday 28 May [1918]

### [*An enormous pocket knife*]

The rush of books was disposed of, & Squire was well drubbed too;
at the same time such a rush of people coincided, that I was clogged
into complete dumbness, I see; but to take up the pen directly upon
coming back from Asheham shows I hope that this book is now a
natural growth of mine—a rather dishevelled, rambling plant,
running a yard of green stalk for every flower. The metaphor comes
from Asheham.

But first let me recall Janet, Desmond, Katherine Mansfield &
Lilian; there were others,—yes, there was Harry Stephen & Clive.[5]
Each left with me a page full of comments, but useless now partly I
think from my habit of telling these incidents over to people, &
once told, I don't want to retell them, the telling leaves a groove in
my mind which gives a hardness to the memory, stereotypes it,
makes it a little dull. But I wandered through Richmond Park in the
moonlight with Desmond. We jumped a palisade into Miss Hick-
man's funeral grove, & found the dark green mounds pointed with

5. Clive Bell (1881–1964), art critic and husband to Vanessa Bell. By this point, the
Bells were friends and still married, each pursuing separate sexual lives. Janet Case
(1862–1937), professor at Girton, Woolf's girlhood Greek tutor, and feminist; Desmond McCarthy (1877–1952), literary journalist and friend; Katherine Mansfield
(1888–1923), writer and friend; Lilian Harris (d. 1949), partner of Margaret Llewe-
lyn Davies, a Girton professor and founder of the Women's Co-operative Guild;
Harry Stephen (1860–1945), Woolf's cousin, a judge in both India and, by this point,
London.

red rosettes. The rhododendron is a lovely flower for the moonlight. And we beheld a china watercloset also lovely in the moonlight, the divinity of a sheltered lodger, wedged in among the ferns & the flowering bushes. Desmond, who has been pestering me with inscrutable persistence, over the telephone in letters in visits to lunch with Prince Bibesco, dropped all that, drank a whole bottle, & bubbled like a tipsy nightingale, amorous, humorous, reminiscent, &, remembering the dead, perhaps melancholy in a happy sort of way. But he spoke rather pointedly of the charm & intelligence of Molly.

"Yes, I've never feared tragedy in *your* lives" I said, nor does one, though from what we hear, they strain at the collar now & then. But modern life has the merit of allowing for that. Katherine was marmoreal, as usual, just married to Murry, & liking to pretend it a matter of convenience. She looks ghastly ill. As usual we came to an oddly complete understanding. My theory is that I get down to what is true rock in her, through the numerous vapours & pores which sicken or bewilder most of our friends. It's her love of writing I think. But she is off to Cornwall. Harry Stephen told his old stories, wrinkled his nose, & alluded several times to his great age. He is 58. An undoubted failure; but that has a freshening effect upon people; they are more irresponsible than the successes; but yet one can't call Harry exactly irresponsible either. He is modest; humorous; all his pride for his father & ancestors. He still takes out an enormous pocket knife, & slowly half opens the blade, & shuts it.[6] Janet was decidely more spirited than of late. She discussed Greek with L. She is still puzzling out theories about Plato: very open minded, & ready to understand whatever one may spring on her. I sprang first, Joyce's novel, then the Murrys; who are to be neighbours. Lilian read a paper to the Guild in a thoroughly co-operative spirit; I think I should take exception to their maternal care of the women's souls, if I were connected with the movement. But I see the terrible temptation of thinking oneself in the right, & wishing to guide & influence.

Then Clive was in his best man-of-the-world vein, fresh from Max Beerbohm, & inclined to think himself one of our foremost. He sent me his book, where I find myself with Hardy & Conrad; & Nessa & Duncan bracketed first. He babbled & prattled & hinted at all his friends & parties & interests—not offensively, to me at least. He gives, or wishes to give the impression that he sits drinking in the Café Royal with Mary, & the young poets & painters drift up, & he knows them all, & between them they settle the business. His

6. See p. 30.

book is stout morality & not very good criticism. He seems to have little natural insight into literature. Roger declares that he doesn't know about pictures. On the other hand, he has the strong English sense of morality. At Asheham we had Roger, a picnic, & I spent a night at Charleston. That is by way of company. But the important thing was the weather. The heat was such that it was intolerable to walk before tea; we sat in the garden, I indolently reading, L. not sitting but gardening. We had the best display of flowers yet seen— wall flowers in profusion, columbines, phlox, & as we went huge scarlet poppies with purple stains in them. The peonies even about to burst. There was a nest of blackbirds against the wall. Last night at Charleston I lay with my window open listening to a nightingale, which beginning in the distance came very near the garden. Fishes splashed in the pond. May in England is all they say—so teeming, amorous, & creative. I talked a good deal with Nessa—much about servants & other possibilities. Roger, of course, came up from Bo-Peep, & there was Mrs B[rereton], burnt brown, solid, stolid, institutional, & very competent. Roger & I croaked a kind of frogs chorus together—how we loved & admired & were only snubbed for our pains—Nessa sitting almost silent, stitching a dress by lamp-light. Roger is growing more egoistical, or it is more apparent to me; & his complaints were more genuine than mine. All interesting people are egoists, perhaps; but it is not in itself desirable. There were numbers of Belgian Hares, & equal numbers of children to judge by the sound, though they are kept to their own rooms & hours by Mrs B. & don't appear at all. Saxon & Barbara arrive at Asheham as we go—this being our compromise, for we didn't want them as visitors as they, coolly enough, proposed that we should have them.

## Tuesday 8 June [1920][†]

### [A complete case of servant's hysteria]

It is quite right to think of June in December, save that its a little over-fresh today, almost as if there were Brighton sea round the corner. One of my field days yesterday—National Gallery—there met Clive—ices at Gunters—much of a spectacle—old black &

---

† This and the following entries are from *The Diary of Virginia Woolf, Vol. 2: 1920–1924*, ed. Anne Olivier Bell assisted by Andrew McNeillie (New York and London: Harcourt Brace Jovanovich, 1978), pp. 47–48, 64–65, 72–73, 112–14, 121–22, 204–06, 247–49, 260–61, 298–300, 321–22. Diary copyright © 1978, 1980 by Quentin Bell and Angelica Garnett. Reprinted by permission of Houghton Mifflin Harcourt Publishing Company and the Society of Authors on behalf of the Estate of Virginia Woolf. All rights reserved. Notes are by Bell unless otherwise indicated.

white lady with a confidante observing manners & customs, benevolently, amused. Young man with a back like a clothes' horse hung
with perfect grey clothes—lithe women or girls with transparent
legs tripping down into the shady caves—ices sucked or sipped in
the strangest silence—two young ladies with their mother eating in
complete silence: not a spark of life, properly dressed, from the
country perhaps. But don't mothers & daughters ever talk? Would a
young man have waked them? I could not say what went forward in
those mute minds. Dine with Nessa. The whole story of Mary was
told me—a complete case of servant's hysteria; all coming, I think,
from her wishing to act a day dream, & then, poor creature, stepping too far & believing it, & now babbling in St Pancras Infirmary.[1]
The sight of her taken off was sinister; & all the servants were looking from all the windows. What horrid people they are! This made
my drive to Waterloo on top of a bus very vivid. A bright night; with
a fresh breeze. An old beggar woman, blind, sat against a stone wall
in Kingsway holding a brown mongrel in her arms & sang aloud.
There was a recklessness about her; much in the spirit of London.
Defiant—almost gay, clasping her dog as if for warmth. How many
Junes has she sat there, in the heart of London? How she came to
be there, what scenes she can go through, I can't imagine. O damn
it all, I say, why cant I know all that too? Perhaps it was the song at
night that seemed strange; she was singing shrilly, but for her own
amusement, not begging. Then the fire engines came by—shrill
too; with their helmets pale yellow in the moonlight. Sometimes
every thing gets into the same mood; how to define this one I don't
know—It was gay, & yet terrible & fearfully vivid. Nowadays I'm
often overcome by London; even think of the dead who have walked
in the city. Perhaps one might visit ⟨city⟩ the churches. The view of
the grey white spires from Hungerford Bridge brings it to me: & yet
I can't say what 'it' is.

## Wednesday 15 September [1920]

*[Especially the satire of the Dalloways]*

Nelly by the way has now had, I suppose every organ in her body
examined, & is pronounced healthy with the exception of her teeth.

1. Vanessa Bell's housemaid, Mary Wilson, suffered a serious nervous breakdown. In May,
she claimed that her mother, father, and brother had died and that her lover had nearly
died, all within a fortnight. She left work, returned shortly, and, as described above, was
hospitalized a few weeks later. The whole story had been a hallucination [*Editor*].

So that shot of mine seems the true one;—but I confess I don't look forward to the winter. The fact is the lower classes *are* detestable.

Something of that reflection I owe to Lytton who has been with us from Friday to Tuesday, & now that the rain is come, I observe maliciously, is with the Hutches at Wittering.[2] (Never does Mary darken my door, or shadow my lawn again, I observe)—And that too comes from Lytton—its a consequence of walking all along the flats with him, on a brilliant evening, so up by Northease farm onto the downs. His admiration of the place made up for all disparagement. But see how many little facts, sayings, points of view I collected from him—that Mary dislikes me 'very feminine', that Clive is a buffoon, that the lower classes are vulgar & stupid, that the Selby Biggs are useless & pretentious,[3] that we only remain—but that the world's very amusing & pleasant, on the whole, society agreeable, 'women essential'; & I think there are one or two doubts of his about the value of his work compared with creating a world of one's own.

Then 'Life is very complex'—this murmured, as if intimate, referring to his own difficulties, which I had explained to me on the Roman Road.[4] A repetition of Nick & Barbara [Bagenal] C[arrington]. lives with P[artridge]. till Christmas, then comes to a decision. And we walked all the way to Kingston, talking, back over the flats, talking. Save for shadows that cross & leave him ruffled, he is now uniformly amiable, & takes pains at table—so that something is always on foot. At night we had the first two or three chapters of Victoria[5]—Disgraceful to say I was twice overcome with sleep, owing to our wood fire; but the liveliness of it is such as to make one forget whether its good or not. I dont know what qualities it has. I suspect it depends too much upon amusing quotations, & is too much afraid of dulness to say anything out of the way. Not at all a meditative or profound book; on the other hand, a remarkably composed & homogeneous book. I doubt whether these portraits are true—whether thats not too much the conventional way of making history—But I think I'm coloured by my own wishes, & experimental mood. A miracle in the matter of condensation & composition I suspect. But we are to read it when done. Blessed with fine weather, I could look from

2. The St John Hutchinsons had a small holiday house, Eleanor Farm, on the Chichester Canal near West Wittering.

3. Sir Amherst Selby-Bigge (1860–1951), Permanent Secretary to the Board of Education, 1911–25, lived at Kingston Manor; the walk on the downs above Northease had brought Lytton and VW down through Kingston, where they had seen Sir Amherst's daughter-in-law in the road.

4. The Roman Road was probably the Woolfs' name for a straight track along the top of the downs. * * *

5. Strachey would have been reading aloud from the manuscript of his biography *Queen Victoria* (1921) [*Editor*].

my window, through the vine leaves, & see Lytton sitting in the deck chair reading Alfieri from a lovely vellum copy, dutifully looking out words. He wore a white felt hat, & the usual grey clothes; was long, & tapering as usual; looking so mild & so ironical, his beard just cut short. As usual; I got my various impressions: of suavity, a gentle but inflexible honesty; lightning speed; something peevish & exacting; something incessantly living, suffering, reflecting moods. Still he can withdraw in that supercilious way that used to gall me; still show himself superior to me, contemptuous of me—of my morality, that is, not of my mind. For my own encouragement, I may note that he praised the Voyage Out voluntarily; "*extremely* good" it seemed to him on re-reading, especially the satire of the Dalloways. Night & Day he judges better, on the whole. Well, I can walk & talk with him by the hour.

\* \* \*

## Monday 25 October (first day of winter time)[6] [1920]

### [A *little strip of pavement over an abyss*]

Why is life so tragic; so like a little strip of pavement over an abyss. I look down; I feel giddy; I wonder how I am ever to walk to the end. But why do I feel this? Now that I say it I don't feel it. The fire burns; we are going to hear the Beggars Opera.[7] Only it lies about me; I can't keep my eyes shut. It's a feeling of impotence: of cutting no ice. Here I sit at Richmond, & like a lantern stood in the middle of a field my light goes up in darkness. Melancholy diminishes as I write. Why then don't I write it down oftener? Well, one's vanity forbids. I want to appear a success even to myself. Yet I dont get to the bottom of it. Its having no children, living away from friends, failing to write well, spending too much on food, growing old—I think too much of whys & wherefores: too much of myself. I dont like time to flap round me. Well then, work. Yes, but I so soon tire of work—can't read more than a little, an hour's writing is enough for me. Out here no one comes in to waste time pleasantly. If they do, I'm cross. The labour of going to London is too great. Nessa's children grow up, & I cant have them in to tea, or go to the Zoo. Pocket money doesn't allow of much. Yet I'm persuaded that these are trivial things: its life itself, I think sometimes, for us in our generation so tragic—no newspaper placard without its shriek of

6. Daylight Saving Time was introduced during World War I [*Editor*].
7. A musical play by John Gay, first produced in 1728 and revived with great success at the Lyric Theatre, Hammersmith, in 1920 by Giles Playfair.

agony from some one. McSwiney this afternoon & violence in Ireland;[8] or it'll be the strike. Unhappiness is everywhere; just beyond the door; or stupidity which is worse. Still I dont pluck the nettle out of me. To write Jacob's Room again will revive my fibres, I feel. Evelyn is done: but I don't like what I write now. And with it all how happy I am—if it weren't for my feeling that its a strip of pavement over an abyss.


## Monday 18 April [1921]

### [*Lunching with a cabinet minister*]

Just back from lunching with a Cabinet Minister. I mean, of course, Herbert Fisher. We think he asked us in order to apologise for—everything. He said he had neither the physical force nor the combativeness to carry things through. He said he hated Parliament. A political life is dull, & wastes all one's time he said; one is always listening to dull speeches, frittering time away. He leaves home at 10, gets back at 11 P.M. & then has a bundle of papers to go through. The upshot of it all was that he couldn't be blamed for his conduct about Ireland.[9] And then he was careful to explain that the public is ridiculously in the dark about everything. Only the cabinet knows the true spring & source of things he said. That is the only solace of the work. A flood tide of business flows incessantly from all quarters of the world through Downing Street; & there are a few miserable men trying desperately to deal with it. They have to make tremendous decisions with insufficient evidence on the spur of the moment. Then he pulled himself up, & said, solemnly, that he is going to Geneva to initiate peace—disarmament.[1] "You are the great authority upon that, I understand", he said to Leonard. Anyhow I confess it seemed to me, sitting opposite to Leonard in that

---

8. Alderman Terence Joseph McSwiney, Lord Mayor of Cork, 1920, MP for mid-Cork since December 1918, died in the early hours of 25 October in Brixton Prison after being on hunger strike since 16 August. McSwiney had been sentenced by court martial to two years imprisonment for holding a Sinn Fein Court in Cork City Hall.

9. This was the period of the most horrific violence between the Irish Republican Army and the Government forces, which was bringing deep discredit upon British rule. VW's cousin H. A. L. Fisher, President of the Board of Trade, a Liberal and a supporter of partition and Home Rule for Ireland, was one of the six members of the Coalition Cabinet's Irish Committee, and as such was, if reluctantly, party to the decision to send the Black and Tans into Ireland in March 1920, and to form the Auxiliary Division of the Royal Irish Constabulary some six months later—'one of those hateful necessities which in exceptional times must be accepted as the lesser of two grave evils' (*An Unfinished Autobiography*, 1940). The Peace Treaty with the Sinn Fein was not signed until December 1921.

1. H. A. L. Fisher attended the annual meeting of the Council of the League of Nations at Geneva, 17–28 June 1921, the proceedings of which he reported to the House of Commons on 5 July.

brown ugly room with its autotypes of Dutch pictures & Aunt Mary
on a donkey,[2] that Leonard was·an authority & Herbert a thin-
shredded thread paper of a man, whose brain has been harrowed in
to sandy streaks like his hair. Never was there a thinner lighter
airier specimen I thought; his words without body, & his head
cocked at a queer angle, & his hands gesticulating, & his eyes so
blue, but almost vacant, & cheerful colourless words, slightly mannered & brushed up in conformity with some official standard of
culture—I daresay Mr Balfour talks something like that.[3] But after
mouthing his meaning behold; it flew away like thistledown, & it
appeared that this Cabinet Minister & representative of Great Britain in whose hands are armies & navies was dry & empty again—&
asking me colloquially whether I remembered Aunt Mary on the
donkey, which I did. 'The donkey is too small', I said 'And the horse
has no ears,' he added. 'Watts has come down in the world' I said,
feeling astonishingly young & juicy beside him.

"Yes, he said. I daresay: But I feel that the man who painted that
picture was a great man—not a great painter, perhaps, but a great
man." After which he descended as usual to badinage about the arts;
& praised a Mr Munnings: wonderful pictures of horses; landscapes
in the 18th century style behind them. "Thats what I like—the
18th century style—old Crome & Cotman. Well, Munnings is that
style—worth going to the Royal Academy to see—quite a young
fellow—fought through the war."[4] But modern art he didn't care for;
& we walked down Victoria Street to the House of Commons; & he
said he was reading Southey's Letters—"first rate reading. There's a
beautiful description of winter. Now who are our promising littera-
teurs?" I said Joyce.[5] Never heard of Joyce. So we parted, Herbert
very amiable, grey & distinguished, in his pea-jacket, going to tackle
the liquor bill, & envying us very much, he said, writing books at

2. Fisher's London home was at 28 Ashley Gardens, Westminster; his mother—VW's
Aunt Mary—had been portrayed as Una by G. F. Watts in his representation of Spen-
ser's 'Una and the Red Cross Knight'. A preparatory drawing and the painting, for which
Mary Jackson sat in 1862 shortly before her marriage to Herbert Fisher, was given to
her by the artist, and is still in the possession of her family. George Frederic Watts, OM
(1817–1904) had been a protégé and neighbour of Mary Jackson's aunt Sara Prinsep,
and frequently called on members of her family—famous for its female beauties—to sit
for him.
3. Arthur James Balfour (1848–1930), philosopher and statesman, was like Fisher (who
admired him immensely) a member of Lloyd-George's coalition cabinet, being at this
time Lord President of the Council.
4. Alfred James Munnings (1878–1959), a Suffolk miller's son, was to become President
of the Royal Academy in 1944. He had been an official war artist attached to the Cana-
dian Cavalry Brigade, and between the wars achieved a tremendous celebrity as a
painter of horses and country scenes.
5. James Joyce (1882–1941), Irish novelist and Woolf's exact contemporary. His *Portrait of
the Artist as a Young Man* (1914) established his reputation. His masterpiece, *Ulysses*,
was appearing in sections. The Woolfs were approached to publish it, but it was too
large a task for their small press [*Editor*].

Richmond.[6] And then we ran into Will Vaughan at the London Library, portly & hearty, & keeping up a laugh like an old sea-captains all the time he talked. Indeed, we had nothing to say.[7]

## Thursday 2 June [1921]

### [*Actually under this roof*]

But this was written a week ago, today being the day after Derby Day, the very height of the season, I suppose: anyhow of leaf & flower.

People turn up regularly though with little planning on our part. Madge [Vaughan] on Friday; Kot on Saturday; Roger; Fredegond; Mr Reginald Morris. Will these names recover anything in 10 years time of the last week of May 1921? I wish I had the same record of 10 years back, when I was a young woman—only then one can't scribble. One takes thought. One gets it too literal.

Madge asked to come; so we had her. She is curiously changed. She has become ordinary. Middle age has thickened her lines, & deepened her colour. In her mind she is grown cheerful, & commonplace. I notice now that her forehead is oddly pinched at the top. She said of herself that she was stunted—which expresses it. She has never grown up, but lived somewhere under shelter, unchastised, talking a great deal about life, but not facing it. Oh she did talk about life—always with reference to herself, which makes the mind squint. She sees nothing in itself. So we vacillated between 'life' & Will: 'my life': 'my odd nature', 'I have no brain' 'I am very psychological'. But then I ought to have broken away, & so on; but as it is quite obvious that she is rich, successful, & happy, these complaints which make the staple of her talk, lack substance; & she easily slides into gossip, & repetition. Indeed you can't keep her to poetry, kitchen, love, art, or children for more than a minute. Yet she has her gaiety & her vitality which protect one from the worst boredom. But not Leonard nor Roger. They were out of hand with misery. And this was the woman I adored! I see myself now standing in the night nursery at Hyde Park Gate, washing my hands, & saying to myself "At this moment she is actually under this roof."

6. H. A. L. Fisher acted as a Government spokesman on matters relating to the Liquor Control Board, established under the Home Office in 1915 as a wartime measure. On 27 April the Government, abandoning a proposed new Licensing Bill, invited the Control Board to continue its existence for another 12 months.
7. William Wyamar Vaughan (1865–1938), now Master of Wellington College, Headmaster of Rugby 1921–31, VW's first cousin.

Fredegond came, all in black (& she dresses very badly). Uncle Hervey is dead, she said.[8] And she was off to bury him, but couldn't find a train (the strike, you see, is still on.) Hervey Fisher was the genius of our youth; & the only fruit of it is a volume of stories which are neither better nor worse than what one reads on a journey in a Red Magazine. They said he was dropped by his nurse; & so for 52 years, poor man, he has been plagued with illness; has been mad; has never done anything he liked, I suppose, even his marriage being called off by Aunt Mary.

# Wednesday 4 October [1922]

### [*I like reading my own writing*]

Our last whole day. From the weather point of view, the summer has been altogether disappointing. It has promised & then withheld. We have not had 7 consecutive good days. There has been a scattering of good ones, but in the midst of rain, wind, & dark London looking skies. Often the Roman road was so muddy I could not walk along it. And often I heard the thunder murmuring as I walked. Grizzel was frightened & ran home—as if God would go out of his way to hurt a mongrel fox terrier walking on the flats at Rodmell! But there's no arguing about these things. I think the garden has never been better, & we have had good crops of apples & pears, & green peas only 2 days ago.

Spiritually speaking we have made some progress in Rodmell society. I was struck by the bloodlessness of philistines the other day at the Rectory. They seem far less alive than we intellectuals. Mr Shanks & the Hoggs [*unidentified*] are, after all, so pale, so watery, so mild. Mrs Hawkesford still discusses the country & London; says, for the 20th time, that she is so glad she kept the tennis court going, even though they turned the pony on it during the war. Boen sits lackadaisical, & helps me to Shanks' cigarettes. Then I don't like underbred young men—Hogg to wit. They seem to me a little peevish & conventional; & talk slang which covers any character they may have.

---

8. Hervey Fisher (1873–1921), seventh of VW's Fisher cousins, died at Sheringham on 26 May. Since childhood he had suffered from crippling spinal tuberculosis and consequent mental derangement, but with tremendous heroism—both his own and his family's—he overcame his disabilities to the extent of being able to lead an active intellectual life. After the death of his mother in 1916 he was looked after by his sister Adeline Vaughan Williams. His one published book was *A Romantic Man and Other Tales* (1920). The fortnightly *Red Magazine* contained nine or ten stories and an instalment of a serial.

I am a little uppish, though, & self assertive, because Brace wrote to me yesterday "We think Jacob's Room[9] an extraordinarily distinguished & beautiful work. You have, of course, your own method, & it is not easy to foretell how many readers it will have; surely it will have enthusiastic ones, & we delight in publishing it"—or words to that effect. As this is my first testimony from an impartial person I am pleased. For one thing it must make *some* impression, as a whole; & cannot be wholly frigid fireworks. We think of publishing on Oct. 27th. I daresay Duckworth is a little cross with me.[1] I snuff my freedom. It is I think true, soberly & not artificially for the public, that I shall go on unconcernedly whatever people say. At last, I like reading my own writing. It seems to me to fit me closer than it did before. I have done my task here better than I expected. Mrs Dalloway & the Chaucer chapter are finished; I have read 5 books of the Odyssey; Ulysses; & now begin Proust. I also read Chaucer & the Pastons. So evidently my plan of the two books running side by side is practicable, & certainly I enjoy my reading with a purpose. I am committed to only one Supt. article—on Essays—& that at my own time; so I am free.[2] I shall read Greek now steadily & begin 'The Prime Minister'[3] on Friday morning. I shall read the Trilogy & some Sophocles & Euripides & a Plato dialogue: also the lives of Bentley & Jebb.[4] At forty I am beginning to learn the mechanism of my own brain—how to get the greatest amount of pleasure & work out of it. The secret is I think always so to contrive that work is pleasant.

## Saturday 8 October [1922]

### [Kitty Maxse's death]

Back again, over the fire at Hogarth House, having read the first chapters of Bentley. Grizzel sits on L.'s knee. Boxall—the kitten, called after Nelly to ingratiate her, is happily off mine; temporarily, or I could not write.

9. Woolf's 1922 novel. She was in negotiations with her American publishing house, Harcourt Brace [*Editor*].

1. The letter from Donald Brace was dated 20 September 1922; it has been very slightly paraphrased by VW. After publishing her first two novels, Gerald Duckworth had agreed to relinquish his option on her third, *Jacob's Room*, to enable the Woolfs to publish it themselves. 290 pages long, it was the Hogarth Press's largest undertaking so far; it was printed for them by R. & R. Clark of Edinburgh.

2. VW's review of *Modern English Essays*, edited by Ernest Rhys, appeared in the *TLS* of 30 November 1922 (Kp C229).

3. An unfinished short story, collected in *The Complete Shorter Fiction*, which is an early version of the second section of *Mrs. Dalloway* [*Editor*].

4. The *Life and Letters* of Sir Richard Claverhouse Jebb (1841–1905), classical scholar renowned for his translations and critical editions of Sophocles in particular, was published by his wife Caroline in 1907. The Oresteian trilogy is by Aeschylus.

But the day has been spoilt for me—so strangely—by Kitty
Maxse's death; & now I think of her lying in her grave at Gunby, &
Leo going home, & all the rest. I read it in the paper. I hadn't seen
her since, I guess, 1908—save at old Davies' funeral, & then I cut
her, which now troubles me—unreasonably I suppose.[5] I could not
have kept up with her; she never tried to see me. Yet yet—these old
friends dying without any notice on our part always—it begins to
happen often—saddens me: makes me feel guilty. I wish I'd met her
in the street. My mind has gone back all day to her; in the queer way
it does. First thinking out how she died, suddenly at 33 Cromwell
Road; she was always afraid of operations. Then visualising her—
her white hair—pink cheeks—how she sat upright—her voice—
with its characteristic tones—her green blue floor—which she
painted with her own hands: her earrings, her gaiety, yet melancholy; her smartness: her tears, which stayed on her cheek. Not that
I ever felt at my ease with her. But she was very charming—very
humorous. She got engaged at St Ives, & Thoby thought it was Paddy
talking to his boy. They sat on the seat by the greenhouse in the
Love Corner.[6] However, I keep going over this very day in my mind.

## Tuesday 19 June [1923]

### [Feeling things deeply]

I took up this book with a kind of idea that I might say something
about my writing—which was prompted by glancing at what K.M.[7]
said about *her* writing in the Dove's Nest. But I only glanced. She
said a good deal about feeling things deeply: also about being pure,
which I wont criticise, though of course I very well could.[8] But now
what do I feel about *my* writing?—this book, that is, The Hours, if
thats its name? One must write from deep feeling, said Dostoevsky.
And do I? Or do I fabricate with words, loving them as I do? No I

5. Kitty Maxse died on 4 October 1922 after a fall at her London home, and was buried
   beside her sister Margaret—whose widower Stephen Massingberd owned Gunby
   Hall—at Gunby Burgh in Lincolnshire on 7 October. Leopold James Maxse (1864–
   1932), whom she had married in 1890, was the owner and editor of the political
   monthly *National Review*. Old Davies was Margaret's father, the Rev. John Llewellyn
   Davies; his funeral took place at Hampstead on 22 May 1916. [Kitty Maxse was an
   important model for Clarissa Dalloway—*Editor*.]
6. This recollection recurs in VW's Memoir Club contribution '22 Hyde Park Gate' written in 1921, and in 'A Sketch of the Past,' 1940; see *Moments of Being*, p 143 and p 111.
7. Katherine Mansfield [*Editor*].
8. J. M. Murry's introductory note to *The Doves' Nest and Other Stories* (1923) by Katherine Mansfield contains several extracts from the author's *Journal*. In these she talks of
   the need for her writing to be '*deeply felt*' and of her feeling not 'pure in heart, not
   humble, not good'. * * *

think not. In this book I have almost too many ideas. I want to give life & death, sanity & insanity; I want to criticise the social system, & to show it at work, at its most intense—But here I may be posing. I heard from Ka this morning that she doesn't like In the Orchard.[9] At once I feel refreshed. I become anonymous, a person who writes for the love of it. She takes away the motive of praise, & lets me feel that without any praise, I should be content to go on. This is what Duncan said of his painting the other night. I feel as if I slipped off all my ball dresses & stood naked—which as I remember was a very pleasant thing to do. But to go on. Am I writing The Hours[1] from deep emotion? Of course the mad part tries me so much, makes my mind squint so badly that I can hardly face spending the next weeks at it. Its a question though of these characters. People, like Arnold Bennett, say I cant create, or didn't in J's R, characters that survive.[2] My answer is—but I leave that to the Nation: its only the old argument that character is dissipated into shreds now: the old post-Dostoevsky argument. I daresay its true, however, that I haven't that 'reality' gift. I insubstantise, wilfully to some extent, distrusting reality—its cheapness. But to get further. Have I the power of conveying the true reality? Or do I write essays about myself? Answer these questions as I may, in the uncomplimentary sense, & still there remains this excitement. To get to the bones, now I'm writing fiction again I feel my force flow straight from me at its fullest. After a dose of criticism I feel that I'm writing sideways, using only an angle of my mind. This is justification; for free use of the faculties means happiness. I'm better company, more of a human being. Nevertheless, I think it most important in this book to go for the central things, even though they dont submit, as they should however, to beautification in language. No, I don't nail my crest to the Murrys, who work in my flesh after the manner of the jigger insect.[3] Its annoying, indeed degrading, to have these bitternesses. Still, think of the 18th Century. But then they were overt, not covert, as now.

I foresee, to return to The Hours, that this is going to be the devil of a struggle. The design is so queer & so masterful. I'm always having to wrench my substance to fit it. The design is certainly

---

9. 'In the Orchard' was published in the *Criterion* in April 1923 (Kp C232). Ka Arnold-Forster wrote from Cornwall on 17 June 1923 (MHP, Sussex): 'No, I don't think I really liked in the Orchard—but then I'm a jealous critic—& I love you very much.'

1. The working title of *Mrs. Dalloway* [*Editor*].

2. Arnold Bennett's article 'Is the Novel Decaying?' appeared in *Cassell's Weekly* on 28 March 1923 (see *M & M*, p 112). 'I have seldom read a cleverer book than Virginia Woolf's *Jacob's Room*. . . . But the characters do not vitally survive in the mind because the author has been obsessed by details of originality and cleverness.'

3. The jigger insect: an americanism—harvester, harvest bug or tick, a very small but troublesome mite.

original, & interests me hugely. I should like to write away & away at it, very quick and fierce. Needless to say, I cant. In three weeks from today I shall be dried up.

Having made this very inadequate confession about the soul, I may turn now to the body—which is money & America & Mr Crowninshield.[4] I'm asked to write for Vanity Fair & shall be paid says Clive £25 for 1500 words: & get £15 from the Nation; & two months ago I was hawking articles of 5,000 words to Jack Squire for £13.

Do you like becoming famous? Marjorie [Joad] asked me yesterday. The truth is I'm being pushed up, but many people are saying that I shant last, & perhaps I shant. So I return to my old feeling of nakedness as the backbone of my existence, which indeed it is.

For the rest, it is observed in Cornwall & the remoter parts of Weybridge[5] that we are living through a storm of obloquy & must be entirely engrossed in the Nation's affairs. It is not so at Hogarth House: I'm no longer so excited about the contents of L.'s dispatch box. But one thing I do feel pretty certain about & here confide it to my diary—we must leave Richmond & set up in London. The arguments are so well known to me that I cant bother to write them down. But when things come upon me in a clap I generally achieve them, because they are then things that matter to me. Leonard remains to be converted, & my God, the move—the horror—the servants. Still this is life—never to be sitting down for longer than one feels inclined.

## Monday 6 August [1923]

*[Hollyhocks, decapitated, swam in a bowl]*

[RODMELL]

I have ruined my mornings work by making bread & buns, which require constant voyages to the kitchen. The demon then always suggests that I shall read The Hours. Sheer weak dribble it seems to me (read in these circumstances). My comfort is that I can have at it in any way I like; & if it still goes wrong, to the fire with it. Nor do I think it wrong altogether. Whenever there is a breach in my content, all disparaging criticisms creep in; meanly enough, the good ones keep off.

---

4. Francis (Frank) Welch Crowninshield (1872–1947), editor of the New York *Vanity Fair* from 1914–35.
5. A further reference to the letter from Ka mentioned above (footnote 9). E. M. Forster lived with his mother at Weybridge; LW no doubt had some talk with him at the Society (Apostles') dinner which was on 15 June.

We went over to Charleston yesterday. Although thinking quite well of ourselves, we were not well received by the painters. There they sat like assid[u]ous children at a task in a bedroom—Roger, Nessa, & Duncan; Roger on chair in foreground; Nessa on sofa, Duncan on bed.[6] In front of them was one jar of flowers, & one arrangement of still live. Roger was picking out his blue flower very brightly. For some reason, the talk was not entirely congenial. I suspect myself of pertness & so on. Clive was sitting in the drawing room window reading Dryden.

A very good edition—I want to ask your husband some questions—Will he take an article. . . . V. O I thought your Lytton article very good. . . . [7] Van. Tea's ready—V. What am I to do with my cigarette?

Hollyhocks, decapitated, swam in a bowl; there was a loaf for tea, & a long slab of cake. Roger, I cant help thinking has become a little querulous with years. His grievances torment him; he talks of them too much. After tea, Angelica had her dolls' tea party in the window, & beat Clive, & when he cried, ran of her own accord & picked him a flower—which was a sensitive womanly act.[8] She is sensitive—minds being laughed at (as I do). She said she wanted a 'slide' in her hair. "Dont laugh at me" she said, petulantly, to Roger.

I should say that the weather is perfect, soft as a cushion, blue to the heart. A gospel caravan has just pitched its tent near, & the other night 10 young men bawled hymns. . . . But I am laying [sic] my mind wander to The Hours. Now its a strange thing that if I have no gift for novel writing, yet it should so absorb me—I cant diagnose my own case—which reminds me that I've started upon the revision of my old articles; & feel rather charitable to that side of my faculty. Leonard is at this moment beginning again his book, which I daresay he has not touched since last Christmas.[9]

6. Charleston was Woolf's sister Vanessa Bell's house, where she lived with her husband, Clive Bell, and her children, Julian, Quentin, and Angelica. The painter Duncan Grant and the painter and critic Roger Fry (both of whom had affairs with Vanessa) are also mentioned here. Duncan was the father of Vanessa Bell's daughter, Angelica [Editor].

7. Clive Bell's edition of Dryden was that prepared by Sir Walter Scott, revised and corrected by George Saintsbury, 18 volumes, 1882–93, of which he owned six. His article 'Lytton Strachey' had appeared in the New Statesman on 4 August 1923.

8. Angelica Bell (1918–2002), Woolf's niece, was five or six at the time. Bell was adopted by Clive Bell, but her biological father was Duncan Grant, a fact the family kept from her for years. She later married David Garnett, Grant's ex-lover [Editor].

9. After 1921, when he published Socialism and Co-operation, LW was too heavily committed to his journalistic and political work and to the Hogarth Press to find much time for his own writing, but he was 'ruminating and slowly writing' After the Deluge, volume I of which was published in 1931. See IV LW, p. 88.

# Saturday 5 April [1924]

## [Angelica's accident]

### 52 TAVISTOCK SQRE

Well, I will make a brief beginning—after 3 weeks silence. But it has not been silence at all. The noise of bus & taxi has worried me, & the noise of the human tongue has disturbed me, pleasantly & otherwise, & now I'm half asleep. Leonard working as usual.

Tonight, & one other, are the only nights I've been in this week; & all this afternoon went in talking to Mr Littell of the New Republic.[1] But can I collect any first impressions? how Marchmont Street[2] was like Paris; how my first night in the basement I saw the moon, with drifting clouds, & it was a terrifying & new [?] London moon; dreadful & exciting; as if the Richmond moon had been veiled. Oh the convenience of this place! & the loveliness too. We walk home from theatres, through the entrails of London. Why do I love it so much? . . . for it is stony hearted, & callous. The tradespeople don't know one—but these disparaging remarks about the shopkeepers of Marchmont Street were interrupted & it is now *Tuesday, April 15th*, & L. & I have been having one of those melancholy middle aged summings up of a situation which occur from time to time, but are seldom recorded. Indeed most of life escapes, now I come to think of it: the texture of the ordinary day. We were to have had a quiet week, & I brought in Mortimer after Gerhardt last night,[3] & he stayed & talked, aimlessly enough, about his money & his uncles; & so L. was desperately gloomy. Not a stroke of work done he says, since we came to London. This is largely imagination anticipating what people say must happen I think, though its true fish keep drifting into the net. Gerald Brenan back; Roger rampant to paint us; Morgan, elflike, mocking, aloof; Nessa & Duncan. Then there was Angelica's accident which, for the psychology of it I should have described. Here was Nessa painting, & I answering the telephone. Positively bad news has to batter down optimism before it reaches one's ears. Louie & Angelica have been knocked down by a motor & are in the Middlesex hospital.[4] Having got that into my head, I had to repeat it to Nessa: to destroy all that simmering everyday comfort, with the smell of paint in the room, & Tom just

---

1. Philip Littell (1868–1943) was the retiring editor of the *New Republic* which he had edited since 1914; it was to become the main American recipient of VW's articles.
2. The local provision centre, full of small shops and bustle.
3. The great German singer Elena Gerhardt (1883–1961) gave a series of song recitals at the Queen's Hall in April 1924; that on the 14th was devoted to Brahms.
4. Louie Dunnet was Angelica's nurse; the Middlesex Hospital in Mortimer Street is one of London's larger teaching hospitals.

coming up stairs to tea. She ran out & away from the telephone instinctively, ran round in an aimless way for a second. Then off they dashed & I after them, & so to the hospital, holding hands in the cab; & then sheer agony, for there was Louie, with her foot bandaged, & no Angelica; only an evasive nurse, parrying enquiries & taking us behind a screen where Angelica lay in bed, still, her face turned away. At last she moved. "She's not dead" Duncan said. They both thought her dead. Then the young Dr came, & seemed silently & considerately but firmly to wish the mother to know that the case was hopeless: very grave; run over across the stomach. Yes there may have to be an operation. The surgeon had been sent for, & was now on the train. So Nessa went back to sit there, & I saw again that extraordinary look of anguish, dumb, not complaining, which I saw in Greece, I think, when she was ill. The feelings of the people who don't talk express themselves thus. My feeling was "a pane of glass shelters me. I'm only allowed to look on at this." at which I was half envious, half grieved. Moreover, I was sent off to find Clive, & so spared, or not allowed, the long wait there, in the chattering ward. Its a queer thing to come so close to agony as this, & just to be saved oneself. What I felt was, not sorrow or pity for Angelica, but that now Nessa would be an old woman; & this would be an indelible mark; & that death & tragedy had once more put down his paw, after letting us run a few paces. People never get over their early impressions of death I think. I always feel pursued. But theres an end of this. Nothing was wrong with Angelica—it was only a joke this time.

It takes a long time to form a habit—the habit of living at 52 Tavistock Sqre is not quite formed, but doing well. Already I have spent a week without being bothered by noise. One ceases to hear or to see. The dominant interests, I suppose assert themselves, make order by triumphing over the lesser. I notice things much less than I did 10 days ago. Soon I shall be making a habit of life in this room.

As for work, I have done the Dr chapter in my novel: & am furbishing up the Greeks; the usual depressions assail me. My criticism seems to me pretty flimsy sometimes. But there is no principle, except to follow this whimsical brain implicitly, pare away the ill fitting, till I have the shape exact, & if thats no good, it is the fault of God, after all. It is He that has made us, not we ourselves. I like that text.[5] I don't at all regret Richmond. Ethel Sands &c think I ought to mourn my beautiful room. But I now behold what is more beautiful—the ⟨Russell⟩ Imperial Hotel in the evening sunshine;

5. From Psalm 100, verse 3.

pink & yellow like the Brighton front.[6] I regret saturday afternoons a little—How I meander & drivel!

Marjorie [Joad] is on her holiday. I keep shop of a morning. Dadie has been—a sensitive vain youth, with considerable grit in him, I judge. Sometimes the future appears perilous; problematical rather, the press that is, but always fruitful & interesting. I have said nothing of my speech at the London Group, which drew tears;[7] or of a host of matters. On Thursday we go to Rodmell, the test of poor Nelly's endurance. And now for the Elizabethans.

Grosvenor Sqre houses are precisely like saloons in Victorian Inns, or glorified boarding houses: handsome ill-proportioned rooms; gilt chairs, fretted tables; urns & vases depicted in pale mauve on the watered silk walls. Each wall has a piece—smugglers, coaching & so on; a little fire burns in a large grate; a glass screen fends it off, & there Nelly & Lord Bob perch, very chilly & formal, a dragoon bringing in little cakes.[8]

# Tuesday 18 November [1924]

## [The mad chapters of Mrs D]

Lady Colefax interrupts. I ask her to call me Virginia—so there.

What I was going to say was that I think writing must be formal. The art must be respected. This struck me reading some of my notes here, for, if one lets the mind run loose, it becomes egotistic: personal, which I detest; like Robert Graves. At the same time the irregular fire must be there; & perhaps to loose it, one must begin by being chaotic, but not appear in public like that. I am driving my way through the mad chapters of Mrs D. My wonder is whether the book would have been better without them. But this is an afterthought, consequent upon learning how to deal with her. Always I think at the end, I see how the whole ought to have been written.

6. Two hotels face towards Russell Square on its north-eastern side, the huge late-Victorian Hotel Russell, in pale terracotta, and the more exuberant dark brick Imperial Hotel, dating from Edwardian times (now demolished). They were both presumably visible from the back windows of 52 Tavistock Square as one side of Woburn Place was demolished at this time.

7. A London Group dinner, presided over by Roger Fry, was held in honour of Bernard Adeney, its retiring president, at Pinoli's Restaurant, Wardour Street, on 31 March 1924. A sympathetic account of VW's terror and triumph as a speaker on this occasion is given by Osbert Sitwell (whose speech preceded hers) in Laughter in the Next Room, 1949, vol. 4 of his autobiography Left Hand, Right Hand. Her theme was the unity of the arts.

8. Lord and Lady Robert Cecil, with whom the Woolfs went to tea on 10 April, were living in the town house of her brother the Earl of Durham at 39 Grosvenor Square, W1.

Lady Colefax has made me tremble. I cannot write. We were, I was rather, at Mary's farewell party last night, & suffer today—[9] having, first, broken my watch, at 3.15 owing to a policeman calling; I having hotted water over the fire in the basement, being infinitely cold & as if rolled in sand, which misery still persists. The upper classes pretended to be clever. Duff Cooper, Lady Diana & all that set, as they say; & my chief amusement came from seeing them as a set. That is the only merit of these parties, that individuals compose differently from what they do in private. One sees groups; gets wholes; general impressions: from the many things being combined. No doubt Proust could say what I mean—that great writer whom I cannot read when I'm correcting, so persuasive is he. He makes it seem easy to write well; which only means that one is slipping along on borrowed skates. So Henry James gives one an unreal impetus; witness my writing after reading him, & Miss Bosanquet.

Dadie came back yesterday & we had a jolly afternoon—oh infinitely better than a party at River House!—lie though I did to Mary on the telephone, doing up Freud.[1] I in two jackets, for it is freezing, & hair down; he in shirtsleeves. Thus one gets to know people; sucks the marrow out, not poised on the edge of a chair on the slippery floor, trying to laugh, & being spurred by wine & sugar cakes. Clive of course changes into an upper class man very loud, familiar, & dashing at once. Lytton sits in his own green shade, only emerging when the gentle youths come in. Philip Ritchie thinks rather too highly of himself, as notice from Lytton always makes them. I was impressed by Nessa, who went to this party for which we were all titivating & dressing up, in her old red brown dress which I think she made herself. (Thinking it over, I believe its getting the rhythm in writing that matters. Could I get my tomorrow mornings rhythm right—take the skip of my sentence at the right moment—I should reel it off;—there is a good deal in this which I should like to think out; its not style exactly—the right words—its a way of levitating the thought out of one—Thank God I hear L.'s key: Grizzle gets up & stands still: now wags; & then trots to the door. A very cold damp foggy night.) But I was saying that I admired Nessa's utter independence of what people say, which triumphs, over all the tubular cropheads.[2]

9. The St John Hutchinsons were moving from River House, Hammersmith to 3 Albert (now Prince Albert) Road, Regent's Park.
1. Volumes I & II of Freud's *Collected Papers* were published by the Hogarth Press in November 1924 (*HP Checklist* 44).
2. Woolf's private nickname for the younger generation of women artists and writers, for their short, cropped hair [*Editor*].

# Tuesday 6 January [1925]†

## [*Proofs will come next week*]

The disgraceful truth is that I shall run year into year, for I cant waste so many blank pages.

What a flourish I began 1924 with! And today, for the 165th time, Nelly has given notice—Won't be dictated to: must do as other girls do. This is the fruit of Bloomsbury.[1] On the whole, I'm inclined to take her at her word. The nuisance of arranging life to suit her fads, & the pressure of 'other girls' is too much, good cook though she is, & honest, crusty old maid too, dependable, in the main, affectionate, kindly, but incurably fussy, nervy, unsubstantial. Anyhow, the servant question no longer much worries me.

Last night we dined at 3 Albert Road Mary's new villa.[2] I like the new year to begin with warm friendly feelings—& it was a superb dinner. There were the children too, a nice girl & boy; a girl with lovely *womans* eyes, sympathetic, startled; & wild like a girl. (I want to begin to describe my own sex.) What do I mean about the expression? Extreme youth, & yet, one felt, this feeling has been existing forever; very feminine. Here I conceive my story—but I'm always conceiving stories now. Short ones—scenes—for instance The Old Man (a character of L.S.) The Professor on Milton—(an attempt at literary criticism)[3] & now The Interruption, women talking alone. However, back to life. Where are we?

I spent this morning writing a note on an E[lizabe]than play—for which I have been reading plays all this year.[4] Then I found the minute hand of my watch had come off (this was talking to Lytton about [Samuel] Richardson last night—I found it off then): so I went into the printing room to see the time—found Angus & Leonard doing Simkin's bill. Stayed & laughed. L. went off to the office, when we had dog-walked round the Square. I came in & set a page

---

† This and the following entries are from *The Diary of Virginia Woolf, Vol. 3: 1925–1930*, ed. Anne Olivier Bell assisted by Andrew McNeillie (New York and London: Harcourt Brace Jovanovich, 1980), pp. 3–4, 9, 32. Diary copyright © 1978, 1980 by Quentin Bell and Angelica Garnett. Reprinted by permission of Houghton Mifflin Harcourt Publishing Company and the Society of Authors on behalf of the Estate of Virginia Woolf. All rights reserved. Notes are by Bell unless otherwise indicated.

1. The Woolfs had employed Nelly Boxall and Lottie Hope as living-in servants since 1916; they took Nelly with them when they moved to Tavistock Square, Bloomsbury, in 1924, and Lottie went to work for the Adrian Stephens in neighbouring Gordon Square.

2. The Hutchinsons had recently moved to 3 Albert (now Prince Albert) Road, Regent's Park, from their previous home at River House, Hammersmith. The children were Barbara (b. 1911) and Jeremy (b. 1915).

3. VW was already envisaging her father Leslie Stephen as the subject of a 'scene' the previous autumn (see *II VW Diary*, 17 October 1924); it was to develop into *To the Lighthouse*. The professor is incorporated in *Mrs Dalloway*, pp 193–4.

4. VW's 'Notes on an Elizabethan Play' was published in the *TLS* of 5 March 1925 (Kp C259).

of Nancy. Then out to Ingersoll to get my watch mended.[5] Then dog
walked. Then here. It being a black grained winter day; lengths of
the pavement ink black where not lighted. Never shall I describe all
the days I have noticed. I cannot hit it off, quite, & yet perhaps if I
read this again I shall see what I meant then.

Rodmell was all gale & flood; these words are exact. The river
overflowed. We had 7 days rain out of 10. Often I could not face a
walk. L. pruned, which needed heroic courage. My heroism was
purely literary. I revised Mrs D[alloway]: the dullest part of the
whole business of writing; the most depressing & exacting. The
worst part is at the beginning (as usual) where the aeroplane has it
all to itself for some pages, & it wears thin. L. read it; thinks it my
best—but then has he not *got* to think so? Still I agree. He thinks it
has more continuity than J[acob]s R[oom]. but is difficult owing to
the lack of connection, visible, between the two themes.

Anyhow it is sent off to Clarks, & proofs will come next week.
This is for Harcourt Brace, who has accepted without seeing &
raised me to 15 p.c.[6]

I did not see very much at Rodmell, having to keep my eyes on
the typewriter.

Angus was with us for Christmas, a very quiet, very considerate,
unselfish deliberate young man, with a charming sense of humour—
colourless, Lytton says: passive. But I think well of him, all the same.


## Sunday 19 April [1925]

### [*Mrs Dalloway is a success*]

It is now after dinner, our first summer time night, & the mood for
writing has left me, only just brushed me & left me. I have not
achieved my sacred half hour yet. But think—in time to come I
would rather read something here than reflect that I did polish off
Mr Ring Lardner successfully.[7] I'm out to make £300 this summer
by writing, & build a bath & hot water range at Rodmell. But, hush,

---

5. Lytton Strachey (1880–1932), author of *Eminent Victorians*, critic, and one of Woolf's
   closest friends. Henry Gordon Davidson (b. 1898), graduate of Magdalene College,
   Cambridge, came to work at the Hogarth Press in December 1924 as successor to
   G. H. W. Rylands and stayed until the end of 1927. Simpkin, Marshall, Hamilton, Kent
   & Co were book wholesalers and distributors. The *Nation* office was at 38 Great James
   Street, WC1. Nancy Cunard (1896–1965), the rebellious daughter of the immensely
   wealthy Sir Bache and Lady Cunard; her long poem *Parallax* was to be published by the
   Hogarth Press in April 1925 (*HP Checklist* 57). The Ingersoll Watch Company had two
   establishments in Kingsway.
6. R & R Clark Ltd, the Edinburgh firm of printers. Harcourt, Brace and Company, VW's
   publishers in America.
7. Ringgold Wilmer (Ring) Lardner (1885–1933), American short-story writer whose
   work is discussed by VW in her article 'American Fiction' (Kp C265).

hush—my books tremble on the verge of coming out, & my future
is uncertain. As for forecasts—its *just* on the cards Mrs Dalloway is
a success (Harcourt thinks it "wonderful"), & sells 2,000—I dont
expect it: I expect a slow silent increase of fame, such has come
about, rather miraculously, since Js R. was published; my value
mounting steadily as a journalist, though scarcely a copy sold. And
I am not very nervous—rather; & I want as usual to dig deep down
into my new stories, without having a looking glass flashed in my
eyes—Todd, to wit; Colefax to wit et cetera.[8]

## Thursday 18 June [1925]

### [*Lytton does not like Mrs Dalloway*]

No, Lytton[9] does not like Mrs Dalloway, &, what is odd, I like him
all the better for saying so, & don't much mind. What he says is that
there is a discordancy between the ornament (extremely beautiful)
& what happens (rather ordinary—or unimportant). This is caused
he thinks by some discrepancy in Clarissa herself; he thinks she is
disagreeable & limited, but that I alternately laugh at her, & cover
her, very remarkably, with myself. So that I think as a whole, the
book does not ring solid; yet, he says, it is a whole; & he says sometimes the writing is of extreme beauty. What can one call it but
genius? he said! Coming when, one never can tell. Fuller of genius,
he said than anything I had done. Perhaps, he said, you have not
yet mastered your method. You should take something wilder &
more fantastic, a frame work that admits of anything, like Tristram
Shandy. But then I should lose touch with emotions, I said. Yes, he
agreed, there must be reality for you to start from. Heaven knows
how you're to do it. But he thought me at the beginning, not at the
end. And he said the C.R.[1] was divine, a classic; Mrs D. being, I
fear, a flawed stone. This is very personal, he said & old fashioned

---

8. VW wrote several 'stories' concerned with 'the party consciousness, the frock consciousness' at this period, seven of which are collected in *Mrs Dalloway's Party* (1973)
edited by Stella McNichol (whose editorial procedures were severely criticised by J. F.
Hulcoop in the *VW Miscellany*, no. 3, Spring 1975, and defended in *ibid*, no. 9, Winter
1977). Manuscript and typescript versions of these stories are both now in the Berg.
Dorothy Todd, who edited British *Vogue* from 1922–26, sought to make it an authoritative and sophisticated guide to high fashion in clothes and culture, and commissioned
contributions from *avant-garde* writers (including VW) and artists in both France and
England. Lady Colefax (*née* Sibyl Halsey, d. 1950) was celebrated for her indefatigable
pursuit of 'interesting' people, whom she and her husband Sir Arthur entertained at
their home, Argyll House, Chelsea. Three of those stories are included in this Norton
Critical Edition [184–200, below].
9. Strachey's praise of the character Mrs. Dalloway in Woolf's first novel, *The Voyage Out*
(1915), had encouraged Woolf to return to the character, but Woolf changed her significantly as the novel evolved [*Editor*].
1. *The Common Reader* (1925), a collection of literary essays [*Editor*].

perhaps; yet I think there is some truth in it. For I remember the night at Rodmell when I decided to give it up, because I found Clarissa in some way tinselly. Then I invented her memories. But I think some distaste for her persisted. Yet, again, that was true to my feeling for Kitty,[2] & one must dislike people in art without its mattering, unless indeed it is true that certain characters detract from the importance of what happens to them. None of this hurts me, or depresses me. Its odd that when Clive & others (several of them) say it is a masterpiece, I am not much exalted; when Lytton picks holes, I get back into my working fighting mood, which is natural to me. I don't see myself a success. I like the sense of effort better. The sales collapsed *July 20th. Have* completely for 3 days; now a little dribble begins *sold about 1550* again. I shall be more than pleased if we sell 1500. Its now 1250.

# LETTERS

## To Emma Vaughan[†]

[*How I do love London*]

[April 1899]

My dearest Toad,                                        *9 St Aubyns, Hove* [*Sussex*]

I have not forgotten your disgraceful behaviour on the platform which amused our fellow passengers highly. But I cannot send back "Madame" because the sheep dog has devoured it, along with a Cheddar cheese, a shoe of mine, a pudding and a bath bun. But our woes are many, nor do I know how to enter upon my discourse, dearly beloved Toad. But imagine our situation. Thoby arrived on Wednesday evening, apparently well save for a cold. He went to bed early, woke with slight fever—we sent for Dr Branfoot who said to our horror that there was Pneumonia in the right lung! We straightaway sent for a nurse for the night, and next day Aunt Mary insisted upon another for the day. Little Branfoot was most depressing—as he always is, the Fishers say; but after giving us all a scare he said it

2. Katherine (Kitty) Maxse, *née* Lushington (1867–1922), a figure of considerable social consequence in VW's Kensington youth, had served as a model for Clarissa Dalloway.

† This and the following letters are from *The Letters of Virginia Woolf, Vol. I: 1888–1912* (*Virginia Stephen*), ed. Nigel Nicolson and Joanne Trautmann (New York and London: Harcourt Brace Jovanovich, 1977), pp. 22–23, 45–46, 173–74, 178–79, 313, 357–58. Letters copyright © 1975, 1976 by Quentin Bell and Angelica Garnett. Reprinted by permission of Houghton Mifflin Harcourt Publishing Company, Penguin Random House UK, and the Society of Authors on behalf of the Estate of Virginia Woolf. All rights reserved. Notes are by Nicolson and Trautmann unless otherwise indicated. Emma Vaughan (1874–1960) was a distant cousin of Woolf and sister of "Madge" Vaughan (1862–1929). Madge was the object of Woolf's intense affection at this time.

was a very slight case and that it would be gone in two or three days. However, Thoby is such a marvellous creature that he is already recovered, save for weakness. His temperature is normal, he is allowed solid food, and his lungs are alright. But you can conceive that this was not altogether the most cheerful way of beginning our holiday. We managed it all in the most businesslike fashion possible and they say that he could not have gone on better. But, my dear Toad, the aggravating and *damnable* (to put it briefly and forcibly) thing about it was that this need never have happened but for the "gross carelessness", to quote Dr. Branfoot, of your blessed Clifton doctor. Thoby was ill in bed with fever and with a slight tendency to pneumonia the day before he started, and yet the doctor allowed him to take the two journeys all the same—it is only a wonder that things were not much worse than they have been, and if Thoby were not as strong as a horse, he would probably have been ill for weeks. So there! We are all furious about it: Father has written very strongly to the man himself, and Aunt Mary is dreading sending Edwin back to such a hole. Really it is rather maddening. We have had a curious time since Wednesday. Miss [Caroline Emelia] Stephen is here and the divine Rosamond. Rosamond came to tea the other day with Charlie and attacked us before him, whom she had never seen before, on our religious faith! It was amusing: then the day after she came at 10.30 and took us out on to the beach and discussed a future life at great length. I think she is a match for dear Aunt Hester. Lord, what a long letter this is—and you will never be able to read it—I purposely write to you and not to Marny so that her eyes may yet survive to tackle with Miss Pater's Greek.

It is a vile wet day, with a wind fit to blow the house down. This is just the hour when you and Marny ought to be sitting at tea with us in the drawing room at home. But this time next week we shall be nearer heaven. Brighton is a very good copy of the other place—what do you think? We have really done nothing—Thoby has upset all our plans so much. Nessa and I struggle out with the sheep dog—whose name is Gurth after the sheep herd in Ivanhoe—at our heels, to buy medicine and cotton wool in Church Road. I had a vision today, Jack [Hills] is here for Sunday—we were sitting in the drawing room after lunch. Suddenly I looked up and saw Nessa sitting writing *in her trousers*!!! My feelings you may imagine—She had forgotten her safety pin—and her skirt had all come undone and this was the result. I laughed so much that I could not say what was the matter. Jack discreetly looked the other way, and Nessa went behind a screen. This is the sort of thing that I have to write to you about. There is nothing else to do.

Oh my dear Toad, how I do love London! It is the most beautiful place on the face of the earth—

The Fishers are all well tho' I have seen very little of them. How are the Andante's? We long for news. And the divinity of the Roseate Nose and Aunt Hester, and Ellen, and Towler, and Marny, and the discreet reptile herself![1] I have a vague idea that your caution is thawed when you take a pen in your hand. Surely it is very different to write secrets than to speak them. I am quite sure that this is your weak point. Please forget your character and write to me as soon as you can. Are you in touch with a curate?

Goodbye at last. I must stop

Your loving,<br>AVS Goat

## To Thoby Stephen[2]

[No true Shakespearian]

Nov 5th [1901]

My dear Grim,                        [22 *Hyde Park Gate*, S.W.]
    Father has had a letter this morning to say that the degree [Hon. D. Litt., Oxford] is put off till the 26 Nov. and he wanted you to know, as you spoke of going there. We have been asked to stay the night by two separate lots of people—but I dont know—Oxford as you can imagine would draw me from my bestial comforts if any place would, but the bestial comforts (they come into Plato this morning, and seemed rather appropriate) are growing rampant. My real object in writing is to make a confession—which is to take back a whole cartload of *goatisms* which I used at Fritham and elsewhere in speaking of a certain great English writer—the greatest: I have been reading Marlow, and I was so much more impressed by him than I thought I should be, that I read Cymbeline just to see if there mightnt be more in the great William [Shakespeare] than I supposed. And I was quite upset! Really and truly I am now let in to [the] company of worshippers—though I still feel a little oppressed by his—greatness I suppose. I shall want a lecture when I see you; to clear up some points about the Plays. I mean about the characters. Why aren't they more human? Imogen and Posthumous and Cymbeline—I find them beyond me—Is this my feminine weakness in the upper region? But really they might have been cut out with a

---

1. The 'Andantes' were the Vaughans: the 'Roseate Nose', Lotta Leaf; Aunt Hester, the younger sister of Henry Halford Vaughan; Ellen and Towler, perhaps servants; Marny, Margaret Vaughan; and 'The discreet reptile', Emma Vaughan herself.
2. Woolf's older brother (1880–1906). He and Woolf shared a love of Shakespeare, as this letter attests. His early death brought together, in mourning, many of his Cambridge friends—including Lytton Strachey and Leonard Woolf—to form what would become the Bloomsbury Group [*Editor*].

pair of scissors—as far as mere humanity goes—Of course they talk divinely. I have spotted the best lines in the play—almost in any play I should think—

Imogen says—Think that you are upon a rock, and now throw me again! and Posthumous answers—Hang there like fruit, my Soul, till the tree die [*Cymbeline*: V. v. 262–5]! Now if that doesn't send a shiver down your spine, even if you are in the middle of cold grouse and coffee—you are no true Shakespearian! Oh dear oh dear—just as I feel in the mood to talk about these things, you go and plant yourself in Cambridge.

Tomorrow I go on to Ben Jonson, but I shant like him as much as Marlow. I read Dr Faustus, and Edward II—I thought them very near the great man—with more humanity I should say—not all on such a grand tragic scale. Of course Shakespeares smaller characters are human; what I say is that superhuman ones *are* superhuman. Just explain this to me—and also why his plots are just cracky things—Marlows are flimsier; the whole thing is flimsier, but there are some very "booming" (Stracheys word[3]) lines and speeches and whole scenes—when Edward dies for instance—and then when Kent is taken away to be executed, and the little King wont have it done, and his mother tries to make him forget and asks him to ride with her in the Park, and he says "And will Uncle Edmund ride with us?" That is a human touch! What a dotard you will think me! but I thought I must just write and tell you—

I write even less connectedly and legibly than usual, because 3 or 400 years ago a wretched Italian tried to blow up the Houses of Parliament! So we English are celebrating the day at this moment—which would be all very well if the children in the muse (see how I spell it!) mews opposite didnt think it necessary to join in with horrible crackers and bonfires and shoutings and whoopings—It seems quite superfluous. Georgie came back last night; and his baggage—made up of Turkey carpets, and Rose leaf jam from the Sultans preserves—and Eastern embroideries and bags of precious stones uncut—and all kinds of extraordinary things—is bumping into the hall at this moment.

Did you go to Miss Noble [of Warboys]?

Yr. Goat

---

3. This could be her first reference to Lytton Strachey, Thoby's great friend at Trinity, whom Virginia had already met in 1901; or possibly Sir Edward Strachey, who wrote extensively on the history of literature.

# To Madge Vaughan

*[Teaching in the Waterloo Road]*

[early January 1905]

Dearest Madge,                              *46 Gordon Square, Bloomsbury*
I hope the 16th, as you say on the flyleaf of your envelope, is the likely date, and not the 13th—and couldn't you make it the 17th—and stay more than 1 night? Adrian is here till the 17th, and we have no extra room: at least we could make an extra room, but we are without a bed, and washing things: so do come on the 17th and stay longer, and then we could do something really amusing.
Our last amusement is a silver point press, which prints off delightful little reddy brown drawings, and even my works of art, which are of the most primitive description being entirely a self taught genius—dont turn out so bad.
Lets have a dinner party for you, and introduce you to some Bohemian lights, after your own heart!
You will be amused to hear that I am going to teach a class of working women in the Waterloo Road [Morley College], upon English Literature! They begged me to give a course of lectures—which I feebly declined, and said I would rather get to know them personally than instruct them—but they are much too keen to let me off—and probably have the whole thing at their fingers ends.
We have just come back from the New Forest, where we spent the loneliest of Christmasses, which was very nice, and barbaric. Thoby and Adrian hunted regularly every day, and Nessa and I wandered about among dead leaves and bogs and forest ponies, and I never once changed for dinner, which is my height of bliss.

\* \* \*

Yr. loving AVS

# To Violet Dickinson[4]

*[Dr Savage's dinner]*

[mid-February 1905]

Wretched Woman,                           *46 Gordon Square, Bloomsbury*
Leo is *delighted* to accept my *charming* article [Street Music]—so there! After your croaks and groans I thought that little job was a

---

4. For many years, Woolf's most intimate friend (1865–1948). Their friendship waned as Woolf's writing career grew [*Editor*].

failure anyhow. I think you must be too good a critic to see what will sell—that is my melancholy conclusion, and if my article had been really good, Leo wouldn't have taken it. But I want a little base popularity at this moment—I spend 5 days of precious time toiling through Henry James' subleties[5] for Mrs Lyttleton, and write a very hardworking review for her; then come orders to cut out quite half of it—*at once*, as it has to go into next weeks Guardian, and the Parsonesses, I suppose, prefer midwifery, to literature. So I gave up 10 minutes, all I had, to laying about me with a pair of scissors: literally I cut two sheets to pieces, wrote a scrawl to mend them together, and so sent the maimed thing off—with a curse. I never hope to see it again. It was quite good before the official eye fell upon it; now it is worthless, and doesn't in the least represent all the toil I put into it—and the book deserved a good, and careful review. However, to make up, the Times has sent me two trashy books, about Thackeray and Dickens and I may write 1500 words or so—Bruce Richmond[6] is generous—and this, with the Nat: give me a little cause for joy in the face of that righteous old Guardian. Really I never read such pedantic commonplace as the Guardianese: it takes up the line of a Governess, and maiden Lady, and high church Parson mixed; how they ever got such a black little goat into their fold, I cant conceive.

I spent all today reading Latin, out of pure virtue; so you needn't preach. What a bore about the Watts article! I think the Outlook and the Independent are the only possible two now—but I dont know that she wants to try elsewhere.

At [Dr] Savages[7] dinner, which was more heavy and dreary than you can conceive, every person I talked to spoke almost with tears of the greatness and beauty of Watts—and wouldn't admit the possibility of criticism, and this, I suppose, is the sample British Public. Savage lives with an odd lot of people; a daughter who is not up to his level, and strange fossils.

I suppose we shant meet till the 1st when I hope to have the pleasure of shaking your hand on the staircase.

We are going to tea with the Horners tomorrow; a long letter from Katharine, insisting on Christian names!

Yr. AVS

---

5. Virginia's review of *The Golden Bowl* appeared in *The Guardian* of 22 February 1905.
6. Editor of *The Times Literary Supplement*. Virginia's reviews of *The Thackeray Country*, by Lewis Melville, and *The Dickens Country*, by F. G. Kitton, appeared on 10 March 1905.
7. Sir George Henry Savage (1842–1921), a psychiatrist and Woolf's doctor. He was an important model for the figure of Sir William Bradshaw [*Editor*].

# To Violet Dickinson

[*The poet Keats*]

Tuesday [1 October 1907]

My Violet,                                        *29 Fitzroy Square, W.*
  God knows where you may be at this moment, and as you dont
write I see no way of beginning or going on with this letter. I cant
tell you for instance how I sat to [Francis] Dodd today—or saw
someone like Katie—only overgrown as a ripe mulberry tree—at
the concert the other night.
  I gave a lecture to 4 working men yesterday: one stutters on his
ms—and another is an Italian and reads English as though it were
mediaeval Latin—and another is my degenerate poet, who rants
and blushes, and almost seizes my hand when we happen to like the
same lines. But I dont have any notes—I can tell you the first sentence of my lecture: "The poet Keats died when he was 25: and he
wrote all his works before that." Indeed—how very interesting,
Miss Stephen.
  By the way. You are a d——d bad woman: I asked you *not* to show
my writing, and you read it to the Crums. Do send it back here at
once. Please never read, or quote or show—it puts me in a misery
only to imagine it.
  We are all driving our pens like so many ploughs: Clive is starting his reviews and articles and novels; Nessa is getting models;
Adrian analyses old ladies wills; I—as usual. To punish you, you
shant know what it is that I'm doing—and yet,—well it needs reading in the British Museum, and a special ticket.
  I am beginning to like this house; and to wish to make—a little
money and buy furniture.
  Now write, or telegraph: I will pay you 6d.

                                                Yr. AVS

# To Vanessa Bell

[*I have no wish to perish*]

Thursday [20 August 1908]

Beloved,                                  *Manorbier [Pembrokeshire]*
  Why did my letter give you the impression of such gloom, I wonder? I cant remember any plaints; but I see that you attribute it to
H[ilton] Y[oung]. I dont think that whatever he could do would
bother me much—might of course make shiver my vanity—but I

expect the real cause was that lodgings are vile, and children shriek.

I am quite happy here, in my big room with a comfortable chair, and no one ever disturbs me.

It pours, beneath a drifting mist, and I have been writing the first pages of Mlle de la Valliere, and snapping my fingers at all the storms and all the lovers (who wont love me) in the world. I always want you; but save for that, I haven't been lonely yet, and I have been away for 20 days.

You dont give me your address, and your punishment will be a severe one. 'No letters? Clive.' 'Yes, my honey jar; one from Snow, from Kitty, from Walter Lamb.' 'Oh I dont count them. No letter from my Apekin I mean?' "No; not a line." 'Oh how I hate Scotch moors.'

I have another letter from good Mary Sheep; the [Bertrand] Russells telegraphed on Monday to ask me to stay with them for four days, but as I had gone the telegram was returned. Ought I to write to Mrs Russell? I have never seen her. Sheep: ends 'The life of the senses is more within my reach than the life of the mind'. Well, it depends what she means by the senses.

I walked along the Cliff yesterday, and found myself slipping on a little ridge just at the edge of a red fissure. I did not remember that they came so near the path; I have no wish to perish. I can imagine sticking out ones arms on the way down, and feeling them tear, and finally whirling over, and cracking ones head. I think I should feel as though I saw a china vase fall from the table; a useless thing to happen—and without any reason or good in it. But numbers of people do fall over; my good landlady tells me stories. Her son in law was found dead in the road, his horses coming home before him, and no one knew how it happened. She is full of saws, and wisdom about making the best of things, and 'here we are, and we must grin and bear it'. She offered me a horn cup, made from an ancestral cow, which I had to refuse as well as I could; and then said that I was like the gentleman she had just had—a true lady.

I dont think the Cliffs are as fine as Cornish cliffs, and the land is certainly tamer, but then Manorbier is practically in the 40ties; there was a school treat on the beach yesterday, and for some reason it seemed to me exactly the kind of thing that happened in the year 1845. They drove off in a two horse waggon, with little bonnets, and side whiskers.

Well—if I am to go out, and I get bitchy if I stay in, I must tramp now, in my great boots and water proof.

Were you sorry to leave Julian? Tell me what Scotland is like.

My book for the Times about Scottish women has just come—a fat dull work, I expect. Write an immense long letter. I pine if they dont come. Kiss your hand.

B.

# To T. S. Eliot[†]

*[As for my own story]*

Good Friday [14 April 1922]

My dear Tom,                    *Monks House, Rodmell, Lewes [Sussex]*
Leonard wants me to say that he could not send you any Russian translations at once,[1] but could be certain of sending something by Aug. 15th. He has in mind some interesting Tchekhov letters, which are hitherto untranslated. Koteliansky also writes to say that there are other materials, but his account is vague: Leonard will find out what he means when he sees him. (As you know, Koteliansky is a fanatic about Russian literature, and rather inarticulate). I'm now translating the newly found chapters of the Possessed, but [J. C.] Squire [of the *London Mercury*] has these under consideration.[2]

As for my own story, I won't anyhow send you anything now. I'm trying to finish off, and send to the printer, a long story;[3] and though I mean to do this in 3 weeks most likely it will take six. If I can, I will try and write something, less than 5,000 words, by Aug. 15th: I should very much like to be edited by you, but you know how ticklish these things are. When one wants to write, one cant. Anyhow, you will not only have to fix the length—you will have to be sincere, and severe. I can never tell whether I'm good or bad; and I promise that I shall respect you all the more for tearing me up and throwing me into the wastepaper basket. When are we to see your poem [*The Waste Land*]?—and then I can have a fling at you.

Did I tell you that I have laid out £4 upon Ulysses, and spent an hour or two yesterday cutting the pages. Leonard began to read last night. I mean to, if it goes on raining. And then, you know, your critical reputation will be at stake.[4]

---

† This and the following letter are from *The Letters of Virginia Woolf, Vol. II: 1912–1922,* ed. Nigel Nicolson and Joanne Trautmann (New York and London: Harcourt Brace Jovanovich, 1976), pp. 521–22, 597–600. Letters copyright © 1975, 1976 by Quentin Bell and Angelica Garnett. Reprinted by permission of Houghton Mifflin Harcourt Publishing Company and the Society of Authors on behalf of the Estate of Virginia Woolf. All rights reserved. Notes are by Nicolson and Trautmann unless otherwise indicated.
1. In 1922 Eliot founded the *Criterion*, the literary magazine which he was to edit until it ceased publication in 1939.
2. In fact the Hogarth Press published them in October 1922. One chapter was also published in the *Criterion* of this month.
3. *Mrs Dalloway in Bond Street*, which was published in the *Dial* (July 1923).
4. Because Eliot had warmly praised *Ulysses*.

# To Gerald Brenan[5]

*[You said you were very wretched]*

Christmas Day 1922

Dear Gerald,                    *Monk's House, Rodmell, Near Lewes, Sussex*
Very stupidly I came away without your letter, though I have
been putting off writing till Christmas, hoping to have time and
some calmness. It interested me, very much, and now I can't take it
up and answer it as I had meant. But no doubt this is as well. What
one wants from a letter is not an answer. So I shall ramble on, until
the cook goes off to tea with Mrs Dedman, when I must scramble
the eggs.

First however, we certainly hope to come to you about the end of
March, or beginning of April. This depends on things that can't be
settled now; so may we leave it, and write definitely later? Apart
from talking to you, as we want to do, at leisure, fully, at night, at
dawn, about people, books, life, and so on and so on, my eyes are
entirely grey with England—nothing but England for 10 years; and
you can't imagine how much of a physical desire it becomes to feed
them on colour and crags—something violent and broken and
dry—not perpetually sloping and sloppy like the country here.
(This is a very wet Christmas day).

I have been thinking a great deal about what you say of writing
novels. One must renounce, you say. I can do better than write novels, you say. I don't altogether understand. I don't see how to write
a book without people in it. Perhaps you mean that one ought not to
attempt a 'view of life'?—one ought to limit oneself to one's own
sensations—at a quartet for instance; one ought to be lyrical,
descriptive: but not set people in motion, and attempt to enter them,
and give them impact and volume? Ah, but I'm doomed! As a matter
of fact, I think that we all are. It is not possible now, and never will
be, to say I renounce. Nor would it be a good thing for literature
were it possible. This generation must break its neck in order that
the next may have smooth going. For I agree with you that nothing
is going to be achieved by us. Fragments—paragraphs—a page perhaps: but no more. Joyce to me seems strewn with disaster. I can't
even see, as you see, his triumphs. A gallant approach, that is all
that is obvious to me: then the usual smash and splinters (I have
only read him, partly, once). The human soul, it seems to me, orien-
tates itself afresh every now and then. It is doing so now. No one
can see it whole, therefore. The best of us catch a glimpse of a nose,

5. Writer (1894–1987), friend of the Woolfs and veteran who moved to Spain after the
   War. Brenan was an important model for Septimus Smith [*Editor*].

a shoulder, something turning away, always in movement. Still, it seems better to me to catch this glimpse, than to sit down with Hugh Walpole, Wells, etc. etc. and make large oil paintings of fabulous fleshy monsters complete from top to toe. Of course, being under 30, this does not apply to you. To you, something more complete may be vouchsafed. If so, it will be partly because I, and some others, have made our attempts first. I have wandered from the point. Never mind. I am only scribbling, more to amuse myself than you, who may never read, or understand: for I am doubtful whether people, the best disposed towards each other, are capable of more than an intermittent signal as they forge past—a sentimental metaphor, leading obviously to ships, and night and storm and reefs and rocks, and the obscured, uncompassionate moon. I wish I had your letter for I could then go ahead; without so many jerks.

You said you were very wretched, didn't you? You described your liver rotting, and how you read all night, about the early fathers; and then walked, and saw the dawn. But were wretched, and tore up all you wrote, and felt you could never, never write—and compared this state of yours with mine, which you imagine to be secure, rooted, benevolent, industrious—you did not say dull—but somehow unattainable, and I daresay, unreal. But you must reflect that I am 40: further, every 10 years, at 20, again at 30, such agony of different sorts possessed me that not content with rambling and reading I did most emphatically attempt to end it all; and should have been often thankful, if by stepping on one flagstone rather than another I could have been annihilated where I stood. I say this partly in vanity that you may not think me insipid; partly as a token (one of those flying signals out of the night and so on) that so we live, all of us who feel and reflect, with recurring cataclysms of horror: starting up in the night in agony: Every ten years brings, I suppose, one of those private orientations which match the vast one which is, to my mind, general now in the race. I mean, life has to be sloughed: has to be faced: to be rejected; then accepted on new terms with rapture. And so on, and so on; till you are 40, when the only problem is how to grasp it tighter and tighter to you, so quick it seems to slip, and so infinitely desirable is it.

As for writing, at 30 I was still writing, reading; tearing up industriously. I had not published a word (save reviews). I despaired. Perhaps at that age one is really most a writer. Then one cannot write, not for lack of skill, but because the object is too near, too vast. I think perhaps it must recede before one can take a pen to it. At any rate, at 20, 30, 40, and I've no doubt 50, 60, and 70, that to me is the task; not particularly noble or heroic, as I see it in my own case, for all my inclinations are to write; but the object of adoration to me, when there comes along someone capable of achieving—if only the page or paragraph; for there are no teachers, saints, prophets, good people, but the artists—as you said—But the last sentence is hopelessly unintelligible. Indeed, I am getting to the end of my letter writing capacity. I have many more things to say; but they cower under their coverlets, and nothing remains but to stare at the fire, and finger some book till the ideas freshen within me, or they once more become impartible.

I think, too, there is a great deal of excitement and fun and pure pleasure and brilliance in one's fellow creatures. I'm not sure that you shouldn't desert your mountain, take your chance, and adventure with your human faculties—friendships, conversations, relations, the mere daily intercourse. Why do young men hold books up before their eyes so long? French literature falls like a blue tint over the landscape.

But I am not saying what I mean, and had better stop. Only you must write to me again—anything that occurs to you—And what about something for the Hogarth Press?

Leonard adds his wishes to mine for the future.

Yours<br>Virginia Woolf

P.S.

I add a postscript, which is intended to explain why I say that one must not renounce. I think I mean that beauty, which you say I sometimes achieve, is only got by the failure to get it; by grinding all the flints together; by facing what must be humiliation—the things one can't do—To aim at beauty deliberately, without this apparently insensate struggle, would result, I think, in little daisies and forget-me-nots—simpering sweetnesses—true love knots—But I agree that one must (we, in our generation must) renounce finally the achievement of the greater beauty: the beauty which comes from completeness, in such books as War and Peace, and Stendhal I suppose, and some of Jane Austen; and Sterne; and I rather suspect in Proust, of whom I have only read one volume. Only now that I have written this, I doubt its truth. Are we not always hoping? and though we fail every time, surely we do not fail so completely as we should have failed if we were not in the beginning, prepared to attack the whole. One must renounce, when the book is finished; but not before it is begun. Excuse me for boring on: you may have said nothing of the kind. I was wondering to myself why it is that though I try sometimes to limit myself to the thing I do well, I am always drawn on and on, by human beings, I think, out of the little circle of safety, on and on, to the whirlpools; when I go under.

# To V. Sackville-West[†]

*[London and the marshes]*

19th August [1924]

My dear Vita,[1]                    *Monk's House, Rodmell, Lewes, Sussex*
Have you come back, and have you finished your book [*Seducers in Ecuador*]—when will you let us have it? Here I am, being a nuisance, with all these questions.

I enjoyed your intimate letter from the Dolomites. It gave me a great deal of pain—which is I've no doubt the first stage of intimacy—no friends, no heart, only an indifferent head. Never mind: I enjoyed your abuse very much.

How could I think mountains and climbing romantic? Wasn't I brought up with alpenstocks in my nursery, and a raised map of the Alps, showing every peak my father had climbed? Of course, London and the marshes are the places I like best.

But I will not go on else I should write you a really intimate letter, and then you would dislike me, more, even more, than you do.

But please let me know about the book.

                                        Yr V.W.

---

† Transcribed by the editor for this Norton Critical Edition from the William Beekman Collection of Virginia Woolf and Her Circle, The Henry W. and Albert A. Berg Collection of English and American Literature, The New York Public Library, Astor, Lenox and Tilden Foundations. Reprinted by permission of The Society of Authors on behalf of the Estate of Virginia Woolf.
1. Vita Sackville-West (1892–1962), writer and gardener. Woolf's friendship with Sackville-West was growing more intimate during the composition of *Mrs. Dalloway*. It blossomed into a brief love affair a few years later. They remained close friends for the rest of Woolf's life [*Editor*].

# Selected Short Stories

## Mrs Dalloway in Bond Street[†]

Mrs Dalloway said she would buy the gloves herself.

Big Ben was striking as she stepped out into the street. It was eleven o'clock and the unused hour was fresh as if issued to children on a beach. But there was something solemn in the deliberate swing of the repeated strokes; something stirring in the murmur of wheels and the shuffle of footsteps.

No doubt they were not all bound on errands of happiness. There is much more to be said about us than that we walk the streets of Westminster. Big Ben too is nothing but steel rods consumed by rust were it not for the care of H. M.'s Office of Works. Only for Mrs Dalloway the moment was complete; for Mrs Dalloway June was fresh. A happy childhood—and it was not to his daughters only that Justin Parry had seemed a fine fellow (weak of course on the Bench); flowers at evening, smoke rising; the caw of rooks falling from ever so high, down down through the October air—there is nothing to take the place of childhood. A leaf of mint brings it back; or a cup with a blue ring.

Poor little wretches, she sighed, and pressed forward. Oh, right under the horses' noses, you little demon! and there she was left on the kerb stretching her hand out, while Jimmy Dawes grinned on the further side.

A charming woman, poised, eager, strangely white-haired for her pink cheeks, so Scope Purvis, C. B., saw her as he hurried to his office. She stiffened a little, waiting for Durtnall's van to pass. Big Ben struck the tenth; struck the eleventh stroke. The leaden circles dissolved in the air. Pride held her erect, inheriting, handing on, acquainted with discipline and with suffering. How people suffered, how they suffered, she thought, thinking of Mrs Foxcroft at the Embassy last night decked with jewels, eating her heart out, because that nice boy was dead, and now the old Manor House (Durtnall's van passed) must go to a cousin.

† From *The Dial* 75 (July 1923): 20–27. This story predates the novel. Notes are by the editor of this Norton Critical Edition.

"Good morning to you!" said Hugh Whitbread raising his hat rather extravagantly by the china shop, for they had known each other as children. "Where are you off to?"

"I love walking in London" said Mrs Dalloway. "Really it's better than walking in the country!"

"We've just come up" said Hugh Whitbread. "Unfortunately to see doctors."

"Milly?" said Mrs Dalloway, instantly compassionate.

"Out of sorts," said Hugh Whitbread. "That sort of thing. Dick all right?"

"First rate!" said Clarissa.

Of course, she thought, walking on, Milly is about my age—fifty—fifty-two. So it is probably *that*,[1] Hugh's manner had said so, said it perfectly—dear old Hugh, thought Mrs Dalloway, remembering with amusement, with gratitude, with emotion, how shy, like a brother—one would rather die than speak to one's brother—Hugh had always been, when he was at Oxford, and came over, and perhaps one of them (drat the thing!) couldn't ride. How then could women sit in Parliament? How could they do things with men? For there is this extraordinarily deep instinct, something inside one; you can't get over it; it's no use trying; and men like Hugh respect it without our saying it, which is what one loves, thought Clarissa, in dear old Hugh.

She had passed through the Admiralty Arch and saw at the end of the empty road with its thin trees Victoria's white mound, Victoria's billowing motherliness, amplitude and homeliness, always ridiculous, yet how sublime, thought Mrs Dalloway, remembering Kensington Gardens and the old lady in horn spectacles and being told by Nanny to stop dead still and bow to the Queen. The flag flew above the Palace. The King and Queen were back then. Dick[2] had met her at lunch the other day—a thoroughly nice woman. It matters so much to the poor, thought Clarissa, and to the soldiers. A man in bronze stood heroically on a pedestal with a gun on her left hand side—the South African war.[3] It matters, thought Mrs Dalloway walking towards Buckingham Palace. There it stood four-square, in the broad sunshine, uncompromising, plain. But it was character she thought; something inborn in the race; what Indians respected. The Queen went to hospitals, opened bazaars—the Queen of England, thought Clarissa, looking at the Palace. Already at this hour a motor car passed out at the gates; soldiers saluted; the

1. Likely meaning menopause. The subsequent reference to being unable to ride seems to refer to old taboos against exercise during menstruation.
2. A common nickname for "Richard," and thus a reference to Clarissa's husband, Richard Dalloway. He is not ever called "Dick" in the novel.
3. A brutal military conflict (1899–1902) between England and two Boer states, Dutch-speaking colonies in the east of what is now South Africa.

gates were shut. And Clarissa, crossing the road, entered the Park, holding herself upright.

June had drawn out every leaf on the trees. The mothers of Westminster with mottled breasts gave suck to their young. Quite respectable girls lay stretched on the grass. An elderly man, stooping very stiffly, picked up a crumpled paper, spread it out flat and flung it away. How horrible! Last night at the Embassy Sir Dighton had said "If I want a fellow to hold my horse, I have only to put up my hand." But the religious question is far more serious than the economic, Sir Dighton had said, which she thought extraordinarily interesting, from a man like Sir Dighton. "Oh, the country will never know what it has lost" he had said, talking, of his own accord, about dear Jack Stewart.

She mounted the little hill lightly. The air stirred with energy. Messages were passing from the Fleet to the Admiralty. Piccadilly and Arlington Street and the Mall seemed to chafe the very air in the Park and lift its leaves hotly, brilliantly, upon waves of that divine vitality which Clarissa loved. To ride; to dance; she had adored all that. Or going long walks in the country, talking, about books, what to do with one's life, for young people were amazingly priggish—oh, the things one had said! But one had conviction. Middle age is the devil. People like Jack'll never know that, she thought; for he never once thought of death, never, they said, knew he was dying. And now can never mourn—how did it go?—a head grown grey. . . . From the contagion of the world's slow stain . . . have drunk their cup a round or two before. . . . From the contagion of the world's slow stain! She held herself upright.

But how Jack would have shouted! Quoting Shelley,[4] in Piccadilly! "You want a pin," he would have said. He hated frumps. "My God Clarissa! My God Clarissa!"—she could hear him now at the Devonshire House party, about poor Sylvia Hunt in her amber necklace and that dowdy old silk. Clarissa held herself upright for she had spoken aloud and now she was in Piccadilly, passing the house with the slender green columns, and the balconies; passing club windows full of newspapers; passing old Lady Burdett Coutts' house where the glazed white parrot used to hang; and Devonshire House, without its gilt leopards; and Claridge's, where she must remember Dick wanted her to leave a card on Mrs Jepson or she would be gone. Rich Americans can be very charming. There was St James palace; like a child's game with bricks; and now—she had passed Bond Street—she was by Hatchard's book shop. The stream was endless—endless—endless. Lords, Ascot, Hurlingham—what was it?

---

4. Percy Bysshe Shelley (1792–1822), English Romantic poet. Clarissa quotes "Adonais: An Elegy on the Death of John Keats."

What a duck, she thought, looking at the frontispiece of some book of memoirs spread wide in the bow window, Sir Joshua perhaps or Romney; arch, bright, demure; the sort of girl—like her own Elizabeth—the only *real* sort of girl. And there was that absurd book, Soapy Sponge, which Jim used to quote by the yard; and Shakespeare's Sonnets. She knew them by heart. Phil and she had argued all day about the Dark Lady, and Dick had said straight out at dinner that night that he had never heard of her. Really, she had married him for that! He had never read Shakespeare! There must be some little cheap book she could buy for Milly—Cranford[5] of course! Was there ever anything so enchanting as the cow in petticoats? If only people had that sort of humour, that sort of self-respect now, thought Clarissa, for she remembered the broad pages; the sentences ending; the characters—how one talked about them as if they were real. For all the great things one must go to the past, she thought. From the contagion of the world's slow stain. . . . Fear no more the heat o' the sun. . . . And now can never mourn, can never mourn, she repeated, her eyes straying over the window; for it ran in her head; the test of great poetry; the moderns had never written anything one wanted to read about death, she thought; and turned.

Omnibuses joined motor cars; motor cars vans; vans taxicabs; taxicabs motor cars—here was an open motor car with a girl, alone. Up till four, her feet tingling, I know, thought Clarissa, for the girl looked washed out, half asleep, in the corner of the car after the dance. And another car came; and another. No! No! No! Clarissa smiled good-naturedly. The fat lady had taken every sort of trouble, but diamonds! orchids! at this hour of the morning! No! No! No! The excellent policeman would, when the time came, hold up his hand. Another motor car passed. How utterly unattractive! Why should a girl of that age paint black round her eyes? And a young man, with a girl, at this hour, when the country—The admirable policeman raised his hand and Clarissa acknowledging his sway, taking her time, crossed, walked towards Bond Street; saw the narrow crooked street, the yellow banners; the thick notched telegraph wires stretched across the sky.

A hundred years ago her great-great-grandfather, Seymour Parry, who ran away with Conway's daughter, had walked down Bond Street. Down Bond Street the Parrys had walked for a hundred years, and might have met the Dalloways (Leighs on the mother's side) going up. Her father got his clothes from Hill's. There was a roll of cloth in the window, and here just one jar on a black table, incredibly expensive; like the thick pink salmon on the ice block at the fishmonger's. The jewels were exquisite—pink and orange stars,

5. Novel (1853) by Elizabeth Gaskell.

paste, Spanish, she thought, and chains of old gold; starry buckles, little brooches which had been worn on sea green satin by ladies with high head-dresses. But no good looking! One must economize. She must go on past the picture dealer's where one of the odd French pictures hung, as if people had thrown confetti—pink and blue—for a joke. If you had lived with pictures (and it's the same with books and music) thought Clarissa, passing the Aeolian Hall, you can't be taken in by a joke.

The river of Bond Street was clogged. There, like a Queen at a tournament, raised, regal, was Lady Bexborough. She sat in her carriage, upright, alone, looking through her glasses. The white glove was loose at her wrist. She was in black, quite shabby, yet, thought Clarissa, how extraordinarily it tells, breeding, self-respect, never saying a word too much or letting people gossip; an astonishing friend; no one can pick a hole in her after all these years, and now, there she is, thought Clarissa, passing the Countess who waited powdered, perfectly still, and Clarissa would have given anything to be like that, the mistress of Clarefield, talking politics, like a man. But she never goes anywhere, thought Clarissa, and it's quite useless to ask her, and the carriage went on and Lady Bexborough was borne past like a Queen at a tournament, though she had nothing to live for and the old man is failing and they say she is sick of it all, thought Clarissa and the tears actually rose to her eyes as she entered the shop.

"Good morning" said Clarissa in her charming voice. "Gloves" she said with her exquisite friendliness and putting her bag on the counter began, very slowly, to undo the buttons. "White gloves" she said. "Above the elbow" and she looked straight into the shopwoman's face—but this was not the girl she remembered? She looked quite old. "These really don't fit" said Clarissa. The shop-girl looked at them. "Madame wears bracelets?" Clarissa spread out her fingers. "Perhaps it's my rings." And the girl took the grey gloves with her to the end of the counter.

Yes, thought Clarissa, if it's the girl I remember she's twenty years older. . . . There was only one other customer, sitting sideways at the counter, her elbow poised, her bare hand drooping, vacant; like a figure on a Japanese fan, thought Clarissa, too vacant perhaps, yet some men would adore her. The lady shook her head sadly. Again the gloves were too large. She turned round the glass. "Above the wrist" she reproached the grey-headed woman; who looked and agreed.

They waited; a clock ticked; Bond Street hummed, dulled, distant; the woman went away holding gloves. "Above the wrist" said the lady, mournfully, raising her voice. And she would have to order chairs, ices, flowers, and cloak-room tickets, thought Clarissa. The people she didn't want would come; the others wouldn't. She would stand by the door. They sold stockings—silk stockings. A lady is known by her gloves and her shoes, old Uncle William used to say. And through the hanging silk stockings quivering silver she looked at the lady, sloping shouldered, her hand drooping, her bag slipping, her eyes vacantly on the floor. It would be intolerable if dowdy women came to her party! Would one have liked Keats if he had worn red socks? Oh, at last—she drew into the counter and it flashed into her mind:

"Do you remember before the war you had gloves with pearl buttons?"

"French gloves, Madame?"

"Yes, they were French" said Clarissa. The other lady rose very sadly and took her bag, and looked at the gloves on the counter. But they were all too large—always too large at the wrist.

"With pearl buttons" said the shop-girl, who looked ever so much older. She split the lengths of tissue paper apart on the counter. With pearl buttons, thought Clarissa, perfectly simple—how French!

"Madame's hands are so slender" said the shop-girl, drawing the glove firmly, smoothly, down over her rings. And Clarissa looked at her arm in the looking glass. The glove hardly came to the elbow. Were there others half an inch longer? Still it seemed tiresome to bother her—perhaps the one day in the month, thought Clarissa, when it's an agony to stand. "Oh, don't bother" she said. But the gloves were brought.

"Don't you get fearfully tired" she said in her charming voice, "standing? When d'you get your holiday?"

"In September, Madame, when we're not so busy."

When we're in the country thought Clarissa. Or shooting. She has a fortnight at Brighton. In some stuffy lodging. The landlady takes the sugar. Nothing would be easier than to send her to Mrs Lumley's right in the country (and it was on the tip of her tongue). But then she remembered how on their honeymoon Dick had shown her the folly of giving impulsively. It was much more important, he said, to get trade with China. Of course he was right. And she could feel the girl wouldn't like to be given things. There she was in her place. So was Dick. Selling gloves was her job. She had her own sorrows quite separate, "and now can never mourn, can never mourn" the words ran in her head, "From the contagion of the world's slow stain" thought Clarissa holding her arm stiff, for there are moments when it seems utterly futile (the glove was drawn off leaving her arm flecked with powder)—simply one doesn't believe, thought Clarissa, any more in God.

The traffic suddenly roared; the silk stockings brightened. A customer came in.

"White gloves," she said, with some ring in her voice that Clarissa remembered.

It used, thought Clarissa, to be so simple. Down down through the air came the caw of the rooks. When Sylvia died, hundreds of years ago, the yew hedges looked so lovely with the diamond webs in the mist before early church. But if Dick were to die to-morrow as for believing in God—no, she would let the children choose, but for herself, like Lady Bexborough, who opened the bazaar, they say, with the telegram in her hand—Roden, her favourite, killed—she would go on. But why, if one doesn't believe? For the sake of others, she thought, taking the glove in her hand. This girl would be much more unhappy if she didn't believe.

"Thirty shillings" said the shopwoman. "No, pardon me Madame, thirty-five. The French gloves are more."

For one doesn't live for oneself, thought Clarissa.

And then the other customer took a glove, tugged it, and it split.

"There!" she exclaimed.

"A fault of the skin," said the grey-headed woman hurriedly. "Sometimes a drop of acid in tanning. Try this pair, Madame."

"But it's an awful swindle to ask two pound ten!"

Clarissa looked at the lady; the lady looked at Clarissa.

"Gloves have never been quite so reliable since the war" said the shop-girl, apologizing, to Clarissa.

But where had she seen the other lady?—elderly, with a frill under her chin; wearing a black ribbon for gold eyeglasses; sensual, clever, like a Sargent drawing. How one can tell from a voice when people are in the habit, thought Clarissa, of making other people—"It's a shade too tight" she said—obey. The shopwoman went off again. Clarissa was left waiting. Fear no more she repeated, playing her finger on the counter. Fear no more the heat o' the sun. Fear no more she repeated. There were little brown spots on her arm. And the girl crawled like a snail. Thou thy wordly task hast done. Thousands of young men had died that things might go on. At last! Half an inch above the elbow; pearl buttons; five and a quarter. My dear slow coach, thought Clarissa, do you think I can sit here the whole morning? Now you'll take twenty-five minutes to bring me my change!

There was a violent explosion in the street outside. The shop-women cowered behind the counters. But Clarissa, sitting very upright, smiled at the other lady. "Miss Anstruther!" she exclaimed.

# The Introduction[†]

Lily Everit saw Mrs Dalloway bearing down on her from the other side of the room, and could have prayed her not to come and disturb her; and yet, as Mrs Dalloway approached with her right hand raised and a smile which Lily knew (though this was her first party) meant: 'But you've got to come out of your corner and talk,' a smile at once benevolent and drastic, commanding, she felt the strangest mixture of excitement and fear, of desire to be left alone and of longing to be taken out and thrown down, down into the boiling depths. But Mrs Dalloway was intercepted; caught by an old gentleman with white moustaches, and thus Lily Everit had two minutes respite in which to hug to herself, like a spar in the sea, to sip, like a glass of wine, the thought of her essay upon the character of Dean Swift[1] which Professor Miller had marked that morning with three red stars; First rate. First rate; she repeated that to herself, but the cordial was ever so much weaker now than it had been when she stood before the long glass being finished off (a pat here, a dab there) by her sister and Mildred, the housemaid. For as their hands moved about her, she felt that they were fidgeting agreeably on the surface but beneath lay untouched like a lump of glowing metal her essay on the character of Dean Swift, and all their praises when she came downstairs and stood in the hall waiting for a cab— Rupert had come out of his room and said what a swell she looked— ruffled the surface, went like a breeze among ribbons, but no more. One divided life (she felt sure of it) into fact, this essay, and into fiction, this going out, into rock and into wave, she thought, driving along and seeing things with such intensity that for ever she would see the truth and herself, a white reflection in the driver's dark back inextricably mixed: the moment of vision. Then as she came into the house, at the very first sight of people moving up stairs, down stairs, this hard lump (her essay on the character of Swift) wobbled, began melting, she could not keep hold of it, and all her being (no longer sharp as a diamond cleaving the heart of life asunder) turned to a mist of alarm, apprehension, and defence as she stood at bay in her corner. This was the famous place: the world.

Looking out, Lily Everit instinctively hid that essay of hers, so ashamed was she now, so bewildered too, and on tiptoe nevertheless

† From *The Complete Shorter Fiction of Virginia Woolf*, Second Edition, ed. Susan Dick (San Diego: Harcourt Brace Jovanovich, 1989), pp. 184–88. Copyright © 1985, 1989 by Quentin Bell and Angelica Garnett. Reprinted by permission of Houghton Mifflin Harcourt Publishing Company and the Society of Authors on behalf of the Estate of Virginia Woolf. All rights reserved. Woolf wrote this short story in 1925, after the completion of *Mrs. Dalloway*, but it was unpublished in her lifetime.
1. Novelist and satirist Jonathan Swift (1667–1745), author of *Gulliver's Travels*, was dean of St. Patrick's Cathedral Dublin, and thus sometimes referred to by the title Dean Swift [*Editor*].

to adjust her focus and get into right proportions (the old having
been shamefully wrong) these diminishing and expanding things
(what could one call them? people—impressions of people's lives?)
which seemed to menace her and mount over her, to turn everything to water, leaving her only—for that she would not resign—
the power to stand at bay.

Now Mrs Dalloway, who had never quite dropped her arm, had
shown by the way she moved it while she stood talking that she
remembered, was only interrupted by the old soldier with the white
moustaches, raised it again definitely and came straight down on
her, and said to the shy charming girl, with her pale skin, her bright
eyes, the dark hair which clustered poetically round her head and
the thin body in a dress which seemed slipping off,

'Come and let me introduce you,' and there Mrs Dalloway hesitated, and then remembering that Lily was the clever one, who read
poetry, looked about for some young man, some young man just
down from Oxford, who would have read everything and could talk
about Shelley. And holding Lily Everit's hand [she] led her towards
a group where there were young people talking, and Bob Brinsley.

Lily Everit hung back a little, might have been the wayward sailing boat curtseying in the wake of a steamer, and felt as Mrs Dalloway led her on, that it was now going to happen; that nothing
could prevent it now; or save her (and she only wanted it to be over
now) from being flung into a whirlpool where either she would perish or be saved. But what was the whirlpool?

Oh it was made of a million things and each was distinct to her;
Westminster Abbey; the sense of enormously high solemn buildings surrounding them; being a woman. Perhaps that was the thing
that came out, that remained, it was partly the dress, but all the
little chivalries and respects of the drawing-room—all made her
feel that she had come out of her chrysalis and was being pro-
claimed what in the comfortable darkness of childhood she had
never been—this frail and beautiful creature, before whom men
bowed, this limited and circumscribed creature who could not do
what she liked, this butterfly with a thousand facets to its eyes and
delicate fine plumage, and difficulties and sensibilities and sad-
nesses innumerable; a woman.

As she walked with Mrs Dalloway across the room she accepted
the part which was now laid on her and, naturally, overdid it a little
as a soldier, proud of the traditions of an old and famous uniform
might overdo it, feeling conscious as she walked, of her finery; of her
tight shoes; of her coiled and twisted hair; and how if she dropped a
handkerchief (this had happened) a man would stoop precipitately
and give it her; thus accentuating the delicacy, the artificiality of her
bearing unnaturally, for they were not hers after all.

Hers it was, rather, to run and hurry and ponder on long solitary walks, climbing gates, stepping through the mud, and through the blur, the dream, the ecstasy of loneliness, to see the plover's wheel and surprise the rabbits, and come in the hearts of woods or wide lonely moors upon little ceremonies which had no audience, private rites, pure beauty offered by beetles and lilies of the valley and dead leaves and still pools, without any care whatever what human beings thought of them, which filled her mind with rapture and wonder and held her there till she must touch the gate post to recollect herself—all this was, until tonight her ordinary being, by which she knew and liked herself and crept into the heart of mother and father and brothers and sisters; and this other was a flower which had opened in ten minutes. As the flower opened so too [came], incontrovertibly, the flower's world, so different, so strange; the towers of Westminster; the high and formal buildings; talk; this civilisation, she felt, hanging back, as Mrs Dalloway led her on, this regulated way of life, which fell like a yoke about her neck, softly, indomitably, from the skies, a statement which there was no gainsaying. Glancing at her essay, the three red stars dulled to obscurity, but peacefully, pensively, as if yielding to the pressure of unquestionable might, that is the conviction that it was not hers to dominate, or to assert; rather to air and embellish this orderly life where all was done already; high towers, solemn bells, flats built every brick of them by men's toil, churches built by men's toil, parliaments too; and even the criss-cross of telegraph wires she thought looking at the window as she walked. What had she to oppose to this massive masculine achievement? An essay on the character of Dean Swift! And as she came up to the group, which Bob Brinsley dominated, (with his heel on the fender, and his head back), with his great honest forehead, and his self-assurance, and his delicacy, and honour and robust physical well being, and sunburn, and airiness and direct descent from Shakespeare, what could she do but lay her essay, oh and the whole of her being, on the floor as a cloak for him to trample on, as a rose for him to rifle. Which she did, emphatically, when Mrs Dalloway said, still holding her hand as if she would run away from this supreme trial, this introduction, 'Mr Brinsley—Miss Everit. Both of you love Shelley.' But hers was not love compared with his.

Saying this, Mrs Dalloway felt, as she always felt remembering her youth, absurdly moved; youth meeting youth at her hands, and there flashing, as at the concussion of steel upon flint (both stiffened to her feeling perceptibly) the loveliest and most ancient of all fires as she saw in Bob Brinsley's change of expression from carelessness to conformity, to formality, as he shook hands, which foreboded Clarissa thought, the tenderness, the goodness, the

carefulness of women latent in all men, to her a sight to bring tears
to the eyes, as it moved her even more intimately, to see in Lily herself the shy look, the startled look, surely the loveliest of all looks
on a girl's face; and man feeling this for woman, and woman that
for man, and there flowing from that contact all those homes,
trials, sorrows, profound joy and ultimate staunchness in the face
of catastrophe, humanity was sweet at its heart, thought Clarissa,
and her own life (to introduce a couple made her think of meeting
Richard for the first time!) infinitely blessed. And on she went.

But, thought Lily Everit. But—but—but what?

Oh nothing, she thought hastily smothering down softly her
sharp instinct. Yes, she said. She did like reading.

'And I suppose you write?' he said, 'poems presumably?'

'Essays,' she said. And she would not let this horror get possession of her. Churches and parliaments, flats, even the telegraph
wires—all, she told herself, made by men's toil, and this young
man, she told herself, is in direct descent from Shakespeare, so she
would not let this terror, this suspicion of something different, get
hold of her and shrivel up her wings and drive her out into loneliness. But as she said this, she saw him—how else could she describe
it—kill a fly. He tore the wings off a fly, standing with his foot on
the fender his head thrown back, talking insolently about himself,
arrogantly, but she didn't mind how insolent and arrogant he was to
her, if only he had not been brutal to flies.

But she said, fidgeting as she smothered down that idea, why not,
since he is the greatest of all worldly objects? And to worship, to
adorn, to embellish was her task, and to be worshipped, her wings
were for that. But he talked; but he looked; but he laughed; he tore
the wings off a fly. He pulled the wings off its back with his clever
strong hands, and she saw him do it; and she could not hide the
knowledge from herself. But it is necessary that it should be so, she
argued, thinking of the churches, of the parliaments and the blocks
of flats, and so tried to crouch and cower and fold the wings down
flat on her back. But—but, what was it why was it? In spite of all
she could do her essay upon the character of Swift became more
and more obtrusive and the three stars burnt quite bright again,
only no longer clear and brilliant, but troubled and bloodstained as
if this man, this great Mr Brinsley, had just by pulling the wings off
a fly as he talked (about his essay, about himself and once laughing,
about a girl there) charged her light being with cloud, and confused
her for ever and ever and shrivelled her wings on her back, and, as
he turned away from her, he made her think of the towers and civilisation with horror, and the yoke that had fallen from the skies onto
her neck crushed her, and she felt like a naked wretch who having
sought shelter in some shady garden is turned out and told—no,

that there are no sanctuaries, or butterflies, in this world, and this civilisation, churches, parliaments and flats—this civilisation, said Lily Everit to herself, as she accepted the kind compliments of old Mrs Bromley on her appearance[, depends upon me,] and Mrs Bromley said later that like all the Everits Lily looked 'as if she had the weight of the world upon her shoulders'.

# The Man Who Loved His Kind[†]

Trotting through Deans Yard that afternoon, Prickett Ellis ran straight into Richard Dalloway, or rather, just as they were passing the covert side glance which each was casting on the other, under his hat, over his shoulder, broadened and burst into recognition; they had not met for twenty years. They had been at school together. And what was Ellis doing? The Bar?[1] Of course, of course—he had followed the case in the papers. But it was impossible to talk here. Wouldn't he drop in that evening. (They lived in the same old place—just round the corner.) One or two people were coming. Joynson perhaps. 'An awful swell now,' said Richard.

'Good—till this evening then,' said Richard, and went his way, 'jolly glad' (that was quite true) to have met that queer chap, who hadn't changed one bit since he had been at school—just the same knobbly, chubby little boy then, with prejudices sticking out all over him, but uncommonly brilliant—won the Newcastle. Well—off he went.

Prickett Ellis, however, as he turned and looked at Dalloway disappearing, wished now he had not met him or, at least, for he had always liked him personally, hadn't promised to come to this party. Dalloway was married, gave parties; wasn't his sort at all. He would have to dress. However, as the evening drew on, he supposed, as he had said that, and didn't want to be rude, he must go there.

But what an appalling entertainment! There was Joynson; they had nothing to say to each other. He had been a pompous little boy; he had grown rather more self-important—that was all; there wasn't a single other soul in the room that Prickett Ellis knew. Not one. So, as he could not go at once, without saying a word to Dalloway, who seemed altogether taken up with his duties, bustling about in a white waistcoat, there he had to stand. It was

† From *The Complete Shorter Fiction of Virginia Woolf*, Second Edition, ed. Susan Dick (San Diego: Harcourt Brace Jovanovich, 1989), pp. 195–200. Copyright © 1985, 1989 by Quentin Bell and Angelica Garnett. Reprinted by permission of Houghton Mifflin Harcourt Publishing Company and the Society of Authors on behalf of the Estate of Virginia Woolf. All rights reserved. Written in 1925, after the completion of *Mrs. Dalloway* and unpublished in Woolf's lifetime, this was first published in *A Haunted House and Other Short Stories* (1944), a collection assembled by Woolf's widower, Leonard.
1. That is, practicing law [*Editor*].

the sort of thing that made his gorge rise. Think of grown up, responsible men and women doing this every night of their lives! The lines deepened on his blue and red shaven cheeks, as he leant against the wall, in complete silence; for though he worked like a horse, he kept himself fit by exercise; and he looked hard and fierce, as if his moustaches were dipped in frost. He bristled; he grated. His meagre dress clothes made him look unkempt, insignificant, angular.

Idle, chattering, overdressed, without an idea in their heads, these fine ladies and gentlemen went on talking and laughing; and Prickett Ellis watched them and compared them with the Brunners who, when they won their case against Fenners' Brewery and got two hundred pounds compensation (it was not half what they should have got) went and spent five of it on a clock for him. That was a decent sort of thing to do; that was the sort of thing that moved one, and he glared more severely than ever at these people, overdressed, cynical, prosperous, and compared what he felt now with what he felt at eleven o'clock that morning when old Brunner and Mrs Brunner in their best clothes, awfully respectable and clean looking old people, had called in to give him that small token, as the old man put it, standing perfectly upright to make his speech of gratitude and respect for the very able way in which you conducted our case, and Mrs Brunner piped up, how it was all due to him they felt. And they deeply appreciated his generosity—because of course he hadn't taken a fee.

And as he took the clock and put it on the middle of his mantelpiece, he had felt that he wished nobody to see his face. That was what he worked for—that was his reward; and he looked at the people who were actually before his eyes as if they danced over that scene in his chambers and were exposed by it, and as it faded—the Brunners faded—there remained as if left of that scene, himself, confronting this hostile population, a perfectly plain unsophisticated man, a man of the people (he straightened himself), very badly dressed, glaring, with not an air or a grace about him, a man who was an ill hand at concealing his feelings, a plain man, an ordinary human being, pitted against the evil, the corruption, the heartlessness of society. But he would not go on staring. Now he put on his spectacles and examined the pictures. He read the titles on a line of books; for the most part poetry. He would have liked well enough to read some of his old favourites again—Shakespeare, Dickens—he wished he ever had time to turn into the National Gallery, but he couldn't—no, one could not. Really one could not—with the world in the state it was in. Not when people all day long wanted your help, fairly clamoured for help. This wasn't an age for luxuries. And he looked at the arm chairs and the paper knives and the well bound books, and shook his head, knowing that he would never have the time, never he was glad to think have the heart, to afford himself such luxuries. The people here would be shocked if they knew what he paid for his tobacco; how he had borrowed his clothes. His one and only extravagance was his little yacht on the Norfolk Broads. And that he did allow himself. He did like once a year to get right away from everybody and lie on his back in a field. He thought how shocked they would be—these fine folk—if they realised the amount of pleasure he got from what he was old fashioned enough to call a love of nature; trees and fields he had known ever since he was a boy.

These fine people would be shocked. Indeed, standing there, putting his spectacles away in his pocket, he felt himself grow more and more shocking every instant. And it was a very disagreeable feeling. He did not feel this—that he loved humanity, that he paid only five pence an ounce for tobacco and loved nature—naturally and quietly. Each of these pleasures had been turned into a protest. He felt that these people whom he despised made him stand and deliver and justify himself. 'I am an ordinary man,' he kept saying. And what he said next he was really ashamed of saying, but he said it. 'I have done more for my kind in one day than the rest of you in all your lives.' Indeed, he could not help himself; he kept recalling scene after scene, like that when the Brunners gave him the clock— he kept reminding himself of the nice things people had said of his humanity, of his generosity, how he had helped them. He kept seeing himself as the wise and tolerant servant of humanity. And he wished he could repeat his praises aloud. It was unpleasant that the sense of his goodness should boil within him. It was still more unpleasant that he could tell no one what people had said about him. Thank the Lord, he kept saying, I shall be back at work tomorrow; and yet he was no longer satisfied simply to slip through the door and go home. He must stay, he must stay until he had justified himself. But how could he? In all that room full of people, he did not know a soul to speak to.

At last Richard Dalloway came up.

'I want to introduce Miss O'Keefe,' he said. Miss O'Keefe looked him full in the eyes. She was a rather arrogant, abrupt mannered woman in the thirties.

Miss O'Keefe wanted an ice or something to drink. And the reason why she asked Prickett Ellis to give it her in what he felt a haughty, unjustifiable manner, was that she had seen a woman and two children, very poor, very tired, pressing against the railings of a square, peering in, that hot afternoon. Can't they be let in? she had thought, her pity rising like a wave; her indignation boiling. No; she rebuked herself the next moment, roughly, as if she boxed her own ears. The whole force of the world can't do it. So she picked up the tennis ball and hurled it back. The whole force of the world can't do it, she said in a fury, and that was why she said so commandingly, to the unknown man:

'Give me an ice.'

Long before she had eaten it, Prickett Ellis, standing beside her without taking anything, told her that he had not been to a party for fifteen years; told her that his dress suit was lent him by his brother-in-law; told her that he did not like this sort of thing, and it would have eased him greatly to go on to say that he was a plain man, who happened to have a liking for ordinary people, and then would have told her (and been ashamed of it afterwards) about the Brunners and the clock, but she said:

'Have you seen the *Tempest*?'

Then, (for he had not seen the *Tempest*) had he read some book? Again no, and then, putting her ice down, did he ever read poetry?

And Prickett Ellis feeling something rise within him which would decapitate this young woman, make a victim of her, massacre her, made her sit down there, where they would not be interrupted, on two chairs, in the empty garden, for everyone was upstairs, only you could hear a buzz and a hum and a chatter and a jingle, like the mad accompaniment of some phantom orchestra to a cat or two slinking across the grass, and the wavering of leaves, and the yellow and red fruit like Chinese lanterns wobbling this way and that—the talk seemed like a frantic skeleton dance music set to something very real, and full of suffering.

'How beautiful!' said Miss O'Keefe.

Oh, it was beautiful, this little patch of grass, with the towers of Westminster massed round it black high in the air, after the drawing-room; it was silent, after that noise. After all, they had that—the tired woman, the children.

Prickett Ellis lit a pipe. That would shock her; he filled it with shag tobacco—five pence halfpenny an ounce. He thought how he would lie in his boat smoking, he could see himself, alone, at night, smoking under the stars. For always tonight he kept thinking how he would look if these people here were to see him. He said to Miss O'Keefe, striking a match on the sole of his boot, that he couldn't see anything particularly beautiful out here.

'Perhaps,' said Miss O'Keefe, 'you don't care for beauty.' (He had told her that he had not seen the *Tempest*; that he had not read a book; he looked ill kempt, all moustache, chin, and silver watch chain.) She thought nobody need pay a penny for this; the Museums are free and the National Gallery; and the country. Of course she knew the objections—the washing, cooking, children; but the root of things, what they were all afraid of saying, was that happiness is dirt cheap. You can have it for nothing. Beauty.

Then Prickett Ellis let her have it—this pale, abrupt, arrogant woman. He told her, puffing his shag tobacco, what he had done that day. Up at six; interviews; smelling a drain in a filthy slum; then to court.

Here he hesitated, wishing to tell her something of his own doings. Suppressing that, he was all the more caustic. He said it made him sick to hear well fed, well dressed women (she twitched her lips, for she was thin, and her dress not up to standard) talk of beauty.

'Beauty!' he said. He was afraid he did not understand beauty apart from human beings.

So they glared into the empty garden where the lights were swaying, and one cat hesitating in the middle, its paw lifted.

Beauty apart from human beings? What did he mean by that? she demanded suddenly.

Well this: getting more and more wrought up, he told her the story of the Brunners and the clock, not concealing his pride in it. That was beautiful, he said.

She had no words to specify the horror his story roused in her. First his conceit; then his indecency in talking about human feelings; it was a blasphemy; no one in the whole world ought to tell a story to prove that they had loved their kind. Yet as he told it—how the old man had stood up and made his speech—tears came into her eyes; ah, if any one had ever said that to her! but then again, she felt how it was just this that condemned humanity for ever; never would they reach beyond affecting scenes with clocks; Brunners making speeches to Prickett Ellises, and the Prickett Ellises would always say how they had loved their kind; they would always be lazy, compromising, and afraid of beauty. Hence sprung revolutions; from laziness and fear and this love of affecting scenes. Still this man got pleasure from his Brunners; and she was condemned to suffer for ever and ever from her poor women shut out from squares. So they sat silent. Both were very unhappy. For Prickett Ellis was not in the least solaced by what he had said; instead of picking her thorn out he had rubbed it in; his happiness of the morning had been ruined. Miss O'Keefe was muddled and annoyed; she was muddy instead of clear.

'I'm afraid I am one of those very ordinary people,' he said, getting up, 'who love their kind.'

Upon which Miss O'Keefe almost shouted, 'So do I.'

Hating each other, hating the whole houseful of people who had given them this painful, this disillusioning evening, these two lovers of their kind got up, and without a word parted for ever.

# Selected Nonfiction

## Review of Dorothy Richardson's *The Tunnel*†

Although *The Tunnel* is the fourth book that Miss Richardson has
written, she must still expect to find her reviewers paying a great
deal of attention to her method. It is a method that demands attention, as a door whose handle we wrench ineffectively calls our attention to the fact that it is locked. There is no slipping smoothly down
the accustomed channels; the first chapters provide an amusing
spectacle of hasty critics seeking them in vain. If this were the result
of perversity, we should think Miss Richardson more courageous
than wise; but being, as we believe, not wilful but natural, it represents a genuine conviction of the discrepancy between what she has
to say and the form provided by tradition for her to say it in. She is
one of the rare novelists who believe that the novel is so much alive
that it actually grows. As she makes her advanced critic, Mr. Wilson, remark: "There will be books with all that cut out—him and
her—all that sort of thing. The book of the future will be clear of all
that." And Miriam Henderson herself reflects: "but if books were
written like that, sitting down and doing it cleverly and knowing just
what you were doing and just how somebody also had done it, there
was something wrong, some mannish cleverness that was only half
right. To write books knowing all about style would be to become
like a man." So "him and her" are cut out, and with them goes the
old deliberate business: the chapters that lead up and the chapters
that lead down; the characters who are always characteristic; the
scenes that are passionate and the scenes that are humorous; the
elaborate construction of reality; the conception that shapes and
surrounds the whole. All these things are cast away, and there is
left, denuded, unsheltered, unbegun and unfinished, the consciousness of Miriam Henderson, the small sensitive lump of matter, half
transparent and half opaque, which endlessly reflects and distorts

† *Times Literary Supplement* (February 13, 1919). *The Tunnel* is the fourth volume in
Richardson's twelve-volume novel sequence, *Pilgrimage*. The first volume, *Pointed Roofs*,
was published by Duckworth's just six months after Woolf's first novel, *The Voyage Out*
(1915).

the variegated procession, and is, we are bidden to believe, the source beneath the surface, the very oyster within the shell.

The critic is thus absolved from the necessity of picking out the themes of the story. The reader is not provided with a story; he is invited to embed himself in Miriam Henderson's consciousness, to register one after another, and one on top of another, words, cries, shouts, notes of a violin, fragments of lectures, to follow these impressions as they flicker through Miriam's mind, waking incongruously other thoughts, and plaiting incessantly the many-coloured and innumerable threads of life. But a quotation is better than description.

> She was surprised now at her familiarity with the details of the room . . . that idea of visiting places in dreams. It was something more than that . . . all the real part of your life has a real dream in it; some of the real dream part of you coming true. You know in advance when you are really following your life. These things are familiar because reality is here. Coming events cast *light*. It is like dropping everything and walking backward to something you know is there. However for you go out you come back. . . . I am back now where I was before I began trying to do things like other people. I left home to get here. None of those things can touch me here. They are mine. . . .

Here we are thinking, word by word, as Miriam thinks. The method, if triumphant, should make us feel ourselves seated at the centre of another mind, and, according to the artistic gift of the writer, we should perceive in the helter-skelter of flying fragments some unity, significance, or design. That Miss Richardson gets so far as to achieve a sense of reality far greater than that produced by the ordinary means is undoubted. But, then, which reality is it, the superficial or the profound? We have to consider the quality of Miriam Henderson's consciousness, and the extent to which Miss Richardson is able to reveal it. We have to decide whether the flying helter-skelter resolves itself by degrees into a perceptible whole. When we are in a position to make up our minds we cannot deny a slight sense of disappointment. Having sacrificed not merely "hims and hers," but so many seductive graces of wit and style for the prospect of some now revelation or greater intensity, we still find ourselves distressingly near the surface. Things look much the same as ever. It is certainly a very vivid surface. The consciousness of Miriam takes the reflection of a dentist's room to perfection. Her senses of touch, sight and hearing are all excessively acute. But sensations, impressions, ideas and emotions glance off her, unrelated and unquestioned, without shedding quite as much light as we had hoped into the hidden depths. We find ourselves in the dentist's room, in the street, in the lodging-house bedroom frequently and convincingly; but never, or only for a tantalizing second, in the reality which underlies these appearances. In particular, the figures of other people on whom Miriam casts her capricious light are vivid enough, but their sayings and doings never reach that degree of significance which we, perhaps unreasonably, expect. The old method seems sometimes the more profound and economical of the two. But it must be admitted that we are exacting. We want to be rid of realism, to penetrate without its help into the regions beneath it, and further require that Miss Richardson shall fashion this new material into something which has the shapeliness of the old accepted forms. We are asking too much; but the extent of our asking proves that *The Tunnel* is better in its failure than most books in their success.

## *From* 22 Hyde Park Gate[†]

As I have said, the drawing room at Hyde Park Gate was divided by black folding doors picked out with thin lines of raspberry red. We were still much under the influence of Titian. Mounds of plush, Watts' portraits, busts shrined in crimson velvet, enriched the gloom of a room naturally dark and thickly shaded in summer by showers of Virginia Creeper.

But it is of the folding doors that I wish to speak. How could family life have been carried on without them? As soon dispense with water-closets or bathrooms as with folding doors in a family of nine men and women, one of whom into the bargain was an idiot. Suddenly there would be a crisis—a servant dismissed, a lover rejected, pass books opened, or poor Mrs Tyndall who had lately poisoned her husband by mistake come for consolation. On one side of the door Cousin Adeline, Duchess of Bedford, perhaps would be on her knees—the Duke had died tragically at Woburn; Mrs Dolmetsch would be telling how she had found her husband in bed with the parlour-maid or Lisa Stillman would be sobbing that Walter Headlam had chalked her nose with a billiard cue—"which", she cried, "is what comes of smoking a pipe before gentlemen"—and my mother had much ado to persuade her that life had still to be faced, and the flower of virginity was still unplucked in spite of a chalk mark on the nose.

---

† From *Moments of Being*, Second Edition, ed. Jeanne Schulkind (San Diego: Harcourt, 1985), pp. 164–66. Copyright © 1976, 1985 by Quentin Bell and Angelica Garnett. Reprinted by permission of Houghton Mifflin Harcourt Publishing Company, Penguin Random House UK, and the Society of Authors on behalf of the Estate of Virginia Woolf. All rights reserved. Woolf delivered this talk likely on November 17, 1920, at the Memoir Club. It details the young Virginia's life after her half-sister Stella's death but before the death of her father in 1904, focusing especially on her half-brother George's efforts to turn her into a "lady" and including a brief account of his abuse.

Though dark and agitated on one side, the other side of the door, especially on Sunday afternoons, was cheerful enough. There round the oval tea table with its pink china shell full of spice buns would be found old General Beadle, talking, of the Indian Mutiny; or Mr Haldane, or Sir Frederick Pollock—talking of all things under the sun; or old C. B. Clarke, whose name is given to three excessively rare Himalayan ferns; and Professor Wolstenholme, capable, if you interrupted him, of spouting two columns of tea not unmixed with sultanas through his nostrils; after which he would relapse into a drowsy ursine torpor, the result of eating opium to which he had been driven by the unkindness of his wife and the untimely death of his son Oliver who was eaten, somewhere off the coast of Coromandel, by a shark. These gentlemen came and came again; and they were often reinforced by Mr Frederick Gibbs, sometime tutor to the Prince of Wales, whose imperturbable common sense and fund of information about the colonies in general and Canada in particular were a perpetual irritation to my father who used to wonder whether a brain fever at college in the year 1863 had not something to do with it. These old gentlemen were generally to be found, eating very slowly, staying very late and making themselves agreeable at Christmas-time with curious presents of Indian silver work, and hand bags made from the skin of the ornithorhynchus—as I seem to remember.

The tea table however was also fertilized by a ravishing stream of female beauty—the three Miss Lushingtons, the three Miss Stillmans, and the three Miss Montgomeries—all triplets, all ravishing, but of the nine the paragon for wit, grace, charm and distinction was undoubtedly the lovely Kitty Lushington—now Mrs Leo Maxse.[1] (Their engagement under the jackmanii in the Love Corner at St Ives was my first introduction to the passion of love.)[*] At the time I speak of she was in process of disengaging herself from Lord Morpeth, and had, I suspect, to explain her motives to my mother, a martinet in such matters, for first promising to marry a man and then breaking it off. My mother believed that all men required an infinity of care. She laid all the blame, I feel sure, upon Kitty. At any rate I have a picture of her as she issued from the secret side of the folding doors bearing on her delicate pink cheeks two perfectly formed pear-shaped crystal tears. They neither fell nor in the least dimmed the lustre of her eyes. She at once became the life and soul of the tea table—perhaps Leo Maxse was there—perhaps Ronny Norman—perhaps Esmé Howard—perhaps Arthur Studd, for the gentlemen were not all old, or all professors by any means—and when my father groaned beneath

---

1. An important model for Clarissa Dalloway [*Editor*].
* In describing the love between Stella and Jack Hills she wrote: "And it was through that engagement that I had my first vision—so intense, so exciting, so rapturous was it that the word vision applies—my first vision then of love between man and woman."

his breath but very audibly, "Oh Gibbs, what a bore you are!" it was Kitty whom my mother instantly threw into the breach. "Kitty wants to tell you how much she loved your lecture", my mother would cry, and Kitty still with the tears on her cheeks would improvise with the utmost gallantry some compliment or opinion which pacified my father who was extremely sensitive to female charm and largely depended upon female praise. Repenting of his irritation he would press poor Gibbs warmly by the hand and beg him to come soon again—which needless to say, poor Gibbs did.

And then there would come dancing into the room rubbing his hands, wrinkling his forehead, the most remarkable figure, as I sometimes think, that our household contained. I have alluded to a grisly relic of another age which we used to disinter from the nursery wardrobe—Herbert Duckworth's wig. (Herbert Duckworth had been a barrister.) Herbert Duckworth's son—George Herbert—was by no means grisly. His hair curled naturally in dark crisp ringlets; he was six foot high; he had been in the Eton Eleven; he was now cramming at Scoones' in the hope of passing the Foreign Office examination. When Miss Willett of Brighton saw him 'throwing off his ulster' in the middle of her drawing room she was moved to write an Ode Comparing George Duckworth to the Hermes of Praxiteles—which Ode my mother kept in her writing table drawer, along with a little Italian medal that George had won for saving a peasant from drowning. Miss Willett was reminded of the Hermes; but if you looked at him closely you noticed that one of his ears was pointed; and the other round; you also noticed that though he had the curls of a God and the ears of a faun he had unmistakably the eyes of a pig. So strange a compound can seldom have existed. And in the days I speak of, God, faun and pig were all in all alive, all in opposition, and in their conflicts producing the most astonishing eruptions.

\* \* \*

## *From* Old Bloomsbury[†]

While I had lain in bed at the Dickinsons' house at Welwyn thinking that the birds were singing Greek choruses and that King Edward was using the foulest possible language among Ozzie

† From *Moments of Being*, Second Edition, ed. Jeanne Schulkind (San Diego: Harcourt, 1985), pp. 184–85. Copyright © 1976, 1985 by Quentin Bell and Angelica Garnett. Reprinted by permission of Houghton Mifflin Harcourt Publishing Company, Penguin Random House UK, and the Society of Authors on behalf of the Estate of Virginia Woolf. All rights reserved. Woolf read this talk in 1922 at the Memoir Club. It tells the story of how, while Woolf was recovering from a breakdown after her father's death, her sister Vanessa moved the three surviving Stephen children to Bloomsbury, where they shed Victorian tradition and set off on a more bohemian life.

Dickinson's azaleas, Vanessa had wound up Hyde Park Gate once and for all. She had sold; she had burnt; she had sorted; she had torn up. Sometimes I believe she had actually to get men with hammers to batter down—so wedged into each other had the walls and the cabinets become. But now all the rooms stood empty. Furniture vans had carted off all the different belongings. For not only had the furniture been dispersed. The family which had seemed equally wedged together had broken apart too. George had married Lady Margaret. Gerald had taken a bachelor flat in Berkeley Street. Laura had been finally incarcerated with a doctor in an asylum; Jack Hills had entered on a political career. The four of us were therefore left alone. And Vanessa—looking at a map of London and seeing how far apart they were—had decided that we should leave Kensington and start life afresh in Bloomsbury.

It was thus that 46 Gordon Square came into existence. When one sees it today, Gordon Square is not one of the most romantic of the Bloomsbury squares. It has neither the distinction of Fitzroy Square nor the majesty of Mecklenburgh Square. It is prosperous middle class and thoroughly mid-Victorian. But I can assure you that in October 1904 it was the most beautiful, the most exciting, the most romantic place in the world. To begin with it was astonishing to stand at the drawing room window and look into all those trees; the tree which shoots its branches up into the air and lets them fall in a shower; the tree which glistens after rain like the body of a seal—instead of looking at old Mrs Redgrave washing her neck across the way. The light and the air after the rich red gloom of Hyde Park Gate were a revelation. Things one had never seen in the darkness there—Watts pictures, Dutch cabinets, blue china—shone out for the first time in the drawing room at Gordon Square. After the muffled silence of Hyde Park Gate the roar of traffic was positively alarming. Odd characters, sinister, strange, prowled and slunk past our windows. But what was even more exhilarating was the extraordinary increase of space. At Hyde Park Gate one had only a bedroom in which to read or see one's friends. Here Vanessa and I each had a sitting room; there was the large double drawing room; and a study on the ground floor. To make it all newer and fresher, the house had been completely done up. Needless to say the Watts-Venetian tradition of red plush and black paint had been reversed; we had entered the Sargent-Furse era; white and green chintzes were everywhere; and instead of Morris wall-papers with their intricate patterns we decorated our walls with washes of plain distemper. We were full of experiments and reforms. We were going to do without table napkins, we were to have [large supplies of] Bromo instead; we were going to paint; to write; to have coffee after dinner instead of tea at nine o'clock. Everything was going to be new; everything was going to be different. Everything was on trial.

\* \* \*

# On Not Knowing Greek[†]

For it is vain and foolish to talk of knowing Greek, since in our ignorance we should be at the bottom of any class of schoolboys, since we do not know how the words sounded, or where precisely we ought to laugh, or how the actors acted, and between this foreign people and ourselves there is not only difference of race and tongue but a tremendous breach of tradition. All the more strange, then, is it that we should wish to know Greek, try to know Greek, feel for ever drawn back to Greek, and be for ever making up some notion of the meaning of Greek, though from what incongruous odds and ends, with what slight resemblance to the real meaning of Greek, who shall say?

It is obvious in the first place that Greek literature is the impersonal literature. Those few hundred years that separate John Paston from Plato, Norwich from Athens, make a chasm which the vast tide of European chatter can never succeed in crossing. When we read Chaucer, we are floated up to him insensibly on the current of our ancestors' lives, and later, as records increase and memories lengthen, there is scarcely a figure which has not its nimbus of association, its life and letters, its wife and family, its house, its character, its happy or dismal catastrophe. But the Greeks remain in a fastness of their own. Fate has been kind there too. She has preserved them from vulgarity, Euripides was eaten by dogs; Aeschylus killed by a stone; Sappho leapt from a cliff. We know no more of them than that. We have their poetry, and that is all.

But that is not, and perhaps never can be, wholly true. Pick up any play by Sophocles, read—

> Son of him who led our hosts at Troy of old, son of Agamemnon,

and at once the mind begins to fashion itself surroundings. It makes some background, even of the most provisional sort, for Sophocles; it imagines some village, in a remote part of the country, near the sea. Even nowadays such villages are to be found in the wilder parts of England, and as we enter them we can scarcely help feeling that here, in this cluster of cottages, cut off from rail or

---

[†] An essay written especially for *The Common Reader* (New York: Harcourt Brace and Company, 1925), pp. 39–59, a collection of literary essays which Woolf published simultaneously with *Mrs. Dalloway*. For fuller notes, see *The Essays, 1925–28*, vol. 4, with notes by editor Andrew McNeillie.

city, are all the elements of a perfect existence. Here is the Rectory; here the Manor house, the farm and the cottages; the church for worship, the club for meeting, the cricket field for play. Here life is simply sorted out into its main elements. Each man and woman has his work; each works for the health or happiness of others. And here, in this little community, characters become part of the common stock; the eccentricities of the clergyman are known; the great ladies' defects of temper; the blacksmith's feud with the milkman, and the loves and matings of the boys and girls. Here life has cut the same grooves for centuries; customs have arisen; legends have attached themselves to hilltops and solitary trees, and the village has its history, its festivals, and its rivalries.

It is the climate that is impossible. If we try to think of Sophocles here, we must annihilate the smoke and the damp and the thick wet mists. We must sharpen the lines of the hills. We must imagine a beauty of stone and earth rather than of woods and greenery. With warmth and sunshine and months of brilliant, fine weather, life of course is instantly changed; it is transacted out of doors, with the result, known to all who visit Italy, that small incidents are debated in the street, not in the sitting-room, and become dramatic; make people voluble; inspire in them that sneering, laughing, nimbleness of wit and tongue peculiar to the Southern races, which has nothing in common with the slow reserve, the low half-tones, the brooding introspective melancholy of people accustomed to live more than half the year indoors.

That is the quality that first strikes us in Greek literature, the lightning-quick, sneering, out-of-doors manner. It is apparent in the most august as well as in the most trivial places. Queens and Princesses in this very tragedy by Sophocles stand at the door bandying words like village women, with a tendency, as one might expect, to rejoice in language, to split phrases into slices, to be intent on verbal victory. The humour of the people was not good natured like that of our postmen and cabdrivers. The taunts of men lounging at the street corners had something cruel in them as well as witty. There is a cruelty in Greek tragedy which is quite unlike our English brutality. Is not Pentheus, for example, that highly respectable man, made ridiculous in the *Bacchæ* before he is destroyed? In fact, of course, these Queens and Princesses were out of doors, with the bees buzzing past them, shadows crossing them, and the wind taking their draperies. They were speaking to an enormous audience rayed round them on one of those brilliant southern days when the sun is so hot and yet the air so exciting. The poet, therefore, had to bethink him, not of some theme which could be read for hours by people in privacy, but of something emphatic, familiar, brief, that would carry, instantly and directly, to an audience of seventeen thousand people, perhaps, with ears and eyes eager and attentive, with bodies whose muscles would grow stiff if they sat too long without diversion. Music and dancing he would need, and naturally would choose one of those legends, like our Tristram and Iseult, which are known to every one in outline, so that a great fund of emotion is ready prepared, but can be stressed in a new place by each new poet.

Sophocles would take the old story of Electra, for instance, but would at once impose his stamp upon it. Of that, in spite of our weakness and distortion, what remains visible to us? That his genius was of the extreme kind in the first place; that he chose a design which, if it failed, would show its failure in gashes and ruin, not in the gentle blurring of some insignificant detail; which, if it succeeded, would cut each stroke to the bone, would stamp each finger-print in marble. His Electra stands before us like a figure so tightly bound that she can only move an inch this way, an inch that. But each movement must tell to the utmost, or, bound as she is, denied the relief of all hints, repetitions, suggestions, she will be nothing but a dummy, tightly bound. Her words in crisis are, as a matter of fact, bare; mere cries of despair, joy, hate

$$\text{Οἲ 'γώ τάλαιν', ὄλωλα τῇδ' ἐν ἡμέρᾳ.}$$

$$\text{Παῖσον, εἰ σθένεις, διπλῆν.}^1$$

But these cries give angle and outline to the play. It is thus, with a thousand differences of degree, that in English literature Jane Austen shapes a novel. There comes a moment—"I will dance with you," says Emma—which rises higher than the rest, which, though not eloquent in itself, or violent, or made striking by beauty of language, has the whole weight of the book behind it. In Jane Austen, too, we have the same sense, though the ligatures are much less tight, that her figures are bound, and restricted to a few definite movements. She, too, in her modest, everyday prose, chose the dangerous art where one slip means death.

But it is not so easy to decide what it is that gives these cries of Electra in her anguish their power to cut and wound and excite. It is partly that we know her, that we have picked up from little turns and twists of the dialogue hints of her character, of her appearance, which, characteristically, she neglected; of something suffering in her, outraged and stimulated to its utmost stretch of capacity, yet, as she herself knows ("my behaviour is unseemly and

---

1. Woolf quotes two of Electra's lines, from quite far apart in the play. The first is spoken upon hearing rumor of her brother's death; the other when she urges him to strike another blow: "Oh, miserable that I am! I am lost this day" (674); "Stab her doubly if you can" (1415) (trans. R. C. Jebb).

becomes me ill"), blunted and debased by the horror of her position, an unwed girl made to witness her mother's vileness and
denounce it in loud, almost vulgar, clamour to the world at large. It
is partly, too, that we know in the same way that Clytemnestra is
no unmitigated villainess. "δεινόν τό τίχειν ἐστίν," she says—"there
is a strange power in motherhood". It is no murderess, violent and
unredeemed, whom Orestes kills within the house, and Electra
bids him utterly destroy—"strike again." No; the men and women
standing out in the sunlight before the audience on the hillside
were alive enough, subtle enough, not mere figures, or plaster
casts of human beings.

Yet it is not because we can analyse them into feelings that they
impress us. In six pages of Proust we can find more complicated
and varied emotions than in the whole of the *Electra*. But in the
*Electra* or in the *Antigone* we are impressed by something different,
by something perhaps more impressive—by heroism itself, by fidelity itself. In spite of the labour and the difficulty it is this that draws
us back and back to the Greeks; the stable, the permanent, the
original human being is to be found there. Violent emotions are
needed to rouse him into action, but when thus stirred by death, by
betrayal, by some other primitive calamity, Antigone and Ajax and
Electra behave in the way in which we should behave thus struck
down; the way in which everybody has always behaved; and thus we
understand them more easily and more directly than we understand the characters in the *Canterbury Tales*. These are the originals, Chaucer's the varieties of the human species.

It is true, of course, that these types of the original man or
woman, these heroic Kings, these faithful daughters, these tragic
Queens who stalk through the ages always planting their feet in the
same places, twitching their robes with the same gestures, from
habit not from impulse, are among the greatest bores and the most
demoralising companions in the world. The plays of Addison, Vol-
taire, and a host of others are there to prove it. But encounter them
in Greek. Even in Sophocles, whose reputation for restraint and
mastery has filtered down to us from the scholars, they are decided,
ruthless, direct. A fragment of their speech broken off would, we
feel, colour oceans and oceans of the respectable drama. Here we
meet them before their emotions have been worn into uniformity.
Here we listen to the nightingale whose song echoes through
English literature singing in her own Greek tongue. For the first
time Orpheus with his lute makes men and beasts follow him.
Their voices ring out clear and sharp; we see the hairy tawny bodies
at play in the sunlight among the olive trees, not posed gracefully
on granite plinths in the pale corridors of the British Museum. And
then suddenly, in the midst of all this sharpness and compression,

Electra, as if she swept her veil over her face and forbade us to think of her any more, speaks of that very nightingale: "that bird distraught with grief, the messenger of Zeus. Ah, queen of sorrow, Niobe, thee I deem divine—thee; who evermore weepest in thy rocky tomb."

And as she silences her own complaint, she perplexes us again with the insoluble question of poetry and its nature, and why, as she speaks thus, her words put on the assurance of immortality. For they are Greek; we cannot tell how they sounded; they ignore the obvious sources of excitement; they owe nothing of their effect to any extravagance of expression, and certainly they throw no light upon the speaker's character or the writer's. But they remain, something that has been stated and must eternally endure.

Yet in a play how dangerous this poetry, this lapse from the particular to the general must of necessity be, with the actors standing there in person, with their bodies and their faces passively waiting to be made use of! For this reason the later plays of Shakespeare, where there is more of poetry than of action, are better read than seen, better understood by leaving out the actual body than by having the body, with all its associations and movements, visible to the eye. The intolerable restrictions of the drama could be loosened, however, if a means could be found by which what was general and poetic, comment, not action, could be freed without interrupting the movement of the whole. It is this that the choruses supply; the old men or women who take no active part in the drama, the undifferentiated voices who sing like birds in the pauses of the wind; who can comment, or sum up, or allow the poet to speak himself or supply, by contrast, another side to his conception. Always in imaginative literature, where characters speak for themselves and the author has no part, the need of that voice is making itself felt. For though Shakespeare (unless we consider that his fools and madmen supply the part) dispensed with the chorus, novelists are always devising some substitute—Thackeray speaking in his own person, Fielding coming out and addressing the world before his curtain rises. So to grasp the meaning of the play the chorus is of the utmost importance. One must be able to pass easily into those ecstasies, those wild and apparently irrelevant utterances, those sometimes obvious and commonplace statements, to decide their relevance or irrelevance, and give them their relation to the play as a whole.

We must "be able to pass easily"; but that of course is exactly what we cannot do. For the most part the choruses, with all their obscurities, must be spelt out and their symmetry mauled. But we can guess that Sophocles used them not to express something outside the action of the play, but to sing the praises of some virtue, or the beauties of some place mentioned in it. He selects what he wishes to emphasise and sings of white Colonus and its nightingale, or of love unconquered in fight. Lovely, lofty, and serene his choruses grow naturally out of his situations, and change, not the point of view, but the mood. In Euripides, however, the situations are not contained within themselves; they give off an atmosphere of doubt, of suggestion, of questioning; but if we look to the choruses to make this plain we are often baffled rather than instructed. At once in the *Bacchæ* we are in the world of psychology and doubt; the world where the mind twists facts and changes them and makes the familiar aspects of life appear new and questionable. What is Bacchus, and who are the Gods, and what is man's duty to them, and what the rights of his subtle brain? To these questions the chorus makes no reply, or replies mockingly, or speaks darkly as if the straitness of the dramatic form had tempted Euripides to violate it in order to relieve his mind of its weight. Time is so short and I have so much to say, that unless you will allow me to place together two apparently unrelated statements and trust to you to pull them together, you must be content with a mere skeleton of the play I might have given you. Such is the argument. Euripides therefore suffers less than Sophocles and less than Aeschylus from being read privately in a room, and not seen on a hillside in the sunshine. He can be acted in the mind; he can comment upon the questions of the moment; more than the others he will vary in popularity from age to age.

If then in Sophocles the play is concentrated in the figures themselves, and in Euripides is to be retrieved from flashes of poetry and questions far flung and unanswered, Aeschylus makes these little dramas (the *Agamemnon* has 1663 lines; *Lear* about 2600), tremendous by stretching every phrase to the utmost, by sending them floating forth in metaphors, by bidding them rise up and stalk eyeless and majestic through the scene. To understand him it is not so necessary to understand Greek as to understand poetry. It is necessary to take that dangerous leap through the air without the support of words which Shakespeare also asks of us. For words, when opposed to such a blast of meaning, must give out, must be blown astray, and only by collecting in companies convey the meaning which each one separately is too weak to express. Connecting them in a rapid flight of the mind we know instantly and instinctively what they mean, but could not decant that meaning afresh into any other words. There is an ambiguity which is the mark of the highest poetry; we cannot know exactly what it means. Take this from the *Agamemnon* for instance—

ὀμμάτων δ' ἐν ἀχηνίαις ἔρρει πᾶσ' Ἀφροδίτα.[2]

2. This is a notoriously difficult line to translate, from *Agamemnon* by Aeschylus. Eduard Fraenkel translated it as "And when the eyes are starved, all charm of love is gone."

The meaning is just on the far side of language. It is the meaning which in moments of astonishing excitement and stress we perceive in our minds without words; it is the meaning that Dostoevsky (hampered as he was by prose and as we are by translation) leads us to by some astonishing run up the scale of emotions and points at but cannot indicate; the meaning that Shakespeare succeeds in snaring.

Aeschylus thus will not give, as Sophocles gives, the very words that people might have spoken, only so arranged that they have in some mysterious way a general force, a symbolic power, nor like Euripides will he combine incongruities and thus enlarge his little space, as a small room is enlarged by mirrors in odd corners. By the bold and running use of metaphor he will amplify and give us, not the thing itself, but the reverberation and reflection which, taken into his mind, the thing has made; close enough to the original to illustrate it, remote enough to heighten, enlarge, and make splendid.

For none of these dramatists had the license which belongs to the novelist, and, in some degree, to all writers of printed books, of modelling their meaning with an infinity of slight touches which can only be properly applied by reading quietly, carefully, and sometimes two or three times over. Every sentence had to explode on striking the ear, however slowly and beautifully the words might then descend, and however enigmatic might their final purport be. No splendour or richness of metaphor could have saved the *Agamemnon* if either images or allusions of the subtlest or most decorative had got between us and the naked cry

ὀτοτοτοτοῖ πόποι δᾶ. ὤπολλον, ὤπολλον,[3]

Dramatic they had to be at whatever cost.

But winter fell on these villages, darkness and extreme cold descended on the hill-side. There must have been some place indoors where men could retire, both in the depths of winter and in the summer heats, where they could sit and drink, where they could lie stretched at their ease, where they could talk. It is Plato, of course, who reveals the life indoors, and describes how, when a party of friends met and had eaten not at all luxuriously and drunk a little wine, some handsome boy ventured a question, or quoted an opinion, and Socrates took it up, fingered it, turned it round, looked at it this way and that, swiftly stripped it of its inconsistencies and falsities and brought the whole company by degrees to gaze with him at the truth. It is an exhausting process; to contract painfully upon the exact meaning of words; to judge what each admission involves; to follow intently, yet critically, the dwindling and changing of opinion

3. "O woe, woe, woe! Alas! Apollo, Apollo!"

as it hardens and intensifies into truth. Are pleasure and good the same? Can virtue be taught? Is virtue knowledge? The tired or feeble mind may easily lapse as the remorseless questioning proceeds; but no one, however weak, can fail, even if he does not learn more from Plato, to love knowledge better. For as the argument mounts from step to step, Protagoras yielding, Socrates pushing on, what matters is not so much the end we reach as our manner of reaching it. That all can feel—the indomitable honesty, the courage, the love of truth which draw Socrates and us in his wake to the summit where, if we too may stand for a moment, it is to enjoy the greatest felicity of which we are capable.

Yet such an expression seems ill fitted to describe the state of mind of a student to whom, after painful argument, the truth has been revealed. But truth is various; truth comes to us in different disguises; it is not with the intellect alone that we perceive it. It is a winter's night; the tables are spread at Agathon's house; the girl is playing the flute; Socrates has washed himself and put on sandals; he has stopped in the hall; he refuses to move when they send for him. Now Socrates has done; he is bantering Alcibiades; Alcibiades takes a fillet and binds it round "this wonderful fellow's head". He praises Socrates. "For he cares not for mere beauty, but despises more than any one can imagine all external possessions, whether it be beauty or wealth or glory, or any other thing for which the multitude felicitates the possessor. He esteems these things and us who honour them, as nothing, and lives among men, making all the objects of their admiration the playthings of his irony. But I know not if any one of you has ever seen the divine images which are within, when he has been opened and is serious. I have seen them, and they are so supremely beautiful, so golden, divine, and wonderful, that everything which Socrates commands surely ought to be obeyed even like the voice of a God." All this flows over the arguments of Plato—laughter and movement; people getting up and going out; the hour changing; tempers being lost; jokes cracked; the dawn rising. Truth, it seems, is various; Truth is to be pursued with all our faculties. Are we to rule out the amusements, the tendernesses, the frivolities of friendship because we love truth? Will truth be quicker found because we stop our ears to music and drink no wine, and sleep instead of talking through the long winter's night? It is not to the cloistered disciplinarian mortifying himself in solitude that we are to turn, but to the well-sunned nature, the man who practises the art of living to the best advantage, so that nothing is stunted but some things are permanently more valuable than others.

So in these dialogues we are made to seek truth with every part of us. For Plato, of course, had the dramatic genius. It is by means of that, by an art which conveys in a sentence or two the setting and the atmosphere, and then with perfect adroitness insinuates itself into the coils of the argument without losing its liveliness and grace, and then contracts to bare statement, and then, mounting, expands and soars in that higher air which is generally reached only by the more extreme measures of poetry—it is this art which plays upon us in so many ways at once and brings us to an exultation of mind which can only be reached when all the powers are called upon to contribute their energy to the whole.

But we must beware. Socrates did not care for "mere beauty", by which he meant, perhaps, beauty as ornament. A people who judged as much as the Athenians did by ear, sitting out-of-doors at the play or listening to argument in the market-place, were far less apt than we are to break off sentences and appreciate them apart from the context. For them there were no Beauties of Hardy, Beauties of Meredith, Sayings from George Eliot. The writer had to think more of the whole and less of the detail. Naturally, living in the open, it was not the lip or the eye that struck them, but the carriage of the body and the proportions of its parts. Thus when we quote and extract we do the Greeks more damage than we do the English. There is a bareness and abruptness in their literature which grates upon a taste accustomed to the intricacy and finish of printed books. We have to stretch our minds to grasp a whole devoid of the prettiness of detail or the emphasis of eloquence. Accustomed to look directly and largely rather than minutely and aslant, it was safe for them to step into the thick of emotions which blind and bewilder an age like our own. In the vast catastrophe of the European war our emotions had to be broken up for us, and put at an angle from us, before we could allow ourselves to feel them in poetry or fiction. The only poets who spoke to the purpose spoke in the sidelong, satiric manner of Wilfrid Owen and Siegfried Sassoon. It was not possible for them to be direct without being clumsy; or to speak simply of emotion without being sentimental. But the Greeks could say, as if for the first time, "Yet being dead they have not died." They could say, "If to die nobly is the chief part of excellence, to us out of all men Fortune gave this lot; for hastening to set a crown of freedom on Greece we lie possessed of praise that grows not old." They could march straight up, with their eyes open; and thus fearlessly approached, emotions stand still and suffer themselves to be looked at.

But again (the question comes back and back), Are we reading Greek as it was written when we say this? When we read these few words cut on a tombstone, a stanza in a chorus, the end or the opening of a dialogue of Plato's, a fragment of Sappho, when we bruise our minds upon some tremendous metaphor in the *Agamemnon* instead of stripping the branch of its flowers instantly as we do in reading *Lear*—are we not reading wrongly? losing our sharp sight in

the haze of associations? reading into Greek poetry not what they
have but what we lack? Does not the whole of Greece heap itself
behind every line of its literature? They admit us to a vision of the
earth unravaged, the sea unpolluted, the maturity, tried but unbro-
ken, of mankind. Every word is reinforced by a vigour which pours
out of olive-tree and temple and the bodies of the young. The nightingale has only to be named by Sophocles and she sings; the grove
has only to be called ἄβατον, "untrodden", and we imagine the
twisted branches and the purple violets. Back and back we are
drawn to steep ourselves in what, perhaps, is only an image of the
reality, not the reality itself, a summer's day imagined in the heart of
a northern winter. Chief among these sources of glamour and perhaps misunderstanding is the language. We can never hope to get
the whole fling of a sentence in Greek as we do in English. We cannot hear it, now dissonant, now harmonious, tossing sound from
line to line across a page. We cannot pick up infallibly one by one all
those minute signals by which a phrase is made to hint, to turn, to
live. Nevertheless it is the language that has us most in bondage; the
desire for that which perpetually lures us back. First there is the
compactness of the expression. Shelley takes twenty-one words in
English to translate thirteen words of Greek.

> πᾶς γοῦν πσιητὴς γίγνεται, "κἂν ἄμουσος ᾖ τὸ πρίν," οὗ ἂν Ἔρως
> ἅψηται.
> . . . For every one, even if before he were ever so undisci-
> plined, becomes a poet as soon as he is touched by love.

Every ounce of fat has been pared off, leaving the flesh firm.
Then, spare and bare as it is, no language can move more quickly,
dancing, shaking, all alive, but controlled. Then there are the words
themselves which, in so many instances, we have made expressive
to us of our own emotions, *thalassa*, *thanatos*, *anthos*, *aster*[4]—to take
the first that come to hand; so clear, so hard, so intense, that to
speak plainly yet fittingly without blurring the outline or clouding
the depths Greek is the only expression. It is useless, then, to read
Greek in translations. Translators can but offer us a vague equivalent; their language is necessarily full of echoes and associations.
Professor Mackail says "wan", and the age of Burne-Jones and Morris is at once evoked. Nor can the subtler stress, the flight and the
fall of the words, be kept even by the most skilful of scholars—

> . . . thee, who evermore weepest in thy rocky tomb is not

> ἅτ᾽ ἐν τάφῳ πετραίῳ,
> αἰαῖ, δακρύεις.

---

4. The words are "sea," "death," "flower," "star," and "moon."

Further, in reckoning the doubts and difficulties there is this important problem—Where are we to laugh in reading Greek? There is a passage in the *Odyssey* where laughter begins to steal upon us, but if Homer were looking we should probably think it better to control our merriment. To laugh instantly it is almost necessary (though Aristophanes may supply us with an exception) to laugh in English. Humour, after all, is closely bound up with a sense of the body. When we laugh at the humour of Wycherley, we are laughing with the body of that burly rustic who was our common ancestor on the village green. The French, the Italians, the Americans, who derive physically from so different a stock, pause, as we pause in reading Homer, to make sure that they are laughing in the right place, and the pause is fatal. Thus humour is the first of the gifts to perish in a foreign tongue, and when we turn from Greek to Elizabethan literature it seems, after a long silence, as if our great age were ushered in by a burst of laughter.

These are all difficulties, sources of misunderstanding, of distorted and romantic, of servile and snobbish passion. Yet even for the unlearned some certainties remain. Greek is the impersonal literature; it is also the literature of masterpieces. There are no schools; no forerunners; no heirs. We cannot trace a gradual process working in many men imperfectly until it expresses itself adequately at last in one. Again, there is always about Greek literature that air of vigour which permeates an "age", whether it is the age of Aeschylus, or Racine, or Shakespeare. One generation at least in that fortunate time is blown on to be writers to the extreme; to attain that unconsciousness which means that the consciousness is stimulated to the highest extent; to surpass the limits of small triumphs and tentative experiments. Thus we have Sappho with her constellations of adjectives, Plato daring extravagant flights of poetry in the midst of prose; Thucydides, constricted and contracted; Sophocles gliding like a shoal of trout smoothly and quietly, apparently motionless, and then with a flicker of fins off and away; while in the *Odyssey* we have what remains the triumph of narrative, the clearest and at the same time the most romantic story of the fortunes of men and women.

The *Odyssey* is merely a story of adventure, the instinctive story-telling of a sea-faring race. So we may begin it, reading quickly in the spirit of children wanting amusement to find out what happens next. But here is nothing immature; here are full-grown people, crafty, subtle, and passionate. Nor is the world itself a small one, since the sea which separates island from island has to be crossed by little hand-made boats and is measured by the flight of the sea-gulls. It is true that the islands are not thickly populated, and the people, though everything is made by hand, are not closely kept at work. They have had time to develop a very dignified, a very stately society, with an ancient tradition of manners behind it, which makes every relation at once orderly, natural, and full of reserve. Penelope crosses the room; Telemachus goes to bed; Nausicaa washes her linen; and their actions seem laden with beauty because they do not know that they are beautiful, have been born to their possessions, are no more self-conscious than children, and yet, all those thousands of years ago, in their little islands, know all that is to be known. With the sound of the sea in their ears, vines, meadows, rivulets about them, they are even more aware than we are of a ruthless fate. There is a sadness at the back of life which they do not attempt to mitigate. Entirely aware of their own standing in the shadow, and yet alive to every tremor and gleam of existence, there they endure, and it is to the Greeks that we turn when we are sick of the vagueness, of the confusion, of the Christianity and its consolations, of our own age.

# Modern Fiction[†]

In making any survey, even the freest and loosest, of modern fiction it is difficult not to take it for granted that the modern practice of the art is somehow an improvement upon the old. With their simple tools and primitive materials, it might be said, Fielding did well and Jane Austen even better, but compare their opportunities with ours! Their masterpieces certainly have a strange air of simplicity. And yet the analogy between literature and the process, to choose an example, of making motor cars scarcely holds good beyond the first glance. It is doubtful whether in the course of the centuries, though we have learnt much about making machines, we have learnt anything about making literature. We do not come to write better; all that we can be said to do is to keep moving, now a little in this direction, now in that, but with a circular tendency should the whole course of the track be viewed from a sufficiently lofty pinnacle. It need scarcely be said that we make no claim to stand, even momentarily, upon that vantage ground. On the flat, in the crowd, half blind with dust, we look back with envy to those happier warriors, whose battle is won and whose achievements wear so serene an air of accomplishment that we can scarcely refrain from whispering that the fight was not so fierce for them as for us. It is for the historian of literature to decide; for him to say if we are now

† A version of this essay was originally published in the *Times Literary Supplement* (April 10, 1919) under the title "Modern Novels." This version was revised for *The Common Reader* (New York: Harcourt Brace and Company, 1925), pp. 207–18.

beginning or ending or standing in the middle of a great period of prose fiction, for down in the plain little is visible. We only know that certain gratitudes and hostilities inspire us; that certain paths seem to lead to fertile land, others to the dust and the desert; and of this perhaps it may be worth while to attempt some account.

Our quarrel, then, is not with the classics, and if we speak of quarrelling with Mr. Wells, Mr. Bennett, and Mr. Galsworthy[1] it is partly that by the mere fact of their existence in the flesh their work has a living, breathing, every-day imperfection which bids us take what liberties with it we choose. But it is also true that, while we thank them for a thousand gifts, we reserve our unconditional gratitude for Mr. Hardy, for Mr. Conrad, and in a much lesser degree for the Mr. Hudson, of *The Purple Land*, *Green Mansions*, and *Far Away and Long Ago*.[2] Mr. Wells, Mr. Bennett, and Mr. Galsworthy have excited so many hopes and disappointed them so persistently that our gratitude largely takes the form of thanking them for having shown us what they might have done but have not done; what we certainly could not do, but as certainly, perhaps, do not wish to do. No single phrase will sum up the charge or grievance which we have to bring against a mass of work so large in its volume and embodying so many qualities, both admirable and the reverse. If we tried to formulate our meaning in one word we should say that these three writers are materialists. It is because they are concerned not with the spirit but with the body that they have disappointed us, and left us with the feeling that the sooner English fiction turns its back upon them, as politely as may be, and marches, if only into the desert, the better for its soul. Naturally, no single word reaches the centre of three separate targets. In the case of Mr. Wells it falls notably wide of the mark. And yet even with him it indicates to our thinking the fatal alloy in his genius, the great clod of clay that has got itself mixed up with the purity of his inspiration. But Mr. Bennett is perhaps the worst culprit of the three, inasmuch as he is by far the best workman. He can make a book so well constructed and solid in its craftsmanship that it is difficult for the most exacting of critics to see through what chink or crevice decay can creep in. There is not so much as a draught between the frames of the windows, or a crack in the boards. And yet—if life

1. Three British novelists of the generation just before Woolf's own. H. G. Wells (1866–1946) was author of *The War of the Worlds* (1898) and *Ann Veronica* (1909; excerpted here), among many other works of fiction and nonfiction; Arnold Bennett (1867–1931) was author of *The Old Wives' Tale* (1908) and was a frequent book reviewer; John Galsworthy (1867–1933) was author of *The Forsyte Saga* (1906–21), among other works. Woolf carried on a literary dispute with Bennett that extended beyond this essay.
2. Thomas Hardy (1840–1928), Joseph Conrad (1857–1924), and William Henry Hudson (1841–1922) were also British novelists of a prior generation, but ones with whom Woolf was less rivalrous. Hardy and Conrad were friendly acquaintances, and Woolf wrote admiring essays about them after their deaths.

should refuse to live there? That is a risk which the creator of *The Old Wives' Tale*, George Cannon, Edwin Clayhanger, and hosts of other figures, may well claim to have surmounted. His characters live abundantly, even unexpectedly, but it remains to ask how do they live, and what do they live for? More and more they seem to us, deserting even the well-built villa in the Five Towns, to spend their time in some softly padded first-class railway carriage, pressing bells and buttons innumerable; and the destiny to which they travel so luxuriously becomes more and more unquestionably an eternity of bliss spent in the very best hotel in Brighton. It can scarcely be said of Mr. Wells that he is a materialist in the sense that he takes too much delight in the solidity of his fabric. His mind is too generous in its sympathies to allow him to spend much time in making things shipshape and substantial. He is a materialist from sheer goodness of heart, taking upon his shoulders the work that ought to have been discharged by Government officials, and in the plethora of his ideas and facts scarcely having leisure to realise, or forgetting to think important, the crudity and coarseness of his human beings. Yet what more damaging criticism can there be both of his earth and of his Heaven than that they are to be inhabited here and hereafter by his Joans and his Peters? Does not the inferiority of their natures tarnish whatever institutions and ideals may be provided for them by the generosity of their creator? Nor, profoundly though we respect the integrity and humanity of Mr. Galsworthy, shall we find what we seek in his pages.

If we fasten, then, one label on all these books, on which is one word materialists, we mean by it that they write of unimportant things; that they spend immense skill and immense industry making the trivial and the transitory appear the true and the enduring.

We have to admit that we are exacting, and, further, that we find it difficult to justify our discontent by explaining what it is that we exact. We frame our question differently at different times. But it reappears most persistently as we drop the finished novel on the crest of a sigh—Is it worth while? What is the point of it all? Can it be that owing to one of those little deviations which the human spirit seems to make from time to time Mr. Bennett has come down with his magnificent apparatus for catching life just an inch or two on the wrong side? Life escapes; and perhaps without life nothing else is worth while. It is a confession of vagueness to have to make use of such a figure as this, but we scarcely better the matter by speaking, as critics are prone to do, of reality. Admitting the vagueness which afflicts all criticism of novels, let us hazard the opinion that for us at this moment the form of fiction most in vogue more often misses than secures the thing we seek. Whether we call it life or spirit, truth or reality, this, the essential thing, has moved off, or on, and refuses to be contained any longer in such ill-fitting vestments as we provide. Nevertheless, we go on perseveringly, conscientiously, constructing our two and thirty chapters after a design which more and more ceases to resemble the vision in our minds. So much of the enormous labour of proving the solidity, the likeness to life, of the story is not merely labour thrown away but labour misplaced to the extent of obscuring and blotting out the light of the conception. The writer seems constrained, not by his own free will but by some powerful and unscrupulous tyrant who has him in thrall to provide a plot, to provide comedy, tragedy, love, interest, and an air of probability embalming the whole so impeccable that if all his figures were to come to life they would find themselves dressed down to the last button of their coats in the fashion of the hour. The tyrant is obeyed; the novel is done to a turn. But sometimes, more and more often as time goes by, we suspect a momentary doubt, a spasm of rebellion, as the pages fill themselves in the customary way. Is life like this? Must novels be like this?

Look within and life, it seems, is very far from being "like this". Examine for a moment an ordinary mind on an ordinary day. The mind receives a myriad impressions—trivial, fantastic, evanescent, or engraved with the sharpness of steel. From all sides they come, an incessant shower of innumerable atoms; and as they fall, as they shape themselves into the life of Monday or Tuesday, the accent falls differently from of old; the moment of importance came not here but there; so that if a writer were a free man and not a slave, if he could write what he chose, not what he must, if he could base his work upon his own feeling and not upon convention, there would be no plot, no comedy, no tragedy, no love interest or catastrophe in the accepted style, and perhaps not a single button sewn on as the Bond Street tailors would have it. Life is not a series of gig lamps symmetrically arranged; but a luminous halo, a semi-transparent envelope surrounding us from the beginning of consciousness to the end. Is it not the task of the novelist to convey this varying, this unknown and uncircumscribed spirit, whatever aberration or complexity it may display, with as little mixture of the alien and external as possible? We are not pleading merely for courage and sincerity; we are suggesting that the proper stuff of fiction is a little other than custom would have us believe it.

It is, at any rate, in some such fashion as this that we seek to define the quality which distinguishes the work of several young writers, among whom Mr. James Joyce is the most notable, from that of their predecessors. They attempt to come closer to life, and to preserve more sincerely and exactly what interests and moves them, even if to do so they must discard most of the conventions which are commonly observed by the novelist. Let us record the atoms as they fall upon the mind in the order in which they fall, let us trace the pattern, however disconnected and incoherent in appearance, which each sight or incident scores upon the consciousness. Let us not take it for granted that life exists more fully in what is commonly thought big than in what is commonly thought small. Any one who has read *The Portrait of the Artist as a Young Man* or, what promises to be a far more interesting work, *Ulysses*,[3] now appearing in the *Little Review*, will have hazarded some theory of this nature as to Mr. Joyce's intention. On our part, with such a fragment before us, it is hazarded rather than affirmed; but whatever the intention of the whole there can be no question but that it is of the utmost sincerity and that the result, difficult or unpleasant as we may judge it, is undeniably important. In contrast with those whom we have called materialists Mr. Joyce is spiritual; he is concerned at all costs to reveal the flickerings of that innermost flame which flashes its messages through the brain, and in order to preserve it he disregards with complete courage whatever seems to him adventitious, whether it be probability, or coherence or any other of these signposts which for generations have served to support the imagination of a reader when called upon to imagine what he can neither touch nor see. The scene in the cemetery, for instance, with its brilliancy, its sordidity, its incoherence, its sudden lightning flashes of significance, does undoubtedly come so close to the quick of the mind that, on a first reading at any rate, it is difficult not to acclaim a masterpiece. If we want life itself here, surely we have it. Indeed, we find ourselves fumbling rather awkwardly if we try to say what else we wish, and for what reason a work of such originality yet fails to compare, for we must take high examples, with *Youth* or *The Mayor of Casterbridge*. It fails because of the comparative poverty of the writer's mind, we might say simply and have done with it. But it is possible to press a little further and wonder whether we may not refer our sense of being in a bright yet narrow room, confined and shut in, rather than enlarged and set free, to some limitation imposed by the method as well as by the mind. Is it the method that inhibits the creative power? Is it due to the method that we feel neither jovial nor magnanimous, but centred in a self which, in spite of its tremor of susceptibility, never embraces or creates what is outside itself and beyond? Does the emphasis laid, perhaps didactically, upon indecency, contribute to the effect of something angular and isolated? Or is it merely that in any effort of such originality it is much easier, for contemporaries especially, to feel what it lacks than to name what it gives? In any case it is a mistake to stand outside examining "methods". Any method is

3. Written April 1919. [Woolf's footnote—*Editor*.]

right, every method is right, that expresses what we wish to express, if we are writers; that brings us closer to the novelist's intention if we are readers. This method has the merit of bringing us closer to what we were prepared to call life itself; did not the reading of *Ulysses* suggest how much of life is excluded or ignored, and did it not come with a shock to open *Tristram Shandy* or even *Pendennis* and be by them convinced that there are not only other aspects of life, but more important ones into the bargain.

However this may be, the problem before the novelist at present, as we suppose it to have been in the past, is to contrive means of being free to set down what he chooses. He has to have the courage to say that what interests him is no longer "this" but "that": out of "that" alone must he construct his work. For the moderns "that", the point of interest, lies very likely in the dark places of psychology. At once, therefore, the accent falls a little differently; the emphasis is upon something hitherto ignored; at once a different outline of form becomes necessary, difficult for us to grasp, incomprehensible to our predecessors. No one but a modern, perhaps no one but a Russian, would have felt the interest of the situation which Tchekov has made into the short story which he calls "Gusev". Some Russian soldiers lie ill on board a ship which is taking them back to Russia. We are given a few scraps of their talk and some of their thoughts; then one of them dies and is carried away; the talk goes on among the others for a time, until Gusev himself dies, and looking "like a carrot or a radish" is thrown overboard. The emphasis is laid upon such unexpected places that at first it seems as if there were no emphasis at all; and then, as the eyes accustom themselves to twilight and discern the shapes of things in a room we see how complete the story is, how profound, and how truly in obedience to his vision Tchekov has chosen this, that, and the other, and placed them together to compose something new. But it is impossible to say "this is comic", or "that is tragic", nor are we certain, since short stories, we have been taught, should be brief and conclusive, whether this, which is vague and inconclusive, should be called a short story at all.

The most elementary remarks upon modern English fiction can hardly avoid some mention of the Russian influence, and if the Russians are mentioned one runs the risk of feeling that to write of any fiction save theirs is waste of time. If we want understanding of the soul and heart where else shall we find it of comparable profundity? If we are sick of our own materialism the least considerable of their novelists has by right of birth a natural reverence for the human spirit. "Learn to make yourself akin to people. . . . But let this sympathy be not with the mind—for it is easy with the mind— but with the heart, with love towards them." In every great Russian

writer we seem to discern the features of a saint, if sympathy for
the sufferings of others, love towards them, endeavour to reach
some goal worthy of the most exacting demands of the spirit constitute saintliness. It is the saint in them which confounds us with a
feeling of our own irreligious triviality, and turns so many of our
famous novels to tinsel and trickery. The conclusions of the Russian mind, thus comprehensive and compassionate, are inevitably,
perhaps, of the utmost sadness. More accurately indeed we might
speak of the inconclusiveness of the Russian mind. It is the sense
that there is no answer, that if honestly examined life presents
question after question which must be left to sound on and on after
the story is over in hopeless interrogation that fills us with a deep,
and finally it may be with a resentful, despair. They are right perhaps; unquestionably they see further than we do and without our
gross impediments of vision. But perhaps we see something that
escapes them, or why should this voice of protest mix itself with our
gloom? The voice of protest is the voice of another and an ancient
civilisation which seems to have bred in us the instinct to enjoy and
fight rather than to suffer and understand. English fiction from
Sterne to Meredith bears witness to our natural delight in humour
and comedy, in the beauty of earth, in the activities of the intellect,
and in the splendour of the body. But any deductions that we may
draw from the comparison of two fictions so immeasurably far
apart are futile save indeed as they flood us with a view of the infinite possibilities of the art and remind us that there is no limit to
the horizon, and that nothing—no "method", no experiment, even
of the wildest—is forbidden, but only falsity and pretence. "The
proper stuff of fiction" does not exist; everything is the proper stuff
of fiction, every feeling, every thought; every quality of brain and
spirit is drawn upon; no perception comes amiss. And if we can
imagine the art of fiction come alive and standing in our midst, she
would undoubtedly bid us break her and bully her, as well as honour
and love her, for so her youth is renewed and her sovereignty assured.

## Introduction to *Mrs. Dalloway*†

It is difficult—perhaps impossible—for a writer to say anything
about his own work. All he has to say has been said as fully and as
well as he can in the body of the book itself. If he has failed to make

† From *Mrs. Dalloway* (New York: Random House, 1928), pp. v–ix. Introduction copyright 1928 by The Modern Library, Inc. Reprinted by permission of the Society of
Authors on behalf of the Estate of Virginia Woolf. Woolf wrote this, the only introduction she ever wrote to one of her novels, for the 1928 American publication of a Modern Library edition of *Mrs. Dalloway*.

his meaning clear there it is scarcely likely that he will succeed in some few pages of preface or postscript. And the author's mind has another peculiarity which is also hostile to introductions. It is as inhospitable to its offspring as the hen sparrow is to hers. Once the young birds can fly, fly they must; and by the time they have fluttered out of the nest the mother bird has begun to think perhaps of another brood. In the same way once a book is printed and published it ceases to be the property of the author; he commits it to the care of other people; all his attention is claimed by some new book which not only thrusts its predecessor from the nest but has a way of subtly blackening its character in comparison with its own.

It is true that the author can if he wishes tell us something about himself and his life which is not in the novel; and to this effort we should do all that we can to encourage him. For nothing is more fascinating than to be shown the truth which lies behind those immense façades of fiction—if life is indeed true, and if fiction is indeed fictitious. And probably the connection between the two is highly complicated. Books are the flowers or fruit stuck here and there on a tree which has its roots deep down in the earth of our earliest life, of our first experiences. But here again to tell the reader anything that his own imagination and insight have not already discovered would need not a page or two of preface but a volume or two of autobiography. Slowly and cautiously one would have to go to work, uncovering, laying bare, and even so when everything had been brought to the surface, it would still be for the reader to decide what was relevant and what not. Of *Mrs. Dalloway* then one can only bring to light at the moment a few scraps, of little importance or none perhaps; as that in the first version Septimus, who later is intended to be her double, had no existence; and that Mrs. Dalloway was originally to kill herself, or perhaps merely to die at the end of the party. Such scraps are offered humbly to the reader in the hope that like other odds and ends they may come in useful.

But if one has too much respect for the reader pure and simple to point out to him what he has missed, or to suggest to him what he should seek one may speak more explicitly to the reader who has put off his innocence and become a critic. For though criticism, whether praise or blame, should be accepted in silence as the legitimate comment which the act of publication invites, now and again a statement is made without bearing on the book's merits or demerits which the writer happens to know to be mistaken. One such statement has been made sufficiently often about *Mrs. Dalloway* to be worth perhaps a word of contradiction. The book, it was said, was the deliberate offspring of a method. The author, it was said, dissatisfied with the form of fiction then in vogue, was determined to beg, borrow, steal or even create another of her own. But, as far as it is possible to be honest about the mysterious process of the mind, the facts are otherwise. Dissatisfied the writer may have been; but her dissatisfaction was primarily with nature for giving an idea, without providing a house for it to live in. The novelists of the preceding generation had done little—after all why should they?—to help. The novel was the obvious lodging, but the novel it seemed was built on the wrong plan. Thus rebuked the idea started as the oyster starts or the snail to secrete a house for itself. And this it did without any conscious direction. The little note book in which an attempt was made to forecast a plan was soon abandoned, and the book grew day by day, week by week, without any plan at all, except that which was dictated each morning in the act of writing. The other way, to make a house and then inhabit it, to develop a theory and then apply it, as Wordsworth did and Coleridge, is, it need not be said, equally good and much more philosophic. But in the present case it was necessary to write the book first and to invent a theory afterwards.

If, however, one singles out the particular point of the book's methods for discussion it is for the reason given—that it has been made the subject of comment by critics, not that in itself it deserves notice. On the contrary, the more successful the method, the less it attracts attention. The reader it is to be hoped will not give a thought to the book's method or to the book's lack of method. He is concerned only with the effect of the book as a whole on his mind. Of that most important question he is a far better judge than the writer. Indeed, given time and liberty to frame his own opinion he is eventually an infallible judge. To him then the writer commends *Mrs. Dalloway* and leaves the court confident that the verdict whether for instant death or for some years more of life and liberty will in either case be just.

VIRGINIA WOOLF.

LONDON,
*June,* 1928.

# Literary Sources

## HOMER

### *From* The Odyssey, Book 5[†]

\* \* \*

The South Wind hurls it, then the North Wind grabs it,
then East Wind yields and lets the West Wind drive it.
But stepping softly, Ino, the White Goddess,
Cadmus' child, once human, human-voiced,
now honored with the gods in salty depths,
noticed that he was suffering and lost,
with pity. Like a gull with wings outstretched
she rose up from the sea, sat on the raft
and said,

      "Poor man! Why does enraged Poseidon
create an odyssey of pain for you?                    340
But his hostility will not destroy you.
You seem intelligent. Do as I say.
Strip off your clothes and leave the raft behind
for winds to take away. With just your arms
swim to Phaeacia. Fate decrees that there
you will survive. Here, take my scarf and tie it
under your chest: with this immortal veil,
you need not be afraid of death or danger.
But when you reach dry earth, untie the scarf
and throw it out to sea, away from land,           350
and turn away." With that, the goddess gave it,
and plunged back down inside the surging sea,
just like a gull. The black wave covered her.

† From *The Odyssey*, trans. Emily Wilson (New York: W. W. Norton, 2018), 5.331–87, 407–35. Copyright © 2018 by Emily Wilson. Used by permission of W. W. Norton & Company, Inc. In this section of Homer's *Odyssey*, Odysseus is saved by the goddess Ino, who gives him a magical veil that protects him from drowning. Nevertheless, his flesh is torn as he tries to land on the rocky shores of Nausicaa's island. Woolf reread *The Odyssey* while writing *Mrs. Dalloway* and drew heavily upon the imagery of this scene for some of her depictions of Septimus in his madness.

The hero who had suffered so much danger
was troubled and confused. He asked himself,
"Some deity has said to leave the raft.
But what if gods are weaving tricks again?
I will not trust her yet: with my own eyes
I saw the land she said I should escape to,
and it is far away. I will do this:      360
as long as these wood timbers hold together,
I will hang on, however hard it is.
But when the waves have smashed my raft to pieces,
then I will have no choice, and I will swim."

While he was thinking this, the Lord of Earthquakes,
Poseidon, roused a huge and dreadful wave
that arched above his head: he hurled it at him.
As when a fierce wind ruffles up a heap
of dry wheat chaff; it scatters here and there;
so were the raft's long timbers flung apart.      370
He climbed astride a plank and rode along
as if on horseback. He took off the clothes
Calypso gave him, but he tied the scarf
around his chest, and dove into the sea,
spreading his arms to swim. The Lord of Earthquakes
saw him and nodded, muttering, "At last
you are in pain! Go drift across the sea,
till you meet people blessed by Zeus, the Sky Lord.
But even then, I think you will not lack
for suffering." He spurred his fine-maned horses,      380
and went to Aegae, where he had his home.

Athena, child of Zeus, devised a plan.
She blocked the path of all the other winds,
told them to cease and made them go to sleep,
but roused swift Boreas and smoothed the waves
in front of him, so that Odysseus
could reach Phaeacia and escape from death.

* * *

Shaken but purposeful, he told himself,

"Zeus went beyond my hopes and let me see
dry land! I made it, cutting the abyss!
But I see no way out from this gray sea.      410
There are steep cliffs offshore, and all around
the rushing water roars; the rock runs sheer;
the sea is deep near shore; there is no way
to set my feet on land without disaster.

If I attempt to scramble out, a wave
will seize and dash me on the jagged rock;
a useless effort. But if I swim on farther,
looking for bays or coves or slanting beaches,
storm winds may seize me once again and drag me,
howling with grief, towards the fish-filled sea.                    420
A god may even send a great sea-monster,
the kind that famous Amphitrite rears.
I know Poseidon wants to do me harm."
As he was thinking this, the waves grew big
and hurled him at the craggy shore. His skin
would have been ripped away, and his bones smashed,
had not Athena given him a thought.
He grabbed a rock as he was swept along
with both hands, and clung to it, groaning, till
the wave passed by. But then the swell rushed back,                    430
and struck him hard and hurled him out to sea.
As when an octopus, dragged from its den,
has many pebbles sticking to its suckers,
so his strong hands were skinned against the rocks.
A mighty wave rolled over him again.

*　*　*

## KING JAMES BIBLE

### *From* The Book of Ruth[†]

*　*　*

Turn again, my daughters, go your way; for I am too old to have an
husband. If I should say, I have hope, if I should have an husband
also to night, and should also bear sons; [13]would ye tarry for them
till they were grown? would ye stay for them from having husbands?
nay, my daughters; for it grieveth me much for your sakes that the

† From Ruth 1.12–17, 1.22–2.1–2 in *The English Bible: The Old Testament: A Norton
Critical Edition* (New York: W. W. Norton, 2012), p. 494. Copyright © 2012 by W. W.
Norton & Company, Inc. Used by permission of W. W. Norton & Company, Inc. Rights
in the Authorized Version in the United Kingdom are vested in the Crown. Reproduced
by permission of the Crown's patentee, Cambridge University Press. The Book of Ruth
opens with a family—parents and two adult sons—from Bethlehem living in Moab
because of famine at home. The sons marry women from Moab. When the father and
sons die, the mother, Naomi, and her daughters-in-law, Orpah and Ruth, are widows.
Rather than remain in Moab, Ruth follows Naomi back to Bethlehem, where, poor and
exiled, she must feed herself by gleaning corn from the fields of the wealthy. Woolf
drew upon the imagery of a poor immigrant widow—and on John Keats's use of this
image in his "Ode to a Nightingale" (see p. 234)—in her description of Rezia in the
moments after Septimus's death. Although Woolf grew up in a secular family, she was
familiar with the Bible.

hand of the LORD is gone out against me. ¹⁴And they lifted up their voice, and wept again: and Orpah kissed her mother in law; but Ruth clave unto her. ¹⁵And she said, Behold, thy sister in law is gone back unto her people, and unto her gods: return thou after thy sister in law. ¹⁶And Ruth said, Intreat me not to leave thee, or to return from following after thee: for whither thou goest, I will go; and where thou lodgest, I will lodge: thy people shall be my people, and thy God my God: ¹⁷where thou diest, will I die, and there will I be buried: the LORD do so to me, and more also, if ought but death part thee and me.

\* \* \*

²²So Naomi returned, and Ruth the Moabitess, her daughter in law, with her, which returned out of the country of Moab: and they came to Bethlehem in the beginning of barley harvest.

²And Naomi had a kinsman of her husband's, a mighty man of wealth, of the family of Elimelech; and his name was Boaz. ²And Ruth the Moabitess said unto Naomi, Let me now go to the field, and glean ears of corn after him in whose sight I shall find grace. And she said unto her, Go, my daughter.

\* \* \*

# WILLIAM SHAKESPEARE

## *From* Richard II 5.5[†]

*Enter* RICHARD.

RICHARD    I have been studying how to compare
    This prison where I live unto the world;
    And, for because the world is populous
    And here is not a creature but myself,
5    I cannot do it. Yet I'll hammer't° out.           *work it*
    My brain I'll prove the female° to my soul,    *(that is, receptive)*
    My soul the father, and these two beget
    A generation of still-breeding° thoughts;    *ever-breeding*

† From *Richard II* 5.5.1–22 in *The Norton Shakespeare: Volume 1, Early Plays and Poems*, gen. eds. Stephen Greenblatt, Walter Cohen, Suzanne Gossett, Jean E. Howard, Katharine Eisaman Maus, Gordon McMullan, 3rd ed. (New York: W. W. Norton, 2016), pp. 952–53. Copyright © 2015, 2008, 1997 by W. W. Norton & Company, Inc. Used by permission of W. W. Norton & Company, Inc. In *Mrs. Dalloway*'s last pages, Sally Seton tries to remember a play where a man scratches on the wall of his cell. She seems to be thinking of *Richard II*. In this speech, Richard's only soliloquy, he compares the cell in which he is imprisoned to the world and imagines clawing his way out. J. M. Dent republished the play in 1923. It was performed in London for two weeks in June 1924. Woolf reread *Richard II* that August (*Diary*, vol. 2, 310).

And these same thoughts people this little world
10  In humors[1] like the people of this world,°          (*the real world*)
For no thought is contented. The better sort,
As thoughts of things divine, are intermixed
With scruples° and do set the faith itself          doubts
Against the faith,[2] as thus: "Come, little ones";[3]
15  And then again,
"It is as hard to come as for a camel
To thread the postern of a needle's eye."[4]
Thoughts° tending to ambition, they do plot          *Other thoughts*
Unlikely wonders:° how these vain weak nails          *miracles*
20  May tear a passage through the flinty ribs
Of this hard world, my raggèd° prison walls;          *rugged*
And, for they cannot, die in their own pride.°          *prime of life; arrogance*


## *From* Othello 2.1[†]

*Enter* OTHELLO *and Attendants.*

CASSIO                              Lo, where he comes!
OTHELLO    O my fair warrior!
DESDEMONA                    My dear Othello!
175  OTHELLO    It gives me wonder great as my content
To see you here before me. O my soul's joy!
If after every tempest come such calms,
May the winds blow till they have wakened death,
And let the laboring bark° climb hills of seas          *small ship*
180  Olympus-high, and duck again as low
As hell's from heaven. If it were now to die,
'Twere now to be most happy—for I fear
My soul hath her content so absolute
That not another comfort like to this
Succeeds° in unknown fate.°          *will follow/future*
185  DESDEMONA                    The heavens forbid

---

1. Temperaments; caprices.
2. *the faith . . . faith*: scriptural passage against scriptural passage.
3. From Matthew 19:14, Mark 10:14, and Luke 18:25, implying the ease of obtaining salvation.
4. Adapting Matthew 19:24, Mark 10:25, or Luke 18:25, which describe the unlikeliness of the rich reaching heaven.
† From *Othello* 2.1.173–93 in *The Norton Shakespeare: Vol. II Later Plays and Poems*, gen. eds. Stephen Greenblatt, Walter Cohen, Suzanne Gossett, Jean E. Howard, Katharine Eisaman Maus, Gordon McMullan, 3rd ed. (New York: W. W. Norton, 2016), p. 400. Copyright © 2015, 2008, 1997 by W. W. Norton & Company, Inc. Used by permission of W. W. Norton & Company, Inc. Several times in *Mrs. Dalloway*, Clarissa compares her joy at being with Sally to Othello's joy upon reuniting with Desdemona. Given Shakespeare's tragic ending, the analogy seems to foreclose long-term happiness between the two.

But that our loves and comforts should increase
Even as our days do grow.
OTHELLO                           Amen to that, sweet powers!
I cannot speak enough of this content;
It° stops me here.° It is too much of joy.      (Emotion)/now, in my kiss
[*They kiss.*]
190    And this, and this, the greatest discords be
That e'er our hearts shall make.
IAGO [*aside*]                        Oh, you are well tuned now,
But I'll set down the pegs that make this music,
As honest as I am.


## *From* Cymbeline 4.2[†]

GUIDERIUS    Fear no more the heat o'th' sun,
             Nor the furious winter's rages.
             Thou thy worldly task hast done,
260          Home art gone and ta'en thy wages.
             Golden lads and girls all must,
             As° chimney-sweepers, come to dust.            Like
ARVIRAGUS    Fear no more the frown o'th' great,
             Thou art past the tyrant's stroke.
265          Care no more to clothe and eat,
             To thee the reed is as the oak.
             The scepter, learning, physic° must     medical knowledge
             All follow this and come to dust.
GUIDERIUS    Fear no more the lightning flash,
270 ARVIRAGUS    Nor th'all-dreaded thunder-stone.°            thunderbolt
GUIDERIUS    Fear not slander, censure rash.
ARVIRAGUS    Thou hast finished joy and moan.
BOTH         All lovers young, all lovers must
             Consign to thee and come to dust.

[†] From *Cymbeline* 4.2.257–80 in *The Norton Shakespeare: Vol. II Later Plays and Poems*,
gen. eds. Stephen Greenblatt, Walter Cohen, Suzanne Gossett, Jean E. Howard, Katharine Eisaman Maus, Gordon McMullan, 3rd ed. (New York: W. W. Norton, 2016),
pp. 1389–90. Copyright © 2015, 2008, 1997 by W. W. Norton & Company, Inc. Used by
permission of W. W. Norton & Company, Inc. Shakespeare's late romance *Cymbeline* has
a terrifically complex plot. This beautiful song is a dirge, or funeral song, which offers
some small comfort in the idea that a dead youth has now passed beyond fear, and will
never again be either too cold or too hot. Clarissa sees *Cymbeline* on display in a bookstore window early in *Mrs. Dalloway*, and both she and Septimus have the song running
through their heads over the course of the day. While this play is fairly obscure, it was
popular in late Victorian England and it is the play that converted Woolf to her lifelong
love of Shakespeare. In this scene, Imogen, a princess in exile, is disguised as a boy and
has taken a potion that makes her appear to be dead. Two huntsmen (actually her long-
lost brothers, living in a separate exile) find her body and, believing the living woman to
be a dead boy, sing the body to rest. All are reunited in the play's bittersweet ending.

| | | | |
|---|---|---|---|
| 275 | GUIDERIUS | No exorciser° harm thee. | *conjurer of spirits* |
| | ARVIRAGUS | Nor no witchcraft charm thee. | |
| | GUIDERIUS | Ghost unlaid forbear thee. | |
| | ARVIRAGUS | Nothing ill come near thee. | |
| | BOTH | Quiet consummation° have, | *ending* |
| 280 | | And renowned be thy grave. | |

# ALEXANDER POPE

## *From* The Rape of The Lock†

But when to mischief mortals bend their will                    125
How soon they find fit instruments of ill!
Just then, Clarissa drew with tempting grace
A two-edged weapon from her shining case:
So ladies in romance assist their knight,
Present the spear, and arm him for the fight.                   130
He takes the gift with rev'rence, and extends
The little engine on his fingers' ends;
This just behind Belinda's neck he spread,
As o'er the fragrant steams she bends her head.
Swift to the lock a thousand sprites repair,                    135
A thousand wings, by turns, blow back the hair;
And thrice they twitched the diamond in her ear;
Thrice she looked back, and thrice the foe drew near.

# JOHN KEATS

## *From* Ode to a Nightingale‡

### 7

Thou wast not born for death, immortal Bird!
No hungry generations tread thee down;
The voice I hear this passing night was heard

---

† From *The Rape of the Lock*, Canto 3.125–38, in *Pope's* The Rape of the Lock, ed. Rev. Arthur Wentworth Eaton (New York: Silver, Burdett and Company, 1901). Pope's bitter satire, first published in 1717, tells the story of a symbolic rape: the efforts by a young man to steal a lock of a woman's hair. As we see in this excerpt, it is a young woman called Clarissa who provides him with the scissors. This Clarissa is one of two famous literary Clarissas who precede Clarissa Dalloway. The other is the heroine of Samuel Richardson's 1748 novel, *Clarissa*, which tells the story in letters of a virtuous young woman, Clarissa Harlowe, who runs off with a notorious womanizer, Robert Lovelace. Although Woolf's father admired and wrote extensively on both Pope and Richardson, Woolf did not. She did not read *Clarissa* until after the publication of *Mrs. Dalloway*.

‡ From "Ode to a Nightingale" lines 61–70, first published in *Lamia, Isabella, The Eve of St. Agnes, and other poems* (1820). Woolf drew upon the imagery here as well as that from the Book of Ruth in her description of Rezia's grief.

In ancient days by emperor and clown:
65    Perhaps the self-same song that found a path
Through the sad heart of Ruth, when, sick for home,
She stood in tears amid the alien corn;
The same that oft-times hath
Charm'd magic casements, opening on the foam
70    Of perilous seas, in faery lands forlorn.

## 8

Forlorn! the very word is like a bell
To toll me back from thee to my sole self!
Adieu! the fancy cannot cheat so well
As she is fam'd to do, deceiving elf.
75    Adieu! adieu! thy plaintive anthem fades
Past the near meadows, over the still stream,
Up the hill-side; and now 'tis buried deep
In the next valley-glades:
Was it a vision, or a waking dream?
80    Fled is that music:—Do I wake or sleep?

# HERMANN VON GILM

## Allerseelen†

Stell auf den Tisch die duftenden Reseden,
Die letzten roten Astern trag herbei
Und lass uns wieder von der Liebe reden,
        Wie einst im Mai.

Gib mir die Hand, dass ich sie heimlich drücke,
Und wenn mans sieht, mir ist es einerlei:
Gib mir nur einen deiner süssen Blicke,
        Wie einst im Mai.

Es blüht und funkelt heut auf jedem Grabe,
Ein Tag im Jahr ist ja den Toten frei;
Komm an mein Herz, dass ich dich wieder habe,
        Wie einst im Mai.

† From *The Ring of Words: An Anthology of Song Texts*, trans. Philip L. Miller (1963; rpt. New York: W. W. Norton, 1973), pp. 54–55. Although the woman by the Tube station singing "ee um fa um so" appears to be singing nonsense, J. Hillis Miller recognized in "*Mrs. Dalloway*: Repetition as the Raising of the Dead" (1982) that the pattern of images in the surrounding paragraphs closely resembles this poem by Hermann Von Gilm. Largely forgotten today, Von Gilm is still remembered for "Allerseelen," as it was set to music by Richard Strauss and continues to be recorded. The Woolfs loved music, and Leonard especially was an admirer of German song.

## All Souls' Day

Place on the table the fragrant mignonettes,
bring in the last red asters,
and let us speak again of love,
as once in May.

Give me your hand, that I may secretly press it,
and if anyone sees, that matters not to me.
Give me only one of your sweet glances,
as once in May.

Every grave blooms and glows tonight:
one day in the year belongs to the dead.
Come to my heart, that I may hold you again,
as once in May.

## H. G. WELLS

## *From* Ann Veronica: A Modern Romance[†]

She decided to go out into the London afternoon again and get something to eat in an Aerated Bread shop or some such place, and perhaps find a cheap room for herself. Of course that was what she had to do; she had to find a cheap room for herself and work! This Room No. 47 was no more than a sort of railway compartment on the way to that.

How does one get work?

She walked along the Strand and across Trafalgar Square, and by the Haymarket to Piccadilly, and so through dignified squares and palatial alleys to Oxford Street; and her mind was divided between a speculative treatment of employment on the one hand, and breezes—zephyr breezes—of the keenest appreciation for London, on the other. The jolly part of it was that for the first time in her life so far as London was concerned, she was not going anywhere in particular; for the first time in her life it seemed to her she was taking London in.

She tried to think how people get work. Ought she to walk into some of these places and tell them what she could do? She

† From *Ann Veronica: A Modern Romance* (New York and London: Harper & Brothers Publishers, 1909). Wells's 1909 novel tells the story of a young woman attempting to make a life for herself in London. This scene describes an unsettling incident in which Ann Veronica is followed by a much older stranger. Woolf wrote the mirror image of this scene into *Mrs. Dalloway*, where Peter delights in stalking a young woman through the same part of London.

hesitated at the window of a shipping-office in Cockspur Street and at the Army and Navy Stores, but decided that perhaps there would be some special and customary hour, and that it would be better for her to find this out before she made her attempt. And, besides, she didn't just immediately want to make her attempt.

She fell into a pleasant dream of positions and work. Behind every one of these myriad fronts she passed there must be a career or careers. Her ideas of women's employment and a modern woman's pose in life were based largely on the figure of Vivie Warren in *Mrs. Warren's Profession*. She had seen *Mrs. Warren's Profession* furtively with Hetty Widgett from the gallery of a Stage Society performance one Monday afternoon. Most of it had been incomprehensible to her, or comprehensible in a way that checked further curiosity, but the figure of Vivien, hard, capable, successful, and bullying, and ordering about a veritable Teddy in the person of Frank Gardner, appealed to her. She saw herself in very much Vivie's position—managing something.

Her thoughts were deflected from Vivie Warren by the peculiar behavior of a middle-aged gentleman in Piccadilly. He appeared suddenly from the infinite in the neighborhood of the Burlington Arcade, crossing the pavement toward her and with his eyes upon her. He seemed to her indistinguishably about her father's age. He wore a silk hat a little tilted, and a morning coat buttoned round a tight, contained figure; and a white slip gave a finish to his costume and endorsed the quiet distinction of his tie. His face was a little flushed perhaps, and his small, brown eyes were bright. He stopped on the curb-stone, not facing her but as if he was on his way to cross the road, and spoke to her suddenly over his shoulder.

"Whither away?" he said, very distinctly in a curiously wheedling voice. Ann Veronica stared at his foolish, propitiatory smile, his hungry gaze, through one moment of amazement, then stepped aside and went on her way with a quickened step. But her mind was ruffled, and its mirror-like surface of satisfaction was not easily restored.

Queer old gentleman!

The art of ignoring is one of the accomplishments of every well-bred girl, so carefully instilled that at last she can even ignore her own thoughts and her own knowledge. Ann Veronica could at the same time ask herself what this queer old gentleman could have meant by speaking to her, and know—know in general terms, at least—what that accosting signified. About her, as she had gone day by day to and from the Tredgold College, she had seen and not seen many an incidental aspect of those sides of life about which girls are expected to know nothing, aspects that were extraordinarily relevant to her own position and outlook on the world, and yet by convention ineffably remote. For all that she was of exceptional intellectual enterprise, she had never yet considered these things with unaverted eyes. She had viewed them askance, and without exchanging ideas with any one else in the world about them.

She went on her way now no longer dreaming and appreciative, but disturbed and unwillingly observant behind her mask of serene contentment.

That delightful sense of free, unembarrassed movement was gone.

* * *

# RUPERT BROOKE

## The Soldier[†]

If I should die, think only this of me:
  That there's some corner of a foreign field
That is for ever England. There shall be
  In that rich earth a richer dust concealed;
A dust whom England bore, shaped, made aware,      5
  Gave, once, her flowers to love, her ways to roam,
A body of England's, breathing English air,
  Washed by the rivers, blest by suns of home.

And think, this heart, all evil shed away,
  A pulse in the eternal mind, no less      10
    Gives somewhere back the thoughts by England given;
Her sights and sounds; dreams happy as her day;
  And laughter, learnt of friends; and gentleness,
    In hearts at peace, under an English heaven.

† From *The Penguin Book of First World War Poetry*, ed. George Walter (New York: Penguin, 2006), p. 108. This sonnet, composed in 1915, is the most famous of several poems by Brooke called "The Soldier." At Clarissa's party, Lady Bruton thinks a mishmash of patriotic thoughts, including "to be not English even among the dead" (p. 127), an idea that recollects this sonnet about dying abroad. Brooke did, in fact, die abroad in 1915. Woolf regretted and was angered by how the nation moved to turn him into a patriotic hero and an encouragement to others to enlist. Brooke had been a friend and is, in part, a model for Septimus.

# T. S. ELIOT

## *From* The Waste Land[†]

### II. A Game of Chess[1]

The Chair she sat in, like a burnished throne,[2]
Glowed on the marble, where the glass
Held up by standards wrought with fruited vines
From which a golden Cupidon peeped out                                    80
(Another hid his eyes behind his wing)
Doubled the flames of sevenbranched candelabra
Reflecting light upon the table as
The glitter of her jewels rose to meet it,
From satin cases poured in rich profusion;                                85
In vials of ivory and coloured glass
Unstoppered, lurked her strange synthetic perfumes,
Unguent, powdered, or liquid—troubled, confused
And drowned the sense in odours; stirred by the air
That freshened from the window, these ascended                            90
In fattening the prolonged candle-flames,
Flung their smoke into the laquearia,[3]
Stirring the pattern on the coffered ceiling.
Huge sea-wood fed with copper
Burned green and orange, framed by the coloured stone,                    95
In which sad light a carvèd dolphin swam.
Above the antique mantel was displayed
As though a window gave upon the sylvan scene[4]

---

† From *The Waste Land: A Norton Critical Edition*, ed. Michael North (New York: W. W. Norton, 2001), p. 8. Copyright © 2001 by W. W. Norton & Company, Inc. Used by permission of W. W. Norton & Company, Inc. Notes are North's unless otherwise indicated. Woolf and Eliot's friendship was at its most intimate while she was writing *Mrs. Dalloway*, and she followed *The Waste Land* closely. She heard him read the poem aloud before she and Leonard saw its publication at the Hogarth Press. *Mrs. Dalloway* contains many echoes of the poem, including an atmospheric sense from this section of "A Game of Chess," in which a wealthy woman sits in a beautifully furnished room, surrounded by cosmetics and a vague sense of looming threat. In this excerpt, Eliot himself shows his debt to both Shakespeare's *Antony and Cleopatra* and Pope's *The Rape of the Lock* (see p. 233 above).

1. Eliot takes the title of this section from a satirical play of the same name by Thomas Middleton (1570?–1627). First produced in 1625, A *Game of Chess* was suppressed because of the biting way in which it allegorized English conflict with Spain as a chess match. The title also alludes to Middleton's *Women Beware Women* (published in 1657), in which a young wife is seduced while her unwitting mother-in-law plays chess.

2. In his own note, Eliot cites Shakespeare's *Antony and Cleopatra*, 2.2.190. In this passage, Enobarbus describes to Agrippa how Cleopatra looked on her first meeting with Mark Antony: "The barge she sat in, like a burnished throne, / Burned on the water: the poop was beaten gold. . . ."

3. The panels of a coffered ceiling. In his note, Eliot cites a passage from Virgil's *Aeneid*: "Burning torches hang from the gold-panelled ceiling, / And vanquish the night with their flames" (Latin).

4. Eliot cites a passage from Milton's *Paradise Lost*, Book 4, in which Satan, approaching Eden, sees it as a "delicious Paradise" and a "Sylvan Scene" overgrown with trees and bushes.

The change of Philomel, by the barbarous king
So rudely forced;[5] yet there the nightingale                    100
Filled all the desert with inviolable voice
And still she cried, and still the world pursues,
"Jug Jug"[6] to dirty ears.

* * *

# KATHERINE MANSFIELD

## The Garden Party[†]

And after all the weather was ideal. They could not have had a more perfect day for a garden party if they had ordered it. Windless, warm, the sky without a cloud. Only the blue was veiled with a haze of light gold, as it is sometimes in early summer. The gardener had been up since dawn, mowing the lawns and sweeping them, until the grass and the dark flat rosettes where the daisy plants had been seemed to shine. As for the roses, you could not help feeling they understood that roses are the only flowers that impress people at garden parties; the only flowers that everybody is certain of knowing. Hundreds, yes, literally hundreds, had come out in a single night; the green bushes bowed down as though they had been visited by archangels.

Breakfast was not yet over before the men came to put up the marquee.

'Where do you want the marquee put, mother?'

'My dear child, it's no use asking me. I'm determined to leave everything to you children this year. Forget I am your mother. Treat me as an honoured guest.'

---

5. Eliot refers in his note to the story of Tereus and Philomela as told in Ovid's *Metamorphoses*. *The Metamorphoses*, an epic poem by Ovid (c. 43 B.C.E.–C. 17 C.E.), recounts the story of Procne and Philomel (among many other myths). Cruel King Tereus married Procne and then raped her sister, Philomel, cutting out Philomel's tongue so she could not tell the story. The sisters avenged the rape by killing Tereus and Procne's son. To end the violence, the gods turned Tereus, Procne, and Philomel into birds. Procne and Philomel became, respectively, a nightingale and a swallow (although earlier, Greek versions of the story have the birds reversed, with Philomel becoming the swallow) [Editor].

6. Conventional literary onomatopoeia for the sound a nightingale supposedly makes.

† From *Katherine Mansfield's Selected Stories: A Norton Critical Edition*, ed. Vincent O'Sullivan (New York: W. W. Norton, 2006), pp. 286–98. Copyright © 2006 by W. W. Norton & Company, Inc. Used by permission of W. W. Norton & Company, Inc. Woolf and Mansfield had a close and competitive friendship until Mansfield's early death from tuberculosis in 1923. "The Garden Party" was written in 1921 and published as the title story in *"The Garden Party" and Other Stories* (1922). *Mrs. Dalloway* takes up many of the themes of the story: the intrusion of death at a party; a young woman's uneasy transition to adulthood; class barriers.

But Meg could not possibly go and supervise the men. She had washed her hair before breakfast, and she sat drinking her coffee in a green turban, with a dark wet curl stamped on each cheek. Jose, the butterfly, always came down in a silk petticoat and a kimono jacket.

'You'll have to go, Laura, you're the artistic one.'

Away Laura flew, still holding her piece of bread-and-butter. It's so delicious to have an excuse for eating out of doors, and besides, she loved having to arrange things; she always felt she could do it so much better than anybody else.

Four men in their shirt-sleeves stood grouped together on the garden path. They carried staves covered with rolls of canvas, and they had big tool-bags slung on their backs. They looked impressive. Laura wished now that she was not holding that piece of bread-and-butter, but there was nowhere to put it, and she couldn't possibly throw it away. She blushed and tried to look severe and even a little bit short-sighted as she came up to them.

'Good morning,' she said, copying her mother's voice. But that sounded so fearfully affected that she was ashamed, and stammered like a little girl, 'Oh—er—have you come—is it about the marquee?'

'That's right, miss,' said the tallest of the men, a lanky, freckled fellow, and he shifted his tool-bag, knocked back his straw hat and smiled down at her. 'That's about it.'

His smile was so easy, so friendly, that Laura recovered. What nice eyes he had, small, but such a dark blue! And now she looked at the others, they were smiling too. 'Cheer up, we won't bite,' their smile seemed to say. How very nice workmen were! And what a beautiful morning! She mustn't mention the morning; she must be business-like. The marquee.

'Well, what about the lily-lawn? Would that do?'

And she pointed to the lily-lawn with the hand that didn't hold the bread-and-butter. They turned, they stared in the direction. A little fat chap thrust out his under-lip, and the tall fellow frowned.

'I don't fancy it,' said he. 'Not conspicuous enough. You see, with a thing like a marquee,' and he turned to Laura in his easy way, 'you want to put it somewhere where it'll give you a bang slap in the eye, if you follow me.'

Laura's upbringing made her wonder for a moment whether it was quite respectful of a workman to talk to her of bangs slap in the eye. But she did quite follow him.

'A corner of the tennis-court,' she suggested. 'But the band's going to be in one corner.'

'H'm, going to have a band, are you?' said another of the workmen. He was pale. He had a haggard look as his dark eyes scanned the tennis-court. What was he thinking?

'Only a very small band,' said Laura gently. Perhaps he wouldn't mind so much if the band was quite small. But the tall fellow interrupted.

'Look here, miss, that's the place. Against those trees. Over there. That'll do fine.'

Against the karakas.[1] Then the karaka-trees would be hidden. And they were so lovely, with their broad, gleaming leaves, and their clusters of yellow fruit. They were like trees you imagined growing on a desert island, proud, solitary, lifting their leaves and fruits to the sun in a kind of silent splendour. Must they be hidden by a marquee?

They must. Already the men had shouldered their staves and were making for the place. Only the tall fellow was left. He bent down, pinched a sprig of lavender, put his thumb and forefinger to his nose and snuffed up the smell. When Laura saw the gesture she forgot all about the karakas in her wonder at him caring for things like that— caring for the smell of lavender. How many men that she knew would have done such a thing. Oh, how extraordinarily nice workmen were, she thought. Why couldn't she have workmen for friends rather than the silly boys she danced with and who came to Sunday night supper? She would get on much better with men like these.

It's all the fault, she decided, as the tall fellow drew something on the back of an envelope, something that was to be looped up or left to hang, of these absurd class distinctions. Well, for her part, she didn't feel them. Not a bit, not an atom. . . . And now there came the chock-chock of wooden hammers. Some one whistled, some one sang out, 'Are you right there, matey?' 'Matey!' The friendliness of it, the—the—Just to prove how happy she was, just to show the tall fellow how at home she felt, and how she despised stupid conventions, Laura took a big bite of her bread-and-butter as she stared at the little drawing. She felt just like a work-girl.

'Laura, Laura, where are you? Telephone, Laura!' a voice cried from the house.

'Coming!' Away she skimmed, over the lawn, up the path, up the steps, across the veranda, and into the porch. In the hall her father and Laurie were brushing their hats ready to go to the office.

'I say, Laura,' said Laurie very fast, 'you might just give a squiz at my coat before this afternoon. See if it wants pressing.'

'I will,' said she. Suddenly she couldn't stop herself. She ran at Laurie and gave him a small, quick squeeze. 'Oh, I do love parties, don't you?' gasped Laura.

'Ra-ther,' said Laurie's warm, boyish voice, and he squeezed his sister too, and gave her a gentle push. 'Dash off to the telephone, old girl.'

1. A tree with glossy dark leaves and large orange-yellow berries.

The telephone. 'Yes, yes; oh yes. Kitty? Good morning, dear. Come to lunch? Do, dear. Delighted of course. It will only be a very scratch meal—just the sandwich crusts and broken meringue-shells and what's left over. Yes, isn't it a perfect morning? Your white? Oh, I certainly should. One moment—hold the line. Mother's calling.' And Laura sat back. 'What, mother? Can't hear.'

Mrs Sheridan's voice floated down the stairs. 'Tell her to wear that sweet hat she had on last Sunday.'

'Mother says you're to wear that *sweet* hat you had on last Sunday. Good. One o'clock. Bye-bye.'

Laura put back the receiver, flung her arms over her head, took a deep breath, stretched and let them fall. 'Huh,' she sighed, and the moment after the sigh she sat up quickly. She was still, listening. All the doors in the house seemed to be open. The house was alive with soft, quick steps and running voices. The green baize door that led to the kitchen regions swung open and shut with a muffled thud. And now there came a long, chuckling absurd sound. It was the heavy piano being moved on its stiff castors. But the air! If you stopped to notice, was the air always like this? Little faint winds were playing chase in at the tops of the windows, out at the doors. And there were two tiny spots of sun, one on the inkpot, one on a silver photograph frame, playing too. Darling little spots. Especially the one on the inkpot lid. It was quite warm. A warm little silver star. She could have kissed it.

The front door bell pealed, and there sounded the rustle of Sadie's print skirt on the stairs. A man's voice murmured; Sadie answered, careless, 'I'm sure I don't know. Wait. I'll ask Mrs Sheridan.'

'What is it, Sadie?' Laura came into the hall.

'It's the florist, Miss Laura.'

It was, indeed. There, just inside the door, stood a wide, shallow tray full of pots of pink lilies. No other kind. Nothing but lilies—canna lilies, big pink flowers, wide open, radiant, almost frighteningly alive on bright crimson stems.

'O-oh, Sadie!' said Laura, and the sound was like a little moan. She crouched down as if to warm herself at that blaze of lilies; she felt they were in her fingers, on her lips, growing in her breast.

'It's some mistake,' she said faintly. 'Nobody ever ordered so many. Sadie, go and find mother.'

But at that moment Mrs Sheridan joined them.

"It's quite right,' she said calmly. 'Yes, I ordered them. Aren't they lovely?' She pressed Laura's arm. 'I was passing the shop yesterday, and I saw them in the window. And I suddenly thought for once in my life I shall have enough canna lilies. The garden party will be a good excuse.'

'But I thought you said you didn't mean to interfere,' said Laura. Sadie had gone. The florist's man was still outside at his van. She put her arm round her mother's neck and gently, very gently, she bit her mother's ear.

'My darling child, you wouldn't like a logical mother, would you? Don't do that. Here's the man.'

He carried more lilies still, another whole tray.

'Bank them up, just inside the door, on both sides of the porch, please,' said Mrs Sheridan. 'Don't you agree, Laura?'

'Oh, I *do*, mother.'

In the drawing-room Meg, Jose and good little Hans had at last succeeded in moving the piano.

'Now, if we put this chesterfield against the wall and move everything out of the room except the chairs, don't you think?'

'Quite.'

'Hans, move these tables into the smoking-room, and bring a sweeper to take these marks off the carpet and—one moment, Hans—' Jose loved giving orders to the servants, and they loved obeying her. She always made them feel they were taking part in some drama. 'Tell mother and Miss Laura to come here at once.'

'Very good, Miss Jose.'

She turned to Meg. 'I want to hear what the piano sounds like, just in case I'm asked to sing this afternoon. Let's try over "This Life is Weary".'

*Pom!* Ta-ta-ta *Tee*-ta! The piano burst out so passionately that Jose's face changed. She clasped her hands. She looked mournfully and enigmatically at her mother and Laura as they came in.

> This Life is *Wee*-ary,
> A Tear—a Sigh.
> A Love that *Chan*-ges,
>    This Life is *Wee*-ary,
> A Tear—a Sigh.
> A Love that *Chan*-ges,
> And then . . . Good-bye!

But at the word 'Good-bye', and although the piano sounded more desperate than ever, her face broke into a brilliant, dreadfully unsympathetic smile.

'Aren't I in good voice, mummy?' she beamed.

> This Life is *Wee*-ary,
> Hope comes to Die.
> A Dream—a *Wa*-kening.

But now Sadie interrupted them. 'What is it, Sadie?'

'If you please, m'm, cook says have you got the flags for the sandwiches?'

'The flags for the sandwiches, Sadie?' echoed Mrs Sheridan dreamily. And the children knew by her face that she hadn't got them. 'Let me see.' And she said to Sadie firmly, 'Tell cook I'll let her have them in ten minutes.'

Sadie went.

'Now, Laura,' said her mother quickly, 'come with me into the smoking-room. I've got the names somewhere on the back of an envelope. You'll have to write them out for me. Meg, go upstairs this minute and take that wet thing off your head. Jose, run and finish dressing this instant. Do you hear me, children, or shall I have to tell your father when he comes home to-night? And—and, Jose, pacify cook if you do go into the kitchen, will you? I'm terrified of her this morning.'

The envelope was found at last behind the dining-room clock, though how it had got there Mrs Sheridan could not imagine.

'One of you children must have stolen it out of my bag, because I remember vividly—cream-cheese and lemon-curd. Have you done that?'

'Yes.'

'Egg and—' Mrs Sheridan held the envelope away from her. 'It looks like mice. It can't be mice, can it?'

'Olive, pet,' said Laura, looking over her shoulder.

'Yes, of course, olive. What a horrible combination it sounds. Egg and olive.'

They were finished at last, and Laura took them off to the kitchen. She found Jose there pacifying the cook, who did not look at all terrifying.

'I have never seen such exquisite sandwiches,' said Jose's rapturous voice. 'How many kinds did you say there were, cook? Fifteen?'

'Fifteen, Miss Jose.'

'Well, cook, I congratulate you.'

Cook swept up crusts with the long sandwich knife, and smiled broadly.

'Godber's has come,' announced Sadie, issuing out of the pantry. She had seen the man pass the window.

That meant the cream puffs had come. Godber's were famous for their cream puffs. Nobody ever thought of making them at home.

'Bring them in and put them on the table, my girl,' ordered cook.

Sadie brought them in and went back to the door. Of course Laura and Jose were far too grown-up to really care about such things. All the same, they couldn't help agreeing that the puffs looked very attractive. Very. Cook began arranging them, shaking off the extra icing sugar.

'Don't they carry one back to all one's parties?' said Laura.

'I suppose they do,' said practical Jose, who never liked to be carried back. 'They look beautifully light and feathery, I must say.'

'Have one each, my dears,' said cook in her comfortable voice. 'Yer ma won't know.'

Oh, impossible. Fancy cream puffs so soon after breakfast. The very idea made one shudder. All the same, two minutes later Jose and Laura were licking their fingers with that absorbed inward look that only comes from whipped cream.

'Let's go into the garden, out by the back way,' suggested Laura. 'I want to see how the men are getting on with the marquee. They're such awfully nice men.'

But the back door was blocked by cook, Sadie, Godber's man and Hans.

Something had happened.

'Tuk-tuk-tuk,' clucked cook like an agitated hen. Sadie had her hand clapped to her cheek as though she had toothache. Hans's face was screwed up in the effort to understand. Only Godber's man seemed to be enjoying himself; it was his story.

'What's the matter? What's happened?'

'There's been a horrible accident,' said cook. 'A man killed.'

'A man killed! Where? How? When?'

But Godber's man wasn't going to have his story snatched from under his very nose.

'Know those little cottages just below here, miss?' Know them? Of course, she knew them. 'Well, there's a young chap living there, name of Scott, a carter. His horse shied at a traction-engine, corner of Hawke Street this morning, and he was thrown out on the back of his head. Killed.'

'Dead!' Laura stared at Godber's man.

'Dead when they picked him up,' said Godber's man with relish. 'They were taking the body home as I come up here.' And he said to the cook, 'He's left a wife and five little ones.'

'Jose, come here.' Laura caught hold of her sister's sleeve and dragged her through the kitchen to the other side of the green baize door. There she paused and leaned against it. 'Jose!' she said, horrified, 'however are we going to stop everything?'

'Stop everything, Laura!' cried Jose in astonishment. 'What do you mean?'

'Stop the garden party, of course.' Why did Jose pretend?

But Jose was still more amazed. 'Stop the garden party? My dear Laura, don't be so absurd. Of course we can't do anything of the kind. Nobody expects us to. Don't be so extravagant.'

'But we can't possibly have a garden party with a man dead just outside the front gate.'

That really was extravagant, for the little cottages were in a lane to themselves at the very bottom of a steep rise that led up to the house. A broad road ran between. True, they were far too near. They were the greatest possible eyesore, and they had no right to be in that neighbourhood at all. They were little mean dwellings painted a chocolate brown. In the garden patches there was nothing but cabbage stalks, sick hens and tomato cans. The very smoke coming out of their chimneys was poverty-stricken. Little rags and shreds of smoke, so unlike the great silvery plumes that uncurled from the Sheridans' chimneys. Washerwomen lived in the lane and sweeps and a cobbler, and a man whose house-front was studded all over with minute bird-cages. Children swarmed. When the Sheridans were little they were forbidden to set foot there because of the revolting language and of what they might catch. But since they were grown up, Laura and Laurie on their prowls sometimes walked through. It was disgusting and sordid. They came out with a shudder. But still one must go everywhere; one must see everything. So through they went.

'And just think of what the band would sound like to that poor woman,' said Laura.

'Oh, Laura!' Jose began to be seriously annoyed. 'If you're going to stop a band playing every time some one has an accident, you'll lead a very strenuous life. I'm every bit as sorry about it as you. I feel just as sympathetic.' Her eyes hardened. She looked at her sister just as she used to when they were little and fighting together. 'You won't bring a drunken workman back to life by being sentimental,' she said softly.

'Drunk! Who said he was drunk?' Laura turned furiously on Jose. She said just as they had used to say on those occasions, 'I'm going straight up to tell mother.'

'Do, dear,' cooed Jose.

'Mother, can I come into your room?' Laura turned the big glass door-knob.

'Of course, child. Why, what's the matter? What's given you such a colour?' And Mrs Sheridan turned round from her dressing-table. She was trying on a new hat.

'Mother, a man's been killed,' began Laura.

'*Not* in the garden?' interrupted her mother.

'No, no!'

'Oh, what a fright you gave me!' Mrs Sheridan sighed with relief, and took off the big hat and held it on her knees.

'But listen, mother,' said Laura. Breathless, half-choking, she told the dreadful story. 'Of course, we can't have our party, can we?' she pleaded. 'The band and everybody arriving. They'd hear us, mother; they're nearly neighbours!'

To Laura's astonishment her mother behaved just like Jose; it was harder to bear because she seemed amused. She refused to take Laura seriously.

'But, my dear child, use your common sense. It's only by accident we've heard of it. If some one had died there normally—and I can't understand how they keep alive in those poky little holes—we should still be having our party, shouldn't we?'

Laura had to say 'yes' to that, but she felt it was all wrong. She sat down on her mother's sofa and pinched the cushion frill.

'Mother, isn't it really terribly heartless of us?' she asked.

'Darling!' Mrs Sheridan got up and came over to her, carrying the hat. Before Laura could stop her she had popped it on. 'My child!' said her mother, 'the hat is yours. It's made for you. It's much too young for me. I have never seen you look such a picture. Look at yourself!' And she held up her hand-mirror.

'But, mother,' Laura began again. She couldn't look at herself; she turned aside.

This time Mrs Sheridan lost patience just as Jose had done.

'You are being very absurd, Laura,' she said coldly. 'People like that don't expect sacrifices from us. And it's not very sympathetic to spoil everybody's enjoyment as you're doing now.'

'I don't understand,' said Laura, and she walked quickly out of the room into her own bedroom. There, quite by chance, the first thing she saw was this charming girl in the mirror, in her black hat trimmed with gold daisies, and a long black velvet ribbon. Never had she imagined she could look like that. Is mother right? she thought. And now she hoped her mother was right. Am I being extravagant? Perhaps it was extravagant. Just for a moment she had another glimpse of that poor woman and those little children, and the body being carried into the house. But it all seemed blurred, unreal, like a picture in the newspaper. I'll remember it again after the party's over, she decided. And somehow that seemed quite the best plan. . . .

Lunch was over by half-past one. By half-past two they were all ready for the fray. The green-coated band had arrived and was established in a corner of the tennis-court.

'My dear!' trilled Kitty Maitland, 'aren't they too like frogs for words? You ought to have arranged them round the pond with the conductor in the middle on a leaf.'

Laurie arrived and hailed them on his way to dress. At the sight of him Laura remembered the accident again. She wanted to tell him. If Laurie agreed with the others, then it was bound to be all right. And she followed him into the hall.

'Laurie!'

'Hallo!' He was half-way upstairs, but when he turned round and saw Laura he suddenly puffed out his cheeks and goggled his eyes at her. 'My word, Laura! You do look stunning,' said Laurie. 'What an absolutely topping hat!'

Laura said faintly 'Is it?' and smiled up at Laurie, and didn't tell him after all.

Soon after that people began coming in streams. The band struck up; the hired waiters ran from the house to the marquee. Wherever you looked there were couples strolling, bending to the flowers, greeting, moving on over the lawn. They were like bright birds that had alighted in the Sheridans' garden for this one afternoon, on their way to—where? Ah, what happiness it is to be with people who all are happy, to press hands, press cheeks, smile into eyes.

'Darling Laura, how well you look!'

'What a becoming hat, child!'

'Laura, you look quite Spanish. I've never seen you look so striking.'

And Laura, glowing, answered softly, 'Have you had tea? Won't you have an ice? The passion-fruit ices really are rather special.' She ran to her father and begged him. 'Daddy darling, can't the band have something to drink?'

And the perfect afternoon slowly ripened, slowly faded, slowly its petals closed.

'Never a more delightful garden party. . . .' 'The greatest success. . . .' 'Quite the most. . . .'

Laura helped her mother with the good-byes. They stood side by side in the porch till it was all over.

'All over, all over, thank heaven,' said Mrs Sheridan. 'Round up the others, Laura. Let's go and have some fresh coffee. I'm exhausted. Yes, it's been very successful. But oh, these parties, these parties! Why will you children insist on giving parties!' And they all of them sat down in the deserted marquee.

'Have a sandwich, daddy dear. I wrote the flag.'

'Thanks.' Mr Sheridan took a bite and the sandwich was gone. He took another. 'I suppose you didn't hear of a beastly accident that happened to-day?' he said.

'My dear,' said Mrs Sheridan, holding up her hand, 'we did. It nearly ruined the party. Laura insisted we should put it off.'

'Oh, mother!' Laura didn't want to be teased about it.

'It was a horrible affair all the same,' said Mr Sheridan. 'The chap was married too. Lived just below in the lane, and leaves a wife and half a dozen kiddies, so they say.'

An awkward little silence fell. Mrs Sheridan fidgeted with her cup. Really, it was very tactless of father. . . .

Suddenly she looked up. There on the table were all those sandwiches, cakes, puffs, all un-eaten, all going to be wasted. She had one of her brilliant ideas.

'I know,' she said. 'Let's make up a basket. Let's send that poor creature some of this perfectly good food. At any rate, it will be the greatest treat for the children. Don't you agree? And she's sure to have neighbours calling in and so on. What a point to have it all ready prepared. Laura!' She jumped up. 'Get me the big basket out of the stairs cupboard.'

'But, mother, do you really think it's a good idea?' said Laura.

Again, how curious, she seemed to be different from them all. To take scraps from their party. Would the poor woman really like that?

'Of course! What's the matter with you to-day? An hour or two ago you were insisting on us being sympathetic, and now—'

Oh well! Laura ran for the basket. It was filled, it was heaped by her mother.

'Take it yourself, darling,' said she. 'Run down just as you are. No, wait, take the arum lilies too. People of that class are so impressed by arum lilies.'

'The stems will ruin her lace frock,' said practical Jose.

So they would. Just in time. 'Only the basket, then. And, Laura!'— her mother followed her out of the marquee—'don't on any account—'

'What mother?'

No, better not put such ideas into the child's head! 'Nothing! Run along.'

It was just growing dusky as Laura shut their garden gates. A big dog ran by like a shadow. The road gleamed white, and down below in the hollow the little cottages were in deep shade. How quiet it seemed after the afternoon. Here she was going down the hill to somewhere where a man lay dead, and she couldn't realize it. Why couldn't she? She stopped a minute. And it seemed to her that kisses, voices, tinkling spoons, laughter, the smell of crushed grass were somehow inside her. She had no room for anything else. How strange! She looked up at the pale sky, and all she thought was, 'Yes, it was the most successful party.'

Now the broad road was crossed. The lane began, smoky and dark. Women in shawls and men's tweed caps hurried by. Men hung over the palings; the children played in the doorways. A low hum came from the mean little cottages. In some of them there was a flicker of light, and a shadow, crab-like, moved across the window. Laura bent her head and hurried on. She wished now she had put on a coat. How her frock shone! And the big hat with the velvet streamer—if only it was another hat! Were the people looking at her? They must be. It was a mistake to have come; she knew all along it was a mistake. Should she go back even now?

No, too late. This was the house. It must be. A dark knot of people stood outside. Beside the gate an old, old woman with a crutch sat in a chair, watching. She had her feet on a newspaper. The voices stopped as Laura drew near. The group parted. It was as though she was expected, as though they had known she was coming here.

Laura was terribly nervous. Tossing the velvet ribbon over her shoulder, she said to a woman standing by, 'Is this Mrs Scott's house?' and the woman, smiling queerly, said, 'It is, my lass.'

Oh, to be away from this! She actually said, 'Help me, God,' as she walked up the tiny path and knocked. To be away from those staring eyes, or to be covered up in anything, one of those women's shawls even. I'll just leave the basket and go, she decided. I shan't even wait for it to be emptied.

Then the door opened. A little woman in black showed in the gloom.

Laura said, 'Are you Mrs Scott?' But to her horror the woman answered, 'Walk in, please, miss,' and she was shut in the passage.

'No,' said Laura, 'I don't want to come in. I only want to leave this basket. Mother sent—'

The little woman in the gloomy passage seemed not to have heard her. 'Step this way, please, miss,' she said in an oily voice, and Laura followed her.

She found herself in a wretched little low kitchen, lighted by a smoky lamp. There was a woman sitting before the fire.

'Em,' said the little creature who had let her in. 'Em! It's a young lady.' She turned to Laura. She said meaningly, 'I'm 'er sister, miss. You'll excuse 'er, won't you?'

'Oh, but of course!' said Laura. 'Please, please don't disturb her. I—I only want to leave—'

But at that moment the woman at the fire turned round. Her face, puffed up, red, with swollen eyes and swollen lips, looked terrible. She seemed as though she couldn't understand why Laura was there. What did it mean? Why was this stranger standing in the kitchen with a basket? What was it all about? And the poor face puckered up again.

'All right, my dear,' said the other. 'I'll thenk the young lady.'

And again she began, 'You'll excuse her, miss, I'm sure,' and her face, swollen too, tried an oily smile.

Laura only wanted to get out, to get away. She was back in the passage. The door opened. She walked straight through into the bedroom where the dead man was lying.

'You'd like a look at 'im, wouldn't you?' said Em's sister, and she brushed past Laura over to the bed. 'Don't be afraid, my lass,'—and now her voice sounded fond and sly, and fondly she drew down the sheet—' 'e looks a picture. There's nothing to show. Come along, my dear.'

Laura came.

There lay a young man, fast asleep—sleeping so soundly, so deeply, that he was far, far away from them both. Oh, so remote, so peaceful. He was dreaming. Never wake him up again. His head was sunk in the pillow, his eyes were closed; they were blind under the closed eyelids. He was given up to his dream. What did garden parties and baskets and lace frocks matter to him? He was far from all those things. He was wonderful, beautiful. While they were laughing and while the band was playing, this marvel had come to the lane. Happy . . . happy. . . . All is well, said that sleeping face. This is just as it should be. I am content.

But all the same you had to cry, and she couldn't go out of the room without saying something to him. Laura gave a loud childish sob.

'Forgive my hat,' she said.

And this time she didn't wait for Em's sister. She found her way out of the door, down the path, past all those dark people. At the corner of the lane she met Laurie.

He stepped out of the shadow. 'Is that you, Laura?'

'Yes.'

'Mother was getting anxious. Was it all right?'

'Yes, quite. Oh, Laurie!' She took his arm, she pressed up against him.

'I say, you're not crying, are you?' asked her brother.

Laura shook her head. She was.

Laurie put his arm round her shoulder. 'Don't cry,' he said in his warm, loving voice. 'Was it awful?'

'No,' sobbed Laura. 'It was simply marvellous. But, Laurie—' She stopped, she looked at her brother. 'Isn't life,' she stammered, 'isn't life—' But what life was she couldn't explain. No matter. He quite understood.

'*Isn't* it, darling?' said Laurie.

# Historical Contexts

## W. H. R. RIVERS

### The Repression of War Experience[†]

I do not attempt to deal in this paper with the whole problem of the part taken by repression in the production and maintenance of the war-neuroses. Repression is so closely bound up with the pathology and treatment of these states that the full consideration of its rôle would amount to a complete study of neurosis in relation to the war.

It is necessary at the outset to consider an ambiguity in the use of the term "repression" as it is now used by writers on the pathology of the mind and nervous system. The term is currently used in two senses which should be carefully distinguished from one another. It is used for the *process* whereby a person endeavours to thrust out of his memory some part of his mental content, and it is also used for the *state* which ensues when, either through this process or by some other means, part of the mental content has become inaccessible to manifest consciousness. In the second sense the word is used for a state which corresponds closely with that known as dissociation, but it is useful to distinguish mere inaccessibility to memory from the special kind of separation from the rest of the mental content which is denoted by the term dissociation. The state of inaccessibility may therefore be called "suppression" in distinction from the process of repression. In this paper I use "repression" for the active or voluntary process by which it is attempted to remove some part of the mental content out of the field of attention with the aim of making it inaccessible to memory and producing the state of suppression.

Using the word in this sense, repression is not in itself a pathological process, nor is it necessarily the cause of pathological states.

[†] Read at a meeting of the Section of Psychiatry, Royal Society of Medicine, December 4, 1917, and published in the *Proceedings of the Royal Society of Medicine*, vol. 11 (1918), Section of Psychiatry, pp. 1–20. See also *Lancet*, vol. 194 (1918). Rivers was a pioneer in the treatment of "shell-shock," or war trauma. Talk therapy of the kind he offered, while effective, was very rare and quite new during and after the War.

On the contrary, it is a necessary element in education and in all social progress. It is not repression in itself which is harmful, but repression under conditions in which it fails to adapt the individual to his environment.

It is in times of special stress that these failures of adaptation are especially liable to occur, and it is not difficult to see why disorders due to this lack of adaptation should be so frequent at the present time. There are few, if any, aspects of life in which repression plays so prominent and so necessary a part as in the preparation for war. The training of a soldier is designed to adapt him to act calmly and methodically in the presence of events naturally calculated to arouse disturbing emotions. His training should be such that the energy arising out of these emotions is partly damped by familiarity, partly diverted into other channels. The most important feature of the present war in its relation to the production of neurosis is that the training in repression normally spread over years has had to be carried out in short spaces of time, while those thus incompletely trained have had to face strains such as have never previously been known in the history of mankind. Small wonder that the failures of adaptation should have been so numerous and so severe.

I do not now propose to consider this primary and fundamental problem of the part played by repression in the original production of the war-neuroses. The process of repression does not cease when some shock or strain has removed the soldier from the scene of warfare, but it may take an active part in the maintenance of the neurosis. New symptoms often arise in hospital or at home which are not the immediate and necessary consequence of war experience, but are due to repression of painful memories and thoughts, or of unpleasant affective states arising out of reflection concerning this experience. It is with the repression of the hospital and of the home rather than with the repression of the trenches that I deal in this paper. I propose to illustrate by a few sample cases some of the effects which may be produced by repression and the line of action by which these effects may be remedied. I hope to show that many of the most trying and distressing symptoms from which the subjects of war-neurosis suffer are not the necessary result of the strain and shocks to which they have been exposed in warfare, but are due to the attempt to banish from the mind distressing memories of warfare or painful affective states which have come into being as the result of their war experience.

Everyone who has had to treat cases of war-neurosis, and especially that form of neurosis dependent on anxiety, must have been faced by the problem what advice to give concerning the attitude the patient should adopt towards his war experience. It is natural to

thrust aside painful memories just as it is natural to avoid dangerous or horrible scenes in actuality. This natural tendency to banish
the distressing or the horrible is especially pronounced in those
whose powers of resistance have been lowered by the long-continued
strains of trench life, the shock of shell explosion, or other catastrophe of warfare. Even if patients were left to themselves, most would
naturally strive to forget distressing memories and thoughts. They
are, however, very far from being left to themselves, the natural
tendency to repress being in my experience almost universally fos-
tered by their relatives and friends, as well as by their medical
advisers. Even when patients have themselves realized the impossibility of forgetting their war experiences and have recognized the
hopeless and enervating character of the treatment by repression,
they are often induced to attempt the task in obedience to medical
orders. The advice which has usually been given to my patients in
other hospitals is that they should endeavour to banish all thoughts
of war from their minds. In some cases all conversation between
patients, or with visitors, about the war is strictly forbidden, and
the patients are instructed to lead their thoughts to other topics, to
beautiful scenery and other pleasant aspects of experience.

To a certain extent this policy is perfectly sound. Nothing annoys
a nervous patient more than the continual inquiries of his relatives
and friends about his experiences of the Front, not only because it
awakens painful memories, but also because of the obvious futility
of most of the questions and the hopelessness of bringing the realities home to his hearers. Moreover, the assemblage together in a
hospital of a number of men with little in common except their war
experiences, naturally leads their conversation far too frequently to
this topic, and even among those whose memories are not especially distressing it tends to enhance the state for which the term
"fed up" seems to be the universal designation.

It is, however, one thing that those who are suffering from the
shocks and strains of warfare should dwell continually on their war
experience or be subjected to importunate inquiries; it is quite
another matter to attempt to banish such experience from their
minds altogether. The cases I am about to record illustrate the evil
influence of this latter course of action and the good effects which
follow its cessation.

The first case is that of a young officer who was sent home from
France on account of a wound received just as he was extricating
himself from a mass of earth in which he had been buried. When
he reached hospital in England he was nervous and suffered from
disturbed sleep and loss of appetite. When his wound had healed
he was sent home on leave, where his nervous symptoms became
more pronounced so that at his next board his leave was extended.

He was for a time an out-patient at a London hospital and was then sent to a convalescent home in the country. Here he continued to sleep badly, with disturbing dreams of warfare, and became very anxious about himself and his prospects of recovery. Thinking he might improve if he rejoined his battalion, he made so light of his condition at his next medical board that he was on the point of being returned to duty when special inquiries about his sleep led to his being sent to Craiglockhart War Hospital for further observation and treatment. On admission he reported that it always took him long to get to sleep at night and that when he succeeded he had vivid dreams of warfare. He could not sleep without a light in his room, because in the dark his attention was attracted by every sound. He had been advised by everyone he had consulted, whether medical or lay, that he ought to banish all unpleasant and disturbing thoughts from his mind. He had been occupying himself for every hour of the day in order to follow this advice and had succeeded in restraining his memories and anxieties during the day, but as soon as he went to bed they would crowd upon him and race through his mind hour after hour, so that every night he dreaded to go to bed.

When he had recounted his symptoms and told me about his method of dealing with his disturbing thoughts, I asked him to tell me candidly his own opinion concerning the possibility of keeping these obtrusive visitors from his mind. He said at once that it was obvious to him that memories such as those he had brought with him from the war could never be forgotten. Nevertheless, since he had been told by everyone that it was his duty to forget them, he had done his utmost in this direction. I then told the patient my own views concerning the nature and treatment of his state. I agreed with him that such memories could not be expected to disappear from the mind and advised him no longer to try to banish them, but that he should see whether it was not possible to make them into tolerable, if not even pleasant, companions instead of evil influences which forced themselves upon his mind whenever the silence and inactivity of the night came round. The possibility of such a line of treatment had never previously occurred to him, but my plan seemed reasonable and he promised to give it a trial. We talked about his war experiences and his anxieties, and following this he had the best night he had had for five months. During the following week he had a good deal of difficulty in sleeping, but his sleeplessness no longer had the painful and distressing quality which had been previously given to it by the intrusion of painful thoughts of warfare. In so far as unpleasant thoughts came to him these were concerned with domestic anxieties rather than with the memories of war, and even these no longer gave rise to the dread which had previously troubled him. His general health improved; his power of sleeping gradually increased and he was able after a time to return to duty, not in the hope that this duty might help him to forget, but with some degree of confidence that he was really fit for it.

The case I have just narrated is a straightforward example of anxiety-neurosis which made no real progress as long as the patient tried to keep out of his mind the painful memories and anxieties which had been aroused in his mind by reflection on his past experience, his present state and the chance of his fitness for duty in the future. When in place of running away from these unpleasant thoughts he faced them boldly and allowed his mind to dwell upon them in the day, they no longer raced through his mind at night and disturbed his sleep by terrifying dreams of warfare.

The next case is that of an officer whose burial as the result of a shell explosion had been followed by symptoms pointing to some degree of cerebral concussion. In spite of severe headache, vomiting and disorder of micturition, he remained on duty for more than two months. He then collapsed altogether after a very trying experience in which he had gone out to seek a fellow officer and had found his body blown into pieces with head and limbs lying separated from the trunk. From that time he had been haunted at night by the vision of his dead and mutilated friend. When he slept he had nightmares in which his friend appeared, sometimes as he had seem him mangled on the field, sometimes in the still more terrifying aspect of one whose limbs and features had been eaten away by leprosy. The mutilated or leprous officer of the dream would come nearer and nearer until the patient suddenly awoke pouring with sweat and in a state of the utmost terror. He dreaded to go to sleep, and spent each day looking forward in painful anticipation of the night. He had been advised to keep all thoughts of war from his mind, but the experience which recurred so often at night was so insistent that he could not keep it wholly from his thoughts, much as he tried to do so. Nevertheless, there is no question but that he was striving by day to dispel memories only to bring them upon him with redoubled force and horror when he slept.

The problem before me in this case was to find some aspect of the painful experience which would allow the patient to dwell upon it in such a way as to relieve its horrible and terrifying character. The aspect to which I drew his attention was that the mangled state of the body of his friend was conclusive evidence that he had been killed outright, and had been spared the prolonged suffering which is too often the fate of those who sustain mortal wounds. He brightened at once, and said that this aspect of the case had never occurred to him, nor had it been suggested by any of those to whom he had previously related his story. He saw at once that this was an aspect of his experience upon which he could allow his thoughts to dwell. He said he would no longer attempt to banish thoughts and memories of his friend from his mind, but would think of the pain and suffering he had been spared. For several nights he had no dreams at all, and then came a night in which he dreamt that he went out into No Man's Land to seek his friend, and saw his mangled body just as in other dreams, but without the horror which had always previously been present. He knelt beside his friend to save for the relatives any objects of value which were upon the body, a pious duty he had fulfilled in the actual scene, and as he was taking off the Sam Browne belt he woke, with none of the horror and terror of the past, but weeping gently, feeling only grief for the loss of a friend. Some nights later he had another dream in which he met his friend, still mangled, but no longer terrifying. They talked together, and the patient told the history of his illness and how he was now able to speak to him in comfort and without horror or undue distress. Once only during his stay in hospital did he again experience horror in connexion with any dream of his friend. During the few days following his discharge from hospital the dream recurred once or twice with some degree of its former terrifying quality, but in his last report to me he had only had one unpleasant dream with a different content, and was regaining his normal health and strength.

In the two cases I have described there can be little question that the most distressing symptoms were being produced or kept in activity by reason of repression. The cessation of the repression was followed by the disappearance of the most distressing symptoms, and great improvement in the general health. It is not always, however, that the line of treatment adopted in these cases is so successful. Sometimes the experience which a patient is striving to forget is so utterly horrible or disgusting, so wholly free from any redeeming feature which can be used as a means of readjusting the attention, that it is difficult or impossible to find an aspect which will make its contemplation endurable. Such a case is that of a young officer who was flung down by the explosion of a shell so that his face struck the distended abdomen of a German several days dead, the impact of his fall rupturing the swollen corpse. Before he lost consciousness the patient had clearly realized his situation, and knew that the substance which filled his mouth and produced the most horrible sensations of taste and smell was derived from the decomposed entrails of an enemy. When he came to himself he vomited profusely, and was much shaken, but "carried on" for several days, vomiting frequently, and haunted by persistent images of taste and smell.

When he came under my care, several months later, suffering from horrible dreams, in which the events I have narrated were faithfully reproduced, he was striving by every means in his power to keep the disgusting and painful memory from his mind. His only period of relief had occurred when he had gone into the country, far from all that could remind him of the war. This experience, combined with the horrible nature of his memory and images, not only made it difficult for him to discontinue the repression, but also made me hesitate to advise this measure with any confidence. During his stay in hospital the dream became less frequent and less terrible, but it still recurred, and it was thought best that he should leave the Army and seek the conditions which had previously given him relief.

A more frequent cause of failure or slight extent of improvement is met with in cases in which the repression has been allowed to continue for so long that it has become a habit. Such a case is that of an officer above the average age who, while looking at the destruction wrought by a shell explosion, lost consciousness, probably as the result of a shock caused by a second shell. He was so ill in France that he could tell little about his state there. When admitted to hospital in England he had lost power and sensation in his legs, and was suffering from severe headache, sleeplessness and terrifying dreams. He was treated by hypnotism and hypnotic drugs, and was advised neither to read the papers nor talk with anyone about the war. After being about two months in hospital he was given three months' leave. On going home he was so disturbed by remarks about the war that he left his relatives and buried himself in the heart of the country, where he saw no one, read no papers, and resolutely kept his mind from all thoughts of war. With the aid of aspirin and bromides he slept better and had less headache, but when at the end of his period of leave he appeared before a medical board and the President asked a question about the trenches, he broke down completely and wept. He was given another two months' leave, and again repaired to the country to continue the treatment by isolation and repression. This went on until the order that all officers must be in hospital or on duty led to his being sent to an inland watering-place, where no inquiries were made about his anxieties or memories, but he was treated by baths, electricity and massage. He rapidly became worse; his sleep, which had improved, became as bad as ever, and he was transferred to Craiglockhart War Hospital. He was then very emaciated, with a constant expression of anxiety and dread. His legs were still weak, and he was able to take very little exercise or apply his mind for any time. His chief complaint was of sleeplessness and frequent dreams in which war scenes were reproduced, while all kinds of distressing thoughts connected with the war would crowd into his mind as he was trying to get to sleep.

He was advised to give up the practice of repression, to read the papers, talk occasionally about the war, and gradually accustom himself to thinking of, and hearing about, war experience. He did so, but in a half-hearted manner, being convinced that the ideal treatment was that he had so long followed. He was reluctant to admit that the success of a mode of treatment which led him to break down and weep when the war was mentioned was of a very superficial kind. Nevertheless, he improved distinctly and slept better. The reproduction of scenes of war in his dreams became less frequent, and were replaced by images the material of which was provided by scenes of home-life. He became able to read the papers without disturbance, but was loth to acknowledge that his improvement was connected with this ability to face thoughts of war, saying that he had been as well when following his own treatment by isolation, and he evidently believed that he would have recovered if he had not been taken from his retreat and sent into hospital. It soon became obvious that the patient would be of no further service in the Army, and he relinquished his commission.

I cite this case not so much as an example of failure, or relative failure, of the treatment by removal of repression, for it is probable that such relaxation of repression as occurred was a definite factor in his improvement. I cite it rather as an example of the state produced by long continued repression and of the difficulties which arise when the repression has had such apparent success as to make the patient believe in it.

In the cases I have just narrated there was no evidence that the process of repression had produced the state of suppression or dissociation. The memories of other painful experience were at hand ready to be recalled or even to obtrude themselves upon consciousness at any moment. A state in which repressed elements of the mental content find their expression in dreams may perhaps be regarded as the first step towards suppression or dissociation, but if so, it forms a very early stage of the process.

There is no question that some people are more liable to become the subjects of dissociation or splitting of consciousness than others. In some persons there is probably an innate tendency in this direction; in others the liability arises through some shock or illness; while other persons become especially susceptible as the result of having been hypnotized.

Not only do shock and illness produce a liability to dissociation, but these factors may also act as its immediate precursors and exciting causes. How far the process of voluntary repression can produce this state is more doubtful. It is probable that it only has this effect in persons who are especially prone to the occurrence of dissociation. The great frequency of the process of voluntary repression in cases of war-neurosis might be expected to provide us with definite evidence on this head and there is little doubt that such evidence is present. As an example I may cite the case of a young officer who had done well in France until he had been deprived of consciousness by a shell explosion. The next thing he remembered was being conducted by his servant towards the base, thoroughly broken down. On admission into hospital he suffered from fearful headaches and had hardly any sleep, and when he slept he had terrifying dreams of warfare. When he came under my care two months later his chief complaint was that whereas ordinarily he felt cheerful and keen on life, there would come upon him at times, with absolute suddenness, the most terrible depression, a state of a kind absolutely different from an ordinary fit of "the blues," having a quality which he could only describe as "something quite on its own."

For some time he had no attack and seemed as if he had not a care in the world. Ten days after admission he came to me one evening, pale and with a tense anxious expression which wholly altered his appearance. A few minutes earlier he had been writing a letter in his usual mood, when there descended upon him a state of deep depression and despair which seemed to have no reason. He had had a pleasant and not too tiring afternoon on some neighbouring hills, and there was nothing in the letter he was writing which could be supposed to have suggested anything painful or depressing. As we talked the depression cleared off and in about ten minutes he was nearly himself again. He had no further attack of depression for nine days, and then one afternoon, as he was standing looking idly from a window, there suddenly descended upon him the state of horrible dread. I happened to be away from the hospital and he had to fight it out alone. The attack was more severe than usual and lasted for several hours. It was so severe that he believed he would have shot himself if his revolver had been accessible. On my return to the hospital some hours after the onset of the attack he was better, but still looked pale and anxious. His state of reasonless dread had passed into one of depression and anxiety natural to one who recognizes that he has been through an experience which has put his life in danger and is liable to recur.

The gusts of depression to which this patient was subject were of the kind which I was then inclined to ascribe to the hidden working of some forgotten yet active experience, and it seemed natural at first to think of some incident during the time which elapsed between the shell explosion which deprived him of consciousness and the moment when he came to himself walking back from the trenches. I considered whether this was not a case in which the lost memory might be recovered by means of hypnotism, but in the presence of the definite tendency to dissociation I did not like to employ this means of diagnosis, and less drastic methods of recovering any forgotten incident were without avail.

It occurred to me that the soldier who was accompanying the patient on his walk from the trenches might be able to supply a clue to some lost memory. While waiting for an answer to this inquiry I discovered that behind his apparent cheerfulness at ordinary times the patient was the subject of grave apprehensions about his fitness for further service in France, which he was not allowing himself to entertain owing to the idea that such thoughts were equivalent to cowardice, or might at any rate be so interpreted by others. It became evident that he had been practising a systematic process of repression of these thoughts and apprehensions, and the question arose whether this repression might not be the source of his attacks of depression rather than some forgotten experience. The patient had already become familiar with the idea that his gusts of depression might be due to the activity of some submerged experience and it was only necessary to consider whether we had not hitherto mistaken the repressed object. Disagreeable as was the situation in which he found himself, I advised him that it was one which it was best to face, and that it was of no avail to pretend that it did not exist. I pointed out that this procedure might produce some discomfort and unhappiness, but that it was far better to suffer so than continue in a course whereby painful thoughts were pushed into hidden recesses of his mind, only to accumulate such force as to make them well up and produce attacks of depression so severe as to put his life in danger from suicide. He agreed to face the situation and no longer to continue his attempt to banish his apprehensions. From this time he had only one transient attack of morbid depression following a minor surgical operation. He became less cheerful generally and his state acquired more closely the usual characters of anxiety-neurosis, and this was so persistent that he was finally passed by a medical board as unfit for military service.

In the cases I have recorded, the elements of the mental content which were the object of repression were chiefly distressing memories. In the case just quoted painful anticipations were prominent, and probably had a place among the objects of repression in other cases. Many other kinds of mental experience may be similarly repressed. Thus, after one of my patients had for long baffled all attempts to discover the source of his trouble, it finally appeared that he was attempting to banish from his mind feelings of shame due to his having broken down. Great improvement rapidly followed a line of action in which he faced this shame and thereby came to see how little cause there was for this emotion. In another case an officer had carried the repression of grief concerning the general loss of life and happiness through the war to the point of suppression, the suppressed emotion finding vent in attacks of weeping, which came on suddenly with no apparent cause. In this case the treatment was less successful, and I cite it only to illustrate the variety of experience which may become the object of repression.

I will conclude my record by a brief account of a case which is interesting in that it might well have occurred in civil practice. A young officer after more than two years' service had failed to get to France, in spite of his urgent desires in that direction. Repeated disappointments in this respect, combined with anxieties connected with his work, had led to the development of a state in which he suffered from troubled sleep, with attacks of somnambulism by night and "fainting fits" by day. Some time after he came under my care I found that, acting under the advice of every doctor he had met, he had been systematically thrusting all thought of his work out of his mind, with the result that when he went to bed battalion orders and other features of his work as an adjutant raced in endless succession through his mind and kept him from sleeping. I advised him to think of his work by day, even to plan what he would do when he returned to his military duties. The troublesome night-thoughts soon went; he rapidly improved and returned to duty. When last he wrote his hopes of general service had at last been realized.

In the cases recorded in this paper the patients had been repressing certain painful elements of their mental content. They had been deliberately practising what we must regard as a definite course of treatment, in nearly every case adopted on medical advice, in which they were either deliberately thrusting certain unpleasant memories or thoughts from their minds or were occupying every moment of the day in some activity in order that these thoughts might not come into the focus of attention. At the same time they were suffering from certain highly distressing symptoms which disappeared or altered in character when the process of repression ceased. Moreover, the symptoms by which they had been troubled were such as receive a natural, if not obvious, explanation as the result of the repression they had been practising. If a person voluntarily represses unpleasant thoughts during the day, it is natural that they should rise into activity when the control of the waking state is removed by sleep or lessened in the state which precedes or follows sleep or occupies its intervals. If the painful thoughts have been kept from the attention throughout the day by means of occupation, it is again natural that they should come into activity when the silence and isolation of the night make occupation no longer possible. It seems as if the thoughts repressed by day assume a painful quality when they come to the surface at night far more intense than is ever attained if they are allowed to occupy the attention during the day. It is as if the process of repression keeps the painful memories or thoughts under a kind of pressure during the day, accumulating such energy by the time night comes that they race through the mind with abnormal speed and violence when the patient is wakeful, or take the most vivid and painful forms when expressed by the imagery of dreams.

When such distressing, if not terrible, symptoms disappear or alter in character as soon as repression ceases, it is natural to conclude that the two processes stand to one another in the relation of cause and effect, but so great is the complexity of the conditions with which we are dealing in the medicine of the mind that it is necessary to consider certain alternative explanations.

The disappearance or improvement of symptoms on the cessation of voluntary repression may be regarded as due to the action of one form of the principle of catharsis. This term is generally used for the agency which is operative when a suppressed or dissociated body of experience is brought to the surface so that it again becomes reintegrated with the ordinary personality. It is no great step from this to the mode of action recorded in this paper, in which experience on its way towards suppression has undergone a similar, though necessarily less extensive, process of reintegration.

There is, however, another form of catharsis which may have been operative in some of the cases I have described. It often happens in cases of war-neurosis, as in neurosis in general, that the sufferers do not suppress their painful thoughts, but brood over them constantly until their experience assumes vastly exaggerated and often distorted importance and significance. In such cases the greatest relief is afforded by the mere communication of these troubles to another. This form of catharsis may have been operative in relation to certain kinds of experience in some of my cases, and this complicates our estimation of the therapeutic value of the cessation of repression. I have, however, carefully chosen for record on this occasion cases in which the second form of catharsis, if present at all, formed an agency altogether subsidiary to that afforded by the cessation of repression.

Another complicating factor which may have entered into the therapeutic processs in some of the cases is re-education. This certainly came into play in the case of the patient who had the terrifying dreams of his mangled friend. In his case the cessation of repression was accompanied by the direction of the attention of the patient to an aspect of his painful memories which he had hitherto completely ignored. The process by which his attention was thus directed to a neglected aspect of his experience introduced a factor which must be distinguished from the removal of repression itself. The two processes are intimately associated, for it was largely, if not altogether, the new view of his experience which made it possible for the patient to dwell upon his painful memories. In some of the other cases this factor of re-education undoubtedly played a part, not merely in making possible the cessation of repression, but also in helping the patient to adjust himself to the situation with which he was faced, thus contributing positively to the recovery or improvement which followed the cessation of repression.

A more difficult and more contentious problem arises when we consider how far the success which attended the cessation of repression may have been, wholly or in part, due to faith and suggestion. Here, as in every branch of therapeutics, whether it be treatment by drugs, diet, baths, electricity, persuasion, re-education or psycho-analysis, we come up against the difficulty raised by the pervasive and subtle influence of these agencies working behind the scenes. In the subject before us, as in every other kind of medical treatment, we have to consider whether the changes which occurred may have been due, not to the agency which lay on the surface and was the motive of the treatment, but at any rate, in part, to the influence, so difficult to exclude, of faith and suggestion. In my later work I have come to believe so thoroughly in the injurious action of repression, and have acquired so lively a faith in the efficacy of my mode of treatment, that this agency cannot be excluded as a factor in any success I may have. In my earlier work, however, I certainly had no such faith, and advised the discontinuance of repression with the utmost diffidence. Faith on the part of the patient may, however, be present even when the physician is diffident. It is of more importance that several of the patients had been under my care for some time without improvement until it was discovered that they were repressing painful experience. It was only when the repression ceased that improvement began.

Definite evidence against the influence of suggestion is provided by the case in which the dream of the mangled friend came to lose its horror, this state being replaced by the far more bearable emotion of grief. The change which followed the cessation of repression in this case could not have been suggested by me, for its possibility had not, so far as I am aware, entered my mind. So far as suggestions, witting or unwitting, were given, these would have had the form that the nightmares would cease altogether, and the change in the affective character of the dream, not having been anticipated by myself, can hardly have been communicated to the patient. It is, of course, possible that my own belief in the improvement which would follow the adoption of my advice acted in a general manner by bringing the agencies of faith and suggestion into action, but these agencies can hardly have produced the specific and definite form which the improvement took. In other of the cases I have recorded, faith and suggestion probably played some part, that of the officer with the sudden and overwhelming attacks of depression being especially open to the possibility of these influences.

Such complicating factors as I have just considered can no more be excluded in this than in any other branch of therapeutics, but I am confident that their part is small beside that due to stopping a course of action whereby patients were striving to carry out an impossible task. In some cases faith and suggestion, re-education and sharing troubles with another, undoubtedly form the chief agents in the removal or amendment of the symptoms of neurosis, but in the cases I have recorded there can be little doubt that they contributed only in a minor degree to the success which attended the giving up of repression.

Before I conclude, a few words must be said about an aspect of my subject to which I have not so far referred. When treating officers or men suffering from war-neurosis, we have not only to think of the restoration of the patient to health, we have also to consider the question of fitness for military service. It is necessary to consider briefly the relation of the prescription of repression to this aspect of military medical practice.

When I find that a soldier is definitely practising repression, I am accustomed to ask him what he thinks is likely to happen if one who has sedulously kept his mind from all thoughts of war, or from special memories of warfare, should be confronted with the reality, or even with such continual reminders of its existence as must inevitably accompany any form of military service at home. If, as often happens in the case of officers, the patient is keenly anxious to remain in the Army, the question at once brings home to him the futility of the course of action he has been pursuing. The deliberate and systematic repression of all thoughts and memories of war by a soldier can have but one result when he is again faced by the realities of warfare.

Several of the officers whose cases I have described or mentioned in this paper were enabled to return to some form of military duty with a degree of success very unlikely if they had persisted in the process of repression. In other cases, either because the repression had been so long continued or for some other reason, return to military duty was deemed inexpedient. Except in one of these cases, no other result could have been expected with any form of treatment. The exception to which I refer is that of the patient who had the sudden attacks of reasonless depression. This officer had a healthy appearance, and would have made light of his disabilities at a Medical Board. He would certainly have been returned to duty and sent to France. The result of my line of treatment was to produce a state of anxiety which led to his leaving the Army. This result, regrettable though it be, is far better than that which would have followed his return to active service, for he would inevitably have broken down under the first stress of warfare, and might have produced some disaster by failure in a critical situation or lowered the morale of his unit by committing suicide.

In conclusion, I must again mention a point to which reference was made at the beginning of this paper. Because I advocate the facing of painful memories, and deprecate the ostrich-like policy of attempting to banish them from the mind, it must not be thought that I recommend the concentration of the thoughts on such memories. On the contrary, in my opinion it is just as harmful to dwell persistently upon painful memories or anticipations, and brood upon feelings of regret and shame, as to attempt to banish them wholly from the mind. It is necessary to be explicit on this matter when dealing with patients. In a recent case in which I neglected to do so, the absence of any improvement led me to inquire into the patient's method of following my advice, and I found that, thinking he could not have too much of a good thing, he had substituted for the system of repression he had followed before coming under my care, one in which he spent the whole day talking, reading, and thinking of war. He even spent the interval between dinner and going to bed in reading a book dealing with warfare.

There are also some victims of neurosis, especially the very young, for whom the horrors of warfare seem to have a peculiar fascination, so that when the opportunity presents itself they cannot refrain from talking by the hour about war experiences, although they know quite well that it is bad for them to do so. Here, as in so many other aspects of the treatment of neurosis, we have to steer a middle course. Just as we prescribe moderation in exercise, moderation at work and play, moderation in eating, drinking, and smoking, so is moderation necessary in talking, reading, and thinking about war experience. Moreover, we must not be content merely to advise our patients to give up repression, we must help them by every means in our power to put this advice into practice. We must show them how to overcome the difficulties which are put in their way by enfeebled volition, and by the distortion of their experience due to its having for long been seen exclusively from some one point of view. It is often only by a process of prolonged re-education that it becomes possible for the patient to give up the practice of repressing war experience.

I am indebted to Major W. H. Bryce, R.A.M.C., for permission to publish the cases recorded in this paper, and for his never-failing support and interest while I was working under his command in Craiglockhart War Hospital.

## DISCUSSION.

Dr. ERNEST JONES: It is gratifying and even novel to hear Dr. Rivers confirm Freud's views that repression, in spite of being a natural defence mechanism, can, in certain circumstances, be exaggerated when it fails in its purpose, and may be harmful. The other main point in Dr. Rivers' paper—namely, that the harmful effects of unsuccessful repression can be partly undone by inculcating an opposite attitude of mind, is practically identical with the cathartic abreaction that constituted the first stage in Freud's psychoanalytic method of treatment. The instinctive resistance mentioned by Dr. Rivers, which is displayed against this attitude both by the patient and by his medical advisers, is a manifestation of the repressive tendency itself. I wish to point out that, although the phenomenon of repression is more easily observed in relation to what may be called external experiences, grief, &c., it is nothing like so extensive or so important pathologically in this sphere as in that of what may be called internal experiences, desires, thoughts, &c., that arise from within, and, indeed, it needs the calamitous happenings of this great war to make the former very manifest at all. It is all the more important, therefore, that the latter group should not be overlooked. They provide the key to the understanding of the individual problems in connexion with the war-neuroses, why one man suffers more than, and differently, from another in the same situation, why particular symptoms appear, and why a case may resist treatment that deals only with the war experience. It is also these previously repressed impulses in the personality that lend the obviously dynamic character to the war traumata, and cause the memory of them to haunt the mind. The intimate relation of pleasure to pain in the primitive unconscious mind has to be remembered in this connexion.

Dr. MAURICE NICOLL: Does Dr. Rivers consider that repression of battle experiences fully accounts for war neuroses? In profound war shock there seems to be a collapse of the whole personality, and a return to a state of infantility of varying degree. The great conception of Freud of the importance of repression in causing neuroses is of immense value in treatment, but the conception of *regression* is also valuable. Regression is to be conceived as a retracing of the path of personal development, and a return to a mode of behaviour that belongs to the past. Dr. Jung, of Zürich, who regards the neurosis as the result of a failure in adaptation, teaches that when reality contains a task that is formidable, regression may occur away from the task, and an inferior mode of function substituted for the superior or adult mode of function. The psychic structure of the individual collapses, and its upper or most recently formed storeys pass into the unconscious. The battle dream—that is, the pure recapitulation of actual battle scenes—is pathognomonic of regression, and once an individual has true battle dreams he is no longer wholly responsible, for regression has begun and part of his "growing fit" has been inverted into the unconscious. Spontaneous recovery is then unlikely on the battlefield. Treatment must now be directed towards finding a *way out* for that part of the personality that has collapsed into the unconscious. In this respect the dream, when it has passed from pure battle incidents, and begins to deal with other material, constitutes a valuable guide as regards the best "way out" for the individual. It must be remembered that Jung takes a view of the unconscious that differs essentially from that of Freud. Jung regards the unconscious in the neurotic as endeavouring to push the individual towards successful adaptation. When regression occurs the unconscious seeks to get rid of the regressed material, and shows the aim of its activity in the dream.

Dr. EDER: Suggestion can, I think, be ruled out in these cases because, as Dr. Rivers has shown, the patients had been long and unsuccessfully treated by suggestions from both medical and lay friends: being strongly urged to try to forget their war experiences. The power of suggestion is, I think, too much of a bugbear to many. In Dr. Rivers' cases the reasonable conclusion must surely be that the success was due to the "abreaction." I agree with Dr. Jones that in some war experiences, where a comrade who has been killed alongside the patient is the subject of painful dreams and reminiscences, there will be found links with earlier ideas or feelings relating to the patient's family. I have published some analyses of cases of this kind. It is noteworthy that in one of the dreams related by Dr. Rivers the mutilated body of the patient's friend became a leprous body. These are instances of regression in Jung's sense. In other cases regression expresses the wish for an earlier (infantile) adaptation or even for death; such wishes being more or less simulated by the symptoms. "Battle dreams" have, I agree with Dr. Nicoll, some diagnostic value. The patient continues to make the manifest content of his dream that of his painful war experiences so long as the symptoms are acute. The manifest content begins to take up its material from his ordinary daily surroundings, as do most dreams, as improvement sets in. This merely means that attention is now being directed to his daily surroundings. It has nothing to do, of course, with the latent content of the dream or its meaning.

Dr. W. H. B. STODDART: I suggest to Dr. Rivers that it would be better to reverse the meanings of the words "repression" and "suppression" as used in the paper, seeing that the present generally accepted meaning of "repression" is that which he has attached to the word "suppression." To continue to use these words in a new sense will lead to confusion. Are the cases diagnosed as "anxiety neurosis" really examples of that disorder, whose characteristic symptoms are such physical disturbances as palpitation, vomiting, diarrhœa, polyuria, difficulties of respiration, tremor, &c., while mental anxiety plays almost a subsidiary role?

Dr. C. M. TUKE: I am glad to hear that Dr. Rivers speaks of "moderation" as regards this treatment. I think that much depends on the special circumstances of each individual case, and the degrees of mental power and previous education and training of the patient. In one case seen, of a young officer invalided home for shell shock without a wound, it was found that he did nothing but talk of his experiences. On being asked if he thought of nothing else, he replied: No, he did not. A few weeks' trout-fishing in the country sufficed to put him right. In a second case, of a private soldier, whose appetite was unimpaired, but who woke shouting in the night frequently, dreaming that he was in the trenches, a few doses of suitable medicine did much to cure him. I think that much depends on the tact and discretion of the medical officer in charge, and that no hard and fast line of treatment can be laid down.

Dr. RIVERS (in reply): The object of my paper was to deal with a practical problem of psycho-therapeutics, and I avoided as far as possible reference to the theoretical side of the subject. I am glad that several speakers have called attention to the bearing of my results on the more fundamental part of Freud's theory of neurosis, a part which, in the heat engendered by the discussion of other aspects, has attracted little notice in this country.

I do not suppose that repression is the only cause of war-neurosis. In my opinion it is a mistake to regard repression and regression as in any way contradictory or mutually exclusive. As my paper shows, repression, in the sense in which I use the term, is a process which produces or aggravates neurosis, while regression is a character of the neurosis itself, a mode of reacting to the environment which is set up, not only by repression, but in other ways. Even when

repression has proceeded to the length of suppression, we still have
to do with a condition underlying the neurosis, and not with a character of the neurosis itself.

I hoped that I had made it clear that I believe faith and suggestion to have taken only a very small part in the improvement shown
by my cases, and that only in some of them. I should have been
neglecting an obvious duty if I had failed to draw attention to the
possibility that these elusive agencies may have had more influence
than I suppose.

When a term has been used for two quite different things, its
limitation to one of the two meanings must always for a time produce a certain amount of confusion. When technical terms are
taken from the language of every day, they should always be used in
a sense approaching as nearly as possible their popular meaning. I
believe that the sense in which I propose to use "repression" and
"suppression" agrees more closely than the reverse with their ordinary meaning.

I believe that the experience arising out of the War has shown
conclusively that the term "anxiety-neurosis" has hitherto been
used by the followers of Freud in too narrow a sense. I follow a
usage now coming widely into vogue according to which anxiety-
neurosis is the most appropriate term for a syndrome of which the
essential underlying condition is anxiety.

# MAY SINCLAIR

## The Novels of Dorothy Richardson[†]

I do not know whether this article is or is not going to be a criticism, for so soon as I begin to think what I shall say I find myself
criticizing criticism, wondering what is the matter with it and what,
if anything, can be done to make it better, to make it alive. Only a
live criticism can deal appropriately with a live art. And it seems to
me that the first step towards life is to throw off the philosophic
cant of the nineteenth century. I don't mean that there is no philosophy of Art, or that if there has been there is to be no more of it;
I mean that it is absurd to go on talking about realism and idealism,
or objective and subjective art, as if the philosophies were sticking
where they stood in the eighties.

† From *The Egoist* (April 1918): 57–59. This review by May Sinclair of one of Dorothy
   Richardson's novels is the first appearance of the phrase "stream of consciousness" to
   refer to a literary work.

In those days the distinction between idealism and realism, between subjective and objective was important and precise. And so long as the ideas they stand for had importance and precision those words were lamps to the feet and lanterns to the path of the critic. Even after they had begun to lose precision and importance they still served him as useful labels for the bewildering phenomena of the arts.

But now they are beginning to give trouble; they obscure the issues. Mr. J. B. Beresford in his admirable Introduction to *Pointed Roofs* confesses to having felt this trouble. When he read it in manuscript he decided that it "was realism, was objective." When he read it in typescript he thought: "This . . . is the most subjective thing I have ever read." It is evident that when first faced with the startling "newness" of Miss Richardson's method, and her form, the issues did seem a bit obscure to Mr. Beresford. It was as if up to one illuminating moment he had been obliged to think of methods and forms as definitely objective or definitely subjective. His illuminating moment came with the third reading, when *Pointed Roofs* was a printed book. The book itself gave him the clue to his own trouble, which is my trouble, the first hint that criticism up till now has been content to think in *clichés,* missing the new trend of the philosophies of the twentieth century. All that we know of reality at first hand is given to us through contacts in which those interesting distinctions are lost. Reality is thick and deep, too thick and too deep, and at the same time too fluid to be cut with any convenient carving-knife. The novelist who would be close to reality must confine himself to this knowledge at first hand. He must, as Mr. Beresford says, simply "plunge in." Mr. Beresford says that Miss Richardson is the first novelist who has plunged in. She has plunged so neatly and quietly that even admirers of her performance might remain unaware of what it is precisely that she has done. She has disappeared while they are still waiting for the splash. So that Mr. Beresford's Introduction was needed.

When first I read *Pointed Roofs* and *Backwater* and *Honeycomb* I too thought, like Mr. Beresford, that Miss Richardson has been the first to plunge. But it seems to me rather that she has followed, independently, perhaps unconsciously, a growing tendency to plunge. As far back as the eighties the de Goncourts plunged completely, finally, in *Sœur Philomène, Germinie Lacerteux,* and *Les Frères Zemgann.* Marguerite Audoux plunged in the best passages of *Marie Claire.* The best of every good novelist's best work is a more or less sustained immersion. The more modern the novelist the longer his capacity to stay under. Miss Richardson has not plunged deeper than Mr. James Joyce in his *Portrait of the Artist as a Young Man.*

By imposing very strict limitations on herself she has brought her art, her method, to a high pitch of perfection, so that her form seems to be newer than it perhaps is. She herself is unaware of the perfection of her method. She would probably deny that she has written with any deliberate method at all. She would say: "I only know there are certain things I mustn't do if I was to do what I wanted." Obviously, she must not interfere; she must not analyse or comment or explain. Rather less obviously, she must not tell a story or handle a situation or set a scene; she must avoid drama as she avoids narration. And there are some things she must not be. She must not be the wise, all-knowing author. She must be Miriam Henderson. She must not know or divine anything that Miriam does not know or divine; she must not see anything that Miriam does not see. She has taken Miriam's nature upon her. She is not concerned, in the way that other novelists are concerned with character. Of the persons who move through Miriam's world you know nothing but what Miriam knows. If Miriam is mistaken, well, she and not Miss Richardson is mistaken. Miriam is an acute observer, but she is very far from seeing the whole of these people. They are presented to us in the same vivid but fragmentary way in which they appeared to Miriam, the fragmentary way in which people appear to most of us. Miss Richardson has only imposed on herself the conditions that life imposes on us all. And if you are going to quarrel with those conditions you will not find her novels satisfactory. But your satisfaction is not her concern.

And I find it impossible to reduce to intelligible terms this satisfaction that I feel. To me these three novels show an art and method and form carried to punctilious perfection. Yet I have heard other novelists say that they have no art and no method and no form, and that it is this formlessness that annoys them. They say that they have no beginning and no middle and no end, and that to have form a novel must have an end and a beginning and a middle. We have come to words that in more primitive times would have been blows on this subject. There is a certain plausibility in what they say, but it depends on what constitutes a beginning and a middle and an end. In this series there is no drama, no situation, no set scene. Nothing happens. It is just life going on and on. It is Miriam Henderson's stream of consciousness going on and on. And in neither is there any grossly discernible beginning or middle or end.

In identifying herself with this life, which is Miriam's stream of consciousness, Miss Richardson produces her effect of being the first, of getting closer to reality than any of our novelists who are trying so desperately to get close. No attitude or gesture of her own is allowed to come between her and her effect. Whatever her sources and her raw material, she is concerned and we ought to be concerned solely with the finished result, the work of art. It is to Miriam's almost painfully acute senses that we owe what in any other novelist would be called the "portraits" of Miriam's mother, of her sister Harriet, of the Corries and Joey Banks in *Honeycomb,* of the Miss Pernes and Julia Doyle, and the North London school-girls in *Backwater,* Fräulein Pfaff and Mademoiselle, of the Martins and Emma Bergmann and Ulrica and "the Australian" in *Pointed Roofs.* The mere "word-painting" is masterly.

> . . . Miriam noticed only the hoarse, hacking laugh of the Australian. Her eyes flew up the table and fixed her as she sat laughing, her chair drawn back, her knees crossed—tea was drawing to an end. The detail of her terrifyingly stylish ruddy brown frieze dress, with its Norfolk jacket bodice and its shiny leather belt, was hardly distinguishable from the dark background made by the folding doors. But the dreadful outline of her shoulders was visible, the squarish oval of her face shone out—the wide forehead from which the wiry black hair was combed to a high puff, the red eyes, black now, the long, straight nose, the wide, laughing mouth with the enormous teeth.

And so on all round the school tea-table. It looks easy enough to "do" until you try it. There are thirteen figures round that table, and each is drawn with the first few strokes, and so well that you see them all and never afterwards can you mistake or confuse them.

You look at the outer world through Miriam's senses, and it is as if you had never seen it so vividly before. Miriam in *Backwater* is on the top of a bus, driving from North London to Piccadilly:

> On the left a tall grey church was coming towards them, spindling up into the sky. It sailed by, showing Miriam a circle of little stone pillars built into its spire. Plumy trees streamed by, standing large and separate on moss-green grass railed from the roadway. Bright, white-faced houses with pillared porches shone through from behind them and blazed white above them against the blue sky. Wide side streets opened, showing high balconied houses. The side streets were feathered with trees and ended mistily.
>
> Away ahead were edges of clean, bright masonry in profile, soft, tufted heads of trees, bright green in the clear light. At the end of the vista the air was like pure saffron-tinted mother-of-pearl.

Or this "interior" from *Honeycomb*:

> . . . the table like an island under the dome of the low-hanging rose-shaded lamp, the table centre thickly embroidered with beetles' wings, the little dishes stuck about, sweets, curiously crusted brown almonds, sheeny grey-green olives; the misty

beaded glass of the finger-bowls—Venetian glass from that shop in Regent street—the four various wine glasses at each right hand, one on a high thin stem, curved and fluted like a shallow tulip, filled with hock: and floating in the warmth amongst all these things the strange, exciting, dry sweet fragrance coming from the mass of mimosa, a forest of little powdery blossoms, little stiff grey—the arms of railway signals at junctions—Japanese looking leaves—standing as if it were growing, in a shallow bowl under the rose-shaded lamp.

It is as if no other writers had ever used their senses so purely and with so intense a joy in their use.

This intensity is the effect of an extreme concentration on the thing seen or felt. Miss Richardson disdains every stroke that does not tell. Her novels are novels of an extraordinary compression, and of an extenuation more extraordinary still. The moments of Miriam's consciousness pass one by one, or overlapping; moments tense with vibration, moments drawn out fine, almost to snapping-point. On one page Miss Richardson seems to be accounting for every minute of Miriam's time. On another she passes over events that might be considered decisive with the merest slur of reference. She is not concerned with the strict order of events in time. Chapter Three of *Pointed Roofs* opens with an air of extreme decision and importance: "Miriam was practising on the piano in the larger of the two English bedrooms," as if something hung on her practising. But no, nothing hangs on it, and if you want to know on what day she is practising you have to read on and back again. It doesn't matter. It is Miriam's consciousness that is going backwards and forwards in time. The time it goes in is unimportant. On the hundredth page out of three hundred and twelve pages Miriam has been exactly two weeks in Hanover. Nothing has happened but the infinitely little affairs of the school, the practising, the *vorspielen*, the English lesson, the *raccommodage,* the hair-washing. At the end of the book Fräulein Pfaff is on the station platform, gently propelling Miriam "up three steps into a compartment marked *Damen-Coupé.* It smelt of biscuits and wine." Miriam has been no more than six months in Hanover. We are not told and Miriam is not told, but we know, as Miriam knows, that she is going because Pastor Lahmann has shown an interest in Miriam very disturbing to Fräulein Pfaff's interest in him. We are not invited to explore the tortuous mind of the pious, sentimental, secretly hysterical Fräulein; but we know, as Miriam knows, that before she can bring herself to part with her English governess she must persuade herself that it is Miriam and not Mademoiselle who is dismissed because she is an unwholesome influence.

In this small world where nothing happens "that dreadful talk with Gertrude," and Fräulein's quarrel with the servant Anna, the sound of her laugh and her scream, "Ja, Sie Können Ihre paar Groschen haben! Ihre paar Groschen!" and Miriam's vision of Mademoiselle's unwholesomeness, stand out as significant and terrifying; they *are* terrifying, they *are* significant; through them we know Gertrude, we know Fräulein Pfaff, we know Mademoiselle as Miriam knows them, under their disguises.

At the end of the third volume, *Honeycomb,* there is, apparently, a break with the design. Something does happen. Something tragic and terrible. We are not told what it is; we know, as Miriam knows, only by inference. Miriam is sleeping in her mother's room.

> Five o'clock. Three more hours before the day began. The other bed was still. "It's going to be a magnificent day," she murmured, pretending to stretch and yawn again. A sigh reached her. The stillness went on and she lay for an hour tense and listening. Some one else must know. . . . At the end of the hour a descending darkness took her suddenly. She woke from it to the sound of violent language, furniture being roughly moved, a swift, angry splashing of water . . . something breaking out, breaking through the confinements of this little furniture-filled room . . . the best gentlest thing she knew openly despairing at last.

Here Miss Richardson "gets" you as she gets you all the time—she never misses once—by her devout adhesion to her method, by the sheer depth of her plunge. For this and this alone is the way things happen. What we used to call the "objective" method is a method of after-thought, of spectacular reflection. What has happened has happened in Miriam's bedroom, if you like; but only by reflection. The first-hand, intimate and intense reality of the happening is in Miriam's mind, and by presenting it thus and not otherwise Miss Richardson seizes reality alive. The intense rapidity of the seizure defies you to distinguish between what is objective and what is subjective either in the reality presented or the art that presents.

Nothing happens. In Miriam Henderson's life there is, apparently, nothing to justify living. Everything she ever wanted was either withheld or taken from her. She is reduced to the barest minimum on which it is possible to support the life of the senses and the emotions at all. And yet Miriam is happy. Her inexhaustible passion for life is fed. Nothing happens, and yet everything that really matters is happening; you are held breathless with the anticipation of its happening. What really matters is a state of mind, the interest or the ecstasy with which we close with life. It can't be explained. To quote Mr. Beresford again: "explanation in this connexion would seem to imply knowledge that only the mystics can faintly realize." But Miss Richardson's is a mysticism apart. It is compatible with, it even encourages such dialogue as this:

> "Tea!" smiled Eve serenely.
> "All right, I'm coming, damn you, aren't I?"
> "Oh, Mimmy!"
> "Well, damn *me*, then. Somebody in the house must swear. I say, Eve!"
> "What?"
> "Nothing, only I *say*."
> "Um."

It is not wholly destroyed when Miriam eats bread and butter—thus:

> When she began at the hard thick edge there always seemed to be tender places on her gums, her three hollow teeth were uneasy and she had to get through worrying thoughts about them—they would get worse as the years went by, and the little places in the front would grow big and painful and disfiguring. After the first few mouthfuls of solid bread a sort of padding seemed to take place and she could go on forgetful.

This kind of thing annoys Kensington. I do not say that it really matters, but that it is compatible with what really matters. Because of such passages it is a pity that Miss Richardson could not use the original title of her series: "Pilgrimage," for it shows what she is really after. Each book marks a stage in Miriam's pilgrimage. We get the first hint of where she is going to in the opening of the tenth chapter of *Pointed Roofs:* "Into all the gatherings at Waldstrasse the outside world came like a presence. It removed the sense of pressure, of being confronted and challenged. Everything that was said seemed to be incidental to it, like remarks dropped in a low tone between individuals at a great conference." In *Backwater* the author's intention becomes still clearer. In *Honeycomb* it is transparently clear:

> Her room was a great square of happy light . . . happy, happy. She gathered up all the sadness she had ever known and flung it from her. All the dark things of the past flashed with a strange beauty as she flung them out. The light had been there all the time; but she had known it only at moments. Now she knew what she wanted. Bright mornings, beautiful bright rooms, a wilderness of beauty all round her all the time—at any cost.

And yet not that:

Something that was not touched, that sang far away down inside the gloom, that cared nothing for the creditors and could get away down and down into the twilight far away from the everlasting accusations of humanity . . . Deeper down was something cool and fresh—endless—an endless garden. In happiness it came up and made everything in the world into a garden. Sorrow blotted it out; but it was always there, waiting and looking on. It had looked on in Germany and had loved the music and the words and the happiness of the German girls, and at Banbury Park, giving her no peace until she got away.

And now it had come to the surface and was with her all the time.

There are two essays of Remy de Gourmont in *Promenades Lit-tèraires,* one on "l'Originalité de Maeterlinck," one on "La Leçon de Saint Antoine." Certain passages might have been written concerning the art of Dorothy Richardson.

Si la vie en sol est un bienfait, et il faut l'accepter comme telle, ou la nier, la fait même de vivre le contient tout entier, et les grands mouvements de la sensibilité, loin de l'enricher, l'appauvrissent au contraire, en concentrant sur quelques partis de nous-mêmes envahies au hazard par la destinée l'effort d'attention qui serait plus uniformement reparti sur l'ensemble de notre conscience vitale. De ce point de vue une vie oú il semblerait ne rien se passer que d'elementaire et quotidien serait mieux remplie qu'une autre vie riche en apparence d'incidents et d'aventures. . . . Il y a peut-être un sentiment nouveau a créer, celui de l'amour de la vie pour la vie elle-même, abstraction faite des grandes joies qu'elle ne donne pas á tous et qu'elle ne donne peut-être á personne . . . Notre paradis, c'est la journée qui passe, la minute qui s'envole, le moment qui n'est déjà plus. Telle est la leçon de Saint Antoine.

# TED BOGACZ

## [The War Office Committee of Enquiry into "Shell-Shock"]†

The first world war fundamentally challenged inherited social and cultural ideas, including traditional views of mental illness and its

† From "War Neurosis and Cultural Change in England, 1914–22: The Work of the War Office Committee of Enquiry into 'Shell-Shock,'" *Journal of Contemporary History* 24.2 (April 1989): 227–28, 231–36, 240–41, 244–49, 251–55. Reprinted by permission of Sage Publications, Ltd. Notes are by Bogacz.

treatment. The hordes of English veterans who suffered from war-induced mental illness, or what was then called 'shell-shock', raised the most complex and disturbing questions. Their sufferings not only challenged long-held medical opinions about the nature and treatment of mental illness, but seemed to demand that the very well-springs of human behaviour be explored anew. Furthermore, so basic were the questions posed by the shell-shock crisis that they ultimately threatened a number of traditional moral values. New views of the mind brought in their wake ambivalence where formerly there had been certainty. An important manifestation of this transformation of values was the *Report of the War Office Committee of Enquiry into 'Shell-Shock'* which was issued in 1922.

On 28 April 1920, Lord Southborough addressed the House of Lords regarding his motion to establish a committee to investigate the nature and treatment of 'shell-shock' in the Great War.

> The subject of shell-shock cannot be referred to with any pleasure. All would desire to forget it—to forget . . . the roll of insanity, suicide, and death; to bury our recollections of the horrible disorder, and to keep on the surface nothing but the cherished memory of those who were the victims of this malignity. But, my Lords, we cannot do this, because a great number of cases of those who suffer from shell-shock and its allied disorders are still upon our hands and they deserve our sympathy and care.[1]

Two years after the Armistice, some 65,000 ex-servicemen were drawing disability pensions for neurasthenia; of these, 9000 were still undergoing hospital treatment.[2] There could scarcely have been a member of the House of Lords who had not heard of someone breaking down as a result of the war. Indeed, it is a signal evidence of the revolution in attitudes toward mental illness in the half-decade since 1914 that in the debate which followed Southborough's statement no one contradicted the existence or seriousness of 'shell-shock', as would likely have been the case in the first years

---

1. Hansard, *House of Lords,* 5th series, 39, 1095. A draft version of Southborough's speech in support of his motion, differing somewhat from Hansard, is to be found in his papers in the possession of his grandson, the current Lord Southborough. I am grateful to Lord Southborough for making these papers available to me.
2. *Report of the War Office Committee of Enquiry into 'Shell-Shock',* Cmd. 1734 (London 1922), 189. (Hereafter referred to as the *Report.*) A further measure of the magnitude of the problem may be gauged from the fact that in March 1939 there were still some 120,000 English Great War veterans receiving pensions or who had received final awards for war-related 'primary psychiatric disability'. These 120,000 cases accounted for 15 per cent of all pensioned disabilities resulting from the first world war. (Robert H. Ahrenfeldt, *Psychiatry in the British Army in the Second World War* [New York 1958], 10.) Clearly, a major reason for government preoccupation with the shell-shock phenomenon was the financial burden of providing pensions and medical care for veterans, some of whom might never get well.

of the war. Lord Horne, formerly a general staff officer, supported the motion, and said: 'I think every one will agree that under the novel conditions that are met with on a modern battlefield there is no man who does not suffer from fright'. Horne was 'much struck' by the possibility of training 'our soldiers to endure the nerve-shattering conditions which lead to this form of shell-shock'.[3]

The relationship between cowardice in battle and 'shell-shock' was a theme which ran all through the debate: Southborough himself had raised it dramatically in his motion. He was not alone. There was widespread fear after the Armistice that among the 3000 soldiers convicted by courts-martial for cowardice, desertion or other crimes (of whom 346 were executed) there were a considerable number who had been suffering from war-induced mental illness and thus had been unjustly sentenced.[4] Viscount Haldane, who had reviewed all court-martial sentences, surprisingly agreed with Southborough that there had been 'injustices done in the early stages of the war' before shell-shock was generally understood.[5] And he revealed that he and the War Office had been much occupied by the problem of shell-shock during the recent conflict.

* * *

Before 1914, some of the ideas of the nascent English psychoanalytic movement had begun to penetrate medical opinion, partially through the efforts of such men as F.W.H. Myers, Havelock Ellis, Bernard Hart and Ernest Jones.[6] However, as a result of the dominant medical and social attitudes described above, many medical practitioners vehemently opposed the new 'depth' psychology of Freud and other continental theorists. The medical journal, *The Lancet,* issued regular broadsides against the parochialism of English psychology.[7]

Yet many doctors thought they had good reason to reject the ideas associated with psychoanalysis. Such therapies, based on the exploration of unconscious motivation and primary processes, seemed to them to encourage rather than alleviate the patient's 'morbid introspection' and 'deficiency of will-power'.[8] Furthermore, Freud's frank discussion of the sexual etiology of neuroses and his stress on

3. Hansard, op. cit., 1101–2.
4. This topic is intelligently treated in Anthony Babington. *For the Sake of Example. Capital Courts-Martial 1914–1920* (New York 1983).
5. Hansard, op. cit., 1105.
6. L. S. Hearnshaw, *A Short History of British Psychology, 1840–1940* (London 1964), 164–5. See also Ronald Clark, *Freud. The Man and the Cause* (New York 1980), 372–5 and Ernest Jones, *Free Associations. Memoirs of a Psycho-Analyst* (New York 1959).
7. See for example *The Lancet* for 6 April 1912; 8 November 1913; 6 June 1914; and 7 November 1914. See also the attacks on the English attitudes toward and treatment of the mentally ill in G. Elliot Smith and T. H. Pear, *Shell-Shock and Its Lessons* (Manchester 1917).
8. Clark, op. cit., 299. Michael J. Clark, 'The Rejection of Psychological Approaches to Mental Disorder in Late Nineteenth-Century British Psychiatry', in *Madhouses,*

infantile sexuality threatened prevailing moral standards, and his emphasis on the continuity between normal and abnormal mental states undermined crucial pre-war legal and medical distinctions. Thus Freud's theories aroused fierce opposition as much for relativizing traditional values and demarcations as for challenging medical orthodoxies.

Such hostile attitudes were still to be found years after the Armistice. Even a doctor sympathetic to victims of war neurosis could write in the official medical history of the war: 'Any soldier above the rank of corporal seemed possessed of too much dignity to become hysterical'.[9] And in 1914 many Englishmen still sharply differentiated between madness and sanity and placed a heavy burden of guilt and shame on those who broke down.

The war on the Western Front helped blur these distinctions. A 1916 editorial in *The Lancet* stated the problem succinctly: in the first two years of the war many 'healthy young males' had suddenly begun to experience the symptoms of neurasthenia. Such cases ought not to be labelled 'sane or insane'. The editorial declared that in medicine there is a 'no-man's-land' which 'defies definition'. 'This nebulous zone shelters many among the sad examples of nervous trouble sent home from the front . . .'[1] The popular catch-all name applied to this muddle of mental affliction arising from the war was 'shell-shock'.

Most Englishmen were utterly unprepared for the stalemate on the Western Front and the triumph of artillery, machine-guns and barbed wire over human 'valour'. For many Britons, after all, the Great War initially had promised to reassert the power of the moral over the mechanical, of the élite over the mass, of spiritual over material forces. All the disintegrative trends of the last sixty years, from the decline of religion to the rise of Labour, would be overcome by courageous men of character who would defeat the enemy through the exertion of their implacable will-power. As an editorial in *The Times* of 25 October 1914 declared, the heroic values of Agincourt would be revived. After November 1914, it was not to be that way at all.

\* \* \*

While soldiers in France were often immediately aware of how these monstrous conditions had contributed to the vast amount of war neurosis on the Western Front, for most civilians in England shell-shock remained an elusive and vaguely threatening

---

*Mad-Doctors and Madmen. The Social History of Psychiatry in the Victorian Era*, ed. Andrew Scull (Philadelphia 1980).

9. *History of the Great War. Medical Services, Diseases of the War*, eds. W.G. MacPherson, W. P. Herringham, T. R. Elliott (London 1923), II, 18.

1. *The Lancet*, 18 March 1916.

phenomenon. They learned of it mainly through the national press, whose articles mirrored the growing English awareness of the nature and intensity of the shell-shock crisis.

In the autumn of 1914, newspapers began to write of the 'uncanny effect of shells', and *The Lancet* reported on October 31: 'More than once in the accounts of the present war reference has been made to the use of shells which on exploding' leave their victims 'in life-like groups . . . the whole suggesting a group of waxwork bodies at Madame Tussaud's'. These early references to shell-shock in the press imply a *mysterious* malady of *physiological* origin resulting from shell bursts which, without leaving a trace, somehow sucked the life out of their victims. By early 1915, however, a clearer picture of war neurosis was beginning to emerge: it soon became obvious even to civilian observers that it was not artillery shells alone which were responsible for the increasing number of breakdowns in France, but rather the general atrocious conditions of the Western Front itself. By early 1915, the English public was reading a startling variety of newspaper stories about shell-shock. A series of articles appeared in *The Times*, for example, referring to hysterical blindness (8 April), 'The Wounded Mind' (24 April), and deafness and paralysis resulting from 'Wounds of consciousness' (25 May) among soldiers in the trenches. By mid-1916, the shell-shocked soldier had become a virtual cliché in the English press.

\* \* \*

[B]y the Armistice, English soldiers and civilians had been exposed for four and a half years to a profound crisis of war-induced mental breakdown on the Western Front. Many, perhaps most, soldiers had heard of or had actually witnessed such cases; the army at all levels from the company commander to the General Staff was concerned about wastage and the effect on morale of shell-shock; the government was drawn in, for it had to create and staff from scratch military mental hospitals and provide pensions for long-term cases; the medical profession was exposed to vigorous debates about the validity of 'mental' explanations of war neurosis; finally, English civilians were bombarded with an array of stories on war neurosis in the national press for the length of the war. By 1918, as a result of the shell-shock crisis, fundamental questions were being raised not only about the origins and treatment of mental illness but also whether formerly firm lines of moral behaviour could continue to be maintained in light of this new knowledge.

The War Office Committee of Enquiry into 'Shell-Shock', under the chairmanship of Lord Southborough, met officially from 7 September 1920 to 22 June 1922. It began its work in a politically-charged atmosphere. Reflecting popular concern and claiming to speak for the other ranks, the Labour Party argued that among those men executed for cowardice were many who had been shell-shock victims and thus had been unjustly sentenced to death. Labour MPs repeatedly raised this issue in parliament and lobbied for the abolition of the military death penalty.[2] Indeed, this mandate, namely, to discover 'whether there was any reason to think that in many cases men executed for cowardice were suffering from some form of this malady', must have weighed heavily on all members of the committee.

\* \* \*

The most important problems and conclusions discussed in the committee's final report may be divided into the following general areas: (1) the nature of shell-shock; (2) who was likely to succumb to it; (3) the general treatment of shell-shock; (4) specific military measures for its prevention and treatment; and (5) cowardice in battle and its relationship to shell-shock.

As on so many other issues, witnesses and committee members were ultimately divided on the nature of shell-shock. Owing perhaps to what the report itself labelled 'the materialistic trend [before 1914] of modern scientific medicine',[3] considerable evidence was given as to the physiological basis of war neurosis. Witnesses explored the relationship of shell-shock to the endocrine glands, the vegetative nervous system, alcoholism, syphilis and other diseases. 'Lesions' of the brain, 'commotional shock', and concussion—all organic wounds stemming from high-explosives—offered opportunities for medical precision in contrast to the muddled categories of what was then called 'emotional' shell-shock.[4]

Yet the committee was fully aware of an alternative explanation of the origins of war neurosis. Perhaps its most crucial statement was that many witnesses, including such respected figures as Drs Henry Head and W. H. R. Rivers, maintained that the origin of the affliction was 'mental'.

How suspect such ideas still were in the early 1920s may be gauged by the committee's discussion of this psychogenic explanation in its 'Summary of Psychological Evidence'.[5] (It is treated, for example, as

2. See Babington, op. cit., 208–10. David Englander's paper on military medicine in the two world wars, delivered before the Wellcome Unit for the Social History of Medicine Seminar, Oxford, November 1979, also gave me insights into this topic. See as well the writings of Ernest Thurtle, a Labour MP who was prominent in the struggle to abolish the military death penalty: *Military Discipline and Democracy* (London 1920) and *Shootings at Dawn. The Army Death Penalty at Work* (London, n.d.). I would like to thank Guff Puttkowski for these references.

3. The *Report*, op. cit., 127.

4. Ibid., 98–109.

5. Ibid., 96–7.

but one of a number of competing theories.) Cautious in its treatment of ideas laden with disturbing implications, the summary resembles in its circumspect language early press reports of the 'shell-shock' crisis. Inevitably, however, some of the vocabulary and ideas found in this summary were indebted to Freud's revolutionary theories. This was evident not only in its emphasis on the unconscious mind but also in the terminology it employed: 'repression' and 'conversion' hysteria, for example, were recent additions to medical and public parlance and were strongly associated with Freud's work.[6] Thus, although later explicitly rejecting his therapy, the committee was repeatedly forced to pay heed to his radical ideas. Furthermore, the committee discovered that some of the most respected psychologists who supported the 'mental' thesis employed some of Freud's insights in their eclectic therapy. (There was, however, no self-proclaimed disciple of Freud among the fifty-nine witnesses.) Thus the tendency of some committee members to favour an organically-based theory of shell-shock was in conflict with the testimony of expert witnesses. In the section on treatment below, we shall see that the committee tried to arrive at a sort of 'half-way house' regarding the origins and treatment of shell-shock.

The report describes in some detail the treatment accorded shell-shock in the regular army at the beginning of the war. The regimental medical officer, trained to see nervous collapse as physiologically-based, either discovered an organic wound which was then treated or, failing that, forced the afflicted soldier to assume 'responsibility' for his condition and return to his unit. Such methods worked well in the regular army, whose officers could properly interpret the 'moral code of honour';[7] but they were no longer suitable for the conscript armies of 1916–18. These 'untrained men', these civilians in uniform, witnesses agreed, had neither the strength nor the endurance of the regular army. With the introduction of such troops in battle shell-shock casualties soared.

\* \* \*

To combat shell-shock in future wars, witnesses and committee members were agreed that improved recruiting and training and

---

6. The concepts of 'repression' and 'conversion' and their role in hysteria, for example, are to be found in Freud and Breuer's famous essay 'On the Psychical Mechanism of Hysterical Phenomena: Preliminary Communication' (1893) and in their *Studies on Hysteria* (1895). For Freud's views on war neuroses, see the discussion of his testimony before the Austrian committee of enquiry into the treatment of 'shell-shock' (1920) in K. R. Eissler, *Freud as an Expert Witness. The Discussion of War Neuroses between Freud and Wagner-Jauregg*, trans. C. Trollope (Madison, Connecticut 1986). For the impact of the war on the Freudian movement, see, for example, Louise E. Hoffman, 'War, Revolution and Psychoanalysis: Freudian Thought Begins to Grapple with Social Reality', *Journal of the History of the Behavioral Sciences*, 17 (1981), 251–69.
7. The *Report*, op. cit., 126–7.

the maintenance of high morale were absolutely essential. The report devoted twenty-nine pages to the crucial problem of military recruiting.[8] It castigated the poor medical selection of the first years of the war which permitted so many 'misfits' to enter the army, men who at the front were liable to break down under stress. Competent medical screening, the committee emphasized, was the key to a healthy army: those with histories of instability or a questionable family background must not be permitted to join the services.[9]

Concluding its discussion of specific military measures, the report declared that all those factors must be combated 'by which a soldier, or even a potential soldier, is encouraged to believe that the weakening or loss of mental control provides an honourable avenue of escape from military service. . . .' [1] Ironically, in its discussion of the relationship of cowardice to shell-shock, the committee itself would provide just such a 'factor'.

There is nothing very startling in the committee's emphasis on a mixed kind of therapy for mental cases, in its periodic references to the 'moral code' and in its insistence on rigorous discipline. What is astonishing is that these certitudes were challenged only a few pages later in the section entitled 'Cowardice and Shell-Shock'.

In some ways, this aspect of the committee's investigation was the most crucial: sustained courage in combat was the most important index of a unit's morale. If the morale of an army were to be maintained, it would seem essential that the man who ran from danger be severely punished. Under the terms of the pre-war 'moral code' referred to repeatedly in the report, cowardice was simply a matter of a failure of 'character', of will-power. Surely, this conservative committee's discussion of cowardice and its relationship to war neurosis ought to be the most straightforward section of the report. That, however, was not the case, for its views on this subject are testimony not to the maintenance but rather to the dilution of the pre-war 'moral code'.

> Cowardice is a military crime for which the death penalty may be exacted.
>
> Some witnesses declined to define it and others did so with reservation.
>
> Major Dowson, a barrister of considerable court-martial experience said: 'Cowardice is showing signs of fear in the face of the enemy'. Such a definition is not helpful to the medical

8. Ibid., 160–89.
9. Ibid., 160–70.
1. Ibid., 149.

officer who may be called on to decide between cowardice and 'shell-shock'.

Cowardice, if regarded as a lack of or failure to show requisite courage, renders discussion more feasible and assists us in comprehending how the brave after much stress may temporarily fail to show their wonted courage without deserving to be called by an opprobrious term.

Fear is the chief factor in both cowardice and emotional 'shell-shock' and it was for this reason that cowardice in the military sense was made a subject of enquiry by the Committee . . .

If the individual exercises his self-control in facing the danger he is not guilty of cowardice, if, however, being capable of doing so, he will not face the situation, he is then a coward. It is here that difficulty arises in cases of war neuroses for it becomes necessary to decide whether the individual has or has not crossed that indefinite line which divides normal emotional reaction from neurosis with impairment of volitional control.[2]

The committee's conclusions regarding cowardice were:

That the military aspect of cowardice is justified.

That seeming cowardice may be beyond the individual's control.

That experienced and specialised medical opinion is required to decide in possible cases of war neurosis of doubtful character.

That a man who has already proved his character should receive special consideration in cases of subsequent lapse.[3]

This section is by far the most revealing of the entire report. It displays all the ambiguities arising from the shell-shock crisis; it demonstrates how impossible it was for the committee to provide neat and tidy conclusions. Although much of their report attempts to determine proper conduct in wartime, to uphold the pre-war 'moral code', and to protect and enhance military morale, on the most important issue for military discipline—namely, cowardice and its relationship to war neurosis—the committee was forced to recognize that the shell-shock phenomenon threw into question some of the most fundamental inherited conceptions of how a man ought to act.

Whereas earlier the report was quick to advocate force to drive the patient back to his duty, here, at the most crucial point, it stressed the difficulty of distinguishing malingering and dereliction

2. Ibid., 138–9.
3. Ibid., 140.

of duty from genuine mental breakdown. The report specifically states that men may be cowards one day and brave the next. As in 1916 when *The Lancet* spoke of a 'no-man's land', a 'nebulous zone' which separated sanity from insanity, so in 1922 the committee offered only an 'indefinite line' between cowardice and 'seeming cowardice' resulting from war neurosis; only an expert could determine the truth. Of necessity, the committee, with its close ties to the War Office, continued to maintain that 'the military aspect of cowardice is justified'; but the effect of its second conclusion, that 'seeming cowardice may be beyond the individual's control', is to negate the first; indeed, it renders cowardice almost impossible to determine with certainty.

This suspension of the 'moral code' with regard to cowardice is an extraordinary demonstration of the power of the shell-shock phenomenon to undermine traditional values. In other more subtle ways, its final report indicates how the committee had arrived at conclusions which challenged some of the very values it may have wished to see upheld. The best example of this is the attention the report paid to the case of an anonymous medical officer, himself a victim of shell-shock on the Western Front. His is the only testimony of a victim of war neurosis to be reported fully. It is certainly no accident that his account was placed last of all the witnesses. Not only is its location significant, so too is the fact that it was not the testimony of some half-educated other rank which was reported at length, but rather that of a regimental medical officer, a member of the articulate classes, a man with whom the committee members could readily identify.

During the second battle of Ypres, this 'gallant officer' had seen his battalion wiped out four times in three months. The medical officer recounted how, after a series of shocks had warned him that he was near breaking-point, it was the sight of a line of horses belonging to dead comrades which had led him to crack; he hid himself and cried for a week.[4]

> Well, I think that was 'shell shock' I had. I lost control when I went into the dugout and concealed myself, and also for that week in which I could not control my tears; but after that, beyond some nightmare [sic] and dreams when I went down the line, after the six months down the line I went up the line again, and I had no difficulty whatever in controlling myself— not the slightest.[5]

By choosing to print this medical officer's eloquent testimony about his breakdown and subsequent recovery, the committee members

4. Ibid., 88–91.
5. Ibid., 91.

revealed that witnesses such as Lord Gort had failed to convince them that shell-shock was all a matter of morale, discipline and especially character. Here was a volunteer, most likely of middle-class origin, who had proved his valour repeatedly in the war—and who had still cracked under the continuous strain of trench warfare.

The testimony of this anonymous officer was a rock against which many pre-war values shattered. Shell-shock could not be tamed, it could not be safely attributed solely to misfits, mental degenerates or weak men of the lower orders; rather it was an impervious leveller of classes.[6] For a generation raised to believe in the exercise of the will, it represented a signal defeat: even the strongest man could fall victim to it. The tortured language of the section on cowardice and other parts of the report is evidence of the committee's struggle to reconcile the modern ambiguous notion of shell-shock with traditional absolutist norms for behaviour in war and peace. The case of a coward ought certainly to be clear-cut. There should be no difficulty in applying the 'moral code' to the man who hid himself during an attack or who walked away from the line. Yet it was on just the issue of cowardice that the committee's efforts to uphold traditional virtues faltered.

The War Office Committee of Enquiry into 'Shell-Shock' concluded its two years of work with a series of recommendations which on the whole seem predictable, even mundane: no soldier should be allowed to think that loss of 'nervous or mental control' provides an 'honourable' escape from the battlefield; if possible, slight cases of mental collapse should be prevented from leaving the front; the 'simplest forms of psycho-therapy' are adequate for the majority of cases; medical officers should be acquainted with the rudiments of psychology; proper medical screening of recruits is of the utmost importance; the term 'shell-shock' should be abolished; concussion victims should be listed as battle casualties, while other types of mental illness should not; shell-shock cases should be treated separately from those with physical wounds; officers should study the psychology of the soldier ('man mastership'); unit morale and discipline are of critical importance in preventing war neurosis; short tours of duty, frequent rotation and home leave are recommended; good sanitation, physical comfort and opportunities for rest of those under strain are encouraged; and so on.[7] Many of these

6. This is not to say that British class distinctions did not find their way into the diagnosis and treatment of shell-shock. On the contrary, physicians were prone to diagnose an officer's mental collapse as neurasthenia (which, before the war, was an 'educated' man's affliction) and to prescribe as treatment a rest cure. They were similarly liable to judge an other rank's mental breakdown as hysteria for which the more punitive treatments (electric shock, etc.) were recommended.

7. The *Report*, op. cit., 190–4.

conclusions defiantly reassert pre-war military values, as if the shell-shock crisis had altered nothing. Pre-war somatic theories of the origins of mental illness are intermittently reasserted and Freud and his 'sexual' theories are explicitly rejected.

The report reflects a period of flux following the Armistice when fundamental values and attitudes of the English educated classes were the target of severe questioning. British politics had undergone a basic shift which saw the decline of the Liberal Party and the rise of Labour; woman's suffrage, a faint hope in 1914, had become a reality as a result of the pressures of total war; trades unions had gained significant power during the prolonged conflict; class lines had begun to blur as a result of the social mobility which the war had encouraged. The arts as well reflected the troubled times: the work of the Western Front painters C. R. W. Nevinson and Paul Nash and the war poetry of Siegfried Sassoon and Wilfred Owen represented profound disillusionment with and sustained attacks on pre-war values; they symbolized a revolt not only against the ideals of an earlier generation but perhaps against authority generally.

It is in this context of social and cultural flux that the investigation of the 'Shell-Shock' Committee must be understood, for in a sense one of the most threatening of all challenges to conventional attitudes was the crisis in mental illness of the recent war. The vast numbers of shell-shock casualties raised the most fundamental human questions; none more so than whether in their wake there were still firm moral laws governing a man's behaviour or whether one must now create a new ethics for each situation.

❊ ❊ ❊

# TRUDI TATE

## [*Mrs Dalloway* and the Armenians]†

❊ ❊ ❊

In *Mrs Dalloway*, Woolf takes a hard look at those who managed the social and economic aspects of the war and treated many survivors so badly afterwards.[1] Power might be concentrated in the hands of men such as Richard Dalloway, but it is held in place by women

---

† From "*Mrs Dalloway* and the Armenian Question" in *Modernism, History and the First World War* (Palgrave-Macmillan, 1998), pp. 166–72. © 1998, 2013 Trudi Tate. Reprinted by permission of the publisher. Notes are by Tate. Page numbers in square brackets refer to this Norton Critical Edition.
1. Alex Zwerdling, *Virginia Woolf and the Real World*, 122, 124.

such as Clarissa and Lady Bruton. Without the domestic and social base provided by women, the political system could not function in the same way. The ruling-class women in the novel are profoundly ignorant. Clarissa, with 'the few twigs of knowledge Fräulein Daniels gave them', knows almost nothing outside her own life: 'no language, no history; she scarcely read a book now' [7]; 'ask her what the Equator was, and she did not know' [87]. She is complacently unaware of the differences between Armenia, Albania and Turkey—nations which faced quite distinct sets of problems after the First World War and which were the subject of a good deal of attention in the British press. Richard Dalloway is sitting on a parliamentary committee on the Armenian Question [85].

Clarissa knows nothing about Richard's work on the Armenians, and regards this as a sign of the strength of their marriage; she congratulates herself that she and Richard have kept their identities as separate persons: 'there is a dignity in people; a solitude; even between husband and wife a gulf; and that one must respect, thought Clarissa' [85]. But more is at stake here than the status of their marriage. Clarissa has no interest in the suffering of the Armenian people as a political or ethical issue in its own right, and the text satirises her mercilessly: 'no, she could feel nothing for the Albanians, or was it the Armenians? but she loved her roses (didn't that help the Armenians?)' [86]. In the same passage, she enjoys being infantilised, 'spoilt', settled on the sofa for an afternoon nap. Yet even as she sinks into this childish posture, she reassures herself that the structure of their marriage secures 'one's independence, one's self-respect—something, after all, priceless' [85]—because she does not remember the details of Richard's committee work.[2]

The Armenian people were victims of the peace as well as the war. Clarissa's refusal to engage with their suffering is masked by proto-feminist statements about marriage. Two separate arguments are elided. It is one thing to refuse to live vicariously through Richard, and quite another to ignore a political issue simply because he happens to be working on it. Clarissa's comments have proved

2. Albania, too faced serious problems during this period, from the Balkan wars immediately preceding the First World War to struggles over its nationhood and borders during and after the war. Miranda Vickers points out that by 1921, 'Albania was devastated and bankrupt, having been continuously at war since 1910'. Britain took a close interest in Albania after oil was found there; according to Vickers, the Anglo-Persian Oil Company provided financial support to Ahmed Zogu, who became prime minister in 1922, then president of the Albanian republic in 1925. In 1928 Albania turned into a monarchy and Zogu became Zog I, King of the Albanians. Vickers, *The Albanians: A Modern History* (London: I. B. Tauris, 1995). There are many brief references to Albania in the British newspapers in the 1920s, but the press is much less sympathetic to the Albanian people than to the Armenians. Clarissa's confusion over the Albanians and Armenians—people who lived in different regions, were caught up in different political questions, and were represented quite differently in the British press—would have been remarkably ignorant for someone in her position in the 1920s, as Woolf's contemporary readers would easily have recognised.

attractive to some later readers, but we need to be cautious about accepting them at face value, for they are cynically employed as an excuse for evading adult responsibility. Here Woolf's satire is rather obvious, as Clarissa tries to hide her complacency and selfishness behind a screen of progressive rhetoric.

The idea that Clarissa's love for roses might help the Armenians is so preposterous that it draws attention to itself. Why does Woolf include this curious scene, and what does it mean in the context of the novel? To understand it, we need to recover something of the history of the Armenian Question in the early 1920s.

### The Armenian Question

What was Britain's interest in Armenia in 1923? For many readers, the matter is almost completely forgotten now, but it was important at the time and widely discussed in the newspapers and political journals. It raised vital issues about human rights and Britain's quasi-imperial responsibilities, and we need to recall the facts of the case if we are to grasp Woolf's satire. Woolf herself was certainly conscious of the Armenians' situation. Indeed, no one who read the newspapers could have been unaware of the issue. Apart from dozens of reports in the press between 1915 and 1923, the Armenian Question was a topic of debate in the early 1920s in the *Nation and Athenaeum,* a journal for which Woolf wrote, and for which Leonard Woolf was literary editor from 1923 to 1929.[3] Lyndall Gordon notes that the massacres of Armenians, like the Dreyfus affair, were fundamental issues in the shaping of Leonard Woolf's political conscience; this was by no means an uncommon response.[4] The historian Arnold Toynbee was an active supporter of the Armenian cause, and published a number of books and articles on the matter. The Toynbees were friends of the Woolfs, and are mentioned several times in Woolf's diary in the early 1920s.[5] During the same period, the Woolfs were in contact with an Armenian friend, Ernest Altounyan, for whom they were literary executors.[6]

Armenia is located between the Black Sea and the Caspian Sea, south of the Caucasian mountains, at the 'crossroads' of eastern

3. Woolf, *Diary,* vol. 2, 23 March 1923, 240; *Diary,* vol. 3, 24 March 1926, 69 and note 14.
4. Gordon, *Virginia Woolf: A Writer's Life* (Oxford: Oxford University Press, 1984), 139. Leonard Woolf also remembers that a teacher in his early schooling was 'obsessed with the horrors and the barbarism of the Armenian massacres'. Quoted in Virginia Woolf, *Diary,* vol. 3, 274 note 9.
5. Toynbee was a member of the British Armenia Committee, and involved in the Political Intelligence Department of the British Foreign Office. Akaby Nassibian, *Britain and the Armenian Question 1915–1923* (London: Croom Helm, 1984), 48, 49, 111. Woolf, *Diary,* vol. 2, 5 December 1920, 18 December 1921, 24 March 1922.
6. Woolf, *Diary,* vol. 1, 22 May 1919, 276; *Diary,* vol. 2, 3 November 1923, 274.

and western empires.[7] The Armenian people, Christians in a largely Muslim area, had been colonised and expelled by various imperial powers since the eleventh century; by 1914, the original area of Armenia lay partly in Russia and partly in Turkey. The history is disputed to this day, but it seems that, during the late nineteenth and early twentieth centuries, the Ottoman authorities made several attempts to clear the area of Armenians, killing and displacing hundreds of thousands of people. In 1878, the Treaty of San Stefano was agreed between Turkey and Russia. Under this treaty, the Armenian lands and population came into the Russian sphere of influence where, historians seem to agree, they would have been safer.

Britain perceived this arrangement as a threat to its interests in the region, and forced a revision of the treaty to keep the Armenian lands within the Ottoman empire. In return, Britain pledged to enforce political reform in Turkey, and to prevent further oppression of minorities. The pledges were not serious, however, and the oppression continued and became more intense. In the 1890s large numbers of Armenians were displaced and killed. Worse massacres occurred during the First World War, in 1915. Some historians consider this the first act of genocide in the twentieth century, and suggest that it provided a useful model for the Nazis in Germany: proof that an entire civilian population could be killed off without reprisal. Britain was partly responsible for this outcome, as Lloyd George later commented:

> Had it not been for our sinister intervention, the great majority of the Armenians would have been placed, by the Treaty of San Stefano, in 1878, under the protection of the Russian flag. [. . .] The action of the British Government led inevitably to the terrible massacres of 1895–7, 1909 and worst of all to the holocausts of 1915.[8]

Many of those displaced died of hunger and exposure. The massacres during the war were widely reported. On 16 September 1915, *The Times* noted that 'It is believed that it is the official intention that this shall be a campaign of extermination, involving the murdering of from 800,000 to 1,000,000 persons'.[9] Often its reports

---

7. For this section I have drawn on Nassibian, *Britain and the Armenian Question*.
8. Lloyd George, *The Truth about the Peace Treaties* (London: Victor Gollancz Ltd, 1938), vol. 2, 1257.
9. *The Times*, 16 September 1915, 7, under the sub-heading 'Exterminating Armenians'. Alan Sharp argues that over a million Armenians were massacred in 1915–16. Evidence of this was used to forge an anti-Turkish consensus in Britain politics. *The Versailles Settlement* (Basingstoke: Macmillan, 1991), 167. *The Times* was actively engaged in creating (or maintaining) public hostility towards Turkey during and after the war, and its reports are not necessarily reliable. Nassibian argues that Britain's publicising of Turkish atrocities was motivated less by concern for human rights than by a desire to

were strongly worded. Historians argue that the massacres were real, but that they were also used as propaganda to discredit Turkey—first, during the war, and later during the final carve-up of the Ottoman Empire. Britain's criticisms of Turkey during this period also need to be read against the long history of the 'Eastern Question' and of European attempts to appropriate portions of the ailing Ottoman Empire.

At the end of September 1915, *The Times* described the 'nauseating and appalling character' of atrocities against Armenians. From many Armenian regions came tales of

> men shot down in cold blood, crucified, mutilated, or dragged off for labour battalions, of children carried off and forcibly converted to Islam, of women violated and enslaved in the interior, shot down, or sent off with their children to the desert west of Mosul, where there is neither water nor food [. . .]. Many of these unfortunates did not reach their destination, because the escort so overdrove their victims that many fell out, and, as flogging and kicking were unavailing, they were left to perish by the roadside, their corpses distinctly defining the route followed. Many were tied back to back in pairs and thrown into rivers alive.[1]

It is difficult to imagine someone in political circles being vague about these matters, especially when they were so widely reported, but the ignorance of ruling-class women is surely one of Woolf's targets in the novel. Sally Seton, too, 'scarcely ever read the papers' [131]. Those who did read the newspapers would have seen a great many references to the Armenian Question during and after the war, especially during 1922 and 1923.

In April 1918, a Transcaucasian Federation was established among the Georgians, Armenians, and Tatars of Azerbaijan; this was dissolved in May 1918 and 'the independent republics of the Caucasus were born'; including an independent Armenia.[2] But it was weak and divided, threatened on all sides, and could not survive.[3] After

---

discredit its enemies. *Britain and the Armenian Question*, 119. Recent Turkish historians emphasise Britain's use of the Armenian Question for propagandistic purposes. Sinasi Orel and Sureyya Yuca, *The Talat Pasha 'Telegrams'* (Nicosia: K. Rustem and Bro., 1986); Kamuran Gürün, *The Armenian File* (1983; London: K. Ruskin and Bro. and Weidenfeld and Nicolson, 1985). See also Michael Gunter, *Armenian History and the Question of Genocide* (New York: Palgrave Macmillan, 2011).

1. 'Wholesale Murder in Armenia: Exterminating a Race', *The Times*, 30 September 1915, 5. *The Times* claims here that Turkish leader Talaat Bey said of the deportations, 'After this for 50 years there will not be an Armenian Question.'
2. Nassibian, *Britain and the Armenian Question*, 104.
3. In December 1922 Armenia became part of the USSR. Michael Dockrill and J. Douglas Goold, *Peace Without Promise* (London: Batsford, 1981), 239. By the mid-1920s, Armenia was internally unstable, 'fatally isolated' and under threat from all sides. Nassibian, *Britain and the Armenian Question*, 207.

the First World War, Britain and its allies entered into complex negotiations with Turkey over the break-up of the Ottoman Empire, culminating in the London and Lausanne Peace Conferences of 1920 and 1923.[4] One aspect of these negotiations involved protection of minorities in Turkish-controlled areas. A number of Armenian support groups had been established in Britain, arguing for permanent Armenian national home. The British government and papers such as *The Times* appeared to support this claim, and argued in favour of human rights for oppressed minority groups in the region.[5] The issue was often mentioned in the *Nation and Athenaeum* during the early 1920s, including in a debate on the Greco-Turkish war between Arnold Toynbee and T. P. O'Connor in the letters pages in December 1921 and January 1922.[6] (Albania, by contrast, received a much less sympathetic press in Britain during this period.)

The Lausanne Treaty was finally signed on 24 July 1923—a few weeks after *Mrs Dalloway* is set. By then, Britain had secured its interests in the region—not in Armenia but in the Persian Gulf, partly by creating the new state of Iraq. The Armenian people were effectively abandoned by the Lausanne Treaty; those in the Soviet Union were to remain citizens of that state, while the remaining survivors were to stay under the rule of Turkey, under a protectorate agreement. The idea of an Armenian national home in the Anatolia region was simply dropped.[7] For many people, this was a grotesque betrayal of the Armenians, who had suffered so much, and for whom Britain had some responsibility.[8]

In *Mrs Dalloway*, Richard Dalloway MP sits on the committee which is negotiating this final act of betrayal in June 1923. That is where he is going after giving Clarissa the roses.

Clarissa's refusal to think about the Armenian problem is a crucial moment in the novel, and provides us with ways into thinking about the relationship between Clarissa and Septimus, the

---

4. Harold Nicolson was involved in the Lausanne negotiations and is another possible source of information for Woolf.
5. The question of an Armenian national home, for example, is mentioned in *The Times* on 13, 14, 15, 16 and 27 December 1922; 8 January and 10 February 1923, 10.
6. 'War on Tap', *Nation and Athenaeum*, 7 October 1922; 'The Meaning of Lausanne', *Nation and Athenaeum*, 10 February 1923. See also 'Events of the Week' in June 1923 for progress reports on the Lausanne Conference.
7. Sharp, *The Versailles Settlement*, 174. Britain's commitment to an independent Armenia was in decline, however, in 1920, and it did not provide material support to the fragile republic. Nassibian, *Britain and the Armenian Question*, 210–13. See also Dockrill and Gould, *Peace without Promise*, 213–14.
8. Arnold Toynbee, *Survey of International Affairs 1920–1923* (Oxford: Oxford University Press, 1925); Nassibian, *Britain and the Armenian Question*, 222. Ernest Hemingway's poem, 'They All Made Peace—What is Peace?,' begins 'All of the turks are gentlemen and Ismet Pasha is a / little deaf. But the Armenians. How about the / Armenians? / Well the Armenians'. *Little Review*, 9, 3 (1923), 20.

war-neurotic soldier. Who is the victim, who the victimiser; who is responsible for the suffering of others? These questions trouble Woolf's text, just as they do HD's *Bid Me to Live*. But where HD's novel retreats into a private place of writing to contemplate the problem, *Mrs Dalloway* takes it into the heart of the political establishment. Even the Prime Minister is present at the Dalloways' party.

* * *

# ALISON LIGHT

## *From* Mrs. Woolf and the Servants[†]

'A servant's life is one long drudgery,' Woolf wrote sympathetically, in a review of a new edition of George Moore's *Esther Waters*, his novel of 1894. Moore's eponymous heroine, a housemaid, is easily pitied, a victim pure and simple—sexual, social and economic; though she rises above circumstances she lives a life of unrelieved toil. The temptation was always to say that servants' lives were ruled by their physical experience, or that their wishes were limited to merely material aspirations: all body and no mind, as it were. But in Bloomsbury the servants were not victims or drudges, and Woolf noted that even her char[1] moved an ornament on the mantelpiece at Monk's House to leave it 'askew' each day, a symptomatic act which, Woolf imagined, showed the desire for ornament and her thirst for art (it might equally have been an assertion of independence). 'Solid Objects', the title of another of Woolf's experimental stories, suggested that in any case 'things' were about far more than the cash invested in them: they became the repository of the immaterial—feelings, obsessions, needs and longings—evidence of a hidden inner life which could not be known or explained.

That servants had souls might have been confirmed by what happened to Mary Wilson, a housemaid who entered Vanessa's service around this time. In February 1920 Vanessa took the top two floors of the Adrian Stephen's house at 50 Gordon Square and travelled with Duncan Grant to Italy and France, leaving the household and children to the care of Sophie Farrell, the old

---

† From "Housemaids' Souls" in *Mrs. Woolf and the Servants: An Intimate History of Domestic Life in Bloomsbury* (London: Penguin Books, 2008), pp. 151–59. Copyright © Alison Light, 2007. Reprinted by permission of Bloomsbury Press and Penguin Books Limited. Notes are Light's unless otherwise indicated.
1. 'The Char', MHP A13f, Sussex, a fragment dated as 'probably 1930s', but the deleted passage in *Jacob's Room* has Mrs Pascoe take 'down the gaudy box placed askew on the mantelpiece', so it may be earlier.

family servant. Vanessa received troubling news of domestic affairs while she was away. Her new housemaid, Mary Wilson, 'had nearly gone off her head', she wrote to Roger Fry, 'owing to the deaths of her mother, father and lover within a fortnight'. Mary's brother was also seriously ill. The bad news had come by telegram or by telephone to Blanche, the maid at 46 Gordon Square, Maynard Keynes's house (the Stephens had as yet no telephone), and relayed to Mary, who had 'terrified Sophie and the 46 servants by raving wildly all night for 3 weeks till it got so bad that [Dr] Moralt had to take her to the infirmary'. Mary was now anxious to come back to work—'I don't think her state was to be wondered at,' Vanessa added. On her return in mid-May, Vanessa took charge of the situation, corresponding with Mary's friends, in particular a Nurse Gibson and a Mr Bracenbury, mysteriously known by the name of 'Nigger'; the former sent a severe letter to Mary, telling her to 'pull herself together', the latter, now effectively Mary's guardian, wrote, telephoned and set up appointments which he did not keep. Meanwhile Mary's condition had deteriorated; she disappeared on errands, going out of her way to avoid strangers and confessing to 'a strange horror of black men'; despite repeated doses of bromide, she lay sobbing and moaning all night. Eventually, when Blanche took Mary across country to find her guardian, Mary bolted. In the event her parents' home was located and they were found to be alive and well, utterly mystified. Mary's letters and calls had all been impersonations. Meanwhile she was at large in London, sending messages in her various characters, until she was captured and brought to Gordon Square. During the long hours of waiting to be admitted to the infirmary she became more and more incoherent. 'Finally she seemed to know no one' and was led tamely away.

In her diary Virginia decided that it was 'a complete case of servant's hysteria; all coming, I think, from her wishing to act a day dream, & then, poor creature, stepping too far & believing it, & now babbling in St Pancras Infirmary'[2] (the old union workhouse). She found the sight of Mary being taken off 'sinister; & all the servants were looking from all the windows. What horrid people they are!', though presumably she too had watched. After this Virginia had taken a bus across London in a heightened state, feeling it was one of those times when 'everything gets into the same mood'. She found another sight which moved her, though differently, an old beggar woman seen from the top of a London bus, singing shrilly 'for her own amusement' up against a stone wall, and 'holding a brown mongrel in her arms':

2. See *Diary*, p. 152 [*Editor*].

There was a recklessness about her; much in the spirit of London. Defiant—almost gay, clasping her dog as if for warmth.
How many Junes has she sat there, in the heart of London? How
she came to be there, what scenes she can go through, I can't
imagine. Oh damn it all, I say, why cant I know all that too?

The inspiring image of the beggar woman was to recur in Woolf's
fiction. The romantic figure of the old vagrant, belonging to the
eternal caste of the poor, so entirely different from oneself, was far
easier to sympathize with than the housemaid, a daydreamer and
hysteric, a poor person in the wrong place, who came much too
close for comfort.

    What, after all, was different about 'servant's hysteria'? Virginia
too feared strangers and heard voices; she too made things up, and
what she daydreamed turned into her reality; she too had been carted
off 'raving', though, like Helen Fry or Vivienne Eliot, to private,
expensive nursing-homes rather than to the old union workhouse.
And though she lost touch entirely with reality, she could recover,
and did. Virginia was always being told—as Helen Fry was—to exercise more self-control, as if her breakdowns were her fault. What if
the difference between 'Mad Mary' and 'Mad Virginia' were one of
degree and not of kind? Everyone, including Virginia, saw her madness as a sign of her specialness; her friends openly referred to it as a
mark of her genius. How could one be a writer and remain in control? In the early 1920s Woolf frequently found metaphors for writing as a process which relied on an active inner life, 'submerged' or
working 'in the dark'; her new method of 'tunnelling' or making
'caves' behind her characters, her interior monologues which read
like free association, and her advice to herself to cultivate a kind of
idle attentiveness, faced with the ebbs and flows of her moods, all
seem to chime with the idea of the unconscious life of the mind.
Psychoanalysis itself had begun with the interpretation of hysterical
symptoms whose origins were believed to lie in forgotten psychical
trauma. But the Freudian analysis which Virginia encountered in her
circle, and tended to mock in the early 20s (in her essay on 'Freudian
Fiction', for example), was potentially as controlling of the patient as
the more conventional treatments she had undergone. Throughout
her life Virginia Woolf experienced many intermediate states of illness, of physical and psychological collapse, which she often found
fruitful for her writing; the border between madness and sanity,
between the life of the mind and of the body, was far more flexible
and porous than any opposition or dissociation might suggest. Perhaps that was why, at least at first, she was antagonistic towards psychoanalysis. She wished to keep her interior to herself and to leave
the body—which anyone could occupy—out of the account.

In the 1920s hysteria was generally a pejorative label, and in her diary and letters Virginia consistently dismissed the servants' illnesses as mysterious, dubious and a bit of a joke. Nellie, though quiet and thoughtful, was prone 'to work herself up into states' or to 'vapours'; Lottie was cheerful and carefree but she was also lazy and 'volatile', liable to be found 'in a state of hysterics'. 'My private wonder is,' Virginia wrote when Nellie was 'seemingly ill' in July 1920, 'how they contrive to live a week—aren't killed by the thunder, like flies. No root in reality is in them; & as for reason, when the mood's on, as soon might one persuade a runaway horse. And nothing the matter save what one of us would call an upset inside & take a pill for.' Too much time was spent talking about 'the insides of women', wrote Virginia. Though Lottie went into hospital for an operation, leaving the Woolfs to carry the coals themselves, the physical toll of the work seems not to have been discussed. Servants' illnesses were the product of unreason, self-induced or just plain malingering. Certainly this was the view canvassed by Mrs Bell when she entertained Bloomsbury's newly established 'Memoir Club' with the whole 'strange story of Mary Elizabeth Wilson', a shilling-shocker in which the economist Maynard Keynes featured as the arch-detective and ultra-rationalist, able instantly to see through the false 'evidence' of the letters, and pre-empting Vanessa Bell's final verdict on Mary's behaviour—'There was no word of truth in her story.' Even the servants agreed that Mary was 'an artful hussy and deceiver'.[3] No wonder Virginia insisted on a clear distance between herself and these other fabricators.

Sooner or later they were all seen as 'temperamental', these girls who cried a lot; who were often frightened and lonely, and a long way from home. Yet their wild insecurity was not unreasonable; they knew they were dispensable, even interchangeable, in the eyes of their employers, and they learnt to live a temporary existence, able to move on at a moment's notice. If they made up stories about themselves, exaggerated and dramatized, just to feel they mattered—to take up more room—what was strange about that? Class was always a matter of fantasy, and 'wishing to act a daydream' the motive-power which underpinned social mobility. Everyone seemed to believe that the upper classes were more important and interesting than the lower orders, and the social hierarchy depended upon that deprivation of self-esteem, which Dickens in *Great Expectations*, with his deep instinct for inferiority feelings, called 'the hurt without a name'. Servants' hysteria might easily have been

---

3. David Garnett, who had known Mary Wilson as a pretty 'English rosebud' of a maid, decided thirty years later that it was a case of 'split personality' and says she later recovered, *The Flowers of the Forest* (Chatto & Windus, 1953), p. 214.

understood as a veiled, unhappy way of asking for more. But in the
early 1920s neither Mary, Nellie nor Lottie could have turned to the
budding psychoanalysts[4] for help. Bloomsbury's clients, like Freud's,
were from their own milieu. In another life intelligent, inventive,
artful 'Mad Mary', doomed to be a housemaid, might well have been
a writer. But who knows what she actually was?

Lottie and Nellie frequently played their employers off against each
other but they never left. In fact many of the Bloomsbury servants
stayed for years, becoming old retainers. According to Virginia, her
household was 'the easiest place in the world' for servants, and there
was some truth in this. In the first place, there was no uniform. Nor
were you called by your surname like the aptly named 'Meek', the
parlourmaid at Cleeve House in Wiltshire, Clive Bell's family home,
where even in the 1930s dinner was served by maids in black alpaca
frocks and spotless white caps and aprons, and no one was allowed
to carry 'anything heavier than a handkerchief'.[5] Virginia and Vanessa were 'Mrs Woolf' and 'Mrs Bell' and not the customary 'Ma'am';
after a row, when Nellie, in later years, began a letter with 'Dear
Madam', Virginia commented that this was 'significant of much'.
These were very informal households. No one dressed for dinner:
hence Virginia's frequent injunction in her letters to her friends telling them 'to bring no clothes' for a stay. A bell would still be rung at
mealtimes at both Monk's House and Charleston but, while food
had to be brought in and plates cleared, there was no waiting at
meals and the Omega dining-tables were used without table linen.
Other fetching and carrying was at a minimum. Neither Mrs Woolf
nor Mrs Bell supervised their servants while they worked, and to
most of their class their manners would have appeared unbelievably
lax. Nor were the servants expected to attend church as was still the
norm—and Bloomsbury was sympathetic and decent towards
unmarried mothers in their employ. In 1919, when Flossie Selwood
had an illegitimate daughter, Mary, Vanessa's friend Faith Henderson kept her on and brought Mary up as one of them, saving them
both from disgrace. Mary 'Henderson' went to private school and
played with the other Bloomsbury children. Only when Flossie married a local man from her Gloucestershire village, and took Mary

4. Including Adrian Stephen and his wife, Karin; Lytton Strachey's brother James and his
   wife, Alix, who were analysed by Freud. They translated his complete works for the
   Hogarth Press. Alix thought it right that Virginia was never psychoanalysed as it might
   have 'stopped' her creativeness, which 'was so interwoven with her fantasies—and
   indeed with her madness': Joan Russell Noble, ed., *Recollections of Virginia Woolf by
   Her Contemporaries* (New York: Harper Collins, 1972), p. 143.
5. Angelica Garnett, *Deceived with Kindness: A Bloomsbury Childhood* (Ann Arbor: University of Michigan Press, 1984), p. 57.

home to live with her new husband, did mother and daughter have to face nastiness and prejudice.

Above all, Bloomsbury was sociable and fun and there were halcyon times, especially in the early 20s. The servants were in and out of each other's places in London and in Sussex; weather permitting, there was much walking and cycling between Charleston and Rodmell, and later to Tilton, the farmhouse near Charleston which became the Keynes's place. There were many parties, including fancy dress, to which the servants were often invited—on one occasion George Harland, who worked for Keynes, was infuriated because 'Mr' had been left off his invitation, despite his having hired a Napoleon costume. Monk's House rang with laughter, Virginia told Roger, with Lottie 'in and out all the time in a transparent white petticoat up to her knees'. Lottie liked to play practical jokes, and caused much hilarity one Christmas by dropping a marzipan mouse in Virginia's tea. 'The girls' saved up for dancing lessons and practised the foxtrot; Virginia bought a kitten and named it 'Boxall' after Nellie—'to ingratiate her'. Servants' relatives often came to stay and there were plenty of treats. Daisy Selwood went travelling abroad with the Adrian Stephens and joined them at parties in her flapper frocks. Grace Germany, who came as a housemaid, aged sixteen, to Charleston and took over as Angelica's nurse after Nelly Brittain left, went several times to Cassis, where Vanessa Bell purchased a farmhouse in the 20s. Grace learnt French and enjoyed wine.

Like servants through the ages, those who worked in Bloomsbury saw how the other half lived and it expanded their horizons. If they were sometimes envious and resentful, they were also grateful and appreciative. But these are two sides of the same coin. They rewarded their employers by becoming snobs, enjoying the borrowed glamour of working for famous people, and in a pathetic tribute to Bloomsbury, mirroring the cliquish world in which they moved, the servants called themselves 'the click'. For all its liberalism, Bloomsbury could be possessive and insular; to others the group acted like a gang. Vanessa wanted to exclude Lydia Lopokova from joining their circle when Maynard Keynes married the Russian ballerina; Lydia was often happiest in the kitchen with Grace or Daisy. Adrian and Karin Stephen were outsiders—no one thought Karin, an American, good enough, and Adrian left Charleston in tears after Duncan Grant, who had once been his lover, made his views plain. After forty years, their daughter, Ann, was still angry and had never, she told Leonard Woolf, understood this 'cold feeling'.[6] As a little girl she had sat in the kitchen listening to

6. 3 June 1964, *LLW*. A typo in the transcription of this letter turns Daisy Selwood into Lottie Hope's sister; the mistake is repeated in MacGibbon's life of Adrian Stephen.

*Nellie Boxall, Lottie Hope, Nelly Brittain, with Angelica Bell, 1922.*
Photograph by Vanessa Bell. Photo © Tate. Image courtesy of
the Tate Modern.

the servants gossip about 'Mr W' and 'Mrs B', and 'there you all
were, larger than life, cracked up by the servants as "great" men
and women and played down by my parents as "no more remarkable
than anyone else for all they think so highly of themselves"'. Yet
Bloomsbury's tribal behaviour was hardly unique to them. Everyone in Britain could find someone to look down on.

No doubt the servants had good times in Bloomsbury. There they
are in Vanessa Bell's remarkably informal photograph, taken in the
early 1920s—Nellie, Lottie and Nelly Brittain, in their ballerina
cardigans and frocks, their hair fashionably bobbed. Lottie laughs
into the camera, her comrades smile; their eyes are hidden beneath

the brim of straw boaters, hands are in pockets. They could be undergraduates or flappers were it not for the chubby toddler and the custodial pose of Angelica's nurse which suggests that they might all be servants in mufti. (And would young ladies grin quite so much?) There are several more portraits of Grace, 'the Angel of Charleston', whose beauty appealed to her painter mistress. Their number is also testimony to Mrs Bell's affection. Yet there is always one photo missing from the Bloomsbury albums. Though mistresses and maids were constantly in each other's company, they seem never to have been photographed together. They never could appear side by side.

## ELIZABETH OUTKA

### [*Mrs. Dalloway* and the Influenza Pandemic]†

Here's what we already know—during the First World War, soldiers and civilians often had remarkably different experiences of the war corpse. Dead bodies were omnipresent on the front line and in the trenches, an inescapable constant for the living soldier. As critic Allyson Booth notes, "Trench soldiers . . . inhabited worlds constructed, literally, of corpses."[1] In Britain and America, however, such corpses were strangely absent; unlike in previous conflicts, bodies were not returned. This dichotomy underscores some of our central assumptions about the differences between the front line and the home front: in the trenches, dead bodies and the ever-present danger of becoming one; at home, the often haunting absence of bodies to mourn, though this mourning occurred in a place of relative safety. These assumptions miss, however, the sudden erosion of these distinctions in 1918, for in the autumn of that year, dead bodies were suddenly everywhere in Britain, in America, and across the globe; some neighborhoods had streets so full of corpses that no one was left alive to bury them. Death came swiftly and with such little warning that mass graves had to be prepared, and as one witness wrote, "Wood for the coffins ran out."[2] The

† From "'Wood for the Coffins Ran Out': Modernism and the Shadowed Afterlife of the Influenza Pandemic," *Modernism/modernity* 21.4 (November 2014): 937–38, 940–43, 953–54, 957–5, 960. © 2015 The Johns Hopkins University Press. Reprinted by permission of The Johns Hopkins University Press. Page numbers in square brackets refer to this Norton Critical Edition.

1. Allyson Booth, *Postcards from the Trenches: Negotiating the Space between Modernism and the First World War* (New York: Oxford University Press, 1996), 50.
2. Letter from Adeline Hill (now Abbitt) to Richard Collier, Item 63/5/5, Richard Collier, Spanish Flu Box of U.K. and France, Imperial War Museum, London. In the 1970s, researcher Richard Collier took out newspaper advertisements asking for letters from those who remembered the pandemic; letters were sent from across Europe and are

influenza pandemic of 1918, which stretched its deathly fingers into 1919, was the most lethal plague in human history, killing somewhere between fifty and one hundred million people worldwide in an astonishingly condensed period.[3] Yet despite inflicting five to ten times more casualties than the First World War, the flu was, for a time at least, seemingly forgotten. British and American literature rarely dwells on it, almost no memorials were built to mark its destruction, and until the last ten years, few historians had told its story; it certainly makes few appearances in modernist studies today.[4]

This neglect, however, should not be taken to mean that the pandemic didn't matter, or didn't matter to modernism, or even that the flu was actually forgotten. The pandemic was the second great traumatic event of the early twentieth century, and even years later, survivors vividly remembered the experience. Modernist writers and painters themselves suffered from the ravages of the flu: Guillaume Apollinaire died; D. H. Lawrence, H.D., Katherine Anne Porter, and Edvard Munch barely survived; even T. S. Eliot felt his brain was affected by his bout with the illness. Our neglect of the pandemic arises, I argue, not because it was insignificant but because it became the shadowed twin to the war, a disaster as unprecedented in its casualties and in its suffering as the war, yet at times locked into a paradoxical relation with it. Because of the pandemic's historical position right at the armistice as well as its unusual constellation of symptoms and aftereffects, it alternatively

now held in the above collection, hereafter cited in the text as *RC*, with letters cited by author. I also quote from narratives about the flu in the U.S. from the Pandemic Influenza Storybook, Centers for Disease Control and Prevention, *http://www.flu.gov /storybook/introduction/index.html*; hereafter cited in the text as S and by storyteller and location.

3. John M. Barry summarizes the evidence for these numbers in *The Great Influenza: The Story of the Deadliest Pandemic in History* (New York: Penguin, 2004), 397–98; hereafter cited in the text as "Barry."

4. Jane Fisher recently published the first book-length study on literature and the flu. (When I submitted this article, Fisher's book had not yet appeared). She takes an interesting look at gender and the pandemic and explores works by modernist authors (Woolf, Porter, Cather) as well as contemporary works from America, Britain, Canada, and Nigeria. There are also a few articles on modernism and the flu, most of which I cite in later endnotes. Joshua Dolezal explores the significance of the flu in Willa Cather's novel *One of Ours*; Caroline Hovanec explores the flu's impact on Katherine Ann Porter, William Maxwell, and John O'Hara, arguing that "influenza serves as a trope for the dehumanizing, denaturalizing, and disjunctive forces of modernity"; Catherine Belling analyzes the challenges the trauma of the pandemic poses to narrative. Fisher, *Envisioning Disease, Gender, and War: Women's Narratives of the 1918 Influenza Pandemic* (New York: Palgrave Macmillan, 2012); hereafter cited in the text as "Fisher." Dolezal, "'Waste in a Great Enterprise': Influenza, Modernism, and *One of Ours*," *Literature and Medicine* 28, no. 1 (Spring 2009): 82–101. Hovanec, "Of Bodies, Families, and Communities: Refiguring the 1918 Influenza Pandemic," *Literature and Medicine* 29, no. 1 (Spring 2011): 178; hereafter cited in the text as "Hovanec." Belling, "Overwhelming the Medium: Fiction and the Trauma of the Pandemic Influenza in 1918," *Literature and Medicine* 28, no. 1 (Spring 2009): 55–81; hereafter cited in the text as "Belling."

became a suspect rival to the "real" trauma of the Great War and (paradoxically) a loss too great to assimilate. Flu deaths were in part drowned out by war deaths, but also in part subsumed into the vast work of mourning that marks the postwar period and modernism itself. The flu's shadowed position continues to hide the profound impacts of the pandemic.

*   *   *

In 1918, much of the world was focused on war, and people everywhere were used to periodic pandemics. Mass outbreaks of disease often spread fear, but the flu was hardly cause for panic, though many in Britain remembered the severe "Russian" influenza that had arrived in the 1890s. So when the 1918 influenza first emerged, it attracted little attention. The virus came in three successive waves between 1918 and 1919, with the first wave concentrated in the spring and summer of the first year.[5] This wave was deadly but comparatively mild. It is difficult to pinpoint where the original outbreak began; at the time, many people believed it had originated in Spain (hence its nickname, "Spanish Influenza"), but this belief likely arose because Spain had less press censorship during the war and thus reported cases earlier (Crosby, 26). The latest thinking among historians is that ground zero was an army base in Kansas (Barry, 98; Honigsbaum, 41). In this early wave, tens of thousands died, including 5,500 British soldiers, but beyond a handful of doctors, few people in these brutal war years paid much attention (Crosby 28; Honigsbaum, 49). The war was so absorbing, and influenza was such a common illness, that there was a collective public shrug. As the *Times* noted, "The man in the street," hearing about Spanish influenza, "cheerfully anticipated its arrival here," and the reporter confidently reported that "epidemic diseases lose force with each successive visitation."[6] While newspapers in June and July described factory closings and the high number of people stricken, the flu didn't seem remarkably different to most people, and public health systems worldwide were not designed to publicize a problematic wave of influenza. A few doctors, though, were noticing one ominous sign: this flu attacked healthy young adults and killed them in high numbers.

5. My discussion of the flu's history is drawn from my own research in newspapers and from survivor accounts, as well as from the work of several excellent flu historians. In addition to Barry, see Alfred W. Crosby, *America's Forgotten Pandemic: The Influenza of 1918*, 2nd ed. (Cambridge: Cambridge University Press, 2003); hereafter cited in the text as "Crosby." See also Mark Honigsbaum, *Living with Enza: The Forgotten Story of Britain and the Great Flu Pandemic of 1918* (London: Macmillan, 2009); hereafter cited in the text as "Honigsbaum." For the timing of the influenza's waves, which varied, see Barry, 180–81, 407–8; Crosby, 17, 45, 202; and Honigsbaum, 35, 65, 107.
6. "The Spanish Influenza: A Sufferer's Symptoms," *Times*, 25 June 1918, 9.

The second wave, however, which came between September and December of 1918, killed millions. As one doctor noted, it produced "the most vicious type of pneumonia that has ever been seen" (Honigsbaum, 71). The war created conditions perfectly designed to spread this strain of flu: millions of men and women in the age range most vulnerable to the virus were living in close quarters and travelling across several continents. In August 1918, outbreaks erupted in three port cities on three continents: Freetown, Sierra Leone; Brest, France; and Boston, Massachusetts (Barry, 182–83). By September, the flu was charging through transport ships, army camps, cities, and towns across the globe. Doctors had never seen anything like it. In France, the flu "swept through the lines so suddenly and with such ferocity that it startled even doctors who'd served in Gallipoli and Salonika and [had] witnessed [hospital] wards overflowing with amoebic dysentery and malaria cases" (Honigsbaum, 19–20). One doctor noted that watching the men "dropping like flies" was worse than "any sight they ever had in France after a battle" (Honigsbaum, 72).

It wasn't just the speed and the targets that made this flu so remarkable; it was also the unusual constellation of symptoms. At first, many doctors assumed the outbreak must be some other disease. While the virus came with a high temperature, headache, and a terrible cough—symptoms not unlike those of the typical flu—it could also cause lethal complications, such as the deadly pneumonia that could quickly develop. The virus often travelled deep into the lung tissue, setting off a grotesque set of symptoms. Doctors noted with alarm that patients suffered from sudden floods of bleeding from the nose, mouth, or ears; such bleeding could continue after death, soaking the death wraps. The cough was bad enough to rip muscles and rib cartilage, and the body aches could feel like bones breaking. Patients gave off a terrible odor that would be remembered by survivors years later. In the final stages, victims often suffered from *heliotrope cyanosis*, a condition that developed when the lungs became so full of fluid that the body turned purple or blue and finally a mahogany color just before death.[7] The devastated lungs, as many doctors noted, were eerily similar to the lungs of soldiers attacked by poison gas (Honigsbaum, 53; Barry, 2). The virus also appeared to be a neurotoxin, capable of invading the brain and the nervous system;

7. Descriptions of symptoms are drawn from survivor letters, the medical literature, and histories of the flu. See, for example, letters from Horace Allen, Betty Barr (formally Boath), and A. Forbes, in *RC*; George Newman, the Chief Medical Officer in Britain, discusses symptoms in the "Report on the Pandemic of Influenza 1918–1919," Ministry of Health, Reports on Public Health and Medical Subjects, 4 (London: HMSO, 1920); online at the "Flu Web Historical Influenza Database," School of Population at the University of Melbourne, Australia, *http://influenza.sph.unimelb.edu.au/data/S0001/chapters/preface.pdf*; hereafter cited in the text as "Newman." Barry, Honigsbaum, and Crosby also describe symptoms (Barry, 2, 224, 232–38, 240–41; Honigsbaum, xii, 4, 15–16, 25, 50; Crosby, 5–9).

patients who recovered frequently reported depression, mental confusion, and even schizophrenia, and the latest research suggests that
the flu was behind the rash of suicides after the war that had previously been attributed to the war itself (Barry, 379–80). One soldier
stationed at Blandford Camp in Dorset would recall years later that
"a small wood below the camp was called 'suicide wood' because of
the number of men, who had flu, committing suicide there; the flu
seemed to leave people with distracted minds" (RC, Frederick Beb-
bington). Newspapers were full of reports of the violent derangement
the flu could produce, with previously peaceful citizens suddenly
erupting in murderous rages.[8]

The virus struck with astonishing speed: people were typically
attacked with no warning. Newspapers in Britain and America
reported every day on the high numbers of people who were simply
dropping in the streets, and survivors frequently recounted that
they had felt fine one moment and were violently ill the next. Death
usually came quickly, in a few hours or days, but the disease could
also linger and kill slowly. And except for caring for the patient's
basic needs, doctors or nurses could do little but let the disease run
its course; indeed, many doctors and nurses died, as well. The third
and final wave came between January and May of 1919, again causing many deaths, but it was not nearly as vicious as the second
wave. And then it disappeared.

Death rates from the flu are staggering. Recent studies suggest
that at least fifty million people died, and quite likely more than
one hundred million. As historian John M. Barry calculates,
between 2.5 and five percent of the world's population died in two
years, mainly in the terrible twelve weeks of the second wave, making it the deadliest pandemic in history in terms of numbers (though
the bubonic plague killed a higher percentage of the existing population) (Barry, 4–5; 396–97). And it was not just the flu's lethality
that made it different; it was the targets. In a typical flu season,
casualties are generally among the very old and the very young, but
this time, the fatalities were high among healthy men and women
between sixteen and forty years of age, and especially among those
between twenty-one and thirty (doctors and scientists were mystified by this anomaly for years; the latest research shows that those
with the strongest immune systems were the most vulnerable, as it was
the immune response that brought the most lethal complications).[9]
Those who lived through the pandemic repeatedly recalled how the
healthiest individuals seemed to be targets; one survivor marveled

8. See, for example, "Triple Murder and Suicide. An Attack of Influenza," Times, 6
   November 1918, 3. See also S, the narrative of Ethel Hubble-Harter, Virginia.
9. See Crosby and Barry on the flu's targets and their explanations of why the virus killed
   young, healthy adults (Crosby, 21–24, 222; Barry, 238–39, 249–50).

at a "big strong healthy looking chap" who died quickly, and another remembered "the heavy weight boxer of Clifton College" being struck down by the flu (*RC*, C. J. Barrow, Horace R. Belcher). As Barry points out, "If the upper estimate of the death toll is true, as many as 8 to 10 percent of all young adults then living may have been killed by the virus" (Barry, 4). The tragedy of this death toll was deepened by the fact that the parents of most young children lay in precisely this age group (Barry, 391).[1] Even at the time, the flu was recognized to be far more devastating than the war. George Newman, the Chief Medical Officer in Britain, noted in his 1920 report on the flu that the pandemic was without a doubt "one of the great historic scourges of our time, a pestilence which affected the well-being of millions of men and women and destroyed more human lives in a few months than did the European war in five years" (Newman, iv).

The flu did not simply unfold behind the closed doors of homes and hospitals; life was visibly changed on the streets, as well. Schools, cinemas, theaters, and factories were all frequently shut down, and many public services simply stopped; too many people were ill—or taking care of the ill—to keep services running. All across the globe, coffins could not be made fast enough, and graves could not be dug quickly enough, to bury all the dead. Few people would come to funerals in any case.[2] Survivors from England noted the eeriness of the streets, with house after house with blinds down—the symbol at the time for a death within. One survivor remembered that in Hambrough Road, Southhall, "so many whole families died that scores of houses became empty" (*RC*, Cairns).[3] In Philadelphia, wagons were pulled through the streets, with priests calling for people to "bring out their dead" (Barry, 5).

The flu was a distinct tragedy, but it was also intimately tied to the tragedy of the war, and the two disasters interacted and overlapped. The war spread the flu and created the perfect conditions for its advance. On the front lines, the flu changed the war, striking millions of soldiers and postponing battles. One of Germany's head generals, Erich von Ludendorff, blamed influenza for contributing to the failed July offensive of 1918, a push that might otherwise have ended the war with the Germans as victors (Crosby, 26–27).

1. The narratives in the Pandemic Influenza Storybook frequently recount how the flu created orphans, single parents, and broken families. See the narratives of Marcella Bobzien, storyteller Marilynn Sutherland, North Dakota; Thomas Langan, storyteller Barbara Reynolds, Nebraska; Arthur and Julienne Scoltic-Valley and Loretta Carmel Crowley, storyteller Kathy Parker, New York.
2. The Collier letters frequently mention the lack of coffins and the piles of bodies, and newspaper accounts constantly note the shutting down of services. Narratives in the Pandemic Influenza Storybook tell of coffins stacked at train stations and the frequent sight of the hearse bringing bodies to the graveyards.
3. See also *RC*, Edith Dilks (now How), and Gladys Hanson (now Bowden).

And in Britain, France, and America, the flu fueled paranoid fears that the Germans had unleashed the virus as part of their war strategy (Barry, 343). Ironically, many people in Britain caught the flu in the crowded and euphoric armistice celebrations (Honigsbaum, 99–101). Some historians argue that the flu even had disastrous consequences for the Treaty of Versailles. Woodrow Wilson was fighting hard for lighter terms for Germany, but on 3 April 1919, he was struck by the flu.[4] After a partial recovery, his mind seemed to be affected, and he became mentally sluggish and paranoid; he suddenly abandoned his goals for Germany and capitulated to the demands of the French (Barry, 385). Lloyd George (who had narrowly survived the flu in September) noted that Wilson had a "nervous and spiritual breakdown in the middle of the Conference" (Barry, 386). The treaty was signed, however, producing the conditions, as many historians argue, for the Second World War.

* * *

Virginia Woolf * * * appeared not only to escape the flu but to scoff at its outbreak. She notes in her diary in 1918 that Lytton Strachey was fleeing London to avoid the disease, and she writes dismissively and parenthetically, "(We are, by the way, in the midst of a plague unmatched since the Black Death, according to the Times, who seem to tremble lest it may seize upon Lord Northcliffe, & thus precipitate us into peace)."[5] Like many people at the start of the pandemic, Woolf feels that hysteria over the flu is absurd and misplaced. In the years after the pandemic, however, when the scope of the destruction was better understood, Woolf seemed to consider the outbreak more seriously and to wonder why illness was so rarely a topic of literature. In her 1926 essay "On Being Ill," she muses that "Novels, one would have thought, would have been devoted to influenza," and she goes on to consider how the body's health influences our perceptions.[6] But it is in *Mrs. Dalloway* that she turns more directly to the pandemic.

*Mrs. Dalloway* is rarely considered in relationship to the 1918 flu. While critics have noted that Clarissa Dalloway is recovering from influenza, the central trauma within the novel has long been considered the war and its devastating effects on the mind of Septimus Smith.[7] The novel is focused on the war, but we should reconceive its

---

4. See Crosby on the flu's effects on Woodrow Wilson and the Treaty of Versailles (Crosby, 171–96). See also Barry's discussion (Barry, 383–88).
5. Woolf, *The Diary of Virginia Woolf*, vol. 1, *1915–1919*, ed. Anne Olivier Bell (New York: Harcourt, 1977), 209.
6. Woolf, "On Being Ill," 317.
7. In Bonnie Kime Scott's excellent introduction to the Harcourt edition of *Mrs. Dalloway*, she notes that Woolf suffered from influenza after publishing *Jacob's Room*: "*Mrs. Dalloway* is the work of a survivor, and indeed takes survival and triumph over illness as a central

structure as built around the *two* central traumas of the early twentieth century. The main characters, Septimus and Clarissa, are both
survivors, one from the battlefield, the other from the pandemic, and
Woolf considers the continued consequences of both tragedies. We
already know a great deal about shell shock and Septimus, but scholars often miss that Clarissa represents a different group of survivors.
Clarissa has, it appears, come close to dying from influenza. At the
start of the novel, she is seen by Scrope Purvis pausing on a London
street corner; she is pale, "very white since her illness," her heart possibly compromised, "affected, they said, by influenza" (*D*, 4)[3]. Certainly, as the novel takes place in 1923, Clarissa could have been
recovering from a more recent outbreak, but any reference to influenza in 1925 would have brought the pandemic to mind, and doctors
were discovering the long-term health consequences of this particular flu. It did indeed often leave the body permanently weakened.[8]

Like Porter's story and Wolfe's novel, *Mrs. Dalloway* is saturated
in an atmosphere of mortality, with the lines between the living
and the dead blurring dangerously. As critics have noted, the minds
of the characters dwell frequently on death, from Clarissa's
repeated musings on her own aging and weakness to Septimus's
mad belief that his dead friend Evans has returned.[9] This atmosphere evokes not simply the aftermath of war but the atmosphere
of the post-pandemic period, as well. Septimus, in his hallucinatory
madness, believes he literally lives in a threshold space, one that
allows him to commune with the dead and to see Evans come back
to life. Traumatized by the war, he repeatedly sees his own death,
his body on fire, his body "macerated until only the nerve fibres
were left" (*D*, 66)[49]. Woolf makes clear, though, that the flu survivor also dwells on this threshold. Throughout the novel, Clarissa
thinks back over her illness, considering the resulting restrictions
on her life: her daily nap, her narrow bed, her tired body, her weakened heart. She broods repeatedly on the Shakespearean line spoken of the dead, "Fear no more the heat o' the sun," and she wonders
how much longer she will survive.

---

subject." I agree with Scott's analysis, but I tie the work to the specific 1918 pandemic.
Fisher also looks at the flu and *Mrs. Dalloway* and observes that Clarissa herself acts as "a
bridge between the living and the dead" (Fisher, 85). Scott, introduction to *Mrs. Dalloway*
(New York: Harcourt, 2005), xli; the novel is hereafter cited in the text as *D*.

8. See Barry, 392, for more on the long-term health consequences of this strain of
influenza.

9. J. Hillis Miller, for example, explores the novel's saturation in death in his "Virginia
Woolf's All Souls' Day: The Omniscient Narrator in *Mrs. Dalloway*," in *The Shaken
Realist: Essays in Honor of F. J. Hoffman*, eds. Melvin Friedman and John Vickery
(Baton Rouge: Louisiana University Press, 1970), 100–27. For a longer discussion of
resurrection and Evans's return, see my article, "Dead Men, Walking: Actors, Net-
works, and Actualized Metaphors in *Mrs. Dalloway* and *Raymond*," *NOVEL: A Forum
on Fiction* 46, no. 2 (Summer 2013): 253–74.

Woolf provides her own scene of dramatic confrontation with the dead in the final pages of the novel, when at her party Clarissa famously hears the news of Septimus's suicide. Here the war intrudes into the domestic space, but this space was not previously a safe zone; the flu had already changed the danger/safety calculus of the home front, and Septimus's death adds to rather than introduces the sense of death already there. Even at her party, Clarissa sees her own death as close, mirrored in the old lady she watches through the window. She thinks how odd it is that her party goes on while "that old woman, quite quietly, go[es] to bed": "She pulled the blind now. The clock began striking. The young man had killed himself" (D, 181) [131]. The description here is full of images of death—sleep, a clock striking, the reference to the suicide, and the pulled-down blinds—a sign, at the time, that a death had taken place (one repeatedly cited by flu survivors as the grim indicator of another casualty). The living Clarissa stares at images of Septimus's death and of her own, one part of her still with the liveliness of the party, one part of her already going to bed.

Yet despite this threshold atmosphere, Clarissa survives, remaining quite clearly alive, but * * * she feels conflicted about living. Woolf depicts in Clarissa a dual climate: the paradoxical sense of astonishment, guilt, and joy at being alive at all after the twin disasters, coupled with the pervasive sense that death and the dead are ever close, intertwined with the living. Learning of Septimus's suicidal leap, Clarissa reviews it in her mind, feeling the leap and the impact in her own body. With the guilty mind of the survivor, she thinks that "somehow it was her disaster—her disgrace": "It was her punishment to see sink and disappear here a man, there a woman, in this profound darkness, and she forced herself to stand here in her evening dress" (D, 181)[130]. Clarissa mourns the deaths of *both* men and women (suggesting not just war deaths) and represents a vivid image of the startled and lonely survivor who is left behind. Part of Clarissa envies Septimus's decision to "throw it all away," and Woolf, like Porter and Wolfe, records the cost of remaining alive while so many had already sunk into death.

* * *

# CRITICISM

# Early Reviews

## ANONYMOUS

### A Long, Long Chapter[†]

This novel is in one chapter, 293 pages of it. That is a normal length, but we like to have places which we can dog-ear when we go to bed, with the certainty of restarting at the exact line. Mrs Dalloway doesn't interest us very much, nor do any of the characters drawn into this somewhat bewildering jumble. Something might have been made of Rezia Warren Smith, the Italian wife of a lunatic ex-soldier, if she had been allowed to evolve naturally. The remainder of the people, who skip into a page and out of it with no apparent purpose, are of no consequence. Great industry has gone into the effort to write wittily, epigrammatically, and with the appearance of ease, and readers of preternaturally nimble intellect may discover a consecutive story. We are only normally endowed.

## ANONYMOUS

### A Novelist's Experiment[‡]

All Mrs Woolf's fiction shows such an instinct for experiment that we may have to show cause why this new book should be called peculiarly experimental. *Jacob's Room*, too, was an adventure. But there is one obvious difference between that novel and *Mrs Dalloway*. While the other, however innovating in its method, observed the usual time-span of a novel, this one describes the passage of a single day. The idea, though new enough to be called an experiment, may not be unique in modern fiction. There was a precedent

---

† From *Western Mail* (May 14, 1925): 9; rpt. in *Virginia Woolf: Critical Assessments, Vol. III*, ed. Eleanor McNees (Mountfield, UK: Helm Information, 1994). p. 265.

‡ From *Times Literary Supplement* (May 21, 1925): 349; rpt. in *Virginia Woolf: Critical Assessments, Vol. III*, ed. Eleanor McNees (Mountfield, UK: Helm Information, 1994), p. 268.

in *Ulysses*. But Mrs Woolf's vision escapes disaster and produces something of her own. People and events here have a peculiar, almost ethereal transparency, as though bathed in a medium where one thing permeates another. Undoubtedly our world is less solid than it was, and our novels may have to shake themselves a little free of matter. Here, Mrs Woolf seems to say, is the stream of life, but reflected always in a mental vision.

Life itself, with the first cool radiance of a June morning in London, is wafted to Clarissa Dalloway as she goes out to buy flowers for her party in the evening—the same Clarissa who made a brief irruption into *The Voyage Out*, so exquisite there and brightly, almost excessively, interested; and now, at fifty-one, a little wiser, more pensive, but adoring life. An hour or two later, and Peter Walsh, whimsically sympathetic, who had been Clarissa's suitor years ago and has just returned from India, is falling asleep on a bench in Regent's Park to dream of memories, and will awake to think them out. Near him is a young couple who seem to be having a grim quarrel; but the man is a war victim who has gone out of his mind, and we shall read the last page of his tragedy before dusk falls. We shall be also at luncheon with Lady Bruton, at tea in the Army and Navy Stores, where Miss Kilman is making her last tense effort to snatch Clarissa's lovely daughter from her mother. But how often these lives and doings seem to distil themselves in something as immaterial as the passing of sunlight or the sound of a clock striking the hour. Distances gleam in the liquid clearness of that drop or bubble. For Mrs Woolf's sensitiveness can retain those wayward flashes as well as the whole chain of mixed images and feelings that unwinds from some tiny coil of memory. If in *Jacob's Room* she suggested the simultaneousness of life, here she paints not only this but its stream-like continuity.

Outwardly, however, the book is a cross-section of life. It does not simplify and concentrate as a play would do, nor does it thread everything on a single mind's experience. On the contrary, Mrs Woolf expands her view with the fullest freedom of a novelist, although she has the briefest limit as regards time; and the fusion of these opposing tendencies into one is a thrilling and hazardous enterprise. Only through sheer vision can it have form and life; and here the finely imaginative substance into which Mrs Woolf has woven it all is certainly reassuring. Moreover, while delineating processes she does not efface persons; on them all the threads depend, and theirs are the values. Theirs, too, that final riddle of separateness, of otherness in the midst of the continuous, thinks Clarissa, watching an old lady in the house opposite:

> The supreme mystery which Kilman might say she had
> solved, or Peter might say he had solved, but Clarissa didn't

believe either of them had the ghost of an idea of solving, was simply this: here was one room: there another. Did religion solve that, or love? [91]

Watching Mrs Woolf's experiment, certainly one of the hardest and very subtly planned, one reckons up its cost. To get the whole value of the present you must enhance it, perhaps, with the past. And with her two chief figures, Clarissa and Peter, meeting after a long severance, Mrs Woolf has a full scope for the use of memories. They are amusing and they illuminate; yet either because of the rest of the design, or one's sense of the probable, or both, one fancies that sometimes these remembrances stretch almost too far. And the tragedy of poor Septimus, the war victim, although poignant in contrast, makes a block in the tideway now and then.

Although there is a surprising characterization in the process, characters must necessarily be shown with the tantalising fluidness of life itself. Lesser figures like Richard Dalloway or Lady Bruton or Miss Kilman, that grimly pathetic vampire, do well enough in outline: but as soon as we are shown more of a character, like Clarissa's or Peter's, we want more still, craving a further dimension that we cannot get. Also the cinemalike speed of the picture robs us of a great deal of the delight in Mrs Woolf's style. It has to be a little clipped, a little breathless; and the reading of her book is not so easy as it seems. Her wit is irresistible when it can escape a little way, as in the vision of those rival goddesses, Proportion and Conversion. In the end no one will complain of her for using all the freedom that she can. All her technical suppleness is needed to cope with the new form. It remains experimental in so far as we are uncertain what more can be done with it, and whether it can give the author's rare gifts full play. But something real has been achieved; for, having the courage of her theme and setting from her vision, Mrs Woolf steeps it in an emotion and irony and delicate imagination which enhance the consciousness and the zest of living.

# E. W. HAWKINS

## The Stream of Consciousness Novel[†]

\* \* \*

*Mrs. Dalloway*, the history of one day in the life of a woman, is stream of consciousness undiluted, and pure pattern. Through it run a primary and a secondary figure, sometimes drawing near,

† From *Atlantic Monthly* (September 1926): 360.

never intersecting, sometimes swerving far apart, always held in relation, as by a woven strip of gold, by the striking of Big Ben through the hours of the day. The primary figure is the heart of Clarissa Dalloway, who loves life with passion, whose only creed is that 'one must pay back from the secret deposit of exquisite moments'; the secondary figure is the heart of poor young Septimus Smith, victim of deferred effects of shell shock, to whom life has become an intolerable horror. The pattern that results is a curiously living thing. As in *Jacob's Room*, sunlight seems poured across the pages; and, more than in *Jacob's Room*, the reader is made aware of a background of innumerable lives. More subtly than either of the other novels, this shows the play of one personality upon another. The method is like the flick of a wing in flight; the revelation is complete. Clarissa's loathing of her own hatred for the fanatical Miss Kilman, who would do anything for the Russians, starved herself for the Austrians, but in private inflicted positive torture, so insensitive was she; the panic and despair of poor Septimus under the robust authoritativeness of the great neurologist; the comfort felt by old Mrs. Hilbery, at Clarissa's party, in the jolly laughter of Sir Harry, 'which, as she heard it across the room, seemed to reassure her on a point which sometimes bothered her if she woke early in the morning and did not like to call her maid for a cup of tea; how it is certain we must die'—countless sharp impressions such as these strike up from the smooth flow of the stream. Smooth, for—though in this novel, too, the point of view constantly shifts—the transitions are made with suavity. The impersonal voice of Big Ben, falling upon different ears, is not the only device used. Clarissa in her exultant morning mood and Septimus in his agony of apprehensiveness are stopped by the same traffic block; the golden sunlight that lifts up the heart of young Elizabeth Dalloway as she rides on the top of a London bus makes patterns on the wall of Septimus's sitting-room, and gives his tormented mind one last moment of vague pleasure; and the bell of the ambulance that is carrying his shattered, unconscious body to the hospital clangs pleasantly to Peter Walsh, speaking to him of the efficiency of London. This novel throws light, as by a prism, not upon a score of lives, but upon life as felt by a score of people; its pursuit of Clarissa Dalloway through one day in London leaves an impression of a real woman, but a stronger impression of a woven fabric of life, gay and tragic and dipped in mystery.

To one reader the highly developed manner of such a novel as *Mrs. Dalloway* seems intolerably artificial; to another it seems an excellent vehicle for wit, for acute sympathy, for the sense of beauty, above all for the sense of life as a thing 'absorbing, mysterious, of infinite richness.' Probably the most vehement apostle of stream of consciousness fiction no more wishes that all novels now and hereafter should he cast in that form than he deplores that *Tom Jones* is not written in the manner of *Fräulein Else*. But he must wonder passionately—and surely it is no fanaticism to wonder—how long so potent a movement in the art of literature will continue to be regarded by a large part of the reading public as an eccentric fad.

# Recent Criticism

## CHRISTINE FROULA

### Sex, Lies, and Selling Out:
### Women and Civilization's Discontents[†]

These words[1] belong to a draft sequence that leads from Rezia's despairing thoughts in Harley Street to Lady Bruton's luncheon. The London medical establishment's "truth" forcibly embraces a "miserable rag & relic" of a soul who comes "fluttering . . . bereft of shelter, shade, or refuge, naked, defenceless," to suffer "the terrific stamp of Sir Williams rage. He swooped; he devoured. . . . Such decision, combined with humanity, . . . endeared Sir William greatly to the relations of his victims" (*H*, 155; cf. *MD*, 99–101) [73]. No reader of Woolf's letters about her incarceration in a home for the insane could fail to sense here the remembered "mad" "me" on which she drew for Septimus nor the "raging furnace" of feelings about "madness and doctors and being forced" that she "kept cooling in [her] mind" for years before she could "touch it without bursting into flame all over."[2] Refracting Septimus's war traumas through her experiences of the social system in action, Woolf discloses and disguises the tangled sources of "madness" in familial and societal dynamics, including her Duckworth half-brothers' incestuous abuse, the reactions of family, friends, and doctors to

† From *Virginia Woolf and the Bloomsbury Avant-garde* (New York: Columbia University Press, 2005), pp. 119–26, 359–60. © 2005 Columbia University Press. Reprinted by permission of the publisher. *H*=*The Hours*; *MD*=*Mrs. Dalloway*; *L* = *Letters*; *D* = *Diary*; *MB* = *Moments of Being*; *CD*=*Civilization and Its Discontents*; page numbers in square brackets refer to this Norton Critical Edition. Notes are Froula's.
1. In an epigraph, the author quotes from Woolf's manuscript draft of the novel, where she wrote "(a delicious idea comes to me that I will write anything I want to write)" as a note to herself [*Editor*].
2. *L*, 3:180, 1 May 1925. See for example the letter to Vanessa/"Dark Devil" in which Woolf begs to be liberated from the home for female lunatics at Twickenham, where her family has installed her to undergo Dr. George Savage's version of S. Weir Mitchell's rest cure. She pays ritual homage to Vanessa and ostentatiously displays good temper and reasonableness while trying to get across that the rest cure is driving her insane (*L*, 1:430–1, 28 July 1910). Woolf's letter to Gwen Raverat about Septimus adds, "You can't think what a raging furnace it still is to me—madness and doctors and being forced. But let's change the subject" (*L*, 3:180, 1 May 1925).

this history, her relations' power over her incarceration, and the pressures of "Proportion" and "Conversion" (*MD*, 100) [71]. In *The Hours* Septimus, like Woolf's "mad . . . me," hears nightingales sing Greek, Philomela's incestuous violation retooled to his war experience: "Evans was a Greek nightingale . . . & now sang this ode, about death . . . 'And so I reached Greece'; where he joined the poets, in Thessaly" (*H*, 66). In *Mrs. Dalloway* nightingales become sparrows singing "in voices prolonged and piercing in Greek words, from trees in the meadow of life beyond a river where the dead walk, how there is no death" (*MD*, 24–5) [19]. Yet Septimus never ceases to be "partly" the ghost of that "me" who signed herself "Sparroy" to Violet Dickinson—one friend who could grasp a "truth" that might as well have been Greek to the society that exalted George Duckworth.[3]

In creating a war veteran "partly" out of that former "me," Woolf foreshadows her analysis in *Three Guineas* of the war at home, the abuses of women under the social law of masculine and heterosexual privilege. In *The Hours* and *Mrs. Dalloway*, women's telling of truth and lies dramatizes their negotiations of elegiac inheritance, sexuality, and social law in a civilization being rebuilt, perhaps, on firmer ground. As Sacks observes, the critical question of communal inheritance from the dead implicates the mourners' sexuality psychically and legally. The old crises of narcissism and sexuality that mourning awakens, inheritance must somehow resolve. Through same-sex attractions, intimations of incest and madness, and conversion dramas, *The Hours* and *Mrs. Dalloway* expose systemic social violence as it governs inheritance, dictates the mourner's sexuality, and provokes the violent energies that the elegy diverts from tragic enactment into social critique. More specifically, women must choose between challenging social law and submitting to it in exchange for socioeconomic rewards. Submission to the Goddess of Conversion, as Clarissa knows, entails lies—silences, omissions, censorship. Thus Lady Bradshaw has "gone under" fifteen years earlier: "a nervous twitch" signals something "really painful to believe—that the poor lady lied"; and Clarissa contrasts Septimus's uncorrupted "treasure" with her youthful passion, renounced and now obscured by "corruption, lies, chatter," as she consoles herself with the pleasures her bargain has bought her (*MD*, 100–1) [130]. This recognition—her legacy from Septimus—weighs conversion's advantages against its costs: "she did not pity him"; she too has felt, "if it were now to die, 'twere now to be most happy"; still, life is enough (*MD*, 186, 184, 35) [131, 130, 24].

---

3. For example, on 22 September 1904, Woolf writes, "You will be glad to hear that your Sparroy feels herself a recovered bird" (*L*, 1:142). See Roger Poole, *The Unknown Virginia Woolf* (Atlantic Highlands, N. J.: Humanities Press, 1982), chapter 13.

*Mrs. Dalloway* depicts a social system in which sexual desire and practice often diverge from law and publicity. Founded, as Freud points out, on the suppression of women's desire, civilization *sanctions*—punishes yet permits—incest and same-sex desire: "incest is anti-social and civilization consists in a progressive renunciation of it" (1897); "we may justly hold our civilization responsible for the spread of neurasthenia" (1898).[4] As Freud explains the contradiction, the incest taboo imposes "perhaps the most drastic mutilation" of erotic life that civilization exacts; it is thus incompletely renounced in modern society. Although civilization polices sexuality as if it were a subject people—it fears revolt, enacts strict precautions, and inflicts "serious injustice" by dictating "a single kind of sexual life for everyone"—it cannot actually enforce its prohibitions and so must "pass over in silence many transgressions which, according to its own rescripts, it ought to have punished" (*CD*, 51–2). When Clarissa judges Sir William "obscurely evil, without sex or lust, extremely polite to women, but capable of some indescribable outrage," her specific exclusion of "sex or lust" in a context that has not raised any such issue invisibly flags a ghost of Woolf's "mad . . . me" who survives the doctor's dead patient. In *The Hours* her owning of Septimus's death as her disaster and disgrace leads to a vehement vow to "fight Sir William Bradshaw. . . . She must go back; breast her enemy. . . . Never would she submit—never, never!" (*H*, 398–9). Later excised, this rather uncharacteristic outburst of social conscience alerts us to other scattered and muted deflections of violated sexuality in both texts, traces of Woolf's own negotiation of social law in the course of writing the novel.

Hard on the heels of the doctor so esteemed by his victims' relations, *The Hours* portrays Hugh Whitbread, who regularly brings his wife Evelyn (frequently visited by Clarissa "in a nursing home") to London "to see doctors" (*MD*, 6) [5]. A freehand portrait of the incestuous George Duckworth, the "admirable Hugh" captures his smug prosperity, sartorial magnificence, "little job at Court," and the "scrupulou[s] little courtesies & old fashioned ways" that have kept him "afloat on the cream of English society for fifty-five years"—just George's age in 1923.[5] Although Hugh is one of the few characters into whose psychic cave the narrator does not venture, the ur-narrator hints sardonically at what his impeccable facade conceals: "a little information about the subconscious self & Dr Freud had leaked into him"; "He had heard of Freud & Stravinsky. . . . His

---

4. See James Strachey, introduction to Sigmund Freud, *Civilization and Its Discontents* (CD) (New York: Norton, 1961), 6.
5. *MD*, 5–6, 103; *H*, 156–7. For Woolf's portraits of George Duckworth see *MB passim*.

affections were understood to be deep"; "one or two humble reforms to his credit" include his undersigning of many long "letters on girls, & stamp out . . . nuisances [*sic*]," "nor did any girl lose her place in his household without being kept sight of" (*H*, 156–7). *Mrs. Dalloway* leaves all this on the cuttingroom floor, substituting a double entendre ("malicious" rumors that Hugh "now kept guard at Buckingham Palace, dressed in silk stockings and knee-breeches, over what nobody knew") and an oblique note that "servant girls had reason to be grateful to him" (*MD*, 103) [73].

The ur-narrator now hands off Hugh, swathed in innuendo, to Lady Bruton's secretary, Milly Brush, who is so irritated by his inquiries after her brother that "she was almost inclined to tell him about her brother, except that she was almost killed her brother [denied once that she] told a lie once about her brother. & would have done so, had it not seemed *margin*: never let on that her brother was not" (*H*, 157). Was the ur-Milly Brush almost killed [by] her brother, or did she almost kill him—or, as her self-interfering grammar suggests, both? What does she deny/lie about, deny lying about, and/or never let on about? Who or what was or is her brother, or was/is he not? *Mrs. Dalloway*'s narrator affects not to know, indeed, tells us less: Hugh always asks "after her brother in South Africa, which, for some reason, Miss Brush . . . so much resented that she said 'Thank you, he's doing very well in South Africa,' when, for half a dozen years, he had been doing badly in Portsmouth" (*MD*, 103) [74]. As the narrative screws down the lid over a site of near-fatal sibling violence, Milly Brush silently mocks her interlocutor with the subaltern's lie.

Nothing in *The Hours* or *Mrs. Dalloway* suggests scattered cinders from Woolf's furnace of white-hot memories more vividly than the narrative convergence of this brother, Milly's incoherent lies, and the George-like Hugh, so solicitous, as it were, of servant girls, in a scene that covertly links the gender dynamics surrounding revelations of sexual violence to women's public speech. The specter of gender-marked "madness" (and familially engineered incarceration) as implements in the social control of "truth" hovers over the ur-Miss Brush, who seems to survive her separate sorrows by sheltering under her powerful employer's wing—a shadowy, diminished double of Lady Millicent Bruton. For her part, Lady Bruton "should have been a general of dragoons" but exhibits her own crippled relation to truth, speech, and social power in her "battle" to compose a letter to the *Times*, for which, feeling "the futility of her own womanhood as she felt it on no other occasion," she finally commandeers the expertise of none other than Hugh (*MD*, 105, 109) [75, 78].

Hugh's sleaziness emerges more explicitly in the drama of truth and lies surrounding a rumor that he once kissed Sally Seton in the smoking-room at Bourton. (Innocuous as it sounds, the furor around this incident suggests that, like Richard's kiss in *The Voyage Out*, it stands in for sexual transgressions ruled unspeakable by actual and internalized censors.) Having fled her "intolerable" home for Bourton, the brilliant young rebel Sally educated the "sheltered" Clarissa in "sex . . . problems . . . life, how they were to reform the world" and "abolish private property" (*H*, 43; *MD*, 33) [25]. In *The Hours* Peter recalls a heated debate on women's suffrage, he and Sally pro, Richard and Hugh con:

> Prostitutes . . . came in; & "the poor women in Piccadilly" she called them; & Hugh flushed, & hitched his trousers up. . . . He said nobody could tell what his mother meant to him . . . & Sally was down right rude & echoed "your mother of course your mother["] . . . she told Hugh that he represented all that was most detestable in the British middle classes. She considered him responsible for the state of those poor girls. [*H*, 76, 86]

Sally, it seems, taxed Hugh with complicity in a social system in which middle- and upper-class men exploit lower-class women to preserve the supposed purity of their disenfranchised mothers, wives, and daughters, and he retaliated by forcing himself on her sexually.[6] Peter's memory is hampered by the fact that "nobody ever knew what happened—it was considered too awful—whether he kissed her or not, merely brushed against her, . . . it had to be hushed up . . . Clarissa murmured something mysterious—but nobody could believe a word against the admirable Hugh, . . . always a perfect gentleman" (*H*, 79). At the party Sally confirms the story and adds that Clarissa "Simply laughed" when she went to her "in a rage" (*H*, 403). In *Mrs. Dalloway* Clarissa sees "her old friend Hugh, talking to the Portuguese Ambassador," and recalls how Sally accused him, "of all people . . . of kissing her in the smoking-room" (that male preserve), so that Clarissa had

> to persuade her not to denounce him at family prayers—which she was capable of doing with her daring, her recklessness, her melodramatic love of being the centre of everything and creating scenes, and it was bound . . . to end in some awful tragedy;

---

6. *H*, 87. In *Mrs. Dalloway* Clarissa recalls that he did it "to punish her for saying that women should have votes" (181) [324]. On prostitution and class see Judith R. Walkowitz, *City of Dreadful Delight: Narratives of Sexual Danger in Late-Victorian London* (Chicago: University of Chicago Press, 1992).

> her death; her martyrdom; instead of which she had married,
> quite unexpectedly, a bald man . . . who owned . . . cotton
> mills at Manchester. And she had five boys! (*MD*, 181–2) [128]

Nowhere to be found in the suffrage debate, Clarissa defended
Hugh "of all people" by silencing Sally at family prayers, of all
places—family piety the cornerstone of a social system that protects men like Hugh by hushing up "truth" in the name of a hypocritical propriety.

Yet in her own mind Clarissa is not simply protecting Hugh but
saving Sally from her own reckless idealism—from "awful tragedy,"
"death," "martyrdom." Her reaction stages the question of what
genre shall govern Sally's life: the revenge tragedy that denouncing
Hugh to a society that is a father might set in motion? a martyrdom
like Septimus's? or an elegiac conversion narrative like her own?
Notwithstanding the ur-Clarissa who vows to fight her "enemy" and
never submit, Clarissa has submitted to social law for the sake of
life, beauty, fun. She recoils from the danger of fighting for truth
and dictates conversation—lies—for Sally, too. And her influence
takes. Sally, "that romantic, that brilliant creature" whose kiss ("a
sudden revelation," "an illumination," "the religious feeling!") holds
out a protestant alternative to the patriarchal religion of family
prayers, and who shares Clarissa's "obscure dread" of marriage
("catastrophe," "doom," "going out to be slaughtered"), marries "a
rich . . . cotton spinner" and has "five enormous boys"—a generic
outcome that strikes Peter as "a little off the mark" (*H*, 80, 47; *MD*,
32, 34–5, 171) [24, 25, 121].

The Goddess of Conversion could display no prouder trophy than
Lady Rosseter. The bold and visionary Sally suppresses her passion for
truth to become a very paragon of conventional prosperous matron-
hood, amply rewarded by social position, the sexual fulfillment her
teeming progeny suggest, and a leisurely country life in which she
rarely reads a newspaper. Her conversion affirms Freud's gendered
divide between a "civilization" that "has become increasingly the business of men," who sustain it through "instinctual sublimations of
which women are little capable," and women's familial and sexual
domain, which civilization "force[s] into the background" (*CD*, 50–1).
Whereas the penniless Sally would "reform the world" on behalf of
women and the poor, the complacent Lady Rosseter has converted her
claim on her civilization's future into individual salvation through a
marriage that indeed spells doom for Sally's "Radical" politics (*MD*,
154) [109].

Lady Rosseter's conversion attests to civilization's deep pockets
in buying off witnesses to the barbarities within—to some extent,
the lying Milly Brush suggests, even that seventh child Virginia,

who hid truth behind fiction's "immense facades" in forging her former "mad . . . me" into Septimus. Yet the sibylline testimony of *The Hours* and *Mrs. Dalloway* intimates the ways Woolf's elegiac art mediated the memories of incest, madness, and social law that threatened to immolate her. The genres open to that remembered "me" would seem to correspond roughly to the fates Clarissa pictures for Sally: a tragic death by unjust social law; unsung martyrdom; suicide as an "embrace" or "attempt to communicate"; revenge, or the eruption of grief into murderous rage; elegiac conversion. In transforming that fluttering, bereft, naked, miserable, defenceless rag and relic of a soul into Septimus—one of the most astonishing characters in modern literature—Woolf wrests from her losses, grief, and life-threatening rage this work of art: a symbolic inheritance that lays her old self to rest (at least for a time) by bringing her to "life." As Clarissa's small elegy for Septimus is also an elegy for a buried self, Woolf's great postwar elegy for "all deaths & sorrows" enfolds a secret elegy for a self her art resurrects from ignominious death for something like tragedy or martyrdom, barely legible as she is in the work's palimpsest.[7] Septimus—not just his death but the life of suffering and witness that endows its gift—is her monument, a fictional facade over autobiographical truth in a work of art that arraigns its civilization and holds it responsible to itself for what it is. In ventriloquizing her "mad" "me" through Septimus, Woolf heeds yet eludes the censors—Dr. Savage, Kitty, Julia, George, even perhaps Vanessa—that her fluttering relic of a soul must have heard cry, Kill yourself, for our sakes.

In vanquishing the life-threatening forces that beset her, Woolf, like Clarissa, emerges as an elegist-hero who fights death and the void and returns from the battlefield bearing trophies of consolation, flaunting her powers of survival: "A new [elegy] by Virginia Woolf"; "This is what I have made of it!" (*MD*, 43, cf. *EE*, 226) [31]. A triumph of elegiac conversion, *Mrs. Dalloway* transforms a destroyed "mad . . . me" into a symbolic consolation in which she, disguised as Septimus, poor devil of both sexes, dies for the sins of the world, dies so that others may live. He does not want it. Why "rage and prophesy? Why fly scourged and outcast?" (*MD*, 142) [101]. Why indeed? Not because he is insane but because the world is; only because the sins and wounds of the world, and its consequent madness and art—not least, this postwar elegy with its

---

7. In 1915 Woolf recorded seeing "a long line of imbeciles," "every one . . . a miserable ineffective shuffling idiotic creature, with no forehead, or no chin, & an imbecile grin, or a wild suspicious stare"; her response, "It was perfectly horrible. They should certainly be killed," suggests disavowal of a suicidal self that she identifies with them, echoed in Septimus's self-mirroring memory of "a maimed file of lunatics" who "ambled and nodded and grinned past him. . . . And would *he* go mad?" (*D*, 1:13, 9 January 1915; *MD*, 90) [64].

arduous celebration of "life"—demand it. No guiltier than anyone else, his only "crime" to have tried to bear (in both senses) witness, Septimus dies for the "terrific" institutionalized violence that Harley Street commits against defenceless naked souls, for the admirable Hugh's less admirable acts, for Milly Brush's suppressed history, Clarissa's defection, and Lady Rosseter's conversion, as well as Europe's vengeful crimes against its future, the Great War and the violent Peace.

But if no one in the novel fully claims the symbolic legacy evoked in Septimus's last words, and if *The Hours* preserves smoldering "truths" that even *Mrs. Dalloway* cannot openly explore, how can anyone think that art might influence the world? What force can art exert toward change, when to fight is out of character for Clarissa, conversion so far the norm that even Sally succumbs, and Septimus's death a silent testimony that leaves even the fictional world unchanged—while the actual world grinds on toward the revenge tragedy for which Versailles set the stage, horrendously enacting Hitler's 1922 vow: "It cannot be that two million Germans should have fallen in vain. . . . No, we do not pardon, we demand—vengeance!"[8]

As powerless as the eloquence of Keynes and Freud to forestall another civil war, Woolf's elegiac art battles alongside them on the side of Love for a future that history had not yet, in 1925, foreclosed. Further, and in keeping with the expansive web of conscious and unconscious being that Clarissa theorizes on the bus, the novel does depict a changing world even if no one seems to be directly changing it. To Peter his dear old civilization seems freer, less repressed and much improved, especially for women: "Newspapers seemed different. Now for instance there was a man writing quite openly in one of the respectable weeklies about water-closets. That you couldn't have done ten years ago" (*MD*, 71) [51]. As a young man on whose "love of abstract principles" "the future of civilization" rests, he advocated women's suffrage; now "women's rights" are an "antediluvian topic" (*MD*, 50, 73) [37, 52]. As he strolls to the party on an evening marvelously lengthened by that postwar innovation "summer time," he delights in the spectacle of beautiful, well-dressed young people and (unlike fellow Anglo-Indians devoted to "biliously summing up the ruin of the world") "more than suspect[s] from the words of a girl, from a housemaid's laughter—intangible things you couldn't lay your hands on—that shift in the whole pyramidal accumulation which

8. Alan Bullock, *Hitler: A Study in Tyranny* (London: Odhams Press, 1952), 79, qtd. in Keegan, *The First World War*, 3.

in his youth had seemed immovable" and had "weighed them down, the women especially" (*MD*, 162) [114]. Echoing Woolf's essay "Mr. Bennett and Mrs. Brown" (1924), which proves by cooks borrowing newspapers and parlor maids trying on hats that "human character" has changed, Peter senses an exhilarating forward motion in postwar civilization that no single life—not his, Sally's, Clarissa's, Septimus's, nor even that of Elizabeth, who would like a profession but is "rather lazy"—can account for (*MD*, 137) [97].[9] Yet there it is.

Lady Rosseter's conversion, moreover, represents no *final* defeat of Sally's reformist hopes, since *Mrs. Dalloway* also immortalizes Sally, ever streaking Bourton's corridor after her sponge like a modern successor to Keats's beleaguered maiden. And of course art may inspire readers to act upon their social worlds not by representing change but by exposing the social system in action. Precisely because its characters defect, convert, fail of speech, die, lie, and "go under," *Mrs. Dalloway* carries the "fight" to rebuild civilization on firmer ground into a future that is always becoming in the wake of the work of art—the future of its readers, whose myriad-minded creativity the skywriting airplane's beholders only suggest. Woolf, meanwhile, triumphed over loss, grief, and maddening rage to reach fresh woods and pastures new—to write her books, found her press, and persevere into the next war as "the only woman in England free to write what I like"—and she felt, on finishing her great communal elegy, no longer "inclined to doff the cap to death": "More & more do I repeat . . . 'Its life that matters'" (*D*, 3:43, 7–8, 8 n. 5; 22 September, 8 April 1925). If water closets in respectable weeklies now, perhaps Milly Brush's brother soon? For the moment, *Mrs. Dalloway* embraces the world as it is, letting Milly, Clarissa, Hugh, and Lady Rosseter live while Septimus dies for his civilization's barbarities—the sexual violence buried in this novel's news of the day no less than the war on its front page.

---

9. *MD*, 137; cf. Claire M. Tylee, *The Great War and Women's Consciousness: Images of Militarism and Womanhood in Women's Writings, 1914–64* (Iowa City: University of Iowa Press, 1990), 166.

# MOLLY HITE

# [Tonal Cues and Character in *Mrs. Dalloway*]†

\* \* \*

*Mrs. Dalloway*, one of the most beloved of Woolf's novels, is also one of the most experimental in terms of the values its third-person narrator complicates or withholds. Its affective indeterminacy leaves elements of the story open to different responses, and these responses cue conscious or unconscious judgments.[1] For instance, to like a character (find him or her sympathetic) is generally to attribute positive qualities to that character, even if these qualities are not immediately perceived as *ethically* positive. As a consequence, *Mrs. Dalloway* has a history of strikingly divergent interpretations that conflict on the value and role assigned to the title character, the nature of the climactic scene, and the attitude readers should have toward the second, shadow protagonist, Septimus Smith. These questions of evaluation arise in the context of perhaps the largest ethical-political question of the twentieth century, egalitarianism. Woolf's ambiguous tonal cues engage this question by stressing both its urgency and its resistance to being understood, much less practiced. Rebecca Walkowitz observes that modernists "sought to imagine models of social critique that would resist social codification" (80).[2] By using third-person narrators who provide insufficient or contradictory tonal cues, Woolf enabled an intense concern with social categories without allowing attentive readers to slot narratorial observations into overall judgments of admiration or censure.

\* \* \*

For example, in *Mrs. Dalloway* Clarissa hears about, reenacts imaginatively, and then reconciles herself to the suicide of a Great War veteran she has never met: "She felt somehow very like him—the

---

† From "Tonal Cues and Uncertain Values: Affect and Ethics in *Mrs. Dalloway*," *Narrative* 18.3 (October 2010): 249–50, 252–55, 269–75. Copyright 2020 by The Ohio State University. Reprinted by permission of The Ohio State University Press. Notes are Hite's unless otherwise indicated. Page numbers in square brackets refer to this Norton Critical Edition.

1. For instance, a lovable scoundrel is lovable because of qualities readers are prompted to value: humor, honesty where it matters, loyalty to certain people or principles validated within the fictional universe, ability to undermine characters whom the narrative does not value, etc. Of course, these qualities may not at all mirror the values that the reader exercises in the world. As Judith Fetterley and many early feminist critics noted, female readers must consciously or unconsciously suspend their resistance to enjoy a narrative that treats misogyny as a positive value. See *The Resisting Reader: A Feminist Approach to American Fiction* (Bloomington: Indiana Univ. Press, 1981).

2. See *Cosmopolitan Style: Modernism Beyond the Nation* (New York: Columbia Univ. Press, 2006).

young man who had killed himself. She felt glad that he had done it; thrown it away. The clock was striking. The leaden circles dissolved in the air. He made her feel the beauty; made her feel the fun. But she must go back" (182) [131]. I quote from the U.S. edition, to which Woolf added the sentence of apparent explanation that I find especially disconcerting: "He made her feel the beauty; made her feel the fun" (Beja 128–38). The thing thrown away is Septimus Smith's life. Clarissa's response is to be "glad"—most evidently because of the contrast to her own life and her party. But . . . glad? Made her feel the beauty? Made her feel the *fun*? Although this reflection, which applies both to Clarissa and Septimus, defies the modern medical professionals whose business is "forcing your soul," Septimus's extreme suffering is hardly comparable to Clarissa's empathetic "disgrace" at hearing of his suicide, or to any other setback in Clarissa's life (180, 181) [130].

We see the tonal ambivalence of this passage even more clearly when we contrast it with a version in the draft, in which Clarissa concludes from Septimus's example that "She must go back; ~~she must~~ breast her enemy; she, ~~must~~ take her rose, Never would she submit—never, never!" (*Hours Ms.* 399, strikeouts in original draft text). Although this battle cry arguably echoes many of Virginia Woolf's own convictions, it also marks an abrupt change in the character of Clarissa Dalloway. It transforms her from a privileged, politically uninvolved society woman into a militant on behalf of the traumatized, and it also seems to identify Clarissa herself as a potential patient of Sir William Bradshaw. Such developments wrench the plot in a different, perhaps melodramatic direction and destroy the carefully developed nuances of the fictional universe and its inhabitants. Ambiguity becomes polemical certainty. In most of the drafts of her novels, Woolf began with such emphatic and value-laden pronouncements in the narrative voice and then revised to mute and complicate these statements, often filling them with conflicting tonal cues that could lead readers to radically different responses to a scene or character (such as sympathy, antipathy, condescension, pity, revulsion) and thus evaluations of this scene or character.

Certainly one implication that a reader of the passage in the final version of the novel might pick up is a callousness aligned with class privilege. Clarissa has reflected on suicide all day. The reiterations of "Fear no more the heat o' the sun" and "If it were now to die, 'twere now to be most happy" affirm the indirect discourse observation when she hears the news of Septimus's suicide. "There was an embrace in death" (180) [130]. The gladness she experiences at the news appears to come from a suicide she can experience without dying, giving new piquancy to her aristocratic party and the presence of the Prime Minister. In a Wildean displacement, it is as though she can let the lower orders do her dying for her.

Yet the scene is the summit of her character development and of the structural and thematic development of the book. It brings Septimus and Clarissa together in a metaphoric "embrace" that never occurs on the metonymic level of action. The thematic reconciliation leads her back to enjoying her life, embodied here in the party.

How should we take Clarissa's assimilation of Septimus's death? No one reads *Mrs. Dalloway* without affectively reacting to and thus interpreting the tone of this passage in some way. But different selections from the tonal cues strewn through the text lead to incompatible readings.

Most published readings minimize the class resonances and stress Clarissa's empathy with Septimus. The novel also emphasizes the interiority of Clarissa, her sense of being "part of people she had never met; being laid out like a mist between the people she knew best" (9) [8], her "extraordinary gift," as Peter Walsh recalls, "of making a world of her own wherever she happened to be" (74) [54], and most of all her intense capacity for pleasure, a hedonia that suffuses the text and helps make possible its vivid celebrations of London streets and shops, skywriting and motorcars, youth, aging, and love. The success of Woolf's reliance on free indirect discourse rules out the kind of distance usual for sustained satire, although it certainly does not rule out satire at certain points, as I discuss in the next section. Most readers who know a character "from inside," without an authorial narrator's value judgments, resist a wholly critical view of that character. Moreover, Clarissa is portrayed in ways that arouse sympathy. Her meditations, along with meditations about her, occupy most of the space in the novel that bears her name. For this reason she is most often read as a sympathetic protagonist, one who for all her failings conveys to others a vivid and vivifying presence: "For there she was" (190) [137]. Clarissa's apparent triumph of being *there*, in the moment, is the culmination of the novel, apparently encompassing or transcending the lesser death of the inevitably lesser character.

But the problem of how to take Clarissa nags at even very nuanced readings that posit her as the central and most sympathetic character. Clarissa develops at this crucial turn because Septimus dies. This account makes him the sacrificial victim of her midlife crisis, in which, as one major critic comments, Clarissa's "grief is not for Septimus but for herself" (Abel 39). Though therapeutic, such grief is selfish, especially given the complex character development of Septimus, and thus may prompt readers to resent and dislike Clarissa.

Such considerations prompt a radically different interpretation of Clarissa. Sally Seton tells Peter Walsh, "Clarissa was at heart a snob" (185) [134]. Clarissa judges a self-supporting female scholar, the politically engaged and distressingly named Miss Kilman, with aesthetic distaste: "Miss Kilman would do anything for the Russians, starved herself for the Austrians, but in private inflicted positive torture, so insensitive was she, dressed in a green mackintosh coat" (11) [10]. And Clarissa notoriously "could feel nothing for the Albanians, or was it the Armenians?" during the Armenian genocide (Woolf 117; see also Tate)[86]. Such details signal how removed she is from the world and how much she takes for granted her own comfort and security. These cues might suggest that Woolf's eponymous protagonist is an object of condemnation. One proponent of this reading writes of "Clarissa's . . . lack of responsiveness to the social system she represents" and concludes, "If Clarissa feels a spiritual bond with Septimus, it is because Woolf makes clear that it is the only kind she is capable of feeling" (Levenback 18). At one extreme of this position, critics have seen class callousness as a deficiency of Virginia Woolf herself, represented (especially in interpretations influenced by the criticism of F. R. and Q. D. Leavis) as a cosseted "snob" who is in many respects identical to Clarissa Dalloway.[3] But scholarship of the last thirty years, involving close readings of Woolf's papers or primary sources, indicates that Woolf bore little resemblance to Clarissa Dalloway in background, education, or opinions.[4]

These different ways of reading *Mrs. Dalloway* indicate how a lack of authoritative tonal cues can lead to conflicting interpretations of a character and even an entire novel. These readings use familiar text-processing strategies: what Brian McHale terms "the pattern-making and pattern-interpreting behavior which the text's formal organization elicits from the reader" ("Modernist Reading"

---

3. See John Carey, *The Intellectuals and the Masses: Pride and Prejudice Among the Literary Intelligentsia, 1880–1939* (New York: St. Martins, 1992), 31–37; Hugh Kenner, *A Sinking Island: The Modern English Writers* (Baltimore: Johns Hopkins Univ. Press, 1989), 161–82; and Frank W. Bradbook, "Virginia Woolf: The Theory and Practice of Fiction," in *The Pelican Guide to English Literature*, ed. Boris Ford, 277–86 (London: Penguin, 1973). For a short history of this strand of criticism, see Regina Marler, *Bloomsbury Pie: The Making of the Bloomsbury Boom* (New York: Henry Holt, 1997).

4. The main source for the character is Kitty Maxse, a society hostess of the preceding generation who tried to introduce the young Vanessa and Virginia Stephen into society and who died under circumstances suggesting suicide shortly before Woolf began writing this novel (*Diary* 2:206–207; *Diary* 3:32; Julia Briggs, *Virginia Woolf: An Inner Life*. (London: Allen Lane/Penguin, 2005), 140–41; Mark Hussey, *Virginia Woolf A to Z: The Essential Reference to Her Life and Writings* (Oxford: Oxford Univ. Press, 1995). Karen Levenback, *Virginia Woolf and the Great War* (Syracuse, NY: Syracuse Univ. Press, 1999), 80, and Hussey (172) also suggest Ottoline Morrell as a partial model; Woolf was deeply ambivalent about Maxse and at least somewhat ambivalent about Morell. She wrote in the cover notes to the U.S. version of *Mrs. Dalloway* that she had initially planned to end the novel with Clarissa's own suicide (*Essays* 4:549) [see the introduction to the 1928 edition, above, pp. 224–26—*Editor*].

63). In the case of Woolf's novels, however, such strategies often are imported to Woolf's texts by readers drawing on their experience of processing other, less tonally ambiguous fiction.[5] How to take Clarissa (or Septimus or Miss Kilman or Peter Walsh) is still an open question because Woolf chose not to be clear about how readers are supposed to judge and respond at certain key points.

How can we interpret strategies that Woolf used to avoid signaling requisite attitudes or positions? If we begin by acknowledging tonal undecidability, we may not jump to a definitive ethical and political "interpretation" that stands in for a whole book or *oeuvre*. I am not suggesting that we abandon a concern with ethical and political issues in the novels of Virginia Woolf. On the contrary, I am suggesting that the novels are tonal labyrinths, conveying varying degrees of authoritativeness, rather than monologic statements of position, and that exploring and even getting lost in these labyrinths allows us to experience the complexity along with the urgency of ethical and political questions.[6]

\* \* \*

In *Mrs. Dalloway* there is one contrast to the general rule of unstable, mixed, or absent tonal cues. No reader can have any question about how to take the general practitioner Holmes or the psychiatrist Sir William Bradshaw. Both try to treat Septimus Smith, and both thereby provoke his suicide. The narrative voice speaks directly about these two medical men, providing clear, thoroughly negative tonal cues—for example, metaphorizing Bradshaw as a bird of prey: "He swooped; he devoured. He shut people up" (Woolf 99; Mezei 83–84) [73].

This narrator appears to be not only authoritative but authorial, a rare instance in Woolf's fiction of a third-person speaker unaffected by any character's point of view, stating what is the case in the narrative universe. "Proportion, divine proportion, Sir William's goddess, was acquired by Sir William walking hospitals, catching salmon, begetting

---

5. They are also imported from Woolf's own nonfictional writing in essays, diaries, and letters and from earlier manuscript drafts of the novels. By looking closely at tonal cues within the published novels, I do not of course recommend a return to the ideological framework of the old New Criticism, with its insistence that biographical and historical material has little or no relevance to the reading of literary texts. Rather, I am interested in Virginia Woolf's own choice, documented in the manuscript drafts, to delete or mute evaluative indicators.

6. In *Virginia Woolf, the Intellectual, and the Public Sphere* (Cambridge: Cambridge Univ. Press, 2003), Melba Cuddy-Keane proposes a slightly different model of ethical complexity for the last two novels, *The Years* and *Between the Acts*, asking, "[H]ow do you communicate any system of values without it becoming propaganda? How do you assert a strong coherent vision without the attendant assumption that your vision encompasses all?" ("Inside and Outside" 178). My sense is that the project of asserting a strong coherent vision is more characteristic of these later 1930s works than of *Jacob's Room*, *Mrs. Dalloway*, *To the Lighthouse*, and *The Waves*.

one son in Harley Street by Lady Bradshaw" (97) [71]. The words—distanced, satiric, and angry—cannot be taken as Bradshaw's own reflections and are too developed to represent Septimus's or Rezia's views. Furthermore, there is no other nearby character whose mental habits could account for their measure and sting. When the narrative voice describes this eminent and powerful doctor, its irony is marked.

In moving into clear satiric attack, the narrator takes on some eighteenth-century traits. Proportion is personified, gendered, and given Augustan capitals, as if to distance this polemical moment even further from the surrounding text. Like Dulness in Alexander Pope's *The Dunciad,* Proportion is a female figure erected for the purpose of vilification. Even more vilified is the next female figure to whom the narrator moves, Conversion. She is at work "in the heat and sands of India, the mud and swamp of Africa, the purlieus of London, wherever in short the climate or the devil tempts men to fall from the true belief which is her own—is even now engaged in dashing down shrines, smashing idols, and setting up in their place her own stern countenance" (Woolf 97) [71]. Bradshaw's imposition of his middle-class and middlebrow ideology on his patients resembles imperialism in the violence it does to existing ways of believing, thinking, feeling, and living.[7] The goddess herself "feasts on the wills of the weakly," casting an ethical shadow over characters like Lady Millicent Bruton and Miss Doris Kilman—threatening, if more ambivalent, portrayals of proto-mothers who wish to direct the mental processes of others (98) [71]. This startling tirade declares the entire novel's antipathy to "normality."[8] This apparent moment of intense authorial emotion erupts into the multi-voiced and tonally nuanced narrative. Certainly it is hard to doubt that it is an expression of authorial opinion. In the *Dalloway* manuscript just before Woolf began to draft the passage about Proportion, she wrote, "(a delicious idea comes to me that I will write anything I want to write)" (*Hours Ms.* 147).

\* \* \*

7. Bradshaw's embodiment of the professional middle class and the values that Woolf in a 1932 letter described as "middlebrow" makes him a powerful agent of social conformity (Woolf, "Middlebrow"). For the complicated situation of the rising professional middle class and its multiple alliances to psychiatric classifications, see David Trotter, *Paranoid Modernism: Literary Experiment, Psychosis, and the Professionalization of English Society* (Oxford: Oxford Univ. Press, 2001).
8. In noting that these objects of invective are women I touch on a concern with women from the generation preceding Virginia Woolf's that I develop to a degree in "Modernism's Other." Readers will observe that both Miss Kilman and Lady Bruton are developed in *Mrs. Dalloway* and that Miss Kilman, especially, is treated finally with a tantalizing mix of pathos and humor (128–31). Molly Hite, "'Modernism's Other' as Mother: Making Room for the Woman of Genius," in *Marketing the Author: Authorial Personae, Narrative Selves and Self-Fashioning, 1880–1930,* ed. Marysa Demoor, 207–33 (Basingstoke, Hamps., UK: Palgrave McMillan, 2004).

# SARA AHMED

## *From* Feminist Killjoys[†]

\*  \*  \*

Feminism involves political consciousness of what women are asked to give up for happiness. Indeed, in even becoming conscious of happiness as loss, feminists have already refused to give up desire, imagination, and curiosity for happiness. There can be sadness simply in the realization of what one has given up. Feminist archives are thus full of housewives becoming conscious of unhappiness as a mood that seems to surround them: think of Virginia Woolf's *Mrs. Dalloway.* The feeling is certainly around, almost as a thickness in the air. We sense the unhappiness seeping through the tasks of the everyday. There she is, about to get flowers, enjoying her walk in London. During that walk, she disappears: "But often now this body she wore (she stopped to look at a Dutch picture), this body, with all its capacities, seemed nothing—nothing at all. She had the oddest sense of being herself invisible; unseen; unknown; there being no more marrying, no more having children now, but only this astonishing and rather solemn progress with the rest of them, up Bond street, this being Mrs. Dalloway; not even Clarissa any more; this being Mrs. Richard Dalloway" ([1925] 1953: 14) [9].

Becoming Mrs. Dalloway is itself a form of disappearance: to follow the paths of life (marriage, reproduction) is to feel that what is before you is a kind of solemn progress, as if you are living somebody else's life, simply going the same way others are going. It is as if you have left the point of life behind you, as if your life is going through motions that were already in motion before you even arrived. As I argued in *Queer Phenomenology* (2006), for a life to count as a good life, it must take on the direction promised as a social good, which means imagining one's futurity in terms of reaching certain points along a life course. If happiness is what allows us to reach certain points, it is not necessarily how you feel when you get there. For Mrs. Dalloway, to reach these points is to disappear. The point of reaching these points seems to be a certain disappearance, a loss of possibility, a certain failure to make use of the body's capacities, to find out what it is that her body can do.[1] To become conscious of possibility can involve mourning for its loss.

† From *The Promise of Happiness* (Durham and London: Duke UP, 2010), pp. 70–76, 245–46. Copyright, 2010, Duke University Press. All rights reserved. Republished by permission of the current copyright holder, Duke University Press. Page numbers in square brackets refer to this Norton Critical Edition. Notes are by the author.

1. It might seem here that I am placing my hope in capacity, as that which is restricted by gender. Capacities are not simply about the joy of opening things up. Capacities also

For Clarissa this rather uncanny sensation of becoming Mrs. Dalloway as a loss of possibility, as an unbecoming, or becoming "nothing at all" does not enter her consciousness in the form of sadness *about* something.[2] The sadness of the book—and it is a sad book—is not one expressed as a point of view. Instead, each sentence of the book takes thoughts and feelings as if they are objects in a shared world: the streets of London, the very oddness of the occasion of passing others by, a feeling of that oddness. Sometimes it can feel like a coincidence, how one coincides with others. To say "it is just a coincidence" can create the impression that the absence of a causal relation between events is the absence of any connection. But feeling a coincidence might mean recognizing that to fall in the same time and place as others, to happen with others or to happen upon others, is a kind of connection. As Clarissa goes out with her task in mind (she has to buy her flowers for her party), she walks into a world with others. You might be in your world (with your own tasks, your own recollections) and yet you share the world of the street, if only for a moment, a fleeting moment, a moment that flees. Things appear as modes of attention: the plane above that writes letters in the sky, the plane that is seen by those who pass each other by. Questions unfold as shared questions: What letter is that? What word is that? "'What are they looking at?' said Clarissa Dalloway" (42) [22]. It is as if the mere direction of a glance is enough to create a shared world. Although each brings to the street a certain kind of moodiness, a preoccupation with this or with that, the street itself can become moody, when an object grabs attention, like the plane that creates words in the sky above, although for each person who looks up, what is seen might be quite different.

If unhappiness becomes a collective impression, then it too is made up of fragments that only loosely attach to points of view. In particular, the proximity between Mrs. Dalloway and the character Septimus is what allows unhappiness to be shared even if it is not

---

make some things possible at the expense of others—even if we don't know yet what a body can do, we can recognize there is only so much this body can do at a given point in time. There is a little misery and loss in every capacity—which does not make capacity miserable. I have been very struck in my participation in conferences by how much "opening up the body's capacity to act" as a kind of weak inheritance of Spinoza has become a mantra in affect studies, as if such openings are necessarily good, or as if they should be installed as an agreed *telos* for politics. We always need to ask capacities for what, and capacities to do what? See the first chapter of my book *Queer Phenomenology* (2006) for a reflection on capacity as a mode of directionality.

2. Mrs. Dalloway's stream of consciousness offers itself as a consciousness of death: "Did it matter, then, she asked herself, as she walked towards Bond Street, did it matter that she must inevitably cease completely; all this must go on without her; did she resent it; or did it not become consoling to believe that death ended absolutely?" (12) [8]. I am offering my own slant by associating consciousness of death with consciousness of gender: so Clarissa in becoming Mrs. Richard Dalloway "must inevitably cease completely."

passed between them; two characters who do not know each other, though they pass each other, but whose worlds are connected by the very jolt of unhappiness. We have the immanence of the shock of how one person's suffering can have an effect on the life world of another. Septimus suffers from shell shock; and we feel his feelings with him, the panic and sadness as the horror of war intrudes as memory. His suffering brings the past into the time of the present, the long time of war, its persistence on the skin as aftermath, its refusal of an after. To those who observe him from a distance, those who share the street on this day, he appears as a madman, at the edge of respectable sociality, a spectacle. To encounter him on the street, you would not know the story behind his suffering. To be near to suffering does not necessarily bring suffering near.

Clarissa and Septimus, as characters who do not meet, thus achieve an odd intimacy: the not-just-private suffering of the housewife and the not-quite-public suffering of the returned soldier are interwoven. Importantly, their sadness is proximate but not contagious. They do not catch sadness from each other; their sadness is what keeps alive histories that are not shared, that cannot be shared, as they pass by on the street. And yet something is shared, perhaps those very things that cannot simply be revealed. Clarissa, thinking of her "odd affinities" with strangers "she had never spoken to," sits on the bus and wonders whether the "unseen part of us" might provide a point of attachment to others and might even be how we survive through others, "perhaps—perhaps" (231–32) [108].

It is Septimus's wife, Rezia, whose musings reflect most directly on the difficulty of experiencing emotions that are simply revealed to proximate others. Rezia is so anxious to reveal her own unhappiness that she "almost felt sometimes that she must stop people in the street, if they looked like good, kind people just to say to them 'I am unhappy'" (125) [59]. She is conscious of how her feelings and Septimus's feelings cannot simply be revealed to passers by: "was there, after all, anything to draw attention to them, anything to make a passer-by suspect here is a young man who carries in him the greatest message in the world, and is, moreover, the happiest man in the world, and the most miserable?" (126) [60]. To inhabit a feeling world does not create a world out of feeling.

Much of the novel is about an event that will happen. For Mrs. Dalloway is planning a party. To some feminist readers, the preoccupation with the party makes the book disappointing. Simone de Beauvoir reads Mrs. Dalloway's enjoyment of parties as a sign that she is trying to turn her "prison into glory," as if as a hostess she can be "the bestower of happiness and gaiety" ([1949] 1997: 554). For de Beauvoir, the gift of the party turns quickly into duty;

such that Mrs. Dalloway, "who loved these triumphs, these sem-blances," still "felt their hollowness" (555). For Kate Millett, Mrs. Dalloway is a rather disappointing figure; she exposes Woolf's failure to turn her own unhappiness into a politics: "Virginia glori-fied two housewives, Mrs. Dalloway and Mrs. Ramsay, recorded the suicidal misery of Rhoda in *The Waves* without ever explaining its causes" (1970: 37). We might say that it is because Mrs. Dalloway is planning a party that we do not have much revealed about her unhappiness, other than the sadness of recalling lost intimacies with Peter and with Sally, who both turn up, unexpectedly during her day, in a way, it is implied, that does not just happen but bears some relation to Mrs. Dalloway's own thoughts: "all day she had been thinking of Bourton, of Peter, of Sally" (280) [130]. Such lost intimacies become lost possibilities, hints of a life she might have lived, if things had not turned out the way they did.

If Mrs. Dalloway is distracted from the causes of unhappiness by the party (and we can have some sympathy with the necessity of distractions), the party is also the event in which unhappiness comes to life. For Mrs. Dalloway, her party is life; it is how she can make things happen; it is a gift, a happening (185) [87]. What hap-pens? That this question is a question is a preservation of the gift. And something does happen. For it is in the party that Septimus's life "touches" Mrs. Dalloway most directly. It touches her through death. Lady Bradshaw says to her: "'Just as we were starting, my husband was called up on the telephone, a very sad case. A young man (that is what Sir William is telling Mr. Dalloway) had killed himself. He had been in the army.' Oh! Thought Clarissa, in the middle of my party, here's death, she thought" (279) [129]. In the middle of the party, words accumulate as a narrative, telling the story of a death. A young man kills himself, and the death itself (and not just the narrating of the death) takes place in the middle of the party, in the middle of the life of the party. The soul of the party is death. The reader has already read about this death; we have witnessed it. Now, we witness the ripples of this death; how it acquires a life of its own, how it takes place somewhere in the middle. For Mrs. Dalloway, this death becomes something to imag-ine, to bring to life by thought:

What business had the Bradshaws to talk of death at her party? A young man had killed himself. And they talked of it at her party—the Bradshaws, talked of death. He had killed himself—but how? Always her body went through it first, when she was told, suddenly, of an accident; her dress flamed, her body burnt. He had thrown himself from a window. Up had flashed the ground; through him, blundering, bruising, went the rusty

spikes. There he lay with a thud, thud, thud in his brain, and
then a suffocation of blackness. So she saw it. But why had he
done it? And the Bradshaws talked of it at her party!

She had once thrown a shilling into the Serpentine, never
anything more. But he had flung it away. They went on living
(she would have to go back; the rooms were still crowded;
people kept on coming). They (all day she had been thinking of
Bourton, of Peter, of Sally), they would grow old. A thing there
was that mattered; a thing, wreathed about with chatter,
defaced, obscured in her own life, let drop every day in corruption, lies, chatter. This he had preserved. Death was defiance.
Death was an attempt to communicate; people feeling the
impossibility of reaching the centre which, mystically, evaded
them; closeness drew apart; rapture faded; one was alone.
There was an embrace in death. (280–81) [129–30]

Septimus's death becomes a question that takes Mrs. Dalloway
away from the party; she attends to his death, wonders about it; she
becomes a retrospective witness even though she was not and could
not have been there. The shudder: the sounds of it; the thud, thud,
thud of it; the ground that flashes; the rusty spikes. His death
becomes material, becomes fleshy through her thoughts. His death
announces not only that sadness can be unbearable but that we
don't have to bear it, that you can fling it away. And in this moment,
when death intervenes in the life of the party, life becomes chatter,
becomes what goes on, "they went on living," what comes and goes,
"people kept on coming." Death comes to embody the suffering that
persists when life becomes chatter.

What is striking about Mrs. Dalloway is how suffering has to
enter her consciousness from the edges, through the arrival of
another, another who is an intruder, who has not been invited to the
party. It is the suffering of an intruder that exposes the emptiness of
life's chatter. Suffering enters not as self-consciousness—as a consciousness of one's own suffering—but as a heightening of consciousness, a world-consciousness in which the suffering of those
who do not belong is allowed to disturb an atmosphere. Even when
unhappiness is a familiar feeling, it can arrive like a stranger, to
disturb the familiar or to reveal what is disturbing in the familiar.

The arrival of suffering from the edges of social consciousness
might teach us about the difficulty of becoming conscious of suffering or teach us about our own resistances to recognizing those
seemingly "little" uneasy feelings of loss or dissatisfaction as unhappiness with one's life. The party might expose the need to keep
busy, to keep going in the face of one's disappearance. So much
sadness revealed in the very need to be busy. So much grief

expressed in the need not to be overwhelmed by grief. It is hard labor just to recognize sadness and disappointment, when you are living a life that is meant to be happy but just isn't, which is meant to be full, but feels empty. It is difficult to give up an idea of one's life, when one has lived a life according to that idea. To recognize loss can mean to be willing to experience an intensification of the sadness that hopefulness postpones.[3]

To inherit feminism can mean to inherit sadness. There is sadness in becoming conscious not only of gender as the restriction of possibility, but also of how this restriction is not necessary. After all, we have inherited the book *Mrs. Dalloway*; we have passed the book around, and the book itself has passed into other cultural forms.[4] Take the film *The Hours* (2002, dir. Stephen Daldry), based on Michael Cunningham's novel *The Hours* (1998), which takes its title from Woolf's original title for *Mrs. Dalloway*. *The Hours* places three generations of women alongside each other and follows their life on a single day: we have a fictionalized account of a day in the life of Virginia Woolf (Nicole Kidman); of Laura Brown (Julianne Moore), an unhappy housewife living in the 1950s as she bakes a cake and reads *Mrs. Dalloway*; and of Clarissa Vaughan (Meryl Streep), who is organizing a party like Mrs. Dalloway, this time for her former lover and friend Richard (Ed Harris), who is dying of AIDS.

*Mrs. Dalloway* the novel is inherited by *The Hours* in multiple ways; we inherit the lost name of the book, the book itself. *The Hours* also mimics the book: following its orientation, its directionality in time, by depicting a whole life in a single day. The film attends closely to gestures which bind each generation to the figure of Mrs. Dalloway: Clarissa, for instance, begins her day by saying she will get the flowers for the party. The gestures or tasks of the everyday become forms of inheritance.

*  *  *

3. To be hopeful can defer recognition that one is not experiencing happiness by following a certain path. You can feel sad but be hopeful that "along the way" things will get better. The more you are hopeful the more you give up by not giving up. In recognizing that situations are hopeless, all those forms of deferred sadness can hit you. Recognition of loss can thus be one of the hardest forms of recognition. It often means being prepared to be undone.

4. Another, more recent book which could be described as an ode to *Mrs. Dalloway* is Rachel Cusk's *Arlington Park* (2006). This book approximates the form of *Mrs. Dalloway*: we have multiple points of consciousness, a sense of an unhappiness that is worldly, that is around; the action of the book takes place on a single day; there is a party, and the different characters of the book meet at the party.

# PAUL K. SAINT-AMOUR

## *Mrs. Dalloway* and the Gaze of Total War[†]

"Nothing ever happens . . . Curse this war; God damn this war!" "The Mark on the Wall"[1] makes wartime an uneventful backdrop before which the eventfulness of thought may be staged, even as thought is laden with displaced recognitions that the war may become eventful at any moment. Among those displacements is the mark itself, whose resistance to identification allies it with the paradigmatic early-twentieth-century object in whose ambiguity terror and ecstasy met:

> "That's where I saw my first aeroplane—there between those chimneys . . . I was standing here, looking out . . . It must have been just after I'd got into the flat, a summer's day, and I saw a black spot in the sky, and . . . I said to Miriam, 'Is it a bird? No, I don't think it can be a bird. It's too big. And yet it moves.' And suddenly it came over me, that's an aeroplane! And it was! You know they'd flown the Channel not so long before. I was staying with you in Dorset at the time: and I remember reading it out in the paper, and someone—your father, I think—said: 'The world will never be the same again!'" (328–29; ellipses added)

This is Eleanor Pargiter in Woolf's *The Years* (1937), speaking during the mid-1930s of a moment in 1909 or 1910 and in terms as direct as "The Mark" is oblique, almost as if the later novel were annotating the earlier story in retrospect. There is more ecstasy than terror in Eleanor's memory, although the remark by "someone"—again the eternal "someone" in proximity to the eternal newspaper—that "the world will never be the same again" has already, in *The Years*, been vividly borne out by the 1917 air raid scene that precedes the above passage by forty pages. I will return later to that scene but want to linger on a few moments of anxious identification in Woolf's First World War diaries. For it is these moments, along with the fictional scenes for which she mined them, that expose the kind of immediate consequentiality of recognition that "The Mark on the Wall" needs to suppress in order to maintain its meditative solitude. By the time that story was published, the airplane had made wartime eventful again for Londoners, foregrounding collective acts of speculation, interpretation,

---

[†] From "Perpetual Suspense: Virginia Woolf's Wartime Gothic" in *Tense Future: Modernism, Total War, Encyclopedic Form* (Oxford: Oxford UP, 2015), pp. 110–20. © Paul K. Saint-Amour 2015. Reprinted by permission of Oxford University Press. Notes are by the author. Page numbers in square brackets refer to this Norton Critical Edition.
1. Short story (1917) by Virginia Woolf. The preceding quotation is the story's final line.

and identification over solitary ones like those detailed in "The Mark." Woolf's first fictive meditation on the civilian's relationship to emergent war forms is also her last to confine itself rigorously to a consciousness defending its solitude. Henceforth, she would adapt both the predicament and the techniques of "The Mark" to communal suspense, public trauma, and the persistence of ethical reciprocity in war.

I [suggest] that the air raid siren had, as a result of the bombing assessments following the First World War, been recognized as a weapon whose power rivaled that of the airborne bomb. This power lay not in the alert's ability to inflict physical damage but in its capacity to disrupt industrial war efforts and shatter a citizenry's peace of mind. The same assessments implied that the panic induced by false alarms was in some ways more disruptive than that caused by actual raids. Unlike the realized physical violence of a raid, a false alarm provides no discharge for the sense of endangerment it produces; it mobilizes anxiety without providing it with a kinetic outlet. Thus the very falsity of the alarm emphasizes a condition of hideously prolonged expectation, a state of emergency that is both perennial, in having been detached from the arrival of violence in a singular event, and horribly deferred—the advance symptom of a disaster still to come. In her diary entry for February 1, 1915, Woolf recorded how the mere threat of Zeppelin raids, four months before bombs actually fell on London, had produced a continuous state of apprehensiveness and frayed nerves among Londoners:

> In St James Street there was a terrific explosion; people came running out of Clubs; stopped still & gazed about them. But there was no Zeppelin or aeroplane—only, I suppose, a very large tyre burst. But it is really an instinct with me, & most people, I suppose, to turn any sudden noise, or dark object in the sky into an explosion, or a German aeroplane. And it always seems utterly impossible that one should be hurt. (*D1*, 32)[2]

Nearly three years later, in March 1918, Woolf records a mirror-image event:

> I'd taken my third & final roll in bed, when there was an explosion. For half a minute a raid seemed so improbable that we made out it was one of the inexplicable outbursts of motor omnibuses. However, next minute the guns went off all round us & we heard the whistles. There was no denying it. (*D1*, 124)

2. The first Zeppelin raids against England occurred in January 1915, but no bombs fell on London until the night of May 31–June 1, 1915.

In the first entry, the everyday urban sounds of a large tire bursting or a car backfiring have been rewritten as signs of bombardment, occasions for scanning the sky even as the writer's sense of her own immunity ("it always seems utterly impossible that one should be hurt") comes to her aid. In the second, months of raids have inverted the earlier responses: after being warded off as a mere backfire, the raid is recognized through a now-routine sequence of sounds, producing a denial of denial ("there was no denying it"). Both incidents can be heard echoing in an early scene in *Mrs. Dalloway*, when "a pistol shot in the street outside," a "violent explosion" coming from a royal car in Bond Street, causes Clarissa to jump and draws the attention of passersby to the car and its exalted passenger (13) [11]. That the events recorded in the diary have been shorn of their air raid referent in the novel, or rather split into an explosion and the subsequent appearance of a sky-writing plane, attests not only to the postwar moment of *Mrs. Dalloway* but also to the fact that the raw material—and the raw nerve—of that postwar moment is still the war itself.

Set in 1923, *Mrs. Dalloway* reminds us early on that "The War was over, except for some one like Mrs. Foxcroft at the Embassy last night eating her heart out because that nice boy was killed and now the old Manor House must go to a cousin; or Lady Bexborough who opened a bazaar, they said, with the telegram in her hand, John, her favourite, killed; but it was over; thank Heaven—over" (4–5) [4]. Four and a half years have elapsed since the war's end, yet the credibility of the pronouncement that "The War was over" is nearly breached by the exceptions the narrator makes for those bereaved civilians whose grief recognizes no Armistice. Mediating Clarissa's thoughts through free indirect discourse, the narrator's "but it was over; thank Heaven—over" asserts closure as an ongoing psychic performance rather than testifying to it as an accomplished historical fact. If "the high singing of some aeroplane overhead" joins brass bands and barrel organs among the sounds Clarissa loves in "this moment of June" (4) [4], it may do so thanks to a similarly forced and uneasy assertion of closure: the war machine is now, thank Heaven, a singer of benign peacetime songs—isn't it? The wartime translation of a burst tire into a bombing raid seems at last to have been reversed, but the demilitarized song of the plane still sounds some overtone of threat in the text, triggering, with all its nervous qualifications, the narrator's insistence in the next paragraph that "The War was over." Though the hostilities have ceased, the funeral for the war dead is clearly still underway—those lost are still mourned as if their loss were fresh, the present is still defined as the aftermath of a war nearly five years gone—and as a consequence any winged objects overhead retain their potential for deadly transformation. It is this sense of future-conditional violence rather than any direct representation of wartime panic that makes *Mrs. Dalloway* the closest analogue in interwar fiction to Douhet's vignette about the bird above the Brescia cemetery. Douhet's point, remember, was less the mourners' terror than the fact that bombardment had reorganized their perceptual reflexes: they were now predisposed to misread an airborne object by the light of past violence or to take on faith the misperceptions of others. Even the interval between raids, or between wars, trembles with the question: is this the return of violence, or just a false alarm? Again, this drawn-out suspension between false and true alarm is not, as Lewis Mumford recognized, just a legacy of violence, but a new incarnation of violence, an uncertainty so dire and so prolonged that the psychic harm it does can outlast a war by many years.

Having sung overhead during Clarissa's morning walk through Westminster, the plane reappears shortly after the "pistol shot" of the motor-car, summoned by that false alarm to a second scene of suspenseful reading. This time the reading is literal: the plane performs a cryptic skywriting that the crowds in Bond Street and Regent's Park attempt, uneasily and inconclusively, to parse.

> Suddenly Mrs. Coates looked up into the sky. The sound of an aeroplane bored ominously into the ears of the crowd. There it was coming over the trees, letting out white smoke from behind, which curled and twisted, actually writing something! making letters in the sky! Every one looked up.
>
> Dropping dead down the aeroplane soared straight up, curved in a loop, raced, sank, rose, and whatever it did, wherever it went, out fluttered behind it a thick ruffled bar of white smoke which curled and wreathed upon the sky in letters. But what letters?
>
> . . . All down the Mall people were standing and looking up into the sky. As they looked the whole world became perfectly silent, and a flight of gulls crossed the sky, first one gull leading, then another, and in this extraordinary silence and peace, in this pallor, in this purity, bells struck eleven times, the sound fading up there among the gulls.
>
> The aeroplane turned and raced and swooped exactly where it liked, swiftly, freely, like a skater. (19–20) [16]

In the hefty amount of commentary it has provoked, the motorcar/skywriting sequence in Woolf's novel has been read as signaling everything from the unseating of human by technological authority to the new ascendancy of commercial over royal spectacle in the national imaginary. For Gillian Beer the skywriting functions as "an image of equalizing as opposed to hierarchy, of freedom and play . . . [t]he aeroplane figures as the free spirit of the modern age returning the eye to the purity of a sky which has 'escaped registration.'" Beer adds that "the aeroplane in *Mrs. Dalloway* is no war-machine. Its frivolity is part of postwar relief."[3] Jennifer Wicke, too, cautions against conflating the skywriter and the warplane: "Precisely what is not meant, it seems to me, is that this airplane is the mere replica of that other engine of destruction. Here the airplane, for good or ill, is an ineluctable feature of modernity capable of hieroglyphic play, of hierophantic writing . . . emblematic of all writing under the sign of mass culture."[4] Vincent Sherry, by contrast, underscores the "ominous" sound of the plane, its "dropping dead down," and the connections between skywriting and the Air Ministry, which saw the practice as a commercially funded way to keep combat pilots in training. Sherry adds that the numerology of the eleventh hour, which strikes as the onlookers strive to read the skywriting, would have had a particular significance for the novel's postwar readership: "The recent war, which ended officially on the eleventh hour of the eleventh day of the eleventh month, still owns this number by rights of association as heavy as those ritualized, already annually ceremonialized memories [i.e., the two minutes of "Great Silence" that yearly commemorate the Armistice]."[5] The bells that break the silence of aerial writing and reading signal, in Sherry's account, mourning and memorialization more than postwar relief.

Given the military origins and potential of skywriting, one might argue that the airplane's significance in *Mrs. Dalloway* is not exclusively commercial or military but a new alloy of the two; the power of the scene would emanate, then, not just from the confluence of consumer culture with gigantic scale and hierophantic mystery, but from the cohering of all three phenomena around a wartime technology that had all too recently terrorized civilians.[6] But the

3. Gillian Beer, "The Island and the Aeroplane: The Case of Virginia Woolf" in *Nation and Narration*, ed. Homi K. Bhabha (London: Routledge, 1990), 275–76.
4. Jennifer Wicke, "Coterie Consumption: Bloomsbury, Keynes, and Modernism as Marketing," in *Marketing Modernisms: Self-Promotion, Canonization, Rereading*, ed. Kevin J. H. Dettmar and Stephen Watts (Ann Arbor: University of Michigan Press, 1996), 122.
5. Vincent Sherry, *The Great War and the Language of Modernism* (Oxford: Oxford University Press, 2003), 265.
6. Skywriting was developed during the First World War by the British flying ace J. C. Savage, who patented the technology; his company, Savage Skywriting, was the first to deploy it commercially, writing "Castrol," "Daily Mail," and "Persil" over Derby in May 1922. As for the military potential of skywriting, here is the Aeronautical Correspondent to the London *Times*, responding on August 18, 1922, to Savage's first skywriting over London: "Vast as the possibilities of advertising by sky-writing are, that is only one of the many purposes to which it may be put, and there can be no doubt that in the near future, generously developed, it might easily rival the tape-machine and wireless telegraphy for the dissemination of news. If one machine can write one or two

tendency in the novel's critics to assign the airplane either a military or a commercial significance confirms the scene's power to transmit the characters' dire uncertainty to its readers, delegating to them the anxious work of assigning a value to a dangerously ambiguous object—the work, that is, of distinguishing between a true and a false alarm. Having depicted the skittishness of the interwar urban civilian, *Mrs. Dalloway* also inflicts that skittishness on its readers by placing them among war survivors in a scene of high-stakes reading: standing on the ground amid the onlookers, the reader struggles alongside them not only to parse the gnomic skywritten message but also to ascertain the intentions of the writing machine. And if, as the London *Times* reported in 1922, skywriting "obviously thrills and fascinates everybody who sees it," it did not succeed in totally overwriting the wartime association of planes over cities with bombardment.[7] As late as 1932, the Air Defenses of Great Britain exercises were moved away from London to allay civilians' anxieties; not only was the Geneva disarmament conference taking place concurrently but, as Tami Davis Biddle notes, "bombers over London seemed to have the effect of underscoring the concerns given voice in the popular fiction of the day."[8] Unlike those popular fictions, one of which I discuss at length in the next chapter, *Mrs. Dalloway* neither describes bombing raids nor imagines the dystopian future of a bombed-out world. Both its memory and its anticipation of the civilian-as-target are more attenuated, etched not in descriptions of realized violence but in scenes of imperiled aerial reading and in the alertness of its war-survivor characters, whose nerves have not yet heard the All Clear.

If the airplane in Woolf's novel is an object of fearful ambiguity, even an embodiment of illegible alterity, what are we to make of the

---

words at an altitude of ten thousand feet, to be read by millions of people simultaneously, there is no reason why sentences should not be produced rapidly by a fleet of these machines. . . . Obviously the uses of the highly developed sky writing in peace and war are manifold. From the spelling out of a single word, or a single sentence, it is easy to foresee the stage when long messages will be written by cooperating machines. Already several experiments have been made with the Morse code, and the purposes to which, over sea or land in wartime, such a system of communication might be put are clearly apparent. One can imagine, too, the new sort of aerial conflict that would arise when, if the operating machines were not successfully attacked, efforts would be made to blot out their messages with heavy smoke clouds. The writing of misleading orders would offer a fascinating occupation to the imaginative, and the possibilities of the use of smoke writing for propaganda purposes over the enemy's lines would be considerable." Unsigned, "Sky-Writing by Aircraft: Wide Scope in War and Peace," *Times* (London), August 18, 1922: 5d.

7. Ibid.

8. Tami Davis Biddle, *Rhetoric and Reality in Air Warfare: The Evolution of British and American Ideas About Strategic Bombing, 1914–1945* (Princeton: Princeton University Press, 2002), 107.

fact that *Mrs. Dalloway*'s narrator seems to sit in its cockpit? One function of the skywriting scene is to tell the story of its readers, the crowd of Londoners and London visitors whose attention is first arrested by the appearance of the royal motorcar and then drawn away by the airplane. Coming from heterogeneous class backgrounds, the members of this crowd briefly constitute an audience thanks to the two spectacles they witness, yet the narrative emphasizes the disunity and variety of their responses to both car and plane. The skywriting, in particular, attracts a collectivized attention without succeeding in totalizing or dominating the collective through a coherent, authoritative message. Through the agency of the narrator, however, the onlookers' unspoken reactions to the spectacles of car and plane are given voice, salted with details about those characters' pasts and class identities and itineraries, and assembled in an image of the social totality; they are the first large-scale illustration of the gossamer social web in which the novel is so interested, and of which the central illustration will be the connection between Clarissa Dalloway and Septimus Smith—between an MP's upper-class wife and a petty-bourgeois Great War veteran she will never meet. *Mrs. Dalloway*'s narrator achieves these radiant portraits of the social matrix by way of extraordinary powers of mobility, penetration, observation, and juxtaposition—by, in effect, turning and racing and swooping exactly where she likes, swiftly, freely, like a skater. Small wonder, then, that the descriptions of the plane over London engage in so much narratorial stunt-pilotry:

> Ah, but that aeroplane! Hadn't Mrs. Dempster always longed to see foreign parts? She had a nephew, a missionary. It soared and shot. She always went on the sea at Margate, not out o'sight of land, but she had no patience with women who were afraid of water. It swept and fell. Her stomach was in her mouth. Up again. There's a fine young feller aboard of it, Mrs. Dempster wagered, and away and away it went, fast and fading, away and away the aeroplane shot; soaring over Greenwich and all the masts; over the little island of grey churches, St. Paul's and the rest till, on either side of London, fields spread out and dark brown woods where adventurous thrushes hopping boldly, glancing quickly, snatched the snail and tapped him on a stone, once, twice, thrice. (27) [21]

Only a narrator who can move effortlessly from Mrs. Dempster's disappointments to a panoramic overview of London airspace to a thrush's tapping a snail on a stone, the passage suggests, is capable of tracing the filaments of feeling, information, and fellow-suffering

across the metropolis to connect Clarissa with Septimus.[9] Affiliated
with the airplane's mobility and capacity for penetrating overview,
the narrator admits the machine into her own airspace in order
either to imitate it or to outperform it in the registers of sympathetic and high-resolution seeing.[1]

To the extent the narrator finds an avatar in the airplane's mobile
point of view, the onlooker's anxious questions of the plane must
also be asked of the narrator: what are the intentions behind this
narratorial reconnaissance? Of what sorts of violent conflations
might this narrator be capable—and to what end? In October 1922,
Woolf recorded in her diary that her short story "Mrs. Dalloway in
Bond Street" had "branched into a book," adding "I adumbrate here
a study of insanity & suicide: the world seen by the sane & the
insane side by side" (*D2*, 207). Whether or not Clarissa and Septimus are exhaustively described as "the sane & the insane," there is
no denying that *Mrs. Dalloway* juxtaposes them. Much work on the
novel during the last two decades has focused on a pairing different
from "the sane & the insane": that of the civilian and the soldier.
The early pages of the novel appear to establish the discreteness of
these categories: if for Clarissa the war is "over; thank Heaven—
over," for the shell-shocked Septimus "the world wavered and quivered and threatened to burst into flames" (15) [12]. He is still visited
by the apparition of his commanding officer Evans, killed in Italy
just before the Armistice; he still sees himself as a "giant mourner"

9. Karen Piper makes a similar point: "[I]ndeed, as a kind of roaming omniscient narrator,
   the airplane appears to determine the logic of the narrative itself. . . . [It] is a means of
   getting perspective, of getting beyond one's house and body and escaping into pure
   thought." Piper observes that the narrator of Woolf's short story "Kew Gardens" (1919)
   also "mimics an aerial perspective—with sudden shifts in altitude and visual resolu-
   tion"; see Karen Piper, *Cartographic Fictions: Maps, Race, and Identity* (New Bruns-
   wick, NJ: Rutgers University Press, 2002), 66. See also Woolf's posthumously
   published essay "Flying Over London" (1928/1950) and discussions of it in my "Over
   Assemblage: *Ulysses* and the *Boîte-en-valise* from Above" in *Cultural Studies of James
   Joyce: European Joyce Studies* 15, ed. R. Brandon Kershner (Amsterdam: Rodopi,
   2003), and in Leo Mellor, *Reading the Ruins: Modernism, Bombsites and British Culture* (Cambridge: Cambridge University Press, 2013), 33–34.
1. It would clearly be an error to read the mobile, omniscient narrator in Woolf's work—
   to say nothing of fiction generally—as a simple emanation or phenomenalization of
   heavier-than-air flight. But we do, I think, need to attend to those rare moments when
   the typically disembodied convention of the omniscient narrator is linked to a specific
   figure or conceit within the diegesis, as when Dickens invokes, in *Dombey and Son*, "a
   good spirit who would take the housetops off, with a more potent and benignant hand
   than the lame demon in the tale, and show a Christian people what dark shapes issue
   from amidst their homes." *Mrs. Dalloway*'s brief projection of omniscient narration
   upon the airplane, I suggest, repurposes the panoramic gaze of total war for counter-
   vailing ends. See Charles Dickens, *Dombey and Son* (London: Penguin, 2002), 702. On
   the convention of the Asmodeus flight (as exemplified in Dickens's "good spirit"), see
   Jonathan Arac, *Commissioned Spirits: The Shaping of Social Motion in Dickens, Car-
   lyle, Melville, and Hawthorne* (New York: Columbia University Press, 1989); Audrey
   Jaffe, *Vanishing Points: Dickens, Narrative, and the Subject of Omniscience* (Berkeley:
   University of California Press, 1991); and David L. Pike, *Metropolis on the Styx: The
   Underworlds of Modern Urban Culture, 1800–2001* (Ithaca, NY: Cornell University
   Press, 2007).

with "legions of men prostrate behind him" (68–69) [50]. For the combatant, the traumatic aftereffects of the war overwhelm the present, whereas noncombatants like Clarissa seem free to buy flowers, mend a dress, meditate on aging, plan a party. Yet, as we have seen, *Mrs. Dalloway* numbers civilians, too, among those for whom the war has not fully ended. Clarissa's aunt, old Miss Parry, is "an indomitable Englishwoman, fretful if disturbed by the War, say, which dropped a bomb at her very door, from her deep meditation over orchids and her own figure journeying in the 'sixties in India" (174) [126]. In the late war the bombs came calling like houseguests, and the domestic threshold, formerly a space for welcoming or warding off social calls, was made to receive more disastrous visitations. Whereas the "indomitable Englishwoman" in mid-Victorian India was at least theoretically protected from military violence by the "figure" she cut—by her gender and by her racial and social consecration as a memsahib—the same woman at home in England during the First World War enjoyed no such protection. With its aftershocks still being felt, the bomb at Miss Parry's door signals the remaking of the civilian as target, and as a bearer of postwar stress.

It would be going too far to say that the novel connects Clarissa and Septimus solely to collapse the distinction between civilian and soldier or to endorse that collapse, although toward the end of her life Woolf would explore the critical possibilities latent in just such a collapse. *Mrs. Dalloway* links its protagonists mostly through their similarities of temperament and experience: they share a history of illness and a dread of doctors who worship the sister goddesses, Proportion and Conversion; they have both witnessed the motorcar in Bond Street and the airplane above it; they can apprehend the coalescence of chatter and accident, occasionally, in a moment of radiant presence that is seldom fully dissociable from a sense of dread. Though they belong to disparate classes, they are brought closer by the vertical relation of patient to physician: at her party, Clarissa learns from the wife of Septimus's doctor that "a young man . . . had killed himself. He had been in the army" (179) [129], and this news precipitates Clarissa's feeling "somehow very like him—the young man who had killed himself. She felt glad that he had done it; thrown it away. . . . He made her feel the beauty; made her feel the fun" (182) [131].[2] Even more intimate is the link forged between Clarissa and Septimus by narratorial echoes in

2. The final sentence in this quotation ("He made her feel the beauty; made her feel the fun") appears in Woolf's American proofs and in all U.S. editions of the novel but *not* in any British ones. For a detailed discussion of this and other variants, see Anne E. Fernald, "Introduction," in Virginia Woolf, *Mrs. Dalloway* (Cambridge: Cambridge University Press, 2014), esp. lxxxiv–xc.

scenes a hundred pages apart. Mending her dress for the party after she has completed her errands, Clarissa recalls a passage ("Fear no more the heat o' the sun") she read earlier that morning in an edition of *Cymbeline* propped open in the window of Hatchards bookshop. The narrator describes Clarissa's calm: "Fear no more, says the heart. Fear no more, says the heart, committing its burden to some sea, which sighs collectively for all sorrows, and renews, begins, collects, lets fall. And the body alone listens to the passing bee; the wave breaking; the dog barking, far away barking and barking" (39) [29]. In a later scene, Septimus experiences a similar moment of peace while his wife decorates a hat: "his hand lay there on the back of the sofa, as he had seen his hand lie when he was bathing, floating, on the top of the waves, while far away on shore he heard dogs barking and barking far away. Fear no more, says the heart in the body; fear no more" (136) [99]. We know that Septimus reveres Shakespeare and may, like Clarissa, have been reminded of the phrase that morning by the same copy of *Cymbeline* in the same Piccadilly shop window; the quotation will sound again in Clarissa's thoughts during the novel's final pages, just as she allows herself to be gladdened by the news of Septimus's death (182) [131]. But in the hat-decorating scene it is not only the phrase itself but also the heart's articulation of the phrase, the oceanic language, and the far away bark of the dog that echo Clarissa's meditations.

One might take these echoes to ratify Clarissa's feeling "very like" Septimus by demonstrating that the states of mind, the interior tableaux, even the mental diction of socially disparate people can be nearly identical. But a more disquieting reading emerges when we return to the narrator through whose agency the momentary fusion of Clarissa and Septimus occurs—a narrator who is conspicuously mobile, surveillant, penetrating, sometimes totalizing, and possessed of an archivist's retentive and cross-referencing powers. This is a narrator, after all, who not only keeps track of individual bodies, phrases, commodities, and thoughts as they circulate in the metropolis but also maps the complex transactions among them in space and time. This narrator traces a Shakespeare quotation that sounds nonsimultaneously in two minds back to a single shop window and forward to their mystical but indirect communion during a party, tracks the ambulance carrying the dying Septimus past Clarissa's old suitor Peter Walsh, in whom, as he stands by the pillar box opposite the British Museum, it triggers "a moment, in which things came together; this ambulance; and life and death" (148) [107]. The *Mrs. Dalloway* narrator ravels the web that joins Shakespeare to shell shock, jam to the war machine, because hers is the gaze of total war. In keeping with an airborne vantage that observes the linkages among discrete things in order to deem them equally legitimate as targets, the narrator's command of particularities leads, chillingly, not to the fortification of discreteness but to its erosion. The sensitive apparatus through which Septimus and Clarissa are observed ends up fusing even the interior language of combatant and noncombatant, threatening to violate the very "privacy of the soul" on which the novel appears to insist (124) [90].

This is not to claim that *Mrs. Dalloway* adopts the gaze of total war for warlike purposes. If the novel's narratorial gaze is the massively interconnective one of a Douhet, it is also, paradoxically, the opposite—a gaze that wants to "travel that spider's thread of attachment" (112) [82] between people, places, things, beliefs, and affects in order to point up the fragility of their interdependence, the susceptibility of the whole social matrix to trauma if even a small part of it is assaulted or destroyed. Woolf's novel, one might say, attempts to capture the logic of total war for redeployment in a deeply pacifist agenda.[3] Yet this is not the same thing as exempting the novel from that logic or the gaze it produces. To protest total war on the grounds that social, cultural, industrial, and military systems are crucially interpenetrative is not to step outside the logic of total war; it is simply to resist one application of that logic. By the same token, the novel's replication of a certain Douhetian gaze does not necessarily weaken its pacifism; it simply attests to the central sorrow of the pacifist in the era of total war: that the architecture of total war proceeds from assumptions few pacifists would reject. These assumptions—e.g., that the war machine is funded and built by civilian workers whose safety, morale, peace of mind, and consent are vulnerable and therefore effective targets—do not, of course, lead inevitably to an endorsement of total war; but to replicate such assumptions, even while deploring the end to which they are put, can seem like a concession of defeat, even an endorsement of that end. Clausewitz argued that whereas the purpose of war is to serve a political end, the nature of war is to serve

3. My tight focus on Woolf leaves to one side the pacifisms of the rest of the Bloomsbury circle, a subject Christine Froula addresses comprehensively in *Virginia Woolf and the Bloomsbury Avant-Garde: War, Civilization, Modernity* (New York: Columbia University Press, 2005). Froula shows (5–6) how prescient John Maynard Keynes and Clive Bell were in arguing that a humiliating peace would increase the likelihood of another war—the central argument not only of Keynes's *The Economic Consequences of the Peace* (1919) but also of Bell's *Peace at Once* (1915). Yet for Froula, these next-war prophecies did not predispose Woolf to a sense of the future's foreclosure, even when, during the final years of the novelist's life, they seemed to have been terribly fulfilled. Of Woolf's suicide, Froula writes, "perhaps it was not that she had ceased to believe in civilization's future but that she could fight no more," adding of *Between the Acts*, "neither the madness to which she attributed her suicide nor her death negate[s] the future that pageant and novel leave open" (324).

only itself.[4] War subjects the self-understanding of all things—ambulances, Bartlett pears, skywriting, Shakespeare, this moment of June—to a military-industrial undertow. As the limit approached by war's centripetal force, the doctrine of total war is susceptible to rejection but not to disproof. The replication of its logic and its gaze in *Mrs. Dalloway*, despite the clearly pacifist vectors along which these are mobilized, may be both the text's primary symptom and its most strategic pacifism: the self-inflicted violence exhibited by the text acts out, at once neurotically and instructively, the brute circularity of war, conspicuously refusing to fabricate some fictive escape from total war's inexorable logic. At the same time, it stages, amid the effects of recent trauma, the persistence of collective but nontotalized reading, thinking, and feeling—which is to say, the persistence of community. As a de facto reading of Douhet, it says that the mourners at Brescia may have had their rite shattered, but they were joined in both the rite and its shattering.

# CELIA MARSHIK

## [Miss Kilman's Mackintosh][†]

*⁂*

In the "Hades" episode of James Joyce's *Ulysses*, the reporter Joe Hynes takes down the names of those who attend the funeral of Paddy Dignam. Hynes asks Leopold Bloom,

> —do you know the fellow in the, fellow was over there in the . . .
> —Macintosh. Yes, I saw him, Mr Bloom said. Where is he now?
> —M'Intosh, Hynes said, scribbling, I don't know who he is. Is that his name?[1]

The mysterious figure, henceforth known as M'Intosh, appears throughout *Ulysses*, known only by the coat that confers a spurious identity. The character's personal history is seemingly a tragic one: he eats dry bread, a clear sign of poverty; he purportedly "loves a lady who is dead," a mark of mourning and loneliness; and he is

4. The elegant paraphrase of Clausewitz is John Keegan's, in *A History of Warfare* (New York: Alfred A. Knopf, 1993), 21.
† From *At the Mercy of Their Clothes: Modernism, the Middlebrow, and British Garment Culture* (New York: Columbia University Press, 2016), pp. 67–72, 79–80, 95–98. © 2016 Columbia University Press. Reprinted by permission of the publisher.
1. James Joyce, *Ulysses* (1922; New York: Vintage, 1990), 110.

identified by medical students as suffering from "trumpery insanity," a sign of ill-health.[2]

\* \* \*

At the opposite cultural pole of *Ulysses,* one finds P. G. Wodehouse's short story "Jeeves and the Dog McIntosh" (1930), in which Bertie Wooster takes care of his Aunt Agatha's beloved Aberdeen terrier. Wooster's canine charge is accidentally given away, but his indefatigable valet, Jeeves, manages to substitute another terrier in his place. As Jeeves explains, "One Aberdeen terrier looks very much like another Aberdeen terrier, sir."[3] To put it another way, one McIntosh looks much like another. In quite different ways, Joyce's and Wodehouse's texts emphasize the ubiquity of the mackintosh *and* of the creatures associated with the coat. Instead of reaching "the absolute finality of fame," M'Intosh and McIntosh find themselves de-particularized through the mac. Becoming a thing, such novels imply, can be much more alienating than Cunnington[4] suggests.

In novels targeted at a variety of readerships, the mackintosh, under its various incarnations, repeatedly turns persons into things. It foments loss of individual identity; it cloaks the unscrupulous, deadly, and cruel. Moreover, the mac seems to have a bull's eye on it, protecting against the elements but attracting the violence of technological warfare. It turns people into units—particularly into uniform entities like soldiers—and into corpses, and it is therefore associated with forms of commemoration. The irony of such activity is increased by the garment's very ordinariness; it was commonplace on the streets of major cities and in the wardrobes of people of all conditions and histories. Although the mackintosh was commercially and popularly aligned with positive traits—including technological innovation, protection, value, and perseverance—writers of the period persistently animated it as enacting violence, anonymity, and the paralysis of characters dwarfed by economic and social structures they could not transcend. While the evening gown demonstrates the way that a bespoke item became acutely problematic in light of changing gender norms, the mackintosh suggests that writers were equally troubled by a mass-produced garment that turned persons into things, making individuals indistinguishable from one another. Evening gowns could and did shame when their wearers failed in bids to achieve singularity, when they failed to become unique and ideal objects; wearers of the mackintosh,

2. Ibid., 254, 333, 427.
3. P. G. Wodehouse, "Jeeves and the Dog McIntosh," in *Very Good, Jeeves* (Garden City, N.Y.: Doubleday, Doran, 1930), 142.
4. C. Wilet Cunnington (1878–1961), fashion historian, author of *Why Women Wear Clothes* (1941) and other books [*Editor*].

I will demonstrate, could seldom aspire to the singular and instead became themselves undifferentiated and threatened material.

Literary scholars have examined representations of the mackintosh in individual novels and have explained what the garment signifies about particular characters, the limits of interpretation, and the social and ethical dimensions of each work.[5] In contrast, this chapter looks at macs across a spectrum of fiction to demonstrate that this most British of garments came to signal the power of clothing to gather connotations and to foment outcomes that individual wearers could seldom control or manipulate. If we consider the mac through the lenses of industrial and military history, children's literature, fashion columns, and advertising *as well as* novels, it becomes clear that the garment was either too innocent or too guilty for an adult to wear. The mackintosh became a mute participant in histories of industrial production and class divisions, in assumptions about which types of people could act on individual volition, and in a historical cataclysm that, until World War II, was unprecedented. Given the presence of the mac in such locations, it is little wonder that writers deployed it as a symptom of—and, eventually, that it became a kind of shorthand for—negative qualities and narratives.

Before turning to a brief biography of the mac, I want to clarify my use of the term throughout this chapter. I subsume a number of words under "mackintosh," including "raincoat," "trench coat," "weather all," and "mackintosh" proper, in part because Charles Macintosh was the first commercial maker of the garment, and the word thus became the British catch-all term for raincoats. According to the *OED*, the mackintosh was "originally: a full-length coat or cloak made of waterproof rubberized material. Subsequently: a rainproof coat made of this or some other material."[6] Manufacturers and retailers did not always differentiate between different kinds of raincoats; the *Harrods General Catalogue* of 1928/1929, for example, does not distinguish between coats made of different textiles, indexing and identifying all raincoats with the term "mackintosh." The *OED* demonstrates the word's universalizing function with an example from *Noblesse Oblige: An Enquiry into Identifiable Characteristics of the English Aristocracy* that follows the definition of "mackintosh": "*Burberry* and *raincoat* are of the same genre, *macintosh* or *mac* being normal." In *Noblesse Oblige*, a footnote to this

5. For example, Jane Marcus argues that "the trench-coat is a class and gender mark covering the body of women at/in this war" (afterword to Helen Zenna Smith [Evadne Price]. *Not So Quiet . . . Stepdaughters of War* [1930; New York: Feminist Press of [NY, 1989], 291). * * *

. . d *English Dictionary Online*, s.v. "mackintosh," http://www.oed.com/view/Entry . . ?redirectedFrom=mackintosh#eid.

definition reads, "This use of *Burberry* no doubt arose because, even before 1914 . . . this was a good and expensive kind of macintosh."[7] This description explains the use of differing terms as an attempt by manufacturers and consumers to assert and maintain class hierarchies in the face of the garment's ubiquity, but "mac" was considered the "normal" term for a waterproof garment.[8] There was, however, nothing "normal" about this garment's deployment in a range of literature, which collectively uses the coat to think about the associations between, and blending of, persons and things.

The commercial history of the mackintosh indicates why negative connotations would gradually accrue to a garment that was (and is) quintessentially British. Charles Macintosh (1766–1843) invented a means of waterproofing fabric and patented it on June 17, 1823. Macintosh's process involved sandwiching rubber, softened by naphtha, between layers of cotton cloth.[9] Although the coats succeeded in keeping out water, they were unattractive and uncomfortable. Nineteenth-century macs were a drab green, long and shapeless, and hard to maneuver. The original material could not be tailored closely to the body because the rubberized fabric did not breathe, and a tight-fitting mac was a prescription for perspiration.[1] The coats themselves also smelled unpleasant. As early as 1839, "*The Gentleman's Magazine* remarked that 'a mackintosh is now become a troublesome thing in town from the difficulty of their being admitted into an omnibus on account of the offensive stench which they emit.'"[2]

Mackintoshes were unique in that they were an early artifact of British mass-production. In a period when most street clothing and outerwear was either home- or custom-made, the production requirements for macs, which had seams that necessitated chemical proofing, meant that "the mackintosh industry was one of the first clothing trades to be substantially carried out in factories."[3] Workers made individual parts of the garment, which was then assembled elsewhere on the premises, rendering the mackintosh a pre-Fordist exemplar of mass-production. Because they were not made to measure for individual customers and were manufactured

7. Nancy Mitford, ed., *Noblesse Oblige: An Enquiry into Identifiable Characteristics of the English Aristocracy* (London: Hamish Hamilton, 1956), 30.
8. The spelling of the word "mackintosh" is varied; writers, perhaps following the spelling of the first manufacturer's name, regularly drop the *k*. I use the "mackintosh" spelling, as this is a standard version offered by the *OED*.
9. Sarah Levitt, "Manchester Mackintoshes: A History of the Rubberised Garment Trade in Manchester," *Textile History* 17 (1986): 51.
1. Ibid., 54.
2. Quoted in Christina Walkley and Vanda Foster, *Crinolines and Crimping Irons: Victorian Clothes: How They Were Cleaned and Cared For* (London: Peter Owen, 1978), 138.
3. Levitt, "Manchester Mackintoshes," 56.

far away from where they were bought and worn, mackintoshes
foreshadowed the eventual popularity of "ready-to-wear" clothing.
The coats were thus an emblem of modernity, but they were also
marked by a lack of exclusivity, as mass-production rendered mackintoshes inexpensive. In 1893, the *India Rubber Journal* asserted,
"Now the servant girl out of her slender means can procure a really
stylish and serviceable waterproof for a mere trifle."[4] Manufacturers
and servant girls were no doubt pleased that the coat had become
so affordable, but such comments led to a growing sense that mackintoshes were cheap, and thus second-rate, articles.

\* \* \*

The first—and, over the long term, best—customer for the mackintosh was the British Army. When other manufacturers entered the
market with different means of waterproofing cloth, they too found
the army to be their best market. Ordinary soldiers wore mass-
produced mackintoshes, but officers wore Aquascutums during the
Crimean War and, later, Burberry waterproofs.[5] These companies
offered tailor-made mackintoshes, but the cut and color of the garments they produced followed military specifications, making the
coats of the officer class visually uniform. Even as the quality of a
mac quietly expressed its wearer's social and economic status, the
coat became a de-individuating garment worn by members of an
institution that functioned because of group behavior, experience,
and history.

\* \* \*

Early advertisements for the mackintosh tended to promote it to
two types of consumer: sportsmen (and, to a lesser extent, women)
and servants. In other words, the upper echelons of British society
would wear their macs while participating in extraordinary leisure
activities, while those in the working class would wear the same
raincoats while performing their ordinary, workaday jobs. During
the nineteenth century, Macintosh touted its waterproofs as a necessary implement for the sporting life, particularly for dangerous
sports. In an advertisement published in the *Illustrated Sporting
and Dramatic News* in 1890, a man and a woman wear the coats
while yachting in rough seas.[6] This advertisement was no doubt
intended to display the protective qualities of the mac—the couple

---

4. Quoted in ibid., 58.
5. *The Aquascutum Story* (London: Aquascutum, 1994), 8.
6. Leonard de Vries, comp., *Victorian Advertisements*, text by James Laver (London: Mur-
ray, 1968), 126.

is endangered but not wet—but it paradoxically aligns the garment with exciting pastimes that verge on the perilous.

\* \* \*

When macs were tailored and marketed for use at the front during the war, the biography of this garment took a dramatic turn; although waterproof coats had long been worn by soldiers, they had never been as ubiquitous—or as abundant—as they became between 1914 and 1918. One of the necessary items in any officer's "kit" was the trench coat, a long belted mackintosh cut differently for each branch of service.[7] Ordinary soldiers and female volunteers also wore such coats, though the cut and quality of individual examples varied, depending on the wearers' financial wherewithal.

The pervasive presence of trench coats during the war is well known, but at our historical remove, it is difficult to imagine the visual impact of the sheer proliferation of these garments. People saw men and women in mackintoshes everywhere: in the streets, at railroad stations, and in the newspapers.

\* \* \*

Because consumers could buy everything from stylish velvet mackintoshes to storm coats in the decades after the war, writers of the 1920s and 1930s had a range of associations to choose from when clothing their characters in mackintoshes. And yet, very few authors chose to depict the coat—and the characters who wear it—as stylish, sporty, comfortable, or modern. More often, mac-clad figures look like *Mrs. Dalloway*'s Doris Kilman, who tutors the Dalloways' daughter, Elizabeth, and "year in year out" wears "a green mackintosh coat."[8] As Clarissa Dalloway speaks to Elizabeth, she senses Kilman's presence:

> [O]utside the door was Miss Kilman, as Clarissa knew; Miss Kilman in her mackintosh, listening to whatever they said.
> Yes, Miss Kilman stood on the landing, and wore a mackintosh; but had her reasons. First, it was cheap; second, she was over forty; and did not, after all, dress to please. She was poor, moreover; degradingly poor.[9]

7. The trench coat was "a waterproofed overcoat worn by officers in the trenches" (*Oxford English Dictionary Online*, 2nd ed., s.v. "trench coat," http://www.oed.com/view/Entry /413383?redirectedFrom=trench+coat#eid). Although trench coats had what might seem to be signature details, including a gun flap, storm pockets, and a belt fastened with D-rings, these coats were produced by different manufacturers and in differing cuts, so any waterproof coat might be seen as a trench coat. The line between trench coats and mackintoshes was thus blurred.
8. Virginia Woolf, *Mrs. Dalloway* (1925: New York: Harcourt Brace Jovanovich, 1981), 12 [10].
9. Ibid., 123 [87].

After Elizabeth and Kilman leave to go shopping, Clarissa muses about "love and religion," which she envisions as "clumsy, hot, domineering, hypocritical, eavesdropping, jealous, infinitely cruel and unscrupulous, dressed in a mackintosh coat."[1] The range of qualities that Clarissa projects onto Kilman—and specifically *into* her coat—points to the tutor's repulsive physicality, to Clarissa's upper-class distaste for the unfashionably dressed, and to Kilman's position as Clarissa's rival for Elizabeth's love and attention. If M'Intosh seems disembodied under his coat, Kilman's abject body is all too present, and her mackintosh underlines rather than disguises that abjection.

There are obvious reasons for Kilman to wear the coat, even if the weather makes it seem unnecessary. Like the characters penned by West, Greene, and Orwell,[2] Kilman's poverty is materialized through the mackintosh. She "could not afford to buy pretty clothes," so Kilman cannot make a striking, distinctive appearance. Instead of a silk or velvet mac, she is likely wearing something like the Blanford or Mattamac coat, in which case price is the garment's sole virtue. Like West's Margaret Grey before her, then, Kilman wears a coat that marks her as out of place in upper-class homes. When wealthy women criticize these characters' coats—Clarissa describes Kilman's appearance as inflicting "positive torture"[3]—such comments reveal as much about upper-class assumptions and values as they do about the women who wear the mackintosh. Horrified reactions to the garment neatly emphasize divisions that neither class can bridge; if the war purportedly unified the nation, reactions to the mackintosh signal deep rifts in postwar unity. Moreover, while Margaret and Jenny kiss "not as women, but as lovers do,"[4] Kilman "genuinely loved" the "beautiful" Elizabeth Dalloway, wishing to "grasp her," "clasp her," and "make her hers absolutely and forever and then die."[5] The female body that is produced by the cheap mac can thus be regarded as queer; economic alterity necessitates the adoption of

---

1. Ibid., 126 [90]. As Laura Gwyn Edson writes, the mac becomes "an encapsulation of everything she [Clarissa] can't stand about Miss Kilman. The hostess figures the tutor as the coat." For Edson, what is most significant about the garment is that "Woolf has submerged clothing into the substrata of multiple consciousness where clothing is claimed as cover or protection but also revealed as a projection of innermost secrets" ("Kicking Off Her Knickers: Virginia Woolf's Rejection of Clothing as Realistic Detail," in *Virginia Woolf and the Arts: Selected Papers from the Sixth Annual Conference on Virginia Woolf*, ed. Diane F. Gillespie and Leslie K. Hankins [New York: Pace University Press, 1997], 122, 123). While the coat certainly functions in this manner, I am interested in how Woolf engages the relationship between person and thing (and between thing and history) through Kilman's garment.
2. Rebecca West (1892–1983), Graham Greene (1904–1991), and George Orwell (1903–1950), British novelists, each of whom wrote novels with characters in mackintosh coats [*Editor*].
3. *Woolf, Mrs. Dalloway*, 12 [10].
4. West, *Return of the Soldier*, 88.
5. Woolf, *Mrs. Dalloway*, 131, 132 [94].

a garment that affords—or, rather, *produces*—a gender identity and sexuality at odds with the femininity and heterosexuality that Kilman finds out of her reach.

The qualities that Clarissa mentally attributes to the mackintosh indicate that it figures more than the garment's persistent class connotations. The coat makes Kilman appear clumsy and awkward in its expression of practicality. While a child might be expected to wear a mackintosh, an adult—particularly a woman—should have other values, whether they are "dress[ing] to please" or personal expression.[6] Although her pragmatic and authentic appearance no doubt contributes to the tutor's appeal to Elizabeth, Kilman herself "minded looking as she did,"[7] and her mackintosh is not so much an attempt to transcend fashion (or a bold assertion of a lesbian identity) as an admission of sartorial defeat.

The power of the negative qualities that Clarissa imagines "in a mackintosh coat" signals, furthermore, that the garment embodies the "cruel and unscrupulous" war that Virginia Woolf and the other writers discussed in this chapter regarded as barbaric and wasteful. It is a reminder of the women and men, including Kilman's brother,[8] who died in their mackintoshes. As the sole character who wears such a coat—even the shell-shocked Septimus Warren Smith wears a "shabby overcoat" instead of a mac[9]—Kilman becomes a perambulating reminder of the war that most people wanted to forget.

No other garment could so succinctly mobilize the range of qualities that make Doris Kilman repulsive to Clarissa Dalloway. Kilman's child-like, unattractive appearance; anger and suppressed violence; and class status are all materialized in the mackintosh, which wears Kilman as much as she wears it. When Kilman stumbles into Westminster Abbey, which contains the "tomb of the Unknown Warrior,"[1] *Mrs. Dalloway* points toward the many traumatizing objects that continue to haunt postwar London. Kilman's coat suggests that the work of mourning continues, and is carried out, across time and space with the help of this one garment.[2]

\* \* \*

6. Ibid., 123 [87].
7. Ibid., 128 [91].
8. Ibid., 123 [88].
9. Ibid., 14 [11].
1. Ibid., 133 [95].
2. As Christine Froula argues, "*Mrs. Dalloway* poses the great question of Europe's future . . . as the fate of collective mourning—a *historic* question of genre for a traumatized Europe poised between elegy and revenge tragedy" (*Virginia Woolf and the Bloomsbury Avant-Garde: War, Civilization, Modernity* [New York: Columbia University Press, 2005], 89). See pp. 318–26 for a different excerpt from this book.

# Virginia Woolf and *Mrs. Dalloway*: A Chronology*

1878   Leslie Stephen and Julia Duckworth (née Jackson) marry (March 26).
1879   Vanessa Stephen born (May 30).
1880   Thoby Stephen born (September 8).
1882   Adeline Virginia Stephen born at 22 Hyde Park Gate, London (January 25). Stephen family begins spending summers in Cornwall. Leslie Stephen begins working on the *Dictionary of National Biography*.
1883   Adrian Stephen born (October 27).
1887   First extant dated VW letter (to American poet James Russell Lowell, February 22).
1891   Along with Vanessa and Thoby, begins writing the family newspaper, *Hyde Park Gate News*.
1895   Julia Stephen dies (May 5).
1896   Begins keeping a diary, briefly, a habit that would stick in 1897 and continue throughout her life.
1897   Half-sister Stella Duckworth marries Jack Hills (April 10) but dies shortly after (July 19). Begins classes in Greek and History at King's College London, where she studies for four years, adding Latin and German.
1904   Leslie Stephen dies. Moves, with siblings, to 46 Gordon Square in the Bloomsbury neighborhood of London. Publishes her first article.
1905   Begins teaching at Morley College in Waterloo Road.
1906   Travels to Greece. Her brother Thoby dies.
1907   Her sister Vanessa marries Clive Bell.
1910   Takes part in the "Dreadnought hoax" (February 7). First Post-Impressionist Exhibition opens (November 8). Volunteers for women's suffrage (January, November, and December).
1912   Marries Leonard Woolf.

---

*D = Diary; L = Letters. * indicates a corresponding diary entry or letter included in this Norton Critical Edition

1915    Her first novel, *The Voyage Out*, which she completed in
        1913, published by Duckworth (March 26).
1916    Meets Katherine Mansfield.
1917    With Leonard, starts the Hogarth Press.
1919    Hogarth publishes "Kew Gardens." Duckworth publishes
        *Night and Day*.
1920    Sees Vanessa Bell's servant, Mary Wilson, driven off to
        St. Pancras Hospital: "a complete case of servant's hysteria"
        (*D2* 47) (June 8).*
        Hears of the "death of a young man" who fell off the roof at
        a party (*D2* 51).
        Lytton Strachey praises *The Voyage Out* (*D2* 65) (September 21).*
1921    Has first Russian lesson with S. S. Koteliansky (*D2* 89)
        (February 5).
        Madge Vaughan visits (*D2* 121–22) (2 June).*
1922    Writes to T. S. Eliot concerning a story (almost certainly
        "Mrs. Dalloway in Bond Street") (*L2* 521) (April 14).*
        States in diary that she plans to finish "Mrs. Dalloway" by
        September 2 and start "Prime Minister" (*D2* 196) (August 28).
        Death of Katherine "Kitty" Maxse (née Lushington) (1868–
        1922) (*D2* 206) (October 8).
        Notes in her manuscript notebook that Mrs. Dalloway and
        Septimus Smith will be central characters: "Mrs. Dalloway
        seeing the truth. S.S. seeing the insane truth" (*The Hours*
        412) (October 16).
        First meets "the lovely gifted aristocratic" Vita Sackville-West
        while dining with Clive Bell (*D2* 216) (December 14).
1923    Katherine Mansfield dies (*D2* 225–26) (January 9).
        The Woolfs depart on a month-long holiday to Spain, traveling by mule to Gerald Brenan's cottage in Yegen, in the
        Sierra Madre (*D2* 240) (March 27).
        LW returns to London; VW stays on alone in Paris, having
        tea with Hope Mirrlees at Rumpelmayer's (*L3* 32) (late April).
        Goes to watch polo at Hurlingham (*L3* 41) (May 21).
        *The Hours* as a possible title; reading Dostoevsky and Mansfield (*D2* 248) (June 19).*
        "Mrs. Dalloway in Bond Street" published in *The Dial* (July).
        "I dig out beautiful caves behind my characters" (*D2* 263)
        (August 30).
        Spends the weekend with John Maynard Keynes and Lydia
        Lopokova, observing her for Rezia (*D2* 266) (September 11).
        Writing the mad scene in Regent's Park (*D2* 272)
        (October 15).

1924    Purchases ten-year lease of 52 Tavistock Square, London (*D2* 282) (January 9).

Woolf's niece, Angelica Bell, hit by a car; Woolf writing the doctor chapter and "On Not Knowing Greek" (D2 299) (April 15).*

Writing Septimus's death (*D2* 307–308) (August 2).

Finishes the draft of *Mrs. Dalloway* (*D2* 316–17) (October 8).

Woolf completes typescript of *Mrs. Dalloway* to give to Leonard over Christmas at Monks House (*D2* 324–25) (December 21).

1925    Revising typescript for printers (*D3* 5) (January 6).*

Begins writing seven short stories related to *Mrs. Dalloway*, including "The Introduction"* and "The Man Who Loved His Kind."*

*The Common Reader* published in Great Britain (April 23).

*Mrs. Dalloway* published in Britain and the United States; *The Common Reader* published in the United States (May 14).

1927    *To the Lighthouse*

1928    *Orlando*

1929    *A Room of One's Own*

1931    *The Waves*

1932    *The Second Common Reader*

1933    *Flush*

1937    *The Years*

1938    *Three Guineas*

1940    *Roger Fry*

1941    Finishes final typescript of *Between the Acts* (February 26). Drowns in the River Ouse (March 28). *Between the Acts* published posthumously (July 17).

# Selected Bibliography

• indicates work included or excerpted in this Norton Critical Edition

## SELECT OTHER WORKS BY WOOLF

• Woolf, Virginia. *A Passionate Apprentice: The Early Journals, 1897–1909*. Ed. Mitchell A. Leaska. Harcourt, 1990.
• ———. *The Complete Shorter Fiction*. Ed. Susan Dick. Harcourt, 1989.
• ———. *The Diary*, 5 vols. Ed. Anne Olivier Bell. Harcourt, 1978–84.
• ———. *The Essays*, 6 vols. Ed. Andrew McNeillie and Stuart M. Clarke. Harcourt, 1988–2011.
———. *The Hours: The British Museum Manuscript of* Mrs. Dalloway. Transcribed and ed. Helen Wussow. Pace UP, 2010.
• ———. *Hyde Park Gate News: The Stephen Family Newspaper*. Ed. Gill Lowe. Hesperus, 2005.
• ———. *The Letters*, 6 vols. Ed. Nigel Nicolson and Joanne Trautmann, vol. 1. Harcourt, 1975–82.
• ———. *Moments of Being*. Ed. Jeanne Schulkind. Harcourt, 1985.
———. *Mrs. Dalloway*. Ed. Anne E. Fernald. Cambridge UP, 2014.

## GENERAL SOURCES ON VIRGINIA WOOLF

Beer, Gillian. *Virginia Woolf: The Common Ground*. Ann Arbor: U of Michigan P, 1996.
Berman, Jessica. *A Companion to Virginia Woolf*. Oxford: Blackwell, 2016.
Briggs, Julia. *Reading Virginia Woolf*. Edinburgh: Edinburgh UP, 2006.
———. *Virginia Woolf: An Inner Life*. London: Penguin, 2005.
• Froula, Christine. *Virginia Woolf and the Bloomsbury Avant-Garde: War, Civilization, Modernity*. New York: Columbia UP, 2005.
Gruber, Ruth. *Virginia Woolf: The Will to Create as a Woman* (1935). New York: Carroll & Graf, 2004.
Holtby, Winifred. *Virginia Woolf*. London: Wishard, 1932.
Lee, Hermione. *Virginia Woolf: A Life*. New York: Vintage, 1999.
Sellers, Susan, ed. *The Cambridge Companion to Virginia Woolf*, 2nd ed. Cambridge: Cambridge UP, 2010.
———, and Jane Goldman, eds. *Virginia Woolf in Context*. Cambridge: Cambridge UP, 2012.
Zwerdling, Alex. *Virginia Woolf and the Real World*. Berkeley: U of California P, 1986.

## SOURCES ON *MRS. DALLOWAY*

• Ahmed, Sara. *The Promise of Happiness*. Durham: Duke UP, 2010.

Bagley, Melissa. "Nature and the Nation in *Mrs. Dalloway.*" *Woolf Studies Annual* 14 (2008): 35–51.

Banfield, Ann. *The Phantom Table: Woolf, Fry, Russell, and Epistemology of Modernism*. Cambridge: Cambridge UP, 2000.

Barrett, Eileen, and Patricia Cramer. *Virginia Woolf: Lesbian Readings*. New York: New York UP, 1997.

Blair, Sara. "Local Modernity, Global Modernism: Bloomsbury and the Places of the Literary." *ELH* 71.3 (Sept. 2004): 813–38.

• Bogacz, Ted. "War Neurosis and Cultural Change in England, 1914–22: The Work of the War Office Committee of Enquiry into 'Shell-Shock.'" *Journal of Contemporary History* 24.2 (April 1989): 227–56.

Bond, Candis E. "Remapping Female Subjectivity in *Mrs. Dalloway*: Scenic Memory and Woolf's 'Bye-Street' Aesthetic." *Woolf Studies Annual* 23 (2017): 63–82.

Bowlby, Rachel. "Untold Stories in *Mrs. Dalloway.*" *Textual Practice* 25.3 (2011): 397–415.

———. "Walking, Women, and Writing: Woolf as Flâneuse." In *New Feminist Discourses*. Ed. Isobel Armstrong. Abingdon: Routledge, 1992, 26–47.

Bradshaw, David. "'Vanished, Like Leaves': The Military, Elegy and Italy in *Mrs. Dalloway.*" *Woolf Studies Annual* 8 (2002): 107–25.

———. "Further Thoughts on Mrs. Dalloway's Hot Wednesday in June 1923," *Virginia Woolf Bulletin* 8 (Sept. 2002): 22–23.

Daiches, David, and John Flower. "A Walking Tour with Mrs. Dalloway." In *Literary Landscapes of the British Isles: A Narrative Atlas*. New York and London: Paddington Press Ltd, 1979.

Dalgarno, Emily. "A British *War and Peace*? Virginia Woolf Reads Tolstoy." *MFS Modern Fiction Studies* 50.1 (Spring 2004): 129–50.

Daugherty, Beth Rigel. "'A Corridor Leading from Mrs. Dalloway to a New Book': Transforming Stories, Bending Genres." In *Trespassing Boundaries: Virginia Woolf's Short Fiction*. Ed. Kathryn N. Benzel and Ruth Hoberman. New York: Palgrave, 2004, 101–24.

———. "The Whole Contention Between Mr. Bennett and Mrs. Woolf, Revisited." In *Virginia Woolf: Centennial Essays*. Ed. Elaine K. Ginsberg and Laura Moss Gottlieb. Troy, NY: Whitson Publishing, 1983, 269–94.

DeMeester, Karen. "Trauma and Recovery in Virginia Woolf's *Mrs. Dalloway.*" *MFS Modern Fiction Studies* 44.3 (Fall 1998): 649–73.

Fernald, Anne E. "A Feminist Public Sphere? Virginia Woolf's Revisions of the Eighteenth Century." *Feminist Studies* 31.1 (Spring 2005): 158–82.

———. "Virginia Woolf and Experimental Fiction." In *Blackwell Companion to British Literature, Vol. IV: Victorian and Twentieth-Century Literature, 1837–2000*. Ed. Robert DeMaria et al. West Sussex: Wiley Blackwell, 2014, 246–59.

Froula, Christine. "*Mrs. Dalloway*'s Postwar Elegy: Women, War, and the Art of Mourning." *Modernism/modernity* 9.1 (January 2002): 125–63.

• Hite, Molly. "Tonal Cues and Uncertain Values: Affect and Ethics in *Mrs. Dalloway.*" *Narrative* 18.3 (October 2010): 249–75.

Levenback, Karen. *Virginia Woolf and the Great War*. Syracuse, NY: Syracuse UP, 1999.

• Light, Alison. *Mrs Woolf and the Servants: An Intimate History of Domestic Life in Bloomsbury*. New York: Bloomsbury, 2010.

Lyon, Janet. "On the Asylum Road with Woolf and Mew." *Modernism/modernity* 18.3 (Sept. 2011): 551–74.

Majumdar, Robin, and Allen McLaurin, eds. *Virginia Woolf: The Critical Heritage*. London and Boston: Routledge & Kegan Paul, 1975.

• Marshik, Celia. *At the Mercy of Their Clothes: Modernism, the Middlebrow, and British Garment Culture*. New York: Columbia UP, 2016.

McNees, Eleanor, ed. *Virginia Woolf: Critical Assessments*, 4 vols. Mountfield: Helm Information, 1994.

Meyer, Jessica. "'Not Septimus Now': Wives of Disabled Veterans and Cultural Memory of the First World War in Britain." *Women's History Review* 13.1 (2004): 117–38.

Miller, J. Hillis. "*Mrs. Dalloway*: Repetition as the Raising of the Dead." In *Fiction and Repetition: Seven English Novels*. Cambridge: Harvard UP, 1982, 176–202.

Monte, Steven. "Ancients and Moderns in *Mrs. Dalloway*." *MLQ: Modern Language Quarterly* 61.4 (Dec. 2000): 587–616.

• Outka, Elizabeth. "'Wood for the Coffins Ran Out': Modernism and the Shadowed Afterlife of the Influenza Pandemic." *Modernism/modernity* 21.4 (November 2014): 937–60.

• Saint-Amour, Paul K. *Tense Future: Modernism, Total War, Encyclopedic Form*. Oxford: Oxford UP, 2015.

Shaffer, Brian W. "Civilization in Bloomsbury: Woolf's *Mrs. Dalloway* and Bell's 'Theory of Civilization.'" *Journal of Modern Literature* 19.1 (Summer 1994): 73–87.

Simpson, Kathryn. *Gifts, Markets and Economies of Desire in Virginia Woolf*. New York: Palgrave, 2008.

Smith, Amy C. "Loving Maidens and Patriarchal Mothers: Revisions of the Homeric Hymn to Demeter and Cymbeline in *Mrs. Dalloway*." *Woolf Studies Annual* 17 (2011): 151–72.

Smith, Patricia Juliana. *Lesbian Panic: Homoeroticism in Modern British Women's Fiction*. New York: Columbia UP, 1997.

Snaith, Anna, and Michael Whitworth. *Locating Woolf: The Politics of Space and Place*. Basingstoke: Macmillan, 2007.

———, and Christine Kenyon-Jones. "Tilting at Universities: Virginia Woolf at King's College London." *Woolf Studies Annual* 16 (2010): 1–44.

• Tate, Trudi. *Modernism, History and the First World War*. Palgrave Macmillan, 1998.